M. W Dunham

Oaklawn Stud of Percherons

Imported and bred by M.W. Dunham, Wayne, DuPage Co., Ill. - catalogue for 1888

M. W Dunham

Oaklawn Stud of Percherons
Imported and bred by M.W. Dunham, Wayne, DuPage Co., Ill. - catalogue for 1888

ISBN/EAN: 9783337195182

Printed in Europe, USA, Canada, Australia, Japan

Cover: Foto ©Andreas Hilbeck / pixelio.de

More available books at **www.hansebooks.com**

OF

PERCHERON HORSES

IMPORTED AND BRED BY

M. W. DUNHAM,

WAYNE, DU PAGE CO., ILLINOIS,

THIRTY-FIVE MILES WEST OF CHICAGO, ON THE GALENA DIVISION OF THE
CHICAGO & NORTHWESTERN RAILWAY.

———————

CATALOGUE FOR 1888.

———————

HENRY O. SHEPARD & CO., PRINTERS, 185-187 MONROE ST., CHICAGO.

INDEX.
STALLIONS.

MARES.

INTRODUCTION.

I trust that the readers of the Oaklawn Catalogue for 1888 will appreciate the benefits to be derived from the complete extension of the pedigree of each animal in such a manner as to give a clear idea of its breeding. As the value of all breeding animals depends largely upon their pedigrees, all who are not perfectly familiar with the origin of the Percheron breed will find the innovation in this issue of great assistance to them, as I have taken pains to make it the most complete in this respect, of any catalogue ever published.

In preparing this catalogue it has been my endeavor to make it represent in every way the growth of the establishment since my beginning with the first Percheron stallion ever imported direct from France to Illinois.

With the birth of the first Percheron foaled in the state Oaklawn began its career as a breeding establishment, in which have been concentrated up to the present time nearly 3,000 imported and pure-bred breeding animals. Its importance among the breeding establishments of the country will be better understood when it is known that for many years its importations exceeded those of all other importers and breeders of draft horses combined. At the present time the actual number imported and bred at Oaklawn exceeds that of any other seven establishments in the country; and at no time, past or present, has there ever been in any other stud in Europe or America, so large a collection of imported and pure-bred Percherons as is now on hand at Oaklawn.

As an evidence that its reputation for possessing the best has not suffered from the purchases made personally by the proprietor the present year I have only to mention the fact that, at the great Percheron Show held in France, thirteen prize-winners were secured for Oaklawn, including every first-prize stallion but one, he being retained in that country. Also at the Illinois State Fair, only other exhibition where the Oaklawn Stud was shown the present year, it was awarded sixteen first prizes out of a possible twenty-one, including the only two breeding prizes offered.

With a determination from the beginning to demonstrate my ability to breed Percherons in America equal to the finest produced in France, I began by selecting the finest mares and the best stallions of the most renowned origin. I have experienced the gratification of seeing the produce of Brilliant (now at the head of Oaklawn Stud) sell for higher prices both in France and America than have ever been paid for the produce of any other Percheron stallion. They have acquired a reputation that makes his service sought after at four times the price paid for that of any other draft stallion in the country.

For many years it has been a fact, acknowledged by all those in a position to know from experience by actual trial, that the crosses from Percheron horses on the stock of the country are superior to those of any other breed. The development of the immense trade in this breed of horses has been the result of this conviction, and it is especially gratifying to the advocates of the Percheron to know that the breed that has given evidence of so much value in this country is receiving greater encouragement and constant expressions of high appreciation from the government and in the country of its nativity.

During the past year the French Minister of Agriculture has issued orders to allow no other government stallions in service in the Perche but those recorded in the "Percheron Stud Book," and to purchase for such service only those that are traceable, through this stud book, to the best families. The high appreciation of the French Government for the Percheron breed will be better understood when it is known (as stated by the Inspector-General of the National Studs, M. La Motte Rouge, who makes the purchases) that Percheron stallions cost double the prices asked for the finest stallions of any other pure draft breed in France.

The action of the Minister of Agriculture and the statement of the Inspector-General are important to purchasers of horses in this country, many of whom have been led to believe that all horses imported from France are equally valuable for breeding purposes and equally appreciated in France.

Every year that passes brings new encouragement to the breeders of Percherons. The fact that the breed is recognized in France as being superior to all other breeds of that country is having a very favorable influence upon our people, whose progressive ideas lead them to demand the best of every breed, being willing always to pay sufficient prices to secure such.

The knowledge that the Percheron is superior to all other breeds, gained by personal investigation at the beginning of the importations of Oaklawn, has been the cause of the unswerving devotion of its proprietor to that race, confident that its supremacy would assert itself when the facts became thoroughly known to our people.

M. W. DUNHAM.

Oaklawn, November 1, 1887.

BRILLIANT 1271 [755], at head of Oaklawn Stud.
From Drawing by Rosa Bonheur.

STALLIONS IN SERVICE AT OAKLAWN.

BRILLIANT 1271 (755).

Black; 16¼ hands; weight 2,000 lbs.; foaled 1876; imported 1881; bred by M. Ernest Perriot, of Cheneliere, near Nogent-le-Rotrou, department of Eure-et-Loir; got by Brilliant 1899 (756); dam Ragout by Favori I (711) out of Aline by Coco (712).

BRILLIANT 1899 (756), by Coco II (714), out of Rosette by Mina, belonging to the French government.

Coco II (714), by Vieux-Chaslin (713), out of La Grise by Vieux-Pierre (883).

VIEUX-CHASLIN (713), by Coco (712).

Coco (712), by Mignon (715), out of Pauline by Vieux-Coco.

MIGNON (715), by Jean-le-Blanc (739), a direct descendant of the famous Arab, Gallipoli.

FAVORI I (711), by Vieux-Chaslin (713), etc.

ALINE by Coco (712), etc., out of Jeanette by Vieux-Coco.

In BRILLIANT we find concentrated the blood of the most noted Percheron stallions, all of which are traceable through their different lines directly to the famous Jean-le-Blanc, and through him possess the blood of the Arab, Gallipoli, thus intensifying in him those powers of reproduction that have made Brilliant the most noted sire of the Perche, his colts selling for far higher prices than the get of any stallion known in that country, and establishing the renown universally acceded to him, as evinced by the avidity with which his progeny are sought after, both in this country and France to place at the heads of the great breeding establishments of both countries.

The confidence I have in this horse has induced me to use him as far as possible on the mares at Oaklawn, and I hope to have, the coming season, at least sixty of his colts from choicest bred dams.

(Hoof No. 272.)　　**BON COEUR 3479 (367).**

Black; 16½ hands; weight, 1,800 lbs.; foaled 1881; imported 1884; got by BRILLIANT 1271 (755); dam Pelote by BRILLIANT 1899 (756) out of Margot by Coco II (714).

BRILLIANT 1271 (755), by Brilliant 1899 (756) out of Ragout by Favori I (711), he by Vieux-Chaslin (713) out of L'Amie by Vieux-Pierre (894), he by Coco (712).

BRILLIANT 1899 (756), by Coco II (714) out of Rosette by Mina, belonging to the French government.

Coco II (714), by Vieux-Chaslin (713) out of La Grise by Vieux-Pierre (883).

VIEUX-CHASLIN, (713) by Coco (712) out of Poule by Sandi.

Coco (712), by Mignon (715) out of Pauline by Vieux-Coco.

MIGNON (715), by Jean-le-Blanc (739).

LA FERTE 5144 (452).

Dapple grey; 16½ hands; weight, 1,910 lbs.; foaled 1881; imported 1886; bred by M. Guillemin of St. Germain-de-la-Coudre, canton of Theil, department of Orne; got by PHILIBERT (760); dam Julie (7594) by BRILLIANT 1899 (756).

PHILIBERT (760), by Superior 454 (730) out of Madelon by Vieux-Vaillant (1383), he by Pierre.

SUPERIOR 454 (730), by Favori I (711) out of Pauline by Vieux-Chaslin (713), he by Coco (712).

Coco (712), by Mignon (715) out of Pauline by Vieux-Coco.

MIGNON (715), by Jean-le-Blanc (739), a direct descendant of the famous Arab stallion Gallipoli.

BRILLIANT 1899 (756), by Coco II (714) out of Rosette by Mina (belonging to the French government).

Coco II (714), by Vieux-Chaslin (713), he by Coco (712), etc.

CATALOGUE FOR 1888,

COMPRISING DESCRIPTIONS AND PEDIGREES OF

IMPORTED AND PURE-BRED PERCHERONS

AT OAKLAWN.

ALL OF WHICH ARE RECORDED IN THE PERCHERON STUD-BOOK OF FRANCE
PUBLISHED UNDER AUTHORITY OF THE FRENCH GOVERNMENT.

The number following the name of the animal is the number as recorded in the Percheron Stud-Book of America; the number within parentheses is the number as recorded in the Percheron Stud-Book of France.

STALLIONS.

(Hoof No. 203.)   **ABOUKIR 3651 (1725).**

[Recorded with pedigree in the Percheron Stud-Books of France and America.]

Dapple grey; 16 hands; weight, 1,700 lbs.; foaled 1882; imported 1884; got by CLEMENT 1965 (936); dam Poule, belonging to M. Fourmy.

CLEMENT 1965 (936) by Philibert (760) out of Rustique by Coco II (714), he by Vieux-Chaslin (713) out of La Grise by Vieux-Pierre (883).
PHILIBERT (760) by Superior 454 (730) out of Madelon by Vieux-Vaillant (1383), he by Pierre out of a daughter of Vieux-Pierre (883).
SUPERIOR 454 (730) by Favori I (711) out of Pauline by Vieux-Chaslin (713).
FAVORI I (711) by Vieux-Chaslin (713) out of L'Amie by Vieux-Pierre (894), he by Coco (712).
VIEUX-CHASLIN (713) by Coco (712) out of Poule by Sandi.
Coco (712) by Mignon (715) out of Pauline by Vieux-Coco.
MIGNON (715) by Jean-le-Blanc (739).

(Hoof No. 54.)   **ABSALON 7017 (8605).**

[Recorded with pedigree in the Percheron Stud-Books of France and America.]

Dark grey; 16½ hands; weight, 1,750 lbs.; foaled February 3, 1885; imported 1887; bred by M. Challier, commune of Vichères, canton of Nogent-le-Rotrou, department of Eure-et-Loir; got by CHILDEBERT 4283 (451); dam Cocotte (5919) by NARBONNE 1334 (777) out of Biche.

CHILDEBERT 4283 (451) by Brilliant 1271 (755) out of Bijou (4644) by Duke of Perche 173 (740), he by Favori I (711) out of Franconie by Vieux-Pierre (883).
FAVORI I (711) by Vieux-Chaslin (713) out of L'Amie by Vieux-Pierre (894), he by Coco (712).
BRILLIANT 1271 (755) by Brilliant 1899 (756) out of Ragout by Favori I (711), etc.
BRILLIANT 1899 (756) by Coco II (714) out of Rosette by Mina, belonging to the French government.
Coco II (714) by Vieux-Chaslin (713) out of La Grise by Vieux-Pierre (883).
VIEUX-CHASLIN (713) by Coco (712) out of Poule by Sandi.
Coco (712) by Mignon (715) out of Pauline by Vieux-Coco.
MIGNON (715) by Jean-le-Blanc (739).
NARBONNE 1334 (777) by Brilliant 1899 (756), etc., out of Madelon (4722) by Favori I (711), etc.

(Hoof No. 125.) **ADORATEUR 6931 (10837).**

[Recorded with pedigree in the Percheron Stud-Books of France and America.]

Black; 16½ hands; weight, 1,710 lbs.; foaled May 15, 1883; imported 1887; bred by M. Mauger, commune of Margon, canton of Nogent-le-Rotrou, department of Eure-et-Loir; got by BRILLANT (710); dam Margot (10836) by BRILLANT (710).

BRILLANT (710) by Brilliant 1899 (756) out of Sophie by Superior 454 (730), he by Favori I (711) out of Pauline by Vieux-Chaslin (713).
FAVORI I (711) by Vieux-Chaslin (713) out of L'Amie by Vieux-Pierre (894), he by Coco (712).
BRILLANT 1899 (756) by Coco II (714) out of Rosette by Mina, belonging to the French government.
Coco II (714) by Vieux-Chaslin (713) out of La Grise by Vieux-Pierre (883).
VIEUX-CHASLIN (713) by Coco (712) out of Poule by Sandi.
Coco (712) by Mignon (715) out of Pauline by Vieux-Coco.
MIGNON (715) by Jean-le-Blanc (739).

(Hoof No. 50.) **ALARIC 6932 (6256).**

[Recorded with pedigree in the Percheron Stud-Books of France and America.]

Steel grey; 16¾ hands; weight, 1,900 lbs.; foaled March 12, 1884; imported 1887; bred by M. E. Bailleau, commune of Coudreceau, canton of Thiron, department of Eure-et-Loir; got by MARQUIS (1394); dam Cocote (6255) by SANSONNET, belonging to M. Ricois, out of Mouvette.

MARQUIS (1394) by Count 643 (736) out of Rosette by Madère.
COUNT 643 (736) by Bayard 26 (717) out of Bijou by Rustique.
BAYARD 26 (717) by Favori I (711) out of Mignonne by Chéri.
FAVORI I (711) by Vieux-Chaslin (713) out of L'Amie by Vieux-Pierre (894), he by Coco (712).
VIEUX-CHASLIN (713) by Coco (712) out of Poule by Sandi.
Coco (712) by Mignon (715) out of Pauline by Vieux-Coco.
MIGNON (715) by Jean-le-Blanc (739).

(Hoof No. 33.) **AMADIS 6933 (5946).**

Dark grey; 16½ hands; weight, 1,895 lbs.; foaled 1884; imported 1887; bred by M. Charles Gouhier, commune of Coudray, canton of Authon, department of Eure-et-Loir; got by RUSTIQUE 3601 (624); dam Robine (5945) by SANSONNET belonging to M. Sagot, out of Robine, belonging to M. Gouhier.

RUSTIQUE 3601 (624) by Raspail [son of Vigoureux (1392)] out of Rose.
VIGOUREUX (1392) by Coco II (714) out of Marguerite by Franconi, belonging to M. Sagot.
Coco II (714) by Vieux-Chaslin (713) out of La Grise by Vieux-Pierre (883).
VIEUX-CHASLIN (713) by Coco (712) out of Poule by Sandi.
Coco (712) by Mignon (715) out of Pauline by Vieux-Coco.
MIGNON (715) by Jean-le-Blanc (739).

(Hoof No. 40.) ### ANDRE 6934 (10531).

[Recorded with pedigree in the Percheron Stud-Books of France and America.]

Dark steel grey; 16¼ hands; weight, 1,750 lbs.; foaled March 24, 1884; imported 1887; bred by M. Renoud, commune of St. Hilaire-sur-Erre, canton of Theil, department of Orne; got by VAILLANT (404); dam Poule (8071) by PORTHOS, belonging to the French government.

VAILLANT (404) by Prosper (893) out of Rosalie by Bienvenu, belonging to the Société Hippique of Eure-et-Loir.
PROSPER (893) by Décidé (892) out of Bourreau by Vieux-Pierre (883).
DÉCIDÉ (892) by Vieux-Pierre (894) out of Pelote, belonging to M. Berjeau, of Courvalien.
VIEUX-PIERRE (894) by Coco (712), he by Mignon (715) out of Pauline by Vieux-Coco.
MIGNON (715) by Jean-le-Blanc (739).

(Hoof No. 32.) ### ARCOLE 6935 (5926).

[Recorded with pedigree in the Percheron Stud-Books of France and America.]

Dapple grey; 16½ hands high; weight, 1,850 lbs.; foaled April, 1884; imported 1887; bred by M. Gasnier, commune of Beaumont, canton of Anthon, department of Eure-et-Loir; got by RUSTIQUE 3601 (624); dam Poule (5925) by PORTHOS, belonging to the French government, out of Pécharde.

RUSTIQUE 3601 (624) by Raspail [son of Vigoureux (1392)] out of Rose.
VIGOUREUX (1392) by Coco II (714) out of Marguerite by Franconi, belonging to M. Sagot.
Coco II (714) by Vieux-Chaslin (713) out of La Grise by Vieux-Pierre (883).
VIEUX-CHASLIN (713) by Coco (712) out of Poule by Sandi.
Coco (712) by Mignon (715) out of Pauline by Vieux-Coco.
MIGNON (715) by Jean-le-Blanc (739).

(Hoof No. 42.) ### ARCOLE 7018 (9346).

[Recorded with pedigree in the Percheron Stud-Books of France and America.]

Dark grey; 16½ hands; weight, 1,760 lbs.; foaled April 28, 1885; imported 1887; bred by Madame Brouard, commune of St. Hilaire-sur-Erre, canton of Theil, department of Orne; got by VAILLANT (404); dam Princess (194) by MADÈRE, he by MARGOT 295 (795); 2d dam Bijou, belonging to M. Ferré.

VAILLANT (404) by Prosper (893) out of Rosalie by Bienvenu, belonging to the Société Hippique of Eure-et-Loir.
PROSPER (893) by Décidé (892) out of Bourreau by Vieux-Pierre (883).
DÉCIDÉ (892) by Vieux-Pierre (894) out of Pelote, belonging to M. Berjeau, of Courvalien.
VIEUX-PIERRE (894) by Coco (712), he by Mignon (715) out of Pauline by Vieux-Coco.
MIGNON (715) by Jean-le-Blanc (739).
MARGOT 295 (795) by Favori I (711), he by Vieux-Chaslin (713) out of L'Amie by Vieux-Pierre (894), etc.
VIEUX-CHASLIN (713) by Coco (712), etc., out of Poule by Sandi.

(Hoof No. 5.)   **ARMAGNAC 7020 (8695).**

[Recorded with pedigree in the Percheron Stud-Books of France and America.]

Dark grey; foaled March 17, 1886; imported 1887; bred by M. Cherré, commune of Préaux, canton of Nocé, department of Orne; got by POTENTAT (495); dam L'Amie (8559) by VIEUX-VAILLANT (1383).

POTENTAT (495) by Vaillant (404) out of Bouro by Favori I (711), he by Vieux-Chaslin (713) out of L'Amie by Vieux-Pierre (894), he by Coco (712).
VAILLANT (404) by Prosper (893) out of Rosalie by Bienvenu, belonging to the Société Hippique of Eure-et-Loir.
PROSPER (893) by Décidé (892) out of Bourreau by Vieux-Pierre (883).
DÉCIDÉ (892) by Vieux-Pierre (894) out of Pelote, belonging to M. Berjean, of Courvalien.
VIEUX-PIERRE (894) by Coco (712), he by Mignon (715) out of Pauline by Vieux-Coco.
MIGNON (715) by Jean-le-Blanc (739).
VIEUX-VAILLANT (1383) by Pierre, belonging to M. Thérin, out of a daughter of Vieux-Pierre (883).

(Hoof No. 212.)   **ARTISAN 5605 (7427).**

[Recorded with pedigree in the Percheron Stud-Books of France and America.]

Dark grey; 16½ hands; weight, 1,560 lbs.; foaled April 28, 1885; imported 1886; bred by M. Domin, commune of Bellavilliers, canton of Pervenchères, department of Orne; got by ROMULUS 3523 (222); dam Sublette (4908) by MOUTON.

ROMULUS 3523 (222) by Prosper (893) out of Bijou by Laboureur (886), he by Jean-le-Blanc (739) out of Sophie by Sandi.
PROSPER (893) by Décidé (892) out of Bourreau by Vieux-Pierre (883).
DÉCIDÉ (892) by Vieux-Pierre (894) out of Pelote, belonging to M. Berjeau, of Courvalien.
VIEUX-PIERRE (894) by Coco (712), he by Mignon (715) out of Pauline by Vieux-Coco.
MIGNON (715) by Jean-le-Blanc (739).

(Hoof No. 140.)   **ATTILA 7015 (6201).**

[Recorded with pedigree in the Percheron Stud-Books of France and America.]

Dark grey; 16½ hands; weight, 1,900 lbs.; foaled April 6, 1884; imported 1887; bred by M. Stanislas Royer, commune of Aunon, canton of Séez, department of Orne; got by LUTHER 4093 (212); dam Cocotte (209) by CHÉRI II, he by CHÉRI; 2d dam Cocotte.

LUTHER 4093 (212) by Luther (792), he by Pierre (887) out of Rosette by Laboureur (886).
PIERRE (887) by Laboureur (886) out of Margot by Faisan.
LABOUREUR (886) by Jean-le-Blanc (739) out of Sophie by Sandi.

(Hoof No. 34.)   **AUBEPIN 7019 (8383).**

[Recorded with pedigree in the Percheron Stud-Books of France and America.]

Steel grey; 16 hands; weight, 1,590 lbs.; foaled April, 1885; imported 1887; bred by M. Bailleau, commune of Argenvilliers, canton of Nogent-le-Rotrou, department of Eure-et-Loir; got by DÉCIDÉ (359); dam Castille (8382) by VAILLANT (2255).

DÉCIDÉ (359) by Vulcain (8003) (son of Vigoureux) out of L'Amie by Vaillant, belonging to Madame Dorchêne.
VAILLANT (2255) by Orizaba out of Pauline (279) by Miramar.

(Hoof No. 185.) **AUBRY 7014 (11542).**

[Recorded with pedigree in the Percheron Stud-Books of France and America.]

Grey ; 16¼ hands ; weight, 1,705 lbs. ; foaled May 2, 1885 ; imported 1887 ; bred by M. Dallier, commune of St. Denis, canton of Mortagne, department of Orne ; got by ROMULUS 3523 (222) ; dam Coquette (10175) by JUPITER 3895 (2253) ; 2d dam Frosine by FAVORI.

ROMULUS 3523 (222) by Prosper (893) out of Bijou by Laboureur (886), he by Jean-le-Blanc (739) out of Sophie by Sandi.
PROSPER (893) by Décidé (892) out of Bourreau by Vieux-Pierre (883).
DÉCIDÉ (892) by Vieux-Pierre (894) out of Pelote, belonging to M. Berjeau, of Courvalien.
VIEUX-PIERRE (894) by Coco (712), he by Mignon (715) out of Pauline by Vieux-Coco.
MIGNON (715) by Jean-le-Blanc (739).
JUPITER 3895 (2253) by Picador I (7330) out of Frosine by Favori.
PICADOR I (7330) by Bayard I (son of Picador) out of Charmante.

(Hoof No. 233.) **BADGER BOY 2490.**

[Recorded with pedigree in the Percheron Stud-Book of America.]

Grey ; 16¼ hands ; weight, 1,520 lbs. ; foaled 1883 ; bred by H. A. Babcock, of Neenah, Wisconsin ; got by VALENTINE 781 ; dam Clara Belle 795 (874) by ESTRABA 187 (796).

ESTRABA 187 (796), a descendant of Jean-le-Blanc (739).

(Hoof No. 259.) **BALLIETT 7161.**

[Recorded with pedigree in the Percheron Stud Book of America.]

Black ; foaled April 4, 1887 ; bred at Oaklawn ; got by BRILLIANT 1271 (755) ; dam Vinette 2752 (1495) by VALENTINE, he by DÉCIDÉ, he by FAVORI I (711) ; 2d dam Marie by CAMBRONNE.

BRILLIANT 1271 (755) by Brilliant 1899 (756) out of Ragout by Favori I (711).
BRILLIANT 1899 (756) by Coco II (714) out of Rosette by Mina, belonging to the French government.
Coco II (714) by Vieux-Chaslin (713) out of La Grise by Vieux-Pierre (883). .
VIEUX-CHASLIN (713) by Coco (712) out of Poule by Sandi.
Coco (712) by Mignon (715) out of Pauline by Vieux-Coco.
MIGNON (715) by Jean-le-Blanc (739).
FAVORI I (711) by Vieux-Chaslin (713), etc., out of L'Amie by Vieux-Pierre (894), he by Coco (712), etc.

(Hoof No 145.) **BAMBINOS 6936 (6428).**

[Recorded with pedigree in the Percheron Stud-Books of France and America.]

Dark dapple grey ; 16½ hands ; weight, 1,700 lbs. ; foaled March 20, 1883 ; imported 1887 ; bred by M. V. Evarard, commune of Barville, canton of Pervenchères, department of Orne ; got by SULTAN (1400) ; dam Docile (6427) by MADÈRE, belonging to Madame Pelletier, out of Mouvette, belonging to M. Evarard.

SULTAN (1400) by Count 643 (736) out of Rosette, belonging to M. Frederic Chouanard, by Madère.
COUNT 643 (736) by Bayard 26 (717) out of Bijou by Rustique.
BAYARD 26 (717) by Favori I (711) out of Mignonne by Chéri.
FAVORI I (711) by Vieux-Chaslin (713) out of L'Amie by Vieux-Pierre (894) he by Coco (712).
VIEUX-CHASLIN (713) by Coco (712) out of Poule by Sandi.
Coco (712) by Mignon (715) out of Pauline by Vieux-Coco.
MIGNON (715) by Jean-le-Blanc (739).

(Hoof No. 222.)   **BANCROFT 3667.**

[Recorded with pedigree in the Percheron Stud-Book of America.]

Brown bay; 16¾ hands; weight, 1,800 lbs.; foaled June 2, 1884; bred at Oaklawn; got by BRILLIANT 1271 (755); dam Constance 1478 (1425) by GRENADIER 688 (726) out of a daughter of TACHEAU 456 (745).

BRILLIANT 1271 (755) by Brilliant 1899 (756) out of Ragout by Favori I (711).
BRILLIANT 1899 (756) by Coco II (714) out of Rosette by Mina, belonging to the French government.
COCO II (714) by Vieux-Chaslin (713) out of La Grise by Vieux-Pierre (883).
VIEUX-CHASLIN (713) by Coco (712) out of Poule by Sandi.
COCO (712) by Mignon (715) out of Pauline by Vieux-Coco.
MIGNON (715) by Jean-le-Blanc (739).
GRENADIER 688 (726) by Comet 104 (719), he by French Monarch 205 (734) out of Suzanne by Cambronne.
FRENCH MONARCH 205 (734) by Ilderim (5302) out of a daughter of Vieux-Pierre (894), he by Coco (712).
ILDERIM (5302) by Valentin (5301) out of Chaton by Vieux-Pierre (894), etc.
VALENTIN (5301) by Vieux-Chaslin (713), etc.
TACHEAU 456 (745) by Favori I (711).
FAVORI I (711) by Vieux-Chaslin (713), etc., out of L'Amie by Vieux-Pierre (894), etc.

BANLIEU 7222.

[Recorded with pedigree in the Percheron Stud-Book of America.]

Black grey; foaled March 24, 1887; bred at Oaklawn; got by BRILLIANT 1271 (755); dam Francine 2744 (1577) by PHILIBERT (760) out of a daughter of MARGOT 295 (795).

BRILLIANT 1271 (755) by Brilliant 1899 (756) out of Ragout by Favori I (711).
BRILLIANT 1899 (756) by Coco II (714) out of Rosette by Mina, belonging to the French government.
COCO II (714) by Vieux-Chaslin (713) out of La Grise by Vieux-Pierre (883).
VIEUX-CHASLIN (713) by Coco (712) out of Poule by Sandi.
COCO (712) by Mignon (715) out of Pauline by Vieux-Coco.
MIGNON (715) by Jean-le-Blanc (739).
PHILIBERT (760) by Superior 454 (730) out of Madelon by Vieux-Vaillant (1383), he by Pierre out of a daughter of Vieux-Pierre (883).
SUPERIOR 454 (730) by Favori I (711) out of Pauline by Vieux-Chaslin (713), etc.
FAVORI I (711) by Vieux-Chaslin (713), etc., out of L'Amie by Vieux-Pierre (894), he by Coco (712), etc.
MARGOT 295 (795) by Favori I (711), etc.

(Hoof No. 249.)   **BANQUO 7235.**

[Recorded with pedigree in the Percheron Stud-Book of America.]

Dark grey; foaled April 15, 1887; bred at Oaklawn; got by BRILLIANT 1271 (755); dam Minda 2354 (1514) by BRILLIANT 1899 (756) out of Frizette by FRENCH MONARCH 205 (734).

BRILLIANT 1271 (755) by Brilliant 1899 (756) out of Ragout by Favori I (711), he by Vieux-Chaslin (713) out of L'Amie by Vieux-Pierre (894), he by Coco (712).
BRILLIANT 1899 (756) by Coco II (714) out of Rosette by Mina, belonging to the French government.
COCO II (714) by Vieux-Chaslin (713) out of La Grise by Vieux-Pierre (883).
VIEUX-CHASLIN (713) by Coco (712) out of Poule by Sandi.
COCO (712) by Mignon (715) out of Pauline by Vieux-Coco.
MIGNON (715) by Jean-le-Blanc (739).
FRENCH MONARCH 205 (734) by Ilderim (5302) out of a daughter of Vieux-Pierre (894), he by Coco (712), etc.
ILDERIM (5302) by Valentin (5301) out of Chaton by Vieux-Pierre (894), etc.
VALENTIN (5301) by Vieux-Chaslin (713), etc.

(Hoof No. 7.) **BAPTISTE 7029 (10088).**

[Recorded with pedigree in the Percheron Stud-Books of France and America.]

Dark grey; foaled April 11, 1886; imported 1887; bred by M. Alphonse Abot, commune of Ballon, canton of Ballon, department of Sarthe; got by VERMOUTH (5574); dam Charmante (10087) by FAVORI II, he by CHARMANT, he by VIGOUREUX, he by FAVORI I, belonging to M. Abot.

VERMOUTH (5574) by Favori II (see above) out of Frosine (5573) by Charmant, he by Vigoureux.

(Hoof No. 23.) **BARABAS 6937 (6027).**

[Recorded with pedigree in the Percheron Stud-Books of France and America.]

Black; 16 hands; weight, 1,750 lbs.; foaled April 28, 1884; imported 1887; bred by M. Roucheray, commune of Melleray, canton of Montmirail, department of Sarthe; got by MARTIN (5541), belonging to M. Lucas of Montmirail; dam Jaune (6026) by L'AMI (1388) out of Brebis.

L'AMI (1388) by Coco [son of Coco II (714)] out of Percheronne, belonging to M. Lucas.
Coco II (714) by Vieux-Chaslin (713) out of La Grise by Vieux-Pierre (883).
VIEUX-CHASLIN (713) by Coco (712) out of Poule by Sandi.
Coco (712) by Mignon (715) out of Pauline by Vieux-Coco.
MIGNON (715) by Jean-le-Blanc (739).

(Hoof No. 36.) **BARBANSON 7028 (8312).**

[Recorded with pedigree in the Percheron Stud-Books of France and America.]

Bay; 16¼ hands; weight, 1,660 lbs.; foaled March 1885; imported 1887; bred by the Count of Souancé, commune of Souancé, canton of Nogent-le-Rotrou, department of Eure-et-Loir; got by CHILDEBERT 4283 (451); dam Stella (62) by DÉCIDÉ, belonging to M. Fardouet père, out of Verveine, belonging to the Count of Souancé.

CHILDEBERT 4283 (451) by Brilliant 1271 (755) out of Bijou (4644) by Duke of Perche 173 (740), he by Favori I (711) out of Franconie by Vieux-Pierre (883).
FAVORI I (711) by Vieux-Chaslin (713) out of L'Amie by Vieux-Pierre (894), he by Coco (712).
BRILLIANT 1271 (755) by Brilliant 1899 (756) out of Ragout by Favori I (711), etc.
BRILLIANT 1899 (756) by Coco II (714), etc., out of Rosette by Mina, belonging to the French government.
Coco II (714) by Vieux-Chaslin (713) out of La Grise by Vieux-Pierre (883).
VIEUX-CHASLIN (713) by Coco (712) out of Poule by Sandi.
Coco (712) by Mignon (715) out of Pauline by Vieux-Coco.
MIGNON (715) by Jean-le-Blanc (739).

(Hoof No. 258.)   **BARRETT 7237.**

[Recorded with pedigree in the Percheron Stud-Book of America.]

Black; foaled May 1, 1887; bred at Oaklawn; got by BRILLIANT 1271 (755); dam Favorita 4360 (4410) by MADÈRE II (2994); 2d dam L'Amie (317) by BAYARD (1385); 3d dam Grenade by DÉCIDÉ.

BRILLIANT 1271 (755) by Brilliant 1899 (756) out of Ragout by Favori I (711), he by Vieux-Chaslin (713) out of L'Amie by Vieux-Pierre (894), he by Coco (712).
BRILLIANT 1899 (756) by Coco II (714) out of Rosette by Mina, belonging to the French government.
COCO II (714) by Vieux-Chaslin (713) out of La Grise by Vieux-Pierre (883).
VIEUX-CHASLIN (713) by Coco (712) out of Poule by Sandi.
COCO (712) by Mignon (715) out of Pauline by Vieux-Coco.
MIGNON (715) by Jean-le-Blanc (739).
MADÈRE II (2994) by Madeira 1546 (770), he by Vidocq 483 (732) out of Jeanne by Favori I (711), etc.
VIDOCQ 483 (732) by Coco II (714), etc., out of a daughter of Chéri, he by Rustique.
BAYARD (1385) by Vidocq 483 (732), etc., out of La Noire by Chéri, he by Coco II (714), etc.

(Hoof No. 265.)   **BASILE 7275.**

[Recorded with pedigree in the Percheron Stud-Book of America.]

Black; foaled October 5, 1887; bred at Oaklawn; got by BRILLIANT 1271 (755); dam Absala 5651 (6718) by BRILLIANT 1271 (755); 2d dam Poule (2032) by BRILLIANT 1899 (756) out of Chaton, belonging to M. Crenier.

BRILLIANT 1271 (755) by Brilliant 1899 (756) out of Ragout by Favori I (711), he by Vieux-Chaslin (713) out of L'Amie by Vieux-Pierre (894), he by Coco (712).
BRILLIANT 1899 (756) by Coco II (714) out of Rosette by Mina, belonging to the French government.
COCO II (714) by Vieux-Chaslin (713) out of La Grise by Vieux-Pierre (883).
VIEUX-CHASLIN (713) by Coco (712) out of Poule by Sandi.
COCO (712) by Mignon (715) out of Pauline by Vieux-Coco.
MIGNON (715) by Jean-le-Blanc (739).

(Hoof No. 16.)   **BAVARD 7030 (10278).**

[Recorded with pedigree in the Percheron Stud-Book of France and America.]

Black; 16½ hands; weight, 1,625 lbs.; foaled April 12, 1885; imported 1887; bred by M. Louis Jamois, commune of Dame-Marie, canton of Bellême, department of Orne; got by MADÈRE 6226 (692); dam Bijou (4378) by DOCILE (4446) out of Cocotte by FAISAN, belonging to M. Jamois, he by CHÉRI.

MADÈRE 6226 (692) by Vidocq (1403) out of Marie.
VIDOCQ (1403) by Utopia 780 (731) out of Bijou by Vieux-Chaslin (713).
UTOPIA 780 (731) by Superior 454 (730) out of Camille by Favori I (711), etc.
SUPERIOR 454 (730) by Favori I (711) out of Pauline by Vieux-Chaslin (713).
FAVORI I (711) by Vieux-Chaslin (713) out of L'Amie by Vieux-Pierre (894), he by Coco (712).
VIEUX-CHASLIN (713) by Coco (712) out of Poule by Sandi.
COCO (712) by Mignon (715) out of Pauline by Vieux-Coco.
MIGNON (715) by Jean-le-Blanc (739).
VIDOCQ 483 (732) by Coco II (714) out of a daughter of Chéri, he by Rustique.
DOCILE (4446) by Faisan (son of Chéri) out of Rose, belonging to M. Simon.

(Hoof No. 206.) **BAVARDO 7236.**

[Recorded with pedigree in the Percheron Stud-Book of America.]

Black ; foaled March 26, 1887 ; bred at Oaklawn, got by BRILL-
IANT 1271 (755) ; dam Bijourie 2759 (1527) by PRODUCTEUR, he by
FAVORA 1542 (765) ; 2d dam by PAPILLON, belonging to M. Miteau.

BRILLIANT 1271 (755) by Brilliant 1899 (756) out of Ragout by Favori I (711), he
    by Vieux-Chaslin (713) out of L'Amie by Vieux-Pierre (894), he by Coco
    (712).
BRILLIANT 1899 (756) by Coco II (714) out of Rosette by Mina, belonging to the
    French government.
Coco II (714) by Vieux-Chaslin (713) out of La Grise by Vieux-Pierre (883).
VIEUX-CHASLIN (713) by Coco (712) out of Poule by Sandi.
Coco (712) by Mignon (715) out of Pauline by Vieux-Coco.
MIGNON (715) by Jean-le-Blanc (739).
FAVORA 1542 (765) by French Monarch 205 (734) out of Marguerite by Favori,
    he by Coco of Mêsle-sur-Sarthe.
FRENCH MONARCH 205 (734) by Ilderim (5302) out of a daughter of Vieux-Pierre
    (894), etc.
ILDERIM (5302) by Valentin (5301) out of Chaton by Vieux-Pierre (894), etc.
VALENTIN (5301) by Vieux-Chaslin (713), etc.

(Hoof No. 206.) **BAYARD 4240 (1772).**

[Recorded with pedigree in the Percheron Stud-Books of France and America.]

Black ; 16½ hands ; weight, 1,705 lbs ; foaled June 20, 1882 ;
imported 1885 ; bred by M. Surcin, commune of Souancé, canton of
Nogent-le-Rotrou, department of Eure-et-Loir ; got by CHEER 2017
(1404) ; dam Lisette (1729) by PORTHOS, belonging to the French
government, out of Malice by ROLAND, belonging to the French government.

CHEER 2017 (1404) by Brilliant 1899 (756) out of Robine by Coco II (714).
BRILLIANT 1899 (756) by Coco II (714) out of Rosette by Mina, belonging to
    the French government.
Coco II (714) by Vieux-Chaslin (713) out of La Grise by Vieux-Pierre (883).
VIEUX-CHASLIN (713) by Coco (712) out of Poule by Sandi.
Coco (712) by Mignon (715) out of Pauline by Vieux-Coco.
MIGNON (715) by Jean-le-Blanc (739).

(Hoof No. 237.) **BEAU NOIR 5741.**

[Recorded with pedigree in the Percheron Stud-Book of America.]

Dapple grey ; 16 hands ; weight, 1,600 lbs.; foaled April 30, 1885 ;
bred by Jacob Hayden, of Sherburnville, Illinois ; got by ARBO 1935
(1031) ; dam Lulia 1494 by BEAU NOIR 913, out of Lucille 976 (1443)
by ORIZABA, belonging to M. Lalouet.

ARBO 1935 (1031) by Adonis 851 (861) out of a daughter of Décidé 126 (720), he
    by Superior 454 (730), he by Favori I (711) out of Pauline by Vieux-Chaslin
    (713).
ADONIS 851 (861) by Bayard 26 (717), he by Favori I (711) out of Mignonne by
    Chéri.
FAVORI I (711) by Vieux-Chaslin (713) out of L'Amie by Vieux-Pierre (894),
    he by Coco (712).
VIEUX-CHASLIN (713) by Coco (712) out of Poule by Sandi.
Coco (712) by Mignon (715) out of Pauline by Vieux-Coco.
MIGNON (715) by Jean-le-Blanc (739).

BEIDLER 7276.

[Recorded with pedigree in the Percheron Stud-Book of America.]

Black ; foaled October 2, 1887 ; bred at Oaklawn ; got by Bismark 5529 (633); dam Sapho 5637 (7030) by Vermouth (6276); 2d dam Rosette (7029) by Madeira 1546 (770) out of Poule.

Bismark 5529 (633) by Sultan (1395) out of Pelotte (7321) by Vigoureux (1392).
Sultan (1395) by Vigoureux (1392) out of Margot by Franconi, belonging to M. Sagot.
Vigoureux (1392) by Coco II (714) out of Marguerite by Franconi.
Coco II (714) by Vieux-Chaslin (713) out of La Grise by Vieux-Pierre (883).
Vieux-Chaslin (713) by Coco (712) out of Poule by Sandi.
Coco (712) by Mignon (715) out of Pauline by Vieux-Coco.
Mignon (715) by Jean-le-Blanc (739).
Vermouth (6276) by Vermouth 1820 (787) out of Rosalie (5986) by Bon Espoir, he by Vidocq 483 (732).
Vermouth 1820 (787) by Vidocq 483 (732) out of Agathe by Vieux-Chaslin (713), etc.
Vidocq 483 (732) by Coco II (714), etc., out of a daughter of Chéri, he by Rustique.
Madeira 1546 (770) by Vidocq 483 (732), etc., out of Jeanne by Favori I (711), he by Vieux-Chaslin (713), etc., out of L'Amie by Vieux-Pierre (894), he by Coco (712), etc.

BELFORT 7031 (8308).

[Recorded with pedigree in the Percheron Stud-Books of France and America.]

Dapple grey ; foaled April 18, 1886 ; imported 1887 ; bred by M. Gouhier, commune of Trizay, canton of Nogent-le-Rotrou, department of Eure-et-Loir ; got by Bismark 5529 (633); dam Rustique (8307) by Brillant (710).

Bismark 5529 (633) by Sultan (1395) out of Pelotte (7321) by Vigoureux (1392).
Sultan (1395) by Vigoureux (1392) out of Margot by Franconi, belonging to M. Sagot.
Vigoureux (1392) by Coco II (714) out of Marguerite by Franconi.
Coco II (714) by Vieux-Chaslin (713) out of La Grise by Vieux-Pierre (883).
Vieux-Chaslin (713) by Coco (712) out of Poule by Sandi.
Coco (712) by Mignon (715) out of Pauline by Vieux-Coco.
Mignon (715) by Jean-le-Blanc (739).
Brillant (710) by Brilliant 1899 (756) out of Sophie by Superior 454 (730), he by Favori I (711) out of Pauline by Vieux-Chaslin (713), etc.
Favori I (711) by Vieux-Chaslin (713), etc., out of L'Amie by Vieux-Pierre (894), he by Coco (712), etc.
Brilliant 1899 (756) by Coco II (714), etc., out of Rosette by Mina, belonging to the French government.

(Hoof No. 128.) **BELLOT 6938 (1635).**

[Recorded with pedigree in the Percheron Stud-Books of France and America.]

Dapple grey; 16½ hands; weight, 1,900 lbs.; foaled 1883; imported 1887; bred by M. Liberge, commune of St. Ouen-de-Cour, canton of Bellême, department of Orne; got by BAYARD (7519); dam Biche (4316) by VIDOCQ II (723) out of Biche.

BAYARD (7519) by Favora 666 (725) out of Pelotte, belonging to M. Noel.
FAVORA 666 (725) by Favori I (711) out of Marie by Coco (712).
FAVORI I (711) by Vieux-Chaslin (713) out of L'Amie by Vieux-Pierre (894), he by Coco (712).
VIEUX-CHASLIN (713) by Coco (712) out of Poule by Sandi.
Coco (712) by Mignon (715) out of Pauline by Vieux-Coco
MIGNON (715) by Jean-le-Blanc (739).
VIDOCQ II (723) by Bayard (1385) out of Brière by Décidé.
BAYARD (1385) by Vidocq 483 (732) out of La Noire by Chéri, he by Coco II (714).
VIDOCQ 483 (732) by Coco II (714) out of a daughter of Chéri, he by Rustique.
Coco II (714) by Vieux-Chaslin (713) out of La Grise by Vieux-Pierre (883).

(Hoof No. 132.) **BEMBO 7024 (7946).**

[Recorded with pedigree in the Percheron Stud-Books of France and America.]

Dark grey; 16¼ hands; weight, 1,690 lbs; foaled March 14, 1885; imported 1887; bred by M. J. Gouhier, commune of Trizay, canton of Nogent-le-Rotrou, department of Eure-et-Loir; got by BURG 4444 (2241); dam Castille (7945) by BRILLANT (710).

BURG 4444 (2241) by Rochambeau (1382) out of Trompette, belonging to M. Rigot.
ROCHAMBEAU (1382) by Brilliant 1899 (756) out of Cocotte by Coco II (714).
BRILLIANT 1899 (756) by Coco II (714) out of Rosette by Mina, belonging to the French government.
Coco II (714) by Vieux-Chaslin (713) out of La Grise by Vieux-Pierre (883).
VIEUX-CHASLIN (713) by Coco (712) out of Poule by Sandi.
Coco (712) by Mignon (715) out of Pauline by Vieux-Coco.
MIGNON (715) by Jean-le-Blanc (739).
BRILLANT (710) by Brilliant 1899 (756), etc., out of Sophie by Superior 454 (730), he by Favori I (711) out of Pauline by Vieux-Chaslin (713), etc.
FAVORI I (711) by Vieux-Chaslin (713), etc., out of L'Amie by Vieux-Pierre (894), he by Coco (712), etc.

(Hoof No. 47.) **BERTRAND 7164 (2924).**

[Recorded with pedigree in the Percheron Stud-Books of France and America.]

Dark grey; 16½ hands; weight, 1,845 lbs.; foaled March 29, 1884; imported 1887; bred by M. Alexandre Morin, commune of La Rouge, canton of Theil, department of Orne; got by ST. LAZARE 2383 (39); dam Margot (4617) by BAYARD, belonging to M. E. Perriot.

ST. LAZARE 2383 (39) by Narbonne 1334 (777) out of Bijou by Coco II (714).
NARBONNE 1334 (777) by Brilliant 1899 (756) out of Madelon (4722) by Favori I (711), he by Vieux-Chaslin (713) out of L'Amie by Vieux-Pierre (894), he by Coco (712).
BRILLIANT 1899 (756) by Coco II (714) out of Rosette by Mina, belonging to the French government.
Coco II (714) by Vieux-Chaslin (713) out of La Grise by Vieux-Pierre (883).
VIEUX-CHASLIN (713) by Coco (712) out of Poule by Sandi.
Coco (712) by Mignon (715) out of Pauline by Vieux-Coco.
MIGNON (715) by Jean-le-Blanc (739).

(Hoof No, 262.)   **BLASON 7230.**

[Recorded with pedigree in the Percheron Stud-Book of America.]

Black; foaled September 30, 1887; bred at Oaklawn; got by BRILLIANT 1271 (755); dam Frosine 4376 (4856) by FAVORA 1542 (765); 2d dam Pauline (4855) by BAYARD 26 (717) out of Rosette.

BRILLIANT 1271 (755) by Brilliant 1899 (756) out of Ragout by Favori I (711).
BRILLIANT 1899 (756) by Coco II (714) out of Rosette by Mina, belonging to the French government.
Coco II (714) by Vieux-Chaslin (713) out of La Grise by Vieux-Pierre (883).
VIEUX-CHASLIN (713) by Coco (712) out of Poule by Sandi.
Coco (712) by Mignon (715) out of Pauline by Vieux-Coco.
MIGNON (715) by Jean-le-Blanc (739).
FAVORA 1542 (765) by French Monarch 205 (734) out of Marguerite by Favori, he by Coco of Mesle-sur-Sarthe, he by Margot, belonging to M. Vallée.
FRENCH MONARCH 205 (734) by Ilderim (5302) out of a daughter of Vieux-Pierre (894), he by Coco (712), etc.
ILDERIM (5302) by Valentin (5301) out of Chaton by Vieux-Pierre (894), etc
VALENTIN (5301) by Vieux-Chaslin (713), etc.
BAYARD 26 (717) by Favori I (711) out of Mignonne by Chéri.
FAVORI I (711) by Vieux-Chaslin (713), etc., out of L'Amie by Vieux-Pierre (894), etc.

(Hoof No. 45.)   **BLEUET 6939 (5712).**

[Recorded with pedigree in the Percheron Stud-Books of France and America.]

Dark grey; 16¼ hands; weight, 1,610 lbs.; foaled March 15, 1884; imported 1887; bred by M. Jumeau, commune of Ceton, canton of Theil, department of Orne; got by VAILLANT (5708); dam Ragotte (5711) by MARGOT 2571 (1160) out of Ragotte.

VAILLANT (5708) by Utopia 780 (731) out of Cocotte, belonging to M. Simon.
UTOPIA 780 (731) by Superior 454 (730) out of Camille by Favori I (711).
SUPERIOR 454 (730) by Favori I (711) out of Pauline by Vieux-Chaslin (713).
FAVORI I (711) by Vieux-Chaslin (713) out of L'Amie by Vieux-Pierre (894), he by Coco (712).
VIEUX-CHASLIN (713) by Coco (712) out of Poule by Sandi.
Coco (712) by Mignon (715) out of Pauline by Vieux-Coco.
MIGNON (715) by Jean-le-Blanc (739).
MARGOT 2571 (1160) by Brilliant 1899 (756) out of Rustique by Vieux-Chaslin (713), etc.
BRILLIANT 1899 (756) by Coco II (714) out of Rosette by Mina, belonging to the French government.
Coco II (714) by Vieux-Chaslin (713) out of La Grise by Vieux-Pierre (883).

(Hoof No. 232.) **BOLINDA 7244.**

[Recorded with pedigree in the Percheron Stud-Book of America.]

Dark grey ; foaled March 20, 1887 ; bred at Oaklawn ; got by
BRILLIANT 1271 (755); dam Linda 2751 (1521) by VAILLANT (404) out
of a daughter of PIERRE (887).

BRILLIANT 1271 (755) by Brilliant 1899 (756) out of Ragout by Favori I (711),
  he by Vieux-Chaslin (713) out of L'Amie by Vieux-Pierre (894), he by
  Coco (712).
BRILLIANT 1899 (756) by Coco II (714) out of Rosette by Mina, belonging to the
  French government.
Coco II (714) by Vieux-Chaslin (713) out of La Grise by Vieux-Pierre (883).
VIEUX-CHASLIN (713) by Coco (712) out of Poule by Sandi.
Coco (712) by Mignon (715) out of Pauline by Vieux-Coco.
MIGNON (715) by Jean-le-Blanc (739).
VAILLANT (404) by Prosper (893) out of Rosalie by Bienvenu, belonging to the
  Société Hippique of Eure-et-Loir.
PROSPER (893) by Décidé (892) out of Bourreau by Vieux-Pierre (883).
DÉCIDÉ (892) by Vieux-Pierre (894) out of Pelote, belonging to M. Berjeau, of
  Courvalien.
VIEUX-PIERRE (894) by Coco (712), etc.
PIERRE (887) by Laboureur (886) out of Margot by Faisan.
LABOUREUR (886) by Jean-le-Blanc (739) out of Sophie by Sandi.

(Hoof No. 175.) **BON ESPOIR 7022 (5618).**

[Recorded with pedigree in the Percheron Stud-Books of France and America.]

Dark dapple grey ; 16½ hands ; weight, 1,800 lbs. ; foaled February 25, 1883 ; imported 1887 ; bred by M. Pelletier, commune of
Souvigny, canton of Mamers, department of Sarthe ; got by SULTAN
(4713); dam Frosine (7444) by PICADOR I, belonging to M. Lefeuvre,
he by BAYARD I ; 2d dam Bijou.

SULTAN (4713) by Bayard I (son of Picador) out of Bijou, belonging to M.
  Lefeuvre.

(Hoof No. 74.) **BON LURON 7027 (9408).**

[Recorded with pedigree in the Percheron Stud-Books of France and America.]

Steel grey ; 16¾ hands ; weight, 1,700 lbs. ; foaled May 15, 1885 ;
imported 1887 ; bred by M. Guillemin, commune of St. Cyr-la-Rosière,
canton of Nocé, department of Orne ; got by MONARCH (365); dam
Vermouth (4663) by DÉCIDÉ, belonging to M. Fardouet père, out of
Pelotte, belonging to M. Guillemin.

MONARCH (365) by Confidence 920 (763) out of Bijou, belonging to M. Fuanon.
CONFIDENCE 920 (763) by Favora 666 (725) out of Marie by Comet 104 (719), he
  by French Monarch 205 (734) out of Suzanne by Cambronne.
  FRENCH MONARCH 205 (734) by Ilderim (5302) out of a daughter of Vieux-
    Pierre (894), he by Coco (712).
  ILDERIM (5302) by Valentin (5301) out of Chaton by Vieux-Pierre (894), etc.
  VALENTIN (5301) by Vieux-Chaslin (713).
FAVORA 666 (725) by Favori I (711) out of Marie by Coco (712).
FAVORI I (711) by Vieux-Chaslin (713) out of L'Amie by Vieux-Pierre (894), etc.
VIEUX-CHASLIN (713) by Coco (712) out of Poule by Sandi.
Coco (712) by Mignon (715) out of Pauline by Vieux-Coco
MIGNON (715) by Jean-le-Blanc (739).

(Hoof No. 238.)   **BORDELAISE 5328.**

[Recorded with pedigree in the Percheron Stud-Book of America.]

Dark grey; foaled April 26, 1886; bred at Oaklawn; got by BRILLIANT 1271 (755); dam Aria 2207 (1414) by FORRESTER 674 (741).

BRILLIANT 1271 (755) by Brilliant 1899 (756) out of Ragout by Favori I (711) he by Vieux-Chaslin (713) out of L'Amie by Vieux-Pierre (894), he by Coco (712).
BRILLIANT 1899 (756) by Coco II (714), out of Rosette by Mina, belonging to the French government.
Coco II (714) by Vieux-Chaslin (713) out of La Grise by Vieux-Pierre (883).
VIEUX-CHASLIN (713) by Coco (712) out of Poule by Sandi.   •
Coco (712) by Mignon (715) out of Pauline by Vieux-Coco.
MIGNON (715) by Jean-le-Blanc (739).
FORRESTER 674 (741) by Vidocq 483 (732), he by Coco II (714), etc., out of a daughter of Chéri, he by Rustique.

(Hoof No. 226.)   **BRACARI 4340.**

[Recorded with pedigree in the Percheron Stud-Book of America.]

Dark grey; 16 hands high; weight, 1,510 lbs.; foaled May 24, 1885; bred at Oaklawn; got by BRILLIANT 1271 (755); dam Ione 2201 (1440) by LUTHER (792) out of a daughter of PORTHOS.

BRILLIANT 1271 (755) by Brilliant 1899 (756) out of Ragout by Favori I (711), he by Vieux-Chaslin (713) out of L'Amie by Vieux-Pierre (894), he by Coco (712).
BRILLIANT 1899 (756), by Coco II (714) out of Rosette by Mina, belonging to the French government.
Coco II (714) by Vieux-Chaslin (713) out of La Grise by Vieux-Pierre (883).
VIEUX-CHASLIN (713) by Coco (712) out of Poule by Sandi.
Coco (712) by Mignon (715) out of Pauline by Vieux-Coco.
MIGNON (715) by Jean-le-Blanc (739).
LUTHER (792) by Pierre (887) out of Rosette by Laboureur (886).
PIERRE (887) by Laboureur (886) out of Margot by Faisan.
LABOUREUR (886) by Jean-le-Blanc (739) out of Sophie by Sandi.

(Hoof No. 240.)   **BRANNOCK 5688.**

[Recorded with pedigree in the Percheron Stud-Book of America.]

Bay; foaled September 16, 1886; bred at Oaklawn; got by BRILLIANT 1271 (755); dam Janecia 2768 (1376) by FAVORI (1401) out of Jubine by PASSE-PARTOUT (1402).

BRILLIANT 1271 (755) by Brilliant 1899 (756) out of Ragout by Favori I (711), he by Vieux-Chaslin (713) out of L'Amie by Vieux-Pierre (894), he by Coco (712).
BRILLIANT 1899 (756) by Coco II (714) out of Rosette by Mina, belonging to the French government.
Coco II (714) by Vieux-Chaslin (713) out of La Grise by Vieux-Pierre (883).
VIEUX-CHASLIN (713) by Coco (712) out of Poule by Sandi.
Coco (712) by Mignon (715) out of Pauline by Vieux-Coco.
MIGNON (715) by Jean-le-Blanc (739).
FAVORI (1401) by Favora 1542 (765) out of Jeannette by Décidé, belonging to M. Vinault.
FAVORA 1542 (765) by French Monarch 205 (734) out of Marguerite by Favori, he by Coco of Mêsle-sur-Sarthe, he by Margot, belonging to M. Vallée.
FRENCH MONARCH 205 (734) by Ilderim (5302) out of a daughter of Vieux-Pierre (894), etc.
ILDERIM (5302) by Valentin (5301) out of Chaton by Vieux-Pierre (894), etc.
VALENTIN (5301) by Vieux-Chaslin (713), etc.
PASSE-PARTOUT (1402) by Comet 104 (719) out of Sophie by Favori I (711), etc.
COMET 104 (719) by French Monarch 205 (734) out of Suzanne by Cambronne.

(Hoof No. 239.) **BRANT 5690.**

[Recorded with pedigree in the Percheron Stud-Book of America.]

Black ; foaled March 28, 1886 ; bred at Oaklawn ; got by BRILL-
IANT 1271 (755) ; dam Rachel 1461 (1460) by SÉLIM (749) out of
Coquette by DUKE-DE-CHARTRES 162 (721).

BRILLIANT 1271 (755) by Brilliant 1899 (756) out of Ragout by Favori I (711), he
by Vieux-Chaslin (713) out of L'Amie by Vieux-Pierre (894), he by Coco
(712).
BRILLIANT 1899 (756) by Coco II (714) out of Rosette by Mina, belonging to the
French government.
Coco II (714) by Vieux-Chaslin (713) out of La Grise by Vieux-Pierre (883).
VIEUX-CHASLIN (713) by Coco (712) out of Poule by Sandi.
Coco (712) by Mignon (715) out of Pauline by Vieux-Coco.
MIGNON (715) by Jean-le-Blanc (739).
SÉLIM (749) by Porthos, belonging to M. Fromentin.
DUKE-DE-CHARTRES 162 (721) by Coco II (714), etc.

(Hoof No. 241.) **BRASTIN 5689.**

[Recorded with pedigree in the Percheron Stud-Book of America.]

Black ; foaled August 7, 1886 ; bred at Oaklawn ; got by BRILL-
IANT 1271 (755) ; dam Faustine 1314 (1431) by SÉLIM (749) out of
Sophia by DUKE-DE-CHARTRES 162 (721).

BRILLIANT 1271 (755) by Brilliant 1899 (756) out of Ragout by Favori I (711),
he by Vieux-Chaslin (713) out of L'Amie by Vieux-Pierre (894), he by
Coco (712).
BRILLIANT 1899 (756) by Coco II (714) out of Rosette by Mina, belonging to the
French government.
Coco II (714) by Vieux-Chaslin (713) out of La Grise by Vieux-Pierre (883).
VIEUX-CHASLIN (713) by Coco (712) out of Poule by Sandi.
Coco (712) by Mignon (715) out of Pauline by Vieux-Coco.
MIGNON (715) by Jean-le-Blanc (739).
SÉLIM (749) by Porthos, belonging to M. Fromentin.
DUKE-DE-CHARTRES 162 (721) by Coco II (714), etc.

(Hoof No. 251.) **BRAVADE 7227.**

[Recorded with pedigree in the Percheron Stud-Book of America.]

Dark grey ; foaled April 10, 1887 ; bred at Oaklawn ; got by
BRILLIANT 1271 (755) ; dam Palma 4359 (4929) by ROMULUS, belonging to M. Lalouet ; 2d dam Rosette (4928) by ROMULUS 873 (785) ; 3d
dam Cocotte, belonging to M. Foulon.

BRILLIANT 1271 (755) by Brilliant 1899 (756) out of Ragout by Favori I (711), he
by Vieux-Chaslin (713) out of L'Amie by Vieux-Pierre (894), he by Coco
(712).
BRILLIANT 1899 (756) by Coco II (714) out of Rosette by Mina, belonging to the
French government.
Coco II (714) by Vieux-Chaslin (713) out of La Grise by Vieux-Pierre (883).
VIEUX-CHASLIN (713) by Coco (712) out of Poule by Sandi.
Coco (712) by Mignon (715) out of Pauline by Vieux-Coco.
MIGNON (715) by Jean-le-Blanc (739).
ROMULUS 873 (785) by the government approved stallion Romulus (son of
Moreuil) out of Fleur-d'Epine by the government approved stallion Chéri,
he by Corbon.

(Hoof No. 142.)   **BRAVO 6940 (6617).**

[Recorded with pedigree in the Percheron Stud-Books of France and America.]

Dark grey ; 16½ hands high ; weight, 1,800 lbs.; foaled February 28, 1884 ; imported 1887 ; bred by M. Bion, commune of Authon-du-Perche, canton of Nogent-le-Rotrou, department of Eure-et-Loir ; got by RUSTIQUE 3601 (624) ; dam Robine (6616) by MOUTON, belonging to M. Sagot, out of Coquette.

RUSTIQUE 3601 (624) by Raspail [son of Vigoureux (1392)] out of Rose.
VIGOUREUX (1392) by Coco II (714) out of Marguerite by Franconi, belonging to M. Sagot.
Coco II (714) by Vieux-Chaslin (713) out of La Grise by Vieux-Pierre (883).
VIEUX-CHASLIN (713) by Coco (712) out of Poule by Sandi.
Coco (712) by Mignon (715) out of Pauline by Vieux-Coco.
MIGNON (715) by Jean-le-Blanc (739).

BREBIO 7231.

[Recorded with pedigree in the Percheron Stud-Book of America.]

Dapple grey ; foaled September 10, 1887 ; bred at Oaklawn ; got by LA FERTÉ 5144 (452) ; dam Brebis 4365 (1753) by BIJOU, belonging to M. Gautier, of Amilly ; 2d dam Brebis (5044) by SOLIDE, belonging to M. Fardouet.

LA FERTÉ 5144 (452) by Philibert (760) out of Julie (7594) by Brilliant 1899 (756) he by Coco II (714) out of Rosette by Mina, belonging to the French government.
Coco II (714) by Vieux-Chaslin (713) out of La Grise by Vieux-Pierre (883).
PHILIBERT (760) by Superior 454 (730) out of Madelon by Vieux-Vaillant (1383), he by Pierre out of a daughter of Vieux-Pierre (883).
SUPERIOR 454 (730) by Favori I (711) out of Pauline by Vieux-Chaslin (713).
FAVORI I (711) by Vieux-Chaslin (713) out of L'Amie by Vieux-Pierre (894), he by Coco (712).
VIEUX-CHASLIN (713) by Coco (712) out of Poule by Sandi.
Coco (712) by Mignon (715) out of Pauline by Vieux-Coco.
MIGNON (715) by Jean-le-Blanc (739).

BREEZE 7224.

[Recorded with pedigree in the Percheron Stud-Book of America.]

Black grey ; foaled April 18, 1887 ; bred at Oaklawn ; got by BRILLIANT 1271 (755); dam Milda 2806 (1542) by MADEIRA 1546 (770), out of a daughter of VIDOCQ 483 (732).

BRILLIANT 1271 (755) by Brilliant 1899 (756) out of Ragout by Favori I (711), he by Vieux-Chaslin (713) out of L'Amie by Vieux-Pierre (894), he by Coco (712).
BRILLIANT 1899 (756) by Coco II (714) out of Rosette by Mina, belonging to the French government.
Coco II (714) by Vieux-Chaslin (713) out of La Grise by Vieux-Pierre (883).
VIEUX-CHASLIN (713) by Coco (712) out of Poule by Sandi.
Coco (712) by Mignon (715) out of Pauline by Vieux-Coco.
MIGNON (715) by Jean-le-Blanc (739).
MADEIRA 1546 (770) by Vidocq 483 (732) out of Jeanne by Favori I (711), etc.
VIDOCQ 483 (732) by Coco II (714), etc., out of a daughter of Chéri, he by Rustique.

(Hoof No. 255.) **BREME 7229.**

[Recorded with pedigree in the Percheron Stud-Book of America.]

Dark grey; foaled April 7, 1887; bred at Oaklawn; got by BRILLIANT 1271 (755); dam Beatrice 4348 (4848) by LAGRANGE 3065 (1334); 2d dam Chopine (4847) by PAPILLON, he by PIERRE; 3d dam Chopine.

BRILLIANT 1271 (755) by Brilliant 1899 (756) out of Ragout by Favori I (711), he by Vieux-Chaslin (713) out of L'Amie by Vieux-Pierre (894), he by Coco (712).
BRILLIANT 1899 (756) by Coco II (714) out of Rosette by Mina, belonging to the French government.
Coco II (714) by Vieux-Chaslin (713) out of La Grise by Vieux-Pierre (883).
VIEUX-CHASLIN (713) by Coco (712) out of Poule by Sandi.
Coco (712) by Mignon (715) out of Pauline by Vieux-Coco.
MIGNON (715) by Jean-le-Blanc (739).
LAGRANGE 3065 (1334) by Brilliant 1271 (755), etc., out of Lydie by Coco II (714), etc.

(Hoof No. 263). **BRETTE 7278.**

[Recorded with pedigree in the Percheron Stud-Book of America.]

Dark grey; foaled October 1, 1887; bred at Oaklawn; got by BRILLIANT 1271 (755); dam Rustique 4367 (2165) by VIDOCQ, he by PICADOR 1254 (780); 2d dam Rustique (4881) by SÉLIM (749) out of Rose, belonging to M. Guillim.

BRILLIANT 1271 (755) by Brilliant 1899 (756) out of Ragout by Favori I (711), he by Vieux-Chaslin (713) out of L'Amie by Vieux-Pierre (894), he by Coco (712).
BRILLIANT 1899 (756) by Coco II (714) out of Rosette by Mina, belonging to the French government.
Coco II (714) by Vieux-Chaslin (713) out of La Grise by Vieux-Pierre (883).
VIEUX-CHASLIN (713) by Coco (712) out of Poule by Sandi.
Coco (712) by Mignon (715) out of Pauline by Vieux-Coco.
MIGNON (715) by Jean-le-Blanc (739).
PICADOR 1254 (780) by Picador (son of Favori, belonging to M. Dupont) out of Marguerite by Sélim (749).
SÉLIM (749) by Porthos, belonging to M. Fromentin.

(Hoof No. 254.) **BREVET 7228.**

[Recorded with pedigree in the Percheron Stud-Book of America.]

Black; foaled April 7, 1887; bred at Oaklawn; got by BRILLIANT 1271 (755); dam Rose 4364 (4330) by BRILLIANT 1899 (756); 2d dam Biche (5087) by PHILIPPE, belonging to M. Perriot père; 3d dam Cocotte, belonging to M. Glon.

BRILLIANT 1271 (755) by Brilliant 1899 (756) out of Ragout by Favori I (711), he by Vieux-Chaslin (713) out of L'Amie by Vieux-Pierre (894), he by Coco (712).
BRILLIANT 1899 (756) by Coco II (714) out of Rosette by Mina, belonging to the French government.
Coco II (714) by Vieux-Chaslin (713) out of La Grise by Vieux-Pierre (883).
VIEUX-CHASLIN (713) by Coco (712) out of Poule by Sandi.
Coco (712) by Mignon (715) out of Pauline by Vieux-Coco.
MIGNON (715) by Jean-le-Blanc (739).

(Hoof No. 250.)   **BREVIAIRE 7225.**

[Recorded with pedigree in the Percheron Stud-Book of America.]

Black ; foaled April 18, 1887 ; bred at Oaklawn ; got by BRILLIANT 1271 (755); dam Macaria 2797 (35) by BRILLIANT 1899 (756) out of Bijou by FAVORA 666 (725).

BRILLIANT 1271 (755) by Brilliant 1899 (756) out of Ragout by Favori I (711).
BRILLIANT 1899 (756) by Coco II (714) out of Rosette by Mina, belonging to the French government.
Coco II (714) by Vieux-Chaslin (713) out of La Grise by Vieux-Pierre (883).
VIEUX-CHASLIN (713) by Coco (712) out of Poule by Sandi.
Coco (712) by Mignon (715) out of Pauline by Vieux-Coco.
MIGNON (715) by Jean-le-Blanc (739).
FAVORA 666 (725) by Favori I (711) out of Marie by Coco (712), etc.
FAVORI I (711) by Vieux-Chaslin (713), etc., out of L'Amie by Vieux-Pierre (894), he by Coco (712), etc.

BRIANT 7223.

[Recorded with pedigree in the Percheron Stud-Book of America.]

Black ; foaled April 1, 1887 ; bred at Oaklawn ; got by BRILLIANT 1271 (755); dam Rachel 1461 (1460) by SÉLIM (749); 2d dam Coquette by DUKE-DE-CHARTRES 162 (721).

BRILLIANT 1271 (755) by Brilliant 1899 (756) out of Ragout by Favori I (711), he by Vieux-Chaslin (713) out of L'Amie by Vieux-Pierre (894), he by Coco (712).
BRILLIANT 1899 (756) by Coco II (714) out of Rosette by Mina, belonging to the French government.
Coco II (714) by Vieux-Chaslin (713) out of La Grise by Vieux-Pierre (883).
VIEUX-CHASLIN (713) by Coco (712) out of Poule by Sandi.
Coco (712) by Mignon (715) out of Pauline by Vieux-Coco.
MIGNON (715) by Jean-le-Blanc (739).
SÉLIM (749) by Porthos, belonging to M. Fromentin.
DUKE-DE-CHARTRES 162 (721) by Coco II (714), etc.

(Hoof No. 247.)   **BRIARDO 7234.**

[Recorded with pedigree in the Percheron Stud-Book of America.]

Dark grey ; foaled March 11, 1887 ; bred at Oaklawn ; got by BRIARD 5317 (1630); dam Peloute 5341 (4962) by CHARTRAIN (1405); 2d dam Cocotte (4961) by BRILLIANT 1899 (756); 3d dam Margot.

BRIARD 5317 (1630) by Brilliant 1271 (755) out of Pelotte (4885) by Brilliant, belonging to M. Thérin.
BRILLIANT 1271 (755) by Brilliant 1899 (756) out of Ragout by Favori I (711).
BRILLIANT 1899 (756) by Coco II (714) out of Rosette by Mina, belonging to the French government.
Coco II (714) by Vieux-Chaslin (713) out of La Grise by Vieux-Pierre (883).
VIEUX-CHASLIN (713) by Coco (712) out of Poule by Sandi.
Coco (712) by Mignon (715) out of Pauline by Vieux-Coco.
MIGNON (715) by Jean-le-Blanc (739).
CHARTRAIN (1405) by Philibert (760) out of Cocotte by Coco II (714), etc.
PHILIBERT (760) by Superior 454 (730) out of Madelon by Vieux-Vaillant (1383), he by Pierre out of a daughter of Vieux-Pierre (883).
SUPERIOR 454 (730) by Favori I (711) out of Pauline by Vieux-Chaslin (713), etc.
FAVORI I (711) by Vieux-Chaslin (713), etc., out of L'Amie by Vieux-Pierre (894), he by Coco (712), etc.

(Hoof No. 257.) **BRICKMAN 7245.**

[Recorded with pedigree in the Percheron Stud-Book of America.]

Dark grey; foaled 1887; bred by J. W. Smith, of Hiattville, Kansas; got by VALENCIENNE 2623 (1163); dam Rigolette 4357 (4931) by CHARTRAIN (1405); 2d dam Ragotte (4930) by SUPERIOR 454 (730) out of Caroline.

VALENCIENNE 2623 (1163) by Valentin out of Brebis by L'Ami.
VALENTIN by Décidé, he by Favori I (711), he by Vieux-Chaslin (713) out of L'Amie by Vieux-Pierre (894), he by Coco (712).
VIEUX-CHASLIN (713) by Coco (712) out of Poule by Sandi.
Coco (712) by Mignon (715) out of Pauline by Vieux-Coco.
MIGNON (715) by Jean-le-Blanc (739).
CHARTRAIN (1405) by Philibert (760) out of Cocotte by Coco II (714), he by Vieux-Chaslin (713), etc., out of La Grise by Vieux-Pierre (883).
PHILIBERT (760) by Superior 454 (730) out of Madelon by Vieux-Vaillant (1383), he by Pierre out of a daughter of Vieux-Pierre (883).
SUPERIOR 454 (730) by Favori I (711), etc., out of Pauline by Vieux-Chaslin (713), etc.

(Hoof No. 266.) **BRIGADIER 7277.**

[Recorded with pedigree in the Percheron Stud-Book of America.]

Dark grey; foaled May, 1887; bred by C. J. Wheeler, of Cedarville, New York; got by SATURN 1208; dam Lura 2793 (37) by BRILLIANT 1271 (755) out of Rosette by BRILLIANT 1899 (756).

BRILLIANT 1271 (755) by Brilliant 1899 (756) out of Ragout by Favori I (711), he by Vieux-Chaslin (713) out of L'Amie by Vieux-Pierre (894), he by Coco (712).
BRILLIANT 1899 (756) by Coco II (714) out of Rosette by Mina, belonging to the French government.
Coco II (714) by Vieux-Chaslin (713) out of La Grise by Vieux-Pierre (883).
VIEUX-CHASLIN (713) by Coco (712) out of Poule by Sandi.
Coco (712) by Mignon (715) out of Pauline by Vieux-Coco.
MIGNON (715) by Jean-le-Blanc (739).

(Hoof No. 159.) **BRILLANT 7021 (9797).**

[Recorded with pedigree in the Percheron Stud-Books of France and America.]

Steel grey; 16 hands; weight, 1,575 lbs.; foaled April 12, 1885; imported 1887; bred by M. Adolphe Miteau, commune of Essai, canton of Mêsle-sur-Sarthe, department of Orne; got by SOPHOCLE 3495 (1669); dam Brillante (6469) by PAPILLON (6800); 2d dam Rose (4032) by MIRAMAR, belonging to M. Lalouet, out of Biche, belonging to M. Germond.

SOPHOCLE 3495 (1669) by Avata 1966 (912) out of Ragotte by Bon Espoir, he by Vidocq 483 (732).
AVATA 1966 (912) by Nogent 738 (729) out of Bicotte by Bayard 26 (717), he by Favori I (711) out of Mignonne by Chéri.
FAVORI I (711) by Vieux-Chaslin (713) out of L'Amie by Vieux-Pierre (894), he by Coco (712).
NOGENT 738 (729) by Vidocq 483 (732) out of a daughter of Favori I (711), etc.
VIDOCQ 483 (732) by Coco II (714) out of a daughter of Chéri, he by Rustique.
Coco II (714) by Vieux-Chaslin (713) out of La Grise by Vieux-Pierre (883).
VIEUX-CHASLIN (713) by Coco (712) out of Poule by Sandi.
Coco (712) by Mignon (715) out of Pauline by Vieux-Coco.
MIGNON (715) by Jean-le-Blanc (739).
PAPILLON (6800) by Moutard (son of Coco of Mêsle-sur-Sarthe) out of Bijou by Coco (712), etc.

(Hoof No. 232.)   **BRISKE 7226.**

[Recorded with pedigree in the Percheron Stud-Book of America.]

Grey; foaled April 3, 1887; bred by M. Tacheau, commune of La Ferté-Bernard, department of Sarthe; got by BISMARK 5529 (633); dam Joyeuse 5682 (2839) by PRIMO (84) out of L'Amie (7461) by VIEUX-CHASLIN (713); 3d dam Rosette.

BISMARK 5529 (633) by Sultan (1395) out of Pelote (7321) by Vigoureux (1392).
SULTAN (1395) by Vigoureux (1392) out of Margot by Franconi, belonging to M. Sagot.
VIGOUREUX (1392) by Coco II (714) out of Marguerite by Franconi, belonging to M. Sagot.
Coco II (714) by Vieux-Chaslin (713) out of La Grise by Vieux-Pierre (883).
VIEUX-CHASLIN (713) by Coco (712) out of Poule by Sandi.
Coco (712) by Mignon (715) out of Pauline by Vieux-Coco.
MIGNON (715) by Jean-le-Blanc (739).
PRIMO (84) by Iago 995 (768) out of Rosalie by Bayard.
IAGO 995 (768) by Utopia 780 (731) out of Cossette by Favora 666 (725), he by Favori I (711) out of Marie by Coco (712).
UTOPIA 780 (731) by Superior 454 (730) out of Camille by Favori I (711).
SUPERIOR 454 (730) by Favori I (711) out of Pauline by Vieux-Chaslin (713), etc.
FAVORI I (711) by Vieux-Chaslin (713), etc., out of L'Amie by Vieux-Pierre (894), he by Coco (712), etc.

(Hoof No. 246.)   **BRISOIR 7233.**

[Recorded with pedigree in the Percheron Stud-Book of America.]

Dark grey; foaled April 12, 1887; bred at Oaklawn; got by BRILLIANT 1271 (755); dam Pecadie 4356 (1712) by BRILLIANT 1271 (755); 2d dam L'Amie (4948) by BAYARD 26 (717); 3d dam Sophie, belonging to M. Guignon.

BRILLIANT 1271 (755) by Brilliant 1899 (756) out of Ragout by Favori I (711).
BRILLIANT 1899 (756) by Coco II (714) out of Rosette by Mina, belonging to the French government.
Coco II (714) by Vieux-Chaslin (713) out of La Grise by Vieux-Pierre (883).
VIEUX-CHASLIN (713) by Coco (712) out of Poule by Sandi.
Coco (712) by Mignon (715) out of Pauline by Vieux-Coco.
MIGNON (715) by Jean-le-Blanc (739).
BAYARD 26 (717) by Favori I (711) out of Mignonne by Chéri.
FAVORI I (711) by Vieux-Chaslin (713), etc., out of L'Amie by Vieux-Pierre (894), he by Coco (712), etc.

(Hoof No. 223.)   **BRISUDAN 5330.**

[Recorded with pedigree in the Percheron Stud-Book of America.]

Black; foaled April 1, 1886; bred at Oaklawn; got by BRILLIANT 1271 (755); dam Isuda 2214 (1442) by BRILLIANT 1271 (755) out of a daughter of BAYARD 26 (717).

BRILLIANT 1271 (755) by Brilliant 1899 (756) out of Ragout by Favori I (711).
BRILLIANT 1899 (756) by Coco II (714) out of Rosette by Mina, belonging to the French government.
Coco II (714) by Vieux-Chaslin (713) out of La Grise by Vieux-Pierre (883).
VIEUX-CHASLIN (713) by Coco (712) out of Poule by Sandi.
Coco (712) by Mignon (715) out of Pauline by Vieux-Coco.
MIGNON (715) by Jean-le-Blanc (739).
BAYARD 26 (717) by Favori I (711) out of Mignonne by Chéri.
FAVORI I (711) by Vieux-Chaslin (713), etc., out of L'Amie by Vieux-Pierre (894), he by Coco (712), etc.

(Hoof No. 59.) **BRITANICUS 7025 (9294).**

[Recorded with pedigree in the Percheron Stud-Books of France and America.]

Grey; 16¼ hands; weight, 1,700 lbs.; foaled April 29, 1885; imported 1887; bred by M. Blanche, commune of St. Bomert, canton of Authon, department of Eure-et-Loir; got by PAMPHILE 6202 (285); dam Rustique (9293) by FAVORA 666 (725).

PAMPHILE 6202 (385) by Roland II (2256) ont of Biche.
ROLAND II (2256) by Roland I (son of Pamphile) out of Pauline (279) by Miramar.
FAVORA 666 (725) by Favori I (711) out of Marie by Coco (712).
FAVORI I (711) by Vieux-Chaslin (713) out of L'Amie by Vieux-Pierre (894), he by Coco (712).
VIEUX-CHASLIN (713) by Coco (712) out of Poule by Sandi.
Coco (712) by Mignon (715) out of Pauline by Vieux-Coco.
MIGNON (715) by Jean-le-Blanc (739).

(Hoof No. 66.) **BROCANTEUR 7026 (9496).**

[Recorded with pedigree in the Percheron Stud-Books of France and America.]

Dark grey; 16¼ hands; weight, 1,725 lbs.; foaled March 12, 1885; imported 1887; bred by M. Deshayes, commune of Préval, canton of La Ferté-Bernard; department of Sarthe; got by LA FERTÉ 5144 (452); dam Pelotte (7700) by BRILLIANT 1271 (755).

LA FERTÉ 5144 (452) by Philibert (760) out of Julie (7594) by Brilliant 1899 (756).
PHILIBERT (760) by Superior 454 (730) out of Madelon by Vieux-Vaillant (1383), he by Pierre out of a daughter of Vieux-Pierre (883).
SUPERIOR 454 (730) by Favori I (711) out of Pauline by Vieux-Chaslin (713).
FAVORI I (711), by Vieux-Chaslin (713) out of L'Amie by Vieux-Pierre (894), he by Coco (712).
VIEUX-CHASLIN (713) by Coco (712) out of Poule by Sandi.
Coco (712) by Mignon (715) out of Pauline by Vieux-Coco.
MIGNON (715) by Jean-le-Blanc (739).
BRILLIANT 1271 (755) by Brilliant 1899 (756) out of Ragout by Favori I (711), etc.
BRILLIANT 1899 (756) by Coco II (714) out of Rosette by Mina, belonging to the French government.
Coco II (714) by Vieux-Chaslin (713), etc., out of La Grise by Vieux-Pierre (883).

(Hoof No. 28.) **BRUTUS 6941 (6019).**

[Recorded with pedigree in the Percheron Stud-Books of France and America.]

Grey; 16¼ hands; weight, 1,920 lbs.; foaled 1884; imported 1887; bred by M. F. Letourneur, commune of Souancé, canton of Nogent-le-Rotrou, department of Eure-et-Loir; got by NOGENT 3769 (435); dam Bijou (6018) by BRILLANT (710) out of Louison.

NOGENT 3769 (435) by Madeira 1546 (770) out of Castille by French Monarch 205 (734), he by Ilderim (5302) out of a daughter of Vieux-Pierre (894), he by Coco (712).
ILDERIM (5302) by Valentin (5301) out of Chaton by Vieux-Pierre (894), etc.
VALENTIN (5301) by Vieux-Chaslin (713).
MADEIRA 1546 (770) by Vidocq 483 (732) out of Jeanne by Favori I (711), he by Vieux-Chaslin (713) out of L'Amie by Vieux-Pierre (894), etc.
VIDOCQ 483 (732) by Coco II (714) out of a daughter of Chéri, he by Rustique.
Coco II (714) by Vieux-Chaslin (713) out of La Grise by Vieux-Pierre (883).
VIEUX-CHASLIN (713) by Coco (712), etc., out of Poule by Sandi.
Coco (712) by Mignon (715) out of Pauline by Vieux-Coco.
MIGNON (715) by Jean-le-Blanc (739).
BRILLANT (710) by Brilliant 1899 (756) out of Sophie by Superior 454 (730), he by Favori I (711), etc., out of Pauline by Vieux-Chaslin (713).
BRILLIANT 1899 (756) by Coco II (714), etc., out of Rosette by Mina, belonging to the French government.

(Hoof No. 245.)   **BUREAUCRATE 7232.**

[Recorded with pedigree in the Percheron Stud-Book of America.]

Black; foaled September 1, 1887; bred at Oaklawn; got by BRILLIANT 1271 (755); dam Bellora 2237 (1415) by BRILLIANT 1271 (755) out of Thérèse by Coco II (714).

BRILLIANT 1271 (755) by Brilliant 1899 (756) out of Ragout by Favori I (711), he by Vieux-Chaslin (713) out of L'Amie by Vieux-Pierre (894), he by Coco (712).
BRILLIANT 1899 (756) by Coco II (714) out of Rosette by Mina, belonging to the French government.
Coco II (714) by Vieux-Chaslin (713) out of La Grise by Vieux-Pierre (883).
VIEUX-CHASLIN (713) by Coco (712) out of Poule by Sandi.
Coco (712) by Mignon (715) out of Pauline by Vieux-Coco.
MIGNON (715) by Jean-le-Blanc (739).

(Hoof No. 181.)   **BUTOR 7023 (9063).**

[Recorded with pedigree in the Percheron Stud-Books of France and America.]

Dark grey; 15¾ hands; weight, 1,600 lbs.; foaled April 20, 1885; imported 1887; bred by M. Jousselin, commune of St. Aubin, canton of Nocé, department of Orne; got by TURC (641); dam Rosette (9063) by MADÈRE, belonging to M. Jamois.

TURC (641) by Brillant (710) out of Sophie.
BRILLANT (710) by Brilliant 1899 (756) out of Sophie by Superior 454 (730), he by Favori I (711) out of Pauline by Vieux-Chaslin (713).
   FAVORI I (711) by Vieux-Chaslin (713) out of L'Amie by Vieux-Pierre (894), he by Coco (712).
BRILLIANT 1899 (756) by Coco II (714) out of Rosette by Mina, belonging to the French government.
Coco II (714) by Vieux-Chaslin (713) out of La Grise by Vieux-Pierre (883).
VIEUX-CHASLIN (713) by Coco (712) out of Poule by Sandi.
Coco (712) by Mignon (715) out of Pauline by Vieux-Coco.
MIGNON (715) by Jean-le-Blanc (739).

(Hoof No. 153.)   **CAMILLE 7034 (9280).**

[Recorded with pedigree in the Percheron Stud-Books of France and America.]

Bay; 16¼ hands; weight, 1,850 lbs.; foaled February 16, 1883; imported 1887; bred by M. Thirouard, commune of Charbonnieres, canton of Authon, department of Eure-et-Loir; got by VAILLANT (6752); dam Jubine (9279) by VIGOUREUX (1392).

VAILLANT (6752) by Bayard (6751) out of Grisette, belonging to M. Brette.
BAYARD (6751) by Mina, belonging to the Société Hippique of Eure-et-Loir, out of Louison by Chéri, belonging to M. Fardouet père, he by Couronne, belonging to M. Sagot.
VIGOUREUX (1392) by Coco II (714) out of Marguerite by Franconi, belonging to M. Sagot.
Coco II (714) by Vieux-Chaslin (713) out of La Grise by Vieux-Pierre (883).
VIEUX-CHASLIN (713) by Coco (712) out of Poule by Sandi.
Coco (712) by Mignon (715) out of Pauline by Vieux-Coco.
MIGNON (715) by Jean-le-Blanc (739).

(Hoof No. 129.) **CANADIEN 7033 (6653).**

[Recorded with pedigree in the Percheron Stud-Books of France and America.]

Grey; 16½ hands; weight, 1,800 lbs.; foaled May 25, 1884; imported 1887; bred by M. Campin, commune of Etilleux, canton of Authon, department of Eure-et-Loir; got by VOLTAIRE 3540 (443); dam Rustique (6652) by FAVORI (4770) out of Rustique.

VOLTAIRE 3540 (443) by Brilliant 1271 (755) out of Cocotte by Coco II (714).
BRILLIANT 1271 (755) by Brilliant 1899 (756) out of Ragout by Favori I (711).
BRILLIANT 1899 (756) by Coco II (714) out of Rosette by Mina, belonging to the French government.
Coco II (714) by Vieux-Chaslin (713) out of La Grise by Vieux-Pierre (883).
VIEUX-CHASLIN (713) by Coco (712) out of Poule by Sandi.
Coco (712) by Mignon (715) out of Pauline by Vieux-Coco.
MIGNON (715) by Jean-le-Blanc (739).
FAVORI (4770) by Superior 454 (730), he by Favori I (711) out of Pauline by Vieux-Chaslin (713), etc.
FAVORI I (711) by Vieux-Chaslin (713), etc., out of L'Amie by Vieux-Pierre (894), he by Coco (712), etc.

(Hoof No. 56.) **CANROBERT 7037 (9260).**

[Recorded with pedigree in the Percheron Stud-Books of France and America.]

Dark grey; 16½ hands; weight, 1,780 lbs.; foaled April 26, 1885; imported 1887; bred by M. Guillemin, commune of Ceton, canton of Theil, department of Orne; got by LA FERTÉ 5144 (452); dam L'Amie (7039) by VALENTIN (5301) out of Margot, belonging to M. Fausse-Abry.

LA FERTÉ 5144 (452) by Philibert (760) out of Julie (7594) by Brilliant 1899 (756), he by Coco II (714) out of Rosette by Mina, belonging to the French government.
  Coco II (714) by Vieux-Chaslin (713) out of La Grise by Vieux-Pierre (883).
PHILIBERT (760) by Superior 454 (730) out of Madelon by Vieux-Vaillant (1383), he by Pierre out of a daughter of Vieux-Pierre (883).
SUPERIOR 454 (730) by Favori I (711) out of Pauline by Vieux-Chaslin (713).
FAVORI I (711) by Vieux-Chaslin (713) out of L'Amie by Vieux-Pierre (894), he by Coco (712).
VIEUX-CHASLIN (713) by Coco (712) out of Poule by Sandi.
Coco (712) by Mignon (715) out of Pauline by Vieux-Coco.
MIGNON (715) by Jean-le-Blanc (739).
VALENTIN (5301) by Vieux-Chaslin (713), etc.

(Hoof No. 142.) **CAPITAINE 6942 (6240).**

[Recorded with pedigree in the Percheron Stud-Books of France and America.]

Dapple grey; 16¾ hands; weight, 2,050 lbs.; foaled April 4, 1883; imported 1887; bred by M. Richard, commune of Melleray, canton of Montmirail, department of Sarthe; got by L'AMI (1388); dam Poule (6239) by FAVORI, belonging to M. Th. Vinault, out of Brebis, belonging to M. Vadé.

L'AMI (1388) by Coco [son of Coco II (714)] out of Percheronne, belonging to M. Lucas.
Coco II (714) by Vieux-Chaslin (713) out of La Grise by Vieux-Pierre (883).
VIEUX-CHASLIN (713) by Coco (712) out of Poule by Sandi.
Coco (712) by Mignon (715) out of Pauline by Vieux-Coco.
MIGNON (715) by Jean-le-Blanc (739).

(Hoof No. 147.)   **CAPORAL 6943 (9568).**

[Recorded with pedigree in the Percheron Stud-Books of France and America.]

Dark grey; 16½ hands; weight, 1,810 lbs.; foaled March 2, 1884; imported 1887; bred by M. Deniau, commune of Authon, department of Eure-et-Loir; got by RUSTIQUE 3601 (624); dam Rosalie (9567) by LE NOIR, belonging to M. Sagot.

RUSTIQUE 3601 (624) by Raspail [son of Vigoureux (1392)] out of Rose.
VIGOUREUX (1392) by Coco II (714) out of Marguerite by Franconi, belonging to M. Sagot.
Coco II (714) by Vieux-Chaslin (713) out of La Grise by Vieux-Pierre (883).
VIEUX-CHASLIN (713) by Coco (712) out of Poule by Sandi.
Coco (712) by Mignon (715) out of Pauline by Vieux-Coco.
MIGNON (715) by Jean-le-Blanc (739).

(Hoof No. 157.)   **CARLOS 7035 (9276).**

[Recorded with pedigree in the Percheron Stud-Books of France and America.]

Steel grey; 16½ hands; weight, 1,705 lbs.; foaled May 22, 1884; imported 1887; bred by M. Gennit, commune of Gréez-sur-Roc, canton of Montmirail, department of Sarthe; got by COLIN (5723); dam Rigolette (9275) by VIEUX-DÉCIDÉ (4569).

COLIN (5723) by Colin, belonging to M. Lucas, out of Margot, belonging to M. Esnault.

(Hoof No. 1.)   **CAROLUS 7032 (8858).**

[Recorded with pedigree in the Percheron Stud-Books of France and America.]

Grey; foaled March 18, 1886; imported 1887; bred by M. Hamelin, commune of La-Chapelle-Souëf, canton of Bellême, department of Orne; got by ROMULUS (1807); dam Parfaite (8857) by PHILIBERT (4634).

ROMULUS (1807) by the government approved stallion Margot, belonging to M. Lucas, out of Biche, belonging to M. Lucas.
PHILIBERT (4634) by Philibert [son of Superior 454 (730)] out of Rustique, belonging to M. Lemesle.
SUPERIOR 454 (730) by Favori I (711) out of Pauline by Vieux-Chaslin (713).
FAVORI I (711) by Vieux-Chaslin (713) out of L'Amie by Vieux-Pierre (894), he by Coco (712).
VIEUX-CHASLIN (713) by Coco (712) out of Poule by Sandi.
Coco (712) by Mignon (715) out of Pauline by Vieux-Coco.
MIGNON (715) by Jean-le-Blanc (739).

(Hoof No. 150.)   **CASTEL 6944 (9278).**

[Recorded with pedigree in the Percheron Stud-Books of France and America.]

Grey; 16¼ hands; weight, 1,800 lbs; foaled March 2, 1884; imported 1887; bred by M. Deniau, commune of Soizé, canton of Authon, department of Eure-et-Loir; got by VAILLANT (6752); dam Rosette (9277) by Vigoureux (1392).

VAILLANT (6752) by Bayard (6751) out of Grisette, belonging to M. Brette.
BAYARD (6751) by Mina, belonging to the French government, out of Louison by Chéri, belonging to M. Fardouet père, he by Couronne, belonging to M. Sagot.
VIGOUREUX (1392) by Coco II (714) out of Marguerite by Franconi, belonging to M. Sagot.
Coco II (714) by Vieux-Chaslin (713) out of La Grise by Vieux-Pierre (883).
VIEUX-CHASLIN (713) by Coco (712) out of Poule by Sandi.
Coco (712) by Mignon (715) out of Pauline by Vieux-Coco.
MIGNON (715) by Jean-le-Blanc (739).

(Hoof No. 85.) ### CATALAN 6945 (10308).

[Recorded with pedigree in the Percheron Stud-Books of France and America.]

Dapple grey ; 16 hands ; weight, 1,795 lbs.; foaled April 15, 1884 ;
imported 1887 ; bred by M. Huet, commune of St. Bomert, canton of
Authon, department of Eure-et-Loir ; got by PAPILLON (2444) ; dam
La Bleue (10304) by SANSONNET, belonging to M. Sagot.

PAPILLON (2444) by Iago 995 (768) out of Sauvons-Nous, belonging to M. Surcin.
IAGO 995 (768) by Utopia 780 (731) out of Cossette by Favora 666 (725), he by
    Favori I (711) out of Marie by Coco (712).
UTOPIA 780 (731) by Superior 454 (730) out of Camille by Favori I (711).
SUPERIOR 454 (730) by Favori I (711) out of Pauline by Vieux-Chaslin (713).
FAVORI I (711) by Vieux-Chaslin (713) out of L'Amie by Vieux-Pierre (894), he
    by Coco (712).
VIEUX-CHASLIN (713) by Coco (712) out of Poule by Sandi.
Coco (712) by Mignon (715) out of Pauline by Vieux-Coco.
MIGNON (715) by Jean-le-Blanc (739).

(Hoof No. 232.) ### CHALDEAN, JR., 3874.

[Recorded with pedigree in the Percheron Stud-Book of America.]

Grey ; 15¾ hands ; weight, 1,520 lbs.; foaled 1884 ; bred by H. A.
Babcock, of Neenah, Wisconsin ; got by CHALDEAN 637 (854) ; dam
Clara Belle 795 (874) by ESTRABA (796).

CHALDEAN 637 (854) by Coco [son of Coco II (714)] out of a daughter of Supe-
    rior 454 (730), he by Favori I (711) out of Pauline by Vieux-Chaslin (713).
    FAVORI I (711) by Vieux-Chaslin (713) out of L'Amie by Vieux-Pierre (894).
Coco II (714) by Vieux-Chaslin (713) out of La Grise by Vieux-Pierre (883).
VIEUX-CHASLIN (713) by Coco (712) out of Poule by Sandi.
Coco (712) by Mignon (715) out of Pauline by Vieux-Coco.
MIGNON (715) by Jean-le-Blanc (739).

(Hoof No. 35.) ### CHANTILLY 7041 (8311).

[Recorded with pedigree in the Percheron Stud-Books of France and America.]

Black grey ; 15½ hands ; weight, 1,510 lbs.; foaled April 15, 1884 ;
imported 1887 ; bred by M. Pelletier, commune of Berd'huis, canton
of Nocé, department of Orne ; got by ADONAIS (83) ; dam Mouvette
(5559) by VIEUX-VAILLANT (1383) out of Rustique, belonging to M.
Coulonges.

ADONAIS (83) by Iago 995 (768) out of Bichette.
IAGO 995 (768) by Utopia 780 (731) out of Cossette by Favora 666 (725), he by
    Favori I (711) out of Marie by Coco (712).
UTOPIA 780 (731) by Superior 454 (730) out of Camille by Favori I (711).
SUPERIOR 454 (730) by Favori I (711) out of Pauline by Vieux-Chaslin (713).
FAVORI I (711) by Vieux-Chaslin (713) out of L'Amie by Vieux-Pierre (894), he
    by Coco (712).
VIEUX-CHASLIN (713) by Coco (712) out of Poule by Sandi.
Coco (712) by Mignon (715) out of Pauline by Vieux-Coco.
MIGNON (715) by Jean-le-Blanc (739).
VIEUX-VAILLANT (1383) by Pierre, belonging to M. Thérin, out of a daughter
    of Vieux-Pierre (883).

(Hoof No. 65.)   **CHAPTAL 7038 (9288).**

[Recorded with pedigree in the Percheron Stud-Books of France and America.]

Dark grey; 16 hands; weight, 1,600 lbs.; foaled March, 1885; imported 1887; bred by M. Besard, commune of Lavarre, canton of Vibraye, department of Sarthe; got by CHARMANT (3073); dam Biche (9287) by FAVORI, belonging to M. Lucas.

CHARMANT (3073) by Passe-Partout (1402) out of Louison, belonging to M. Lucas.
PASSE-PARTOUT (1402) by Comet 104 (719) out of Sophie by Favori I (711), he by Vieux-Chaslin (713) out of L'Amie by Vieux-Pierre (894), he by Coco (712).
COMET 104 (719) French Monarch 205 (734) out of Suzanne by Cambronne.
FRENCH MONARCH 205 (734) by Ilderim (5302) out of a daughter of Vieux-Pierre (894), he by Coco (712).
ILDERIM (5302) by Valentin (5301) out of Chaton by Vieux-Pierre (894), etc.
VALENTIN (5301) by Vieux-Chaslin (713), he by Coco (712) out of Poule by Sandi.
Coco (712) by Mignon (715) out of Pauline by Vieux-Coco.
MIGNON (715) by Jean-le-Blanc (739).

(Hoof No. 27.)   **CHARMANT 7042 (7334).**

[Recorded with pedigree in the Percheron Stud-Books of France and America.]

Black; 16¾ hands; weight, 1,850 lbs.; foaled February 5, 1881; imported 1887; bred by M. Arsené Lefeuvre, commune of Marolles-les-Braux, department of Sarthe; got by Coco, belonging to M. Lefeuvre; dam Rose (7450) by PICADOR, he by BAYARD; 2d dam Coquette by CHARMANT.

(Hoof No. 270.)   **CHÉRI 5148 (5614).**

[Recorded with pedigree in the Percheron Stud-Books of France and America.]

Bay; foaled April 8, 1882; imported 1886; bred by M. Lefeuvre, commune of Marolles-les-Braux, canton of Marolles-les-Braux, department of Sarthe; got by VERMOUTH (5497); dam Biche (7328) by BAYARD I out of Marianne, belonging to M. Lefeuvre.

VERMOUTH (5497) by Picador I (7330) out of Charmante by Oscar.
PICADOR I (7330) by Bayard I (son of Picador) out of Rose.

(Hoof No. 107.) **CHERUBIN 6946 (11241).**

[Recorded with pedigree in the Percheron Stud-Books of France and America.]

Black; 16 hands; weight, 1,590 lbs.; foaled March 19, 1883; imported 1887; bred by M. Delcuzé, commune of Sérigny, canton of Bellême, department of Orne; got by AVATA 1966 (912); dam Bijou (11240) by VIDOCQ II (723).

AVATA 1966 (912) by Nogent 738 (729) out of Bicotte by Bayard 26 (717), he by
    Favori I (711) out of Mignonne by Chéri.
    FAVORI I (711) by Vieux-Chaslin (713) out of L'Amie by Vieux-Pierre (894),
      he by Coco (712).
NOGENT 738 (729) by Vidocq 483 (732) out of a daughter of Favori I (711), etc.
VIDOCQ 483 (732) by Coco II (714) out of a daughter of Chéri, he by Rustique.
Coco II (714) by Vieux-Chaslin (713) out of La Grise by Vieux-Pierre (883).
VIEUX-CHASLIN (713) by Coco (712) out of Poule by Sandi.
Coco (712) by Mignon (715) out of Pauline by Vieux-Coco.
MIGNON (715) by Jean-le-Blanc (739).
VIDOCQ II (723) by Bayard (1385) out of Brière by Décidé, belonging to M.
    Vinault.
BAYARD (1385) by Vidocq 483 (732), etc., out of La Noire by Chéri, he by Coco
    II (714), etc.

(Hoof No. 110.) **CHICAGO 6947 (7485).**

[Recorded with pedigree in the Percheron Stud-Books of France and America.]

Black; 16¾ hands; weight, 1,900 lbs.; foaled May, 1883; imported 1887; bred by M. Boulay, commune of Dame-Marie, canton of Bellême, department of Orne; got by AVATA 1966 (912); dam Bijou (302) by VIDOCQ 483 (732).

AVATA 1966 (912) by Nogent 738 (729) out of Bicotte by Bayard 26 (717), he by
    Favori I (711) out of Mignonne by Cheri.
    FAVORI I (711) by Vieux-Chaslin (713) out of L'Amie by Vieux-Pierre (894), he
      by Coco (712).
NOGENT 738 (729) by Vidocq 483 (732) out of a daughter of Favori I (711), etc.
VIDOCQ 483 (732) by Coco II (714) out of a daughter of Chéri, he by Rustique.
Coco II (714) by Vieux-Chaslin (713) out of La Grise by Vieux-Pierre (883).
VIEUX-CHASLIN (713) by Coco (712) out of Poule by Sandi.
Coco (712) by Mignon (715) out of Pauline by Vieux-Coco.
MIGNON (715) by Jean-le-Blanc (739).

(Hoof No. 72.) **CHRAM 6948 (9406).**

[Recorded with pedigree in the Percheron Stud-Books of France and America.]

Black; 16 hands; weight, 1,700 lbs.; foaled April 14, 1884; imported 1887; bred by M. Berger, commune of Vichères, canton of Nogent-le-Rotrou, department of Eure-et-Loir; got by MARQUIS (1394); dam Poule (9405) by ROLAND II (7279).

MARQUIS (1394) by Count 643 (736) out of Rosette (belonging to M. F. Choua-
    nard) by Madère.
COUNT 643 (736) by Bayard 26 (717) out of Bijou by Rustique.
BAYARD 26 (717) by Favori I (711), etc., out of Mignonne by Chéri.
FAVORI I (711) by Vieux-Chaslin (713) out of L'Amie by Vieux-Pierre (894), he
    by Coco (712).
VIEUX-CHASLIN (713) by Coco (712) out of Poule by Sandi.
Coco (712) by Mignon (715) out of Pauline by Vieux-Coco.
MIGNON (715) by Jean-le-Blanc (739).
ROLAND II (7279) by Roland I (son of Pamphile, belonging to the Société
    Hippique of Eure-et-Loir) out of Poule, belonging to M. Bouvereau.

(Hoof No. 176.) **CLOVIS IV 7036 (11350).**

[Recorded with pedigree in the Percheron Stud-Books of France and America.]

Dark grey; 15½ hands; weight, 1,425 lbs.; foaled April 5, 1885; imported 1887; bred by M. E. Morin, commune of Marolles-les-Braux, department of Sarthe; got by PICADOR II (5606); dam Charmante (7326) by FAVORI II (7332) out of Rose, belonging to M. Morin.

PICADOR II (5606) by Picador I (7330) out of Rose.
PICADOR I (7330) by Bayard I (son of Picador) out of Charmante.
FAVORI II (7332) by Favori I, belonging to M. Lefeuvre, out of Frosine.

(Hoof No. 75.) **COLBERT 7039 (9410).**

[Recorded with pedigree in the Percheron Stud-Books of France and America.]

Black; 16½ hands; weight, 1,650 lbs.; foaled April 1, 1885; imported 1887; bred by M. Simon, commune of Gué-de-la-Chaine, canton of Bellême, department of Orne; got by BRILLANT 4285 (2252); dam Pelotte (9409) by PHILIBERT (4634).

BRILLANT 4285 (2252) by Picador I (7330) out of Josephine (4787) by Miramar.
PICADOR I (7330) by Bayard I (son of Picador) out of Charmante.
PHILIBERT (4634) by Philibert [son of Superior 454 (730)] out of Rustique, belonging to M. Lemesle.
SUPERIOR 454 (730) by Favori I (711) out of Pauline by Vieux-Chaslin (713), etc.
FAVORI I (711) by Vieux-Chaslin (713) out of L'Amie by Vieux-Pierre (894), he by Coco (712).
VIEUX-CHASLIN (713) by Coco (712) out of Poule by Sandi.
Coco (712) by Mignon (715) out of Pauline by Vieux-Coco.
MIGNON (715) by Jean-le-Blanc (739).

(Hoof No. 124.) **COLIN 6949 (10833).**

[Recorded with pedigree in the Percheron Stud-Books of France and America.]

Dark grey; 16½ hands; weight, 1,800 lbs.; foaled March 8, 1883; imported 1887; bred by M. Berger, commune of Thiron, department of Eure-et-Loir; got by BRILLANT (4737); dam Poule (10832).

BRILLANT (4737) by L'Ami (1388), he by Coco [son of Coco II (714)] out of Percheronne, belonging to M. Lucas.
Coco II (714) by Vieux-Chaslin (713) out of La Grise by Vieux-Pierre (883).
VIEUX-CHASLIN (713) by Coco (712) out of Poule by Sandi.
Coco (712) by Mignon (715) out of Pauline by Vieux-Coco.
MIGNON (715) by Jean-le-Blanc (739).

(Hoof No. 210.) **COMTE LOBAU 5531 (5490).**

[Recorded with pedigree in the Percheron Stud-Books of France and America.]

Dapple grey; 16¼ hands; weight, 1,685 lbs.; foaled May 1, 1882; imported 1886; bred by M. Seguin, commune of Brunelles, canton of Nogent-le-Rotrou, department of Eure-et-Loir; got by CHÉRI (4137); dam L'Amie (5489) by RUSTIQUE, he by VAILLANT.

CHÉRI (4137) by Bijou, belonging to M. Fardouet père, out of Biche, belonging to M. Debray.

(Hoof No. 82.) **CORUBERT 6950 (10239).**

[Recorded with pedigree in the Percheron Stud-Books of France and America.]

Black; 15½ hands; weight, 1,625 lbs.; foaled March 25, 1884; imported 1887; bred by M. Chartrain, commune of Corubert, canton of Nocé, department of Orne; got by Gérome 3655 (436); dam Biche (9861) by Madeira 1542 (770).

Gérome 3655 (436) by Vidocq II (723) out of Pelote by Superior 454 (730), he by Favori I (711) out of Pauline by Vieux-Chaslin (713).
    Favori I (711) by Vieux-Chaslin (713) out of L'Amie by Vieux-Pierre (894), he by Coco (712).
Vidocq II (723) by Bayard (1385) out of Brière by Décidé.
Bayard (1385) by Vidocq 483 (732) out of La Noire by Chéri, he by Coco II (714).
Vidocq 483 (732) by Coco II (714) out of a daughter of Chéri, he by Rustique.
Coco II (714) by Vieux-Chaslin (713) out of La Grise by Vieux-Pierre (883).
Vieux-Chaslin (713) by Coco (712) out of Poule by Sandi.
Coco (712) by Mignon (715) out of Pauline by Vieux-Coco.
Mignon (715) by Jean-le-Blanc (739).
Madeira 1546 (770) by Vidocq 483 (732), etc., out of Jeanne by Favori I (711), etc.

(Hoof No. 78.) **COURCERAULT 7040 (9327).**

[Recorded with pedigree in the Percheron Stud-Books of France and America.]

Dark grey; 16 hands; weight, 1,700 lbs.; foaled April 15, 1885; imported 1887; bred by M. Chaumier, commune of Courcerault, canton of Nocé, department of Orne; got by Bon Cœur 3479 (367); dam Chaton (9326) by Coco 1269 (762).

Bon Cœur 3479 (367) by Brilliant 1271 (755) out of Pelote by Brilliant 1899 (756).
Brilliant 1271 (755) by Brilliant 1899 (756) out of Ragout by Favori I (711).
Brilliant 1899 (756) by Coco II (714) out of Rosette by Mina, belonging to the French government.
Coco II (714) by Vieux-Chaslin (713) out of La Grise by Vieux-Pierre (883).
Vieux-Chaslin (713) by Coco (712) out of Poule by Sandi.
Coco (712) by Mignon (715) out of Pauline by Vieux-Coco.
Mignon (715) by Jean-le-Blanc (739).
Coco 1269 (762) by Favora 666 (725) out of a daughter of Duke-de-Chartres 162 (721), he by Coco II (714), etc.
Favora 666 (725) by Favori I (711) out of Marie by Coco (712), etc.
Favori I (711) by Vieux-Chaslin (713), etc., out of L'Amie by Vieux-Pierre (894), he by Coco (712), etc.

(Hoof No. 100.)   **CYGNE 6951 (6956).**

[Recorded with pedigree in Percheron Stud-Books of France and America.]

Light dapple grey ; 16¾ hands ; weight, 2,100 lbs. ; foaled March 15, 1883 ; imported 1887 ; bred by M. Brouard, commune of St. Martin, canton of La Ferté-Bernard, department of Sarthe ; got by COLIN (1390) ; dam Favorite (6955) by FAVORA 1542 (765) out of Vieille-Favorite.

COLIN (1390) by Passe-Partout (1402) out of a daughter of Vieux-Chaslin (713).
PASSE-PARTOUT (1402) by Comet 104 (719) out of Sophie by Favori I (711), he by Vieux-Chaslin (713) out of L'Amie by Vieux-Pierre (894), he by Coco (712).
COMET 104 (719) by French Monarch 205 (734) out of Suzanne by Cambronne.
FRENCH MONARCH 205 (734) by Ilderim (5302) out of a daughter of Vieux-Pierre (894), etc.
ILDERIM (5302) by Valentin (5301) out of Chaton by Vieux-Pierre (894), etc.
VALENTIN (5301) by Vieux-Chaslin (713), he by Coco (712) out of Poule by Sandi.
Coco (712) by Mignon (715) out of Pauline by Vieux-Coco.
MIGNON (715) by Jean-le-Blanc (739).
FAVORA 1542 (765) by French Monarch 205 (734), etc., out of Marguerite by Favori, he by Coco of Mêsle-sur-Sarthe, he by Margot, belonging to M. Vallée.

(Hoof No. 204.)   **DANTE 2158 (941).**

[Recorded with pedigree in the Percheron Stud-Books of France and America.]

Dapple grey ; 16½ hands ; weight, 1,820 lbs. ; foaled 1882 ; imported 1882 ; got by AVATA 1966 (912) ; dam by FAVORA 666 (725).

AVATA 1966 (912) by Nogent 738 (729) out of Bicotte by Bayard 26 (717), he by Favori I (711) out of Mignonne by Chéri.
    FAVORI I (711) by Vieux-Chaslin (713) out of L'Amie by Vieux-Pierre (894), he by Coco (712).
NOGENT 738 (729) by Vidocq 483 (732) out of a daughter of Favori I (711), etc.
VIDOCQ 483 (732) by Coco II (714) out of a daughter of Chéri, he by Rustique.
Coco II (714) by Vieux-Chaslin (713) out of La Grise by Vieux-Pierre (883).
VIEUX-CHASLIN (713) by Coco (712) out of Poule by Sandi.
Coco (712) by Mignon (715) out of Pauline by Vieux-Coco.
MIGNON (715) by Jean-le-Blanc (739).
FAVORA 666 (725) by Favori I (711), etc., out of Marie by Coco (712), etc.

(Hoof No. 95.)   **DAVID 7045 (9059).**

[Recorded with pedigree in the Percheron Stud-Books of France and America.]

Steel grey ; 16¾ hands ; weight, 1,625 lbs.; foaled April 24, 1885 ; imported 1887 ; bred by M. Blin, commune of Frazé, canton of Thiron, department of Eure-et-Loir ; got by PAPILLON (2444); dam Pelotte (8956) by FAVORI, belonging to M. Bouvard.

PAPILLON (2444) by Iago 995 (768) out of Sauvons-Nous, belonging to M. Surcin.
IAGO 995 (768) by Utopia 780 (731) out of Cossette by Favora 666 (725), he by Favori I (711) out of Marie by Coco (712).
UTOPIA 780 (731) by Superior 454 (730) out of Camille by Favori I (711).
SUPERIOR 454 (730) by Favori I (711) out of Pauline by Vieux-Chaslin (713).
FAVORI I (711) by Vieux-Chaslin (713) out of L'Amie by Vieux-Pierre (894), he by Coco (712).
VIEUX-CHASLIN (713) by Coco (712) out of Poule by Sandi.
Coco (712) by Mignon (715) out of Pauline by Vieux-Coco.
MIGNON (715) by Jean-le-Blanc (739).

(Hoof No. 80.)   **DÉCIDÉ 6952 (9325).**

[Recorded with pedigree in the Percheron Stud-Books of France and America.]

Dark grey; 16½ hands; weight, 1,800 lbs.; foaled 1883; imported 1887; bred by M. Virlouvet, commune of Souancé, canton of Nogent-le-Rotrou, department of Eure-et-Loir; got by VAILLANT (404); dam Rustique (9254) by CHÉRI, he by Coco II (714).

VAILLANT (404) by Prosper (893) out of Rosalie by Bienvenu, belonging to the Société Hippique of Eure-et-Loir.
PROSPER (893) by Décidé (892) out of Bourreau by Vieux-Pierre (883).
DÉCIDÉ (892) by Vieux-Pierre (894) out of Pelote, belonging to M. Berjeau, of Courvalien.
VIEUX-PIERRE (894) by Coco (712), he by Mignon (715) out of Pauline by Vieux-Coco.
MIGNON (715) by Jean-le-Blanc (739).
Coco II (714) by Vieux-Chaslin (713) out of La Grise by Vieux-Pierre (883).
VIEUX-CHASLIN (713) by Coco (712), etc., out of Poule by Sandi.

(Hoof No. 84.)   **DELVINO 6953 (6623).**

[Recorded with pedigree in the Percheron Stud-Books of France and America.]

Dapple grey; 16½ hands; weight, 1,900 lbs.; foaled April 25, 1884; imported 1887; bred by M. Besnard, commune of Ceton, canton of Theil, department of Orne; got by JOLY (4171); dam Rosalie (6620) by CHÉRI, he by Coco II (714); 2d dam Bijou.

JOLY (4171) by Brilliant 1899 (756), he by Coco II (714) out of Rosette by Mina, belonging to the French government.
Coco II (714) by Vieux-Chaslin (713) out of La Grise by Vieux-Pierre (883).
VIEUX-CHASLIN (713) by Coco (712) out of Poule by Sandi.
Coco (712) by Mignon (715) out of Pauline by Vieux-Coco.
MIGNON (715) by Jean-le-Blanc (739).

(Hoof No. 44.)   **DEMOSTHENE 6954 (5710).**

[Recorded with pedigree in the Percheron Stud-Books of France and America.]

Steel grey; 16½ hands; weight, 1,805 lbs.; foaled 1883; imported 1887; bred by M. Gautier, commune of Ceton, canton of Theil, department of Orne; got by JOLY (4171); dam Bijou (5709) by UTOPIA 780 (731).

JOLY (4171) by Brilliant 1899 (756), he by Coco II (714) out of Rosette by Mina, belonging to the French government.
Coco II (714) by Vieux-Chaslin (713) out of La Grise by Vieux-Pierre (883).
VIEUX-CHASLIN (713) by Coco (712) out of Poule by Sandi.
Coco (712) by Mignon (715) out of Pauline by Vieux-Coco.
MIGNON (715) by Jean-le-Blanc (739).
UTOPIA 780 (731) by Superior 454 (730) out of Camille by Favori I (711).
SUPERIOR 454 (730) by Favori I (711) ont of Pauline by Vieux-Chaslin (713), etc.
FAVORI I (711) by Vieux-Chaslin (713), etc., out of L'Amie by Vieux-Pierre (894), he by Coco (712), etc.

(Hoof No. 227.)　　　　　　**DEY 5556 (6572).**

[Recorded with pedigree in the Percheron Stud-Books of France and America.]

Reddish grey; 16 hands; weight, 1,600 lbs.; foaled May 9, 1885; imported 1886; bred by M. Saunier, commune of Lamnay, canton of Montmirail, department of Sarthe; got by AVANT-COUREUR 4641 (449); dam Chaton (6571) by PHILIBERT (760) out of Julie, belonging to M. Saunier.

AVANT-COUREUR 4641 (449) by Narbonne 1334 (777) out of Robine by Mina.
NARBONNE 1334 (777) by Brilliant 1899 (756) out of Madelon (4722) by Favori I (711).
BRILLIANT 1899 (756) by Coco II (714) out of Rosette by Mina, belonging to the French government.
Coco II (714) by Vieux-Chaslin (713) out of La Grise by Vieux-Pierre (883).
VIEUX-CHASLIN (713) by Coco (712) out of Poule by Sandi.
Coco (712) by Mignon (715) out of Pauline by Vieux-Coco.
MIGNON (715) by Jean-le-Blanc (739).
PHILIBERT (760) by Superior 454 (730) out of Madelon by Vieux-Vaillant (1383), he by Pierre, belonging to M. Thérin, out of a daughter of Vieux-Pierre (883).
SUPERIOR 454 (730) by Favori I (711) out of Pauline by Vieux-Chaslin (713), etc.
FAVORI I (711) by Vieux-Chaslin (713), etc., out of L'Amie by Vieux-Pierre (894), he by Coco (712), etc.

(Hoof No. 164.)　　　　　　**DISTINGUE 7043 (9574).**

[Recorded with pedigree in the Percheron Stud-Books of France and America.]

Steel grey; 16 hands; weight, 1,590 lbs.; foaled April 10, 1885; imported 1887; bred by M. Royer, commune of La Chapelle Souëf, canton of Bellême, department of Orne; got by PAUL 3478 (364); dam Biche (9573) by ARCOLA, belonging to M. Perpère.

PAUL 3478 (364) by Vaillant (404) out of Cocotte by Vieux-Vaillant (1383), he by Pierre, belonging to M. Thérin, out of a daughter of Vieux-Pierre (883).
VAILLANT (404) by Prosper (893) out of Rosalie by Bienvenu, belonging to the Société Hippique of Eure-et-Loir.
PROSPER (893) by Décidé (892) out of Bourreau by Vieux-Pierre (883).
DÉCIDÉ (892) by Vieux-Pierre (894) out of Pelote, belonging to M. Berjeau, of Courvalien.
VIEUX-PIERRE (894) by Coco (712), he by Mignon (715) out of Pauline by Vieux-Coco.
MIGNON (715) by Jean-le-Blanc (739).

(Hoof No. 118.)　　　　　　**DOMINANT 6955 (6776).**

[Recorded with pedigree in the Percheron Stud-Books of France and America.]

Black; foaled April 1, 1884; imported 1887; bred by M. Deleuze, commune of Serigny, canton of Bellême, department of Orne; got by MADÈRE II (2994); dam Poule (4060) by VIDOCQ 483 (732) out of Lisette.

MADÈRE II (2994) by Madeira 1546 (770), he by Vidocq 483 (732) out of Jeanne by Favori I (711), he by Vieux-Chaslin (713) out of L'Amie by Vieux-Pierre (894), he by Coco (712).
VIDOCQ 483 (732) by Coco II (714) out of a daughter of Chéri, he by Rustique.
Coco II (714) by Vieux-Chaslin (713) out of La Grise by Vieux-Pierre (883).
VIEUX-CHASLIN (713) by Coco (712) out of Poule by Sandi.
Coco (712) by Mignon (715) out of Pauline by Vieux-Coco.
MIGNON (715) by Jean-le-Blanc (739).

(Hoof No. 137.) **DOMPTEUR 6956 (9765).**

[Recorded with pedigree in the Percheron Stud-Books of France and America.]

Dark grey; 16½ hands; weight, 1,720; foaled June 8, 1884; imported 1887; bred by M. Celeste Lefevre, commune of Almenêches, canton of Séez, department of Orne; got by CHÉRI 5079 (2423); dam La Poule (9763) by SÉLIM (749).

CHÉRI 5079 (2423) by Bayard (9661) out of Mignonne by Coco II (714).
BAYARD (9661) by Duke-de-Chartres 162 (721), he by Coco II (714), he by Vieux-Chaslin (713) out of La Grise by Vieux-Pierre (883).
VIEUX-CHASLIN (713) by Coco (712) out of Poule by Sandi.
Coco (712) by Mignon (715) out of Pauline by Vieux-Coco.
MIGNON (715) by Jean-le-Blanc (739).
SÉLIM (749) by Porthos, belonging to M. Fromentin.

(Hoof No. 136.) **DUC-NOIR 6957 (10204).**

[Recorded with pedigree in the Percheron Stud-Books of France and America.]

Black; foaled March 8, 1884; imported 1887; bred by M. Honoré Desprez, commune of Godisson, canton of Merlerault, department of Orne; got by SÉLIM III (4820); dam Mignonnette (5224) by CHERE 855 (791) 2d dam Rosette (4319) by SÉLIM (749); 3d dam L'Amie by PIERRE (887).

SÉLIM III (4820) by Sélim (749) (son of Porthos) out of Sophie by Duke-de-Chartres 162 (721), he by Coco II (714), he by Vieux-Chaslin (713) out of La Grise by Vieux-Pierre (883).
VIEUX-CHASLIN (713) by Coco (712) out of Poule by Sandi.
Coco (712) by Mignon (715) out of Pauline by Vieux-Coco.
MIGNON (715) by Jean-le-Blanc (739).
CHERE 855 (791) by Favori, belonging to M. Dupont, out of Maria by Horisabat.
PIERRE (887) by Laboureur (886) out of Margot by Faisan.
LABOUREUR (886) by Jean-le-Blanc (739) out of Sophie by Sandi.

(Hoof No. 21.) **DUMAS 7046 (10396).**

[Recorded with pedigree in the Percheron Stud-Books of France and America.]

Grey; 16 hands; weight, 1,600 lbs., foaled April, 1885; imported 1887; bred by M. Pelletier, commune of Préaux, canton of Nocé, department of Orne; got by VAILLANT (404); dam Lisette (272) by PROSPER (893) out of Chaloupe.

VAILLANT (404) by Prosper (893) out of Rosalie by Bienvenu, belonging to the Société Hippique of Eure-et-Loir.
PROSPER (893) by Décidé (892) out of Bourreau by Vieux-Pierre (883).
DÉCIDÉ (892) by Vieux-Pierre (894) out of Pelote, belonging to M. Berjeau, of Courvalien.
VIEUX-PIERRE (894) by Coco (712), he by Mignon (715) out of Pauline by Vieux-Coco.
MIGNON (715) by Jean-le-Blanc (739).

(Hoof No. 6.) **DU-ROCHER 7044 (8864).**

[Recorded with pedigree in the Percheron Stud-Books of France and America.]

Dark grey; foaled February 8, 1886; imported 1887; bred by M. Baptiste Besonnier, commune of Souligné, canton of Ballon, department of Sarthe; got by SANSONNET (8767); dam Biche (8863) by CHARMANT, belonging to M. Chaudet.

SANSONNET (8767) by Mouton, belonging to M. Poilpre.

(Hoof No. 169.)   **EXTRADOR III 6958 (11224).**

[Recorded with pedigree in the Percheron Stud-Books of France and America.]

Black ; 16 hands ; weight, 1,520 lbs. ; foaled April 15, 1885 ; imported 1887 ; bred by M. Philippe Adam, commune of La Fresnaye, canton of La Fresnaye, department of Sarthe ; got by MARGOT 4147 (426); dam Rosette (11223) by FACILE (5404).

MARGOT 4147 (426) by Favora 1542 (765), he by French Monarch 205 (734) out of Marguerite by Favori, he by Coco of Mêsle-sur-Sarthe, he by Margot, belonging to M. Vallée.
FRENCH MONARCH 205 (734) by Ilderim (5302) out of a daughter of Vieux-Pierre (894), he by Coco (712).
ILDERIM (5302) by Valentin (5301) out of Chaton by Vieux-Pierre (894), etc.
VALENTIN (5301) by Vieux-Chaslin (713), he by Coco (712) out of Poule by Sandi.
Coco (712) by Mignon (715) out of Pauline by Vieux-Coco.
MIGNON (715) by Jean-le-Blanc (739).
FACILE 5404 by Orizaba, he by Miramar, belonging to M. Lalouet.

(Hoof No. 68.)   **FARAOUCK 7052 (3009).**

[Recorded with pedigree in the Percheron Stud-Books of France and America.]

Dapple grey ; 16½ hands ; weight, 1,820 lbs. ; foaled April 11, 1883 ; imported 1887 ; bred by M. Coulonges, commune of Dancé, canton of Nocé, department of Orne ; got by AVATA 1966 (912); dam Rustique (3008) by PROSPER (893) out of L'Amie, belonging to M. Ferré.

AVATA 1966 (912) by Nogent 738 (729) out of Bicotte by Bayard 26 (717), he by Favori I (711) out of Mignonne by Chéri.
  FAVORI I (711) by Vieux-Chaslin (713) out of L'Amie by Vieux-Pierre (894), he by Coco (712).
NOGENT 738 (729) by Vidocq 483 (732) out of a daughter of Favori I (711), etc.
VIDOCQ 483 (732) by Coco II (714) out of a daughter of Chéri, he by Rustique.
Coco II (714) by Vieux-Chaslin (713) out of La Grise by Vieux-Pierre (883).
VIEUX-CHASLIN (713) by Coco (712) out of Poule by Sandi.
Coco (712) by Mignon (715) out of Pauline by Vieux-Coco.
MIGNON (715) by Jean-le-Blanc (739).
PROSPER (893) by Décidé (892) out of Bourreau by Vieux-Pierre (883).
DÉCIDÉ (892) by Vieux-Pierre (894) out of Pelote, belonging to M. Berjeau, of Courvalien.
VIEUX-PIERRE (894) by Coco (712), etc.

(Hoof No. 230.)   **FERRAND 5152 (6950)**

[Recorded with pedigree in the Percheron Stud-Books of France and America.]

Steel grey ; 16½ hands ; weight, 1,760 lbs.; foaled June 5, 1883 ; imported 1886 ; bred by M. Ferré, commune of Préaux, canton of Nocé, department of Orne ; got by BAYARD (7519) ; dam Bijou (4992) by PROSPER (893) out of L'Amie, belonging to M. Ferré.

BAYARD (7519) by Favora 666 (725) out of Pelotte, belonging to M. Noël.
FAVORA 666 (725) by Favori I (711) out of Marie by Coco (712).
FAVORI I (711) by Vieux-Chaslin (713) out of L'Amie by Vieux-Pierre (894), he by Coco (712).
VIEUX-CHASLIN (713) by Coco (712) out of Poule by Sandi.
Coco (712) by Mignon (715) out of Pauline by Vieux-Coco.
MIGNON (715) by Jean-le-Blanc (739).
PROSPER (893) by Décidé (892) out of Bourreau by Vieux-Pierre (883).
DÉCIDÉ (892) by Vieux-Pierre (894) out of Pelote, belonging to M. Berjeau, of Courvalien.
VIEUX-PIERRE (894) by Coco (712), etc.

(Hoof No. 98.) **FIER 6959 (10662).**

[Recorded with pedigree in the Percheron Stud-Books of France and America.]

Dapple grey; 16½ hands; weight, 1,800 lbs.; foaled March 10, 1884; imported 1887; bred by M. F. Bourgivet, commune of Vouvray-sur-Huisne, canton of Tuffé, department of Sarthe; got by FAVORI III (1381); dam Margot (10661) by MOUTON (1640).

FAVORI III (1381) by Utopia 780 (731) out of La Noire, belonging to M. Letourneur.
UTOPIA 780 (731) by Superior 454 (730) out of Camille by Favori I (711).
SUPERIOR 454 (730) by Favori I (711) out of Pauline by Vieux-Chaslin (713).
FAVORI I (711) by Vieux-Chaslin (713), etc., out of L'Amie by Vieux-Pierre (894), he by Coco (712).
VIEUX-CHASLIN (713) by Coco (712) out of Poule by Sandi.
Coco (712) by Mignon (715) out of Pauline by Vieux-Coco.
MIGNON (715) by Jean-le-Blanc (739).
MOUTON (1640) by French Monarch 205 (734), etc., out of Rose by Décidé, belonging to M. Vinault.
FRENCH MONARCH 205 (734) by Ilderim (5302) out of a daughter of Vieux-Pierre (894), etc.
ILDERIM (5302) by Valentin (5301) out of Chaton by Vieux-Pierre (894), etc.
VALENTIN (5301) by Vieux-Chaslin (713), etc.

(Hoof No. 4.) **FIRMIN 7047 (8011).**

[Recorded with pedigree in the Percheron Stud-Books of France and America.]

Dark grey; foaled March 1, 1886; imported 1887; bred by M. Frederic Souvre, commune of Préaux, canton of Nocé, department of Orne; got by POTENTAT (495); dam Bijou (8010) by BIENVENU, belonging to the Société Hippique of Eure-et-Loir.

POTENTAT (495) by Vaillant (404) out of Bouro by Favori I (711), he by Vieux-Chaslin (713) out of L'Amie by Vieux-Pierre (894).
VIEUX-CHASLIN (713) by Coco (712) out of Poule by Sandi.
VAILLANT (404) by Prosper (893) out of Rosalie by Bienvenu, belonging to the Société Hippique of Eure-et-Loir.
PROSPER (893) by Décidé (892) out of Bourreau by Vieux-Pierre (883).
DÉCIDÉ (892) by Vieux-Pierre (894) out of Pelote, belonging to M. Berjeau, of Courvalien.
VIEUX-PIERRE (894) by Coco (712), he by Mignon (715) out of Pauline by Vieux-Coco.
MIGNON (715) by Jean-le-Blanc (739).

(Hoof No. 13.) **FRANC CŒUR 7048 (10829).**

[Recorded with pedigree in the Percheron Stud-Books of France and America.]

Dark grey; 16 hands; weight, 1,605 lbs.; foaled May 4, 1885; imported 1887; bred by M. Robert, commune of Dancé, canton of Nocé, department of Orne; got by BRILLANT (4737); dam Bijou (10828) by MADÈRE (2847).

BRILLANT (4737) by L'Ami (1388), he by Coco [son of Coco II (714)] out of Percheronne, belonging to M. Lucas.
Coco II (714) by Vieux-Chaslin (713) out of La Grise by Vieux-Pierre (883).
VIEUX-CHASLIN (713) by Coco (712) out of Poule by Sandi.
Coco (712) by Mignon (715) out of Pauline by Vieux-Coco.
MIGNON (715) by Jean-le-Blanc (739).
MADÈRE (2847) by Brillant, belonging to M. Thérin, out of Bibi, by Vaillant, belonging to M. Dorchéne.

(Hoof No. 209.)   **FRANC PICARD 3706 (2469).**

[Recorded with pedigree in the Percheron Stud-Books of France and America.]

Dark grey ; foaled March 14, 1881 ; imported 1884 ; bred by M. Guillin, commune of Eperrais, canton of Pervenchères, department of Orne ; got by BAYARD, he by BAYARD 26 (717) ; dam Mignonne by MARGOT 295 (795).

BAYARD 26 (717) by Favori I (711) out of Mignonne by Chéri.
FAVORI I (711) by Vieux-Chaslin (713) out of L'Amie by Vieux-Pierre (894), he by Coco (712).
VIEUX-CHASLIN (713) by Coco (712) out of Poule by Sandi.
COCO (712) by Mignon (715) out of Pauline by Vieux-Coco.
MIGNON (715) by Jean-le-Blanc(739).
MARGOT 295 (795) by Favori I (711), etc.

(Hoof No. 87.)   **FRANCOIS I 7051 (8772).**

[Recorded with pedigree in the Percheron Stud-Books of France and America.]

Dark grey ; 16¾ hands ; weight, 1,750 lbs. ; foaled April 26, 1885 ; imported 1887 ; bred by M. Michaudel, commune of Préaux, canton of Nocé, department of Orne ; got by HERCULE 3714 (2354) ; dam Charmante (5904) by MADÈRE 1263 (772) ; 2d dam Rosette (1911) by BIENVENU, belonging to the Société Hippique, of Eure-et-Loir ; 3d dam, Bijou, belonging to M. Michaudel.

HERCULE 3714 (2354) by Chéri out of Castille (2362) by Bon Espoir, he by Chéri, he by Coco II (714).
CHÉRI by Rustique, he by Vidocq 483 (732), he by Coco II (714) out of a daughter of Chéri, he by Rustique.
COCO II (714) by Vieux-Chaslin (713) out of La Grise by Vieux-Pierre (883).
VIEUX-CHASLIN (713) by Coco (712) out of Poule by Sandi.
COCO (712) by Mignon (715) out of Pauline by Vieux-Coco.
MIGNON (715) by Jean-le-Blanc (739).
MADÈRE 1263 (772) by Brilliant 1899 (756) out of Hortense by Duke-de-Chartres 162 (721), he by Coco II (714), etc.
BRILLIANT 1899 (756) by Coco II (714), etc., out of Rosette by Mina, belonging to the French government.

(Hoof No. 231.)   **FRANCONI 5578 (6401).**

[Recorded with pedigree in the Percheron Stud-Books of France and America.]

Grey ; 16¼ hands ; weight, 1,690 lbs. ; foaled April 20, 1883 ; imported 1886 ; bred by M. Sicot, commune of Bazoches-sur-Hoëne, department of Orne ; got by SULTAN (1400) ; dam Rose (6400) by ROMULUS 873 (785) out of Rose, belonging to M. Sicot.

SULTAN (1400) by Count 643 (736) out of Rosette by Madère.
COUNT 643 (736) by Bayard 26 (717) out of Bijou by Rustique.
BAYARD 26 (717) by Favori I (711) out of Mignonne by Chéri.
FAVORI I (711) by Vieux-Chaslin (713) out of L'Amie by Vieux-Pierre (894), he by Coco (712).
VIEUX-CHASLIN (713) by Coco (712) out of Poule by Sandi.
COCO (712) by Mignon (715) out of Pauline by Vieux-Coco.
MIGNON (715) by Jean-le-Blanc (739).
ROMULUS 873 (785) by the government approved stallion Romulus (son of Moreuil) out of Fleur-d'Épine by the government approved stallion Chéri, he by Corbon.

(Hoof No. 135.) **FRANCONI 6960 (10203).**

[Recorded with pedigree in the Percheron Stud-Books of France and America.]

Grey ; 16½ hands ; weight, 1,790 lbs.,; foaled May 5, 1884 ; imported 1887 ; bred by M. M. Belhomme, commune of Merlerault, department of Orne ; got by Bon Espoir (213); dam La Petite (8198) by Sélim (749).

Bon Espoir (213) by Brilliant 1899 (756) out of Poule, belonging to M. Barbet.
Brilliant 1899 (756) by Coco II (714) out of Rosette by Mina, belonging to the French government.
Coco II (714) by Vieux-Chaslin (713) out of La Grise by Vieux-Pierre (883).
Vieux-Chaslin (713) by Coco (712) out of Poule by Sandi.
Coco (712) by Mignon (715) out of Pauline by Vieux-Coco.
Mignon (715) by Jean-le-Blanc (739).
Sélim (749) by Porthos, belonging to M. Fromentin.

(Hoof No. 89.) **FRAZÉ 7050 (9449).**

[Recorded with pedigree in the Percheron Stud-Books of France and America.]

Dark grey ; 16½ hands ; weight, 1,600 lbs.; foaled March 24, 1885 ; imported 1887; bred by M. E. Lavie, commune of Frazé, canton of Thiron, department of Eure-et-Loir ; got by Brillantin (1945); dam Brebis (9448) by Bismark, belonging to M. Bouvard-Brebion.

Brillantin (1945) by Décidé, belonging to M. Perriot, out of Pelote, belonging to M. Pichard.

(Hoof No. 48.) **FRITZ 6961 (5458).**

[Recorded with pedigree in the Percheron Stud-Books of France and America.]

Black ; 16½ hands ; weight, 1,850 lbs.; foaled April 30, 1884 ; imported 1887 ; bred by M. Hervé, commune of Voudray-sur-Huisne, canton of Tuffé, department of Sarthe ; got by Papillon 3559 (379); dam Rose (5457) by French Monarch 205 (734) out of Juliette, belonging to M. Eugène Tacheau.

Papillon 3559 (379) by Brillant (710) out of Cocotte by Coco II (714).
Brillant (710) by Brilliant 1899 (756) out of Sophie by Superior 454 (730), he by Favori I (711) out of Pauline by Vieux-Chaslin (713).
Favori I (711) by Vieux-Chaslin (713) out of L'Amie by Vieux-Pierre (894), he by Coco (712).
Brilliant 1899 (756) by Coco II (714) out of Rosette by Mina, belonging to the French government.
Coco II (714) by Vieux-Chaslin (713) out of La Grise by Vieux-Pierre (883).
Vieux-Chaslin (713) by Coco (712) out of Poule by Sandi.
Coco (712) by Mignon (715) out of Pauline by Vieux-Coco.
Mignon (715) by Jean-le-Blanc (739).
French Monarch 205 (734) by Ilderim (5302) out of a daughter of Vieux-Pierre (894), he by Coco (712).
Ilderim (5302) by Valentin (5301) out of Chaton by Vieux-Pierre (894), etc.
Valentin (5301) by Vieux-Chaslin (713), etc.

(Hoof No. 77.)   **FULMINANT 7049 (11916).**

[Recorded with pedigree in the Percheron Stud-Books of France and America.]

Dark grey; 16¼ hands; weight, 1,650 lbs.; foaled 1885; imported 1887; bred by M. Bigot, commune of Gemages, canton of Theil, department of Orne; got by MONARCH (365); dam Rosette (10251) by PIERRE, belonging to M. Tacheau.

MONARCH (365) by Confidence 920 (763) out of Bijou, belonging to M. Fouanon.
CONFIDENCE 920 (763) by Favora 666 (725) out of Marie by Comet 104 (719), he by French Monarch 205 (734) out of Suzanne by Cambronne.
  FRENCH MONARCH 205 (734) by Ilderim (5302) out of a daughter of Vieux-Pierre (894), he by Coco (712).
    ILDERIM (5302) by Valentin (5301) out of Chaton by Vieux-Pierre (894), etc.
    VALENTIN (5301) by Vieux-Chaslin (713).
FAVORA 666 (725) by Favori I (711) out of Marie by Coco (712).
FAVORI I (711) by Vieux-Chaslin (713) out of L'Amie by Vieux-Pierre (894), etc.
VIEUX-CHASLIN (713) by Coco (712) out of Poule by Sandi.
Coco (712) by Mignon (715) out of Pauline by Vieux-Coco.
MIGNON (715) by Jean-le-Blanc (739).

(Hoof No. 101.)   **GASTRONOME 7054 (8270).**

[Recorded with pedigree in the Percheron Stud-Books of France and America.]

Dark grey; foaled February 20, 1886; imported 1887; bred by M. Guillemin, commune of Berd'huis, canton of Nocé, department of Orne; got by MADRID 5153 (441); dam Ragotte (8269) by VIEUX-PIERRE, belonging to M. Thérin, of La Massuette.

MADRID 5153 (441) by Avata 1966 (912) out of Jeannette (7597) by Vidocq 483 (732).
AVATA 1966 (912) by Nogent 738 (729) out of Bicotte by Bayard 26 (717), he by Favori I (711) out of Mignonne by Chéri.
  FAVORI I (711) by Vieux-Chaslin (713) out of L'Amie by Vieux-Pierre (894), he by Coco (712).
NOGENT 738 (729) by Vidocq 483 (732) out of a daughter of Favori I (711), etc.
VIDOCQ 483 (732) by Coco II (714) out of a daughter of Chéri, he by Rustique.
Coco II (714) by Vieux-Chaslin (713) out of La Grise by Vieux-Pierre (883).
VIEUX-CHASLIN (713) by Coco (712) out of Poule by Sandi.
Coco (712) by Mignon (715) out of Pauline by Vieux-Coco.
MIGNON (715) by Jean-le-Blanc (739).

(Hoof No. 94.)   **GASTRONOME 7058 (8952).**

[Recorded with pedigree in the Percheron Stud-Books of France and America.]

Dapple grey; 16 hands; weight, 1,800 lbs.; foaled April 9, 1885; imported 1887; bred by M. Truquet, commune of Frazé, canton of Thiron, department of Eure-et-Loir; got by PAPILLON (2444); dam Souris (8786) by BRILLANT (710).

PAPILLON (2444) by Iago 995 (768) out of Sauvons-Nous.
IAGO 995 (768) by Utopia 780 (731) out of Cossette by Favora 666 (725), he by Favori I (711) out of Marie by Coco (712).
UTOPIA 780 (731) by Superior 454 (730) out of Camille by Favori I (711).
SUPERIOR 454 (730) by Favori I (711) out of Pauline by Vieux-Chaslin (713).
FAVORI I (711) by Vieux-Chaslin (713) out of L'Amie by Vieux-Pierre (894), he by Coco (712).
VIEUX-CHASLIN (713) by Coco (712) out of Poule by Sandi.
Coco (712) by Mignon (715) out of Pauline by Vieux-Coco.
MIGNON (715) by Jean-le-Blanc (739).
BRILLANT (710) by Brilliant 1899 (756) out of Sophie by Superior 454 (730), etc.
BRILLIANT 1899 (756) by Coco II (714) out of Rosette by Mina, belonging to the French government.
Coco II (714) by Vieux-Chaslin (713), etc., out of La Grise by Vieux-Pierre (883).

(Hoof No. 91.) **GESTATOR 6962 (8957).**

[Recorded with pedigree in the Percheron Stud-Books of France and America.]

Dark grey; 16¼ hands; weight, 1,750 lbs.; foaled April 13, 1884; imported 1887; bred by M. Blin, commune of Frazé, canton of Thiron, department of Eure-et-Loir; got by PAPILLON (2444); dam Pelotte (8956) by FAVORI, belonging to M. Bouvard.

PAPILLON (2444) by Iago 995 (768) out of Sauvons-Nous, belonging to M. Surcin.
IAGO 995 (768) by Utopia 780 (731) out of Cossette by Favora 666 (725), he by Favori I (711) out of Marie by Coco (712).
UTOPIA 780 (731) by Superior 454 (730) out of Camille by Favori I (711).
SUPERIOR 454 (730) by Favori I (711) out of Pauline by Vieux-Chaslin (713).
FAVORI I (711) by Vieux-Chaslin (713) out of L'Amie by Vieux-Pierre (894), he by Coco (712).
VIEUX-CHASLIN (713) by Coco (712) out of Poule by Sandi.
Coco (712) by Mignon (715) out of Pauline by Vieux-Coco.
MIGNON (715) by Jean-le-Blanc (739).

(Hoof No. 103.) **GIBRALTAR 7053 (7826).**

[Recorded with pedigree in the Percheron Stud-Books of France and America.]

Dark grey; foaled April 8, 1886; imported 1887; bred by M. M. P. Avisseau, commune of St. Maixent, canton of Montmirail, department of Sarthe; got by Coco 4250 (234); dam Pelotte (6143) by OSCAR, belonging to M. Avisseau, out of Bleue.

Coco 4250 (234) by Martin, belonging to M. Lucas, out of Grisette (4917) by Marquis (4696), he by Guiloiseau, belonging to M. Noireau, out of Pelotte.

(Hoof No. 105.) **GLORIA 7055 (7827).**

[Recorded with pedigree in the Percheron Stud-Books of France and America.]

Dark grey; foaled February 25, 1886; bred by M. Bourgue, commune of Villaines, canton of La Ferté-Bernard, department of Sarthe; got by PASSE-A-PIC (2403); dam Pelotte (6577) by COLIN-ROUX, belonging to M. Th. Vinault, out of Rose.

PASSE-A-PIC (2403) by Passe-Partout (1402) out of Boule by Colin-Roux.
PASSE-PARTOUT (1402) by Comet 104 (719) out of Sophie by Favori I (711), he by Vieux-Chaslin (713) out of L'Amie by Vieux-Pierre (894), he by Coco (712).
COMET 104 (719) by French Monarch 205 (734) out of Suzanne by Cambronne.
FRENCH MONARCH 205 (734) by Ilderim (5302) out of a daughter of Vieux-Pierre (894), he by Coco (712).
ILDERIM (5302) by Valentin (5301) out of Chaton by Vieux-Pierre (894), etc.
VALENTIN (5301) by Vieux-Chaslin (713), he by Coco (712) out of Poule by Sandi.
Coco (712) by Mignon (715) out of Pauline by Vieux-Coco.
MIGNON (715) by Jean-le-Blanc (739).

(Hoof No. 179.)   **GODICHON 7056 (6342).**

[Recorded with pedigree in the Percheron Stud-Books of France and America.]

Black; 16 hands; weight, 1,700 lbs.; foaled May 16, 1885; imported 1887; bred by M. Provost, commune of St. Antoine, canton of La Ferté-Bernard, department of Sarthe; got by LORD BYRON 3648 (398); dam Biche (6341) by FLEURUS, he by FRENCH MONARCH 205 (734); 2d dam Suzanne, belonging to M. Provost.

LORD BYRON 3648 (398) by Favora 1542 (765) out of Suzanne by French Monarch 205 (734).
FAVORA 1542 (765) by French Monarch 205 (734) out of Marguerite by Favori, he by Coco of Mêsle-sur-Sarthe, he by Margot, belonging to M. Vallée.
FRENCH MONARCH 205 (734) by Ilderim (5302) out of a daughter of Vieux-Pierre (894), he by Coco (712).
ILDERIM (5302) by Valentin (5301) out of Chaton by Vieux-Pierre (894), etc.
VALENTIN (5301) by Vieux-Chaslin (713), he by Coco (712) out of Poule by Sandi.
COCO (712) by Mignon (715) out of Pauline by Vieux-Coco.
MIGNON (715) by Jean-le-Blanc (739).

(Hoof No. 57.)   **GOLIATH 7057 (9290).**

[Recorded with pedigree in the Percheron Stud-Books of France and America.]

Black; 15¾ hands; weight, 1,600 lbs.; foaled May 12, 1885; imported 1887; bred by M. Bourdin, commune of Serigny, canton of Bellême, department of Orne; got by BRILLANT 3767 (607); dam Mignonne (9289) by DOCILE (4446).

BRILLANT 3767 (607) by Bon Espoir [son of Superior 454 (730)] out of Julie.
SUPERIOR 454 (730) by Favori I (711) out of Pauline by Vieux-Chaslin (713).
FAVORI I (711) by Vieux-Chaslin (713) out of L'Amie by Vieux-Pierre (894), he by Coco (712).
VIEUX-CHASLIN (713) by Coco (712) out of Poule by Sandi.
COCO (712) by Mignon (715) out of Pauline by Vieux-Coco.
MIGNON (715) by Jean-le-Blanc (739).
DOCILE (4446) by Faisan (son of Chéri) out of Rose, belonging to M. Simon.

(Hoof No. 71.)   **GRIS GRIS 6963 (9912).**

[Recorded with pedigree in the Percheron Stud-Books of France and America.]

Dark grey; 16 hands; weight, 1,798 lbs.; foaled March 1, 1884; imported 1887; bred by M. Touchard, commune of Choué, canton of Mondoubleau, department of Loir-et-Cher; got by BAYARD (9910); dam Lisette (9911) by PAUL, belonging to M. Chauvin.

BAYARD (9910) by Colin, belonging to M. Chauvin.

(Hoof No. 30.) **HAROLD 7060 (8386).**

[Recorded with pedigree in the Percheron Stud-Books of France and America.]

Grey ; foaled March 19, 1886 ; imported 1887 ; bred by M. Brunet, commune of Trizay, canton of Nogent-le-Rotrou, department of Eure-et-Loir ; got by CHAMPEAUX 6218 (2248); dam Bijou (7238) by BRILLIANT 1899 (756) out of Chaton, belonging to M. Brunet.

CHAMPEAUX 6218 (2248) by Iago 995 (768) out of Madeleine, belonging to M. Guillemin.
IAGO 995 (768) by Utopia 780 (731) out of Cossette by Favora 666 (725), he by Favori I (711) out of Marie by Coco (712).
UTOPIA 780 (731) by Superior 454 (730) out of Camille by Favori I (711).
SUPERIOR 454 (730) by Favori I (711) out of Pauline by Vieux-Chaslin (713).
FAVORI I (711) by Vieux-Chaslin (713) out of L'Amie by Vieux-Pierre (894), he by Coco (712).
VIEUX-CHASLIN (713) by Coco (712) out of Poule by Sandi.
Coco (712) by Mignon (715) out of Pauline by Vieux-Coco.
MIGNON (715) by Jean-le-Blanc (739).
BRILLIANT 1899 (756) by Coco II (714) out of Rosette by Mina, belonging to the French government.
Coco II (714) by Vieux-Chaslin (713), etc., out of La Grise by Vieux-Pierre (883).

(Hoof No. 3.) **HELVETIUS 7061 (8854).**

[Recorded with pedigree in the Percheron Stud-Books of France and America.]

Brown bay ; weight, 1,450 lbs.; foaled April 8, 1886 ; imported 1887 ; bred by Madame Dreux, commune of Luce, canton of Marolles-les-Branx, department of Sarthe ; got by CHARMANT (5575); dam Brebis (8853) by CHARMANT I, he by VIGOUREUX, he by L'AMI, belonging to M. Abot.

CHARMANT (5575) by Favory out of Rosalie (5572) by Vigoureux, he by L'Ami.
FAVORY by Charmant I, he by Vigoureux, he by L'Ami.

(Hoof No. 138.) **HENRI 6964 (8129).**

[Recorded with pedigree in the Percheron Stud-Books of France and America.]

Dapple grey ; 16½ hands ; weight, 1,725 lbs.; foaled March 17, 1883 ; imported 1887 ; bred by M. Guitton, commune of Alménêches, canton of Mortrée, department of Orne ; got by BERNARD 5075 (5501) ; dam Adelaine (6924) by CHÉRI (5464) out of Charmante.

BERNARD 5075 (5501) by Chéri (5464) out of Mignonne (5240) by Picador, belonging to M. Vimont.
CHÉRI (5464) by Mouton (son of Coco of Mesle-sur-Sarthe) out of Cocotte by Corbon.

(Hoof No. 162.) **HERCULANUM 6965 (4027).**

[Recorded with pedigree in the Percheron Stud-Books of France and America.]

Black ; 16¾ hands ; weight, 1,700 lbs.; foaled May 3, 1884 ; imported 1887 ; bred by M. Caget, commune of Lonrai, canton of Alençon, department of Orne ; got by MADÈRE 3693 (424); dam Bijou (4026) by PAUL, belonging to M. Miteau, out of Célina.

MADÈRE 3693 (424) by Madère [son of Romulus 873 (785)] out of Castille by Paul.
ROMULUS 873 (785) by the government approved stallion Romulus (son of Moreuil) out of Fleur-d'Epine by the government approved stallion Chéri, he by Corbon.

(Hoof No. 183.)   **HOLOPHERNE 7059 (8542).**

[Recorded with pedigree in the Percheron Stud-Books of France and America.]

Dark grey; 16 hands; weight, 1,575 lbs.; foaled May 12, 1885; imported 1887; bred by M. Pelletier, commune of St.-Aubin-des-Grois, canton of Nocé, department of Orne; got by GÉROME 3655 (436); dam Rosette (8541) by VERMOUTH 1820 (787).

GÉROME 3655 (436) by Vidocq II (723) out of Pelote by Superior 454 (730), he by Favori I (711) out of Pauline by Vieux-Chaslin (713).
    FAVORI I (711) by Vieux-Chaslin (713) out of L'Amie by Vieux-Pierre (894), he by Coco (712).
VIDOCQ II (723) by Bayard (1385) out of Brière by Décidé.
BAYARD (1385) by Vidocq 483 (732) out of La Noire by Chéri, he by Coco II (714).
VIDOCQ 483 (732) by Coco II (714) out of a daughter of Chéri, he by Rustique.
Coco II (714) by Vieux-Chaslin (713) out of La Grise by Vieux-Pierre (883).
VIEUX-CHASLIN (713) by Coco (712) out of Poule by Sandi.
Coco (712) by Mignon (715) out of Pauline by Vieux-Coco.
MIGNON (715) by Jean-le-Blanc (739).
VERMOUTH 1820 (787) by Vidocq 483 (732), etc., out of Agathe by Vieûx-Chaslin 713, etc.

(Hoof No. 126.)   **JAPONAIS 6966 (6636).**

[Recorded with pedigree in the Percheron Stud-Books of France and America.]

Dapple grey; 16 hands; weight, 1,800 lbs.; foaled May 1, 1884; imported 1887; bred by M. Gouhier, commune of St. Agnan-sur-Erre, canton of Theil, department of Orne; got by VAILLANT (404); dam Bijou (6635) by BRILLIANT (710) out of Rosette belonging to M. Gouhier, by PROSPER (893).

VAILLANT (404) by Prosper (893) out of Rosalie by Bienvenu, belonging to the Société Hippique of Eure-et-Loir.
PROSPER (893) by Décidé (892) out of Bourreau by Vieux-Pierre (883).
DÉCIDÉ (892) by Vieux-Pierre (894) out of Pelote, belonging to M. Berjeau, of Courvalien.
VIEUX-PIERRE (894) by Coco (712), he by Mignon (715) out of Pauline by Vieux-Coco.
MIGNON (715) by Jean-le-Blanc (739).
BRILLANT (710) by Brilliant 1899 (756) out of Sophie by Superior 454 (730), he by Favori I (711) out of Pauline by Vieux-Chaslin (713).
    FAVORI I (711) by Vieux-Chaslin (713) out of L'Amie by Vieux-Pierre (894), etc.
BRILLIANT 1899 (756) by Coco II (714) out of Rosette by Mina, belonging to the French government.
Coco II (714) by Vieux-Chaslin (713) out of La Grise by Vieux-Pierre (883).
VIEUX-CHASLIN (713) by Coco (712), etc., out of Poule by Sandi.

(Hoof No. 225.) **JEAN-BART 5502 (6789).**
[Recorded with pedigree in the Percheron Stud-Books of France and America.]

Dapple grey; 16¾ hands; weight, 1,925 lbs.; foaled March 21, 1883; imported 1886; bred by M. Legendre, commune of Vaunoise, canton of Bellême, department of Orne; got by MADÈRE II (2994); dam Gentille (4062) by PORTHOS, belonging to M. Fromentin, out of Gentille.

MADÈRE II (2994) by Madeira 1546 (770), he by Vidocq 483 (732) out of Jeanne by Favori I (711), he by Vieux-Chaslin (713) out of L'Amie by Vieux-Pierre (894), he by Coco (712).
VIDOCQ 483 (732) by Coco II (714) out of a daughter of Chéri, he by Rustique.
Coco II (714) by Vieux-Chaslin (713) out of La Grise by Vieux-Pierre (883).
VIEUX-CHASLIN (713) by Coco (712) out of Poule by Sandi.
Coco (712) by Mignon (715) out of Pauline by Vieux-Coco.
MIGNON (715) by Jean-le-Blanc (739).

(Hoof No. 17.) **JEAN JACQUES 7062 (10395).**
[Recorded with pedigree in the Percheron Stud-Books of France and America.]

Black; 16 hands; weight, 1,610 lbs.; foaled April 3, 1885; imported 1887; bred by M. P. Aubry, commune of Champaissant, canton of Mamers, department of Sarthe; got by VERMOUTH (5497); dam Sophie (10394) by PICADOR I (7330).

VERMOUTH (5497) by Picador I (7330) out of Charmante by Oscar.
PICADOR I (7330) by Bayard I (son of Picador) out of Charmante.

(Hoof No. 166). **JEAN-LE-BON 6967 (6047).**
[Recorded with pedigree in the Percheron Stud-Books of France and America.]

Black; 16¼ hands; weight, 1,900 lbs.; foaled May 10, 1884; imported 1887; bred by M. Gravier, commune of Echauffour, department of Orne; got by LUTHER (1792); dam Pusse (6044) by LUTHER (792); 2d dam Élise (6042) by JEAN-BART (716) out of Poule, belonging to M. Heron.

LUTHER (1792) by Luther (792) out of Mignonne by Mondoubleau, belonging to M. Géru.
LUTHER (792) by Pierre (887) out of Rosette (belonging to M. Miard) by Laboureur (886).
PIERRE (887) by Laboureur (886) out of Margot by Faisan.
LABOUREUR (886) by Jean-le-Blanc (739).
JEAN-BART (716) by Bayard, belonging to M. Perpère, out of Jeanne by Porthos.

(Hoof No. 234.) **JOHN A. LOGAN 4111.**
[Recorded with pedigree in the Percheron Stud-Book of America.]

Dapple grey; 15½ hands; weight, 1,430 lbs.; foaled June 2, 1885; bred by H. A. Babcock, of Neenah, Wisconsin; got by CHALDEAN 637 (854); dam Ina B 1773 by CHERE 855 (791); 2d dam Clara Belle 795 (874) by ESTRABA 187 (796), a descendant of JEAN-LE-BLANC (739).

CHALDEAN 637 (854) by Coco [son of Coco II (714)] out of a daughter of Superior 454 (730) he by Favori I (711) out of Pauline by Vieux-Chaslin (713).
Favori I (711) by Vieux-Chaslin (713) out of L'Amie by Vieux-Pierre (894), he by Coco (712).
Coco II (714) by Vieux-Chaslin (713) out of La Grise by Vieux-Pierre (883).
VIEUX-CHASLIN (713) by Coco (712) out of Poule by Sandi.
Coco (712) by Mignon (715) out of Pauline by Vieux-Coco.
MIGNON (715) by Jean-le-Blanc (739).
CHERE 855 (791) by Favori, belonging to M. Dupont, out of Maria by Horisabat.

(Hoof No. 271.)   **KANSAS 7246.**

[Recorded with pedigree in the Percheron Stud-Book of America.]

Black ; foaled 1886 ; bred by J. W. Smith, of Hiattville, Kansas ; got by VALENCIENNE 2623 (1163); dam Margot 4361 (4230) by LUCO 1940 (1058); 2d dam Pelote (4229) by SANSONNET ; 3d dam Rosalie.

VALENCIENNE 2623 (1163) by Valentin out of Brebis by L'Ami.
VALENTIN by Décidé, he by Favori I (711), he by Vieux-Chaslin (713) out of
   L'Amie by Vieux-Pierre (894), he by Coco (712).
VIEUX-CHASLIN (713) by Coco (712) out of Poule by Sandi.
Coco (712) by Mignon (715) out of Pauline by Vieux-Coco.
MIGNON (715) by Jean-le-Blanc (739).
LUCO 1940 (1058) by Merlin 723 out of Marguerite by Bayard 26 (717), he by
   Favori I (711), etc., out of Mignonne by Chéri.

(Hoof No. 111.)   **KLEBER 7063 (10270).**

[Recorded with pedigree in the Percheron Stud-Books of France and America.]

Black ; 16 hands ; weight, 1,675 lbs. ; foaled February 22, 1885 ; imported 1887 ; bred by M. Moulin, commune of Igé, canton of Bellême, department of Orne ; got by GÉROME 3655 (436); dam Charmante (1920) by MADEIRA 1546 (770) out of Rosette, belonging to M. Moulin.

GÉROME 3655 (436) by Vidocq II (723) out of Pelote by Superior 454 (730), he
   by Favori I (711) out of Pauline by Vieux-Chaslin (713).
   FAVORI I (711) by Vieux-Chaslin (713) out of L'Amie by Vieux-Pierre (894),
      he by Coco (712).
VIDOCQ II (723) by Bayard (1385) out of Brière by Décidé.
BAYARD (1385) by Vidocq 483 (732) out of La Noire by Chéri, he by Coco II
   (714).
VIDOCQ 483 (732) by Coco II (714) out of a daughter of Chéri, he by Rustique.
Coco II (714) by Vieux-Chaslin (713) out of La Grise by Vieux-Pierre (883).
VIEUX-CHASLIN (713) by Coco (712) out of Poule by Sandi.
Coco (712) by Mignon (715) out of Pauline by Vieux-Coco.
MIGNON (715) by Jean-le-Blanc (739).
MADEIRA 1546 (770) by Vidocq 483 (732), etc., out of Jeanne by Favori I (711),
   etc.

(Hoof No. 214.)   **LABRIE 7247.**

[Recorded with pedigree in the Percheron Stud-Book of America.]

Dapple grey ; foaled September 1, 1887 ; bred at Oaklawn ; got by LA FERTÉ 5144 (452); dam Brie 2777 (1568) by BRILLIANT 1899 (756) out of a daughter of FAVORI I (711).

LA FERTÉ 5144 (452) by Philibert (760) out of Julie (7594) by Brilliant 1899 (756).
PHILIBERT (760) by Superior 454 (730) out of Madelon by Vieux-Vaillant
   (1383), he by Pierre out of a daughter of Vieux-Pierre.
SUPERIOR 454 (730) by Favori I (711) out of Pauline by Vieux-Chaslin (713).
FAVORI I (711) by Vieux-Chaslin (713) out of L'Amie by Vieux-Pierre (894),
   he by Coco (712).
VIEUX-CHASLIN (713) by Coco (712) out of Poule by Sandi.
Coco (712) by Mignon (715) out of Pauline by Vieux-Coco.
MIGNON (715) by Jean-le-Blanc (739).
BRILLIANT 1899 (756) by Coco II (714) out of Rosette by Mina, belonging to
   the French government.
Coco II (714) by Vieux-Chaslin (713), etc., out of La Grise by Vieux-Pierre
   (883).

L'AMI 6968 (6775).

(Hoof No. 113.)

[Recorded with pedigree in the Percheron Stud-Books of France and America.]

Dapple grey; 16 hands; weight, 1,700 lbs.; foaled March 25, 1883; imported 1887; bred by M. Jean-de-Leuze, commune of Scriguy, canton of Bellême, department of Orne; got by MADÈRE II (2994); dam L'Amie (6772) by VIDOCQ 483 (732) out of Bijou.

MADÈRE II (2994) by Madeira 1546 (770), he by Vidocq 483 (732) out of Jeanne by Favori I (711), he by Vieux-Chaslin (713) out of L'Amie by Vieux-Pierre (894), he by Coco (712).
VIDOCQ 483 (732) by Coco II (714) out of a daughter of Chéri, he by Rustique.
Coco II (714) by Vieux-Chaslin (713) out of La Grise by Vieux-Pierre (883).
VIEUX-CHASLIN (713) by Coco (712) out of Poule by Sandi.
Coco (712) by Mignon (715) out of Pauline by Vieux-Coco.
MIGNON (715) by Jean-le-Blanc (739).

L'AMI 7068 (9532).

(Hoof No. 152.)

[Recorded with pedigree in the Percheron Stud-Books of France and America.]

Dapple grey; 16½ hands; weight, 1,750 lbs.; foaled April 10, 1884; imported 1887; bred by M. Poupard, commune of St. Hilaire-sur-Erre, canton of Theil, department of Orne; got by ADONAIS (83); dam Bijou (4844) by PAPILLON, belonging to M. Thérin, he by PIERRE; 2d dam Cocotte, belonging to M. Meunier.

ADONAIS (83) by Iago 995 (768) out of Bichette.
IAGO 995 (768) by Utopia 780 (731) out of Cossette by Favora 666 (725), he by Favori I (711) out of Marie by Coco (712).
UTOPIA 780 (731) by Superior 454 (730) out of Camille by Favori I (711).
SUPERIOR 454 (730) by Favori I (711) out of Pauline by Vieux-Chaslin (713).
FAVORI I (711) by Vieux-Chaslin (713) out of L'Amie by Vieux-Pierre (894), he by Coco (712).
VIEUX-CHASLIN (713) by Coco (712) out of Poule by Sandi.
Coco (712) by Mignon (715) out of Pauline by Vieux-Coco.
MIGNON (715) by Jean-le-Blanc (739).

L'AMIRAL 7067 (9570).

(Hoof No. 154.)

[Recorded with pedigree in the Percheron Stud-Books of France and America.]

Black; 16¾ hands; weight, 2,000 lbs.; foaled April 18, 1883; imported 1887; bred by M. Virlouvette, commune of Souancé, canton of Nogent-le-Rotrou, department of Eure-et-Loir; got by VAILLANT (404); dam Pelotte (9569) by VAILLANT (404).

VAILLANT (404) by Prosper (893) out of Rosalie by Bienvenu, belonging to the Société Hippique of Eure-et-Loir.
PROSPER (893) by Décidé (892) out of Bourreau by Vieux-Pierre (883).
DÉCIDÉ (892) by Vieux-Pierre (894) out of Pelote, belonging to M. Berjeau, of Courvalien.
VIEUX-PIERRE (894) by Coco (712), he by Mignon (715) out of Pauline by Vieux-Coco.
MIGNON (715) by Jean-le-Blanc (739).

LE BLOND 7066 (7270).

(Hoof No. 132.)

[Recorded with pedigree in the Percheron Stud-Books of France and America.]

Dark steel grey; 16 hands; weight, 1,605 lbs.; foaled April 2, 1884; imported 1887; bred by M. Le Blond, commune of Choué, canton of Mondoubleau, department of Loir-et-Cher; got by O'CONNEL, belonging to the French government; dam Poule (7269) by MARTIN, belonging to M. Hayes, out of La Rouge, belonging to M. Le Blond.

(Hoof No. 38.) **LEMNOS 7071 (8399).**

[Recorded with pedigree in the Percheron Stud-Books of France and America.]

Grey ; foaled April 11, 1886 ; imported 1887 ; bred by M. Gaulard, commune of Coudray-au-Perche, canton of Authon, department of Eure-et-Loir ; got by BISMARCK 5529 (633) ; dam Coquette (4264) by FAVORI, belonging to M. Gouhier, out of Castille.

BISMARCK 5529 (633) by Sultan (1395) out of Pelote (7322) by Vigoureux (1392).
SULTAN (1395) by Vigoureux (1392) out of Margot by Franconi, belonging to M. Sagot.
VIGOUREUX (1392) by Coco II (714) out of Marguerite by Franconi.
Coco II (714) by Vieux-Chaslin (713) out of La Grise by Vieux-Pierre (883).
VIEUX-CHASLIN (713) by Coco (712) out of Poule by Sandi.
Coco (712) by Mignon (715) out of Pauline by Vieux-Coco.
MIGNON (715) by Jean-le-Blanc (739).

(Hoof No. 116.) **LERIDA 6969 (6780).**

[Recorded with pedigree in the Percheron Stud-Books of France and America.]

Grey ; 16¼ hands ; weight, 1,825 lbs. ; foaled April 10, 1884 ; imported 1887 ; bred by M. Guit, commune of St. Aubin, canton of Nocé, department of Orne ; got by GÉROME 3655 (436) ; dam L'Amie (6779) by BAYARD (1385).

GÉROME 3655 (436) by Vidocq II (723) out of Pelotte by Superior 454 (730), he by Favori I (711) out of Pauline by Vieux-Chaslin (713).
    FAVORI I (711) by Vieux-Chaslin (713) out of L'Amie by Vieux-Pierre (894), he by Coco (712).
VIDOCQ II (723) by Bayard (1385) out of Brière by Décidé.
BAYARD (1385) by Vidocq 483 (732) out of La Noire by Chéri, he by Coco II (714).
VIDOCQ 483 (732) by Coco II (714) out of a daughter of Chéri, he by Rustique.
Coco II (714) by Vieux-Chaslin (713) out of La Grise by Vieux-Pierre (883).
VIEUX-CHASLIN (713) by Coco (712) out of Poule by Sandi.
Coco (712) by Mignon (715) out of Pauline by Vieux-Coco.
MIGNON (715) by Jean-le-Blanc (739).

(Hoof No. 180.) **L'ERMITAGE 7070 (9437).**

[Recorded with pedigree in the Percheron Stud-Books of France and America.]

Brown ; 16 hands ; weight, 1,620 lbs. ; foaled April 12, 1885 ; imported 1887 ; bred by M. Mauger, commune of L'Hermitiere, canton of Theil, department of Orne ; got by SULTAN 3548 (356) ; dam L'Amie (9438) by FAVORI, belonging to M. Ernest Perriot.

SULTAN 3548 (356) by Narbonne 1334 (777) out of L'Amie by Count 643 (736), he by Bayard 26 (717) out of Bijou by Rustique.
    BAYARD 26 (717) by Favori I (711) out of Mignonne by Chéri.
    FAVORI I (711) by Vieux-Chaslin (713) out of L'Amie by Vieux-Pierre (894), he by Coco (712).
NARBONNE 1334 (777) by Brilliant 1899 (756) out of Madelon (4722) by Favori I (711), etc.
BRILLIANT 1899 (756) by Coco II (714) out of Rosette by Mina, belonging to the French government.
Coco II (714) by Vieux-Chaslin (713) out of La Grise by Vieux-Pierre (883).
VIEUX-CHASLIN (713) by Coco (712) out of Poule by Sandi.
Coco (712) by Mignon (715) out of Pauline by Vieux-Coco.
MIGNON (715) by Jean-le-Blanc (739).

(Hoof No. 139.)   **LION-D'OR 6970 (8583).**

[Recorded with pedigree in the Percheron Stud-Books of France and America.]

Dapple grey ; 16 hands ; weight, 1,795 lbs.; foaled May 4, 1884 ; imported 1887 ; bred by M. Boulay, commune of Eperrais, canton of Pervenchères, department of Orne ; got by PHILIBERT 5732 (1632); dam Rustique (8582) by MADÈRE 1263 (772).

PHILIBERT 5732 (1632) by Favori, belonging to M. Epinette, out of Caraby, belonging to M. Liberge.
MADÈRE 1263 (772) by Brilliant 1899 (756) out of Hortense by Duke-de-Chartres 162 (721), he by Coco II (714).
BRILLIANT 1899 (756) by Coco II (714) out of Rosette by Mina, belonging to the French government.
Coco II (714) by Vieux-Chaslin (713) out of La Grise by Vieux-Pierre (883).
VIEUX-CHASLIN (713) by Coco (712) out of Poule by Sandi.
Coco (712) by Mignon (715) out of Pauline by Vieux-Coco.
MIGNON (715) by Jean-le-Blanc (739).

(Hoof No. 90.)   **LODI 6971 (9451).**

[Recorded with pedigree in the Percheron Stud-Books of France and America.]

Light dapple grey ; 16¼ hands ; weight, 1,690 lbs.; foaled April 15, 1884 ; imported 1887 ; bred by M. Legout, commune of St. Germain-des-Grois, canton of Rémalard, department of Orne ; got by ADONAIS (83); dam Biche (9450) by IAGO 995 (768).

ADONAIS (83) by Iago 995 (768) out of Bichette.
IAGO 995 (768) by Utopia 780 (731) out of Cossette by Favora 666 (725), he by Favori I (711) out of Marie by Coco (712).
UTOPIA 780 (731) by Superior 454 (730) out of Camille by Favori I (711).
SUPERIOR 454 (730) by Favori I (711) out of Pauline by Vieux-Chaslin (713).
FAVORI I (711) by Vieux-Chaslin (713) out of L'Amie by Vieux-Pierre (894), he by Coco (712).
VIEUX-CHASLIN (713) by Coco (712) out of Poule by Sandi.
Coco (712) by Mignon (715) out of Pauline by Vieux-Coco.
MIGNON (715) by Jean-le-Blanc (739).

(Hoof No. 130.)   **LOKE 7065 (9885).**

[Recorded with pedigree in the Percheron Stud-Books of France and America.]

Dapple grey ; 16¼ hands ; weight, 1,760 lbs. ; foaled March 15, 1884 ; imported 1887 ; bred by M. Caillon, commune of La-Ferté-Bernard, department of Sarthe ; got by LAGRANGE 3065 (1334) ; dam Cocotte (9884) by FAVORA 1542 (765).

LAGRANGE 3065 (1334) by Brilliant 1271 (755) out of Lydie by Coco II (714).
BRILLIANT 1271 (755) by Brilliant 1899 (756) out of Ragout by Favori I (711), he by Vieux-Chaslin (713) out of L'Amie by Vieux-Pierre (894), he by Coco (712).
BRILLIANT 1899 (756) by Coco II (714) out of Rosette by Mina, belonging to the French government.
Coco II (714) by Vieux-Chaslin (713) out of La Grise by Vieux-Pierre (883).
VIEUX-CHASLIN (713) by Coco (712) out of Poule by Sandi.
Coco (712) by Mignon (715) out of Pauline by Vieux-Coco.
MIGNON (715) by Jean-le-Blanc (739).
FAVORA 1542 (765) by French Monarch 205 (734) out of Marguerite by Favori, he by Coco of Mêsle-sur-Sarthe, he by Margot.
FRENCH MONARCH 205 (734) by Ilderim (5302) out of a daughter of Vieux-Pierre (894), etc.
ILDERIM (5302) by Valentin (5301) out of Chaton by Vieux-Pierre (894), etc.
VALENTIN (5301) by Vieux-Chaslin (713), etc.

(Hoof No. 123.)   **LOTO 7064 (10649).**

[Recorded with pedigree in the Percheron Stud-Books of France and America.]

Bay; 16½ hands; weight, 1,775 lbs.; foaled February 17, 1885; imported 1887; bred by M. Vallée, commune of Coulonges, canton of Rémalard, department of Sarthe; got by DÉCIDÉ (359); dam Victorine (6951) by FAVORA 666 (725).

DÉCIDÉ (359) by Vulcain (8003) out of L'Amie, by Vaillant, belonging to Madame Dorchêne.
VULCAIN (8003) by Vigoureux.
FAVORA 666 (725) by Favori I (711), out of Marie by Coco (712).
FAVORI I (711) by Vieux-Chaslin (713) out of L'Amie by Vieux-Pierre (894), he by Coco (712).
VIEUX-CHASLIN (713) by Coco (712) out of Poule by Sandi.
Coco (712) by Mignon (715) out of Pauline by Vieux-Coco.
MIGNON (715) by Jean-le-Blanc (739).

(Hoof No. 20.)   **LUCIEN 7072 (8681).**

[Recorded with pedigree in the Percheron Stud-Books of France and America.]

Dark grey; 16¼ hands; weight, 1,650 lbs.; foaled April 16, 1885; imported 1887; bred by M. Forges, commune of Dame-Marie, canton of Bellême, department of Orne; got by SUPÉRIEUR (2169); dam Biche (5243) by PHILIBERT (4634) out of L'Amie, belonging to M. Mouthean.

SUPÉRIEUR (2169) by Avata 1966 (912) out of Christine by Superior 454 (730), he by Favori I (711) out of Pauline by Vieux-Chaslin (713).
   FAVORI I (711) by Vieux-Chaslin (713) out of L'Amie by Vieux-Pierre (894), he by Coco (712).
AVATA 1966 (912) by Nogent 738 (729) out of Bicotte by Bayard 26 (717), he by Favori I (711), etc., out of Mignonne by Chéri.
NOGENT 738 (729) by Vidocq 483 (732) out of a daughter of Favori I (711), etc.
VIDOCQ 483 (732) by Coco II (714) out of a daughter of Chéri, he by Rustique.
Coco II (714) by Vieux-Chaslin (713) out of La Grise by Vieux-Pierre (883).
VIEUX-CHASLIN (713) by Coco (712) out of Poule by Sandi.
Coco (712) by Mignon (715) out of Pauline by Vieux-Coco.
MIGNON (715) by Jean-le-Blanc (739).
PHILIBERT (4634) by Philibert [son of Superior 454 (730)] out of Rustique, belonging to M. Lemesle.
SUPERIOR 454 (730) by Favori I (711), etc., out of Pauline by Vieux-Chaslin (713), etc.

(Hoof No. 93.)   **LUCIUS 7010 (6873).**

[Recorded with pedigree in the Percheron Stud-Books of France and America.]

Dark brown; 16½ hands; weight, 1,750 lbs.; foaled May 22, 1882; imported 1887; bred by M. Thomas, commune of Brunelles, department of Eure-et-Loir; got by MARQUIS (1394); dam Robine (6872) by BRILLANT (710) out of L'Amie, belonging to M. Coudray.

MARQUIS (1394) by Count 643 (736) out of Rosette by Madere.
COUNT 643 (736) by Bayard 26 (717) out of Bijou by Rustique.
BAYARD 26 (717) by Favori I (711) out of Mignonne by Chéri.
FAVORI I (711) by Vieux-Chaslin (713), out of L'Amie by Vieux-Pierre (894), he by Coco (712).
VIEUX-CHASLIN (713) by Coco (712) out of Poule by Sandi.
Coco (712) by Mignon (715) out of Pauline by Vieux-Coco.
MIGNON (715) by Jean-le-Blanc (739).
BRILLANT (710) by Brilliant 1899 (756) out of Sophie by Superior 454 (730), he by Favori I (711), etc., out of Pauline by Vieux-Chaslin (713), etc.

(Hoof No. 178.) **LURON 7069 (6346).**

[Recorded with pedigree in the Percheron Stud-Books of France and America.]

Black ; 16 hands ; weight, 1,670 lbs.; foaled May 10, 1885 ; imported 1887 ; bred by M. Louis Poivre, commune of Courgenard, department of Sarthe ; got by PAPILLON 3559 (379) ; dam Poulotte (6345) by PASSE-PARTOUT (1402) out of Biche, belonging to M. Poivre.

PAPILLON 3559 (379) by Brilliant (710) out of Cocotte by Coco II (714).
BRILLANT (710) by Brilliant 1899 (756) out of Sophie by Superior 454 (730), he by Favori I (711) out of Pauline by Vieux-Chaslin (713).
    FAVORI I (711) by Vieux-Chaslin (713) out of L'Amie by Vieux-Pierre (894), he by Coco (712).
BRILLIANT 1899 (756) by Coco II (714) out of Rosette by Mina, belonging to the French government.
Coco II (714) by Vieux-Chaslin (713) out of La Grise by Vieux-Pierre (883).
VIEUX-CHASLIN (713) by Coco (712) out of Poule by Sandi.
Coco (712) by Mignon (715) out of Pauline by Vieux-Coco.
MIGNON (715) by Jean-le-Blanc (739).
PASSE-PARTOUT (1402) by Comet 104 (719) out of Sophie by Favori I (711), he by Vieux-Chaslin (713) out of L'Amie by Vieux-Pierre (894), he by Coco (712).
COMET 104 (719) by French Monarch 205 (734) out of Suzanne by Cambronne.
FRENCH MONARCH 205 (734) by Ilderim (5302) out of a daughter of Vieux-Pierre (894). etc.
ILDERIM (5302) by Valentin (5301) out of Chaton by Vieux-Pierre (894), etc.
VALENTIN (5301) by Vieux-Chaslin (713), he by Coco (712) out of Poule by Sandi.

(Hoof No. 114.) **MAGENTA 6972 (10476).**

[Recorded with pedigree in the Percheron Stud-Books of France and America.]

Grey ; 16 hands ; weight, 1,540 lbs.; foaled March 15, 1884 ; imported 1887 ; bred by M. Gouhier, commune of Colonard, department of Orne ; got by GÉROME 3655 (436) ; dam Rosette (151) by BAYARD (1385) out of Castille.

GÉROME 3655 (436) by Vidocq II (723) out of Pelote by Superior 454 (730), he by Favori I (711) out of Pauline by Vieux-Chaslin (713).
    FAVORI I (711) by Vieux-Chaslin (713) out of L'Amie by Vieux-Pierre (894), he by Coco (712).
VIDOCQ II (723) by Bayard (1385) out of Brière by Décidé.
BAYARD (1385) by Vidocq 483 (732) out of La Noire by Chéri, he by Coco II (714).
VIDOCQ 483 (732) by Coco II (714) out of a daughter of Chéri, he by Rustique.
Coco II (714) by Vieux-Chaslin (713) out of La Grise by Vieux-Pierre (883).
VIEUX-CHASLIN (713) by Coco (712) out of Poule by Sandi.
Coco (712) by Mignon (715) out of Pauline by Vieux-Coco.
MIGNON (715) by Jean-le-Blanc (739).

(Hoof No. 102.) **MAGENTA 7073 (7817).**

[Recorded with pedigree in the Percheron Stud-Books of France and America.]

Black ; foaled April 25, 1886 ; imported 1887 ; bred by M. Guede, commune of Theligny, canton of La Ferté-Bernard, department of Sarthe ; got by Coco 4250 (234); dam Frosine (7816) by SANSONNET (4350).

Coco 4250 (234) by Martin, belonging to M. Lucas, out of Grisette (4917) by Marquis (4696), he by Guiloiseau, belonging to M. Noireau, out of Pelotte.
SANSONNET (4350) by Décidé (4569) out of Cocotte, belonging to M. Courturier.

(Hoof No. 224.)   **MAHDI 5594 (6171)**.

[Recorded with pedigree in the Percheron Stud-Books of France and America.]

Dark grey ; 16½ hands ; weight, 1,705 lbs.; foaled March.11, 1884 ; imported 1886 ; bred by M. Fleury, commune of Anguaise, canton of Moulins-la-Marche, department of Orne ; got by DÉSIRÉ (6170); dam Mademoiselle Anguaise (2171) by BRILLANT (6165) out of Bijou, belonging to M. Fleury.

DÉSIRÉ (6170), belonging to the French government.
BRILLANT (6165) by Brillant, belonging to M. Jousset, out of Vaillante by Vaillant.

(Hoof No. 2.)   **MANDRIN 7079 (10582)**.

[Recorded with pedigree in the Percheron Stud-Books of France and America.]

Dark grey ; foaled April, 1886 ; bred by M. Sclicien Tessier, commune of Dame-Marie, canton of Bellême, department of Orne ; got by TURCO (604); dam Cadette (4469) by PICADOR, he by CHÉRI, belonging to M. Jamois, 2d dam Jeannette.

TURCO (604) by Philibert (4634) out of Victorine, belonging to M. Boisseau.
PHILIBERT (4634) by Philibert [son of Superior 454 (730)] out of Rustique, belonging to M. Lemesle.
SUPERIOR 454 (730) by Favori I (711) out of Pauline by Vieux-Chaslin (713).
FAVORI I (711) by Vieux-Chaslin (713) out of L'Amie by Vieux-Pierre (894), he by Coco (712).
VIEUX-CHASLIN (713) by Coco (712) out of Poule by Sandi.
Coco (712) by Mignon (715) out of Pauline by Vieux-Coco.
MIGNON (715) by Jean-le-Blanc (739).

(Hoof No. 15.)   **MARJOY 7078 (11088)**.

[Recorded with pedigree in the Percheron Stud-Books of France and America.]

Grey ; 16¼ hands ; weight, 1,575 lbs. ; foaled March 28, 1885 ; imported 1887 ; bred by M. E. Velard, commune of Dancé, canton of Nocé, department of Orne ; got by CHÉRI 6183 (358); dam Franconie (11087) by CHÉRI, belonging to M. Fardouet fils.

CHÉRI 6183 (358) by Vermouth 1820 (787) out of Chaton.
VERMOUTH 1820 (787) by Vidocq 483 (732) out of Agathe by Vieux-Chaslin (713).
VIDOCQ 483 (732) by Coco II (714) out of a daughter of Chéri, he by Rustique.
Coco II (714) by Vieux-Chaslin (713) out of La Grise by Vieux-Pierre (883).
VIEUX-CHASLIN (713) by Coco (712) out of Poule by Sandi.
Coco (712) by Mignon (715) out of Pauline by Vieux-Coco.
MIGNON (715) by Jean-le-Blanc (739).

(Hoof No. 81.) ### MEAUCÉ 6973 (7410).

[Recorded with pedigree in the Percheron Stud-Books of France and America.]

Steel grey; 16 hands; weight, 1,790 lbs., foaled April 15, 1884; imported 1887; bred by M. Jean Boulay, commune of Berd'huis, canton of Nocé, department of Orne; got by Gérome 3655 (436); dam Margot (7409) by Brilliant (710), out of Castille, belonging to M. Jousselin.

Gérome 3655 (436) by Vidocq II (723) out of Pelote by Superior 454 (730), he by Favori I (711) out of Pauline by Vieux-Chaslin (713).
  Favori I (711) by Vieux-Chaslin (713) out of L'Amie by Vieux-Pierre (894), he by Coco (712).
Vidocq II (723) by Bayard (1385) out of Brière by Décidé.
Bayard (1385) by Vidocq 483 (732) out of La Noire by Chéri, he by Coco II (714).
Vidocq 483 (732) by Coco II (714) out of a daughter of Chéri, he by Rustique.
Coco II (714) by Vieux-Chaslin (713) out of La Grise by Vieux-Pierre (883).
Vieux-Chaslin (713) by Coco (712) out of Poule by Sandi.
Coco (712) by Mignon (715) out of Pauline by Vieux-Coco.
Mignon (715) by Jean-le-Blanc (739).
Brillant (710) by Brilliant 1899 (756) out of Sophie by Superior 454 (730), etc.
Brilliant 1899 (756) by Coco II (714), etc., out of Rosette by Mina, belonging to the French government.

(Hoof No. 39.) ### MEDARD 7076 (7065).

[Recorded with pedigree in the Percheron Stud-Books of France and America.]

Dark grey; 16¼ hands; weight, 1,650 lbs.; foaled March 4, 1884; imported 1887; bred by M. Pelletier, commune of St. Agnan-sur-Erre, canton of Theil, department of Orne; got by Vaillant (404); dam L'Amie (7064) by Vieux-Vaillant (1383).

Vaillant (404) by Prosper (893) out of Rosalie by Bienvenu, belonging to the Société Hippique of Eure-et-Loir.
Prosper (893) by Décidé (892) out of Bourreau by Vieux-Pierre (883).
Décidé (892) by Vieux-Pierre (894) out of Pelote, belonging to M. Berjeau, of Courvalien.
Vieux-Pierre (894) by Coco (712), he by Mignon (715) out of Pauline by Vieux-Coco.
Mignon (715) by Jean-le-Blanc (739).
Vieux-Vaillant (1383) by Pierre, belonging to M. Thérin, out of a daughter of Vieux-Pierre (883).

(Hoof No. 11.)   **MONTAGNARD 7077 (10281).**

[Recorded with pedigree in the Percheron Stud-Books of France and America.]

Dark grey ; foaled March 12, 1886 ; imported 1887 ; bred by M. Louis Jamois, commune of Dame-Marie, canton of Bellême, department of Orne ; got by Turco (604); dam Rosette (10280) by Vidocq II (723).

Turco (604) by Philibert (4634) out of Victorine, belonging to M. Boisseau.
Philibert (4634) by Philibert [son of Superior 454 (730)] out of Rustique, belonging to M. Lemesle.
Superior 454 (730) by Favori I (711) out of Pauline by Vieux-Chaslin (713).
Favori I (711) by Vieux-Chaslin (713) out of L'Amie by Vieux-Pierre (894), he by Coco (712).
Vieux-Chaslin (713) by Coco (712) out of Poule by Sandi.
Coco (712) by Mignon (715) out of Pauline by Vieux-Coco.
Mignon (715) by Jean-le-Blanc (739).
Vidocq II (723) by Bayard (1385) out of Brière by Décidé.
Bayard (1385) by Vidocq 483 (732) out of La Noire by Chéri, he by Coco II (714).
Vidocq 483 (732) by Coco II (714) out of a daughter of Chéri, he by Rustique.
Coco II (714) by Vieux-Chaslin (713), etc., out of La Grise by Vieux-Pierre (883).

(Hoof No. 134.)   **MONT D'OR 7074 (10684).**

[Recorded with pedigree in the Percheron Stud-Books of France and America.]

Dapple grey ; 16¼ hands ; weight, 1,670 lbs. ; foaled March 7, 1885 ; imported 1887 ; bred by M. Guillaume, commune of Sargé, canton of Mondoubleau, department of Loir-et-Cher ; got by Vermouth 5134 (2004); dam Julie (10683) by Coco, belonging to M. Derais.

Vermouth 5134 (2004) by Paul (7433) out of Poule (7434) by Paul, belonging to M. Dubois.
Paul (7434) by Paul, belonging to M. Dubois, out of Biche by Pierre.

(Hoof No. 148.)   **MOUTON 6974 (6768).**

[Recorded with pedigree in the Percheron Stud-Books of France and America.]

Black ; 16¼ hands ; weight, 1,900 lbs. ; foaled February 15, 1882 ; imported 1887 ; bred by M. Junier, commune of St. Marc-du-Cor, canton of Mondoubleau, department of Loir-et-Cher ; got by Fort-a-Bras, belonging to the French government ; dam Petite (6767) by Vigoureux, belonging to M. Landron, out of Julie.

(Hoof No. 146.)   **MOUTON 6975 (10475).**

[Recorded with pedigree in the Percheron Stud-Books of France and America.]

Dark grey ; 16½ hands ; weight, 1,800 lbs. ; foaled April 28, 1883; imported 1887 ; bred by M. Rousseau, commune of St. Pierre-Fixe, canton of Nogent-le-Rotrou, department of Eure-et-Loir ; got by Philibert II 2684 (1310) ; dam Bleue (10474) by Vieux-Chaslin (713).

Philibert II 2684 (1310) by Philibert (760) out of Fannie by Favori I (711).
Philibert (760) by Superior 454 (730) out of Madelon by Vieux-Vaillant (1383), he by Pierre out of a daughter of Vieux-Pierre (883).
Superior 454 (730) by Favori I (711) out of Pauline by Vieux-Chaslin (713).
Favori I (711) by Vieux-Chaslin (713) out of L'Amie by Vieux-Pierre (894), he by Coco (712).
Vieux-Chaslin (713) by Coco (712) out of Poule by Sandi.
Coco (712) by Mignon (715) out of Pauline by Vieux-Coco.
Mignon (715) by Jean-le-Blanc (739).

(Hoof No. 112.) **MOUVETTE 6976 (59).**

[Recorded with pedigree in the Percheron Stud-Books of France and America.]

Dapple grey; 15½ hands; weight, 1,600 lbs.; foaled 1882; imported 1887; bred by M. Gouhier, commune of Colonard, canton of Nocé, department of Orne; got by AVATA 1966 (912); dam Bijou (150) by CHÉRI, he by Coco II (714); 2d dam L'Amie.

AVATA 1966 (912) by Nogent 738 (729) out of Bicotte by Bayard 26 (717), he by Favori I (711) out of Mignonne by Chéri.
FAVORI I (711) by Vieux-Chaslin (713) out of L'Amie by Vieux-Pierre (894), he by Coco (712).
NOGENT 738 (729) by Vidocq 483 (732) out of a daughter of Favori I (711), etc.
VIDOCQ 483 (732) by Coco II (714) out of a daughter of Chéri, he by Rustique.
Coco II (714) by Vieux-Chaslin (713) out of La Grise by Vieux-Pierre (883).
VIEUX-CHASLIN (713) by Coco (712) out of Poule by Sandi.
Coco (712) by Mignon (715) out of Pauline by Vieux-Coco.
MIGNON (715) by Jean-le-Blanc (739).

(Hoof No. 9.) **NEPTUNE 7080 (8862).**

[Recorded with pedigree in the Percheron Stud-Books of France and America.]

Grey; foaled April 9, 1886; imported 1887; bred by M. Blot, commune of Mezières, canton of Marolles-les-Braux, department of Sarthe; got by BAYARD II (5612); dam Bleue (8861).

BAYARD II (5612) by Picador I (7330) out of Sophia.
PICADOR (7330) by Bayard I (son of Picador) out of Charmante.

(Hoof No. 215.) **NORWAY 5691.**

[Recorded with pedigree in the Percheron Stud-Book of America.]

Grey; 16¼ hands; weight, 1,660 lbs.; foaled April 13, 1884; bred by Daniel Cushman, of Champaign, Illinois; got by NORVAL 1369 (794); dam La Bella 974.

NORVAL 1369 (794) by Brilliant 1899 (756) out of Frosine by Décidé, belonging to M. Fardouet.
BRILLIANT 1899 (756) by Coco II (714) out of Rosette by Mina, belonging to the French government.
Coco II (714) by Vieux-Chaslin (713) out of La Grise by Vieux-Pierre (883).
VIEUX-CHASLIN (713) by Coco (712) out of Poule by Sandi.
Coco (712) by Mignon (715) out of Pauline by Vieux-Coco.
MIGNON (715) by Jean-le-Blanc (739).

(Hoof No. 218.) **OBÉRON 2184 (991).**

[Recorded with pedigree in the Percheron Stud-Books of France and America.]

Dark grey; 15¾ hands; weight, 1,550 lbs.; foaled 1882; imported 1882; got by DOCILE, he by BRILLIANT 1899 (756); dam Coquette by Coco II (714.)

BRILLIANT 1899 (756) by Coco II (714) out of Rosette by Mina, belonging to the French government.
Coco II (714) by Vieux-Chaslin (713) out of La Grise by Vieux-Pierre (883).
VIEUX-CHASLIN (713), he by Coco (712) out of Poule by Sandi.
Coco (712) by Mignon (715) out of Pauline by Vieux-Coco.
MIGNON (715) by Jean-le-Blanc (739).

(Hoof No. 167.)   **ORGUEILLEUX 7013 (6051).**

[Recorded with pedigree in the Percheron Stud-Books of France and America.]

Steel grey ; 16 hands ; weight, 1,660 lbs.; foaled April 15, 1884 ; imported 1887 ; bred by M. Gibory, commune of Echauffour, canton of Merlerault, department of Orne ; got by LUTHER III (1792); dam Lisette (6050) by LUTHER (792) out of Sophie.

LUTHER III (1792) by Luther (792) out of Mignonne by Mondoubleau, belong- ing to M. Geru.
LUTHER (792) by Pierre (887) out of Rosette by Laboureur (886).
PIERRE (887) by Laboureur (886) out of Margot by Faisan.
LABOUREUR (886) by Jean-le-Blanc (739) out of Sophie by Sandi.

(Hoof No. 21.   **ORPHELIN 5521 (6980).**

[Recorded with pedigree in the Percheron Stud-Books of France and America.]

Dark grey ; 16½ hands ; weight, 1,720 lbs.; foaled February 15, 1884 ; imported 1886 ; bred by M. Aubert, commune of St. Cyr-la-Rosière, canton of Nocé, department of Orne ; got by CHÉRI (7702); dam Rustique (7464) by COUNT 643 (736).

CHÉRI (7702) by Fleurus, he by French Monarch 205 (734), he by Ilderim (5302) out of a daughter of Vieux-Pierre (894), he by Coco (712).
ILDERIM (5302) by Valentin (5301) out of Chaton by Vieux-Pierre (894), etc.
VALENTIN (5301) by Vieux-Chaslin (713), he by Coco (712) out of Poule by Sandi.
COCO (712) by Mignon (715) out of Pauline by Vieux-Coco.
MIGNON (715) by Jean-le-Blanc (739).
COUNT 643 (736) by Bayard 26 (717) out of Bijou by Rustique.
BAYARD 26 (717) by Favori I (711) out of Mignonne by Chéri.
FAVORI I (711) by Vieux-Chaslin (713), etc., out of L'Amie by Vieux-Pierre (894), etc.

(Hoof No. 83.)   **PACHA 6977 (4368).**

[Recorded with pedigree in the Percheron Stud-Books of France and America.]

Silver grey; 16¼ hands ; weight, 1,875 lbs. ; foaled May 12, 1884 ; imported 1887 ; bred by M. Victor Gouhier, commune of Colonard, canton of Nocé, department of Orne ; got by GÉROME 3655 (436); dam Castille (6334) by DÉCIDÉ, belonging to M. Fardouet père, out of Chérie, belonging to M. Gouhier, of Plessis.

GÉROME 3655 (436) by Vidocq II (723) out of Pelote by Superior 454 (730), he by Favori I (711) out of Pauline by Vieux-Chaslin (713).
    FAVORI I (711) by Vieux-Chaslin (713) out of L'Amie by Vieux-Pierre (894), he by Coco (712).
VIDOCQ II (723) by Bayard (1385) out of Brière by Décidé.
BAYARD (1385) by Vidocq 483 (732) out of La Noire by Chéri, he by Coco II (714).
VIDOCQ 483 (732) by Coco II (714) out of a daughter of Chéri, he by Rustique.
COCO II (714) by Vieux-Chaslin (713) out of La Grise by Vieux-Pierre (883).
VIEUX-CHASLIN (713) by Coco (712) out of Poule by Sandi.
COCO (712) by Mignon (715) out of Pauline by Vieux-Coco.
MIGNON (715) by Jean-le-Blanc (739).

(Hoof No. 141.) **PALEFRENIER 6978 (6314).**

[Recorded with pedigree in the Percheron Stud-Books of France and America.]

Dark grey; 16 hands; weight, 1,700 lbs.; foaled April 10, 1884; imported 1887; bred by M. Melet, commune of Chapelle Royale, canton of Authon, department of Eure-et-Loir; got by TACONET 2581 (1307); dam Brebis (6313) by SANDY, belonging to M. Melet, out of Barrée, belonging to M. Melet.

TACONET 2581 (1307) by Brillant (710) out of Bonne by Coco II (714).
BRILLANT (710) by Brilliant 1899 (756) out of Sophie by Superior 454 (730), he by Favori I (711) out of Pauline by Vieux-Chaslin (713).
 FAVORI I (711) by Vieux-Chaslin (713) out of L'Amie by Vieux-Pierre (894), he by Coco (712).
BRILLIANT 1899 (756) by Coco II (714) out of Rosette by Mina, belonging to the French government.
Coco II (714) by Vieux-Chaslin (713) out of La Grise by Vieux-Pierre (883).
VIEUX-CHASLIN (713) by Coco (712) out of Poule by Sandi.
Coco (712) by Mignon (715) out of Pauline by Vieux-Coco.
MIGNON (715) by Jean-le-Blanc (739).

(Hoof No. 298.) **PAMPEIRO 5564 (6580).**

[Recorded with pedigree in the Percheron Stud-Books of France and America.]

Dark grey; 16¼ hands;. weight, 1,620 lbs.; foaled April 4, 1882; imported 1886; bred by M. Renoud, commune of St. Agnan-sur-Erre, canton of Theil, department of Orne; got by VAILLANT (404); dam Poule (6579) by VAILLANT (4271) out of Lucie, belonging to M. Pelletier.

VAILLANT (404) by Prosper (893) out of Rosalie by Bienvenu, belonging to the Société Hippique of Eure-et-Loir.
PROSPER (893) by Décidé (892) out of Bourreau by Vieux-Pierre (883).
DÉCIDÉ (892) by Vieux-Pierre (894) out of Pelote, belonging to M. Berjeau, of Courvalien.
VIEUX-PIERRE (894) by Coco (712), he by Mignon (715) out of Pauline by Vieux-Coco.
MIGNON (715) by Jean-le-Blanc (739).
VAILLANT (4271) by Favori I (711), he by Vieux-Chaslin (713) out of L'Amie by Vieux-Pierre (894), etc.
VIEUX-CHASLIN (713) by Coco (712), etc., out of Poule by Sandi.

(Hoof No. 186.) **PANORAMA 7085 (12010).**

[Recorded with pedigree in the Percheron Stud-Books of France and America.]

Black; 16 hands; weight, 1,700 lbs.; foaled March 17, 1883; imported 1887; bred by M. Leleuze, commune of Serigny, canton of Bellême, department of Orne; got by AVATA 1966 (912); dam Poule (6774) by MADEIRA 1546 (770) out of Poule.

AVATA 1966 (912) by Nogent 738 (729) out of Bicotte by Bayard 26 (717), he by Favori I (711) out of Mignonne by Chéri.
 FAVORI I (711) by Vieux-Chaslin (713) out of L'Amie by Vieux-Pierre (894), he by Coco (712).
NOGENT 738 (729) by Vidocq 483 (732) out of a daughter of Favori I (711), etc.
VIDOCQ 483 (732) by Coco II (714) out of a daughter of Chéri, he by Rustique.
Coco II (714) by Vieux-Chaslin (713) out of La Grise by Vieux-Pierre (883).
VIEUX-CHASLIN (713) by Coco (712) out of Poule by Sandi.
Coco (712) by Mignon (715) out of Pauline by Vieux-Coco.
MIGNON (715) by Jean-le-Blanc (739).
MADEIRA 1546 (770) by Vidocq 483 (732), etc., out of Jeanne by Favori I (711), etc.

(Hoof No. 8.)   **PANORAMA 7091 (7920).**

[Recorded with pedigree in the Percheron Stud-Books of France and America.]

Dark grey; foaled April 12, 1886; imported 1887; bred by M. Bonhomme, commune of La Rouge, canton of Theil, department of Orne; got by ROCHAMBORT 4328 (172); dam Melie (7472) by NARBONNE 1334 (777) out of Biche.

ROCHAMBORT 4328 (172) by Rochambeau (1382) out of L'Amie (4838) by Favori I (711), he by Vieux-Chaslin (713) out of L'Amie by Vieux-Pierre (894), he by Coco (712).
ROCHAMBEAU (1382) by Brilliant 1899 (756) out of Cocotte by Coco II (714).
BRILLIANT 1899 (756) by Coco II (714) out of Rosette by Mina, belonging to the French government.
Coco II (714) by Vieux-Chaslin (713) out of La Grise by Vieux-Pierre (883).
VIEUX-CHASLIN (713) by Coco (712) out of Poule by Sandi.
Coco (712) by Mignon (715) out of Pauline by Vieux-Coco.
MIGNON (715) by Jean-le-Blanc (739).
NARBONNE 1334 (777) by Brilliant 1899 (756), etc., out of Madelon (4722) by Favori I (711), etc.

(Hoof No. 162.)   **PAPILLON 6979 (9572).**

[Recorded with pedigree in the Percheron Stud-Books of France and America.]

Light dapple grey; 16½ hands; weight, 1,750 lbs.; foaled April 15, 1884; imported 1887; bred by M. Elmire Chantepie, commune of Marche-Maisons, canton of Mêsle-sur-Sarthe, department of Orne; got by PAPILLON (6800); dam Biche (9571) by CÉSAR, belonging to M. Chevrier.

PAPILLON (6800) by Moutard (son of Coco of Mêsle-sur-Sarthe) out of Bijou, belonging to M. Miteau, by Coco (712), he by Mignon (715) out of Pauline by Vieux-Coco.
MIGNON (715) by Jean-le-Blanc (739).

(Hoof No. 92.)   **PAPILLON 7089 (5753).**

[Recorded with pedigree in the Percheron Stud-Books of France and America.]

Light dapple grey; 16½ hands; weight, 1,820 lbs.; foaled March 27, 1882; imported 1887; bred by M. Auguste Vadé, commune of Melleray, canton of Montmirail, department of Sarthe; got by MOUTON (4602), he by Coco, belonging to M. Louis Perriot; dam Pelotte (5752).

(Hoof No. 46.) **PAPILLON III 7086 (11409).**

[Recorded with pedigree in the Percheron Stud-Books of France and America.]

Grey; 16¼ hands; weight, 1,700 lbs.; foaled March 5, 1885; imported 1887; bred by M. Alexandre Souchay, commune of Ceton, canton of Theil, department of Orne; got by PAPILLON 3559 (379); dam Marianne (6879) by MOUTON (1640) out of Bijou.

PAPILLON 3559 (379) by Brillant (710) out of Cocotte by Coco II (714).
BRILLANT (710) by Brilliant 1899 (756) out of Sophie by Superior 454 (730), he by Favori I (711) out of Pauline by Vieux-Chaslin (713).
FAVORI I (711) by Vieux-Chaslin (713) out of L'Amie by Vieux-Pierre (894), he by Coco (712).
BRILLANT 1899 (756) by Coco II (714) out of Rosette by Mina, belonging to the French government.
Coco II (714) by Vieux-Chaslin (713) out of La Grise by Vieux-Pierre (883).
VIEUX-CHASLIN (713) by Coco (712) out of Poule by Sandi.
Coco (712) by Mignon (715) out of Pauline by Vieux-Coco.
MIGNON (715) by Jean-le-Blanc (739).
MOUTON (1640) by French Monarch 205 (734) out of Rose by Décidé.
FRENCH MONARCH 205 (734) by Ilderim (5302) out of a daughter of Vieux-Pierre (894), etc.
ILDERIM (5302) by Valentin (5301) out of Chaton by Vieux-Pierre (894), etc.
VALENTIN (5301) by Vieux-Chaslin (713), etc.

(Hoof No. 260.) **PAROLE 7240.**

[Recorded with pedigree in the Percheron Stud-Book of America.]

Grey; foaled May 15, 1887, bred at Oaklawn; got by PRODUCTEUR 4280 (68); dam Alma 3672 by BRILLIANT 1271 (755); 2d dam Agnes 1477 (1409) by PICADOR, belonging to the French government, he by FAVORI; 3d dam by BAYARD 26 (717).

PRODUCTEUR 4280 (68) by Madeira 1546 (770) out of Gentille (4062) by Porthos.
MADEIRA 1546 (770) by Vidocq 483 (732) out of Jeanne by Favori I (711).
VIDOCQ 483 (732) by Coco II (714) out of a daughter of Chéri, he by Rustique.
Coco II (714) by Vieux-Chaslin (713) out of La Grise by Vieux-Pierre (883).
VIEUX-CHASLIN (713) by Coco (712) out of Poule by Sandi.
Coco (712) by Mignon (715) out of Pauline by Vieux-Coco.
MIGNON (715) by Jean-le-Blanc (739).
BRILLIANT 1271 (755) by Brilliant 1899 (756) out of Ragout by Favori I (711).
BRILLIANT 1899 (756) by Coco II (714), etc., out of Rosette by Mina, belonging to the French government.
BAYARD 26 (717) by Favori I (711) out of Mignonne by Chéri.
FAVORI I (711) by Vieux-Chaslin (713), etc., out of L'Amie by Vieux-Pierre (894), he by Coco (712), etc.

(Hoof No. 122.)   **PAROLI 6980 (6521).**

[Recorded with pedigree in the Percheron Stud-Books of France and America.]

Dapple grey; 16½ hands; weight, 1,550 lbs.; foaled March 8, 1884; imported 1887; bred by M. Désiré Ducœurjoly, commune of Brunelles, canton of Nogent-le-Rotrou, department of Eure-et-Loir; got by VAINQUEUR 4288 (284); dam Perlette (282) by ROLAND II (2256) out of Bichette; 2d dam Pauline (279) by MIRAMAR.

VAINQUEUR 4288 (284) by Bayard (6751) out of Grisette (280) by Médoc, he by
    French Monarch 205 (734), he by Ilderim out of a daughter of Vieux-
    Pierre (894), he by Coco (712).
ILDERIM (5302) by Valentin (5301) out of Chaton by Vieux-Pierre (894), etc.
VALENTIN (5301) by Vieux-Chaslin (713), he by Coco (712) out of Poule by
    Sandi.
Coco (712) by Mignon (715) out of Pauline by Vieux-Coco.
MIGNON (715) by Jean-le-Blanc (739).
BAYARD (6751) by Mina, belonging to the Société Hippique of Eure-et-Loir, out
    of Louison by Chéri, belonging to M. Fardouet père, he by Couronne,
    belonging to M. Sagot.

PARTHENON 7241.

[Recorded with pedigree in the Percheron Stud-Book of America.]

Grey; foaled September 9, 1887; bred at Oaklawn; got by PRO-
DUCTEUR 4280 (68); dam Madelon 5669 (2174) by CHARTRAIN (1405);
2d dam L'Amie (7039) by VALENTIN (5301); 3d dam Margot, belonging to M. Fausse-Abry.

PRODUCTEUR 4280 (68) by Madeira 1546 (770) out of Gentille (4062) by Porthos.
MADEIRA 1546 (770) by Vidocq 483 (732) out of Jeanne by Favori I (711).
VIDOCQ 483 (732) by Coco II (714) out of a daughter of Chéri, he by Rustique.
Coco II (714) by Vieux-Chaslin (713) out of La Grise by Vieux-Pierre (883).
VIEUX-CHASLIN (713) by Coco (712) out of Poule by Sandi.
Coco (712) by Mignon (715) out of Pauline by Vieux-Coco.
MIGNON (715) by Jean-le-Blanc (739).
CHARTRAIN (1405) by Philibert (760) out of Cocotte by Coco II (714), etc.
PHILIBERT (760) by Superior 454 (730) out of Madelon by Vieux-Vaillant (1383),
    he by Pierre out of a daughter of Vieux-Pierre (883).
SUPERIOR 454 (730) by Favori I (711) out of Pauline by Vieux-Chaslin (713), etc.
FAVORI I (711) by Vieux-Chaslin (713), etc., out of L'Amie by Vieux-Pierre
    (894), he by Coco (712), etc.
VALENTIN (5301) by Vieux-Chaslin (713), etc.

PAS NOMMÉ 7083 (9799).

[Recorded with pedigree in the Percheron Stud-Books of France and America.]

Dark grey; foaled May 2, 1886; imported 1887; bred by M. Adolphe Miteau, commune of Essai, canton of Mêsle-sur-Sarthe, department of Orne; got by PRODUCTEUR (429); dam Rosette (4039) by SÉLIM (749); 2d dam Biche (4038) by PAPILLON, belonging to M. Miteau, he by Coco of Mêsle-sur-Sarthe, he by MARGOT, belonging to M. Vallée; 3d dam Rose, belonging to M. Essai.

PRODUCTEUR (429) by Producteur [son of Favora 1542 (765)] out of Poule by Solide.
FAVORA 1542 (765) by French Monarch 205 (734) out of Marguerite by Favori, he by Coco of Mêsle-sur-Sarthe, etc.
FRENCH MONARCH 205 (734) by Ilderim (5302) out of a daughter of Vieux-Pierre (894), he by Coco (712).
ILDERIM (5302) by Valentin (5301) out of Chaton by Vieux-Pierre (894), etc.
VALENTIN (5301) by Vieux-Chaslin (713), he by Coco (712) out of Poule by Sandi.
Coco (712) by Mignon (715) out of Pauline by Vieux-Coco.
MIGNON (715) by Jean-le-Blanc (739.)
SÉLIM (749) by Porthos, belonging to M. Fromentin.

PATCHOULI 6981 (6541).

[Recorded with pedigree in the Percheron Stud-Books of France and America.]

Dapple grey; 16¼ hands; weight, 1,630 lbs.; foaled 1884; imported 1887; bred by M. Bouvry, commune of Coulonges-les-Sablons, canton of Rémalard, department of Orne; got by CHÉRI 6183 (358); dam Mouvette (6540) by VERMOUTH 1820 (787); 2d dam Mouvette (5466) by FAVORI, he by FAVORI I (711); 3d dam Robine.

CHÉRI 6183 (358) by Vermouth 1820 (787) out of Chaton.
VERMOUTH 1820 (787) by Vidocq 483 (732) out of Agathe by Vieux-Chaslin (713).
VIDOCQ 483 (732) by Coco II (714) out of a daughter of Chéri, he by Rustique.
Coco II (714) by Vieux-Chaslin (713) out of La Grise by Vieux-Pierre (883).
VIEUX-CHASLIN (713) by Coco (712) out of Poule by Sandi.
Coco (712) by Mignon (715) out of Pauline by Vieux-Coco.
MIGNON (715) by Jean-le-Blanc (739).
FAVORI I (711) by Vieux-Chaslin (713), etc., out of L'Amie by Vieux-Pierre (894), he by Coco (712), etc.

(Hoof No. 55.)   **PATURIN 7087 (9292).**

[Recorded with pedigree in the Percheron Stud-Books of France and America.]

Grey; 16¼ hands; weight, 1,685 lbs.; foaled March 15, 1885; imported 1887; bred by M. Nion, commune of Mâsles, canton of Theil, department of Orne; got by Champeaux 6218 (2248); dam Favorite (9291) by Vermouth 1820 (787).

Champeaux 6218 (2248) by Iago 995 (768) out of Madeleine, belonging to M. Guillemin.
Iago 995 (768) by Utopia 780 (731) out of Cossette by Favora 666 (725), he by Favori I (711) out of Marie by Coco (712).
Utopia 780 (731) by Superior 454 (730) out of Camille by Favori I (711).
Superior 454 (730) by Favori I (711) out of Pauline by Vieux-Chaslin (713).
Favori I (711) by Vieux-Chaslin (713) out of L'Amie by Vieux-Pierre (894), he by Coco (712).
Vieux-Chaslin (713) by Coco (712) out of Poule by Sandi.
Coco (712) by Mignon (715) out of Pauline by Vieux-Coco.
Mignon (715) by Jean-le-Blanc (739).
Vermouth 1820 (787) by Vidocq 483 (732) out of Agathe by Vieux-Chaslin (713), etc.
Vidocq 483 (732) by Coco II (714) out of a daughter of Chéri, he by Rustique.
Coco II (714), he by Vieux-Chaslin (713), etc., out of La Grise by Vieux-Pierre (883).

(Hoof No. 171.)   **PAUL 7084 (10971).**

[Recorded with pedigree in the Percheron Stud-Books of France and America.]

Dapple grey; 16 hands; weight, 1,675 lbs.; foaled March 10, 1883; bred by M. De Proussel, commune of St. Hilaire-la-Gerard, canton of Séez, department of Orne; got by Berrard 3689 (2603); dam Rosette (10970) by Mouton, belonging to M. Vimont.

Berrard 3689 (2603) by Le Duc [son of Hercule (884)] out of Margot by Duke-de-Chartres, 162 (721) he by Coco II (714).
Hercule (884) by Coco II (714), he by Vieux-Chaslin (713) out of La Grise by Vieux-Pierre (883).
Vieux-Chaslin (713) by Coco (712) out of Poule by Sandi.
Coco (712) by Mignon (715) out of Pauline by Vieux-Coco.
Mignon (715) by Jean-le-Blanc (739).

(Hoof No. 133.)   **PAULUS 7081 (10685).**

[Recorded with pedigree in the Percheron Stud-Books of France and America.]

Steel grey; 15¾ hands; weight, 1,525 lbs.; foaled February 15, 1885; imported 1887; bred by M. Loyau, commune of Bessé, canton of St. Calais, department of Sarthe; got by Florent II (5950); dam Marquise (10686) by Pierre, belonging to M. Maupu.

Florent II (5950) by Philibert (760) out of Favorite, belonging to M. Gasnier.
Philibert (760) by Superior 454 (730) out of Madelon by Vieux-Vaillant (1383), he by Pierre out of a daughter of Vieux-Pierre (883).
Superior 454 (730) by Favori I (711) out of Pauline by Vieux-Chaslin (713).
Favori I (711) by Vieux-Chaslin (713) out of L'Amie by Vieux-Pierre (894), he by Coco (712).
Vieux-Chaslin (713) by Coco (712) out of Poule by Sandi.
Coco (712) by Mignon (715) out of Pauline by Vieux-Coco.
Mignon (715) by Jean-le-Blanc (739).

(Hoof No. 261.) **PELLICO 3506 (1715).**

. [Recorded with pedigree in the Percheron Stud-Books of France and America.

Black ; 16¼ hands ; weight, 1,600 lbs.; foaled 1882 ; imported 1884 ; got by FLORENT, he by COMET 104 (719); dam Sophie by MINA, belonging to the French government.

COMET 104 (719) by French Monarch 205 (734) out of Suzanne by Cambronne.
FRENCH MONARCH 205 (734) by Ilderim (5302) out of a daughter of Vieux-Pierre (894), he by Coco (712).
ILDERIM (5302) by Valentin (5301) out of Chaton by Vieux-Pierre (894), etc.
VALENTIN (5301) by Vieux-Chaslin (713), he by Coco (712) out of Poule by Sandi.
Coco (712) by Mignon (715) out of Pauline by Vieux-Coco.
MIGNON (715) by Jean-le-Blanc (739).

(Hoof No. 207.) **PERVENCHERES 5604 (7426).**

[Recorded with pedigree in the Percheron Stud-Books of France and America.]

Dark grey ; 16¾ hands ; weight, 1,700 lbs.; foaled March 10, 1885 ; imported 1886 ; bred by M. Boudon, commune of St. Jouin-de-Blazou, canton of Pervenchères, department of Orne ; got by ROMULUS 3523 (222); dam Biche 4104 by HENRI out of Rose, belonging to M. Boudon.

ROMULUS 3523 (222) by Prosper (893) out of Bijou by Laboureur (886), he by Jean-le-Blanc (739) out of Sophie by Sandi.
PROSPER (893) by Décidé (892) out of Bourreau by Vieux-Pierre (883).
DÉCIDÉ (892) by Vieux-Pierre (894) out of Pelote, belonging to M. Berjeau.
VIEUX-PIERRE (894) by Coco (712), he by Mignon (715) out of Pauline by Vieux-Coco.
MIGNON (715) by Jean-le-Blanc (739).

(Hoof No. 109.) **PHILIBERT IV 6982 (11239).**

[Recorded with pedigree in the Percheron Stud-Books of France and America.]

Steel grey ; 15½ hands ; weight, 1,700 lbs. ; foaled May 18, 1884 ; imported 1887 ; bred by M. Francois Massard, commune of Igé, canton of Bellême, department of Orne ; got by GÉROME 3655 (436) ; dam Poule (11238) by SUPERIEUR, belonging to M. Fardouet père, he by VIDOCQ 483 (732).

GÉROME 3655 (436) by Vidocq II (723) out of Pelote by Superior 454 (730), he by Favori I (711) out of Pauline by Vieux-Chaslin (713).
  FAVORI I (711) by Vieux-Chaslin (713) out of L'Amie by Vieux-Pierre (894), he by Coco (712).
VIDOCQ II (723) by Bayard (1385) out of Brière by Décidé.
BAYARD (1385) by Vidocq 483 (732) out of La Noire by Chéri, he by Coco II (714).
VIDOCQ 483 (732) by Coco II (714) out of a daughter of Chéri, he by Rustique.
Coco II (714) by Vieux-Chaslin (713) out of La Grise by Vieux-Pierre (883).
VIEUX-CHASLIN (713) by Coco (712) out of Poule by Sandi.
Coco (712) by Mignon (715) out of Pauline by Vieux-Coco.
MIGNON (715) by Jean-le-Blanc (739).

(Hoof No. 229.) **PHILIPPE 5552 (4200).**

[Recorded with pedigree in the Percheron Stud-Books of France and America.]

Black ; 15½ hands ; weight, 1,650 lbs. ; foaled March 1, 1884 ; imported 1886 ; bred by M. Louis Moreau, commune of Ceton, canton of Theil, department of Orne ; got by SANDI 3803 (444) ; dam Pelote (327) by BRILLIANT 1899 (756) out of Poule by Coco II (714).

SANDI 3803 (444) by Brilliant 1271 (755) out of Calot by Coco II (714).
BRILLIANT 1271 (755) by Brilliant 1899 (756) out of Ragout by Favori I (711), he by Vieux-Chaslin (713) out of L'Amie by Vieux-Pierre (894), he by Coco (712).
BRILLIANT 1899 (756) by Coco II (714) out of Rosette by Mina, belonging to the French government.
Coco II (714) by Vieux-Chaslin (713) out of La Grise by Vieux-Pierre (883).
VIEUX-CHASLIN (713) by Coco (712) out of Poule by Sandi.
Coco (712) by Mignon (715) out of Pauline by Vieux-Coco.
MIGNON (715) by Jean-le-Blanc (739).

(Hoof No. 64.) **PHILIPPE AUGUSTE 7088 (8642).**

[Recorded with pedigree in the Percheron Stud-Books of France and America.]

Black ; 16¼ hands ; weight, 1,705 lbs.; foaled April 15, 1885 ; imported 1887 ; bred by M. Deshayes, commune of Préval, canton of La Ferté-Bernard, department of Sarthe ; got by LA FERTÉ 5144 (452); dam Pelotte (8640) by BRILLIANT 1899 (756).

LA FERTÉ 5144 (452) by Philibert (760) out of Julie (7594) by Brilliant 1899 (756).
PHILIBERT (760) by Superior 454 (730) out of Madelon by Vieux-Vaillant (1383), he by Pierre, out of a daughter of Vieux-Pierre (883).
SUPERIOR 454 (730) by Favori I (711) out of Pauline by Vieux-Chaslin (713).
FAVORI I (711) by Vieux-Chaslin (713) out of L'Amie by Vieux-Pierre (894), he by Coco (712).
VIEUX-CHASLIN (713) by Coco (712) out of Poule by Sandi.
Coco (712) by Mignon (715) out of Pauline by Vieux-Coco.
MIGNON (715) by Jean-le-Blanc (739).
BRILLIANT 1899 (756) by Coco II (714) out of Rosette by Mina, belonging to the French government.
Coco II (714) by Vieux-Chaslin (713), etc., out of La Grise by Vieux-Pierre (883).

(Hoof No. 221.) **PILLIER 5177 (6445).**

[Recorded with pedigree in the Percheron Stud-Books of France and America.]

Dark grey ; 16¾ hands ; weight, 1,790 lbs.; foaled May 3, 1883 ; imported 1886 ; bred by M. Gouhier, commune of Colonard, canton of Nocé, department of Orne ; got by MADÈRE II (2994); dam Chaton (153) by PAPILLON.

MADÈRE II (2994) by Madeira 1546 (770), he by Vidocq 483 (732) out of Jeanne by Favori I (711), he by Vieux-Chaslin (713) out of L'Amie by Vieux-Pierre (894), he by Coco (712).
VIDOCQ 483 (732) by Coco II (714) out of a daughter of Chéri, he by Rustique.
Coco II (714) by Vieux-Chaslin (713) out of La Grise by Vieux-Pierre (883).
VIEUX-CHASLIN (713) by Coco (712) out of Poule by Sandi.
Coco (712) by Mignon (715) out of Pauline by Vieux-Coco.
MIGNON (715) by Jean-le-Blanc (739).

(Hoof No. 99.) **PILLON 6983 (4227).**

[Recorded with pedigree in the Percheron Stud-Books of France and America.]

Black; 16¾ hands; weight, 2,150 lbs.; foaled May 7, 1884; imported 1887; bred by M. Michael Girard, commune of Sceaux, canton of Tuffé, department of Sarthe; got by PAPILLON 3559 (379); dam Biche (4226) by FLEURUS, he by FRENCH MONARCH 205 (734); 2d dam Christine.

PAPILLON 3559 (379) by Brillant (710) out of Cocotte by Coco II (714).
BRILLANT (710) by Brilliant 1899 (756) out of Sophie by Superior 454 (730), he
    by Favori I (711) out of Pauline by Vieux-Chaslin (713).
    FAVORI I (711) by Vieux-Chaslin (713) out of L'Amie by Vieux-Pierre (894),
      he by Coco (712).
BRILLIANT 1899 (756) by Coco II (714) out of Rosette by Mina, belonging to the
    French government.
Coco II (714) by Vieux-Chaslin (713) out of La Grise by Vieux-Pierre (883).
VIEUX-CHASLIN (713) by Coco (712) out of Poule by Sandi.
Coco (712) by Mignon (715) out of Pauline by Vieux-Coco.
MIGNON (715) by Jean-le-Blanc (739).
FRENCH MONARCH 205 (734) by Ilderim (5302) out of a daughter of Vieux-Pierre
    (894), etc.
ILDERIM (5302) by Valentin (5301) out of Chaton by Vieux-Pierre (894), etc.
VALENTIN (5301) by Vieux-Chaslin (713), etc.

(Hoof No. 242.) **PLUTARQUE 5220.**

[Recorded with pedigree in the Percheron Stud-Book of America.]

Grey; foaled March 8, 1886; bred by Ballachey Brothers, of Brantford, Ontario; got by ARTHUR 904 (847); dam Maud Templeton 5223 by DAUNTLESS 648 (823) out of Peerless 744.

ARTHUR 904 (847) by Favora 1542 (765) out of a daughter of Décidé 126 (720),
    he by Superior 454 (730), he by Favori I (711) out of Pauline by Vieux-
    Chaslin (713).
    FAVORI I (711) by Vieux-Chaslin (713) out of L'Amie by Vieux-Pierre (894),
      he by Coco (712).
FAVORA 1542 (765) by French Monarch 205 (734) out of Marguerite by Favori,
    he by Coco of Mésle-sur-Sarthe, he by Margot, belonging to M. Vallée.
FRENCH MONARCH 205 (734) by Ilderim (5302) out of a daughter of Vieux-
    Pierre (894), he by Coco (712).
ILDERIM (5302) by Valentin (5301) out of Chaton by Vieux-Pierre (894), etc.
VALENTIN (5301) by Vieux-Chaslin (713), he by Coco (712) out of Poule by
    Sandi.
Coco (712) by Mignon (715) out of Pauline by Vieux-Coco.
MIGNON (715) by Jean-le-Blanc (739).
DAUNTLESS 648 (823) by Duke-de-Chartres 162 (721) out of a daughter of Sélim
    (749), he by Porthos.
DUKE-DE-CHARTRES 162 (721) by Coco II (714), he by Vieux-Chaslin (713), etc.,
    out of La Grise by Vieux-Pierre (883).

(Hoof No. 79.)   **POLLUX 6984 (6880).**

[Recorded with pedigree in the Percheron Stud-Books of France and America.]

Dark steel grey ; 16½ hands ; weight, 2,000 lbs. ; foaled March 1, 1884 ; imported 1887 ; bred by M. Souchay, commune of Ceton, canton of Theil, department of Orne ; got by PAPILLON 3559 (379); dam Marianne (6879) by MOUTON (1640) out of Bijou.

PAPILLON 3559 (379) by Brillant (710) out of Cocotte by Coco II (714).
BRILLANT (710) by Brilliant 1899 (756) out of Sophie by Superior 454 (730), he by Favori I (711) out of Pauline by Vieux-Chaslin (713).
    FAVORI I (711) by Vieux-Chaslin (713) out of L'Amie by Vieux-Pierre (894), he by Coco (712).
BRILLIANT 1899 (756) by Coco II (714) out of Rosette by Mina, belonging to the French government.
Coco II (714) by Vieux-Chaslin (713) out of La Grise by Vieux-Pierre (883).
VIEUX-CHASLIN (713) by Coco (712) out of Poule by Sandi.
Coco (712) by Mignon (715) out of Pauline by Vieux-Coco.
MIGNON (715) by Jean-le-Blanc (739).
MOUTON (1640) by French Monarch 205 (734) out of Rose by Décidé.
FRENCH MONARCH 205 (734) by Ilderim (5302) out of a daughter of Vieux-Pierre (894), etc.
ILDERIM (5302) by Valentin (5301) out of Chaton by Vieux-Pierre (894), etc.
VALENTIN (5301) by Vieux-Chaslin (713), etc.

(Hoof No. 219.)   **PONCEAU 5512 (6682).**

[Recorded with pedigree in the Percheron Stud-Books of France and America.]

Dapple grey ; 16¾ hands ; weight, 1,750 lbs. ; foaled April 15, 1884 ; imported 1886 ; bred by M. Bourdon, commune of St. Hilaire-sur-Erre, canton of Theil, department of Orne; got by VAILLANT (404); dam Biche (6881) by VIEUX-VAILLANT (1383) out of L'Amie.

VAILLANT (404) by Prosper (893) out of Rosalie by Bienvenu, belonging to the Société Hippique of Eure-et-Loir.
PROSPER (893) by Décidé (892) out of Bourreau by Vieux-Pierre (883).
DÉCIDÉ (892) by Vieux-Pierre (894) out of Pelote, belonging to M. Berjeau, of Courvalien.
VIEUX-PIERRE (894) by Coco (712), he by Mignon (715) out of Pauline by Vieux-Coco.
MIGNON (715) by Jean-le-Blanc (739).
VIEUX-VAILLANT (1383) by Pierre, belonging to M. Thérin, out of a daughter of Vieux-Pierre (883).

(Hoof No. 248.)   **PRECEPT 7239.**

[Recorded with pedigree in the Percheron Stud-Book of America.]

Dark grey ; foaled April 23, 1887 ; bred at Oaklawn ; got by PRODUCTEUR 4280 (68); dam Frasie 4358 (4740) by SULTAN (4713); 2d dam Bamboche (4766) by BAYARD I, belonging to M. Lefeuvre, he by PICADOR ; 3d dam Coquette, belonging to M. Jouaux.

PRODUCTEUR 4280 (68) by Madeira 1546 (770) out of Gentille (4062) by Porthos.
MADEIRA 1546 (770) by Vidocq 483 (732) out of Jeanne by Favori I (711), he by Vieux-Chaslin (713) out of L'Amie by Vieux-Pierre (894), he by Coco (712).
VIDOCQ 483 (732) by Coco II (714) out of a daughter of Chéri, he by Rustique.
Coco II (714) by Vieux-Chaslin (713) out of La Grise by Vieux-Pierre (883).
Coco (712) by Mignon (715) out of Pauline by Vieux-Coco.
MIGNON (715) by Jean-le-Blanc (739).
SULTAN (4713) by Bayard I (son of Picador) out of Bijou, belonging to M. Lefeuvre.

(Hoof No. 243.) **PRODIGE 7238.**

[Recorded with pedigree in the Percheron Stud-Book of America.]

Dark grey ; foaled April 8, 1887 ; bred at Oaklawn ; got by
PRODUCTEUR 4280 (68) ; dam Coletia 2730 (1537) by BRILLIANT 1899
(756) out of a daughter of NARBONNE 1334 (777).

PRODUCTEUR 4280 (68) by Madeira 1546 (770) out of Gentille (4062) by Porthos.
MADEIRA 1546 (770) by Vidocq 483 (732) out of Jeanne by Favori I (711), he by
    Vieux-Chaslin (713) out of L'Amie by Vieux-Pierre (894), he by Coco (712).
VIDOCQ 483 (732) by Coco II (714) out of a daughter of Chéri, he by Rustique.
COCO II (714) by Vieux-Chaslin (713) out of La Grise by Vieux-Pierre (883).
VIEUX-CHASLIN (713) by Coco (712) out of Poule by Sandi.
COCO (712) by Mignon (715) out of Pauline by Vieux-Coco.
MIGNON (715) by Jean-le-Blanc (739).
BRILLIANT 1899 (756) by Coco II (714), etc., out of Rosette by Mina, belonging
    to the French government.
NARBONNE 1334 (777) by Brilliant 1899 (756), etc., out of Madelon (4722) by
    Favori I (711), etc.

PRODUCTEUR 7242.

[Recorded with pedigree in the Percheron Stud-Book of America.]

Grey ; foaled April 27, 1887 ; bred at Oaklawn ; got by PRODUC-
TEUR 4280 (68) ; dam Verbéna 2278 by BRILLIANT 1271 (755) ; 2d dam
Fleur-de-Lis 971 (1432) by DÉCIDÉ ; 3d dam by BAYARD 26 (717).

PRODUCTEUR 4280 (68) by Madeira 1546 (770) out of Gentille (4062) by Porthos.
MADEIRA 1546 (770) by Vidocq 483 (732) out of Jeanne by Favori I (711).
VIDOCQ 483 (732) by Coco II (714) out of a daughter of Chéri, he by Rustique.
COCO II (714) by Vieux-Chaslin (713) out of La Grise by Vieux-Pierre (883).
VIEUX-CHASLIN (713) by Coco (712) out of Poule by Sandi.
COCO (712) by Mignon (715) out of Pauline by Vieux-Coco.
MIGNON (715) by Jean-le-Blanc (739).
BAYARD 26 (717) by Favori I (711) out of Mignonne by Chéri.
FAVORI I (711) by Vieux-Chaslin (713), etc., out of L'Amie by Vieux-Pierre, he
    by Coco (712), etc.

(Hoof No. 156.) **PROTECTEUR 7082 (9272).**

[Recorded with pedigree in the Percheron Stud-Books of France and America.]

Dapple grey ; 16¾ hands ; weight, 1,800 lbs. ; foaled May 1, 1883 ;
imported 1887 ; bred by M. Guilleaux, commune of Romilly, canton
of Broué, department of Loir-et-Cher ; got by ROLAND II (7279) ; dam
Bijou (12089) by ROLAND II (7279).

ROLAND II (7279) by Roland I (son of Pamphile, belonging to the Société Hip-
    pique of Eure-et-Loir) out of Boule, belonging to M. Bouvereau.

(Hoof No. 37.)   **PROUDHON 7090 (10643).**

[Recorded with pedigree in the Percheron Stud-Books of France and America.]

Brown grey ; foaled March 25, 1886 ; bred by M. Thibault, commune of Nogent-le-Rotrou, department of Eure-et-Loir; got by GILBERT 5154 (461); dam Bijou (1748) by PROSPER (893) out of L'Amie, belonging to M. Souvre.

GILBERT 5154 (461) by Brilliant 1271 (755) out of Sophie.
BRILLIANT 1271 (755) by Brilliant 1899 (756) out of Ragout by Favori I (711), he by Vieux-Chaslin (713) out of L'Amie by Vieux-Pierre (894).
BRILLIANT 1899 (756) by Coco II (714) out of Rosette by Mina, belonging to the French government.
Coco II (714) by Vieux-Chaslin (713) out of La Grise by Vieux-Pierre (883).
VIEUX-CHASLIN (713) by Coco (712) out of Poule by Sandi.
Coco (712) by Mignon (715) out of Pauline by Vieux-Coco.
MIGNON (715) by Jean-le-Blanc (739).
PROSPER (893) by Décidé (892) out of Bourreau by Vieux-Pierre (883).
DÉCIDÉ (892) by Vieux-Pierre (894), out of Pelote, belonging to M. Berjeau of Courvalien.
VIEUX-PIERRE (894) by Coco (712), etc.

(Hoof No. 60.)   **QUIPROQUO 7092 (9602).**

[Recorded with pedigree in the Percheron Stud-Books of France and America.]

Black ; 16 hands; weight, 1,600 lbs.; foaled March 25, 1885 ; imported 1887 ; bred by M. L. Blin, commune of Savigné-l'Evêque, department of Sarthe ; got by POLYDOR (5443); dam Bijou (9601) by FAVORI, belonging to M. Gueranger.

POLYDOR (5443) by Charmant I out of Biche by Vigoureux, belonging to M. Abot.
CHARMANT I by Vigoureux, he by Favori, belonging to M. Abot.

(Hoof No. 108.)   **RAPHAEL 6985 (11242).**

[Recorded with pedigree in the Percheron Stud-Books of France and America.]

Dapple grey; 16½ hands ; weight, 1,900 lbs.; foaled February 4, 1884 ; imported 1887 ; bred by M. Gouhier, commune of Colonard, canton of Nocé, department of Orne ; got by MADÈRE II (2994); dam Rosette (151) by BAYARD (1385) out of Castille.

MADÈRE II (2994) by Madeira 1546 (770), he by Vidocq 483 (732) out of Jeanne by Favori I (711), he by Vieux-Chaslin (713) out of L'Amie by Vieux-Pierre (894), he by Coco (712).
VIDOCQ 483 (732) by Coco II (714) out of a daughter of Chéri, he by Rustique.
Coco II (714) by Vieux-Chaslin (713) out of La Grise by Vieux-Pierre (883).
VIEUX-CHASLIN (713) by Coco (712) out of Poule by Sandi.
Coco (712) by Mignon (715) out of Pauline by Vieux-Coco.
MIGNON (715) by Jean-le-Blanc (739).
BAYARD (1385) by Vidocq 483 (732), etc., out of La Noire by Chéri, he by Coco II (714), etc.

(Hoof No. 88.) ### RAVAGEUR 7094 (8673).

[Recorded with pedigree in the Percheron Stud-Books of France and America.]

Light grey; 15¾ hands; weight, 1,575 lbs.; foaled April 25, 1885; imported 1887; bred by M. E. Pelletier, commune of Préaux, canton of Nocé, department of Orne; got by VAILLANT (404); dam Bijou (8672) by Coco, belonging to M. Bajeon.

VAILLANT (404) by Prosper (893) out of Rosalie by Bienvenu, belonging to the Société Hippique of Eure-et-Loir.
PROSPER (893) by Décidé (892) out of Bourreau by Vieux-Pierre (883).
DÉCIDÉ (892) by Vieux-Pierre (894) out of Pelote, belonging to M. Berjeau, of Courvalien.
VIEUX-PIERRE (894) by Coco (712), he by Mignon (715) out of Pauline by Vieux-Coco.
MIGNON (715) by Jean-le-Blanc (739).

(Hoof No. 96.) ### REGENT 7095 (5167).

[Recorded with pedigree in the Percheron Stud-Books of France and America.]

Black; 15¾ hands; weight, 1,580 lbs.; foaled May 1, 1885; imported 1887; bred by M. Bigot, commune of Sceaux, canton of Tuffé, department of Sarthe; got by DÉSIRÉ (1946); dam Margot (5166) by MOUTON (1640) out of Margot.

DÉSIRÉ (1946) by Mouton (1640) out of Poule, belonging to M. Tuvache.
MOUTON (1640) by French Monarch 205 (734) out of Rose by Décidé.
FRENCH MONARCH 205 (734) by Ilderim (5302) out of a daughter of Vieux-Pierre (894), he by Coco (712).
ILDERIM (5302) by Valentin (5301) out of Chaton by Vieux-Pierre (894), etc.
VALENTIN (5301) by Vieux-Chaslin (713), he by Coco (712) out of Poule by Sandi.
Coco (712) by Mignon (715) out of Pauline by Vieux-Coco.
MIGNON (715) by Jean-le-Blanc (739).

(Hoof No. 119.) ### REQUIN 6986 (6014).

[Recorded with pedigree in the Percheron Stud-Books of France and America.]

Dark steel grey; 16½ hands; weight, 1,790 lbs.; foaled March 26, 1884; imported 1887; bred by M. Houssay, commune of Vidai, canton of Pervenchères, department of Orne; got by SULTAN (1400); dam Margot (6013) by MADÈRE, belonging to Madame Pelletier, out of Percheronne.

SULTAN (1400) by Count 643 (736) out of Rosette by Madère.
COUNT 643 (736) by Bayard 26 (717) out of Bijou by Rustique.
BAYARD 26 (717) by Favori I (711) out of Mignonne by Chéri.
FAVORI I (711) by Vieux-Chaslin (713) out of L'Amie by Vieux-Pierre (894), he by Coco (712).
VIEUX-CHASLIN (713) by Coco (712) out of Poule by Sandi.
Coco (712) by Mignon (715) out of Pauline by Vieux-Coco.
MIGNON (715) by Jean-le-Blanc (739).

(Hoof No. 121.)   **REVOLTÉ 6987 (5485).**

[Recorded with pedigree in the Percheron Stud-Books of France and America.]

Black grey; 16 hands; weight, 1,725 lbs.; foaled April 11, 1884 ; imported 1887 ; bred by M. Jasse, commune of St. Hilaire-de-Lierru, canton of Tuffé, department of Sarthe ; got by DÉSIRÉ (1946) ; dam Madelon (5484) by Coco II (714) out of Cocotte belonging to M. Deshayes.

DÉSIRÉ (1946) by Mouton (1640) out of Poule, belonging to M. Tuvache.
MOUTON (1640) by French Monarch 205 (734) out of Rose by Décidé, belonging to M. Vinault.
FRENCH MONARCH 205 (734) by Ilderim (5302) out of a daughter of Vieux-Pierre (894), he by Coco (712).
ILDERIM (5302) by Valentin (5301) out of Chaton by Vieux-Pierre (894), etc.
VALENTIN (5301) by Vieux-Chaslin (713), he by Coco (712) out of Poule by Sandi.
Coco (712) by Mignon (715) out of Pauline by Vieux-Coco.
MIGNON (715) by Jean-le-Blanc (739).
Coco II (714) by Vieux-Chaslin (713), etc., out of La Grise by Vieux-Pierre (883).

(Hoof No. 101.)   **RICHELIEU 7096 (7803).**

[Recorded with pedigree in the Percheron Stud-Books of France and America.]

Dark grey; foaled May 9, 1886 ; imported 1887 ; bred by M. Leon Lecomte, commune of Cherré, canton of La Ferté-Bernard, department of Sarthe ; got by ABD-EL-KADER (232); dam Pelotte (7802) by PASSE-PARTOUT (1402).

ABD-EL-KADER (232) by Passe-Partout (1402) out of Biche by Comet 104 (719).
PASSE-PARTOUT (1402) by Comet 104 (719) out of Sophie by Favori I (711), he by Vieux-Chaslin (713) out of L'Amie by Vieux-Pierre (894), he by Coco (712).
COMET 104 (719) by French Monarch 205 (734) out of Suzanne by Cambronne.
FRENCH MONARCH 205 (734) by Ilderim (5302) out of a daughter of Vieux-Pierre (894).
ILDERIM (5302) by Valentin (5301) out of Chaton by Vieux-Pierre (894), etc.
VALENTIN (5301) by Vieux-Chaslin (713), he by Coco (712) out of Poule by Sandi.
Coco (712) by Mignon (715) out of Pauline by Vieux-Coco.
MIGNON (715) by Jean-le-Blanc (739).

(Hoof No. 168.)   **ROITELET 7093 (11222).**

[Recorded with pedigree in the Percheron Stud-Books of France and America.]

Dapple grey; 16¼ hands; weight, 1,650 lbs.; foaled April 14, 1885 ; imported 1887 ; bred by M. A. Moinet, commune of Roulée, canton of Fresnaye, department of Sarthe; got by PERVENCHÈRES, belonging to the French government ; dam Brebis (11221) by MIRA-MAR, belonging to M. Lalouet.

(Hoof No. 14.) **ROMANO 7098 (11090).**

[Recorded with pedigree in the Percheron Stud-Books of France and America.]

Black; 16 hands; weight, 1,575 lbs.; foaled March, 1885; imported 1887; bred by M. Jules Sotteau, commune of La Chapelle, canton of Bellême, department of Orne; got by SUPÉRIEUR (2169); dam Jubine (11089) by DOCILE (4446).

SUPÉRIEUR (2169) by Avata 1966 (912) out of Christine by Superior 454 (730), he by Favori I (711) out of Pauline by Vieux-Chaslin (713).
  FAVORI I (711) by Vieux-Chaslin (713) out of L'Amie by Vieux-Pierre (894), he by Coco (712).
AVATA 1966 (912) by Nogent 738 (729) out of Bicotte by Bayard 26 (717), he by Favori I (711), etc., out of Mignonne by Chéri.
NOGENT 738 (729) by Vidocq 483 (732) out of a daughter of Favori I (711), etc.
VIDOCQ 483 (732) by Coco II (714) out of a daughter of Chéri, he by Rustique.
COCO II (714) by Vieux-Chaslin (713) out of La Grise by Vieux-Pierre (883).
VIEUX-CHASLIN (713) by Coco (712) out of Poule by Sandi.
COCO (712) by Mignon (715) out of Pauline by Vieux-Coco.
MIGNON (715) by Jean-le-Blanc (739).
DOCILE (4446) by Faisan (son of Chéri, belonging to M. Jamois) out of Rose, belonging to M. Simon.

(Hoof No. 200.) **ROMULUS 3523 (222).**

[Recorded with pedigree in the Percheron Stud-Books of France and America.]

Light grey; 16½ hands; weight, 2,020 lbs.; foaled 1879; imported 1884; got by PROSPER (893); dam Bijou by LABOUREUR (886).

PROSPER (893) by Décidé (892) out of Bourreau by Vieux-Pierre (883).
DÉCIDÉ (892) by Vieux-Pierre (894) out of Pelote, belonging to M. Berjeau, of Courvalien.
VIEUX-PIERRE (894) by Coco (712), he by Mignon (715) out of Pauline by Vieux-Coco.
MIGNON (715) by Jean-le-Blanc (739).
LABOUREUR (886) by Jean-le-Blanc (739) out of Sophie by Sandi.

(Hoof No. 18.) **ROULAND 7099 (10393).**

[Recorded with pedigree in the Percheron Stud-Books of France and America.]

Iron grey; 16 hands; weight, 1,665 lbs.; foaled April 4, 1885; imported 1887; bred by M. Menager, commune of Berd'huis, canton of Nocé, department of Orne; got by HERCULE 3714 (2354); dam L'Amie (10392) by CHÉRI, belonging to M. Fardouet père.

HERCULE 3714 (2354) by Chéri out of Castille (2362) by Bon Espoir, he by Chéri, he by Coco II (714).
CHÉRI by Rustique, he by Vidocq 483 (732), he by Coco II (714) out of a daughter of Chéri, he by Rustique.
COCO II (714) by Vieux-Chaslin (713) out of La Grise by Vieux-Pierre (883).
VIEUX-CHASLIN (713) by Coco (712) out of Poule by Sandi.
COCO (712) by Mignon (715) out of Pauline by Vieux-Coco.
MIGNON (715) by Jean-le-Blanc (739).

(Hoof No. 127.)   **ROUSTAN 6988 (4105).**

[Recorded with pedigree in the Percheron Stud-Books of France and America.]

Light dapple grey; 16¼ hands; weight, 1,725 lbs.; foaled 1883; imported 1887; bred by M. Boudon, commune of St. Jouin-de-Blavou, canton of Pervenchères, department of Orne; got by ROMULUS 3523 (222); dam Biche (4104) by HENRI, belonging to M. Perpère, out of Rose, belonging to M. Boudon.

ROMULUS 3523 (222) by Prosper (893) out of Bijou by Laboureur (886), he by
    Jean-le-Blanc (739) out of Sophie by Sandi.
PROSPER (893) by Décidé (892) out of Bourreau by Vieux-Pierre (883).
DÉCIDÉ (892) by Vieux-Pierre (894) out of Pelote, belonging to M. Berjeau, of
    Courvalien.
VIEUX-PIERRE (894) by Coco (712), he by Mignon (715) out of Pauline by Vieux-
    Coco.
MIGNON (715) by Jean-le-Blanc (739).

(Hoof No. 12.)   **ROUVIER 7097 (10831).**

[Recorded with pedigree in the Percheron Stud-Books of France and America.]

Light grey; 16 hands; weight, 1,575 lbs.; foaled April 28, 1885; imported 1887; bred by M. Michel Legay, commune of Champaissant, canton of Mamers, department of Sarthe; got by EPINETTE 2698 (1267); dam Pelagie (10830) by VERMOUTH, belonging to M. L. Epinette.

EPINETTE 2698 (1267) by Brilliant 1899 (756) out of Rustique by Prosper (893),
    he by Décidé (892) out of Bourreau by Vieux-Pierre (883).
    DÉCIDÉ (892) by Vieux-Pierre (894) out of Pelote, belonging to M. Berjeau, of
        Courvalien.
    VIEUX-PIERRE (894) by Coco (712).
BRILLIANT 1899 (756) by Coco II (714) out of Rosette by Mina, belonging to the
    French government.
Coco II (714) by Vieux-Chaslin (713) out of La Grise by Vieux-Pierre (883).
VIEUX-CHASLIN (713) by Coco (712) out of Poule by Sandi.
Coco (712) by Mignon (715) out of Pauline by Vieux-Coco.
MIGNON (715) by Jean-le-Blanc (739).

(Hoof No. 86.)   **SALVADOR 6989 (4370).**

[Recorded with pedigree in the Percheron Stud-Books of France and America.]

Dapple grey; 16½ hands; weight, 1,775 lbs.; foaled April 15, 1884; imported 1887; bred by M. Nion, commune of Coudray, canton of Authon, department of Eure-et-Loir; got by BEAU-CŒUR 5421 (49); dam L'Amie (4299) by MADÈRE (son of Coco) out of Lisette.

BEAU-CŒUR 5421 (49) by Prosper (893) out of Cocotte by De-Duc.
PROSPER (893) by Décidé (892) out of Bourreau by Vieux-Pierre (883).
DÉCIDÉ (892) by Vieux-Pierre (894) out of Pelote, belonging to M. Berjeau
    of Courvalien.
VIEUX-PIERRE (894) by Coco (712) he by Mignon (715) out of Pauline by Vieux-
    Coco.
MIGNON (715) by Jean-le-Blanc (739).

(Hoof No. 97.)   **SAMSON.**

Dapple grey ; 16¼ hands ; weight, 1,525 lbs.; foaled 1883 ; imported 1887 ; breeding unknown.

(Hoof No. 267.)   **SANDY 3464 (55).**

[Recorded with pedigree in the Percheron Stud-Books of France and America.]

Dark grey ; foaled 1881 ; imported 1884 ; got by MADEIRA 1546 (770); dam Rigolette by REGOUIN, belonging to M. Regouin.

MADEIRA 1546 (770) by Vidocq 483 (732) out of Jeanne by Favori I (711), he by
    Vieux-Chaslin (713) out of L'Amie by Vieux-Pierre (894), he by Coco (712).
VIDOCQ 483 (732) by Coco II (714) out of a daughter of Chéri, he by Rustique.
Coco II (714) by Vieux-Chaslin (713) out of La Grise by Vieux-Pierre (883).
VIEUX-CHASLIN (713) by Coco (712) out of Poule by Sandi.
Coco (712) by Mignon (715) out of Pauline by Vieux-Coco.
MIGNON (715) by Jean-le-Blanc (739).

SANDY 5162 (2225).

[Recorded with pedigree in the Percheron Stud-Books of France and America.]

Grey ; foaled April 18, 1883 ; imported 1886 ; bred by M. Bois, commune of Theil, department of Orne ; got by SANDY (4954) ; dam Rosette (7431) by PAPILLION.

SANDY (4954) by Sandy, he by Superior 454 (730), he by Favori I (711) out of
    Pauline by Vieux-Chaslin (713).
FAVORI I (711) by Vieux-Chaslin (713) out of L'Amie by Vieux-Pierre (894),
    he by Coco (712).
VIEUX-CHASLIN (713) by Coco (712) out of Poule by Sandi.
Coco (712) by Mignon (715) out of Pauline by Vieux-Coco.
MIGNON (715) by Jean-le-Blanc (739).

(Hoof No. 165.)   **SANDY 6990 (7801).**

[Recorded with pedigree in the Percheron Stud-Books of France and America.]

Black grey ; 16¼ hands ; weight, 1,750 lbs.; foaled April 7, 1883 ; imported 1887 ; bred by M. Lesage, commune of St. Aubin, canton of Mesle-sur-Sarthe, department of Orne ; got by BON ESPOIR (213) ; dam Célina (7800) by SÉLIM (749).

BON ESPOIR (213) by Brilliant 1899 (756) out of Poule, belonging to M. Barbet.
BRILLIANT 1899 (756) by Coco II (714) out of Rosette by Mina, belonging to the
    French government.
Coco II (714) by Vieux-Chaslin (713) out of La Grise by Vieux-Pierre (883).
VIEUX-CHASLIN (713) by Coco (712) out of Poule by Sandi.
Coco (712) by Mignon (715) out of Pauline by Vieux-Coco.
MIGNON (715) by Jean-le-Blanc (739).
SÉLIM (749) by Porthos, belonging to M. Fromentin.

(Hoof No. 129.)   **SANSONNET 6991 (8811).**

[Recorded with pedigree in the Percheron Stud-Books of France and America.]

Black; 16½ hands; weight, 1,875 lbs.; foaled April 21, 1884; imported 1887; bred by M. Neveu, commune of St. Landis, canton of Mortagne, department of Orne; got by FAVORI III (1381); dam Bleue (8810) by MOUTON (1640).

FAVORI III (1381) by Utopia 780 (731) out of La Noire, belonging to M. Letourneur.
UTOPIA 780 (731) by Superior 454 (730) out of Camille by FAVORI I (711).
SUPERIOR 454 (730) by Favori I (711) out of Pauline by Vieux-Chaslin (713).
FAVORI I (711) by Vieux-Chaslin (713) out of L'Amie by Vieux-Pierre (894), he by Coco (712).
VIEUX-CHASLIN (713) by Coco (712) out of Poule by Sandi.
COCO (712) by Mignon (715) out of Pauline by Vieux-Coco.
MIGNON (715) by Jean-le-Blanc (739).
MOUTON (1640) by French Monarch 205 (734) out of Rose by Décidé, belonging to M. Vinault.
FRENCH MONARCH 205 (734) by Ilderim (5302) out of a daughter of Vieux-Pierre, (894), etc.
ILDERIM (5302) by Valentin (5301) out of Chaton by Vieux-Pierre (894), etc.
VALENTIN (5301) by Vieux-Chaslin (713), etc.

(Hoof No. 143.)   **SANS SOUCI 7100 (6070).**

[Recorded with pedigree in the Percheron Stud-Books of France and America.]

Dapple grey; 16¼ hands; weight, 1,730 lbs.; foaled May 7, 1884; imported 1887; bred by M. Pohu, commune of Epuisay, canton of Savigny, department of Loir-et-Cher; got by SNOWFLAKE (107); dam Marquise (6069) by SOLFERINO, belonging to M. Ruet, out of Margot.

SNOWFLAKE (107) by Iago 995 (768) out of Bijou.
IAGO 995 (763) by Utopia 780 (731) out of Cossette by Favora 666 (725), he by Favori I (711) out of Marie by Coco (712).
UTOPIA 780 (731) by Superior 454 (730) out of Camille by Favori I (711).
SUPERIOR 454 (730) by FAVORI I (711) out of Pauline by Vieux-Chaslin (713).
FAVORI I (711) by Vieux-Chaslin (713) out of L'Amie by Vieux-Pierre (894), he by Coco (712).
VIEUX-CHASLIN (713) by Coco (712), etc., out of Poule by Sandi.
COCO (712) by Mignon (715) out of Pauline by Vieux-Coco.
MIGNON (715) by Jean-le-Blanc (739).

(Hoof No. 106.)   **SANS TACHE 7114 (10073).**

[Recorded with pedigree in the Percheron Stud-Books of France and America.]

Iron grey; foaled April 28, 1886; imported 1887; bred by M. Vigot, commune of Sceaux, canton of Tuffé, department of Sarthe; got by DÉSIRÉ (1946); dam Rose (10072) by L'AMI (1388).

DÉSIRÉ (1946) by Mouton (1640) out of Ponle, belonging to M. Tuvache.
MOUTON (1640) by French Monarch 205 (734) out of Rose by Décidé.
FRENCH MONARCH 205 (734) by Ilderim (5302) out of a daughter of Vieux-Pierre (894), he by Coco (712).
ILDERIM (5302) by Valentin (5301) out of Chaton by Vieux-Pierre (894), etc.
VALENTIN (5301) by Vieux-Chaslin (713), he by Coco (712) out of Poule by Sandi.
COCO (712) by Mignon (715) out of Pauline by Vieux-Coco.
MIGNON (715) by Jean-le-Blanc (739).
L'AMI (1388) by Coco [son of Coco II (714)] out of Percheronne, belonging to M. Lucas.
COCO II (714) by Vieux-Chaslin (713), etc., out of La Grise by Vieux-Pierre (883).

(Hoof No. 151.) **SATURNE 7102 (6236).**

[Recorded with pedigree in the Percheron Stud-Books of France and America.]

Black; 16 hands; weight, 1,600 lbs.; foaled February 13, 1883; imported 1887; bred by M. Challier, commune of Dompierre, canton of Brou, department of Eure-et-Loir; got by VAILLANT (4271); dam Cocotte (6235) by SANSONNET, belonging to M. Sagot, out of Margot.

VAILLANT (4271) by Favori I (711), he by Vieux-Chaslin (713) out of L'Amie by Vieux-Pierre (894), he by Coco (712).
VIEUX-CHASLIN (713) by Coco (712) out of Poule by Sandi.
Coco (712) by Mignon (715) out of Pauline by Vieux-Coco.
MIGNON (715) by Jean-le-Blanc (739).

(Hoof No. 177.) **SAVARIN 7113 (11544).**

[Recorded with pedigree in the Percheron Stud-Books of France and America.]

Dapple grey; 16¼ hands; weight, 1,700 lbs.; foaled May 25, 1885; imported 1887; bred by M. Legros, commune of Montgaudry, canton of Pervenchères, department of Orne; got by ROMULUS 3523 (222); dam Céline (11543) by L'AMI, belonging to M. Moreuil.

ROMULUS 3523 (222) by Prosper (893) out of Bijou by Laboureur (886), he by Jean-le-Blanc (739) out of Sophie by Sandi.
PROSPER (893) by Décidé (892) out of Bourreau by Vieux-Pierre (883).
DÉCIDÉ (892) by Vieux-Pierre (894) out of Pelote, belonging to M. Berjeau, of Courvalien.
VIEUX-PIERRE (894) by Coco (712), he by Mignon (715) out of Pauline by Vieux-Coco.
MIGNON (715) by Jean-le-Blanc (739).

(Hoof No. 26.) **SCIPION 6992 (10096).**

[Recorded with pedigree in the Percheron Stud-Books of France and America.]

Black; 16 hands; weight, 1,800 lbs.; foaled April 29, 1883; imported 1887; bred by M. Lucien Epinette, commune of Gué-de-la-Chaine, canton of Bellême, department of Orne; got by ACHILLE 3708 (421); dam Rosette (4095) by PHILIBERT (4634) out of Sophie by MOUTON, belonging to M. Epinette.

ACHILLE 3708 (421) by Décidé, belonging to M. Ricois, out of Bamboche, by Vidocq 483 (732), he by Coco II (714) out of a daughter of Chéri, he by Rustique.
Coco II (714) by Vieux-Chaslin (713) out of La Grise by Vieux-Pierre (883).
PHILIBERT (4634) by Philibert [son of Superior 454 (730)] out of Rustique, belonging to M. Lemesle.
SUPERIOR 454 (730) by Favori I (711) out of Pauline by Vieux-Chaslin (713).
FAVORI I (711), by Vieux-Chaslin (713) out of L'Amie by Vieux-Pierre (894), he by Coco (712).
VIEUX-CHASLIN (713) by Coco (712) out of Poule by Sandi.
Coco (712) by Mignon (715) out of Pauline by Vieux-Coco.
MIGNON (715) by Jean-le-Blanc (739).

(Hoof No. 61.)   **SIMONNEAU 7108 (9020).**

[Recorded with pedigree in the Percheron Stud-Books of France and America.]

Black ; 16 hands ; weight, 1,700 lbs.; foaled May 24, 1885 ; imported 1887 by M. Simon, commune of Masles, canton of Theil, department of Orne ; got by CHILDEBERT 4283 (451); dam Rosette (9019) by NARBONNE 1334 (777).

CHILDEBERT 4283 (451) by Brilliant 1271 (755) out of Bijon (4644) by Duke of
    Perche 173 (740), he by Favori I (711) out of Franconie by Vieux-Pierre
    (883).
    FAVORI I (711) by Vieux-Chaslin (713) out of L'Amie by Vieux-Pierre (894),
    he by Coco (712).
BRILLIANT 1271 (755) by Brilliant 1899 (756) out of Ragout by Favori I
    (711), etc.
BRILLIANT 1899 (756) by Coco II (714) out of Rosette by Mina, belonging to the
    French government.
Coco II (714) by Vieux-Chaslin (713) out of La Grise by Vieux-Pierre (883).
VIEUX-CHASLIN (713) by Coco (712) out of Poule by Sandi.
Coco (712) by Mignon (715) out of Pauline by Vieux-Coco.
MIGNON (715) by Jean-le-Blanc (739).
NARBONNE 1334 (777) by Brilliant 1899 (756), etc., out of Madelon (4722) by
    Favori I (711), etc.

(Hoof No. 174.)   **SOLIDE 7104 (9808).**

[Recorded with pedigree in the Percheron Stud-Books of France and America.]

Black ; 16½ hands ; weight, 1,825 lbs.; foaled March 3, 1882 ; imported 1887 ; bred by M. Lefeuvre, commune of Marolles-les-Braux, department of Sarthe ; got by Coco-DEUX (5607); dam Sophie (7437) by CHARMANT, belonging to M. Lefeuvre, he by FAVORI, belonging to M. Lefeuvre ; 2d dam Rosette by BAYARD I, belonging to M. Lefeuvre.

Coco-DEUX (5607) by Coco I, belonging to M. Lefeuvre, out of Charmant.

(Hoof No. 62.)   **SOLIMAN 7109 (8652).**

[Recorded with pedigree in the Percheron Stud-Books of France and America.]

Brown bay ; 16 hands ; weight, 1,595 lbs. ; foaled February 25, 1885 ; imported 1887 ; bred by M. Beale, commune of Vichères, canton of Nogent-le-Rotrou, department of Eure-et-Loir, got by CHILDEBERT 4283 (451); dam Coline (6795) by NORBERT, belonging to M. Ernest Perriot.

CHILDEBERT 4283 (451) by Brilliant 1271 (755) out of Bijou (4644) by Duke of
    Perche 173 (740), he by Favori I (711) out of Franconie by Vieux-Pierre
    (883).
    FAVORI I (711) by Vieux-Chaslin (713) out of L'Amie by Vieux-Pierre (894),
    he by Coco (712).
BRILLIANT 1271 (755) by Brilliant 1899 (756) out of Ragout by Favori I (711),
    etc.
BRILLIANT 1899 (756) by Coco II (714) out of Rosette by Mina, belonging to the
    French government.
Coco II (714) by Vieux-Chaslin (713) out of La Grise by Vieux-Pierre (883).
VIEUX-CHASLIN (713) by Coco (712) out of Poule by Sandi.
Coco (712) by Mignon (715) out of Pauline by Vieux-Coco.
MIGNON (715) by Jean-le-Blanc (739).

(Hoof No. 49.) **SOPHOCLE 7105 (4548).**

[Recorded with pedigree in the Percheron Stud-Books of France and America.]

Light dapple grey ; 16¾ hands ; weight, 1,890 lbs. ; foaled May 10, 1884 ; imported 1887 ; bred by M. Guinebert, commune of Ceton, canton of Theil, department of Orne ; got by Primo (84); dam Rosalie (4547) by Favora 666 (725) out of Cocotte by Vieux-Chaslin (713).

Primo (84) by Iago 995 (768) out of Rosalie by Bayard.
Iago 995 (768) by Utopia 780 (731) out of Cossette by Favora 666 (725).
Utopia 780 (731) by Superior 454 (730) out of Camille by Favori I (711).
Superior 454 (730) by Favori I (711) out of Pauline by Vieux-Chaslin (713).
Favori I (711) by Vieux-Chaslin (713) out of L'Amie by Vieux-Pierre (894), he by Coco (712).
Vieux-Chaslin (713) by Coco (712) out of Poule by Sandi.
Coco (712) by Mignon (715) out of Pauline by Vieux-Coco.
Mignon (715) by Jean-le-Blanc (739).
Favora 666 (725) by Favori I (711), etc., out of Marie by Coco (712).

(Hoof No. 69.) **SOUANCÉ 7111 (9104).**

[Recorded with pedigree in the Percheron Stud-Books of France and America.]

Dark grey ; 16¼ hands ; weight, 1,690 lbs.; foaled March 20, 1885 ; imported 1887 ; bred by M. D. Richardeau, commune of Souancé, canton of Nogent-le-Rotrou, department of Eure-et-Loir ; got by Adonais (83); dam Pelotte (582) by Bayard (6751) out of Pelote, belonging to M. Richardeau.

Adonais (83) by Iago 995 (768) out of Bichette.
Iago 995 (768) by Utopia 780 (731) out of Cossette by Favora 666 (725), he by Favori I (711) out of Marie by Coco (712).
Utopia 780 (731) by Superior 454 (730) out of Camille by Favori I (711).
Superior 454 (730) by Favori I (711) out of Pauline by Vieux-Chaslin (713).
Favori I (711) by Vieux-Chaslin (713) out of L'Amie by Vieux-Pierre (894), he by Coco (712).
Vieux-Chaslin (713) by Coco (712) out of Poule by Sandi.
Coco (712) by Mignon (715) out of Pauline by Vieux-Coco.
Mignon (715) by Jean-le-Blanc (739).
Bayard (6751) by Mina, belonging to the Société Hippique of Eure-et-Loir, out of Louison by Chéri, belonging to M. Fardouet père, he by Couronne, belonging to M. Sagot.

(Hoof No. 22.) **SOUVENIR 6993 (4500).**

[Recorded with pedigree in the Percheron Stud-Books of France and America.]

Dark grey ; 16½ hands ; weight, 1,760 lbs. ; foaled March, 1884 ; imported 1887 ; bred by M. Charron, commune of St. Hilaire-sur-Erre, canton of Theil, department of Orne ; got by Vaillant (404); dam Gamine (4499) by Prosper (893) out of Catherine, belonging to M. Charron.

Vaillant (404) by Prosper (893) out of Rosalie by Bienvenu, belonging to the Société Hippique of Eure-et-Loir.
Prosper (893) by Décidé (892) out of Bourreau by Vieux-Pierre (883).
Décidé (892) by Vieux-Pierre (894) out of Pelote, belonging to M. Berjean, of Courvalien.
Vieux-Pierre (894) by Coco (712), he by Mignon (715) out of Pauline by Vieux-Coco.
Mignon (715) by Jean-le-Blanc (739).

(Hoof No. 52.)   **SOUVERAIN 7106 (6214).**

[Recorded with pedigree in the Percheron Stud-Books of France and America.]

Dark grey ; 16¼ hands ; weight, 1,700 lbs. ; foaled April 20, 1885 ; imported 1887 ; bred by M. Epinette, commune of Souvigné-sur-Même, canton of La Ferté-Bernard, department of Sarthe ; got by LA FERTÉ 5144 (452) ; dam La Biche (5081) by BRILLIANT 1899 (756) out of Pelotte.

LA FERTÉ 5144 (452) by Philibert (760) out of Julie (7594) by Brilliant 1899 (756).
PHILIBERT (760) by Superior 454 (730) out of Madelon by Vieux-Vaillant, he by
    Pierre out of a daughter of Vieux-Pierre (883).
SUPERIOR 454 (730) by Favori I (711) out of Pauline by Vieux-Chaslin (713).
FAVORI I (711) by Vieux-Chaslin (713) out of L'Amie by Vieux-Pierre (894),
    he by Coco (712).
VIEUX-CHASLIN (713) by Coco (712) out of Poule by Sandi.
Coco (712) by Mignon (715) out of Pauline by Vieux-Coco.
MIGNON (715) by Jean-le-Blanc (739).
BRILLIANT 1899 (756) by Coco II (714) out of Rosette by Mina, belonging to the
    French government.
Coco II (714) by Vieux-Chaslin (713), etc., out of La Grise by Vieux-Pierre (883).

(Hoof No. 58.)   **SPARTACUS 7107 (9296).**

[Recorded with pedigree in the Percheron Stud-Books of France and America.]

Steel grey ; 16¼ hands ; weight, 1,600 lbs. ; foaled April 17, 1885 ; imported 1887 ; bred by M. Pinagot, commune of Courgeout, canton of Bazoches-sur-Hoesne, department of Orne ; got by BRILLANT 5427 (215) ; dam Mignonne (9295) by VOLTAIRE (5728).

BRILLANT 5427 (215) by Décidé out of Rustique.
VOLTAIRE (5728) by Coco, belonging to M. Bignon, son of Margot, belonging to
    M. Vallée, out of Rosette by Vieux-Coco, belonging to M. Bignon.

(Hoof No. 24.)   **STRADAT 7112 (2463).**

[Recorded with pedigree in the Percheron Stud-Books of France and America.]

Black ; 16¾ hands ; weight, 1,920 lbs. ; foaled 1880 ; imported 1887 ; bred by M. Marin Chartrain, commune of Courgenard, canton of La Ferté-Bernard, department of Sarthe ; got by PASSE-PARTOUT (1402); dam Biche (12004) by a son of Coco II (714).

PASSE-PARTOUT (1402) by Comet 104 (719) out of Sophie by Favori I (711), he
    by Vieux-Chaslin (713) out of L'Amie by Vieux-Pierre (894), he by Coco
    (712).
COMET 104 (719) by French Monarch 205 (734) out of Suzanne by Cambronne.
FRENCH MONARCH 205 (734) by Ilderim (5302) out of a daughter of Vieux-Pierre
    (894), etc.
ILDERIM (5302) by Valentin (5301) out of Chaton by Vieux-Pierre (894); etc.
VALENTIN (5301) by Vieux-Chaslin (713), he by Coco (712) out of Poule by Sandi.
Coco (712) by Mignon (715) out of Pauline by Vieux-Coco.
MIGNON (715) by Jean-le-Blanc (739).
Coco II (714) by Vieux-Chaslin, (713), etc., out of La Grise by Vieux-Pierre (883).

(Hoof No. 201.) **SUCCESS 5613 (6864).**

[Recorded with pedigree in the Percheron Stud-Books of France and America.]

Dapple grey; 16½ hands; weight, 1,705 lbs.; foaled April 12, 1882; imported 1886; bred by M. Moreau, commune of Ceton, canton of Theil, department of Orne; got by CLEMENT 1965 (936); dam Carabie (6863) by BRILLIANT 1899 (756) out of Carabie.

CLEMENT 1965 (936) by Philibert (760) out of Rustique by Coco II (714).
PHILIBERT (760) by Superior 454 (730) out of Madelon by Vieux-Vaillant (1383), he by Pierre out of a daughter of Vieux-Pierre (883).
SUPERIOR 454 (730) by Favori I (711) out of Pauline by Vieux-Chaslin (713).
FAVORI I (711) by Vieux-Chaslin (713) out of L'Amie by Vieux-Pierre (894), he by Coco (712).
VIEUX-CHASLIN (713) by Coco (712) out of Poule by Sandi.
Coco (712) by Mignon (715) out of Pauline by Vieux-Coco.
MIGNON (715) by Jean-le-Blanc (739).
BRILLIANT 1899 (756) by Coco II (714) out of Rosette by Mina, belonging to the French government.
Coco II (714) by Vieux-Chaslin (713), etc., out of La Grise by Vieux-Pierre (883).

(Hoof No. 160.) **SULTAN IV 7103 (9798).**

[Recorded with pedigree in the Percheron-Stud-Books of France and America.]

Black; 16 hands; weight, 1,460 lbs.; foaled June 5, 1885; imported 1887; bred by M. Adolphe Miteau, commune of Essai, canton of Mesle-sur-Sarthe, department of Orne; got by SULTAN 3683 (1610); dam Biche (4038) by PAPILLON (6800) out of Rose, belonging to M. Essai.

SULTAN 3683 (1610) by Vaillant (404) out of Julie by Prosper (893).
VAILLANT (404) by Prosper (893) out of Rosalie by Bienvenu, belonging to the Société Hippique of Eure-et-Loir.
PROSPER (893) by Décidé (892) out of Bourreau by Vieux-Pierre (883).
DÉCIDÉ (892) by Vieux-Pierre (894) out of Pelote, belonging to M. Berjeau, of Courvalien.
VIEUX-PIERRE (894) by Coco (712), he by Mignon (715) out of Pauline by Vieux-Coco.
MIGNON (715) by Jean-le-Blanc (739).
PAPILLON (6800) by Moutard (son of Coco of Mêsle-sur-Sarthe) out of Bijon, belonging to M. Miteau, by Coco (712), etc.

(Hoof No. 67.) **SYLVIO 7110 (10776).**

[Recorded with pedigree in the Percheron Stud-Books of France and America.]

Iron grey; foaled April 8, 1886; bred by M. Auguste Benoist, commune of Nogent-le-Rotrou, department of Eure-et-Loir; got by CHAMPEAUX 6218 (2248); dam Cocotte (10774) by MARGOT 2571 (1160).

CHAMPEAUX 6218 (2248) by Iago 995 (768) out of Madeleine, belonging to M. Guillemin.
IAGO 995 (768) by Utopia 780 (731) out of Cossette by Favora 666 (725), he by Favori I (711) out of Marie by Coco (712).
UTOPIA 780 (731) by Superior 454 (730) out of Camille by Favori I (711).
SUPERIOR 454 (730) by Favori I (711) out of Pauline by Vieux-Chaslin (713).
FAVORI I (711) by Vieux-Chaslin (713) out of L'Amie by Vieux-Pierre (894), he by Coco (712).
VIEUX-CHASLIN (713) by Coco (712) out of Poule by Sandi.
Coco (712) by Mignon (715) out of Pauline by Vieux-Coco.
MIGNON (715) by Jean-le-Blanc (739).
MARGOT 2571 (1160) by Brilliant 1899 (756) out of Rustique by Vieux-Chaslin (713), etc.
BRILLIANT 1899 (756) by Coco II (714) out of Rosette by Mina, belonging to the French government.
Coco II (714) by Vieux-Chaslin (713), etc., out of La Grise by Vieux-Pierre (883).

(Hoof No. 10.)   **TAMARIN 7118 (10586).**

[Recorded with pedigree in the Percheron Stud-Books of France and America.]

Dark grey; foaled May, 1886; imported 1887; bred by M. M. Selicien Tessier, commune of Dame-Marie, canton of Bellême, department of Orne; got by TURCO (604); dam Lisette (10578) by PICADOR, belonging to M. Jamois.

TURCO (604) by Philibert (4634) out of Victorine, belonging to M. Boisseau.
PHILIBERT (4634) by Philibert [son of Superior 454 (730)] out of Rustique, belonging to M. Lemesle.
SUPERIOR 454 (730) by Favori I (711) out of Pauline by Vieux-Chaslin (713).
FAVORI I (711) by Vieux-Chaslin (713) out of L'Amie by Vieux-Pierre (894), he by Coco (712).
VIEUX-CHASLIN (713) by Coco (712) out of Poule by Sandi.
COCO (712) by Mignon (715) out of Pauline by Vieux-Coco.
MIGNON (715) by Jean-le-Blanc (739).

(Hoof No. 19.)   **TAMBOUR MAJOR 7119 (10091).**

[Recorded with pedigree in the Percheron Stud-Books of France and America.]

Dark grey; 16¼ hands; weight, 1,620 lbs.; foaled April 5, 1885; imported 1887; bred by M. Legout, commune of Dame-Marie, canton of Bellême, department of Orne; got by PAUL 3478 (364); dam Mignonne (5207) by DÉCIDÉ, belonging to M. Fardouet père, out of Mignonne.

PAUL 3478 (364) by Vaillant (404) out of Cocotte by Vieux-Vaillant (1383), he by Pierre out of a daughter of Vieux-Pierre (883).
VAILLANT (404) by Prosper (893) out of Rosalie by Bienvenu, belonging to the Société Hippique of Eure-et-Loir.
PROSPER (893) by Décidé (892) out of Bourreau by Vieux-Pierre (883).
DÉCIDÉ (892) by Vieux-Pierre (894) out of Pelote, belonging to M. Berjeau, of Courvalien.
VIEUX-PIERRE (894) by Coco (712), he by Mignon (715) out of Pauline by Vieux-Coco.
MIGNON (715) by Jean-le-Blanc (739).

(Hoof No. 209.)   **TEMERAIRE 5567 (6371).**

[Recorded with pedigree in the Percheron Stud-Books of France and America.]

Grey; 16½ hands; weight, 1,625 lbs.; foaled March 22, 1884; imported 1886; bred by M. Thibault, commune of Coudray-au-Perche, canton of Authon, department of Eure-et-Loir; got by JOINVILLE 4070 (104); dam Poule by BAPTISTE 22 (737).

JOINVILLE 4070 (104) by Brilliant 1899 (756) out of Cocotte.
BRILLIANT 1899 (756) by Coco II (714) out of Rosette by Mina, belonging to the French government.
COCO II (714) by Vieux-Chaslin (713) out of La Grise by Vieux-Pierre (883).
VIEUX-CHASLIN (713) by Coco (712) out of Poule by Sandi.
COCO (712) by Mignon (715) out of Pauline by Vieux-Coco.
MIGNON (715) by Jean-le-Blanc (739).
BAPTISTE 22 (737) by Brilliant 1899 (756), etc.

(Hoof No. 181.) **TIMONNIER 7116 (8616).**

[Recorded with pedigree in the Percheron Stud-Books of France and America.]

Dark grey; 16 hands; weight, 1,650 lbs.; foaled April 28, 1885; imported 1887; bred by M. Virlouvette, commune of Ceton, canton of Theil, department of Orne; got by BRILLANT (710); dam Coquette (8615) by FAVORI I (711).

BRILLANT (710) by Brilliant 1899 (756) out of Sophie by Superior 454 (730), he by Favori I (711) out of Pauline by Vieux-Chaslin (713).
BRILLANT 1899 (756) by Coco II (714) out of Rosette by Mina, belonging to the French government.
Coco II (714) by Vieux-Chaslin (713) out of La Grise by Vieux-Pierre (883).
VIEUX-CHASLIN (713) by Coco (712) out of Poule by Sandi.
Coco (712) by Mignon (715) out of Pauline by Vieux-Coco.
MIGNON (715) by Jean-le-Blanc (739).
FAVORI I (711) by Vieux-Chaslin (713), etc., out of L'Amie by Vieux-Pierre (894), he by Coco (712), etc.

(Hoof No. 217.) **TOCSIN 5534 (6223).**

[Recorded with pedigree in the Percheron Stud-Books of France and America.]

Dapple grey; 16 hands; weight, 1,670 lbs.; foaled April 4, 1885; imported 1886; bred by M. Julliard, commune of Ceton, canton of Theil, department of Orne; got by SANDI 3803 (444); dam Docile (6222) by DOCILE out of Sophie.

SANDI 3803 (444) by Brilliant 1271 (755) out of Calot by Coco II (714).
BRILLANT 1271 (755) by Brilliant 1899 (756) out of Ragout by Favori I (711), he by Vieux-Chaslin (713) out of L'Amie by Vieux-Pierre (894), he by Coco (712).
BRILLANT 1899 (756) by Coco II (714) out of Rosette by Mina, belonging to the French government.
Coco II (714) by Vieux-Chaslin (713) out of La Grise by Vieux-Pierre (883).
VIEUX-CHASLIN (713) by Coco (712) out of Poule by Sandi.
Coco (712) by Mignon (715) out of Pauline by Vieux-Coco.
MIGNON (715) by Jean-le-Blanc (739).

(Hoof No. 131.) **TRAGEDIEN 6994 (10126).**

[Recorded with pedigree in the Percheron Stud-Books of France and America.]

Grey; 16 hands; weight, 1,640 lbs.; foaled March 15, 1884; imported 1887; bred by M. Lebret, commune of Le Gault, canton of Droué, department of Loir-et-Cher; got by ADONAIS (83); dam Pelotte (10125) by SANSONNET, belonging to M. Bataille.

ADONAIS (83) by Iago 995 (768) out of Bichette.
IAGO 995 (768) by Utopia 780 (731) out of Cossette by Favora 666 (725), he by Favori I (711) out of Marie by Coco (712), etc.
UTOPIA 780 (731) by Superior 454 (730) out of Camille by Favori I (711).
SUPERIOR 454 (730) by Favori I (711) out of Pauline by Vieux-Chaslin (713).
FAVORI I (711) by Vieux-Chaslin (713) out of L'Amie by Vieux-Pierre (894), he by Coco (712).
VIEUX-CHASLIN (713) by Coco (712) out of Poule by Sandi.
Coco (712) by Mignon (715) out of Pauline by Vieux-Coco.
MIGNON (715) by Jean-le-Blanc (739).

(Hoof No. 228.)   **TRIANON 5525 (6508).**

[Recorded with pedigree in the Percheron Stud-Books of France and America.]

Dapple grey; 16¾ hands; weight, 1,760 lbs.; foaled February 25, 1883; imported 1886; bred by M. Bruneau, commune of Sargé, canton of Mondoubleau, department of Loir-et-Cher; got by FLORENCE II (5950); dam Poule (6507) by JOSEPH out of Louise.

FLORENCE II (5950) by Philibert (760) out of Favorite, belonging to M. Gasnier.
PHILIBERT (760) by Superior 454 (730) out of Madelon by Vieux-Vallant (1383),
    he by Pierre out of a daughter of Vieux-Pierre (883).
SUPERIOR 454 (730) by Favori I (711) out of Pauline by Vieux-Chaslin (713).
FAVORI I (711) by Vieux-Chaslin (713) out of L'Amie by Vieux-Pierre (894), he
    by Coco (712).
VIEUX-CHASLIN (713) by Coco (712) out of Poule by Sandi.
Coco (712) by Mignon (715) out of Pauline by Vieux-Coco.
MIGNON (715) by Jean-le-Blanc (739).

(Hoof No. 173.)   **TRILBY 7115 (8417).**

[Recorded with pedigree in the Percheron Stud-Books of France and America.]

Black; foaled March 24, 1886; imported 1887; bred by M. Fleury, commune of Auguaise, canton of Moulins-la-Marche, department of Orne; got by SULTAN (1400); dam Bijou (6168) by SANSONNET, belonging to the French government, out of Bicotte.

SULTAN (1400) by Count 643 (736) out of Rosette by Madère.
COUNT 643 (736) by Bayard 26 (717) out of Bijou by Rustique.
BAYARD 26 (717) by Favori I (711) out of Mignonne by Chéri.
FAVORI I (711) by Vieux-Chaslin (713) out of L'Amie by Vieux-Pierre (894), he
    by Coco (712).
VIEUX-CHASLIN (713) by Coco (712) out of Poule by Sandi.
Coco (712) by Mignon (715) out of Pauline by Vieux-Coco.
MIGNON (715) by Jean-le-Blanc (739).

(Hoof No. 211.)   **TROCU 3497 (2498).**

[Recorded with pedigree in the Percheron Stud-Books of France and America.]

Dapple grey; 15½ hands; weight, 1,500 lbs.; foaled 1878; imported 1884; got by L'AMI, he by HERCULE (884); dam Biche by HERCULE (884).

HERCULE (884) by Coco II (714), he by Vieux-Chaslin (713) out of La Grise by
    Vieux-Pierre (883).
VIEUX-CHASLIN (713) by Coco (712) out of Poule by Sandi.
Coco (712) by Mignon (715) out of Pauline by Vieux-Coco.
MIGNON (715) by Jean-le-Blanc (739).

(Hoof No. 235.)   **TROPHY 4006.**

[Recorded with pedigree in the Percheron Stud-Book of America.]

Black; 15¾ hands; weight, 1,550 lbs.; foaled March 2, 1885; bred by Parsons & Baldwin, of Watervliet, Michigan; got by TROJAN 1205 (832); dam Floreda 1490 (1433) by ROMULUS 873 (785) out of a daughter of JEAN-BART (716).

TROJAN 1205 (832) by Vivian 785 (831) out of Franconie by Vieux-Pierre (894),
    he by Coco (712), he by Mignon (715) out of Pauline by Vieux-Coco.
MIGNON (715) by Jean-le-Blanc (739).
VIVIAN 785 (831) by Jean-Bart (716), he by Bayard out of Jeanne by Porthos.
ROMULUS 873 (785) by the government approved stallion Romulus (son of
    Moreuil) out of Fleur-d'Épine by the government approved stallion Chéri,
    he by Corbon.

(Hoof No. 220.) **ULYSSE 5551 (6747).**

[Recorded with pedigree in the Percheron Stud-Books of France and America.]

Dapple grey; 16½ hands; weight, 1,610 lbs.; foaled March 1, 1885; imported 1886; bred by M. Moreau, commune of Ceton, canton of Theil, department of Orne; got by SANDI 3803 (444); dam Chatton (4195) by FAVORI I (711), out of Chatton by COCO II (714).

SANDI 3803 (444) by Brilliant 1271 (755) out of Calot by Coco II (714).
BRILLIANT 1271 (755) by Brilliant 1899 (756) out of Ragout by Favori I (711).
BRILLIANT 1899 (756) by Coco II (714) out of Rosette by Mina, belonging to the French government.
Coco II (714) by Vieux-Chaslin (713) out of La Grise by Vieux-Pierre (883).
VIEUX-CHASLIN (713) by Coco (712) out of Poule by Sandi.
Coco (712) by Mignon (715) out of Pauline by Vieux-Coco.
MIGNON (715) by Jean-le-Blanc (739).
FAVORI I (711) by Vieux-Chaslin (713), etc., out of L'Amie by Vieux-Pierre (894), he by Coco (712), etc.

(Hoof No. 202.) **VAINQUEUR 4288 (284).**

[Recorded with pedigree in the Percheron Stud-Books of France and America.]

Dapple grey; foaled April 10, 1881; imported 1885; bred by M. Désiré Duccœurjoly, commune of Brunelles, canton of Nogent-le-Rotrou, department of Eure-et-Loir; got by BAYARD (6751); dam Grisette (280) by MEDOC, he by FRENCH MONARCH 205 (734); 2d dam Pauline (279) by MIRAMAR.

BAYARD (6751) by Mina, belonging to the Société Hippique of Eure-et-Loir.
FRENCH MONARCH 205 (734) by Ilderim (5302) out of a daughter of Vieux-Pierre (894), he by Coco (712).
ILDERIM (5302) by Valentin (5301) out of Chaton by Vieux-Pierre (894), etc.
VALENTIN (5301) by Vieux-Chaslin (713), he by Coco (712) out of Poule by Sandi.
Coco (712) by Mignon (715) out of Pauline by Vieux-Coco.
MIGNON (715) by Jean-le-Blanc (739).

(Hoof No. 236.) **VALENCIENNE 2623 (1163).**

[Recorded with pedigree in the Percheron Stud-Books of France and America.]

Dark grey; 16½ hands; weight, 1,720 lbs.; foaled 1882; imported 1883; got by VALENTIN, he by DÉCIDÉ, he by FAVORI I (711); dam Brebis by L'AMI.

FAVORI I (711) by Vieux-Chaslin (713) out of L'Amie by Vieux-Pierre (894), he by Coco (712).
VIEUX-CHASLIN (713) by Coco (712) out of Poule by Sandi.
Coco (712) by Mignon (715) out of Pauline by Vieux-Coco.
MIGNON (715) by Jean-le-Blanc (739).

(Hoof No. 155.) **VAUCLAIR 7122 (9274).**

[Recorded with pedigree in the Percheron Stud-Books of France and America.]

Steel grey; 16¼ hands; weight, 1,740 lbs.; foaled April 24, 1884; imported 1887; bred by M. Fisseau, commune of Danzé, canton of Morée, department of Loir-et-Cher; got by ROLAND II (7279); dam Cocotte (9273) by ROLAND II (7279).

ROLAND II (7279) by Roland I (son of Pamphile, belonging to the Société Hippique of Eure-et-Loir) out of Poule, belonging to M. Bouvereau.

(Hoof No. 43.)   **VENTEUR 6995 (6182).**

[Recorded with pedigree in the Percheron Stud-Books of France and America.]

Light grey; 16½ hands; weight, 1,800 lbs.; foaled 1884; imported 1887; bred by M. Ferré, commune of Souancé, canton of Nogent-le-Rotrou, department of Eure-et-Loir; got by RUSTIQUE 3601 (624); dam Rustique (6181) by VAILLANT (4271) out of La Pelotte.

RUSTIQUE 3601 (624) by Raspail [son of Vigoureux (1391)] out of Rose.
VIGOUREUX (1392) by Coco II (714) out of Marguerite by Franconi, belonging to M. Sagot.
Coco II (714) by Vieux-Chaslin (713) out of La Grise by Vieux-Pierre (883).
VIEUX-CHASLIN (713) by Coco (712) out of Poule by Sandi.
Coco (712) by Mignon (715) out of Pauline by Vieux-Coco.
MIGNON (715) by Jean-le-Blanc (739).
VAILLANT (4271) by Favori I (711), he by Vieux-Chaslin (713), etc., out of L'Amie by Vieux-Pierre (894), he by Coco (712), etc.

(Hoof No. 205.)   **VERMOUTH 4266 (608).**

[Recorded with pedigree in the Percheron Stud-Books of France and America.]

Grey; 16½ hands; weight, 1,860 lbs.; foaled June 17, 1882; imported 1885; bred by M. Simon, commune of Serigny, canton of Bellême, department of Orne; got by VERMOUTH; dam Sophie (4841) by JACQUES, belonging to M. Lucien Epinette, out of Jeannette.

(Hoof No. 268.)   **VIGOUREUX 3516 (2372).**

[Recorded with pedigree in the Percheron Stud-Books of France and America.]

Black; foaled 1879; imported 1884; got by SANSONNET, he by VIDOCQ 483 (732); dam Brunette by ROYAL, he by BAYARD, he by SOLIDE.

VIDOCQ 483 (732) by Coco II (714) out of a daughter of Chéri, he by Rustique.
Coco II (714) by Vieux-Chaslin (713) out of La Grise by Vieux-Pierre (883).
VIEUX-CHASLIN (713) by Coco (712) out of Poule by Sandi.
Coco (712) by Mignon (715) out of Pauline by Vieux-Coco.
MIGNON (715) by Jean-le-Blanc (739).

(Hoof No. 117.)   **VOLTA 6996 (6777).**

[Recorded with pedigree in the Percheron Stud-Books of France and America.]

Dark grey; 16¼ hands; weight, 1,800 lbs.; foaled February 10, 1884; imported 1887; bred by M. Arsene Guesneau, commune of La Chapelle-Souëf, canton of Bellême, department of Orne; got by GÉROME 3655 (436); dam Madeleine (2452) by MADEIRA 1546 (770) out of Rigolette, belonging to M. Guenot.

GÉROME 3655 (436) by Vidocq II (723) out of Pelotte by Superior 454 (730), he by Favori I (711) out of Pauline by Vieux-Chaslin (713).
     FAVORI I (711) by Vieux-Chaslin (713) out of L'Amie by Vieux-Pierre (894), he by Coco (712).
VIDOCQ II (723) by Bayard (1385) out of Brière by Décidé.
BAYARD (1385) by Vidocq 483 (732) out of La Noire by Chéri, he by Coco II (714).
VIDOCQ 483 (732) by Coco II (714), etc., out of a daughter of Chéri, he by Rustique.
Coco II (714) by Vieux-Chaslin (713) out of La Grise by Vieux-Pierre (883).
VIEUX-CHASLIN (713) by Coco (712) out of Poule by Sandi.
Coco (712) by Mignon (715) out of Pauline by Vieux-Coco.
MIGNON (715) by Jean-le-Blanc (739).
MADEIRA 1546 (770) by Vidocq 483 (732), etc., out of Jeanne by Favori I (711), etc.

(Hoof No. 144.) **VOLTAIRE 7121 (5431).**

[Recorded with pedigree in the Percheron Stud-Books of France and America.]

Dark grey; 16 hands; weight, 1,800 lbs.; foaled March 28, 1883; imported 1887; bred by M. Avice, commune of Théligny, canton of La Ferté-Bernard, department of Sarthe; got by VERMOUTH (6276); dam Bijou (5430) by Coco, belonging to M. Bajeon, he by VIEUX-CHASLIN (713); 2d dam Chatton, belonging to M. Grémillou.

VERMOUTH (6276) by Vermouth 1820 (787) out of Rosalie (5986) by Bon Espoir, he by Vidocq 483 (732).
VERMOUTH 1820 (787) by Vidocq 483 (732) out of Agathe by Vieux-Chaslin (713).
VIDOCQ 483 (732) by Coco II (714) out of a daughter of Chéri, he by Rustique.
Coco II (714) by Vieux-Chaslin (713) out of La Grise by Vieux-Pierre (883).
VIEUX-CHASLIN (713) by Coco (712) out of Poule by Sandi.
Coco (712) by Mignon (715) out of Pauline by Vieux-Coco.
MIGNON (715) by Jean-le-Blanc (739).

(Hoof No. 51.) **VOLTAIRE II 6997 (2920).**

[Recorded with pedigree in the Percheron Stud-Books of France and America.]

Dark grey; 16½ hands; weight, 1,850 lbs.; foaled February 17, 1884; bred by M. Eugène François, commune of Coudray, canton of Nogent-le-Rotrou, department of Eure-et-Loir; got by VOLTAIRE 3540 (443) dam Sophie (11163) by VAILLANT (6752) out of Couronne, belonging to M. François.

VOLTAIRE 3540 (443) by Brilliant 1271 (755) out of Cocotte by Coco II (714).
BRILLIANT 1271 (755) by Brilliant 1899 (756) out of Ragout by Favori I (711). he by Vieux-Chaslin (713) out of L'Amie by Vieux-Pierre (894), he by Coco (712).
BRILLIANT 1899 (756) by Coco II (714) out of Rosette by Mina, belonging to the French government.
Coco II (714) by Vieux-Chaslin (713) out of La Grise by Vieux-Pierre (883).
VIEUX-CHASLIN (713) by Coco (712) out of Poule by Sandi.
Coco (712) by Mignon (715) out of Pauline by Vieux-Coco.
MIGNON (715) by Jean-le-Blanc (739).
VAILLANT (6752) by Bayard (6751) (son of Mina) out of Grisette, belonging to M. Brette.

(Hoof No. 172.) **VOLTAIRE VII 7123 (11948).**

[Recorded with pedigree in the Percheron Stud-Books of France and America.]

Dark grey; 16½ hands; weight, 1,680 lbs.; foaled May 1, 1882; imported 1887; bred by M. Bachelier, commune of Mortrée, canton of Mortrée, department of Orne; got by SÉLIM (749); dam Pauline (4777) by MOUTON, belonging to M. Aubry.

SÉLIM (749) by Porthos, belonging to M. Fromentin.

(Hoof No. 70.)   **VOLTIGEUR 6998 (6102).**

[Recorded with pedigree in the Percheron Stud-Books of France and America.]

Dapple grey ; 16¼ hands ; weight, 1,900 lbs.; foaled May 4, 1884 ;
imported 1887 ; bred by M. Desert, commune of St. Hilaire-sur-Erre,
canton of Theil, department of Orne ; got by VAILLANT (404); dam
Mignonne (4205) by MOUTON, belonging to M. Bouvart, out of La
Bleue, belonging to M. Mousset.

VAILLANT (404) by Prosper (893) out of Rosalie by Bienvenu, belonging to the
   Société Hippique of Eure-et-Loir.
PROSPER (893) by Décidé (892) out of Bourreau by Vieux-Pierre (883).
DÉCIDÉ (892) by Vieux-Pierre (894) out of Pelote, belonging to M. Berjeau, of
   Courvalien.
VIEUX-PIERRE (894) by Coco (712), he by Mignon (715) out of Pauline by Vieux-
   Coco.
MIGNON (715) by Jean-le-Blanc (739).

(Hoof No. 115.)   **VOLTIGEUR 7120 (6778).**

[Recorded with pedigree in the Percheron Stud-Books of France and America.]

Dark grey ; 15¾ hands ; weight, 1,700 lbs.; foaled April 25, 1884 ;
imported 1887 ; bred by M. Guillemin, commune of Berd'huis, department of Orne ; got by GÉROME 3655 (436); dam Castille (635) by
VIDOCQ II (723) out of La Poule.

GÉROME 3655 (436) by Vidocq II (723) out of Pelote by Superior 454 (730), he
   by Favori I (711) out of Pauline by Vieux-Chaslin (713).
   FAVORI I (711) by Vieux-Chaslin (713) out of L'Amie by Vieux-Pierre (894),
   he by Coco (712).
VIDOCQ II (723) by Bayard (1385) out of Brière by Décidé.
BAYARD (1385) by Vidocq 483 (732) out of La Noire by Chéri, he by Coco II
   (714).
VIDOCQ 483 (732) by Coco II (714) out of a daughter of Chéri, he by Rustique.
Coco II (714) by Vieux-Chaslin (713) out of La Grise by Vieux-Pierre (883).
VIEUX-CHASLIN (713) by Coco (712) out of Poule by Sandi.
Coco (712) by Mignon (715) out of Pauline by Vieux-Coco.
MIGNON (715) by Jean-le-Blanc (739).

(Hoof No. 76.)   **VOYAGEUR 6999 (9407).**

[Recorded with pedigree in the Percheron Stud-Books of France and America.]

Dapple grey ; 16 hands ; weight, 1,670 lbs. ; foaled February 28,
1883 ; imported 1887 ; bred by M. Legout, commune of Dame-Marie,
canton of Bellême, department of Orne ; got by VOLNEY 2584 (2);
dam Mignonne (5207) by DÉCIDÉ, belonging to M. Fardouet père, out
of Mignonne.

VOLNEY 2584 (2) by Vidocq II (723) out of Célestine by Coco II (714).
VIDOCQ II (723) by Bayard (1385) out of Brière by Décidé.
BAYARD (1385) by Vidocq 483 (732) out of La Noire by Chéri, he by Coco II
   (714).
Coco II (714) by Vieux-Chaslin (713) out of La Grise by Vieux-Pierre (883).
VIEUX-CHASLIN (713) by Coco (712) out of Poule by Sandi.
Coco (712) by Mignon (715) out of Pauline by Vieux-Coco.
MIGNON (715) by Jean-le-Blanc (739).

(Hoof No. 41.) **VULCAIN 7124 (5515).**

[Recorded with pedigree in the Percheron Stud-Books of France and America.]

Dark grey; 16 hands; weight, 1,600 lbs.; foaled May 12, 1885; imported 1887; bred by M. Louis Maute, commune of L'Hermitiere, canton of Theil, department of Orne; got by VAILLANT (404); dam Lisette (5514) by PROSPER (893) out of Castille.

VAILLANT (404) by Prosper (893) out of Rosalie by Bienvenu, belonging to the Société Hippique of Eure-et-Loir.
PROSPER (893) by Décidé (892) out of Bourreau by Vieux-Pierre (883).
DÉCIDÉ (892) by Vieux-Pierre (894) out of Pelote, belonging to M. Berjeau, of Courvalien.
VIEUX-PIERRE (894) by Coco (712), he by Mignon (715) out of Pauline by Vieux-Coco.
MIGNON (715) by Jean-le-Blanc (739).

(Hoof No. 63.) **WEBER 7125 (9016).**

[Recorded with pedigree in the Percheron Stud-Books of France and America.]

Dark grey; 16 hands; weight, 1,600 lbs.; foaled April 25, 1885; imported 1887; bred by M. Aveline, commune of Mâsles, canton of Theil, department of Orne; got by VOLTAIRE 3540 (443); dam Rosetta (4429) by MARVEL 1922 (1061) out of L'Amie (4426) by TRANQUIL, belonging to M. Thérin; 3d dam Castille.

VOLTAIRE 3540 (443) by Brilliant 1271 (755) out of Cocotte by Coco II (714).
BRILLIANT 1271 (755) by Brilliant 1899 (756) out of Ragout by Favori I (711), he by Vieux-Chaslin (713) out of L'Amie by Vieux-Pierre (894), he by Coco (712).
BRILLIANT 1899 (756) by Coco II (714) out of Rosette by Mina, belonging to the French government.
Coco II (714) by Vieux-Chaslin (713) out of La Grise by Vieux-Pierre (883).
VIEUX-CHASLIN (713) by Coco (712) out of Poule by Sandi.
Coco (712) by Mignon (715) out of Pauline by Vieux-Coco.
MIGNON (715) by Jean-le-Blanc (739).
MARVEL 1922 (1061) by Brilliant 1899 (756), etc., out of a daughter of French Monarch 205 (734), he by Ilderim (5302) out of a daughter of Vieux-Pierre (894), etc.
ILDERIM (5302) by Valentin (5301) out of Chaton by Vieux-Pierre (894), etc.
VALENTIN (5301) by Vieux-Chaslin (713), etc.

(Hoof No. 31.) **WESTERMAN 7000 (5932).**

[Recorded with pedigree in the Percheron Stud-Books of France and America.]

Bay; 16¾ hands; weight, 1,710 lbs.; foaled March 19, 1884; imported 1887; bred by M. Lecomte, commune of Trizay, canton of Nogent-le-Rotrou, department of Eure-et-Loir; got by MADÈRE (363); dam Julie (5931) by VAILLANT (2255) out of Rustique, belonging to M. Levier.

MADÈRE (363) by Prosper (893) out of L'Amie by Papillon, belonging to M. Thérin.
PROSPER (893) by Décidé (892) out of Bourreau by Vieux-Pierre (883).
DÉCIDÉ (892) by Vieux-Pierre (894) out of Pelote, belonging to M. Berjeau, of Courvalien.
VIEUX-PIERRE (894) by Coco (712), he by Mignon (715) out of Pauline by Vieux-Coco.
MIGNON (715) by Jean-le-Blanc (739).
VAILLANT (2255) by Orizaba, belonging to M. Lalouet, out of Pauline (279) by Miramar.

(Hoof No. 214.)   **WILIAM 5583 (6333).**

[Recorded with pedigree in the Percheron Stud-Book of France and America.]

Dark grey; 16½ hands; weight, 1,650 lbs.; foaled April 12, 1883; imported 1886; bred by M. Guerin, commune of Margon, canton of Nogent-le-Rotrou, department of Eure-et-Loir; got by Chéri 6183 (358); dam Chaton (7394) by Brillant (4951).

Chéri 6183 (358) by Vermouth 1820 (787) out of Chaton.
Vermouth 1820 (787) by Vidocq 483 (732) out of Agathe by Vieux-Chaslin (713).
Vidocq 483 (732) by Coco II (714) out of a daughter of Chéri, he by Rustique.
Coco II (714) by Vieux-Chaslin (713) out of La Grise by Vieux-Pierre (883).
Vieux-Chaslin (713) by Coco (712) out of Poule by Sandi.
Coco (712) by Mignon (715) out of Pauline by Vieux-Coco.
Mignon (715) by Jean-le-Blanc (739).
Brillant (4951) by Vaillant out of Poule by Colin (6949).

IMPORTED AND PURE BRED

PERCHERON MARES.

(Hoof No. 40.)   **ABSALA 5651 (6718).**

[Recorded with pedigree in the Percheron Stud-Books of France and America.]

Black ; foaled May 18, 1871 ; imported 1886 ; bred by M. Charles Rigot, commune of St. Bomert, canton of Authon, department of Orne ; got by BRILLIANT 1271 (755); dam Poule (2032) by BRILLIANT 1899 (756) out of Chaton.

BRILLIANT 1271 (755) by Brilliant 1899 (756) out of Ragout by Favori I (711), he by Vieux-Chaslin (713) out of L'Amie by Vieux-Pierre (894), he by Coco (712).
BRILLIANT 1899 (756) by Coco II (714) out of Rosette by Mina, belonging to the French government.
Coco II (714) by Vieux-Chaslin (713) out of La Grise by Vieux-Pierre (883).
VIEUX-CHASLIN (713) by Coco (712) out of Poule by Sandi.
Coco (712) by Mignon (715) out of Pauline by Vieux-Coco.
MIGNON (715) by Jean-le-Blanc (739).

Bred to LA FERTÉ 5144 (452), October 12, 1887.

(Hoof No. 262.)   **ACTINE 7316.**

[Recorded with pedigree in the Percheron Stud-Book of America.]

Black ; foaled April 25, 1887 ; bred at Oaklawn ; got by BRILLIANT 1271 (755); dam Actress 961 (1406) by SÉLIM (749) out of a daughter of PORTHOS, belonging to M. Fromentin.

BRILLIANT 1271 (755) by Brilliant 1899 (756) out of Ragout by Favori I (711), he by Vieux-Chaslin (713) out of L'Amie by Vieux-Pierre (894), he by Coco (712).
BRILLIANT 1899 (756) by Coco II (714) out of Rosette by Mina, belonging to the French government.
Coco II (714) by Vieux-Chaslin (713) out of L'Amie by Vieux-Pierre (883).
VIEUX-CHASLIN (713) by Coco (712) out of Poule by Sandi.
Coco (712) by Mignon (715) out of Pauline by Vieux-Coco.
MIGNON (715) by Jean-le-Blanc (739).
SÉLIM (749) by Porthos, belonging to M. Fromentin.

(Hoof No. 127.)   **ACTRESS 961 (1406).**

[Recorded with pedigree in the Percheron Stud-Books of France and America.]

Light dapple grey ; foaled 1877 ; imported 1880 ; got by SÉLIM (749), he by PORTHOS ; dam by PORTHOS, belonging to M. Fromentin.

Bred to BRILLIANT 1271 (755), April 10, 1887.

(Hoof No. 128.)   **ACTRINE 5697.**

[Recorded with pedigree in the Percheron Stud-Book of America.]

Dark grey; foaled April 3, 1886; bred at Oaklawn; got by
Brilliant 1271 (755); dam Actress 961 (1406) by Sélim (749); 2d
dam by Porthos.

Brilliant 1271 (755) by Brilliant 1899 (756), out of Ragout by Favori I (711),
he by Vieux-Chaslin (713) out of L'Amie by Vieux-Pierre (894), he by
Coco (712).
Brilliant 1899 (756) by Coco II (714) out of Rosette by Mina, belonging to
the French government.
Coco II (714) by Vieux-Chaslin (713) out of La Grise by Vieux-Pierre (883).
Vieux-Chaslin (713) by Coco (712) out of Poule by Sandi.
Coco (712) by Mignon (715) out of Pauline by Vieux-Coco.
Mignon (715) by Jean-le-Blanc (739).
Sélim (749) by Porthos, belonging to M. Fromentin.

(Hoof No. 114.)   **ADELAIDE 519 (1407).**

[Recorded with pedigree in the Percheron Stud-Books of France and America.]

Black; foaled 1872; imported 1875; got by Duke-de-Chartres
162 (721); dam by Favori I (711).

Duke-de-Chartres 162 (721) by Coco II (714), he by Vieux-Chaslin (713) out of
La Grise by Vieux-Pierre (883).
Vieux-Chaslin (713) by Coco (712) out of Poule by Sandi.
Coco (712) by Mignon (715) out of Pauline by Vieux-Coco.
Mignon (715) by Jean-le-Blanc (739).
Favori I (711) by Vieux-Chaslin (713), etc., out of L'Amie by Vieux-Pierre
(894), he by Coco (712), etc.

Bred to La Ferté 5144 (452), October 4, 1887.

(Hoof No. 297.)   **ADELAIDE 5221.**

[Recorded with pedigree in the Percheron Stud-Book of America.]

Grey; foaled June, 1886; bred by Brickman & Baker, of Rednerville, Ontario; got by Romulus 1300; dam Fannie 2750 (1522) by
Sélim (749) out of Sophie by Duke-de-Chartres 162 (721).

Sélim (749) by Porthos, belonging to M. Fromentin.
Duke-de-Chartres 162 (721) by Coco II (714), he by Vieux-Chaslin (713) out
of La Grise by Vieux-Pierre (883).
Vieux-Chaslin (713) by Coco (712) out of Poule by Sandi.
Coco (712) by Mignon (715) out of Pauline by Vieux-Coco.
Mignon (715) by Jean-le-Blanc (739).

(Hoof No. 195.)   **ADRIENNE 2781 (1565).**

[Recorded with pedigree in the Percheron Stud-Books of France and America.]

Brown bay; foaled 1880; imported 1883; got by Adonis 851
(861); dam by Introuvable.

Adonis 851 (861) by Bayard 26 (717), he by Favori I (711) out of Mignonne
by Chéri.
Favori I (711) by Vieux-Chaslin (713) out of L'Amie by Vieux-Pierre (894), he
by Coco (712).
Vieux-Chaslin (713) by Coco (712) out of Poule by Sandi.
Coco (712) by Mignon (715) out of Pauline by Vieux-Coco.
Mignon (715) by Jean-le-Blanc (739).

Bred to Brilliant 1271 (755), August 26, 1887.

(Hoof No. 280.)   **AGRIPPINE 5652 (6489).**

[Recorded with pedigree in the Percheron Stud-Books of France and America.]

Black ; foaled May 1, 1885 ; imported 1886 ; bred by M. Peuvret, commune of Ceton, canton of Theil, department of Orne ; got by LA FERTÉ 5144 (452) ; dam Coquette (5689) by BRILLIANT 1899 (756) out of Poule.

LA FERTÉ 5144 (452) by Philibert (760) out of Julie (7594) by Brilliant 1899 (756).

PHILIBERT (760) by Superior 454 (730) out of Madelon by Vieux-Vaillant (1383), he by Pierre out of a daughter of Vieux-Pierre (883).

SUPERIOR 454 (730) by Favori I (711) out of Pauline by Vieux-Chaslin (713).

FAVORI I (711) by Vieux-Chaslin (713) out of L'Amie by Vieux-Pierre (894), he by Coco (712).

VIEUX-CHASLIN (713) by Coco (712) out of Poule by Sandi.

Coco (712) by Mignon (715) out of Pauline by Vieux-Coco.

MIGNON (715) by Jean-le-Blanc (739).

BRILLIANT 1899 (756) by Coco II (714) out of Rosette by Mina, belonging to the French government.

Coco II (714) by Vieux-Chaslin (713) out of La Grise by Vieux-Pierre (883).

Bred to SANDY 5162 (2225), August 20, 1887.

(Hoof No. 221.)   **ALBERTINE 6923 (10792).**

[Recorded with pedigree in the Percheron-Stud Books of France and America.]

Black ; foaled March 27, 1885 ; imported 1887 ; bred by M. Louis Guillemin, commune of Ceton, canton of Theil, department of Orne ; got by LA FERTÉ 5144 (452) ; dam Cocotte (10781) by PHILIBERT (760).

LA FERTÉ 5144 (452) by Philibert (760) out of Julie (7594) by Brilliant 1899 (756), he by Coco II (714) out of Rosette by Mina, belonging to the French government.

Coco II (714) by Vieux-Chaslin (713) out of La Grise by Vieux-Pierre (883).

PHILIBERT (760) by Superior 454 (730) out of Madelon by Vieux-Vaillant (1383), he by Pierre out of a daughter of Vieux-Pierre (883).

SUPERIOR 454 (730) by Favori I (711) out of Pauline by Vieux-Chaslin (713).

FAVORI I (711) by Vieux-Chaslin (713) out of L'Amie by Vieux-Pierre (894), he by Coco (712).

VIEUX-CHASLIN (713) by Coco (712) out of Poule by Sandi.

Coco (712) by Mignon (715) out of Pauline by Vieux-Coco.

MIGNON (715) by Jean-le-Blanc (739).

Bred to BRILLIANT 1271 (755), September 2, 1887.

(Hoof No. 186.)   **ALÊNE 4392.**

[Recorded with pedigree in the Percheron Stud-Book of America.]

Black ; foaled April 2, 1885 ; bred at Oaklawn ; got by BRILLIANT 1271 (755) ; dam Amelia 2733 (1533) by ROMULUS, he by WATERLOO 2199 (733) out of a daughter of JEAN-BART (716).

BRILLIANT 1271 (755) by Brilliant 1899 (756) out of Ragout by Favori I (711), he by Vieux-Chaslin (713) out of L'Amie by Vieux-Pierre (894), he by Coco (712).

BRILLIANT 1899 (756) by Coco II (714) out of Rosette by Mina, belonging to the French government.

Coco II (714) by Vieux-Chaslin (713) out of La Grise by Vieux-Pierre (883).

VIEUX-CHASLIN (713) by Coco (712) out of Poule by Sandi.

Coco (712) by Mignon (715) out of Pauline by Vieux-Coco.

MIGNON (715) by Jean-le-Blanc (739).

WATERLOO 2199 (733) by Jean-Bart (716) out of Poule, belonging to M. Bourdin.

JEAN-BART (716) by Bayard, belonging to M. Perpère, out of Jeanne by Porthos.

Bred to LA FERTÉ 5144 (452), July 7, 1887.

(Hoof No. 149.)   **ALMA 3672.**

[Recorded with pedigree in the Percheron Stud-Book of America.]

Black; foaled March 26, 1884; bred at Oaklawn; got by BRILL-
IANT 1271 (755); dam Agnes 1477 (1409) by PICADOR, he by FAVORI;
2d dam by BAYARD 26 (717).

BRILLIANT 1271 (755) by Brilliant 1899 (756) out of Ragout by Favori I (711).
BRILLIANT 1899 (756) by Coco II (714) out of Rosette by Mina, belonging to the
    French government.
Coco II (714) by Vieux-Chaslin (713) out of La Grise by Vieux-Pierre (883).
VIEUX-CHASLIN (713) by Coco (712) out of Poule by Sandi.
Coco (712) by Mignon (715) out of Pauline by Vieux-Coco.
MIGNON (715) by Jean-le-Blanc (739).
BAYARD 26 (717) by Favori I (711) out of Mignonne by Chéri.
FAVORI I (711) by Vieux-Chaslin (713), etc., out of L'Amie by Vieux-Pierre
    (894), he by Coco (712), etc.

Bred to LA FERTÉ 5144 (452), August 30, 1887.

                          ALVENA 7319.

[Recorded with pedigree in the Percheron Stud-Book of America.]

Grey; foaled April 28, 1887; bred at Oaklawn; got by PRODUC-
TEUR 4280 (68); dam Vena 2276 by BRILLIANT 1271 (755); 2d dam
Geraldine 1433 (1437) by ROMULUS 873 (785); 3d dam by JEAN-BART
(716)

PRODUCTEUR 4280 (68) by Madeira 1546 (770) out of Gentille (4062) by Porthos.
MADEIRA 1546 (770) by Vidocq 483 (732) out of Jeanne by Favori I (711), he by
    Vieux-Chaslin (713) out of L'Amie by Vieux-Pierre (894), he by Coco (712).
VIDOCQ 483 (732) by Coco II (714) out of a daughter of Chéri, he by Rustique.
Coco II (714) by Vieux-Chaslin (713) out of La Grise by Vieux-Pierre (883).
VIEUX-CHASLIN (713) by Coco (712) out of Poule by Sandi.
Coco (712) by Mignon (715) out of Pauline by Vieux-Coco.
MIGNON (715) by Jean-le-Blanc (739).
BRILLIANT 1271 (755) by Brilliant 1899 (756) out of Ragout by Favori I (711),
    etc.
BRILLIANT 1899 (756) by Coco II (714), etc., out of Rosette by Mina, belonging to
    the French government.
ROMULUS 873 (785) by the government approved stallion Romulus (son of
    Moreuil) out of Fleur-d'Épine by Chéri, he by Corbon.
JEAN-BART (716) by Bayard, belonging to M. Perpère, out of Jeanne by Porthos.

(Hoof No. 158.)   **MELIA 2733 (1533).**

[Recorded with pedigree in the Percheron Stud-Books of France and America.]

Black; foaled 1882; imported 1883; got by ROMULUS, he by
WATERLOO 2199 (733); dam by JEAN-BART (716).

WATERLOO 2199 (733) by Jean-Bart (716) out of Poule, belonging to M. Bourdin.
JEAN-BART (716) by Bayard, belonging to M. Perpère, out of Jeanne by Porthos.

Bred to BRILLIANT 1271 (755), April 10, 1887.

(Hoof No. 263.) **AMIE 7337.**

[Recorded with pedigree in the Percheron Stud-Book of America.]

Black; foaled April 3, 1887; bred at Oaklawn; got by BRILLIANT 1271 (755); dam Amelia 2733 (1533) by ROMULUS, he by WATERLOO 2199 (733); 2d dam by JEAN-BART (716).

BRILLIANT 1271 (755) by Brilliant 1899 (756) out of Ragout by Favori I (711), he by Vieux-Chaslin (713) out of L'Amie by Vieux-Pierre (894), he by Coco (712).

BRILLIANT 1899 (756) by Coco II (714) out of Rosette by Mina, belonging to the French government.

Coco II (714) by Vieux-Chaslin (713) out of La Grise by Vieux-Pierre (883).

VIEUX-CHASLIN (713) by Coco (712) out of Poule by Sandi.

Coco (712) by Mignon (715) out of Pauline by Vieux-Coco.

MIGNON (715) by Jean-le-Blanc (739).

WATERLOO 2199 (733) by Jean-Bart (716) out of Poule, belonging to M. Bourdin.

JEAN-BART (716) by Bayard, belonging to M. Perpère, out of Jeanne by Porthos.

(Hoof No. 35.) **AMIRAUTÉ 5646 (6719).**

[Recorded with pedigree in the Percheron Stud-Books of France and America.]

Grey; foaled May 15, 1884; imported 1886; bred by M. Charles Rigot, commune of St. Bomert, canton of Authon, department of Eure-et-Loir; got by SANDI 3803 (444); dam Poule (2032) by BRILLIANT 1899 (756) out of Chaton.

SANDI 3803 (444) by Brilliant 1271 (755) out of Calot by Coco II (714).

BRILLIANT 1271 (755) by Brilliant 1899 (756) out of Ragout by Favori I (711), he by Vieux-Chaslin (713) out of L'Amie by Vieux-Pierre (894), he by Coco (712).

BRILLIANT 1899 (756) by Coco II (714) out of Rosette by Mina, belonging to the French government.

Coco II (714) by Vieux-Chaslin (713) out of La Grise by Vieux-Pierre (883).

VIEUX-CHASLIN (713) by Coco (712) out of Poule by Sandi.

Coco (712) by Mignon (715) out of Pauline by Vieux-Coco.

MIGNON (715) by Jean-le-Blanc (739).

Bred to BRILLIANT 1271 (755), April 21, 1887.

(Hoof No. 175.) **ANGÈLE 4342 (4850).**

[Recorded with pedigree in the Percheron Stud-Books of France and America.]

Reddish grey; foaled March 21, 1883; imported 1885; bred by M. Bourgeteau, commune of Cerories, canton of La Ferté-Bernard, department of Sarthe; got by FAVORI III (1381); dam Marmotte (4849) by PASSE-PARTOUT (1402) out of Suzon.

FAVORI III (1381) by Utopia 780 (731) out of La Noire, belonging to M. Letourneur.

UTOPIA 780 (731) by Superior 454 (730) out of Camille by Favori I (711).

SUPERIOR 454 (730) by Favori I (711) out of Pauline by Vieux-Chaslin (713).

FAVORI I (711) by Vieux-Chaslin (713) out of L'Amie by Vieux-Pierre (894), he by Coco (712).

VIEUX-CHASLIN (713) by Coco (712) out of Poule by Sandi.

Coco (712) by Mignon (715) out of Pauline by Vieux-Coco.

MIGNON (715) by Jean-le-Blanc (739).

PASSE-PARTOUT (1402) by Comet 104 (719) out of Sophie by Favori I (711), etc.

COMET 104 (719) by French Monarch 205 (734) out of Suzanne by Cambronne.

FRENCH MONARCH 205 (734) by Ilderim (5302) out of a daughter of Vieux-Pierre (894), etc.

ILDERIM (5302) by Valentin (5301) out of Chaton by Vieux-Pierre (894), etc.

VALENTIN (5301) by Vieux-Chaslin (713), etc.

Bred to BRILLIANT 1271 (755), April 21, 1887.

(Hoof No. 251.)   **ANGELIC 7336.**

[Recorded with pedigree in the Percheron Stud-Book of America.]

Dark grey; foaled April 17, 1887; bred at Oaklawn; got by BRILLIANT 1271 (755); dam Angele 4342 (4850) by FAVORI III (1381); 2d dam Marmotte (4849) by PASSE-PARTOUT (1402); 3d dam Suzon.

BRILLIANT 1271 (755) by Brilliant 1899 (756) out of Ragout by Favori I (711).
BRILLIANT 1899 (756) by Coco II (714) out of Rosette by Mina, belonging to the French government.
Coco II (714) by Vieux-Chaslin (713) out of La Grise by Vieux-Pierre (883).
VIEUX-CHASLIN (713) by Coco (712) out of Poule by Sandi.
Coco (712) by Mignon (715) out of Pauline by Vieux-Coco.
MIGNON (715) by Jean-le-Blanc (739).
FAVORI III (1381) by Utopia 780 (731) out of La Noire, belonging to M. Letourneur.
UTOPIA 780 (731) by Superior 454 (730) out of Camille by Favori I (711).
SUPERIOR 454 (730) by Favori I (711) out of Pauline by Vieux-Chaslin (713), etc.
FAVORI I (711) by Vieux-Chaslin (713), etc., out of L'Amie by Vieux-Pierre (894), he by Coco (712), etc.
PASSE-PARTOUT (1402) by Comet 104 (719) out of Sophie by Favori I (711), etc.
COMET 104 (719) by French Monarch 205 (734) out of Suzanne by Cambronne.
FRENCH MONARCH 205 (734) by Ilderim (5302) out of a daughter of Vieux-Pierre (894), etc.
ILDERIM (5302) by Valentin (5301) out of Chaton by Vieux-Pierre (894), etc.
VALENTIN (5301) by Vieux-Chaslin (713), etc.

(Hoof No. 307)   **ANNA 4371 (4262).**

[Recorded with pedigree in the Percheron Stud-Books of France and America.]

Dark grey; foaled May 4, 1883; imported 1885; bred by M. Just Brouard, commune of St. Hilaire-sur-Erre, canton of Theil, department of Orne; got by VAILLANT (404); dam Franconie (4260) by VIEUX-VAILLANT (1383); 2d dam Pélagie (7428) by LOULOU out of Madelon.

VAILLANT (404) by Prosper (893) out of Rosalie by Bienvenu, belonging to the Société Hippique of Eure-et-Loir.
PROSPER (893) by Décidé (892) out of Bourreau by Vieux-Pierre (883).
DÉCIDÉ (892) by Vieux-Pierre (894) out of Pelote, belonging to M. Berjeau, of Courvalien.
VIEUX-PIERRE (894) by Coco (712), he by Mignon (715) out of Pauline by Vieux-Coco.
MIGNON (715) by Jean-le-Blanc (739).
VIEUX-VAILLANT (1383) by Pierre, belonging to M. Thérin, out of a daughter of Vieux-Pierre (883).

Bred to LA FERTÉ 5144 (452), July 3, 1887.

(Hoof No. 129.)   **ARIA 2207 (1414).**

[Recorded with pedigree in the Percheron Stud-Books of France and America.]

Light dapple grey; foaled 1877; imported 1882; got by FORRESTER 674 (741).

FORRESTER 674 (741) by Vidocq 483 (732), he by Coco II (714) out of a daughter of Chéri, he by Rustique.
Coco II (714) by Vieux-Chaslin (713) out of L'Amie by Vieux-Pierre (894), he by Coco (712).
VIEUX-CHASLIN (713) by Coco (712) out of Poule by Sandi.
Coco (712) by Mignon (715) out of Pauline by Vieux-Coco.
MIGNON (715) by Jean-le-Blanc (739).

Bred to LA FERTÉ 5144 (452), April 12, 1887.

(Hoof No. 90.) **AVENA 7162.**

[Recorded with pedigree in the Percheron Stud-Book of America.]

Brown bay; foaled March 13, 1887; bred at Oaklawn; got by
BRILLIANT 1271 (755); dam Avenante 2783 (1562) by AVATA 1966
(912) out of Adelaide by VIDOCQ 483 (732).

BRILLIANT 1271 (755) by Brilliant 1899 (756) out of Ragout by Favori I (711), he
by Vieux-Chaslin (713) out of L'Amie by Vieux-Pierre (894), he by Coco
(712).
BRILLIANT 1899 (756) by Coco II (714) out of Rosette by Mina, belonging to the
French government.
Coco II (714) by Vieux-Chaslin (713) out of La Grise by Vieux-Pierre (883).
VIEUX-CHASLIN (713) by Coco (712) out of Poule by Sandi.
Coco (712) by Mignon (715) out of Pauline by Vieux-Coco.
MIGNON (715) by Jean-le-Blanc (739).
AVATA 1966 (912) by Nogent 738 (729) out of Bicotte by Bayard 26 (717), he by
Favori I (711), etc., out of Mignonne by Chéri.
NOGENT 738 (729) by Vidocq 483 (732) out of a daughter of Favori I (711), etc.
VIDOCQ 483 (732) by Coco II (714), etc., out of a daughter of Chéri, he by
Rustique.

(Hoof No. 140.) **AVENANTE 2783 (1562).**

[Recorded with pedigree in the Percheron Stud-Books of France and America.]

Brown bay; foaled 1882; imported 1883; got by AVATA 1966
(912); dam Adelaide by VIDOCQ 483 (732).

AVATA 1966 (912) by Nogent 738 (729) out of Bicotte by Bayard 26 (717), he by
Favori I (711) out of Mignonne by Chéri.
FAVORI I (711) by Vieux-Chaslin (713) out of L'Amie by Vieux-Pierre (894),
he by Coco (712).
NOGENT 738 (729) by Vidocq 483 (732) out of a daughter of Favori I (711), etc.
VIDOCQ 483 (732) by Coco II (714) out of a daughter of Chéri, he by Rustique.
Coco II (714) by Vieux-Chaslin (713) out of La Grise by Vieux-Pierre (883).
VIEUX-CHASLIN (713) by Coco (712) out of Poule by Sandi.
Coco (712) by Mignon (715) out of Pauline by Vieux-Coco.
MIGNON (715) by Jean-le-Blanc (739).

Bred to BRILLIANT 1271 (755), March 23, 1887.

(Hoof No. 213.) **BABIE 7127 (9508).**

[Recorded with pedigree in the Percheron Stud-Books of France and America.]

Steel grey; foaled April 22, 1885; imported 1887; bred by M.
Denis Pelletier, commune of Préaux, canton of Nocé, department of
Orne; got by VAILLANT (404); dam Bijou (271) by DÉCIDÉ, belonging
to M. Fardouet.

VAILLANT (404) by Prosper (893) out of Rosalie by Bienvenu, belonging to the
Société Hippique of Eure-et-Loir.
PROSPER (893) by Décidé (892) out of Bourreau by Vieux-Pierre (883).
DÉCIDÉ (892) by Vieux-Pierre (894) out of Pelote, belonging to M. Berjeau, of
Courvalien.
VIEUX-PIERRE (894) by Coco (712), he by Mignon (715) out of Pauline by Vieux-
Coco.
MIGNON (715) by Jean-le-Blanc (739)

Bred in France to MALAKOFF (8275).

(Hoof No. 219.)   **BABIE 7129 (8721).**

[Recorded with pedigree in the Percheron Stud-Books of France and America.]

Black; foaled April 5, 1884; imported 1887; bred by M. J. Gautret, commune of La Ferté-Bernard, department of Sarthe; got by Désiré (1946); dam Bleue (8720) by Favora 1542 (765).

Désiré (1946) by Mouton (1640) out of Poule, belonging to M. Tuvache.
Mouton (1640) by French Monarch 205 (734) out of Rose by Décidé.
French Monarch 205 (734) by Ilderim (5302) out of a daughter of Vieux-Pierre (894), he by Coco (712).
Ilderim (5302) by Valentin (5301) out of Chaton by Vieux-Pierre (894), etc.
Valentin (5301) by Vieux-Chaslin (713), he by Coco (712) out of Poule by Sandi.
Coco (712) by Mignon (715) out of Pauline by Vieux-Coco.
Mignon (715) by Jean-le-Blanc (739).
Favora 1542 (765) by French Monarch 205 (734), etc., out of Marguerite by Favori, he by Coco of Mésle-sur-Sarthe.

Bred to MALAKOFF (8275), April 13, 1887.

(Hoof No. 220.)   **BALSAMINE 6924 (5998).**

[Recorded with pedigree in the Percheron Stud-Books of France and America.]

Dark grey; foaled April 10, 1885; imported 1887; bred by M. Hubert, commune of Préaux, canton of Nocé, department of Orne; got by Vaillant (404); dam Favorite (5997) by Vaillant (404); 2d dam Brebis (4004) by French Monarch 205 (734); 3d dam Riquette, belonging to M. Hubert.

Vaillant (404) by Prosper (893) out of Rosalie by Bienvenu, belonging to the Société Hippique of Eure-et-Loir.
Prosper (893) by Décidé (892) out of Bourreau by Vieux-Pierre (883).
Décidé (892) by Vieux-Pierre (894) out of Pelote, belonging to M. Berjeau, of Courvalien.
Vieux-Pierre (894) by Coco (712), he by Mignon (715) out of Pauline by Vieux-Coco.
Mignon (715) by Jean-le-Blanc (739).
French Monarch 205 (734) by Ilderim (5302) out of a daughter of Vieux-Pierre (894), etc.
Ilderim (5302) by Valentin (5301) out of Chaton by Vieux-Pierre (894), etc.
Valentin (5301) by Vieux-Chaslin (713), etc.

Bred to LA FERTÉ 5144 (452), September 7, 1887.

(Hoof No. 46.) **BARBICHE 5337 (6488).**

[Recorded with pedigree in the Percheron Stud-Books of France and America.]

Light grey; foaled June 3, 1882; imported 1886; bred by M. Jean Baptiste Dumur, commune of St. Jean-des-Echelles, canton of Montmirail, department of Sarthe; got by PASSE-PARTOUT (1402); dam Cocotte (7584) by Coco II (714) out of La Grise, belonging to M. Leroy.

PASSE-PARTOUT (1402) by Comet 104 (719) out of Sophie by Favori I (711), he by Vieux-Chaslin (713) out of L'Amie by Vieux-Pierre (894), he by Coco (712).
COMET 104 (719) by French Monarch 205 (734) out of Suzanne by Cambronne.
FRENCH MONARCH 205 (734) by Ilderim (5302) out of a daughter of Vieux-Pierre (894), etc.
ILDERIM (5302) by Valentin (5301) out of Chaton by Vieux-Pierre (894), etc.
VALENTIN (5301) by Vieux-Chaslin (713), he by Coco (712) out of Poule by Sandi.
Coco (712) by Mignon (715) out of Pauline by Vieux-Coco.
MIGNON (715) by Jean-le-Blanc (739).
Coco II (714) by Vieux-Chaslin (713), etc., out of La Grise by Vieux-Pierre (883).

Bred to BRILLIANT 1271 (755), December 4, 1886.

(Hoof No. 162.) **BÉATRICE 4348 (4848).**

[Recorded with pedigree in the Percheron Stud-Books of France and America.]

Dark grey; foaled April 28, 1884; imported 1885; bred by M. Joseph Tuvache, commune of Cormes, canton of La Ferté-Bernard, department of Sarthe; got by LAGRANGE 3065 (1334); dam Chopine (4847) by PAPILLON, he by PIERRE out of Chopine.

LAGRANGE 3065 (1334) by Brilliant 1271 (755) out of Lydie by Coco II (714).
BRILLIANT 1271 (755) by Brilliant 1899 (756) out of Ragout by Favori I (711), he by Vieux-Chaslin (713) out of L'Amie by Vieux-Pierre (894), he by Coco (712).
BRILLIANT 1899 (756) by Coco II (714) out of Rosette by Mina, belonging to the French government.
Coco II (714) by Vieux-Chaslin (713) out of La Grise by Vieux-Pierre (883).
VIEUX-CHASLIN (713) by Coco (712) out of Poule by Sandi.
Coco (712) by Mignon (715) out of Pauline by Vieux-Coco.
MIGNON (715) by Jean-le-Blanc (739).

Bred to BRILLIANT 1271 (755), May 12, 1887.

(Hoof No. 254.) **BELINDA 7334.**

[Recorded with pedigree in the Percheron Stud-Book of America.]

Dark grey; foaled April 1, 1887; bred at Oaklawn; got by BRILLIANT 1271 (755); dam Bellina 2801 (1548) by CHALUMEAU out of a daughter of the government approved stallion ROMULUS, he by MOREUIL.

BRILLIANT 1271 (755) by Brilliant 1899 (756) out of Ragout by Favori I (711), he by Vieux-Chaslin (713) out of L'Amie by Vieux-Pierre (894), he by Coco (712).
BRILLIANT 1899 (756) by Coco II (714) out of Rosette by Mina, belonging to the French government.
Coco II (714) by Vieux-Chaslin (713) out of La Grise by Vieux-Pierre (883).
VIEUX-CHASLIN (713) by Coco (712) out of Poule by Sandi.
Coco (712) by Mignon (715) out of Pauline by Vieux-Coco.
MIGNON (715) by Jean-le-Blanc (739).

BELLA 7335.

[Recorded with pedigree in the Percheron Stud-Book of América.]

Black ; foaled May 29, 1887 ; bred at Oaklawn ; got by BRILLIANT 1271 (755); dam Belle 4352 (4852) by LAGRANGE 3065 (1334); 2d dam Biche (4851) by MOUTON (4602); 3d dam Bichette, belonging to M. Dumur.

BRILLIANT 1271 (755) by Brilliant 1899 (756) out of Ragout by Favori I (711), he by Vieux-Chaslin (713) out of L'Amie by Vieux-Pierre (894), he by Coco (712).
BRILLIANT 1899 (756) by Coco II (714) out of Rosette by Mina, belonging to the French government.
Coco II (714) by Vieux-Chaslin (713) out of La Grise by Vieux-Pierre (883).
VIEUX-CHASLIN (713) by Coco (712) out of Poule by Sandi.
Coco (712) by Mignon (715) out of Pauline by Vieux-Coco.
MIGNON (715) by Jean-le-Blanc (739).
LAGRANGE 3065 (1334) by Brilliant 1271 (755), etc., out of Lydie by Coco II (714), etc.
MOUTON (4602) by Coco, belonging to M. Louis Perriot.

(Hoof No. 109.)   **BELLE 4352 (4852).**

[Recorded with pedigree in the Percheron Stud-Books of France and America.]

Black ; foaled April 12, 1884 ; imported 1885 ; bred by M. Dumur, commune of Champroud, canton of Montmirail, department of Sarthe ; got by LAGRANGE 3065 (1334); dam Biche (4851) by MOUTON (4602) out of Bichette.

LAGRANGE 3065 (1334) by Brilliant 1271 (755) out of Lydie by Coco II (714).
BRILLIANT 1271 (755) by Brilliant 1899 (756) out of Ragout by Favori I (711), he by Vieux-Chaslin (713) out of L'Amie by Vieux-Pierre (894), he by Coco (712).
BRILLIANT 1899 (756) by Coco II (714) out of Rosette by Mina, belonging to the French government.
Coco II (714) by Vieux-Chaslin (713) out of La Grise by Vieux-Pierre (883).
VIEUX-CHASLIN (713) by Coco (712) out of Poule by Sandi.
Coco (712) by Mignon (715) out of Pauline by Vieux-Coco.
MIGNON (715) by Jean-le-Blanc (739).
MOUTON (4602) by Coco, belonging to M. Louis Perriot.

Bred to LA FERTÉ 5144 (452), June 8, 1887.

(Hoof No. 161.)   **BELLINA 2801 (1548).**

[Recorded with pedigree in the Percheron Stud-Books of France and America.]

Black ; foaled 1881 ; imported 1883 ; got by CHALUMEAU ; dam by ROMULUS, he by MOREUIL.

Bred to BRILLIANT 1271 (755), April 9, 1887.

(Hoof No. 105.) **BELLORA 2237 (1415).**

[Recorded with pedigree in the Percheron Stud-Books of France and America.]

Black; foaled 1882; imported 1882; got by BRILLIANT 1271 (755); dam Thérèse by Coco II (714).

BRILLIANT 1271 (755) by Brilliant 1899 (756) out of Ragout by Favori I (711), he by Vieux-Chaslin (713) out of L'Amie by Vieux-Pierre (894), he by Coco (712).
BRILLIANT 1899 (756) by Coco II (714) out of Rosette by Mina, belonging to the French government.
Coco II (714) by Vieux-Chaslin (713) out of La Grise by Vieux-Pierre (883).
VIEUX-CHASLIN (713) by Coco (712) out of Poule by Sandi.
Coco (712) by Mignon (715) out of Pauline by Vieux-Coco.
MIGNON (715) by Jean-le-Blanc (739).

Bred to LA FERTÉ 5144 (452), September 9, 1887.

(Hoof No. 238.) **BERGÈRE 7130 (6046).**

[Recorded with pedigree in the Percheron Stud-Books of France and America.]

Dark grey; foaled June 3, 1883; imported 1887; bred by M. Gravier, commune of Echauffour, canton of Merlerault, department of Orne; got by BIJOU (6076); dam Pusse (6044) by LUTHER (792); 2d dam Elise (6042) by JEAN-BART (716); 3d dam Poule, belonging to M. Heron.

BIJOU (6076) by Luther (792) out of Mignonne, belonging to M. Chemin, by Leblanc, belonging to M. Géru.
LUTHER (792) by Pierre (887) out of Rosette by Laboureur (886).
PIERRE (887) by Laboureur (886) out of Margot by Faisan.
LABOUREUR (886) by Jean-le-Blanc (739) out of Sophie by Sandi.
JEAN-BART (716) by Bayard, belonging to M. Perpère, out of Jeanne by Porthos.

Bred to BRILLIANT 1271 (755), September 20, 1887.

(Hoof No. 74.) **BERTHA 5340 (7008).**

[Recorded with pedigree in the Percheron Stud-Books of France and America.]

Black; foaled April 15, 1881; imported 1886; bred by M. Jules Fossey, commune of Courcival, canton of Bonnétable, department of Sarthe; got by PICADOR II (5606); dam Rosette (7007) by VIGOUREUX, he by FAVORI; 2d dam Frosine.

PICADOR II (5606) by Picador I (7330) out of Rose.
PICADOR I (7330) by Bayard I (son of Picador) out of Charmante.

Bred to BRILLIANT 1271 (755), July 19, 1887.

(Hoof No. 270.)   **BERTHINE 7333.**

[Recorded with pedigree in the Percheron Stud-Book of America.]

Grey ; foaled August 10, 1887 ; bred by M. Moreau, commune of
Ceton, canton of Theil, department of Orne ; got by DANCÉ (5622);
dam Bichonne 5644 (6721) by CHEER 2017 (1404); 2d dam Cocotte
(6720) by FAVORI I (711); 3d dam Bijou, belonging to M. Glond.

DANCÉ (5622) by Vidocq (1403) out of Cocotte (4701) by Superior 454 (730).
VIDOCQ (1403) by Utopia 780 (731) out of Bijou by Vieux-Chaslin (713).
UTOPIA 780 (731) by Superior 454 (730) out of Camille by Favori I (711).
SUPERIOR 454 (730) by Favori I (711) out of Pauline by Vieux-Chaslin (713).
FAVORI I (711) by Vieux-Chaslin (713) out of L'Amie by Vieux-Pierre (894),
    he by Coco (712).
VIEUX-CHASLIN (713) by Coco (712) out of Poule by Sandi.
COCO (712) by Mignon (715) out of Pauline by Vieux-Coco.
MIGNON (715) by Jean-le-Blanc (739).
CHEER 2017 (1404) by Brilliant 1899 (756) out of Robine by Coco II (714).
BRILLIANT 1899 (756) by Coco II (714) out of Rosette by Mina, belonging to the
    French government.
COCO II (714) by Vieux-Chaslin (713), etc., out of La Grise by Vieux-Pierre
    (883).

(Hoof No. 267.)   **BETHOUNE 7332.**

[Recorded with pedigree in the Percheron Stud-Book of America.]

Black ; foaled August 7, 1887 ; bred at Oaklawn ; got by BRILLIANT
1271 (755); dam Bijou 5657 (7023) by IAGO 995 (768); 2d dam Fraisine
(7022) by Coco, belonging to M. Trottier ; 3d dam Michelle, belonging to M. Hubert.

BRILLIANT 1271 (755) by Brilliant 1899 (756) out of Ragout by Favori I (711).
BRILLIANT 1899 (756) by Coco II (714) out of Rosette by Mina, belonging to
    the French government.
COCO II (714) by Vieux-Chaslin (713) out of La Grise by Vieux-Pierre (883).
VIEUX-CHASLIN (713) by Coco (712) out of Poule by Sandi.
COCO (712) by Mignon (715) out of Pauline by Vieux-Coco.
MIGNON (715) by Jean-le-Blanc (739).
IAGO 995 (768) by Utopia 780 (731) out of Cossette by Favora 666 (725), he by
    Favori I (711) out of Marie by Coco (712), etc.
UTOPIA 780 (731) by Superior 454 (730) out of Camille by Favori I (711).
SUPERIOR 454 (730) by Favori I (711) out of Pauline by Vieux-Chaslin (713), etc.
FAVORI I (711) by Vieux-Chaslin (713), etc., out of L'Amie by Vieux-Pierre
    (894), he by Coco (712), etc.

(Hoof No. 216.)   **BIBI 7128 (10248).**

[Recorded with pedigree in the Percheron Stud-Books of France and America.]

Black ; foaled May 28, 1886 ; imported 1887 ; bred by M. B. Morin,
commune of St. Hilaire-sur-Erre, canton of Theil, department of Orne ;
got by VIGOUREUX 4262 (406); dam Rosette (10247) by PROSPER (893).

VIGOUREUX 4262 (406) by Vaillant (404) out of Poule (4159) by Vieux-Vaillant
    (1383), he by Pierre out of a daughter of Vieux-Pierre (883).
VAILLANT (404) by Prosper (893) out of Rosalie by Bienvenu, belonging to the
    Société Hippique of Eure-et-Loir.
PROSPER (893) by Décidé (892) out of Bourreau by Vieux-Pierre (883).
DÉCIDÉ (892) by Vieux-Pierre (894) out of Pelote, belonging to M. Berjeau, of
    Courvalien.
VIEUX-PIERRE (894) by Coco (712), he by Mignon (715) out of Pauline by
    Vieux-Coco.
MIGNON (715) by Jean-le-Blanc (739).

(Hoof No. 33.) **BICHONNE 5644 (6721).**

[Recorded with pedigree in the Percheron Stud-Books of France and America.]

Grey; foaled May 4, 1882; imported 1886; bred by M. Louis Grenéche, commune of Ceton, canton of Theil, department of Orne; got by CHEER 2017 (1404); dam Cocote (6720) by FAVORI I (711) out of Bijou.

CHEER 2017 (1404) by Brilliant 1899 (756) out of Robine by Coco II (714).
BRILLIANT 1899 (756) by Coco II (714) out of Rosette by Mina, belonging to the French government.
Coco II (714) by Vieux-Chaslin (713) out of La Grise by Vieux-Pierre (883).
VIEUX-CHASLIN (713) by Coco (712) out of Poule by Sandi.
Coco (712) by Mignon (715) out of Pauline by Vieux-Coco.
MIGNON (715) by Jean-le-Blanc (739).
FAVORI I (711) by Vieux-Chaslin (713), etc., out of L'Amie by Vieux-Pierre (894), he by Coco (712), etc.

Bred to BRILLIANT 1271 (755), August 27, 1887.

(Hoof No. 291.) **BIJOU 3658 (2083).**

[Recorded with pedigree in the Percheron Stud-Books of France and America.]

Grey; foaled March 12, 1882; imported 1884; bred by M. Guibert, commune of Souancé, canton of Nogent-le-Rotrou, department of Eure-et-Loir; got by RUSTIQUE, he by BRILLIANT 1899 (756); dam Chaton by ROYAL, he by BAYARD, he by SOLIDE.

BRILLIANT 1899 (756) by Coco II (714) out of Rosette by Mina, belonging to the French government.
Coco II (714) by Vieux-Chaslin (713) out of La Grise by Vieux-Pierre (883).
VIEUX-CHASLIN (713) by Coco (712) out of Poule by Sandi.
Coco (712) by Mignon (715) out of Pauline by Vieux-Coco.
MIGNON (715) by Jean-le-Blanc (739).

Bred to SANDY 5162 (2225), August 17, 1887.

(Hoof No. 47.) **BIJOU 5657 (7023).**

[Recorded with pedigree in the Percheron Stud-Books of France and America.]

Black; foaled March 20, 1881; imported 1886; bred by M. Ségouin, commune of Ceton, canton of Theil, department of Orne; got by IAGO 995 (768); dam Fraisine (7022) by Coco out of Michelle, belonging to M. Hubert.

IAGO 995 (768) by Utopia 780 (731) out of Cossette by Favora 666 (725), he by Favori I (711) out of Marie by Coco (712).
UTOPIA 780 (731) by Superior 454 (730) out of Camille by Favori I (711).
SUPERIOR 454 (730) by Favori I (711) out of Pauline by Vieux-Chaslin (713).
FAVORI I (711) by Vieux-Chaslin (713) out of L'Amie by Vieux-Pierre (894), he by Coco (712).
VIEUX-CHASLIN (713) by Coco (712) out of Poule by Sandi.
Coco (712) by Mignon (715) out of Pauline by Vieux-Coco.
MIGNON (715) by Jean-le-Blanc (739).

Bred to BRILLIANT 1271 (755), September 7, 1887.

(Hoof No. 243.)   **BIJOU 7126 (10601).**

[Recorded with pedigree in the Percheron Stud-Books of France and America.]

Dapple grey; foaled April 5, 1883; imported 1887; bred by M. F. Renoud, commune of St. Aignan, canton of Theil, department of Orne; got by VAILLANT (404); dam Bourreau (10600), belonging to M. Renoud.

VAILLANT (404) by Prosper (893) out of Rosalie by Bienvenu, belonging to the Société Hippique of Eure-et-Loir.
PROSPER (893) by Décidé (892) out of Bourreau by Vieux-Pierre (883).
DÉCIDÉ (892) by Vieux-Pierre (894) out of Pelote, belonging to M. Berjeau, of Courvalien.
VIEUX-PIERRE (894) by Coco (712), he by Mignon (715) out of Pauline by Vieux-Coco.
MIGNON (715) by Jean-le-Blanc (739).

Bred in France to MOUTON 6975 (10475).

(Hoof No. 154.)   **BIJOURIE 2759 (1527).**

[Recorded with pedigree in the Percheron Stud-Books of France and America.]

Grey; foaled 1882; imported 1883; got by PRODUCTEUR, he by FAVORA 1542 (765); dam by PAPILLON.

FAVORA 1542 (765) by French Monarch 205 (734) out of Marguerite by Favori, he by Coco of Mêsle-sur-Sarthe.
FRENCH MONARCH 205 (734) by Ilderim (5302) out of a daughter of Vieux-Pierre (894), he by Coco (712).
ILDERIM (5302) by Valentin (5301) out of Chaton by Vieux-Pierre (894), etc.
VALENTIN (5301) by Vieux-Chaslin (713), he by Coco (712) out of Poule by Sandi.
COCO (712) by Mignon (715) out of Pauline by Vieux-Coco.
MIGNON (715) by Jean-le-Blanc (739).

Bred to BRILLIANT 1271 (755), May 17, 1887.

(Hoof No. 281.)   **BLEUETTE 5621 (6148).**

[Recorded with pedigree in the Percheron Stud-Books of France and America.]

Grey; foaled March 1, 1885; imported 1886; bred by M. Auguste Vadé, commune of Duneau, canton of Tuffé, department of Sarthe; got by PAPILLON 3559 (379); dam Bleue (6147) by FLEURUS, he by FRENCH MONARCH 205 (734); 2d dam Pelotte, belonging to M. Goufray.

PAPILLON 3559 (379) by Brilliant (710) out of Cocotte by Coco II (714).
BRILLANT (710) by Brilliant 1899 (756) out of Sophie by Superior 454 (730), he by Favori I (711) out of Pauline by Vieux-Chaslin (713).
    FAVORI I (711) by Vieux-Chaslin (713) out of L'Amie by Vieux-Pierre (894), he by Coco (712).
BRILLIANT 1899 (756) by Coco II (714) out of Rosette by Mina, belonging to the French government.
COCO II (714) by Vieux-Chaslin (713) out of La Grise by Vieux-Pierre (883).
VIEUX-CHASLIN (713) by Coco (712) out of Poule by Sandi.
COCO (712) by Mignon (715) out of Pauline by Vieux-Coco.
MIGNON (715) by Jean-le-Blanc (739).
FRENCH MONARCH 205 (734) by Ilderim (5302) out of a daughter of Vieux-Pierre (894), he by Coco (712).
ILDERIM (5302) by Valentin (5301) out of Chaton by Vieux-Pierre (894), etc.
VALENTIN (5301) by Vieux-Chaslin (713), etc.

Bred to SANDY 5162 (2225), July 5, 1887.

(Hoof No. 196.) **BREBIS 4365 (1753).**

[Recorded with pedigree in the Percheron Stud-Books of France and America.]

' Dapple grey; foaled 1880; imported 1885; bred by M. Duval, commune of Ceton, canton of Theil, department of Orne; got by BIJOU, belonging to M. Gautier, of Amilly; dam Brebis (5044) by SOLIDE, belonging to M. Fardouet.

Bred to LA FERTÉ 5144 (452), September 8, 1887.

(Hoof No. 191.) **BRIE 2777 (1568).**

[Recorded with pedigree in the Percheron Stud-Books of France and America.]

Grey; foaled 1877; imported 1883; got by BRILLIANT 1899 (756); dam by FAVORI I (711).

BRILLIANT 1899 (756) by Coco II (714) out of Rosette by Mina, belonging to the French government.
Coco II (714) by Vieux-Chaslin (713) out of La Grise by Vieux-Pierre (883).
VIEUX-CHASLIN (713) by Coco (712) out of Poule by Sandi.
Coco (712) by Mignon (715) out of Pauline by Vieux-Coco.
MIGNON (715) by Jean-le-Blanc (739).
FAVORI I (711) by Vieux-Chaslin (713), etc., out of L'Amie by Vieux-Pierre (894), he by Coco (712), etc.

Bred to LA FERTÉ 5144 (452), September 17, 1887.

(Hoof No. 21.) **BRILLANTE 5634 (4057)**

[Recorded with pedigree in the Percheron Stud-Books of France and America.]

Black; foaled April 22, 1883; imported 1886; bred by M. Bourdin, commune of Igé, canton of Bellême, department of Orne; got by AVATA 1966 (912); dam Lisette (4056) by VIDOCQ 483 (732) out of Rose.

AVATA 1966 (912) by Nogent 738 (729) out of Bicotte by Bayard 26 (717), he by Favori I (711) out of Mignonne by Chéri.
FAVORI I (711) by Vieux-Chaslin (713) out of L'Amie by Vieux-Pierre (894), he by Coco (712).
NOGENT 738 (729) by Vidocq 483 (732) out of a daughter of Favori I (711), etc.
VIDOCQ 483 (732) by Coco II (714) out of a daughter of Chéri, he by Rustique.
Coco II (714) by Vieux-Chaslin (713) out of La Grise by Vieux-Pierre (883).
VIEUX-CHASLIN (713) by Coco (712) out of Poule by Sandi.
Coco (712) by Mignon (715) out of Pauline by Vieux-Coco.
MIGNON (715) by Jean-le-Blanc (739).

Bred to BRILLIANT 1271 (755), October 5, 1887.

(Hoof No. 66.)   **BRILLANTINE 5675 (6948).**

[Recorded with pedigree in the Percheron Stud-Books of France and America.]

Dark grey ; foaled March 28, 1884 ; imported 1886 ; bred by M. Loiseau, commune of La Rouge, canton of Theil, department of Orne ; got by VOLTAIRE 3540 (443) ; dam Rustique (6947) by FAVORI (4770) out of Bijou by VIEUX-VAILLANT (1383).

VOLTAIRE 3540 (443) by Brilliant 1271 (755) out of Cocotte by Coco II (714).
BRILLIANT 1271 (755) by Brilliant 1899 (756) out of Ragout by Favori I (711).
BRILLIANT 1899 (756) by Coco II (714) out of Rosette by Mina, belonging to the French government.
COCO II (714) by Vieux-Chaslin (713) out of La Grise by Vieux-Pierre (883).
VIEUX-CHASLIN (713) by Coco (712) out of Poule by Sandi.
COCO (712) by Mignon (715) out of Pauline by Vieux-Coco.
MIGNON (715) by Jean-le-Blanc (739).
FAVORI (4770) by Superior 454 (730) by Favori I (711).out of Pauline by Vieux-Chaslin (713), etc.
FAVORI I (711) by Vieux-Chaslin (713), etc., out of L'Amie by Vieux-Pierre (894), he by Coco (712), etc.
VIEUX-VAILLANT (1383) by Pierre, belonging to M. Thérin, out of a daughter of Vieux-Pierre (883).

Bred to LA FERTÉ 5144 (452), May 28, 1887.

(Hoof No. 269.)   **BRILLETTE 7343.**

[Recorded with pedigree in the Percheron Stud-Book of America.]

Black ; foaled September 25, 1887 ; bred at Oaklawn ; got by GOLIATH 4302 (2944) ; dam Brillante 5634 (4057) by AVATA 1966 (912) ; 2d dam Lisette (4056) by VIDOCQ 483 (732) out of Rose.

GOLIATH 4302 (2944) by Clement 1965 (936) out of Pauline (5014) by Favora 1542 (765), he by French Monarch 205 (734) out of Marguerite by Favori, he by Coco of Mêsle-sur-Sarthe, he by Margot.
  FRENCH MONARCH 205 (734) by Ilderim (5302) out of a daughter of Vieux-Pierre (894), he by Coco (712).
  ILDERIM (5302) by Valentin (5301) out of Chaton by Vieux-Pierre (894), etc.
  VALENTIN (5301) by Vieux-Chaslin (713).
CLEMENT 1965 (936) by Philibert (760) out of Rustique by Coco II (714).
PHILIBERT (760) by Superior 454 (730) out of Madelon by Vieux-Vaillant (1383), he by Pierre out of a daughter of Vieux-Pierre (883).
SUPERIOR 454 (730) by Favori I (711) out of Pauline by Vieux-Chaslin (713).
FAVORI I (711) by Vieux-Chaslin (713) out of L'Amie by Vieux-Pierre (894), etc.
VIEUX-CHASLIN (713) by Coco (712) out of Poule by Sandi.
COCO (712) by Mignon (715) out of Pauline by Vieux-Coco.
MIGNON (715) by Jean-le-Blanc (739).
AVATA 1966 (912) by Nogent 738 (729) out of Bicotte by Bayard 26 (717), he by Favori I (711), etc., out of Mignonne by Chéri.
NOGENT 738 (729) by Vidocq 483 (732) out of a daughter of Favori I (711), etc.
VIDOCQ 483 (732) by Coco II (714) out of a daughter of Chéri, he by Rustique.
COCO II (714) by Vieux-Chaslin (713), etc., out of La Grise by Vieux-Pierre (883).

(Hoof No 125.) **CALETTE 5696.**

[Recorded with pedigree in the Percheron Stud-Book of America.]

Black ; foaled April 2, 1886 ; bred at Oaklawn ; got by BRILLIANT
1271 (755); dam Calecia 2776 (1496) by VIDOCQ ; 2d dam Julie by
FLEURUS.

BRILLIANT 1271 (755) by Brilliant 1899 (756), out of Ragout by Favori I (711), he
by Vieux-Chaslin (713) out of L'Amie by Vieux-Pierre (894), he by Coco
(712).
BRILLIANT 1899 (756) by Coco II (714) out of Rosette by Mina, belonging to the
French government.
Coco II (714) by Vieux-Chaslin (713) out of La Grise by Vieux-Pierre (883).
VIEUX-CHASLIN (713) by Coco (712) out of Poule by Sandi.
Coco (712) by Mignon (715) out of Pauline by Vieux-Coco.
MIGNON (715) by Jean-le-Blanc (739).

(Hoof No. 79.) **CAMILLE 5339 (6894).**

[Recorded with pedigree in the Percheron Stud-Books of France and America.]

Dark grey ; foaled May 10, 1884 ; imported 1886 ; bred by M.
Loiseau, commune of La Rouge, canton of Theil, department of Orne ;
got by VOLTAIRE 3540 (443); dam Poule (6893) by VAILLANT out of
Rosette.

VOLTAIRE 3540 (443) by Brilliant 1271 (755) out of Cocotte by Coco II (714).
BRILLIANT 1271 (755) by Brilliant 1899 (756) out of Ragout by Favori I (711), he
by Vieux-Chaslin 713 out of L'Amie by Vieux-Pierre (894), he by Coco
(712).
BRILLIANT 1899 (756) by Coco II (714) out of Rosette by Mina, belonging to
the French government.
Coco II (714) by Vieux-Chaslin (713) out of La Grise by Vieux-Pierre (883).
VIEUX-CHASLIN (713) by Coco (712) out of Poule by Sandi.
Coco (712) by Mignon (715) out of Pauline by Vieux-Coco.
MIGNON (715) by Jean-le-Blanc (739).

Bred to BRILLIANT 1271 (755), August 31, 1887.

(Hoof No. 240.) **CAMILLE 7134 (8561).**

[Recorded with pedigree in the Percheron Stud-Books of France and America.]

Grey ; foaled February 26, 1886 ; imported 1887 ; bred by M.
Bajeon, commune of Souvigné-sur-Même, canton of La Ferté-Bernard,
department of Sarthe ; got by LA FERTÉ 5144 (452); dam Brillante
(2014) by BRILLIANT 1271 (755) out of Saphir, belonging to M.
Foreau.

LA FERTÉ 5144 (452) by Philibert (760) out of Julie (7594) by Brilliant 1899
(756).
PHILIBERT (760) by Superior 454 (730) out of Madelon by Vieux-Vaillant (1383),
he by Pierre out of a daughter of Vieux-Pierre (883).
SUPERIOR 454 (730) by Favori I (711) out of Pauline by Vieux-Chaslin (713).
FAVORI I (711) by Vieux-Chaslin (713) out of L'Amie by Vieux-Pierre (894),
he by Coco (712).
VIEUX-CHASLIN (713) by Coco (712) out of Poule by Sandi.
Coco (712) by Mignon (715) out of Pauline by Vieux-Coco.
MIGNON (715) by Jean-le-Blanc (739).
BRILLIANT 1271 (755) by Brilliant 1899 (756) out of Ragout by Favori I (711),
etc.
BRILLIANT 1899 (756) by Coco II (714) out of Rosette by Mina, belonging to the
French government.
Coco II (714) by Vieux-Chaslin (713), etc., out of La Grise by Vieux-Pierre
(883).

(Hoof No. 177.)   **CARAVANE 4385.**
[Recorded with pedigree in the Percheron Stud-Books of France and America.]

Bay ; foaled May 7, 1885 ; bred at Oaklawn ; got by VIDOCQ 483 (732) ; dam Coletia 2730 (1537) by BRILLIANT 1271 (755) ; 2d dam by NARBONNE 1334 (777).

VIDOCQ 483 (732) by Coco II (714) out of a daughter of Cheri, he by Rustique.
Coco II (714) by Vieux-Chaslin (713) out of La Grise by Vieux-Pierre (883).
VIEUX-CHASLIN (713) by Coco (712), etc., out of Poule by Sandi.
Coco (712) by Mignon (715) out of Pauline by Vieux-Coco.
MIGNON (715) by Jean-le-Blanc (739).
BRILLIANT 1271 (755) by Brilliant 1899 (756) out of Ragout by Favori I (711), he by Vieux-Chaslin (713), etc., out of L'Amie by Vieux-Pierre (894), he by Coco (712).
BRILLIANT 1899 (756) by Coco II (714), etc., out of Rosette by Mina, belonging to the French government.
NARBONNE 1334 (777) by Brilliant 1899 (756), etc., out of Madelon (4722) by Favori I (711), etc.

Bred to LA FERTÉ 5144 (452), June 28, 1887.

(Hoof No. 65.)   **CAROLINE 5674 (7034).**
[Recorded with pedigree in the Percheron Stud-Books of France and America.]

Black ; foaled May 1, 1885 ; imported 1886 ; bred by M. Louvancoun, commune of St. Pierre Fixé, canton of Nogent-le-Rotrou, department of Eure-et-Loir ; got by VOLTAIRE 3540 (443) ; dam Collette (7033) by NARBONNE 1334 (777) out of Rustique.

VOLTAIRE 3540 (443) by Brilliant 1271 (755) out of Cocotte by Coco II (714).
BRILLIANT 1271 (755) by Brilliant 1899 (756) out of Ragout by Favori I (711), he by Vieux-Chaslin (713) out of L'Amie by Vieux-Pierre (894), he by Coco (712).
BRILLIANT 1899 (756) by Coco II (714) out of Rosette by Mina, belonging to the French government.
Coco II (714) by Vieux-Chaslin (713) out of La Grise by Vieux-Pierre (883).
VIEUX-CHASLIN (713) by Coco (712) out of Poule by Sandi.
Coco (712) by Mignon (715) out of Pauline by Vieux-Coco.
MIGNON (715) by Jean-le-Blanc (739).
NARBONNE 1334 (777) by Brilliant 1899 (756), etc., out of Madelon (4722) by Favori I (711), etc.

Bred to BRILLIANT 1271 (755), September 16, 1887.

(Hoof No. 214.)   **CHALOUPE 7131 (9507).**
[Recorded with pedigree in the Percheron Stud-Books of France and America.]

Steel grey ; foaled April, 1885 ; imported 1887 ; bred by M. Denis-Pelletier, commune of Preaux, canton of Nocé, department of Orne ; got by VAILLANT (404) ; dam Rustique (274) by PROSPER (893) out of Chaloupe.

VAILLANT (404) by Prosper (893) out of Rosalie by Bienvenu, belonging to the Société Hippique of Eure-et-Loir.
PROSPER (893) by Décidé (892) out of Bourreau by Vieux-Pierre (883).
DÉCIDÉ (892) by Vieux-Pierre (894) out of Pelote, belonging to M. Berjeau, of Courvalien.
VIEUX-PIERRE (894) by Coco (712), he by Mignon (715) out of Pauline by Vieux-Coco.
MIGNON (715) by Jean-le-Blanc (739).

Bred in France to MALAKOFF (8275).

(Hoof No. 206.) **CHANSONNETTE 5630 (6394).**

[Recorded with pedigree in the Percheron Stud-Books of France and America.]

Black; foaled March 20, 1884; imported 1886; bred by M. Durant, commune of Souancé, canton of Nogent-le-Rotrou, department of Eure-et-Loir; got by MARVEL 1922 (1061); dam Pelotte (1883) by VAILLANT (4271) out of Moutonne.

MARVEL 1922 (1061) by Brilliant 1899 (756) out of a daughter of French Monarch 205 (734), he by Ilderim (5302) out of a daughter of Vieux-Pierre (894), he by Coco (712).
  ILDERIM (5302) by Valentin (5301) out of Chaton by Vieux-Pierre (894), etc.
  VALENTIN (5301) by Vieux-Chaslin (713).
BRILLIANT 1899 (756) by Coco II (714) out of Rosette by Mina, belonging to the French government.
Coco II (714) by Vieux-Chaslin (713) out of La Grise by Vieux-Pierre (883).
VIEUX-CHASLIN (713) by Coco (712) out of Poule by Sandi.
Coco (712) by Mignon (715) out of Pauline by Vieux-Coco.
MIGNON (715) by Jean-le-Blanc (739).
VAILLANT (4271) by Favori I (711), he by Vieux-Chaslin (713), etc., out of L'Amie by Vieux-Pierre (894), etc.

Bred to BRILLIANT 1271 (755), June 1, 1887.

(Hoof No. 157.) **CHARMANTE 2734 (1540).**

Dapple grey; foaled 1879; imported 1883; got by LUTHER (792); dam by JEAN-BART (716).

LUTHER (792) by Pierre (887) out of Rosette by Laboureur (886).
PIERRE (887) by Laboureur (886) out of Margot by Faisan.
LABOUREUR (886) by Jean-le-Blanc (739) out of Sophie by Sandi.
JEAN-BART (716) by Bayard, belonging to M. Perpère, out of Jeanne by Porthos.

Bred to BRILLIANT 1271 (755), May 4, 1887.

(Hoof No. 299.) **CINNA 7133 (10124).**

[Recorded with pedigree in the Percheron Stud-Books of France and America.]

Black; foaled April 18, 1885; imported 1887; bred by M. Albert Quatravaux, commune of Villiers-en-Ouche, canton of La Ferté-Fresnel, department of Orne; got by COLOSSE (10097); dam Rosette (10106) by FAVORI, belonging to M. Panthou.

COLOSSE (10097) by Brilliant 1271 (755), he by Brilliant 1899 (756) out of Ragout by Favori I, (711), he by Vieux-Chaslin (713) out of L'Amie by Vieux-Pierre (894), he by Coco (712).
BRILLIANT 1899 (756) by Coco II (714) out of Rosette by Mina, belonging to the French government.
Coco II (714) by Vieux-Chaslin (713) out of La Grise by Vieux-Pierre (883).
VIEUX-CHASLIN (713) by Coco (712) out of Poule by Sandi.
Coco (712) by Mignon (715) out of Pauline by Vieux-Coco.
MIGNON (715) by Jean-le-Blanc (739).

Bred in France to SULTAN (1400).

(Hoof No. 217.)   **CLOTHILDE 7132 (10655).**

[Recorded with pedigree in the Percheron Stud-Books of France and America.]

Grey ; foaled March 24, 1886 ; imported 1887 ; bred by M. Louis Surcin, commune of Coudray, canton of Authon, department of Eure-et-Loir ; got by CHAMPEAUX 6218 (2248) ; dam Chaton (1728) by PERCHERON, belonging to the French government, out of Pelote by ROLAND, belonging to the French government.

CHAMPEAUX 6218 (2248) by Iago 995 (768) out of Madeleine, belonging to M. Guillemin.
IAGO 995 (768) by Utopia 780 (731) out of Cossette by Favora 666 (725), he by Favori I (711) out of Marie by Coco (712).
UTOPIA 780 (731) by Superior 454 (730) out of Camille by Favori I (711).
SUPERIOR 454 (730) by FAVORI I (711) out of Pauline by Vieux-Chaslin (713).
FAVORI I (711) by Vieux-Chaslin (713) out of L'Amie by Vieux-Pierre (894), he by Coco (712).
VIEUX-CHASLIN (713) by Coco (712) out of Poule by Sandi.
Coco (712) by Mignon (715) out of Pauline by Vieux-Coco.
MIGNON (715) by Jean-le-Blanc (739).

(Hoof No. 282.)   **COCODETTE 4362 (4658).**

[Recorded with pedigree in the Percheron Stud-Books of France and America.]

Black ; foaled May 20, 1883 ; imported 1885 ; bred by M. Groux, commune of St. Hilaire-sur-Erre, canton of Theil, department of Orne ; got by VAILLANT (404) ; dam L'Amie (4187) by DOCILE (4446).

VAILLANT (404) by Prosper (893) out of Rosalie by Bienvenu, belonging to the Société Hippique of Eure-et-Loir.
PROSPER (893) by Décidé (892) out of Bourreau by Vieux-Pierre (883).
DÉCIDÉ (892) by Vieux-Pierre (894) out of Pelote, belonging to M. Berjeau, of Courvalien.
VIEUX-PIERRE (894) by Coco (712), he by Mignon (715) out of Pauline by Vieux-Coco.
MIGNON (715) by Jean-le-Blanc (739).
DOCILE (4446) by Faisan (son of Chéri) out of Rose.

Bred to SANDY 5162 (2225), August 30, 1887.

(Hoof No. 235.)   **COCOTTE 6925 (10560).**

[Recorded with pedigree in the Percheron Stud-Books of France and America.]

Dapple grey ; foaled March 20, 1882 ; imported 1887 ; bred by M. Mauclerc, commune of La Chapelle Huon, canton of St. Calais, department of Sarthe ; got by PAUL (7433) ; dam Rosie (10559) by PIERRE, belonging to M. Mauclerc.

PAUL (7433) by Paul, belonging to M. Dubois, out of Biche by Pierre, belonging to M. Mauclerc.

Bred to La FERTÉ 5144 (452), August 19, 1887.

(Hoof No. 141.) **COLETIA 2730 (1537).**

[Recorded with pedigree in the Percheron Stud-Books of France and America.]

Bay; foaled 1882; imported 1883; got by BRILLIANT 1899 (756); dam by NARBONNE 1334 (777).

BRILLIANT 1899 (756) by Coco II (714) out of Rosette by Mina, belonging to the French government.
Coco II (714) by Vieux-Chaslin (713) out of La Grise by Vieux-Pierre (883).
VIEUX-CHASLIN (713) by Coco (712) out of Poule by Sandi.
Coco (712) by Mignon (715) out of Pauline by Vieux-Coco.
MIGNON (715) by Jean-le-Blanc (739).
NARBONNE 1334 (777) by Brilliant 1899 (756), etc., out of Madelon (4722) by Favori I (711), he by Vieux-Chaslin (713), etc., out of L'Amie by Vieux-Pierre (894), he by Coco (712), etc.

Bred to La FERTÉ 5144 (452), April 17, 1887.

COLINE 7339.

[Recorded with pedigree in the Percheron Stud-Book of America.]

Black; foaled May 30, 1887; bred at Oaklawn; got by BRILLIANT 1271 (755); dam Constance 1478 (1425) by GRENADIER 688 (726) out of a daughter of TACHEAU 456 (745).

BRILLIANT 1271 (755) by Brilliant 1899 (756) out of Ragout by Favori I (711).
BRILLIANT 1899 (756) by Coco II (714) out of Rosette by Mina, belonging to the French government.
Coco II (714) by Vieux-Chaslin (713) out of La Grise by Vieux-Pierre (883).
VIEUX-CHASLIN (713) by Coco (712) out of Poule by Sandi.
Coco (712) by Mignon (715) out of Pauline by Vieux-Coco.
MIGNON (715) by Jean-le-Blanc (739).
GRENADIER 688 (726) by Comet 104 (719), he by French Monarch 205 (734) out of Suzanne by Cambronne.
FRENCH MONARCH 205 (734) by Ilderim (5302) out of a daughter of Vieux-Pierre (894), he by Coco (712), etc.
ILDERIM (5302) by Valentin (5301) out of Chaton by Vieux-Pierre (894), etc.
VALENTIN (5301) by Vieux-Chaslin (713), etc.
TACHEAU 456 (745) by Favori I (711), he by Vieux-Chaslin (713), etc., out of L'Amie by Vieux-Pierre (894), etc.

(Hoof No. 172.) **CONSTANCE 1478 (1425).**

[Recorded with pedigree in the Percheron Stud-Books of France and America.]

Bay; foaled 1878; imported 1881; got by GRENADIER 688 (726); dam by TACHEAU 456 (745).

GRENADIER 688 (726) by Comet 104 (719), he by French Monarch 205 (734) out of Suzanne by Cambronne.
FRENCH MONARCH 205 (734) by Ilderim (5302) out of a daughter of Vieux-Pierre (894), he by Coco (712).
ILDERIM (5302) by Valentin (5301) out of Chaton by Vieux-Pierre (894), etc.
VALENTIN (5301) by Vieux-Chaslin (713), he by Coco (712) out of Poule by Sandi.
Coco (712) by Mignon (715) out of Pauline by Vieux-Coco.
MIGNON (715) by Jean-le-Blanc (739).
TACHEAU 456 (745) by Favori I (711), he by Vieux-Chaslin (713), etc., out of L'Amie by Vieux-Pierre (894), etc.

Bred to BRILLIANT 1271 (755), June 8, 1887.

(Hoof No. 68.)   **COQUETTA 5677 (7366).**

[Recorded with pedigree in the Percheron Stud-Books of France and America.]

Dapple grey ; foaled March 15, 1882 ; imported 1886 ; bred by M. Grassin, commune of Lucé-sous-Ballon, canton of Marolles-les-Braux, department of Sarthe ; got by PICADOR II (5606); dam Rose (7365) by FAVORI I, belonging to M. Lefeuvre, out of Charmante.

PICADOR II (5606) by Picador I (7330) out of Rose.
PICADOR I (7330) by Bayard I (son of Picador) out of Charmante.

Bred to BRILLIANT 1271 (755), June 24, 1887.

(Hoof No. 139.)   **COQUETTE 2774 (1538).**

[Recorded with pedigree in the Percheron Stud-Books of France and America.]

Dapple grey ; foaled 1882 ; imported 1883 ; got by NARBONNE 1334 (777); dam by SANSONNET.

NARBONNE 1334s(777) by Brilliant 1899 (756) out of Madelon (4722) by Favori I (711), he by Vieux-Chaslin (713) out of L'Amie by Vieux-Pierre (894), he by Coco (712).
BRILLIANT 1899 (756) by Coco II (714) out of Rosette by Mina, belonging to the French government.
Coco II (714) by Vieux-Chaslin (713) out of La Grise by Vieux-Pierre (883).
VIEUX-CHASLIN (713) by Coco (712) out of Poule by Sandi.
Coco (712) by Mignon (715) out of Pauline by Vieux-Coco.
MIGNON (715) by Jean-le-Blanc (739).

Bred to BRILLIANT 1271 (755), August 15, 1887.

(Hoof No. 160.)   **COQUETTE 4366 (5310).**

[Recorded with pedigree in the Percheron Stud-Books of France and America.]

Brown bay ; foaled April 7, 1883 ; imported 1885 ; bred by M. Boucher, commune of St. Cyr-la-Rosière, canton of Nocé, department of Orne ; got by MADÈRE (5308) ; dam Rosette (5309) by VIEUX-VAILLANT (1383).

MADÈRE (5308) by Mouton (1640) out of Cocote.
MOUTON (1640) by French Monarch 205 (734) out of Rose by Décidé.
FRENCH MONARCH 205 (734) by Ilderim (5302) out of a daughter of Vieux-Pierre (894), he by Coco (712).
ILDERIM (5302) by Valentin (5301) out of Chaton by Vieux-Pierre (894), etc.
VALENTIN (5301) by Vieux-Chaslin (713), he by Coco (712) out of Poule by Sandi.
Coco (712) by Mignon (715) out of Pauline by Vieux-Coco.
MIGNON (715) by Jean-le-Blanc (739).
VIEUX-VAILLANT (1383) by Pierre, belonging to M. Thérin, out of a daughter of Vieux-Pierre (883).

Bred to BRILLIANT 1271 (755), September 6, 1887.

(Hoof No. 258.) **COQUILLE 7331.**

[Recorded with pedigree in the Percheron Stud-Book of America.]

Bay ; foaled June 17, 1887 ; bred at Oaklawn ; got by BRILLIANT 1271 (755); dam Coquette 2774 (1538) by NARBONNE 1334 (777) out of a daughter of SANSONNET.

BRILLIANT 1271 (755) by Brilliant 1899 (756) out of Ragout by Favori I (711), he by Vieux-Chaslin (713) out of L'Amie by Vieux-Pierre (894), he by Coco (712).
BRILLIANT 1899 (756) by Coco II (714) out of Rosette by Mina, belonging to the French government.
Coco II (714) by Vieux-Chaslin (713) out of La Grise by Vieux-Pierre (883).
VIEUX-CHASLIN (713) by Coco (712) out of Poule by Sandi.
Coco (712) by Mignon (715) out of Pauline by Vieux-Coco.
MIGNON (715) by Jean-le-Blanc (739).
NARBONNE 1334 (777) by Brilliant 1899 (756), etc., out of Madelon (4722) by Favori I (711), etc.

(Hoof No. 283.) **CORBEILLE 5645 (6674).**

[Recorded with pedigree in the Percheron Stud-Books of France and America.]

Black ; foaled April 22, 1884 ; imported 1886 ; bred by M. Auguste Julliard, commune of Cormes, canton of La Ferté-Bernard, department of Sarthe ; got by SANDI 3803 (444); dam Madelon (6367) by SANDY I out of Sophie, belonging to M. Julliard.

SANDI 3803 (444) by Brilliant 1271 (755) out of Calot by Coco II (714).
BRILLIANT 1271 (755) by Brilliant 1899 (756) out of Ragout by Favori I (711), he by Vieux-Chaslin (713) out of L'Amie by Vieux-Pierre (894), he by Coco (712).
BRILLIANT 1899 (756) by Coco II (714) out of Rosette by Mina, belonging to the French government.
Coco II (714) by Vieux-Chaslin (713) out of La Grise by Vieux-Pierre (883).
VIEUX-CHASLIN (713) by Coco (712) out of Poule by Sandi.
Coco (712) by Mignon (715) out of Pauline by Vieux-Coco.
MIGNON (715) by Jean-le-Blanc (739).

Bred to SANDY 5162 (2225), August 3, 1887.

(Hoof No. 103.) **DAISY 1893.**

[Recorded with pedigree in the Percheron Stud-Books of France and America.]

Black ; foaled 1882 ; bred by James M. Dunn, of Waseca, Minnesota ; got by MARMADUKE 297 ; dam Minerva 585.

Bred to BRILLIANT 1271 (755), May 24, 1887.

(Hoof No. 203.) **DAMEMARIE 7135 (11296).**

[Recorded with pedigree in the Percheron Stud-Books of France and America.]

Steel grey ; foaled April 20, 1885 ; imported 1887 ; bred by M. Manguin, commune of Dame-Marie canton of Bellême, department of Orne ; got by MADÈRE 6226 (692); dam Poule (11295) by PICADOR, belonging to M. Jamois.

MADÈRE 6226 (692) by Vidocq (1403) out of Marie.
VIDOCQ (1403) by Utopia 780 (731) out of Bijou by Vieux-Chaslin (713).
UTOPIA 780 (731) by Superior 454 (730) out of Camille by Favori I (711).
SUPERIOR 454 (730) by Favori I (711) out of Pauline by Vieux-Chaslin (713).
FAVORI I (711) by Vieux-Chaslin (713) out of L'Amie by Vieux-Pierre (894), he by Coco (712).
VIEUX-CHASLIN (713) by Coco (712) out of Poule by Sandi.
Coco (712) by Mignon (715) out of Pauline by Vieux-Coco.
MIGNON (715) by Jean-le-Blanc (739).

Bred to STRADAT 7112 (2463), June 28, 1887.

(Hoof No. 264.) **DELIGHT 7330.**

[Recorded with pedigree in the Percheron Stud-Book of America.]

Black; foaled April 3, 1887; bred at Oaklawn; got by BRILL-
IANT 1271 (755); dam Delora 2756 (1530) by CHALLENGE 987 (758) out
of a daughter of SÉLIM (749).

BRILLIANT 1271 (755) by Brilliant 1899 (756) out of Ragout by Favori I (711).
BRILLIANT 1899 (756) by Coco II (714) out of Rosette by Mina, belonging to the
    French government.
Coco II (714) by Vieux-Chaslin (713) out of La Grise by Vieux-Pierre (883).
VIEUX-CHASLIN (713) by Coco (712) out of Poule by Sandi.
Coco (712) by Mignon (715) out of Pauline by Vieux-Coco.
MIGNON (715) by Jean-le-Blanc (739).
CHALLENGE 987 (758) by Décidé 126 (720), he by Superior 454 (730), he by Favori
    I (711) out of Pauline by Vieux-Chaslin (713), etc.
FAVORI I (711) by Vieux-Chaslin (713), etc., out of L'Amie by Vieux-Pierre
    (894), he by Coco (712), etc.
SÉLIM (749) by Porthos, belonging to M. Fromentin.

(Hoof No. 138.) **DELORA 2756 (1530).**

[Recorded with pedigree in the Percheron Stud-Books of France and America.]

Black; foaled 1881; imported 1883; got by CHALLENGE 987
(758); dam by SÉLIM (749).

CHALLENGE 987 (758) by Décidé 126 (720), he by Superior 454 (730), he by
    Favori I (711) out of Pauline by Vieux-Chaslin (713).
FAVORI I (711) by Vieux-Chaslin (713) out of L'Amie by Vieux-Pierre (894), he
    by Coco (712).
VIEUX-CHASLIN (713) by Coco (712) out of Poule by Sandi.
Coco (712) by Mignon (715) out of Pauline by Vieux-Coco.
MIGNON (715) by Jean-le-Blanc (739).
SÉLIM (749) by Porthos, belonging to M. Fromentin.

Bred to BRILLIANT 1271 (755), June 15, 1887.

(Hoof No. 150.) **DELPHINETTE 4375 (4982).**

[Recorded with pedigree in the Percheron Stud-Books of France and America.]

Black; foaled March 15, 1883; imported 1885; bred by M. Alex.
Morin, commune of La Rouge, canton of Theil, department of Orne;
got by MARVEL 1922 (1061); dam Margot (4617) by BAYARD, belonging to M. Ernest Perriot.

MARVEL 1922 (1061) by Brilliant 1899 (756) out of a daughter of French
    Monarch 205 (734), he by Ilderim (5302) out of a daughter of Vieux-Pierre
    (894), he by Coco (712).
  ILDERIM (5302) by Valentin (5301) out of Chaton by Vieux-Pierre (894), etc.
  VALENTIN (5301) by Vieux-Chaslin (713).
BRILLIANT 1899 (756) by Coco II (714) out of Rosette by Mina, belonging to the
    French government.
Coco II (714) by Vieux-Chaslin (713) out of La Grise by Vieux-Pierre (883).
VIEUX-CHASLIN (713) by Coco (712) out of Poule by Sandi.
Coco (712) by Mignon (715) out of Pauline by Vieux-Coco.
MIGNON (715) by Jean-le-Blanc (739).

Bred to LA FERTÉ 5144 (452), April 13, 1887.

(Hoof No. 110.) **DIANA 2765 (1378).**

[Recorded with pedigree in the Percheron Stud-Books of France and America.]

Black ; foaled 1882 ; imported 1883 ; got by FAVORI (1401); dam Lise by FAVORA 1542 (765).

FAVORI (1401) by Favora 1542 (765) out of Jeannette by Décidé.
FAVORA 1542 (765) by French Monarch 205 (734) out of Marguerite by Favori, he by Coco of Mêsle-sur-Sarthe.
FRENCH MONARCH 205 (734) by Ilderim (5302) out of a daughter of Vieux-Pierre (894), he by Coco (712).
ILDERIM (5302) by Valentin (5301) out of Chaton by Vieux-Pierre (894), etc.
VALENTIN (5301) by Vieux-Chaslin (713), he by Coco (712) out of Poule by Sandi.
Coco (712) by Mignon (715) out of Pauline by Vieux-Coco.
MIGNON (715) by Jean-le-Blanc (739).

Bred to BRILLIANT 1271 (755), July 19, 1887.

(Hoof No. 82.) **ÉGALITÉ 5685 (7233).**

[Recorded with pedigree in the Percheron Stud-Books of France and America.]

Black ; foaled April 25, 1884 ; imported 1886 ; bred by M. Rottier, commune of Igé, department of Orne ; got by WATERLOO (4874) ; dam Julie (5030) by PHILIBERT (4634) out of Rose.

WATERLOO (4874) by Passe-Partout (1402) out of Margot (4873) by Coco II (714), he by Vieux-Chaslin (713) out of La Grise by Vieux-Pierre (883).
PASSE-PARTOUT (1402) by Comet 104 (719) out of Sophie by Favori I (711).
COMET 104 (719) by French Monarch 205 (734) out of Suzanne by Cambronne.
FRENCH MONARCH 205 (734) by Ilderim (5302) out of a daughter of Vieux-Pierre (894), he by Coco (712).
ILDERIM (5302) by Valentin (5301) out of Chaton by Vieux-Pierre (894), etc.
VALENTIN (5301) by Vieux-Chaslin (713), he by Coco (712) out of Poule by Sandi.
Coco (712) by Mignon (715) out of Pauline by Vieux-Coco.
MIGNON (715) by Jean-le-Blanc (739).
PHILIBERT (4634) by Philibert [son of Superior 454 (730)] out of Rustique, belonging to M. Lemesle.
SUPERIOR 454 (730) by Favori I (711) out of Pauline by Vieux-Chaslin (713), etc.
FAVORI I (711) by Vieux-Chaslin (713), etc., out of L'Amie by Vieux-Pierre (894), etc.

Bred to BRILLIANT 1271 (755), April 13, 1887

(Hoof No. 31.) **ÉGERIÉ 5642 (6748).**

[Recorded with pedigree in the Percheron Stud-Books of France and America.]

Grey ; foaled February 10, 1883 ; imported 1886 ; bred by M. Moreau, commune of Ceton, canton of Theil, department of Orne ; got by PHILIBERT II 2684 (1310) ; dam Chatton (4195) by Favori I (711) out of Chatton by Coco II (714).

PHILIBERT II 2684 (1310) by Philibert (760) out of Fannie by Favori I (711).
PHILIBERT (760) by Superior 454 (730) out of Madelon by Vieux-Valliant (1383), he by Pierre out of a daughter of Vieux-Pierre (883).
SUPERIOR 454 (730) by Favori I (711) out of Pauline by Vieux-Chaslin (713).
FAVORI I (711) by Vieux-Chaslin (713) out of L'Amie by Vieux-Pierre (894), he by Coco (712).
VIEUX-CHASLIN (713) by Coco (712) out of Poule by Sandi.
Coco (712) by Mignon (715) out of Pauline by Vieux-Coco.
MIGNON (715) by Jean-le-Blanc (739).
Coco II (714) by Vieux-Chaslin (713), etc., out of La Grise by Vieux-Pierre (883).

Bred to BRILLIANT 1271 (755), May 11, 1887.

(Hoof No. 62.) **EGLANTINE 5338 (7028).**

[Recorded with pedigree in the Percheron Stud-Books of France and America.]

Black; foaled May 2, 1881; imported 1886; bred by M. Deshayes, commune of Préval, canton of La Ferté-Bernard, department of Sarthe; got by Brilliant 1271 (755); dam Jubine II (7027) by Coco II (714) out of Jubine I.

Brilliant 1271 (755) by Brilliant 1899 (756) out of Ragout by Favori I (711), he by Vieux-Chaslin (713) out of L'Amie by Vieux-Pierre (894), he by Coco (712).
Brilliant 1899 (756) by Coco II (714) out of Rosette by Mina, belonging to the French government.
Coco II (714) by Vieux-Chaslin (713) out of La Grise by Vieux-Pierre (883).
Vieux-Chaslin (713) by Coco (712) out of Poule by Sandi.
Coco (712) by Mignon (715) out of Pauline by Vieux-Coco.
Mignon (715) by Jean-le-Blanc (739).

Bred to La Ferté 5144 (452), June 8, 1887.

(Hoof No. 55.) **ELDORADO 5665 (7178).**

[Recorded with pedigree in the Percheron Stud-Books of France and America.]

Black; foaled March 5, 1881; imported 1886; bred by M. Louis Veau, commune of St. Germain-de-la-Coudre, canton of Theil, department of Orne; got by Brilliant 1271 (755); dam L'Amie (7177) by Brilliant 1899 (756) out of Bijou.

Brilliant 1271 (755) by Brilliant 1899 (756) out of Ragout by Favori I (711), he by Vieux-Chaslin (713) out of L'Amie by Vieux-Pierre (894), he by Coco (712).
Brilliant 1899 (756) by Coco II (714) out of Rosette by Mina, belonging to the French government.
Coco II (714) by Vieux-Chaslin (713) out of La Grise by Vieux-Pierre (883).
Vieux-Chaslin (713) by Coco (712) out of Poule by Sandi.
Coco (712) by Mignon (715) out of Pauline by Vieux-Coco.
Mignon (715) by Jean-le-Blanc (739).

Bred to La Ferté 5144 (452), April 18, 1887.

(Hoof No. 293.) **ÉLISE 5618 (7094).**

[Recorded with pedigree in the Percheron Stud-Books of France and America.]

Grey; foaled April 8, 1884; imported 1886; bred by M. Ligot, commune of Cherreau, canton of La Ferté-Bernard, department of Sarthe; got by Lagrange 3065 (1334); dam Frosine (7093) by French Monarch 205 (734) out of Poule.

Lagrange 3065 (1334) by Brilliant 1271 (755) out of Lydie by Coco II (714).
Brilliant 1271 (755) by Brilliant 1899 (756) out of Ragout by Favori I (711), he by Vieux-Chaslin (713) out of L'Amie by Vieux-Pierre (894), he by Coco (712).
Brilliant 1899 (756) by Coco II (714) out of Rosette by Mina, belonging to the French government.
Coco II (714) by Vieux-Chaslin (713) out of La Grise by Vieux-Pierre (883).
Vieux-Chaslin (713) by Coco (712) out of Poule by Sandi.
Coco (712) by Mignon (715) out of Pauline by Vieux-Coco.
Mignon (715) by Jean-le-Blanc (739).
French Monarch 205 (734) by Ilderim (5302) out of a daughter of Vieux-Pierre (894), etc.
Ilderim (5302) by Valentin (5301) out of Chaton by Vieux-Pierre (894), etc.
Valentin (5301) by Vieux-Chaslin (713), etc.

Bred to Sultan 4291 (4052), September 29, 1887.

(Hoof No. 83.) **ÉLISE 5686 (7387).**

[Recorded with pedigree in the Percheron Stud-Books of France and America.]

Grey; foaled April 24, 1884; imported 1886; bred by M. Oury, commune of Mamers, department of Sarthe; got by PICADOR (7173); dam Lucrèce (7386) by TAUPIN, belonging to M. Philibin, out of Bleue.

PICADOR (7173) by Papillon, belonging to M. Brunet, out of Biche.

Bred to BRILLIANT 1271 (755), August 20, 1887.

(Hoof No. 284.) **ENTERPRISE 5648 (6485).**

[Recorded with pedigree in the Percheron Stud-Books of France and America.]

Grey; foaled May 25, 1883; imported 1886; bred by M. Rigot, commune of St. Bomert, canton of Authon, department of Eure-et-Loir; got by CHARTRAIN (1405); dam Poule (2032) by BRILLIANT 1899 (756) out of Chaton, belonging to M. Crenier.

CHARTRAIN (1405) by Philibert (760) out of Cocotte by Coco II (714).
PHILIBERT (760) by Superior 454 (730) out of Madelon by Vieux-Vaillant (1383), he by Pierre out of a daughter of Vieux-Pierre (883).
SUPERIOR 454 (730) by Favori I (711) out of Pauline by Vieux-Chaslin (713).
FAVORI I (711) by Vieux-Chaslin (713) out of L'Amie, by Vieux-Pierre (894), he by Coco (712).
VIEUX-CHASLIN (713) by Coco (712) out of Poule by Sandi.
COCO (712) by Mignon (715) out of Pauline by Vieux-Coco.
MIGNON (715) by Jean-le-Blanc (739).
BRILLIANT 1899 (756) by Coco II (714) out of Rosette by Mina, belonging to the French government.
Coco II (714) by Vieux-Chaslin (713), etc., out of La Grise by Vieux-Pierre (883).

Bred to SANDY 5162 (2225), August 12, 1887.

(Hoof No. 192.) **ERCILLA 2211 (1429).**

[Recorded with pedigree in the Percheron Stud-Books of France and America.]

Light grey; foaled 1879; imported 1882; got by WATERLOO 2199 (733); dam by LUTHER (792).

WATERLOO 2199 (733) by Jean-Bart (716) out of Poule, belonging to M. Bourdin.
JEAN-BART (716) by Bayard, belonging to M. Perpère, out of Jeanne by Porthos.
LUTHER (792) by Pierre (887) out of Rosette by Laboureur (886).
PIERRE (887) by Laboureur (886) out of Margot by Faisan.
LABOUREUR (886) by Jean-le-Blanc (739) out of Sophie by Sandi.

Bred to BRILLIANT 1271 (755), April 16, 1887.

(Hoof No. 224.)   **ÉTOILE DU PERCHE 6926 (8887).**

[Recorded with pedigree in the Percheron Stud-Books of France and America.]

Grey; foaled May 25, 1884; imported 1887; bred by M. Riguet, commune of St. Hilaire-sur-Erre, canton of Theil, department of Orne; got by VOLTAIRE 3540 (443); dam Cocotte (8886) by PAPILLON, belonging to M. Thérin.

VOLTAIRE 3540 (443) by Brilliant 1271 (755) out of Cocotte by Coco II (714).
BRILLIANT 1271 (755) by Brilliant 1899 (756) out of Ragout by Favori I (711), he
    by Vieux-Chaslin (713) out of L'Amie by Vieux-Pierre (894), he by Coco
    (712).
BRILLIANT 1899 (756) by Coco II (714) out of Rosette by Mina, belonging to the
    French government.
Coco II (714) by Vieux-Chaslin (713) out of La Grise by Vieux-Pierre (883).
VIEUX-CHASLIN (713) by Coco (712) out of Poule by Sandi.
Coco (712) by Mignon (715) out of Pauline by Vieux-Coco.
MIGNON (715) by Jean-le-Blanc (739).

Bred to LA FERTÉ 5144 (452), October 13, 1887.

(Hoof No. 208.)   **EULALIE 3670.**

[Recorded with pedigree in the Percheron Stud-Books of France and America.]

Grey; foaled 1884; bred at Oaklawn; got by BRILLIANT 1271 (755); dam Ercilla 2211 (1429) by WATERLOO 2199 (733) out of a daughter of LUTHER (792).

BRILLIANT 1271 (755) by Brilliant 1899 (756) out of Ragout by Favori I (711), he
    by Vieux-Chaslin (713) out of L'Amie by Vieux-Pierre (894), he by Coco
    (712).
BRILLIANT 1899 (756) by Coco II (714) out of Rosette by Mina, belonging to the
    French government.
Coco II (714) by Vieux-Chaslin (713) out of La Grise by Vieux-Pierre (883).
VIEUX-CHASLIN (713) by Coco (712) out of Poule by Sandi.
Coco (712) by Mignon.(715) out of Pauline by Vieux-Coco.
MIGNON (715) by Jean-le-Blanc (739).
WATERLOO 2199 (733) by Jean-Bart (716) ont of Poule, belonging to M. Bourdin.
JEAN-BART (716) by Bayard, belonging to M. Perpère, out of Jeanne by Porthos.
LUTHER (792) by Pierre (887) out of Rosette by Laboureur (886).
PIERRE (887) by Laboureur (886) out of Margot by Faisan.
LABOUREUR (886) by Jean-le-Blanc (739) out of Sophie by Sandi.

Bred to LA FERTÉ 5144 (452), August 24, 1887.

(Hoof No. 148.)   **EUNICE 2206.**

Dapple grey; foaled November, 1882; bred at Oaklawn; got by BRILLIANT 1271 (755); dam Eloise 2216 (1427) by VIDOCQ 483 (732).

BRILLIANT 1271 (755) by Brilliant 1899 (756) out of Ragout by Favori I (711),
    he by Vieux-Chaslin (713) out of L'Amie by Vieux-Pierre (894), he by
    Coco (712).
BRILLIANT 1899 (756) by Coco II (714) out of Rosette by Mina, belonging to the
    French government.
Coco II (714) by Vieux-Chaslin (713) out of La Grise by Vieux-Pierre (883).
VIEUX-CHASLIN (713) by Coco (712) out of Poule by Sandi.
Coco (712) by Mignon (715) out of Pauline by Vieux-Coco.
MIGNON (715) by Jean-le-Blanc (739).
VIDOCQ 483 (732) by Coco II (714), etc., out of a daughter of Chéri, he by Rus-
    tique.

Bred to LA FERTÉ 5144 (452), etc., July 27, 1887.

(Hoof No. 218.) **FATMA 7136 (9512).**

[Recorded with pedigree in the Percheron Stud-Books of France and America.]

Black ; foaled February 14, 1886 ; imported 1887 ; bred by M. Eugène Moreau, commune of Souancé, canton of Nogent-le-Rotrou, department of Eure-et-Loir ; got by BISMARK 5529 (633); dam Rosette (9511) by BRILLANT (710).

BISMARK 5529 (633) by Sultan (1395) out of Pelote (7321) by Vigoureux (1392).
SULTAN (1395) by Vigoureux (1392) out of Margot by Franconi, belonging to M. Sagot.
VIGOUREUX (1392) by Coco II (714) out of Marguerite by Franconi.
Coco II (714) by Vieux-Chaslin (713) out of La Grise by Vieux-Pierre (883).
VIEUX-CHASLIN (713) by Coco (712) out of Poule by Sandi.
Coco (712) by Mignon (715) out of Pauline by Vieux-Coco.
MIGNON (715) by Jean-le-Blanc (739).
BRILLANT (710) by Brilliant 1899 (756) out of Sophie by Superior 454 (730), he by Favori I (711) out of Pauline by Vieux-Chaslin (713), etc.
FAVORI I (711) by Vieux-Chaslin (713), etc., out of L'Amie by Vieux-Pierre (894), he by Coco (712), etc.
BRILLIANT 1899 (756) by Coco II (714) out of Rosette by Mina, belonging to the French government.

(Hoof No. 122.) **FAUSTINE 1314 (1431).**

[Recorded with pedigree in the Percheron Stud-Books of France and America.]

Light grey ; foaled 1876 ; imported 1880 ; got by SÉLIM (749); dam Sophia by DUKE-DE-CHARTRES 162 (721).

SÉLIM (749) by Porthos, belonging to M. Fromentin.
DUKE-DE-CHARTRES 162 (721) by Coco II (714), he by Vieux-Chaslin (713) out of La Grise by Vieux-Pierre (883).
VIEUX-CHASLIN (713) by Coco (712) out of Poule by Sandi.
Coco (712) by Mignon (715) out of Pauline by Vieux-Coco.
MIGNON (715) by Jean-le-Blanc (739).

Bred to BRILLIANT 1271 (755), June 6, 1887.

(Hoof No. 174.) **FAUVETTE 4388.**

[Recorded with pedigree in the Percheron Stud-Book of America.]

Black ; foaled June 15, 1885 ; bred at Oaklawn ; got by BRILLIANT 1271 (755); dam Fadette 2780 (1558) by FAVORI, he by BRILLIANT 1899 (756); 2d dam Julie by COMET 104 (719).

BRILLIANT 1271 (755) by Brilliant 1899 (756) out of Ragout by Favori I (711, he by Vieux-Chaslin (713) out of L'Amie by Vieux-Pierre (894), he by Coco (712).
BRILLIANT 1899 (756) by Coco II (714) out of Rosette by Mina, belonging to the French government.
Coco II (714) by Vieux-Chaslin (713) out of La Grise by Vieux-Pierre (883).
VIEUX-CHASLIN (713) by Coco (712) out of Poule by Sandi.
Coco (712) by Mignon (715) out of Pauline by Vieux-Coco.
MIGNON (715) by Jean-le-Blanc (739).
COMET 104 (719) by French Monarch 205 (734) out of Suzanne by Cambronne.
FRENCH MONARCH 205 (734) by Ilderim (5302) out of a daughter of Vieux-Pierre (894), etc.
ILDERIM (5302) by Valentin (5301) out of Chaton by Vieux-Pierre (894), etc.
VALENTIN (5301) by Vieux-Chaslin (713), etc.

Bred to LA FERTÉ 5144 (452), September 3, 1887.

(Hoof No. 102.)   **FAVORITA 4360 (4410).**
[Recorded with pedigree in the Percheron Stud-Books of France and America.,

Black; foaled April 12, 1882; imported 1885; bred by M. Avignon, commune of Préaux, canton of Nocé, department of Orne; got by MADÈRE II (2994); dam L'Amie (317) by VIDOCQ II (723) out of Grenade by DÉCIDÉ.

MADÈRE (2994) by Madeira 1546 (770), he by Vidocq 483 (732) out of Jeanne by Favori I (711), he by Vieux-Chaslin (713) out of L'Amie by Vieux-Pierre (894), he by Coco (712).
VIDOCQ 483 (732) by Coco II (714) out of a daughter of Chéri, he by Rustique.
COCO II (714) by Vieux-Chaslin (713) out of La Grise by Vieux-Pierre (883).
VIEUX-CHASLIN (713) by Coco (712) out of Poule by Sandi.
COCO (712) by Mignon (715) out of Pauline by Vieux-Coco.
MIGNON (715) by Jean-le-Blanc (739).
VIDOCQ II (723) by Bayard (1385) out of Brière by Décidé.
BAYARD (1385) by Vidocq 483 (732), etc., out of La Noire by Chéri, he by Coco II (714), etc.

Bred to BRILLIANT 1271 (755), June 9, 1887.

(Hoof No. 170.)   **FRANCAISE 3669.**
[Recorded with pedigree in the Percheron Stud-Book of America.]

Light grey; foaled 1884; bred at Oaklawn; got by GÉROME 3655 (436); dam Francine 2744 (1577) by PHILIBERT (760); 2d dam by MARGOT 295 (795).

GÉROME 3655 (436) by Vidocq II (723) out of Pelotte by Superior 454 (730), he by Favori I (711) out of Pauline by Vieux-Chaslin (713).
    FAVORI I (711) by Vieux-Chaslin (713) out of L'Amie by Vieux-Pierre (894), he by Coco (712).
VIDOCQ II (723) by Bayard (1385) out of Brière by Décidé.
BAYARD (1385) by Vidocq 483 (732) out of La Noire by Chéri, he by Coco II (714).
VIDOCQ 483 (732) by Coco II (714) out of a daughter of Chéri, he by Rustique.
COCO II (714) by Vieux-Chaslin (713) out of La Grise by Vieux-Pierre (883).
VIEUX-CHASLIN (713) by Coco (712) out of Poule by Sandi.
COCO (712) by Mignon (715) out of Pauline by Vieux-Coco.
MIGNON (715) by Jean-le-Blanc (739).
PHILIBERT (760) by Superior 454 (730) out of Madelon by Vieux-Vaillant (1383), he by Pierre out of a daughter of Vieux-Pierre (883).
SUPERIOR 454 (730) by Favori I (711), etc., out of Pauline by Vieux-Chaslin (713), etc.
MARGOT 295 (795) by Favori I (711), etc.

Bred to LA FERTÉ 5144 (452), June 16, 1887.

(Hoof No. 167.)   **FRANCINE 2744 (1577).**
[Recorded with pedigree in the Percheron Stud-Books of France and America.]

Dapple grey; foaled 1878; imported 1883; got by PHILIBERT (760); dam by MARGOT 295 (795).

PHILIBERT (760) by Superior 454 (730) out of Madelon by Vieux-Vaillant (1383), he by Pierre out of a daughter of Vieux-Pierre (883).
SUPERIOR 454 (730) by Favori I (711) out of Pauline by Vieux-Chaslin (713).
FAVORI I (711) by Vieux-Chaslin (713) out of L'Amie by Vieux-Pierre (894), he by Coco (712).
VIEUX-CHASLIN (713) by Coco (712) out of Poule by Sandi.
COCO (712) by Mignon (715) out of Pauline by Vieux-Coco.
MIGNON (715) by Jean-le-Blanc (739).
MARGOT 295 (795) by Favori I (711), etc.

Bred to BRILLIANT 1271 (755), April 2, 1887.

(Hoof No. 252.) **FRANCESCA 7328.**

[Recorded with pedigree in the Percheron Stud-Book of America.]

Dark grey ; foaled April 30, 1887 ; bred at Oaklawn ; got by BRILLIANT 1271 (755); dam Francaise 3669 by GÉROME 3655 (436); 2d dam Francine 2744 (1577) by PHILIBERT (760); 3d dam by MARGOT 295 (795).

BRILLIANT 1271 (755) by Brilliant 1899 (756) out of Ragout by Favori I (711).
BRILLIANT 1899 (756) by Coco II (714) out of Rosette by Mina, belonging to the French government.
Coco II (714) by Vieux-Chaslin (713) out of La Grise by Vieux-Pierre (883).
VIEUX-CHASLIN (713) by Coco (712) out of Poule by Sandi.
Coco (712) by Mignon (715) out of Pauline by Vieux-Coco.
MIGNON (715) by Jean-le-Blanc (739).
GÉROME 3655 (436) by Vidocq II (723) out of Pelotte by Superior 454 (730).
VIDOCQ II (723) by Bayard (1385) out of Brière by Décidé.
BAYARD (1385) by Vidocq 483 (732) out of La Noire by Chéri, he by Coco II (714), etc.
VIDOCQ 483 (732) by Coco II (714), etc., out of a daughter of Chéri, he by Rustique.
PHILIBERT (760) by Superior 454 (730) out of Madelon by Vieux-Vaillant (1383), he by Pierre, out of a daughter of Vieux-Pierre (883).
SUPERIOR 454 (730) by Favori I (711) out of Pauline by Vieux-Chaslin (713).
FAVORI I (711) by Vieux-Chaslin (713), etc., out of L'Amie by Vieux-Pierre (894), he by Coco (712), etc.
MARGOT 295 (795) by Favori I (711), etc.

(Hoof No. 101.) **FRASIE 4358 (4740).**

[Recorded with pedigree in the Percheron Stud-Books of France and America.]

Black ; foaled April 14, 1883 ; imported 1885 ; bred by M. Jouaux, commune of St. Longis, canton of Mamers, department of Sarthe ; got by SULTAN (4713); dam Bamboche (4766) by BAYARD, belonging to M. Lefeuvre, he by PICADOR ; 2d dam Cocotte, belonging to M. Jouaux.

SULTAN (4713) by Bayard I (son of Picador) out of Bijou, belonging to M. Lefeuvre.

Bred to BRILLIANT 1271 (755), May 3, 1887.

(Hoof No. 26.) **FRÉGATE 5639 (5974).**

[Recorded with pedigree in the Percheron Stud-Books of France and America.]

Dark grey ; foaled May 15, 1884 ; imported 1886 ; bred by M. Paul Pelletier, commune of St. Agnan, canton of Theil, department of Orne ; got by VAILLANT (404); dam Pelotte (5973) by FAVORI I (711) out of Bijou, belonging to M. Bajeon.

VAILLANT (404) by Prosper (893) out of Rosalie by Bienvenu, belonging to the Société Hippique of Eure-et-Loir.
PROSPER (893) by Décidé (892) out of Bourreau by Vieux-Pierre (883).
DÉCIDÉ (892) by Vieux-Pierre (894) out of Pelote, belonging to M. Berjeau, of Courvalien.
VIEUX-PIERRE (894) by Coco (712), he by Mignon (715) out of Pauline by Vieux-Coco.
MIGNON (715) by Jean-le-Blanc (739).
FAVORI I (711) by Viéux-Chaslin (713) out of L'Amie by Vieux-Pierre (894), etc.
VIEUX-CHASLIN (713) by Coco (712), etc., out of Poule by Sandi.

Bred to BRILLIANT 1271 (755), June 29, 1887.

(Hoof No. 173.)   **FROSINE 4376 (4856).**

[Recorded with pedigree in the Percheron Stud-Books of France and America.]

Bay ; foaled March 20, 1881 ; imported 1885 ; bred by M. Hubert, commune of Cormes, canton of La Ferté-Bernard, department of Sarthe ; got by FAVORA 1542 (765); dam Pauline (4855) by BAYARD 26 (717) out of Rosette.

FAVORA 1542 (765) by French Monarch 205 (734) out of Marguerite by Favori, he by Coco of Mêsle-sur-Sarthe.
FRENCH MONARCH 205 (734) by Ilderim (5302) out of a daughter of Vieux-Pierre (894), he by Coco (712).'
ILDERIM (5302) by Valentin (5301) out of Chaton by Vieux-Pierre (894), etc.
VALENTIN (5301) by Vieux-Chaslin (713), he by Coco (712) out of Poule by Sandi.
Coco (712) by Mignon (715) out of Pauline by Vieux-Coco.
MIGNON (715) by Jean-le-Blanc (739).
BAYARD 26 (717) by Favori I (711) out of Mignonne by Chéri.
FAVORI I (711) by Vieux-Chaslin (713), etc., out of L'Amie by Vieux-Pierre (894), etc.

Bred to BRILLIANT 1271 (755), October 7, 1887.

(Hoof No. 189.)   **FULIDA 1456 (1435).**

[Recorded with pedigree in the Percheron Stud-Books of France and America.]

Dapple grey ; foaled 1877 ; imported 1881 ; got by DÉCIDÉ 126 (720); dam by DUKE OF PERCHE 173 (740).

DÉCIDÉ 126 (720) by Superior 454 (730), he by Favori I (711) out of Pauline by Vieux-Chaslin (713).
FAVORI I (711) by Vieux-Chaslin (713) out of L'Amie by Vieux-Pierre (894), he by Coco (712).
VIEUX-CHASLIN (713) by Coco (712) out of Poule by Sandi.
Coco (712) by Mignon (715) out of Pauline by Vieux-Coco.
MIGNON (715) by Jean-le-Blanc (739).
DUKE OF PERCHE 173 (740) by Favori I (711), etc., out of Franconie by Vieux-Pierre (883).

Bred to BRILLIANT 1271 (754), May 28, 1887.

(Hoof No. 57.)   **GALLIMA 5667 (6791).**

[Recorded with pedigree in the Percheron Stud-Books of France and America.]

Dapple grey ; foaled April 15, 1881 ; imported 1886 ; bred by M. Leroy, commune of Champroud, canton of Nogent-le-Rotrou, department of Eure-et-Loir ; got by SULTAN (1395) ; dam Cocote (6790) by PARISIEN, belonging to M. Sagot, out of Cocote.

SULTAN (1395) by Vigoureux (1392) out of Margot by Franconi, belonging to M. Sagot.
VIGOUREUX (1392) by Coco II (714) out of Marguerite by Franconi.
Coco II (714) by Vieux-Chaslin (713) out of La Grise by Vieux-Pierre (883).
VIEUX-CHASLIN (713) by Coco (712) out of Poule by Sandi.
Coco (712) by Mignon (715) out of Pauline by Vieux-Coco.
MIGNON (715) by Jean-le-Blanc (739).

Bred to BRILLIANT 1271 (755), September 3, 1887.

(Hoof No. 44.) **GENTILLE 5655 (1754).**

[Recorded with pedigree in the Percheron Stud-Books of France and America.]

Grey; foaled March 20, 1883; imported 1886; bred by M. Guillotin, commune of Ceton, canton of Theil, department of Orne; got by VIDOCQ (1403); dam Margot (7323) by FAVORI I (711) out of Chaton, belonging to M. Guillotin.

VIDOCQ (1403) by Utopia 780 (731) out of Bijou by Vieux-Chaslin (713).
UTOPIA 780 (731) by Superior 454 (730) out of Camille by Favori I (711).
SUPERIOR 454 (730) by Favori I (711) out of Pauline by Vieux-Chaslin (713).
FAVORI I (711) by Vieux-Chaslin (713) out of L'Amie by Vieux-Pierre (894), he by Coco (712).
VIEUX-CHASLIN (713) by Coco (712) out of Poule by Sandi.
COCO (712) by Mignon (715) out of Pauline by Vieux-Coco.
MIGNON (715) by Jean-le-Blanc (739).

Bred to BRILLIANT 1271 (755), May 20, 1887.

(Hoof No. 212.) **GENTILLETTE 7137 (9811).**

[Recorded with pedigree in the Percheron Stud-Books of France and America.]

Black; foaled February 20, 1884; imported 1887; bred by M. Lefeuvre, commune of Marolles-les-Braux, department of Sarthe; got by COCO-DEUX (5607); dam Rose (7450) by PICADOR, he by BAYARD, belonging to M. Lefeuvre; 2d dam Coquette by CHARMANT, belonging to M. Lefeuvre.

COCO-DEUX (5607) by Coco I, belonging to M. Lefeuvre, out of Charmante.

(Hoof No. 190.) **GERALDINE 1433 (1437).**

[Recorded with pedigree in the Percheron Stud-Books of France and America.]

Light grey; foaled 1878; imported 1881; got by ROMULUS 873 (785); dam by JEAN-BART (716).

ROMULUS 873 (785) by the government approved stallion Romulus (son of Moreun, out of Fleur-d'Epine by the government approved stallion Chéri, he by Corbon.
JEAN-BART (716) by Bayard, belonging to M. Ferrère, out of Jeanne by Porthos.

Bred to BRILLIANT 1271 (755), September 5, 1887.

(Hoof No. 76.) **GERMAINE 5681 (6833).**

[Recorded with pedigree in the Percheron Stud-Books of France and America.]

Dapple grey; foaled April 5, 1883; imported 1886; bred by M. Alexandre Duval, commune of St. Germain-de-la-Coudre, canton of Theil, department of Orne; got by CHARTRAIN (1405); dam Lisette (5094) by FAVORI (4770) out of Blanchette.

CHARTRAIN (1405) by Philibert (760) out of Cocotte by Coco II (714), he by Vieux-Chaslin (713) out of La Grise by Vieux-Pierre (883).
PHILIBERT (760) by Superior 454 (730) out of Madelon by Vieux-Vaillant (1383), he by Pierre.
SUPERIOR 454 (730) by Favori I (711) out of Pauline by Vieux-Chaslin (713).
FAVORI I (711) by Vieux-Chaslin (713) out of L'Amie by Vieux-Pierre (894), he by Coco (712).
VIEUX-CHASLIN (713) by Coco (712) out of Poule by Sandi.
COCO (712) by Mignon (715) out of Pauline by Vieux-Coco.
MIGNON (715) by Jean-le-Blanc (739).
FAVORI (4770) by Superior 454 (730), etc.

Bred to BRILLIANT 1271 (755), August 12, 1887.

(Hoof No. 7.)   **GERVAISE 5620 (6146).**

[Recorded with pedigree in the Percheron Stud-Books of France and America.]

Grey; foaled March 8, 1885; imported 1886; bred by M. Henri Guillemin, commune of St. Germain-de-la-Coudre, canton of Theil, department of Orne; got by LA FERTÉ 5144 (452); dam Pelotte (6145) by BRILLIANT 1271 (755) out of Madelon.

LA FERTÉ 5144 (452) by Philibert (760) out of Julie (7594) by Brilliant 1899 (756).
PHILIBERT (760) by Superior 454 (730) out of Madelon by Vieux-Vaillant (1383), he by Pierre out of a daughter of Vieux-Pierre (883).
SUPERIOR 454 (730) by Favori I (711) out of Pauline by Vieux-Chaslin (713).
FAVORI I (711) by Vieux-Chaslin (713) out of L'Amie by Vieux-Pierre (894), he by Coco (712).
VIEUX-CHASLIN (713) by Coco (712) out of Poule by Sandi.
Coco (712) by Mignon (715) out of Pauline by Vieux-Coco.
MIGNON (715) by Jean-le-Blanc (739).
BRILLIANT 1271 (755) by Brilliant 1899 (756) out of Ragout by Favori I (711), etc.
BRILLIANT 1899 (756) by Coco II (714) out of Rosette by Mina, belonging to the French government.
Coco II (714) by Vieux-Chaslin (713), etc., out of La Grise by Vieux-Pierre (883).

Bred to BRILLIANT 1271 (755), July 13, 1887.

(Hoof No. 107.)   **GIARIA 2755 (1531).**

[Recorded with pedigree in the Percheron Stud-Books of France and America.]

Black; foaled 1882; imported 1883; got by EMIGRANT 1241 (764); dam by GLADIATOR 683 (742).

EMIGRANT 1241 (764) by Gladiator 683 (742), he by Brilliant 1899 (756), he by Coco II (714) out of Rosette by Mina, belonging to the French government.
Coco II (714) by Vieux-Chaslin (713) out of La Grise by Vieux-Pierre (883).
VIEUX-CHASLIN (713) by Coco (712) out of Poule by Sandi.
Coco (712) by Mignon (715) out of Pauline by Vieux-Coco.
MIGNON (715) by Jean-le-Blanc (739).

Bred to LA FERTÉ 5144 (452), April 10, 1887.

(Hoof No. 233.)   **GIPSY GIRL 7329.**

[Recorded with pedigree in the Percheron Stud-Book of America.]

Black; foaled April 3, 1887; bred at Oaklawn; got by BRILLIANT 1271 (755); dam Giaria 2755 (1531) by EMIGRANT 1241 (764) out of a daughter of GLADIATOR 683 (742).

BRILLIANT 1271 (755) by Brilliant 1899 (756) out of Ragout by Favori I (711), he by Vieux-Chaslin (713) out of L'Amie by Vieux-Pierre (894), he by Coco (712).
BRILLIANT 1899 (756) by Coco II (714) out of Rosette by Mina, belonging to the French government.
Coco II (714) by Vieux-Chaslin (713) out of La Grise by Vieux-Pierre (883).
VIEUX-CHASLIN (713) by Coco (712) out of Poule by Sandi.
Coco (712) by Mignon (715) out of Pauline by Vieux-Coco.
MIGNON (715) by Jean-le-Blanc (739).
EMIGRANT 1241 (764) by Gladiator 683 (742), he by Brilliant 1899 (756), etc.

(Hoof No. 29.)   **GUERANDE 5641 (6568).**

[Recorded with pedigree in the Percheron Stud-Books of France and America.]

Dark grey ; foaled May 19, 1885 ; imported 1886 ; bred by M. Brouard, commune of St. Hilaire-sur-Erre, canton of Theil, department of Orne ; got by Vaillant (404); dam Franconie (4260) by Vieux-Vaillant (1383).

Vaillant (404) by Prosper (893) out of Rosalie by Bienvenu, belonging to the Société Hippique of Eure-et-Loir.
Prosper (893) by Décidé (892) out of Bourreau by Vieux-Pierre (883).
Décidé (892) by Vieux-Pierre (894) out of Pelote, belonging to M. Berjeau, of Courvalien.
Vieux-Pierre (894) by Coco (712), he by Mignon (715) out of Pauline by Vieux-Coco.
Mignon (715) by Jean-le-Blanc (739).
Vieux-Vaillant (1383) by Pierre, belonging to M. Thérin, out of a daughter of Vieux-Pierre (883).

Bred to Brilliant 1271 (755), September 8, 1887.

(Hoof No. 299.)   **HIRONDELLE 7138 (10398).**

[Recorded with pedigree in the Percheron Stud-Books of France and America.]

Dark grey ; foaled September 30, 1886 ; imported 1887 ; bred by M. Moitez, commune of Bonnétable, department of Sarthe ; got by Coco-Deux (5607); dam Marie (10397) by Pierre, belonging to M. Juguin.

Coco-Deux (5607) by Coco I, belonging to M. Lefeuvre, out of Charmante.

(Hoof No. 116.)   **IDEALITY 4393.**

[Recorded with pedigree in the Percheron Stud-Book of America.]

Grey ; foaled 1883 ; imported in dam 1883 ; bred by M. Anatold Miard, commune of Echauffour, canton of Merlerault, department of Orne ; got by Producteur 2371 (1256); dam Irena 2739 (1587) by Favora 666 (725); 2d dam Poule by Margot 295 (795).

Producteur 2371 (1256) by Jean-Bart (716) out of Louise by Waterloo 2199 (733), he by Jean-Bart (716) out of Poule, belonging to M. Bourdin.
Jean-Bart (716) by Bayard, belonging to M. Perpère, out of Jeanne by Porthos.
Favora 666 (725) by Favori I (711) out of Marie by Coco (712).
Favori I (711) by Vieux-Chaslin (713) out of L'Amie by Vieux-Pierre (894), he by Coco (712).
Vieux-Chaslin (713) by Coco (712) out of Poule by Sandi.
Coco (712) by Mignon (715) out of Pauline by Vieux-Coco.
Mignon (715) by Jean-le-Blanc (739).
Margot 295 (795) by Favori I (711), etc.

Bred to La Ferté 5144 (452), September 9, 1887.

(Hoof No. 294.)   **IMPATIENTE 5670 (5993).**

[Recorded with pedigree in the Percheron Stud-Books of France and America.]

Grey ; foaled April 17, 1884 ; imported 1886 ; bred by M. Louis Guillemin, commune of Préaux, canton of Nocé, department of Orne ; got by MADÈRE II (2994); dam Lisette (5992) by PROSPER (893) out of Rustique, belonging to M. Avignon.

MADÈRE II (2994) by Madeira 1546 (770), he by Vidocq 483 (732) out of Jeanne by Favori I (711), he by Vieux-Chaslin (713) out of L'Amie by Vieux-Pierre (894), he by Coco (712).
VIDOCQ 483 (732) by Coco II (714) out of a daughter of Chéri, he by Rustique.
COCO II (714) by Vieux-Chaslin (713) out of La Grise by Vieux-Pierre (883).
VIEUX-CHASLIN (713) by Coco (712) out of Poule by Sandi.
COCO (712) by Mignon (715) out of Pauline by Vieux-Coco.
MIGNON (715) by Jean-le-Blanc (739).
PROSPER (893) by Décidé (892) out of Bourreau by Vieux-Pierre (883).
DÉCIDÉ (892) by Vieux-Pierre (894) out of Pelote, belonging to M. Berjeau, of Courvalien.
VIEUX-PIERRE (894) by Coco (712), etc.

Bred to SULTAN 4291 (4052), September 3, 1887.

(Hoof No. 188.)   **IONE 2201 (1440).**

[Recorded with pedigree in the Percheron Stud-Books of France and America.]

Dapple grey ; foaled 1878 ; imported 1882 ; got by LUTHER (792); dam by PORTHOS, belonging to M. Fromentin.

LUTHER (792) by Pierre (887) out of Rosette by Laboureur (886).
PIERRE (887) by Laboureur (886) out of Margot by Faisan.
LABOUREUR (886) by Jean-le-Blanc (739) out of Sophie by Sandi.

Bred to BRILLIANT 1271 (755), May 23, 1887.

(Hoof No. 124.)   **ISUDA 2214 (1442).**

[Recorded with pedigree in the Percheron Stud-Books of France and America.]

Black ; foaled 1882 ; imported 1882 ; got by BRILLIANT 1271 (755); dam by BAYARD 26 (717).

BRILLIANT 1271 (755) by Brilliant 1899 (756) out of Ragout by Favori I (711).
BRILLIANT 1899 (756) by Coco II (714) out of Rosette by Mina, belonging to the French government.
COCO II (714) by Vieux-Chaslin (713) out of La Grise by Vieux-Pierre (883).
VIEUX-CHASLIN (713) by Coco (712) out of Poule by Sandi.
COCO (712) by Mignon (715) out of Pauline by Vieux-Coco.
MIGNON (715) by Jean-le-Blanc (739).
BAYARD 26 (717) by Favori I (711) out of Mignonne by Chéri.
FAVORI I (711) by Vieux-Chaslin (713), etc., out of L'Amie by Vieux-Pierre (894), he by Coco (712), etc.

Bred to LA FERTÉ 5144 (452), May 22, 1887.

(Hoof No. 261.) **ISUDINE 7327.**
[Recorded with pedigree in the Percheron Stud-Book of America.]

Black ; foaled April 2, 1887 ; bred at Oaklawn ; got by BRILLIANT 1271 (755); dam Isuda 2214 (1442) by BRILLIANT 1271 (755) out of a daughter of BAYARD 26 (717).

BRILLIANT 1271 (755) by Brilliant 1899 (756) out of Ragout by Favori I (711).
BRILLIANT 1899 (756) by Coco II (714) out of Rosette by Mina, belonging to the French government.
Coco II (714) by Vieux-Chaslin (713) out of La Grise by Vieux-Pierre (883).
VIEUX-CHASLIN (713) by Coco (712) out of Poule by Sandi.
Coco (712) by Mignon (715) out of Pauline by Vieux-Coco.
MIGNON (715) by Jean-le-Blanc (739).
BAYARD 26 (717) by Favori I (711), etc., out of Mignonne by Chéri.
FAVORI I (711) by Vieux-Chaslin (713), etc., out of L'Amie by Vieux-Pierre (894), he by Coco (712), etc.

(Hoof No. 123.) **JANECIA 2768 (1376).**
[Recorded with pedigree in the Percheron Stud-Books of France and America.]

Bay ; foaled 1882 ; imported 1883 ; got by FAVORI (1401); dam Jubine by PASSE-PARTOUT (1402).

FAVORI (1401) by Favora 1542 (765) out of Jeannette by Décidé, belonging to M. Vinault.
FAVORA 1542 (765) by French Monarch 205 (734) out of Marguerite by Favori, he by Coco of Mésle-sur-Sarthe.
FRENCH MONARCH 205 (734) by Ilderim (5302) out of a daughter of Vieux-Pierre (894), he by Coco (712).
ILDERIM (5302) by Valentin (5301) out of Chaton by Vieux-Pierre (894), etc.
VALENTIN (5301) by Vieux-Chaslin (713), he by Coco (712) out of Poule by Sandi.
Coco (712) by Mignon (715) out of Pauline by Vieux-Coco.
MIGNON (715) by Jean-le-Blanc (739).
PASSE-PARTOUT (1402) by Comet 104 (719) out of Sophie by Favori I (711), he by Vieux-Chaslin (713), etc., out of L'Amie by Vieux-Pierre (894), etc.
COMET 104 (719) by French Monarch 205 (734), etc., out of Suzanne by Cambronne.

Bred to BRILLIANT 1271 (755), May 19, 1887.

(Hoof No. 234.) **JENNY 7157 (8553).**
[Recorded with pedigree in the Percheron Stud-Books of France and America.]

Dark grey ; foaled May 25, 1886 ; imported 1887 ; bred by M. Guillemin, commune of St. Germain-de-la-Coudre, canton of Theil, department of Orne ; got by LA FERTÉ 5144 (452); dam Pelotte 5671 (1706) by BRILLIANT 1271 (755) out of Pelote (4093) by SUPERIOR 454 (730).

LA FERTÉ 5144 (452) by Philibert (760) out of Julie (7594) by Brilliant 1899 (756).
PHILIBERT (760) by Superior 454 (730) out of Madelon by Vieux-Vaillant (1383), he by Pierre out of a daughter of Vieux-Pierre (883).
SUPERIOR 454 (730) by Favori I (711) out of Pauline by Vieux-Chaslin (713).
FAVORI I (711) by Vieux-Chaslin (713) out of L'Amie by Vieux-Pierre (894), he by Coco (712).
VIEUX-CHASLIN (713) by Coco (712) out of Poule by Sandi.
Coco (712) by Mignon (715) out of Pauline by Vieux-Coco.
MIGNON (715) by Jean-le-Blanc (739).
VIDOCQ 483 (732) by Coco II (714) out of a daughter of Chéri, he by Rustique.
BRILLIANT 1271 (755) by Brilliant 1899 (756) out of Ragout by Favori I (711), etc.
BRILLIANT 1899 (756) by Coco II (714) out of Rosette by Mina, belonging to the French government.
Coco II (714) by Vieux-Chaslin (713), etc., out of La Grise by Vieux-Pierre (883).

(Hoof No. 201.)   **JOUVENCELLE 7158 (8836).**

[Recorded with pedigree in the Percheron Stud-Books of France and America.]

Black ; foaled March 30, 1884 ; imported 1887; bred by M. Henry, commune of Tréhet, canton of Montoire, department of Loir-et-Cher ; got by Coco (4796); dam Margot (8835) by Coco, belonging to the French government.

Coco (4796) by Paul, belonging to M. Dubois, out of Rosette, belonging to M. L'Hermitte.

Bred to BRILLIANT 1271 (755), October 19, 1887.

(Hoof No. 77.)   **JOYEUSE 5682 (2839).**

[Recorded with pedigree in the Percheron Stud-Books of France and America.]

Grey ; foaled March 18, 1884 ; imported 1886 ; bred by M. Glond, commune of Masles, canton of Theil, department of Orne ; got by PRIMO (84); dam L'Amie (7461) by VIEUX-CHASLIN (713) out of Rosette.

PRIMO (84) by Iago 995 (768) out of Rosalie by Bayard.
IAGO 995 (768) by Utopia 780 (731) out of Cossette by Favora 666 (725), he by Favori I (711) out of Marie by Coco (712).
UTOPIA 780 (731) by Superior 454 (730) out of Camille by Favori I (711).
SUPERIOR 454 (730) by Favori I (711) out of Pauline by Vieux-Chaslin (713).
FAVORI I (711) by Vieux-Chaslin (713) out of L'Amie by Vieux-Pierre (894), he by Coco (712).
VIEUX-CHASLIN (713) by Coco (712) out of Poule by Sandi.
Coco (712) by Mignon (715) out of Pauline by Vieux-Coco.
MIGNON (715) by Jean-le-Blanc (739).

Bred to BRILLIANT 1271 (755), April 12, 1887.

(Hoof No. 67.)   **JULIA 5676 (7015).**

[Recorded with pedigree in the Percheron Stud-Books of France and America.]

Black ; foaled April 20, 1885 ; imported 1886 ; bred by M. Guille-min, commune of St. Germain-de-la-Coudre, canton of Theil, department of Orne ; got by LA FERTÉ 5144 (452); dam Brillante (7014) by BRILLIANT 1899 (756) out of Brillante.

LA FERTÉ 5144 (452) by Philibert (760) out of Julie (7594) by Brilliant 1899 (756).
PHILIBERT (760) by Superior 454 (730) out of Madelon by Vieux-Vaillant (1383), he by Pierre.
SUPERIOR 454 (730) by Favori I (711) out of Pauline by Vieux-Chaslin (713).
FAVORI I (711) by Vieux-Chaslin (713) out of L'Amie by Vieux-Pierre (894), he by Coco (712).
VIEUX-CHASLIN (713) by Coco (712) out of Poule by Sandi.
Coco (712) by Mignon (715) out of Pauline by Vieux-Coco.
MIGNON (715) by Jean-le-Blanc (739).
BRILLIANT 1899 (756) by Coco II (714) out of Rosette by Mina, belonging to the French government.
Coco II (714) by Vieux-Chaslin (713), etc., out of La Grise by Vieux-Pierre (883).

Bred to BRILLIANT 1271 (755), August 3, 1887.

JULIE 5656 (2961).

(Hoof No. 285.)

[Recorded with pedigree in the Percheron Stud-Books of France and America.]

Black; foaled May 1, 1883; imported 1886; bred by M. Bourlier, commune of St. Bomert, canton of Authon, department of Eure-et-Loir; got by CHARTRAIN (1405); dam Cocotte (6226) by BRILLIANT 1899 (756) out of Brebis.

CHARTRAIN (1405) by Philibert (760) out of Cocotte by Coco II (714).
PHILIBERT (760) by Superior 454 (730) out of Madelon by Vieux-Vaillant (1383), he by Pierre out of a daughter of Vieux-Pierre (883).
SUPERIOR 454 (730) by Favori I (711) out of Pauline by Vieux-Chaslin (713).
FAVORI I (711) by Vieux-Chaslin (713) out of L'Amie by Vieux-Pierre (894), he by Coco (712).
VIEUX-CHASLIN (713) by Coco (712) out of Poule by Sandi.
Coco (712) by Mignon (715) out of Pauline by Vieux-Coco.
MIGNON (715) by Jean-le-Blanc (739).
BRILLIANT 1899 (756) by Coco II (714) out of Rosette by Mina, belonging to the French government.
Coco II (714) by Vieux-Chaslin (713), etc., out of La Grise by Vieux-Pierre (883).

Bred to SANDY 5162 (2225), May 16, 1887.

LA BOURDONNIÈRE 7139 (8842).

(Hoof No. 202.)

[Recorded with pedigree in the Percheron Stud-Books of France and America.]

Dark grey; foaled March 12, 1885; imported 1887; bred by M. Gasnier fils, commune of Pervenchères, department of Orne; got by ROMULUS 3523 (222); dam L'Amie (8332) by BLAINVILLE, belonging to the French government.

ROMULUS 3523 (222) by Prosper (893) out of Bijou by Laboureur (886), he by Jean-le-Blanc (739) out of Sophie by Sandi.
PROSPER (893) by Décidé (892) out of Bourreau by Vieux-Pierre (883).
DÉCIDÉ (892) by Vieux-Pierre (894) out of Pelote, belonging to M. Berjeau, of Courvalien.
VIEUX-PIERRE (894) by Coco (712), he by Mignon (715) out of Pauline by Vieux-Coco.
MIGNON (715) by Jean-le-Blanc (739).

Bred to STRADAT 7112 (2463), May 28, 1887.

LANCETTE 5672 (6994).

(Hoof No. 63.)

[Recorded with pedigree in the Percheron Stud-Books of France and America.]

Black grey; foaled March 15, 1885; imported 1886; bred by M. François Justice, commune of Souvigné-sur-Même, canton of La Ferté-Bernard, department of Sarthe; got by LA FERTÉ 5144 (452); dam Pelotte (6993) by BRILLIANT 1899 (756) out of Bijou, belonging to M. Moulin.

LA FERTÉ 5144 (452) by Philibert (760) out of Julie (7594) by Brilliant 1899 (756).
PHILIBERT (760) by Superior 454 (730) out of Madelon by Vieux-Vaillant (1383), he by Pierre out of a daughter of Vieux-Pierre (883).
SUPERIOR 454 (730) by Favori I (711) out of Pauline by Vieux-Chaslin (713).
FAVORI I (711) by Vieux-Chaslin (713) out of L'Amie by Vieux-Pierre (894), he by Coco (712).
VIEUX-CHASLIN (713) by Coco (712) out of Poule by Sandi.
Coco (712) by Mignon (715) out of Pauline by Vieux-Coco.
MIGNON (715) by Jean-le-Blanc (739).
BRILLIANT 1899 (756) by Coco II (714) out of Rosette by Mina, belonging to the French government.
Coco II (714) by Vieux-Chaslin (713), etc., out of La Grise by Vieux-Pierre (883).

Bred to BRILLIANT 1271 (755), October 12, 1887.

(Hoof No. 206.)   **LÉA 7141 (8841).**

[Recorded with pedigree in the Percheron Stud-Books of France and America.]

Light grey; foaled April 15, 1885; imported 1887; bred by M. Montheau, commune of Appenay, canton of Bellême, department of Orne; got by PAUL 3478 (364); dam Mouvette (8840) by MADEIRA 1546 (770).

PAUL 3478 (364) by Vaillant (404) out of Cocotte by Vieux-Vaillant (1383), he by Pierre out of a daughter of Vieux-Pierre (883).
VAILLANT (404) by Prosper (893) out of Rosalie by Bienvenu, belonging to the Société Hippique of Eure-et-Loir.
PROSPER (893) by Décidé (892) out of Bourreau by Vieux-Pierre (883).
DÉCIDÉ (892) by Vieux-Pierre (894) out of Pelote, belonging to M. Berjeau, of Courvallen.
VIEUX-PIERRE (894) by Coco (712), he by Mignon (715) out of Pauline by Vieux-Coco.
MIGNON (715) by Jean-le-Blanc (739).
MADEIRA 1546 (770) by Vidocq 483 (732) out of Jeanne by Favori I (711), he by Vieux-Chaslin (713) out of L'Amie by Vieux-Pierre (894), etc.
VIDOCQ 483 (732) by Coco II (714) out of a daughter of Chéri, he by Rustique.
COCO II (714) by Vieux-Chaslin (713) out of La Grise by Vieux-Pierre (883).
VIEUX-CHASLIN (713) by Coco (712), etc., out of Poule by Sandi.

Bred to STRADAT 7112 (2463), June 25, 1887.

(Hoof No. 232.)   **LÉONA 7144 (9768).**

[Recorded with pedigree in the Percheron Stud-Books of France and America.]

Dark grey; foaled April 15, 1885; imported 1887; bred by M. Lesault, commune of St. Germain-de-la-Condre, canton of Theil, department of Orne; got by LA FERTÉ 5144 (452); dam Jubine (9767) by BRILLIANT 1899 (756).

LA FERTÉ 5144 (452) by Philibert (760) out of Julie (7594) by Brilliant 1899 (756).
PHILIBERT (760) by Superior 454 (730) out of Madelon by Vieux-Vaillant (1383), he by Pierre out of a daughter of Vieux-Pierre (883).
SUPERIOR 454 (730) by Favori I (711) out of Pauline by Vieux-Chaslin (713).
FAVORI I (711) by Vieux-Chaslin (713) out of L'Amie by Vieux-Pierre (894), he by Coco (712).
VIEUX-CHASLIN (713) by Coco (712) out of Poule by Sandi.
COCO (712) by Mignon (715) out of Pauline by Vieux-Coco.
MIGNON (715) by Jean-le-Blanc (739).
BRILLIANT 1899 (756) by Coco II (714) out of Rosette by Mina, belonging to the French government.
COCO II (714) by Vieux-Chaslin (713), etc., out of La Grise by Vieux-Pierre (883).

Bred to BRILLIANT 1271 (755), October 19, 1887.

(Hoof No. 205.)   **LÉVRETTE 7140 (8838).**

[Recorded with pedigree in the Percheron Stud-Books of France and America.]

Grey; foaled April 2, 1884; imported 1887; bred by M. Henry, commune of Troô, canton of Montoire, department of Loir-et-Cher; got by Coco (4796); dam Martine (8837) by PAPILLON, belonging to M. Chalumeau.

COCO (4796) by Paul, belonging to M. Dubois, out of Rosette, belonging to M. L'Hermitte.

Bred to STRADAT 7112 (2463), May 29, 1887.

(Hoof No. 286.)   **LIBÉRIA 5629 (7046).**

[Recorded with pedigree in the Percheron Stud-Books of France and America.]

Grey ; foaled April 11, 1885 ; imported 1886 ; bred by M. Lisieur, commune of Ceton, canton of Theil, department of Orne ; got by PAPILLON 3559 (379); dam Manette (7045) by BRILLANT (4951) out of Bijou, belonging to M. Lebraye.

PAPILLON 3559 (379) by Brillant (710) out of Cocotte by Coco II (714).
BRILLANT (710) by Brilliant 1899 (756), he by Coco II (714) out of Rosette by
    Mina, belonging to the French government.
Coco II (714) by Vieux-Chaslin (713) out of La Grise by Vieux-Pierre (883).
VIEUX-CHASLIN (713) by Coco (712) out of Poule by Sandi.
Coco (712) by Mignon (715) out of Pauline by Vieux-Coco.
MIGNON (715) by Jean-le-Blanc (739).
BRILLANT (4951) by Vaillant, belonging to M. Dorchène, out of Poule by Colin
    (6949).

Bred to SANDY 5162 (2225), July 29, 1887.

(Hoof No. 233.)   **LILIANE 7145 (8554).**

[Recorded with pedigree in the Percheron Stud-Books of France and America.]

Black ; foaled March 1, 1886 ; imported 1887 ; bred by M. Guillemin, commune of St. Germain, canton of Theil, department of Orne ; got by LA FERTÉ 5144 (452) ; dam Pauline (1705) by BRILLIANT 1899 (756) out of L'Amie by Coco II (714).

LA FERTÉ 5144 (452) by Philibert (760) out of Julie (7594) by Brilliant 1899
    (756).
PHILIBERT (760) by Superior 454 (730) out of Madelon by Vieux-Vaillant (1383),
    he by Pierre out of a daughter of Vieux-Pierre (883).
SUPERIOR 454 (730) by Favori I (711) out of Pauline by Vieux-Chaslin (713).
FAVORI I (711) by Vieux-Chaslin (713), etc., out of L'Amie by Vieux-Pierre
    (894), he by Coco (712).
VIEUX-CHASLIN (713) by Coco (712) out of Poule by Sandi.
Coco (712) by Mignon (715) out of Pauline by Vieux-Coco.
MIGNON (715) by Jean-le-Blanc (739).
BRILLIANT 1899 (756) by Coco II (714) out of Rosette by Mina, belonging to the
    French government.
Coco II (714) by Vieux-Chaslin (713), etc., out of La Grise by Vieux-Pierre (883).

(Hoof No. 303.)   **LINDA 2751 (1521).**

[Recorded with pedigree in the Percheron Stud-Books of France and America.]

Dark dapple grey ; foaled 1881 ; imported 1883 ; got by VAILLANT (404) ; dam by PIERRE (887).

VAILLANT (404) by Prosper (893) out of Rosalie by Bienvenu, belonging to the
    Société Hippique of Eure-et-Loir.
PROSPER (893) by Décidé (892) out of Bourreau by Vieux-Pierre (883).
DÉCIDÉ (892) by Vieux-Pierre (894) out of Pelote, belonging to M. Berjeau, of
    Courvalien.
VIEUX-PIERRE (894) by Coco (712), he by Mignon (715) out of Pauline by Vieux-
    Coco.
MIGNON (715) by Jean-le-Blanc (739).
PIERRE (887) by Laboureur (886) out of Margot by Faisan.
LABOUREUR (886) by Jean-le-Blanc (739) out of Sophie by Sandi.

Bred to BRILLIANT 1271 (755), April 21, 1887.

(Hoof-No. 227.)'   **LOISELLE 7143 (8661).**
[Recorded with pedigree in the Percheron Stud-Books of France and America.]

Steel grey ; foaled April 10, 1885 ; imported 1887 ; bred by M. Michael Loiseau, commune of La Louve, canton of Theil, department of Orne ; got by VOLTAIRE 3540 (443) ; dam Poule (6893) by VAILLANT, belonging to M. Tacheau, out of Rosette, belonging to M. Louis Lambert.

VOLTAIRE 3540 (443) by Brilliant 1271 (755) out of Cocotte by Coco II (714).
BRILLIANT 1271 (755) by Brilliant 1899 (756) out of Ragout by Favori I (711), he by Vieux-Chaslin (713) out of L'Amie by Vieux-Pierre (894), he by Coco (712).
BRILLIANT 1899 (756) by Coco II (714) out of Rosette by Mina, belonging to the French government.
Coco II (714) by Vieux-Chaslin (713) out of La Grise by Vieux-Pierre (883).
VIEUX-CHASLIN (713) by Coco (712) out of Poule by Sandi.
Coco (712) by Mignon (715) out of Pauline by Vieux-Coco.
MIGNON (715) by Jean-le-Blanc (739).

Bred to LA FERTÉ 5144 (452), October 19, 1887.

(Hoof No. 208.)   **LOULOUTE 7142 (10093).**
[Recorded with pedigree in the Percheron Stud-Books of France and America.]

Black ; foaled April 8, 1886 ; imported 1887 ; bred by M. Auguste Leguillon, commune of Souligné, canton of Ballon, department of Sarthe ; got by POLYDOR (5443) ; dam Pelotte (10092) by CHARMANT, belonging to M. Chauder.

POLYDOR (5443) by Charmant I out of Biche by Vigoureux, belonging to M. Abot.
CHARMANT I by Vigoureux, he by Favory, belonging to M. Abot.

(Hoof No. 131.)   **MACARIA 2797 (35).**
[Recorded with pedigree in the Percheron Stud-Books of France and America.]

Dapple grey; foaled 1878 ; imported 1883 ; got by BRILLIANT 1899 (756); dam Bijou by FAVORA 666 (725).

BRILLIANT 1899 (756) by Coco II (714) out of Rosette by Mina, belonging to the French government.
Coco II (714) by Vieux-Chaslin (713) out of La Grise by Vieux-Pierre (883).
VIEUX-CHASLIN (713) by Coco (712) out of Poule by Sandi.
Coco (712) by Mignon (715) out of Pauline by Vieux-Coco.
MIGNON (715) by Jean-le-Blanc (739).
FAVORA 666 (725) by Favori I (711) out of Marie by Coco (712), etc.
FAVORI I (711) by Vieux-Chaslin (713), etc., out of L'Amie by Vieux-Pierre (894), he by Coco (712), etc.

Bred to LA FERTÉ 5144 (452), April 27, 1887.

(Hoof No. 292.)   **MADONNA 1474.**
[Recorded with pedigree in the Percheron Stud-Book of America.]

Dapple grey; foaled 1882 ; bred at Oaklawn ; got by VIDOCQ 483 (732); dam Mid-Ocean 583 ; 2d dam La Belle France 570.

VIDOCQ 483 (732) by Coco II (714), etc., out of a daughter of Chéri, he by Rustique.
Coco II (714) by Vieux-Chaslin (713) out of La Grise by Vieux-Pierre (883).
VIEUX-CHASLIN (713) by Coco (712) out of Poule by Sandi.
Coco (712) by Mignon (715) out of Pauline by Vieux-Coco.
MIGNON (715) by Jean-le-Blanc (739).

Bred to SANDY 5162 (2225), August 23, 1887.

(Hoof No. 171.) **MAITRESSE 2778** (1560).

[Recorded with pedigree in the Percheron Stud-Books of France and America.]

Grey ; foaled 1877 ; imported 1883 ; got by MADEIRA 1546 (770); dam by VIDOCQ 483 (732).

MADEIRA 1546 (770) by Vidocq 483 (732) out of Jeanne by Favori I (711), he by
 Vieux-Chaslin (713) out of L'Amie by Vieux-Pierre (894), he by Coco (712).
VIDOCQ 483 (732) by Coco II (714) out of a daughter of Chéri, he by Rustique.
Coco II (714) by Vieux-Chaslin (713) out of La Grise by Vieux-Pierre (883).
VIEUX-CHASLIN (713) by Coco (712) out of Poule by Sandi.
Coco (712) by Mignon (715) out of Pauline by Vieux-Coco.
MIGNON (715) by Jean-le-Blanc (739).

Bred to BRILLIANT 1271 (755), October 6, 1887.

(Hoof No. 152.) **MARALIA 2769** (1499).

[Recorded with pedigree in the Percheron Stud-Books of France and America.]

Dark grey ; foaled 1882 ; imported 1883 ; got by ESMERALDA ; dam Madeline by FRENCH MONARCH 205 (734).

FRENCH MONARCH 205 (734) by Ilderim (5302) out of a daughter of Vieux-Pierre
 (894).
ILDERIM (5302) by Valentin (5301) out of Chaton by Vieux-Pierre (894), etc.
VALENTIN (5301) by Vieux-Chaslin (713), he by Coco (712) out of Poule by
 Sandi.
Coco (712) by Mignon (715) out of Pauline by Vieux-Coco.
MIGNON (715) by Jean-le-Blanc (739).

Bred to BRILLIANT 1271 (755), October 4, 1887.

(Hoof No. 301.) **MARGOT 4361** (4230).

[Recorded with pedigree in the Percheron Stud-Books of France and America.]

Black ; foaled March 15, 1883 ; imported 1885 ; bred by M. Blotos, commune of Souday, canton of Mondoubleau, department of Loir-et-Cher ; got by SANSONNET (4593); dam Pelotte (4229) by SANSONNET, belonging to M. Bataille, out of Rosalie.

SANSONNET (4593) by Vigoureux (1392), he by Coco II (714) out of Marguerite
 by Franconi, belonging to M. Sagot.
Coco II (714) by Vieux-Chaslin (713) out of La Grise by Vieux-Pierre (883).
VIEUX-CHASLIN (713) by Coco (712) out of Poule by Sandi.
Coco (712) by Mignon (715) out of Pauline by Vieux-Coco.
MIGNON (715) by Jean-le-Blanc (739).

Bred to LA FERTÉ 5144 (452), October 8, 1887.

(Hoof No. 48.)   **MARGOT 5658 (7021).**

[Recorded with pedigree in the Percheron Stud-Books of France and America.]

Black; foaled May 20, 1885; imported 1886; bred by M. Simon, commune of Ceton, canton of Theil, department of Orne; got by LA FERTÉ 5144 (452); dam Chatton (7020) by BRILLIANT 1271 (755) out of Bijou.

LA FERTÉ 5144 (452) by Philibert (760) out of Julie (7594) by Brilliant 1899 (756).
PHILIBERT (760) by Superior 454 (730) out of Madelon by Vieux-Vaillant (1383), he by Pierre out of a daughter of Vieux-Pierre (883).
SUPERIOR 454 (730) by Favori I (711) out of Pauline by Vieux-Chaslin (713).
FAVORI I (711) by Vieux-Chaslin (713) out of L'Amie by Vieux-Pierre (894), he by Coco (712).
VIEUX-CHASLIN (713) by Coco (712) out of Poule by Sandi.
Coco (712) by Mignon (715) out of Pauline by Vieux-Coco.
MIGNON (715) by Jean-le-Blanc (739).
BRILLIANT 1271 (755) by Brilliant 1899 (756) out of Ragout by Favori I (711), etc.
BRILLIANT 1899 (756) by Coco II (714) out of Rosette by Mina, belonging to the French government.
Coco II (714) by Vieux-Chaslin (713), etc., out of La Grise by Vieux-Pierre (883).

Bred to BRILLIANT 1271 (755), September 15, 1887.

(Hoof No. 287.)   **MARGOT 5662 (1734).**

[Recorded with pedigree in the Percheron Stud-Books of France and America.]

Grey; foaled 1882; imported 1886; bred by M. Surcin, commune of Souancé, canton of Nogent-le-Rotrou, department of Eure-et-Loir; got by BRILLANT (710); dam Rustique (1727) by DÉCIDÉ, belonging to M. L. Perriot, out of Lisette by ROLAND, belonging to the French government.

BRILLANT (710) by Brilliant 1899 (756), out of Sophie by Superior 454 (730), he by Favori I (711) out of Pauline by Vieux-Chaslin (713).
   FAVORI I (711) by Vieux-Chaslin (713) out of L'Amie by Vieux-Pierre (894), he by Coco (712).
BRILLIANT 1899 (756) by Coco II (714) out of Rosette by Mina, belonging to the French government.
Coco II (714) by Vieux-Chaslin (713) out of La Grise by Vieux-Pierre (883).
VIEUX-CHASLIN (713) by Coco (712) out of Poule by Sandi.
Coco (712) by Mignon (715) out of Pauline by Vieux-Coco.
MIGNON (715) by Jean-le-Blanc (739).

Bred to SANDY 5162 (2225), April 18, 1887.

(Hoof No. 229.) **MARTHA 7148 (11965).**

[Recorded with pedigree in the Percheron Stud-Books of France and America.]

Dark grey; foaled March 17, 1886; imported 1887; bred by M. Romet, commune of Cherré, canton of La Ferté-Bernard, department of Sarthe; got by King of Perche 4975 (6738); dam Frosine (11964) by Passe-Partout (1402).

King of Perche 4975 (6738) by Chéri (6441) out of Rustique (6737) by Superior 454 (730), he by Favori I (711) out of Pauline by Vieux-Chaslin (713).
Chéri (6441) by Favora 666 (725) out of Bijou, belonging to M. Simon.
Favora 666 (725) by Favori I (711) out of Marie by Coco (712).
Favori I (711) by Vieux-Chaslin (713) out of L'Amie by Vieux-Pierre (894), he by Coco (712).
Vieux-Chaslin (713) by Coco (712) out of Poule by Sandi.
Coco (712) by Mignon (715) out of Pauline by Vieux-Coco.
Mignon (715) by Jean-le-Blanc (739).
Vidocq 483 (732) by Coco II (714) out of a daughter of Chéri, he by Rustique.
Coco II (714) by Vieux-Chaslin (713) out of La Grise by Vieux-Pierre (883).
Passe-Partout (1402) by Comet 104 (719) out of Sophie by Favori I (711), etc.
Comet 104 (719) by French Monarch 205 (734) out of Suzanne by Cambronne.
French Monarch 205 (734) by Ilderim (5302) out of a daughter of Vieux-Pierre (894), etc.
Ilderim (5302) by Valentin (5301) out of Chaton by Vieux-Pierre (894), etc.
Valentin (5301) by Vieux-Chaslin (713), etc.

(Hoof No. 215.) **MASCOTTE 6927 (4265).**

[Recorded with pedigree in the Percheron Stud-Books of France and America.]

Light dapple grey; foaled April, 1882; imported 1887; bred by M. Gaulard, commune of Coudray-au-Perche, canton of Authon, department of Eure-et-Loir; got by Papillon 3511 (2141); dam Lisette (4263) by Favori, belonging to M. L. Perriot, out of Sophie.

Papillon 3511 (2141) by Marquis 868 (774) out of Sophie by Vidocq 483 (732), he by Coco II (714) out of a daughter of Chéri, he by Rustique.
Coco II (714) by Vieux-Chaslin (713) out of La Grise by Vieux-Pierre (883).
Marquis 868 (774) by Superior 454 (730) out of Bijou by Coco II (714), etc.
Superior 454 (730) by Favori I (711) out of Pauline by Vieux-Chaslin (713).
Favori I (711) by Vieux-Chaslin (713) out of L'Amie by Vieux-Pierre (894), he by Coco (712).
Vieux-Chaslin (713) by Coco (712) out of Poule by Sandi.
Coco (712) by Mignon (715) out of Pauline by Vieux-Coco.
Mignon (715) by Jean-le-Blanc (739).

Bred to Brilliant, August 21, 1887.

(Hoof No. 230.) **MATHILDE 7149 (11927).**

[Recorded with pedigree in the Percheron Stud-Books of France and America.]

Dark grey; foaled January 18, 1886; imported 1887; bred by M. Touzard, commune of St. Calez, canton of Mamers, department of Sarthe; got by Sultan (4713); dam Phrosine (11699) by Coco-Deux (5607).

Sultan (4713) by Bayard (son of Picador) out of Bijou, belonging to M. Lefeuvre.
Coco-Deux (5607) by Coco I, belonging to M. Lefeuvre, out of Charmante.

(Hoof No. 119.)   **MATIE 2795 (1591).**

[Recorded with pedigree in the Percheron Stud-Books of France and America.]

Dapple grey; foaled 1882; imported 1883; got by BRILLIANT 1271 (755); dam by BRILLIANT 1899 (756).

BRILLIANT 1271 (755) by Brilliant 1899 (756) out of Ragout by Favori I (711), he by Vieux-Chaslin (713) out of L'Amie by Vieux-Pierre (894), he by Coco (712).
BRILLIANT 1899 (756) by Coco II (714) out of Rosette by Mina, belonging to the French government.
Coco II (714) by Vieux-Chaslin (713) out of La Grise by Vieux-Pierre (883).
VIEUX-CHASLIN (713) by Coco (712) out of Poule by Sandi.
Coco (712) by Mignon (715) out of Pauline by Vieux-Coco.
MIGNON (715) by Jean-le-Blanc (739).

Bred to LA FERTÉ 5144 (452), September 21, 1887.

(Hoof No. 182.)   **MEDORA 4386.**

[Recorded with pedigree in the Percheron Stud-Book of America.]

Black; foaled April 16, 1885; bred at Oaklawn; got by VIDOCQ 483 (732); dam Mère 2775 (1497) by MOUTON (1640) out of Jeannette by FRENCH MONARCH 205 (734).

VIDOCQ 483 (732) by Coco II (714) out of a daughter of Chéri, he by Rustique.
Coco II (714) by Vieux-Chaslin (713) out of La Grise by Vieux-Pierre (883).
VIEUX-CHASLIN (713) by Coco (712) out of Poule by Sandi.
Coco (712) by Mignon (715) out of Pauline by Vieux-Coco.
MIGNON (715) by Jean-le-Blanc (739).
MOUTON (1640) by French Monarch 205 (734) out of Rose by Décidé.
FRENCH MONARCH 205 (734) by Ilderim (5302) out of a daughter of Vieux-Pierre (894), he by Coco (712).
ILDERIM (5302) by Valentin (5301) out of Chaton by Vieux-Pierre (894), etc.
VALENTIN (5301) by Vieux-Chaslin (713), etc.

Bred to LA FERTÉ 5144 (452), August 12, 1887.

(Hoof No. 132.)   **MÈRE 2775 (1497).**

[Recorded with pedigree in the Percheron Stud-Books of France and America.]

Grey; foaled 1882; imported 1883; got by MOUTON (1640); dam Jeannette by FRENCH MONARCH 205 (734).

MOUTON (1640) by French Monarch 205 (734) out of Rose by Décidé.
FRENCH MONARCH 205 (734) by Ilderim (5302) out of a daughter of Vieux-Pierre (894), he by Coco (712).
ILDERIM (5302) by Valentin (5301) out of Chaton by Vieux-Pierre (894), etc.
VALENTIN (5301) by Vieux-Chaslin (713), he by Coco (712) out of Poule by Sandi.
Coco (712) by Mignon (715) out of Pauline by Vieux-Coco.
MIGNON (715) by Jean-le-Blanc (739).

Bred to BRILLIANT 1271 (755), October 3, 1887.

(Hoof No. 133.) **MERINE 5698.**

[Recorded with pedigree in the Percheron Stud-Book of America.]

Black ; foaled April 15, 1886 ; bred at Oaklawn ; got by Brilliant 1271 (755) ; dam Mère 2775 (1497) by Mouton (1640) out of
Jeannette by French Monarch 205 (734).

Brilliant 1271 (755) by Brilliant 1899 (756) out of Ragout by Favori I (711), he
by Vieux-Chaslin (713) out of L'Amie by Vieux-Pierre (894), he by Coco
(712).
Brilliant 1899 (756) by Coco II (714) out of Rosette by Mina, belonging to the
French government.
Coco II (714) by Vieux-Chaslin (713) out of La Grise by Vieux-Pierre (883).
Vieux-Chaslin (713) by Coco (712) out of Poule by Sandi.
Coco (712) by Mignon (715) out of Pauline by Vieux-Coco.
Mignon (715) by Jean-le-Blanc (739).
Mouton (1640) by French Monarch 205 (734) out of Rose by Décidé.
French Monarch 205 (734) by Ilderim (5302) out of a daughter of Vieux-Pierre
(894), etc.
Ilderim (5302) by Valentin (5301) out of Chaton by Vieux-Pierre (894), etc.
Valentin (5301) by Vieux-Chaslin (713), etc.

(Hoof No. 271.) **MERIT 7326.**

[Recorded with pedigree in the Percheron Stud-Book of America.]

Grey black ; foaled September 24, 1887 ; bred at Oaklawn ; got by
Brilliant 1271 (755); dam Mere 2775 (1497) by Mouton (1640); 2d
dam Jeannette by French Monarch 205 (734).

Brilliant 1271 (755) by Brilliant 1899 (756) out of Ragout by Favori I (711),
he by Vieux-Chaslin (713) out of L'Amie by Vieux-Pierre (894), he by
Coco (712).
Brilliant 1899 (756) by Coco II (714) out of Rosette by Mina, belonging to the
French government.
Coco II (714) by Vieux-Chaslin (713) out of La Grise by Vieux-Pierre (883).
Vieux-Chaslin (713) by Coco (712) out of Poule by Sandi.
Coco (712) by Mignon (715) out of Pauline by Vieux-Coco.
Mignon (715) by Jean-le-Blanc (739).
Mouton (1640) by French Monarch 205 (734) out of Rose by Décidé, belonging
to M. Vinault.
French Monarch 205 (734) by Ilderim (5302) out of a daughter of Vieux-Pierre
(894), he by Coco (712), etc.
Ilderim (5302) by Valentin (5301) out of Chaton by Vieux-Pierre (894), etc.
Valentin (5301) by Vieux-Chaslin (713), etc.

(Hoof No. 193.) **MIGNONNE 4349 (2962).**

[Recorded with pedigree in the Percheron Stud-Books of France and America.]

Black ; foaled April 15, 1881 ; imported 1885 ; bred by M. Duval,
commune of St. Germain-de-la-Coudre, canton of Theil, department of
Orne ; got by Brilliant 1271 (755); dam Lisette (5094) by Favori
(4770) out of Blanchette.

Brilliant 1271 (755) by Brilliant 1899 (756) out of Ragout by Favori I (711).
Brilliant 1899 (756) by Coco II (714) out of Rosette by Mina, belonging to
the French government.
Coco II (714) by Vieux-Chaslin (713) out of La Grise by Vieux-Pierre (883).
Vieux-Chaslin (713) by Coco (712) out of Poule by Sandi.
Coco (712) by Mignon (715) out of Pauline by Vieux-Coco.
Mignon (715) by Jean-le-Blanc (739).
Favori (4770) by Superior 454 (730), he by Favori I (711) out of Pauline by
Vieux-Chaslin (713), etc.
Favori I (711) by Vieux-Chaslin (713), etc., out of L'Amie by Vieux-Pierre
(894) he by Coco (712), etc.

Bred to La Ferté 5144 (452), September 16, 1887.

(Hoof No. 145.)   **MILDA 2806 (1542).**

[Recorded with pedigree in the Percheron Stud-Books of France and America.]

Grey ; foaled 1881 ; imported 1883 ; got by MADEIRA 1546 (770);
dam by VIDOCQ 483 (732).

MADEIRA 1546 (770) by Vidocq 483 (732) out of Jeanne by Favori I (711), he by
      Vieux-Chaslin (713) out of L'Amie by Vieux-Pierre (894), he by Coco (712).
VIDOCQ 483 (732) by Coco II (714) out of a daughter of Chéri, he by Rustique.
COCO II (714) by Vieux-Chaslin (713) out of La Grise by Vieux-Pierre (883).
VIEUX-CHASLIN (713) by Coco (712) out of Poule by Sandi.
COCO (712) by Mignon (715) out of Pauline by Vieux-Coco.
MIGNON (715) by Jean-le-Blanc (739).

Bred to BRILLIANT 1271 (755), April 27, 1887.

(Hoof No 115.)   **MINDA 2354 (1514).**

[Recorded with pedigree in the Percheron Stud-Books of France and America.]

Light dapple grey ; foaled 1877 ; imported 1883 ; got by BRILLIANT
1899 (756); dam Frisette by FRENCH MONARCH 205 (734).

BRILLIANT 1899 (756) by Coco II (714), out of Rosette by Mina, belonging to the
      French government.
COCO II (714) by Vieux-Chaslin (713) out of La Grise by Vieux-Pierre (883).
VIEUX-CHASLIN (713) by Coco (712) out of Poule by Sandi.
COCO (712) by Mignon (715) out of Pauline by Vieux-Coco.
MIGNON (715) by Jean-le-Blanc (739).
FRENCH MONARCH 205 (734) by Ilderim (5302) out of a daughter of Vieux-
      Pierre (894), he by Coco (712), etc.
ILDERIM (5302) by Valentin (5301) out of Chaton by Vieux-Pierre (894), etc.
VALENTIN (5301) by Vieux-Chaslin (713), etc.

Bred to BRILLIANT 1271 (755), May 30, 1887.

(Hoof No. 237.)   **MINETTE 7150 (4059).**

[Recorded with pedigree in the Percheron Stud-Books of France and America.]

Grey ; foaled May 20, 1884 ; imported 1887 ; bred by M. Th.
Bourdin, commune of Igé, canton of Bellême, department of Orne ;
got by GÉROME 3655 (436); dam Lisette (4056) by VIDOCQ 483 (732)
out of Rose.

GÉROME 3655 (436) by Vidocq II (723) out of Pelote by Superior 454 (730), he
      by Favori I (711) out of Pauline by Vieux-Chaslin (713).
   FAVORI I (711) by Vieux-Chaslin (713) out of L'Amie by Vieux-Pierre (894),
      he by Coco (712).
VIDOCQ II (723) by Bayard (1385) ont of Brière by Décidé.
BAYARD (1385) by Vidocq 483 (732) out of La Noire by Chéri, he by Coco II
      (714).
VIDOCQ 483 (732) by Coco II (714) out of a daughter of Chéri, he by Rustique.
COCO II (714) by Vieux-Chaslin (713) out of La Grise by Vieux-Pierre (883).
VIEUX-CHASLIN (713) by Coco (712) out of Poule by Sandi.
COCO (712) by Mignon (715) out of Pauline by Vieux-Coco.
MIGNON (715) by Jean-le-Blanc (739).

Bred to MALAKOFF (8275), May 7, 1887.

(Hoof No. 207.) **MIRA 7146 (8627).**

[Recorded with pedigree in the Percheron Stud-Books of France and America.]

Blue grey; foaled March 15, 1884; imported 1887; bred by M. François Guillet, commune of La Ferté-Bernard, department of Sarthe; got by Mouton (1640); dam Sophie (8626) by Pierre, belonging to M. Benoist.

Mouton (1640) by French Monarch 205 (734) out of Rose by Décidé.
French Monarch 205 (734) by Ilderim (5302) out of a daughter of Vieux-Pierre (894), he by Coco (712).
Ilderim (5302) by Valentin (5301) out of Chaton by Vieux-Pierre (894), etc.
Valentin (5301) by Vieux-Chaslin (713), he by Coco (712) out of Poule by Sandi.
Coco (712) by Mignon (715) out of Pauline by Vieux-Coco.
Mignon (715) by Jean-le-Blanc (739).

Bred to La Ferté 5144 (452), July 3, 1887.

(Hoof No. 183.) **MIRANE 4379.**

[Recorded with pedigree in the Percheron Stud-Book of America.]

Black; foaled April 2, 1885; bred at Oaklawn; got by Brilliant 1271 (755); dam Millicent 2791 (1578) by Chalumeau; 2d dam by Favora 666 (725).

Brilliant 1271 (755) by Brilliant 1899 (756) out of Ragout by Favori I (711).
Brilliant 1899 (756) by Coco II (714) out of Rosette by Mina, belonging to the French government.
Coco II (714) by Vieux-Chaslin (713) out of La Grise by Vieux-Pierre (883).
Vieux-Chaslin (713) by Coco (712) out of Poule by Sandi.
Coco (712) by Mignon (715) out of Pauline by Vieux-Coco.
Mignon (715) by Jean-le-Blanc (739).
Favora 666 (725) by Favori I (711) out of Marie by Coco (712), etc.
Favori I (711) by Vieux-Chaslin (713), etc., out of L'Amie by Vieux-Pierre (894), he by Coco (712), etc.

Bred to La Ferté 5144 (452), August 18, 1887.

(Hoof No. 210.) **MISS 7147 (10083).**

[Recorded with pedigree in the Percheron Stud-Books of France and America.]

Black; foaled March 9, 1886; imported 1887; bred by M. Cournard, commune of Dehault, canton of La Ferté-Bernard, department of Sarthe; got by Henri le Blanc 4542 (2433), dam Poule (10082) by Comet 104 (719).

Henri le Blanc 4542 (2433) by Rustique, belonging to M. Sagot, out of Malice, belonging to M. Girard.
Comet 104 (719) by French Monarch 205 (734) out of Suzanne by Cambronne.
French Monarch 205 (734) by Ilderim (5302) out of a daughter of Vieux-Pierre (894), he by Coco (712).
Ilderim (5302) by Valentin (5301) out of Chaton by Vieux-Pierre (894), etc.
Valentin (5301) by Vieux-Chaslin (713), he by Coco (712) out of Poule by Sandi.
Coco (712) by Mignon (715) out of Pauline by Vieux-Coco.
Mignon (715) by Jean-le-Blanc (739).

(Hoof No. 241.)   **MLLE. D'AUGUAISE 7151 (2171).**

[Recorded with pedigree in the Percheron Stud-Books of France and America.]

Dapple grey; foaled April 10, 1880; imported 1887; bred by M. Fleury, commune of Auguaise, canton of Moulins, department of Orne; got by BRILLANT (6165); dam Bijou (6168) by SANSONNET, belonging to the French government, out of Bicotte.

BRILLANT (6165) by Brillant, belonging to M. Jousset, out of Vaillante by Vaillant.

Bred in France to SULTAN (1400).

(Hoof No. 244.)   **MOUVANTE 7163 (10303).**

[Recorded with pedigree in the Percheron Stud-Books of France and America.]

Black; foaled April 1, 1884; imported 1887; bred by M. Lubrun, commune of Marchemaisons, canton of Mêsle-sur-Sarthe, department of Orne; got by CHÉRI 2384 (18); dam Bijou (10302) by MARGOT, belonging to M. Vallée.

CHÉRI 2384 (18) by Favora 1542 (765) out of Joséphine by Valentine, be by Décidé, he by Favori I (711), he by Vieux-Chaslin (713) out of L'Amie by Vieux-Pierre (894), he by Coco (712).
FAVORA 1542 (765) by French Monarch 205 (734) out of Marguerite by Favori, he by Coco of Mésle-sur-Sarthe, he by Margot, belonging to M. Vallée.
FRENCH MONARCH 205 (734) by Ilderim (5302) out of a daughter of Vieux-Pierre (894), etc.
ILDERIM (5302) by Valentin (5301) out of Chaton by Vieux-Pierre (894), etc.
VALENTIN (5301) by Vieux-Chaslin (713), he by Coco (712) out of Poule by Sandi.
Coco (712) by Mignon (715) out of Pauline by Vieux-Coco.
MIGNON (715) by Jean-le-Blanc (739).

Bred in France to ATILLA 7015 (6201).

(Hoof No. 153.)   **NIAMI 2229 (1455).**

[Recorded with pedigree in the Percheron Stud-Books of France and America.]

Dapple grey; foaled 1882; imported 1882; got by AVATA 1966 (912); dam by DÉCIDÉ 126 (720).

AVATA 1966 (912) by Nogent 738 (729) out of Bicotte by Bayard 26 (717), he by Favori I (711) out of Mignonne by Chéri.
NOGENT 738 (729) by Vidocq 483 (732) out of a daughter of Favori I (711).
VIDOCQ 483 (732) by Coco II (714) out of a daughter of Chéri, he by Rustique.
Coco II (714) by Vieux-Chaslin (713) out of La Grise by Vieux-Pierre (883).
VIEUX-CHASLIN (713) by Coco (712) out of Poule by Sandi.
Coco (712) by Mignon (715) out of Pauline by Vieux-Coco.
MIGNON (715) by Jean-le-Blanc (739).
DÉCIDÉ 126 (720) by Superior 454 (730), he by Favori I (711) out of Pauline by Vieux-Chaslin (713), etc.
FAVORI I (711) by Vieux-Chaslin (713), etc., out of L'Amie by Vieux-Pierre (894), he by Coco (712), etc.

Bred to BRILLIANT 1271 (755), August 30, 1887.

(Hoof No. 304.) **NITA 3671.**

[Recorded with pedigree in the Percheron Stud-Book of America.]

Dark grey; foaled 1884; bred at Oaklawn; got by BRILLIANT 1271 (755); dam Navolia 2209 (1454) by WATERLOO 2199 (733) out of a daughter of PORTHOS.

BRILLIANT 1271 (755) by Brilliant 1899 (756) out of Ragout by Favori I (711), he by Vieux-Chaslin (713) out of L'Amie by Vieux-Pierre (894), he by Coco 712.
BRILLIANT 1899 (756) by Coco II (714), etc., out of Rosette by Mina, belonging to the French government.
Coco II (714) by Vieux-Chaslin (713), etc., out of La Grise by Vieux-Pierre (883).
VIEUX-CHASLIN (713) by Coco (712) out of Poule by Sandi.
Coco (712) by Mignon (715) out of Pauline by Vieux-Coco.
MIGNON (715) by Jean-le-Blanc (739).
WATERLOO 2199 (733) by Jean-Bart (716) out of Poule, belonging to M. Bourdin.
JEAN-BART (716) by Bayard, belonging to M. Perpère, out of Jeanne by Porthos.

Bred to LA FERTÉ 5144 (452), August 16, 1887.

(Hoof No. 257.) **NITANTE 7325.**

[Recorded with pedigree in the Percheron Stud-Book of America.]

Black; foaled May 10, 1887; bred at Oaklawn; got by PRODUCTEUR 4280 (68); dam Nita 3671 by BRILLIANT 1271 (755); 2d dam Navolia 2209 (1454) by WATERLOO 2199 (733); 3d dam by PORTHOS.

PRODUCTEUR 4280 (68) by Madeira 1546 (770) out of Gentille (4062) by Porthos.
MADEIRA 1546 (770) by Vidocq 483 (732) out of Jeanne by Favori I (711), he by Vieux-Chaslin (713) out of L'Amie by Vieux-Pierre (894), he by Coco (712).
VIDOCQ 483 (732) by Coco II (714) out of a daughter of Chéri, he by Rustique.
Coco II (714) by Vieux-Chaslin (713) out of La Grise by Vieux-Pierre (883).
VIEUX-CHASLIN (713) by Coco (712) out of Poule by Sandi.
Coco (712) by Mignon (715) out of Pauline by Vieux-Coco.
MIGNON (715) by Jean-le-Blanc (739).
BRILLIANT 1271 (755) by Brilliant 1899 (756) out of Ragout by Favori I (711), etc.
BRILLIANT 1899 (756) by Coco II (714), etc., out of Rosette by Mina, belonging to the French government.
WATERLOO 2199 (733) by Jean-Bart (716) out of Poule, belonging to M. Bourdin.
JEAN-BART (716) by Bayard, belonging to M. Perpère, out of Jeanne by Porthos.

(Hoof No. 256.) **NORA 7324.**

[Recorded with pedigree in the Percheron Stud-Book of America.]

Brown bay; foaled March 24, 1887; bred at Oaklawn; got by BRILLIANT 1271 (755); dam Norvaline 2233 (1457) by NORVAL 1369 (794) out of Poule by Coco II (714).

BRILLIANT 1271 (755) by Brilliant 1899 (756) out of Ragout by Favori I (711), he by Vieux-Chaslin (713) out of L'Amie by Vieux-Pierre (894), he by Coco (712).
BRILLIANT 1899 (756) by Coco II (714) out of Rosette by Mina, belonging to the French government.
Coco II (714) by Vieux-Chaslin (713) out of La Grise by Vieux-Pierre (883).
VIEUX-CHASLIN (713) by Coco (712) out of Poule by Sandi.
Coco (712) by Mignon (715) out of Pauline by Vieux-Coco.
MIGNON (715) by Jean-le-Blanc (739).
NORVAL 1369 (794) by Brilliant 1899 (756), etc., out of Frosine by Décidé, belonging to M. Fardouet.

(Hoof No. 134.)   **NORVALINE 2233 (1457).**

[Recorded with pedigree in the Percheron Stud-Books of France and America.]

Brown bay; foaled 1882; imported 1882; got by NORVAL 1369 (794); dam Poule by Coco II (714).

NORVAL 1369 (794) by Brilliant 1899 (756) out of Frosine by Décidé, belonging to M. Fardouet.
BRILLIANT 1899 (756) by Coco II (714) out of Rosette by Mina, belonging to the French government.
Coco II (714) by Vieux-Chaslin (713) out of La Grise by Vieux-Pierre (883).
VIEUX-CHASLIN (713) by Coco (712) out of Poule by Sandi.
Coco (712) by Mignon (715) out of Pauline by Vieux-Coco.
MIGNON (715) by Jean-le-Blanc (739).

Bred to BRILLIANT 1271 (755), May 3, 1887.

(Hoof No. 135.)   **NORVETTE 5699.**

[Recorded with pedigree in the Percheron Stud-Book of America.]

Bay; foaled March 28, 1886; bred at Oaklawn; got by BRILLIANT 1271 (755); dam Norvaline 2233 (1457) by NORVAL 1369 (794) out of Poule by Coco II (714).

BRILLIANT 1271 (755) by Brilliant 1899 (756) out of Ragout by Favori I (711), he by Vieux-Chaslin (713) out of L'Amie by Vieux-Pierre (894), he by Coco (712).
BRILLIANT 1899 (756) by Coco II (714) out of Rosette by Mina, belonging to the French government.
Coco II (714) by Vieux-Chaslin (713) out of La Grise by Vieux-Pierre (883).
VIEUX-CHASLIN (713) by Coco (712) out of Poule by Sandi.
Coco (712) by Mignon (715) out of Pauline by Vieux-Coco.
MIGNON (715) by Jean-le-Blanc (739).
NORVAL 1369 (794) by Brilliant 1899 (756), etc., out of Frosine by Décidé, belonging to M. Fardouet.

(Hoof No. 108.)   **NUDA 2761 (1491).**

[Recorded with pedigree in the Percheron Stud-Books of France and America.]

Black; foaled 1881; imported 1883; got by IAGO 995 (768); dam by DÉCIDÉ 126 (720).

IAGO 995 (768) by Utopia 780 (731) out of Cossette by Favora 666 (725), he by Favori I (711) out of Marie by Coco (712).
UTOPIA 780 (731) by Superior 454 (730) out of Camille by Favori I (711).
SUPERIOR 454 (730) by Favori I (711) out of Pauline by Vieux-Chaslin (713).
FAVORI I (711) by Vieux-Chaslin (713) out of L'Amie by Vieux-Pierre (894), he by Coco (712).
VIEUX-CHASLIN (713) by Coco (712) out of Poule by Sandi.
Coco (712) by Mignon (715) out of Pauline by Vieux-Coco.
MIGNON (715) by Jean-le-Blanc (739).
DÉCIDÉ 126 (720) by Superior 454 (730), etc.

Bred to BRILLIANT 1271 (755), September 8, 1887.

(Hoof No. 265.)   **NUDINE 7323.**

[Recorded with pedigree in the Percheron Stud-Book of America.]

Black ; foaled September 2, 1887 ; bred at Oaklawn ; got by BRILL-IANT 1271 (755) ; dam Nuda 2761 (1491) by IAGO 995 (768) out of a daughter of DÉCIDÉ 126 (720).

BRILLIANT 1271 (755) by Brilliant 1899 (756) out of Ragout by Favori I (711).
BRILLIANT 1899 (756) by Coco II (714) out of Rosette by Mina, belonging to the French government.
Coco II (714) by Vieux-Chaslin (713) out of La Grise by Vieux-Pierre (883).
VIEUX-CHASLIN (713) by Coco (712) out of Poule by Sandi.
Coco (712) by Mignon (715) out of Pauline by Vieux-Coco.
MIGNON (715) by Jean-le-Blanc (739).
IAGO 995 (768) by Utopia 780 (731) out of Cossette by Favora 666 (725), he by Favori I (711) out of Marie by Coco (712), etc.
UTOPIA 780 (731) by Superior 454 (730) out of Camille by Favori I (711).
SUPERIOR 454 (730) by Favori I (711) out of Pauline by Vieux-Chaslin (713), etc.
FAVORI I (711) by Vieux-Chaslin (713), etc., out of L'Amie by Vieux-Pierre (894), he by Coco (712), etc.
DÉCIDÉ 126 (720) by Superior 454 (730), etc.

(Hoof No. 204.)   **ONDINE 7152 (8839).**

[Recorded with pedigree in the Percheron Stud-Books of France and America.]

Dark grey ; foaled April 1, 1885 ; imported 1887 ; bred by M. P. Vadé, commune of Vibraye, department of Sarthe ; got by PASSE-A-PIC (2403) ; dam Sophie III (6937) by L'AMIE (1388) out of Sophie, belonging to M. Vadé.

PASSE-A-PIC (2403) by Passe-Partout (1402) out of Boule by Colin-Roux.
PASSE-PARTOUT (1402) by Comet 104 (719) out of Sophie by Favori I (711), he by Vieux-Chaslin (713) out of L'Amie by Vieux-Pierre (894) he by Coco (712).
COMET 104 (719) by French Monarch 205 (734) out of Suzanne by Cambronne.
FRENCH MONARCH 205 (734) by Ilderim (5302) out of a daughter of Vieux-Pierre (894), etc.
ILDERIM (5302) by Valentin (5301) out of Chaton by Vieux-Pierre (894), etc.
VALENTIN (5301) by Vieux-Chaslin (713), he by Coco (712) out of Poule by Sandi.
Coco (712) by Mignon (715) out of Pauline by Vieux-Coco.
MIGNON (715) by Jean-le-Blanc (739).
L'AMI (1388) by Coco [son of Coco II (714)] out of Percheronne, belonging to M. Lucas.
Coco II (714) by Vieux-Chaslin (713), etc., out of La Grise by Vieux-Pierre (883).

Bred to STRADAT 7112 (2463), May 29, 1887.

(Hoof No. 23.)   **PALLAS 5636 (2258).**

[Recorded with pedigree in the Percheron Stud-Books of France and America.]

Dark grey ; foaled February 18, 1884 ; imported 1886 ; bred by M. Désiré Ducœurjoly, commune of Brunelles, canton of Nogent-le-Rotrou, department of Eure-et-Loir ; got by MADÈRE II (2994); dam Pauline by MIRAMAR out of Rustique.

MADÈRE II (2994) by Madeira 1545 (770), he by Vidocq 483 (732) out of Jeanne by Favori I (711), he by Vieux-Chaslin (713) out of L'Amie by Vieux-Pierre (894), he by Coco (712).
VIDOCQ 483 (732) by Coco II (714) out of a daughter of Chéri, he by Rustique.
Coco II (714) by Vieux-Chaslin (713) out of La Grise by Vieux-Pierre (883).
VIEUX-CHASLIN (713) by Coco (712) out of Poule by Sandi.
Coco (712) by Mignon (715) out of Pauline by Vieux-Coco.
MIGNON (715) by Jean-le-Blanc (739).

Bred to BRILLIANT 1271 (755), September 12, 1887.

(Hoof No. 143.)   **PALMA 4359 (4929).**

[Recorded with pedigree in the Percheron Stud-Books of France and America.]

Dapple grey ; foaled May 15, 1882 ; imported 1885 ; bred by M. Denis, commune of Alençon, department of Orne ; got by ROMULUS, belonging to M. Lalouet ; dam Rosette (4928) by ROMULUS 873 (785) out of Cocotte, belonging to M. Foulon.

ROMULUS 873 (785) by the government approved stallion Romulus (son of Moreuil) out of Fleur-d'Épine by the government approved stallion Chéri, he by Corbon.

Bred to BRILLIANT 1271 (755), June 10, 1887.

(Hoof No. 22.)   **PANDORA 5635 (6669).**

[Recorded with pedigree in the Percheron Stud-Books of France and America.]

Black ; foaled May 22, 1883 ; imported 1886 ; bred by M. Maillard, commune of Marolles-les-Buits, canton of Thiron, department of Eure-et-Loir ; got by BIENFAISANT (1397); dam Faisante (2254) by VAILL-ANT (2255) out of Câline by FLEURI, belonging to M. Sagot.

BIENFAISANT (1397) by Vermouth 1820 (787) out of Rustique by Favori I (711), he by Vieux-Chaslin (713) out of L'Amie by Vieux-Pierre (894), he by Coco (712).
VERMOUTH 1820 (787) by Vidocq 483 (732) out of Agathe by Vieux-Chaslin (713).
VIDOCQ 483 (732) by Coco II (714) out of a daughter of Chéri, he by Rustique.
Coco II (714) by Vieux-Chaslin (713) out of La Grise by Vieux-Pierre (883).
VIEUX-CHASLIN (713) by Coco (712) out of Poule by Sandi.
Coco (712) by Mignon (715) out of Pauline by Vieux-Coco.
MIGNON (715) by Jean-le-Blanc (739).
VAILLANT (2255) by Orizaba, belonging to M. Lalouet, out of Pauline (279) by Miramar.

Bred to BRILLIANT 1271 (755), May 5, 1887.

(Hoof No. 223.)   **PANDORE 7153 (10780).**

[Recorded with pedigree in the Percheron Stud-Books of France and America.]

Dark grey ; foaled February 27, 1886 ; imported 1887 ; bred by Madame Guillemin, commune of Berd'huis, canton of Nocé, department of Orne ; got by MADRID 5153 (441); dam Bijou (10779) by VIDOCQ 1917 (1084).

MADRID 5153 (441) by Avata 1966 (912) out of Jeannette (7597) by Vidocq 483 (732).
AVATA 1966 (912) by Nogent 738 (729) out of Bicotte by Bayard 26 (717), he by Favori I (711) out of Mignonne by Chéri.
 FAVORI I (711) by Vieux-Chaslin (713) out of L'Amie by Vieux-Pierre (894), he by Coco (712).
NOGENT 738 (729) by Vidocq 483 (732) out of a daughter of Favori I (711), etc.
VIDOCQ 483 (732) by Coco II (714) out of a daughter of Chéri, he by Rustique.
Coco II (714) by Vieux-Chaslin (713) out of La Grise by Vieux-Pierre (883).
VIEUX-CHASLIN (713) by Coco (712) out of Poule by Sandi.
Coco (712) by Mignon (715) out of Pauline by Vieux-Coco.
MIGNON (715) by Jean-le-Blanc (739).
VIDOCQ 1917 (1084) by Nogent 738 (729), etc., out of Fannie by Bayard 26 (717), etc.

(Hoof No. 73.) **PAQUERETTE 5680 (6834).**

[Recorded with pedigree in the Percheron Stud-Books of France and America.]

Black; foaled May 5, 1882; imported 1886; bred by M. Duval, commune of St. Germain-de-la-Coudre, canton of Theil, department of Orne; got by BRILLIANT 1271 (755); dam Lisette (5094) by FAVORI (4770) out of Blanchette.

BRILLIANT 1271 (755) by Brilliant 1899 (756) out of Ragout by Favori I (711).
BRILLIANT 1899 (756) by Coco II (714) out of Rosette by Mina, belonging to the French government.
Coco II (714) by Vieux-Chaslin (713) out of La Grise by Vieux-Pierre (883).
VIEUX-CHASLIN (713) by Coco (712) out of Poule by Sandi.
Coco (712) by Mignon (715) out of Pauline by Vieux-Coco.
MIGNON (715) by Jean-le-Blanc (739).
FAVORI (4770) by Superior 454 (736), he by Favori I (711) out of Pauline by Vieux-Chaslin (713), etc.
FAVORI I (711) by Vieux-Chaslin (713), etc., out of L'Amie by Vieux-Pierre (894), he by Coco (712), etc.

Bred to LA FERTÉ 5144 (452), June 27, 1887.

(Hoof No. 164.) **PECADIE 4356 (1712).**

[Recorded with pedigree in the Percheron Stud-Books of France and America.]

Dapple grey; foaled 1881; imported 1885; bred by M. Luvignon, commune of Cherreau, canton of La Ferté-Bernard, department of Sarthe; got by BRILLIANT 1271 (755); dam L'Amie (4948) by BAYARD 26 (717) out of Sophie, belonging to M. Guignon.

BRILLIANT 1271 (755) by Brilliant 1899 (756) out of Ragout by Favori I (711).
BRILLIANT 1899 (756) by Coco II (714) out of Rosette by Mina, belonging to the French government.
Coco II (714) by Vieux-Chaslin (713) out of La Grise by Vieux-Pierre (883).
VIEUX-CHASLIN (713) by Coco (712) out of Poule by Sandi.
Coco (712) by Mignon (715) out of Pauline by Vieux-Coco.
MIGNON (715) by Jean-le-Blanc (739).
BAYARD 26 (717) by Favori I (711) out of Mignonne by Chéri.
FAVORI I (711) by Vieux-Chaslin (713), etc., out of L'Amie by Vieux-Pierre (894), he by Coco (712), etc.

Bred to LA FÉRTÉ 5144 (452), April 28, 1887.

(Hoof No. 296.) **PEERLESS 5222.**

[Recorded with pedigree in the Percheron Stud-Book of America.]

Black; foaled May 10, 1886; bred by Brickman & Baker, of Rednerville, Ontario; got by ROMULUS 1300; dam Pelotte 3659 (1809) by BAPTISTE, he by COMET 104 (719): 2d dam Margot by VIEUX-VAILLANT (1383).

COMET 104 (719) by French Monarch 205 (734) out of Suzanne by Cambronne.
FRENCH MONARCH 205 (734) by Ilderim (5302) out of a daughter of Vieux-Pierre (894), he by Coco (712).
ILDERIM (5302) by Valentin (5301) out of Chaton by Vieux-Pierre (894), etc.
VALENTIN (5301) by Vieux-Chaslin (713), he by Coco (712) out of Poule by Sandi.
Coco (712) by Mignon (715) out of Pauline by Vieux-Coco.
MIGNON (715) by Jean-le-Blanc (739).
VIEUX-VAILLANT (1383) by Pierre, belonging to M. Thérin, out of a daughter of Vieux-Pierre (883).

150 M. W. DUNHAM'S CATALOGUE

(Hoof No. 312.) **PELOTTE 4369 (1923).**
[Recorded with pedigree in the Percheron Stud-Books of France and America.]

Dark dapple grey; foaled March 20, 1883; imported 1885; bred by M. Ferdinand Garreau, commune of St. Pierre-la-Bruyère, canton of Nocé, department of Orne; got by VAILLANT (404); dam Rustique (1924) by VIEUX-VAILLANT (1383) out of Pelote by PIERRE, belonging to M. Thérin.

VAILLANT (404) by Prosper (893) out of Rosalie by Bienvenu, belonging to the Société Hippique of Eure-et-Loir.
PROSPER (893) by Décidé (892) out of Bourreau by Vieux-Pierre (883).
DÉCIDÉ (892) by Vieux-Pierre (894) out of Pelote, belonging to M. Berjeau, of Courvalien.
VIEUX-PIERRE (894) by Coco (712), he by Mignon (715) out of Pauline by Vieux-Coco.
MIGNON (715) by Jean-le-Blanc (739).
VIEUX-VAILLANT (1383) by Pierre, belonging to M. Thérin, out of a daughter of Vieux-Pierre (883).

Bred to BRILLIANT 1271 (755), August 12, 1887.

(Hoof No. 236.) **PELOTTE 6928 (157).**
[Recorded with pedigree in the Percheron Stud-Books of France and America.

Reddish dapple grey; foaled 1883; imported 1887; bred by M. Gouhier, commune of Colonard, canton of Nocé, department of Orne; got by AVATA 1966 (912); dam Bijou, belonging to M. Gouhier, by CHÉRI, he by Coco II (714).

AVATA 1966 (912) by Nogent 738 (729) out of Bicotte by Bayard 26 (717), he by Favori I (711) out of Mignonne by Chéri.
FAVORI I (711) by Vieux-Chaslin (713) out of L'Amie by Vieux-Pierre (894), he by Coco (712).
NOGENT 738 (729) by Vidocq 483 (732) out of a daughter of Favori I (711), etc.
VIDOCQ 483 (732) by Coco II (714) out of a daughter of Chéri, he by Rustique.
COCO II (714) by Vieux-Chaslin (713) out of La Grise by Vieux-Pierre (883).
VIEUX-CHASLIN (713) by Coco (712) out of Poule by Sandi.
COCO (712) by Mignon (715) out of Pauline by Vieux-Coco.
MIGNON (715) by Jean-le-Blanc (739).

Bred in France to BRUTUS 6941 (6019).

(Hoof No. 75.) **PELOUTE 5341 (4962).**
[Recorded with pedigree in the Percheron Stud-Books of France and America.]

Dark dapple grey; foaled March 1, 1883; imported 1886; bred by Madame Poussin, commune of Ceton, canton of Theil, department of Orne; got by CHARTRAIN (1405); dam Cocotte (4961) by BRILLIANT 1899 (756) out of Margot.

CHARTRAIN (1405) by Philibert (760) out of Cocotte by Coco II (714).
PHILIBERT (760) by Superior 454 (730) out of Madelon by Vieux-Vaillant (1383), he by Pierre out of a daughter of Vieux-Pierre (883).
SUPERIOR 454 (730) by Favori I (711) out of Pauline by Vieux-Chaslin (713).
FAVORI I (711) by Vieux-Chaslin (713) out of L'Amie by Vieux-Pierre (894), he by Coco (712).
VIEUX-CHASLIN (713) by Coco (712) out of Poule by Sandi.
COCO (712) by Mignon (715) out of Pauline by Vieux-Coco.
MIGNON (715) by Jean-le-Blanc (739).
BRILLIANT 1899 (756) by Coco II (714), etc., out of Rosette by Mina, belonging to the French government.
COCO II (714) by Vieux-Chaslin (713), etc., out of La Grise by Vieux-Pierre (883).

Bred to BRILLIANT 1271 (755), April 12, 1887.

(Hoof No. 288.) **POULETTE 5615 (6713).**

[Recorded with pedigree in the Percheron Stud-Books of France and America.]

Light dapple grey; foaled February 5, 1883; imported 1886; bred by M. Gautier, commune of Marcei, canton of Mortrée, department of Orne; got by VIDOCQ (1403); dam Rosette (5273) by MONDOUBLEAU out of Coquette, belonging to M. Gautier père.

VIDOCQ (1403) by Utopia 780 (731) out of Bijou by Vieux-Chaslin (713).
UTOPIA 780 (731) by Superior 454 (730) out of Camille by Favori I (711).
SUPERIOR 454 (730) by Favori I (711) out of Pauline by Vieux-Chaslin (713).
FAVORI I (711) by Vieux-Chaslin (713) out of L'Amie by Vieux-Pierre (894), he by Coco (712).
VIEUX-CHASLIN (713) by Coco (712) out of Poule by Sandi.
Coco (712) by Mignon (715) out of Pauline by Vieux-Coco.
MIGNON (715) by Jean-le-Blanc (739).

Bred to SANDY 5162 (2225), April 19, 1887.

(Hoof No. 1.) **POULOTTE 5614 (6677).**

[Recorded with pedigree in the Percheron Stud-Books of France and America.]

Black; foaled March 25, 1883; imported 1886; bred by M. Gouhier, commune of Coulonges-les-Sablons, canton of Rémalard, department of Orne; got by THOMAS (4786); dam Brebis (4941) by VIDOCQ (1403) out of Biche.

THOMAS (4786) by Sansonnet, belonging to M. Bellessort, out of Bijou, belonging to M. Boiteau.
VIDOCQ (1403) by Utopia 780 (731) out of Bijou by Vieux-Chaslin (713).
UTOPIA 780 (731) by Superior 454 (730) out of Camille by Favori I (711).
SUPERIOR 454 (730) by Favori I (711) out of Pauline by Vieux-Chaslin (713).
FAVORI I (711) by Vieux-Chaslin (713) out of L'Amie by Vieux-Pierre (894), he by Coco (712).
VIEUX-CHASLIN (713) by Coco (712) out of Poule by Sandi.
Coco (712) by Mignon (715) out of Pauline by Vieux-Coco.
MIGNON (715) by Jean-le-Blanc (739).

Bred to LA FERTÉ 5144 (452), August 17, 1887.

(Hoof No. 310.) **PROFUSION 5664 (6614).**

[Recorded with pedigree in the Percheron Stud-Books of France and America.]

Grey; foaled April 6, 1884; imported 1886; bred by M. Thibault, commune of Nogent-le-Rotrou, department of Eure-et-Loir; got by BAYARD 3555 (687); dam Poule (1752) by PERCHERON, belonging to M. Sagot, out of Brebis, belonging to M. Thibault.

BAYARD 3555 (687) by Narbonne 1334 (777) out of Ragotte by Bon Cœur d'Amilly.
NARBONNE 1334 (777) by Brilliant 1899 (756) out of Madelon (4722) by Favori I (711), he by Vieux-Chaslin (713) out of L'Amie by Vieux-Pierre (894), he by Coco (712).
BRILLIANT 1899 (756) by Coco II (714) out of Rosette by Mina, belonging to the French government.
Coco II (714) by Vieux-Chaslin (713) out of La Grise by Vieux-Pierre (883).
VIEUX-CHASLIN (713) by Coco (712) out of Poule by Sandi.
Coco (712) by Mignon (715) out of Pauline by Vieux-Coco.
MIGNON (715) by Jean-le-Blanc (739).

Bred to BRILLIANT 1271 (755), June 22, 1887.

(Hoof No. 185.)   **RAFALE 4391.**
[Recorded with pedigree in the Percheron Stud-Book of America.]

Black ; foaled April 17, 1885 ; bred at Oaklawn ; got by BRILLIANT 1271 (755); dam Rachel 1461 (1460) by SÉLIM (749); 2d dam Coquette by DUKE-DE-CHARTRES 162 (721).

BRILLIANT 1271 (755) by Brilliant 1899 (756) out of Ragout by Favori I (711), he by Vieux-Chaslin (713) out of L'Amie by Vieux-Pierre (894), he by Coco (712).
BRILLIANT 1899 (756), by Coco II (714) out of Rosette by Mina, belonging to the French government.
Coco II (714) by Vieux-Chaslin (713) out of La Grise by Vieux-Pierre (883).
VIEUX-CHASLIN (713) by Coco (712) out of Poule by Sandi.
Coco (712) by Mignon (715) out of Pauline by Vieux-Coco.
MIGNON (715) by Jean-le-Blanc (739).
SÉLIM (749) by Porthos, belonging to M. Fromentin.
DUKE-DE-CHARTRES 162 (721) by Coco II (714), etc.

Bred to LA FERTÉ 5144 (452), August 11, 1887.

(Hoof No. 305).   **RAGOTTE 4374 (2026).**
[Recorded with pedigree in the Percheron Stud-Books of France and America.]

Dark grey ; foaled April 1, 1883 ; imported 1885 ; bred by Madame Brouard, commune of St. Hilaire-sur-Erre, canton of Theil, department of Orne ; got by VAILLANT (404) ; dam Rustique (4068) by VIEUX-VAILLANT (1383) out of Rosalie.

VAILLANT (404) by Prosper (893) out of Rosalie by Bienvenu, belonging to the Société Hippique of Eure-et-Loir.
PROSPER (893) by Décidé (892) out of Bourreau by Vieux-Pierre (883).
DÉCIDÉ (892) by Vieux-Pierre (894) out of Pelote, belonging to M. Berjeau, of Courvalien.
VIEUX-PIERRE (894) by Coco (712), he by Mignon (715) out of Pauline by Vieux-Coco.
MIGNON (715) by Jean-le-Blanc (739).
VIEUX-VAILLANT (1383) by Pierre, belonging to M. Thérin, out of a daughter of Vieux-Pierre (883).

Bred to BRILLIANT 1271 (755), June 7, 1887.

(Hoof No. 235.)   **REINE DES PRÉS 6929 (8889).**
[Recorded with pedigree in the Percheron Stud-Books of France and America.]

Dark grey ; foaled May 24, 1885 ; imported 1887 ; bred by M. Pouissin, commune of La Rouge, canton of Theil, department of Orne ; got by VOLTAIRE 3540 (443); dam Cocotte (8888) by PROSPER (893).

VOLTAIRE 3540 (443) by Brilliant 1271 (755) out of Cocotte by Coco II (714).
BRILLIANT 1271 (755) by Brilliant 1899 (756) out of Ragout by Favori I (711), he by Vieux-Chaslin (713) out of L'Amie by Vieux-Pierre (894), he by Coco (712).
BRILLIANT 1899 (756) by Coco II (714) out of Rosette by Mina, belonging to the French government.
Coco II (714) by Vieux-Chaslin (713) out of La Grise by Vieux-Pierre (883).
VIEUX-CHASLIN (713) by Coco (712) out of Poule by Sandi.
Coco (712) by Mignon (715) out of Pauline by Vieux-Coco.
MIGNON (715) by Jean-le-Blanc (739).
PROSPER (893) by Décidé (892) out of Bourreau by Vieux-Pierre (883).
DÉCIDÉ (892) by Vieux-Pierre (894) out of Pelote, belonging to M. Berjeau, of Courvalien.
VIEUX-PIERRE (894) by Coco (712), etc.

Bred to LA FERTÉ 5144 (452), October 15, 1887.

(Hoof No. 302.) **RIGOLETTE 4357 (4931).**

[Recorded with pedigree in the Percheron Stud-Books of France and America.]

Dark grey; foaled March 15, 1883; imported 1885; bred by M. Gasnier, commune of Avezé, canton of La Ferté-Bernard, department of Sarthe; got by Chartrain (1405); dam Ragotte (4930) by Superior 454 (730) out of Caroline.

Chartrain (1405) by Philibert (760) out of Cocotte by Coco II (714), he by Vieux-Chaslin (713) out of La Grise by Vieux-Pierre (883).
Philibert (760) by Superior 454 (730) out of Madelon by Vieux-Vaillant (1383), he by Pierre out of a daughter of Vieux-Pierre (883).
Superior 454 (730) by Favori I (711) out of Pauline by Vieux-Chaslin (713).
Favori I (711) by Vieux-Chaslin (713) out of L'Amie by Vieux-Pierre (894), he by Coco (712).
Vieux-Chaslin (713) by Coco (712) out of Poule by Sandi.
Coco (712) by Mignon (715) out of Pauline by Vieux-Coco.
Mignon (715) by Jean-le-Blanc (739).

Bred to Brilliant 1271 (755), August 23, 1887.

(Hoof No. 289.) **RISETTE 5653 (5511).**

[Recorded with pedigree in the Percheron Stud-Books of France and America.]

Black; foaled April 20, 1885; imported 1886; bred by M. Bajeon, commune of Théligny, canton of La Ferté-Bernard, department of Sarthe; got by Voltaire 3540 (443); dam Margot (5510) by Brilliant 1899 (756) out of Margot by Coco II (714).

Voltaire 3540 (443) by Brilliant 1271 (755) out of Cocotte by Coco II (714).
Brilliant 1271 (755) by Brilliant 1899 (756) out of Ragout by Favori I (711), he by Vieux-Chaslin (713) out of L'Amie by Vieux-Pierre (894), he by Coco (712).
Brilliant 1899 (756) by Coco II (714) out of Rosette by Mina, belonging to the French government.
Coco II (714) by Vieux-Chaslin (713) out of La Grise by Vieux-Pierre (883).
Vieux-Chaslin (713) by Coco (712) out of Poule by Sandi.
Coco (712) by Mignon (715) out of Pauline by Vieux-Coco.
Mignon (715) by Jean-le-Blanc (739).

Bred to Sandy 5162 (2225), September 21, 1887.

(Hoof No. 222.) **ROLA 7154 (10784).**

[Recorded with pedigree in the Percheron Stud-Books of France and America.]

Dark dapple grey; foaled March 1, 1885; imported 1887; bred by M. Vinsot, commune of Bouffry, canton of Droué, department of Loir-et-Cher; got by Roland II (7279); dam Marquis (10783) by Vigoureux, belonging to M. Landron.

Roland II (7279) by Roland I (son of Pamphile, belonging to the French government) out of Poule, belonging to M. Bouvereau.

Bred in France to Malakoff (8275).

(Hoof No. 184.)   **ROSALENE 5176.**

[Recorded with pedigree in the Percheron Stud-Book of America.]

Black ; foaled 1885 ; bred at Oaklawn ; got by BRILLIANT 1271 (755); dam Rose 2771 (1542) by MADEIRA 1546 (770) out of a daughter of VIDOCQ 483 (732).

BRILLIANT 1271 (755) by Brilliant 1899 (756) out of Ragout by Favori I (711), he by Vieux-Chaslin (713) out of L'Amie by Vieux-Pierre (894), he by Coco (712).

BRILLIANT 1899 (756) by Coco II (714) out of Rosette by Mina, belonging to the French government.

Coco II (714) by Vieux-Chaslin (713) out of La Grise by Vieux-Pierre (883).

VIEUX-CHASLIN (713) by Coco (712) out of Poule by Sandi.

Coco (712) by Mignon (715) out of Pauline by Vieux-Coco.

MIGNON (715) by Jean-le-Blanc (739).

MADEIRA 1546 (770) by Vidocq 483 (732), etc., out of Jeanne by Favori I (711), etc.

VIDOCQ 483 (732) by Coco II (714) out of a daughter of Chéri, he by Rustique.

Bred to LA FERTÉ 5144 (452), August 19, 1887.

(Hoof No. 111.)   **ROSE 4364 (4330).**

[Recorded with pedigree in the Percheron Stud-Books of France and America.]

Black ; foaled March 8, 1883 ; imported 1885 ; bred by M. Henri Pouissin, commune of Avezé, canton of La Ferté-Bernard, department of Sarthe ; got by BRILLIANT 1899 (756); dam Biche (5087) by PHILIPPE, belonging to M. Perriot père, out of Cocotte, belonging to M. Glon.

BRILLIANT 1899 (756) by Coco II (714) out of Rosette by Mina, belonging to the French government.

Coco II (714) by Vieux-Chaslin (713) out of La Grise by Vieux-Pierre (883).

VIEUX-CHASLIN (713) by Coco (712) out of Poule by Sandi.

Coco (712) by Mignon (715) out of Pauline by Vieux-Coco.

MIGNON (715) by Jean-le-Blanc (739).

Bred to LA FERTÉ 5144 (452), May 11, 1887.

(Hoof No. 147.)   **ROSE ATHERTON 3675.**

[Recorded with pedigree in the Percheron Stud-Book of America.]

Dark grey ; foaled May 1, 1883 ; bred by W. D. Gruber, of Grand Ridge, Illinois ; got by OSPREY 1268 (779); dam Céleste 963.

OSPREY 1268 (779) by Waterloo 2199 (733) out of Flora by Sélim (749), he by Porthos.

WATERLOO 2199 (733) by Jean-Bart (716) out of Poule, belonging to M. Bourdin.

JEAN-BART (716) by Bayard, belonging to M. Perpère, out of Jeanne by Porthos.

Bred to BRILLIANT 1271 (755), May 6, 1887.

(Hoof No. 150.)   **ROSEDALE 1463.**

[Recorded with pedigree in the Percheron Stud-Book of America.]

Steel grey ; foaled November, 1881 ; bred at Oaklawn ; got by MOLIÈRE 936 ; dam Rosabelle 599 (1474) by Coco (712).

Coco (712) by Mignon (715) out of Pauline by Vieux-Coco.

MIGNON (715) by Jean-le-Blanc (739).

Bred to BRILLIANT 1271 (755), August 9, 1887.

(Hoof No. 295.) **ROSETTE 5650 (6717).**

[Recorded with pedigree in the Percheron Stud-Books of France and America.]

Black ; foaled April 28, 1881 ; imported 1886 ; bred by M. Esnault, commune of Théligny, canton of La Ferté-Bernard, department of Sarthe ; got by BRILLIANT 1271 (755); dam Margot (6716) by BRILLIANT 1899 (756) out of Bijou.

BRILLIANT 1271 (755) by Brilliant 1899 (756) out of Ragout by Favori I (711), he by Vieux-Chaslin (713) out of L'Amie by Vieux-Pierre (894), he by Coco (712).
BRILLIANT 1899 (756) by Coco II (714) out of Rosette by Mina, belonging to the French government.
Coco II (714) by Vieux-Chaslin (713) out of La Grise by Vieux-Pierre (883).
VIEUX-CHASLIN (713) by Coco (712) out of Poule by Sandi.
Coco (712) by Mignon (715) out of Pauline by Vieux-Coco.
MIGNON (715) by Jean-le-Blanc (739).

Bred to SOLIDE 7104 (9808), October 14, 1887.

(Hoof No. 81.) **ROSETTE 5684 (7345).**

[Recorded with pedigree in the Percheron Stud-Books of France and America.]

Brown bay ; foaled April 18, 1883 ; imported 1886 ; bred by M. Voisin, commune of St. Aignan, canton of Marolles-les-Braux, department of Sarthe ; got by PAPILLON (7344); dam Charmante (7343) by PAPILLON (7344) out of Bamboche I, belonging to M. Voisin.

PAPILLON (7344) by Coco I out of Rose.

Bred to BRILLIANT 1271 (755), May 4, 1887.

(Hoof No. 226.) **ROSIÈRE 7155 (9119).**

[Recorded with pedigree in the Percheron Stud-Books of France and America.]

Grey ; foaled April 4, 1885 ; imported 1887 ; bred by M. Bergeot, commune of Cormes, canton of La Ferté-Bernard, department of Sarthe; got by VOLTAIRE 3540 (443); dam Jubine (9118) by Coco II (714).

VOLTAIRE 3540 (443) by Brilliant 1271 (755) out of Cocotte by Coco II (714).
BRILLIANT 1271 (755) by Brilliant 1899 (756) out of Ragout by Favori I (711), he by Vieux-Chaslin (713) out of L'Amie by Vieux-Pierre (894), he by Coco (712).
BRILLIANT 1899 (756) by Coco II (714) out of Rosette by Mina, belonging to the French government.
Coco II (714) by Vieux-Chaslin (713) out of La Grise by Vieux-Pierre (883).
VIEUX-CHASLIN (713) by Coco (712) out of Poule by Sandi.
Coco (712) by Mignon (715) out of Pauline by Vieux-Coco.
MIGNON (715) by Jean-le-Blanc (739).

Bred to VOLTAIRE II 6997 (2920), June 9, 1887.

(Hoof No. 113.)   **ROSINE 5692.**

[Recorded with pedigree in the Percheron Stud-Book of America.]

Dark grey ; foaled February 3, 1886 ; bred at Oaklawn ; got by MOUSSE 4232 (458); dam Rose 4364 (4330) by BRILLIANT 1899 (756) out of Biche (5087) by PHILIPPE.

MOUSSE 4232 (458) by Brilliant 1271 (755) out of Bouro (5078) by Margot 295 (795) he by Favori I (711), he by Vieux-Chaslin (713) out of L'Amie by Vieux-Pierre (894) he by Coco (712).
BRILLIANT 1271 (755) by Brilliant 1899 (756) out of Ragout by Favori I (711), etc.
BRILLIANT 1899 (756) by Coco II (714) out of Rosette by Mina, belonging to the French government.
Coco II (714) by Vieux-Chaslin (713) out of La Grise by Vieux-Pierre (883).
VIEUX-CHASLIN (713) by Coco (712) out of Poule by Sandi.
Coco (712) by Mignon (715) out of Pauline by Vieux-Coco.
MIGNON (715) by Jean-le-Blanc (739).

(Hoof No. 194.)   **RUSTIQUE 4367 (2165).**

[Recorded with pedigree in the Percheron Stud-Books of France and America.]

Light grey ; foaled April 4, 1882 ; imported 1885 ; bred by M. Joseph Guillin, canton of Mortagne, department of Orne ; got by VIDOCQ (belonging to M. Pelletier), he by PICADOR 1254 (780); dam Rustique (4881) by SÉLIM (749) out of Rose, belonging to M. Guillin.

PICADOR 1254 (780) by Picador (son of Favori, belonging to M. Dupont) out of Marguerite by Sélim (749).
SÉLIM (749) by Porthos, belonging to M. Fromentin.

Bred to BRILLIANT 1271 (755), October 11, 1887.

(Hoof No. 24.)   **SAPHO 5637 (7030).**

[Recorded with pedigree in the Percheron Stud-Books of France and America.]

Black ; foaled May 27, 1883 ; imported 1886 ; bred by M. Eugène Hée, commune of Coudray, canton of Authon, department of Eure-et-Loir ; got by VERMOUTH (6276); dam Rosette (7029) by MADEIRA 1546 (770) out of Poule.

VERMOUTH (6276) by Vermouth 1820 (787) out of Rosalie (5986) by Bon Espoir, he by Vidocq 483 (732).
VERMOUTH 1820 (787) by Vidocq 483 (732) out of Agathe by Vieux-Chaslin (713).
VIDOCQ 483 (732) by Coco II (714) out of a daughter of Chéri, he by Rustique.
Coco II (714) by Vieux-Chaslin (713) out of La Grise by Vieux-Pierre (883).
VIEUX-CHASLIN (713) by Coco (712) out of Poule by Sandi.
Coco (712) by Mignon (715) out of Pauline by Vieux-Coco.
MIGNON (715) by Jean-le-Blanc (739).
MADEIRA 1546 (770) by Vidocq 483 (732) out of Jeanne by Favori I (711), he by Vieux-Chaslin (713), etc., out of L'Amie by Vieux-Pierre (894), he by Coco (712).

Bred to BRILLIANT 1271 (755), October 4, 1887.

(Hoof No. 228.) **SARAH 7156 (8660).**

[Recorded with pedigree in the Percheron Stud-Books of France and America.]

Black ; foaled March 18, 1885 ; imported 1887 ; bred by M. Clocheau, commune of La Ferté-Bernard, department of Sarthe ; got by CONFIDENT 3647 (397) ; dam Bijou (5743) by FLEURUS, belonging to M. Tacheau, he by FRENCH MONARCH 205 (734) ; 2d dam Cocotte.

CONFIDENT 3647 (397) by Brilliant 1271 (755) out of Rose by Coco II (714).
BRILLIANT 1271 (755) by Brilliant 1899 (756) out of Ragout by Favori I (711), he by Vieux-Chaslin (713) out of L'Amie by Vieux-Pierre (894), he by Coco (712).
BRILLIANT 1899 (756) by Coco II (714) out of Rosette by Mina, belonging to the French government.
Coco II (714) by Vieux-Chaslin (713) out of La Grise by Vieux-Pierre (883).
VIEUX-CHASLIN (713) by Coco (712) out of Poule by Sandi.
Coco (712) by Mignon (715) out of Pauline by Vieux-Coco.
MIGNON (715) by Jean-le-Blanc (739).
FRENCH MONARCH 205 (734) by Ilderim (5302) out of a daughter of Vieux-Pierre (894), etc.
ILDERIM (5302) by Valentin (5301) out of Chaton by Vieux-Pierre (894), etc.
VALENTIN (5301) by Vieux-Chaslin (713), etc.

Bred to LA FERTÉ 5144 (452), October 20, 1887. X

(Hoof No. 71.) **SULTANE 5678 (4099).**

[Recorded with pedigree in the Percheron Stud-Books of France and America.]

Black grey ; foaled May 1, 1884 ; imported 1886 ; bred by M. Chauvin, commune of Le Plantis, canton of Courtomer, department of Orne ; got by MADÈRE 4653 (2421) ; dam Cocotte (4098) by SÉLIM (749).

MADÈRE 4653 (2421) by D'Artagnan [son of Sélim (749)] out of Rosette by Porthos, belonging to M. Fromentin.
SÉLIM (749) by Porthos, belonging to M. Fromentin.

Bred to LA FERTÉ 5144 (452), May 13, 1887.

(Hoof No. 32.) **SUZANNE 5643 (6808).**

[Recorded with pedigree in the Percheron Stud-Books of France and America.]

Grey ; foaled March 8, 1883 ; imported 1886 ; bred by M. Moreau, commune of Ceton, canton of Theil, department of Orne ; got by PHILIBERT II 2684 (1310) ; dam Brebis (4194) by Coco II (714).

PHILIBERT II 2684 (1310) by Philibert (760) out of Fannie by Favori I (711).
PHILIBERT (760) by Superior 454 (730) out of Madelon by Vieux-Vaillant (1383), he by Pierre out of a daughter of Vieux-Pierre (883).
SUPERIOR 454 (730) by Favori I (711) out of Pauline by Vieux-Chaslin (713).
FAVORI I (711) by Vieux-Chaslin (713) out of L'Amie by Vieux-Pierre (894), he by Coco (712).
VIEUX-CHASLIN (713) by Coco (712) out of Poule by Sandi.
Coco (712) by Mignon (715) out of Pauline by Vieux-Coco.
MIGNON (715) by Jean-le-Blanc (739).
Coco II (714) by Vieux-Chaslin (713), etc., out of La Grise by Vieux-Pierre (883).

Bred to BRILLIANT 1271 (755), July 29, 1887.

(Hoof No. 290.)   **SYLVA 5633 (6600).**

[Recorded with pedigree in the Percheron Stud-Books of France and America.]

Grey; foaled March 18, 1883; imported 1886; bred by M. Clocheau, commune of Cormes, canton of La Ferté-Bernard, department of Sarthe; got by FAVORI III (1381); dam Biche (6599) by FAVORA 1542 (765) out of Camille, belonging to M. Clocheau père.

FAVORI III (1381) by Utopia 780 (731) out of La Noire, belonging to M. Letourneur.
UTOPIA 780 (731) by Superior 454 (730) out of Camille by Favori I (711).
SUPERIOR 454 (730) by Favori I (711) out of Pauline by Vieux-Chaslin (713).
FAVORI I (711) by Vieux-Chaslin (713) out of L'Amie by Vieux-Pierre (894), he by Coco (712).
VIEUX-CHASLIN (713) by Coco (712) out of Poule by Sandi.
Coco (712) by Mignon (715) out of Pauline by Vieux-Coco.
MIGNON (715) by Jean-le-Blanc (739).
FAVORA 1542 (765) by French Monarch 205 (734) out of Marguerite by Favori, he by Coco of Mêsle-sur-Sarthe.
FRENCH MONARCH 205 (734) by Ilderim (5302) out of a daughter of Vieux-Pierre (894), etc.
ILDERIM (5302) by Valentin (5301) out of Chaton by Vieux-Pierre (894), etc.
VALENTIN (5301) by Vieux-Chaslin (713), etc.

Bred to SANDY 5162 (2225), August 30, 1887.

(Hoof No. 155.)   **TAMBOURETTE 4363 (4409).**

[Recorded with pedigree in the Percheron Stud-Books of France and America.]

Black; foaled April 22, 1882; imported 1885; bred by M. Tuffier, commune of St. Cyr-la-Rosière, canton of Nocé, department of Orne; got by MADÈRE 1263 (772); dam Mignonne (4407) by CHÉRI out of Tambour.

MADÈRE 1263 (772) by Brilliant 1899 (756) out of Hortense by Duke-de-Chartres 162 (721), he by Coco II (714).
BRILLIANT 1899 (756) by Coco II (714) out of Rosette by Mina, belonging to the French government.
Coco II (714) by Vieux-Chaslin (713) out of La Grise by Vieux-Pierre (883).
VIEUX-CHASLIN (713) by Coco (712) out of Poule by Sand'
Coco (712) by Mignon (715) out of Pauline by Vieux-Coco
MIGNON (715) by Jean-le-Blanc (739).

Bred to BRILLIANT 1271 (755), August 15, 1887

(Hoof No. 259.)   **TAMBOURINE 7321.**

[Recorded with pedigree in the Percheron Stud-Book of America.]

Black; foaled July 11, 1887; bred at Oaklawn; got by BRILLIANT 1271 (755); dam Tambourette 4363 (4409) by MADÈRE 1263 (772); 2d dam Mignonne (4407) by CHÉRI, belonging to M. E. Perriot, out of Tambour.

BRILLIANT 1271 (755) by Brilliant 1899 (756) out of Ragout by Favori I (711), he by Vieux-Chaslin (713) out of L'Amie by Vieux-Pierre (894), he by Coco (712).
BRILLIANT 1899 (756) by Coco II (714) out of Rosette by Mina, belonging to the French government.
Coco II (714) by Vieux-Chaslin (713) out of La Grise by Vieux-Pierre (883).
VIEUX-CHASLIN (713) by Coco (712) out of Poule by Sandi.
Coco (712) by Mignon (715) out of Pauline by Vieux-Coco.
MIGNON (715) by Jean-le-Blanc (739).
MADÈRE 1263 (772) by Brilliant 1899 (756), etc., out of Hortense by Duke-de-Chartres 162 (721), he by Coco II (714), etc.

(Hoof No. 311.) **THÉRÈSE 5647 (2960).**

[Recorded with pedigree in the Percheron Stud-Books of France and America.]

Grey; foaled April 20, 1884; imported 1886; bred by M. Rouis, commune of St. Antoine, canton of La Ferté-Bernard, department of Sarthe; got by CLEMENT 1965 (936); dam Poule (7112) by BRILLIANT 1899 (756) out of RUSTIQUOTTE.

CLEMENT 1965 (936) by Philibert (760) out of Rustique by Coco II (714).
PHILIBERT (760) by Superior 454 (730) out of Madelon by Vieux-Vaillant (1383), he by Pierre out of a daughter of Vieux-Pierre (883).
SUPERIOR 454 (730) by Favori I (711) out of Pauline by Vieux-Chaslin (713).
FAVORI I (711) by Vieux-Chaslin (713) out of L'Amie by Vieux-Pierre (894), he by Coco (712).
VIEUX-CHASLIN (713) by Coco (712) out of Poule by Sandi.
COCO (712) by Mignon (715) out of Pauline by Vieux-Coco.
MIGNON (715) by Jean-le-Blanc (739).
BRILLIANT 1899 (756) by Coco II (714) out of Rosette by Mina, belonging to the French government.
Coco II (714) by Vieux-Chaslin (713), etc., out of La Grise by Vieux-Pierre (883).

Bred to BRILLIANT 1271 (755), July 26, 1887.

(Hoof No. 137.) **TRANQUETTE 5700.**

[Recorded with pedigree in the Percheron Stud-Book of America.]

Bay; foaled March 28, 1886; bred at Oaklawn; got by BRILLIANT 1271 (755); dam Tranquille 2729 (1525) by ROMULUS 1938 (1078); 2d dam by WATERLOO 2199 (733). .

BRILLIANT 1271 (755) by Brilliant 1899 (756) out of Ragout by Favori I (711), he by Vieux-Chaslin (713) out of L'Amie by Vieux-Pierre (894), he by Coco (712).
BRILLIANT 1899 (756) by Coco II (714) out of Rosette by Mina, belonging to the French government.
Coco II (714) by Vieux-Chaslin (713) out of La Grise by Vieux-Pierre (883).
VIEUX-CHASLIN (713) by Coco (712) out of Poule by Sandi.
Coco (712) by Mignon (715) out of Pauline by Vieux-Coco.
MIGNON (715) by Jean-le-Blanc (739).
ROMULUS 1938 (1078) by Romulus 873 (785) out of Catherine by Moreuil.
ROMULUS 873 (785) by the government approved stallion Romulus (son of Moreuil) out of Fleur-d'Épine by the government approved stallion Chéri, he by Corbon.
WATERLOO 2199 (733) by Jean-Bart (716) out of Poule, belonging to M. Bourdin.
JEAN-BART (716) by Bayard, belonging to M. Perpère, out of Jeanne by Porthos.

(Hoof No. 255.)   **TRANQUILITY 7322.**

[Recorded with pedigree in the Percheron Stud-Book of America.]

Bay ; foaled March 20, 1887 ; bred at Oaklawn ; got by GOLIATH 4302 (2944); dam Tranquille 2729 (1525) by ROMULUS 1938 (1078); 2d dam by WATERLOO 2199 (733).

GOLIATH 4302 (2944) by Clement 1965 (936) out of Pauline (5014) by Favora 1542 (765), he by French Monarch 205 (734) out of Marguerite by Favori, he by Coco of Mêsle-sur-Sarthe, he by Margot, belonging to M. Vallée.
FRENCH MONARCH 205 (734) by Ilderim (5302) out of a daughter of Vieux-Pierre (894), he by Coco (712).
ILDERIM (5302) by Valentin (5301) out of Chaton by Vieux-Pierre (894), etc.
VALENTIN (5301) by Vieux-Chaslin (713).
CLEMENT 1965 (936) by Philibert (760) out of Rustique by Coco II (714) he by Vieux-Chaslin (713) out of La Grise by Vieux-Pierre (883).
PHILIBERT (760) by Superior 454 (730) out of Madelon by Vieux-Vaillant (1383), he by Pierre out of a daughter of Vieux-Pierre (883).
SUPERIOR 454 (730) by Favori I (711) ont of Pauline by Vieux-Chaslin (713).
FAVORI I (711) by Vieux-Chaslin (713) out of L'Amie by Vieux-Pierre (894), etc.
VIEUX-CHASLIN (713) by Coco (712) out of Poule by Sandi.
COCO (712) by Mignon (715) out of Pauline by Vieux-Coco.
MIGNON (715) by Jean-le-Blanc (739).
ROMULUS 1938 (1078) by Romulus 873 (785) out of Catherine by Moreuil.
ROMULUS 873 (785) by the government approved stallion Romulus (son of Moreuil) out of Fleur-d'Epine by the government approved stallion Chéri, he by Corbon.
WATERLOO 2199 (733) by Jean-Bart (716) out of Poule, belonging to M. Bourdin.
JEAN-BART (716) by Bayard out of Jeanne by Porthos.

(Hoof No. 136.)   **TRANQUILLE 2729 (1525).**

[Recorded with pedigree in the Percheron Stud-Books of France and America.]

Bay ; foaled 1882 ; imported 1883 ; got by ROMULUS 1938 (1078); dam by WATERLOO 2199 (733).

ROMULUS 1938 (1078) by Romulus 873 (785) out of Catherine by Moreuil.
ROMULUS 873 (785) by the government approved stallion Romulus (son of Moreuil) out of Fleur-d'Epine by the government approved stallion Chéri, he by Corbon.
WATERLOO 2199 (733) by Jean-Bart (716) out of Poule, belonging to M. Bourdin.
JEAN-BART (716) by Bayard, belonging to M. Perpère, out of Jeanne by Porthos.

Bred to BRILLIANT 1271 (755), March 29, 1887.

(Hoof No. 242.)   **TRIANA 7159 (9841).**

[Recorded with pedigree in the Percheron Stud-Books of France and America.]

Black ; foaled April 26, 1885 ; imported 1887 ; bred by M. Felix Grenier, commune of Coulonges, canton of Mêsle-sur-Sarthe, department of Orne ; got by SUPERIEUR 5752 (2188); dam Frisette (9390), belonging to M. Felix Grenier.

SUPERIEUR 5752 (2188) by Vidocq (son of Brilliant) out of Margot by Bon Espoir.

Bred in France to SULTAN (1400).

(Hoof No. 399.) **UBEDA 1470 (1465).**

[Recorded with pedigree in the Percheron Stud-Books of France and America.]

Light grey; foaled 1877; imported 1881; got by UTOPIA 780 (731) dam by BLACK CHIEF 45 (735).

UTOPIA 780 (731) by Superior 454 (730) out of Camille by Favori I (711).
SUPERIOR 454 (730) by Favori I (711) out of Pauline by Vieux-Chaslin (713).
FAVORI I (711) by Vieux-Chaslin (713) out of L'Amie by Vieux-Pierre (894), he by Coco (712).
VIEUX-CHASLIN (713) by Coco (712) out of Poule by Sandi.
COCO (712) by Mignon (715) out of Pauline by Vieux-Coco.
MIGNON (715) by Jean-le-Blanc (739).
BLACK CHIEF 45 (735) by Brilliant 1899 (756), he by Coco II (714) out of Rosette by Mina, belonging to the French government.
COCO II (714) by Vieux-Chaslin (713), etc., out of La Grise by Vieux-Pierre (883).

Bred to BRILLIANT 1271 (755), September 7, 1887.

(Hoof No. 250.) **UMBRIA 7320.**

[Recorded with pedigree in the Percheron Stud-Book of America.]

Bay; foaled August 19, 1887; bred at Oaklawn; got by BRILLIANT 1271 (755); dam Ubeda 1470 (1465) by UTOPIA 780 (731) out of a daughter of BLACK CHIEF 45 (735).

BRILLIANT 1271 (755) by Brilliant 1899 (756) out of Ragout by Favori I (711).
BRILLIANT 1899 (756) by Coco II (714) out of Rosette by Mina, belonging to the French government.
COCO II (714) by Vieux-Chaslin (713) out of La Grise by Vieux-Pierre (883).
VIEUX-CHASLIN (713) by Coco (712) out of Poule by Sandi.
COCO (712) by Mignon (715) out of Pauline by Vieux-Coco.
MIGNON (715) by Jean-le-Blanc (739).
UTOPIA 780 (731) by Superior 454 (730) out of Camille by Favori I (711).
SUPERIOR 454 (730) by Favori I (711) out of Pauline by Vieux-Chaslin (713), etc.
FAVORI I (711) by Vieux-Chaslin (713), etc., out of L'Amie by Vieux-Pierre (894), he by Coco (712), etc.
BLACK CHIEF 45 (735) by Brilliant 1899 (756), etc.

VALENTIA 7317.

[Recorded with pedigree in the Percheron Stud-Book of America.]

Grey black; foaled April 12, 1887; bred at Oaklawn; got by BRILLIANT 1271 (755); dam Valentine 3663 (2778) by AVATA 1966 (912) out of Poule by BAYARD 1520 (790).

BRILLIANT 1271 (755) by Brilliant 1899 (756) out of Ragout by Favori I (711).
BRILLIANT 1899 (756) by Coco II (714) out of Rosette by Mina, belonging to the French government.
COCO II (714) by Vieux-Chaslin (713) out of La Grise by Vieux-Pierre (883).
VIEUX-CHASLIN (713) by Coco (712) out of Poule by Sandi.
COCO (712) by Mignon (715) out of Pauline by Vieux-Coco.
MIGNON (715) by Jean-le-Blanc (739).
AVATA 1966 (912) by Nogent 738 (729) out of Bicotte by Bayard 26 (717).
NOGENT 738 (729) by Vidocq 483 (732) out of a daughter of Favori I (711).
VIDOCQ 483 (732) by Coco II (714), etc., out of a daughter of Chéri, he by Rustique.
BAYARD 1520 (790) by Bayard 26 (717) out of a daughter of Exile 196 (724), he by Favori I (711).
BAYARD 26 (717) by Favori I (711) out of Mignonne by Chéri.
FAVORI I (711) by Vieux-Chaslin (713), etc., out of L'Amie by Vieux-Pierre (894), he by Coco (712), etc.

(Hoof No. 101.)   **VALENTINE 3663 (2778).**

[Recorded with pedigree in the Percheron Stud-Books of France and America.]

Black; foaled March, 1882; imported 1884; bred by M. Hamelin, commune of St. Martin, canton of Bellême, department of Orne; got by AVATA 1966 (912); dam Poule by BAYARD 1520 (790).

AVATA 1966 (912) by Nogent 738 (729) out of Bicotte by Bayard 26 (717).
NOGENT 738 (729) by Vidocq 483 (732) out of a daughter of Favori I (711), etc.
VIDOCQ 483 (732) by Coco II (714) out of a daughter of Chéri, he by Rustique.
COCO II (714) by Vieux-Chaslin (713) out of La Grise by Vieux-Pierre (883).
VIEUX-CHASLIN (713) by Coco (712) out of Poule by Sandi.
COCO (712) by Mignon (715) out of Pauline by Vieux-Coco.
MIGNON (715) by Jean-le-Blanc (739).
BAYARD 1520 (790) by Bayard 26 (717) out of a daughter of Exile 193 (724), he by Favori I (711).
BAYARD 26 (717) by Favori I (711) out of Mignonne by Chéri.
FAVORI I (711) by Vieux-Chaslin (713), etc., out of L'Amie by Vieux-Pierre (894), he by Coco (712), etc.

Bred to BRILLIANT 1271 (755), April 22, 1887.

(Hoof No. 156.)   **VANITY 2275.**

[Recorded with pedigree in the Percheron Stud-Book of America.]

Black; foaled April 21, 1883; bred at Oaklawn; got by BRILLIANT 1271 (755); dam Rachel 1461 (1460) by SÉLIM (749) out of Coquette by DUKE-DE-CHARTRES 162 (721).

BRILLIANT 1271 (755) by Brilliant 1899 (756) out of Ragout by Favori I (711), he by Vieux-Chaslin (713) out of L'Amie by Vieux-Pierre (894), he by Coco (712).
BRILLIANT 1899 (756) by Coco II (714) out of Rosette by Mina, belonging to the French government.
COCO II (714) by Vieux-Chaslin (713) out of La Grise by Vieux-Pierre (883).
VIEUX-CHASLIN (713) by Coco (712) out of Poule by Sandi.
COCO (712) by Mignon (715) out of Pauline by Vieux-Coco.
MIGNON (715) by Jean-le-Blanc (739).
SÉLIM (749) by Porthos, belonging to M. Fromentin.
DUKE-DE-CHARTRES 162 (721) by Coco II (714), etc.

Bred to LA FERTÉ 5144 (452), September 6, 1887.

(Hoof No. 163.)   **VENA 2276.**

[Recorded with pedigree in the Percheron Stud-Book of America.]

Reddish grey; foaled May 29, 1883; bred at Oaklawn; got by BRILLIANT 1271 (755); dam Geraldine 1433 (1437) by ROMULUS 873 (785) out of a daughter of JEAN-BART.

BRILLIANT 1271 (755) by Brilliant 1899 (756) out of Ragout by Favori I (711), he by Vieux-Chaslin (713) out of L'Amie by Vieux-Pierre (894), he by Coco (712).
BRILLIANT 1899 (756) by Coco II (714) out of Rosette by Mina, belonging to the Société Hippique of Eure-et-Loir.
COCO II (714) by Vieux-Chaslin (713) out of La Grise by Vieux-Pierre (883).
VIEUX-CHASLIN (713) by Coco (712) out of Poule by Sandi.
COCO (712) by Mignon (715) out of Pauline by Vieux-Coco.
MIGNON (715) by Jean-le-Blanc (739).
ROMULUS 873 (785) by the government approved stallion Romulus (son of Moreuil) out of Fleur-d'Épine by the government approved stallion Chéri, he by Corbon.
JEAN-BART (716) by Bayard, belonging to M. Perpère, out of Jeanne by Porthos.

Bred to LA FERTÉ 5144 (452), August 26, 1887.

(Hoof No. 146.) **VERBENA 2278.**

[Recorded with pedigree in the Percheron Stud-Book of America.]

Dapple grey; foaled April 27, 1883; bred at Oaklawn; got by BRILLIANT 1271 (755); dam Fleur-de-Lis 971 (1432) by DÉCIDÉ, belonging to M. Fardouet père, out of a daughter of BAYARD 26 (717).

BRILLIANT 1271 (755) by Brilliant 1899 (756) out of Ragout by Favori I (711).
BRILLIANT 1899 (756) by Coco II (714) out of Rosette by Mina, belonging to the French government.
Coco II (714) by Vieux-Chaslin (713) out of La Grise by Vieux-Pierre (883).
VIEUX-CHASLIN (713) by Coco (712) out of Poule by Sandi.
Coco (712) by Mignon (715) out of Pauline by Vieux-Coco.
MIGNON (715) by Jean-le-Blanc (739).
BAYARD 26 (717) by Favori I (711) out of Mignonne by Chéri.
FAVORI I (711) by Vieux-Chaslin (713), etc., out of L'Amie by Vieux-Pierre (894), he by Coco (712).

Bred to LA FERTÉ 5144 (452), July 13, 1887.

(Hoof No. 25.) **VESTALE 5638 (5972).**

[Recorded with pedigree in the Percheron Stud-Books of France and America.]

Dapple grey; foaled March 15, 1884; imported 1886; bred by M. François Gouhier, commune of Ceton, canton of Theil, department of Orne; got by FAVRIL 2387 (1122); dam Coquette (5971) by BRILLIANT 1899 (756) out of Percheronne.

FAVRIL 2387 (1122) by Iago 995 (768) out of Charmante by Margot 295 (795), he by Favori I (711).
IAGO 995 (768) by Utopia 780 (731) out of Cossette by Favora 666 (725), he by Favori I (711) out of Marie by Coco (712).
UTOPIA 780 (731) by Superior 454 (730) out of Camille by Favori I (711).
SUPERIOR 454 (730) by Favori I (711) out of Pauline by Vieux-Chaslin (713).
FAVORI I (711) by Vieux-Chaslin (713) out of L'Amie by Vieux-Pierre (894), he by Coco (712).
VIEUX-CHASLIN (713) by Coco (712) out of Poule by Sandi.
Coco (712) by Mignon (715) out of Pauline by Vieux-Coco.
MIGNON (715) by Jean-le-Blanc (739).
BRILLIANT 1899 (756) by Coco II (714) out of Rosette by Mina, belonging to the French government.
Coco II (714) by Vieux-Chaslin (713), etc., out of La Grise by Vieux-Pierre (883).

Bred to BRILLIANT 1271 (755), May 7, 1887.

(Hoof No. 106.) **VINETTE 2752 (1495).**

[Recorded with pedigree in the Percheron Stud-Books of France and America.]

Black; foaled 1882; imported 1883; got by VALENTINE, he by DÉCIDÉ, belonging to M. Sagot, he by FAVORI I (711); dam Marie by CAMBRONNE, belonging to M. Tacheau.

FAVORI I (711), by Vieux-Chaslin (713) out of L'Amie by Vieux-Pierre (894), he by Coco (712).
VIEUX-CHASLIN (713) by Coco (712) out of Poule by Sandi.
Coco (712) by Mignon (715) out of Pauline by Vieux-Coco.
MIGNON (715) by Jean-le-Blanc (739).

Bred to LA FERTÉ 5144 (452), April 12, 1887.

(Hoof No. 198.)   **VIOLA 5739.**

[Recorded with pedigree in the Percheron Stud-Book of America.]

Grey ; foaled May 6, 1886 ; bred by Jacob Hayden, of Sherburnville, Illinois ; got by ARBO 1935 (1031) ; dam Lulia 1494 by BEAU NOIR 913 ; 2d dam Lucille 976 (1443) by ORIZABAT.

ARBO 1935 (1031) by Adonis 851 (861) out of a daughter of Décidé 126 (720), he by Superior 454 (730), he by Favori I (711) out of Pauline by Vieux-Chaslin (713).
ADONIS 851 (861) by Bayard 26 (717), he by Favori I (711) out of Mignonne by Chéri.
FAVORI I (711) by Vieux-Chaslin (713) out of L'Amie by Vieux-Pierre (894), he by Coco (712).
VIEUX-CHASLIN (713) by Coco (712) out of Poule by Sandi.
Coco (712) by Mignon (715) out of Pauline by Vieux-Coco.
MIGNON (715) by Jean-le-Blanc (739).

(Hoof No. 53.)   **VIOLETTE 5663 (6358).**

[Recorded with pedigree in the Percheron Stud-Books of France and America.]

Black ; foaled May 10, 1884 ; imported 1886 ; bred by M. Debray, commune of Nocé, canton of Nocé, department of Orne ; got by BRILLANT (710) ; dam L'Amie (6357) by ROMULUS (4443).

BRILLANT (710) by Brilliant 1899 (756) out of Sophie by Superior 454 (730), he by Favori I (711) out of Pauline by Vieux-Chaslin (713).
   FAVORI I (711) by Vieux-Chaslin (713) out of L'Amie by Vieux-Pierre (894), he by Coco (712).
BRILLIANT 1899 (756) by Coco II (714) out of Rosette by Mina, belonging to the French government.
Coco II (714) by Vieux-Chaslin (713) out of La Grise by Vieux-Pierre (883).
VIEUX-CHASLIN (713) by Coco (712) out of Poule by Sandi.
Coco (712) by Mignon (715) out of Pauline by Vieux-Coco.
MIGNON (715) by Jean-le-Blanc (739).
ROMULUS (4443) by Sansonnet, belonging to M. Auguste Tacheau, out of Rustique, belonging to M. Lemesle.

Bred to LA FERTÉ 5144 (452), May 23, 1887.

(Hoof No. 50.)   **VOLTAIRIENNE 5660 (6154).**

[Recorded with pedigree in the Percheron Stud-Books of France and America.]

Steel grey ; foaled April 8, 1884 ; imported 1886 ; bred by M. Leprout, commune of Ceton, canton of Theil, department of Orne ; got by VOLTAIRE 3540 (443) ; dam Rosalie (6153) by FLEURUS, he by FRENCH MONARCH 205 (734) ; 2d dam Sophie, belonging to M. Julliard.

VOLTAIRE 3540 (443) by Brilliant 1271 (755) out of Cocotte by Coco II (714).
BRILLIANT 1271 (755) by Brilliant 1899 (756) out of Ragout by Favori I (711), he by Vieux-Chaslin (713) out of L'Amie by Vieux-Pierre (894), he by Coco (712).
BRILLIANT 1899 (756) by Coco II (714) out of Rosette by Mina, belonging to the French government.
Coco II (714) by Vieux-Chaslin (713) out of La Grise by Vieux-Pierre (883).
VIEUX-CHASLIN (713) by Coco (712) out of Poule by Sandi.
Coco (712) by Mignon (715) out of Pauline by Vieux-Coco.
MIGNON (715) by Jean-le-Blanc (739).
FRENCH MONARCH 205 (734) by Ilderim (5302) out of a daughter of Vieux-Pierre (894), etc.
ILDERIM (5302) by Valentin (5301) out of Chaton by Vieux-Pierre (894), etc.
VALENTIN (5301) by Vieux-Chaslin (713), etc.

Bred to LA FERTÉ 5144 (452), May 11, 1887.

(Hoof No. 72.) **YDA 5679 (4064).**

[Recorded with pedigree in the Percheron Stud-Books of France and America.]

Black ; foaled April 5, 1883 ; imported 1886 ; bred by M. Bourdin, commune of Bellême, department of Orne ; got by AVATA 1966 (912); dam Bijou (6656) by MADEIRA 1546 (770) out of Percheronne, belonging to M. Gouhier.

AVATA 1966 (912) by Nogent 738 (729) out of Bicotte by Bayard 26 (717), he by Favori I (711) out of Mignonne by Chéri.
   FAVORI I (711) by Vieux-Chaslin (713) out of L'Amie by Vieux-Pierre (894), he by Coco (712).
NOGENT 738 (729) by Vidocq 483 (732) out of a daughter of Favori I (711), etc.
VIDOCQ 483 (732) by Coco II (714) out of a daughter of Chéri, he by Rustique.
Coco II (714) by Vieux-Chaslin (713) out of La Grise by Vieux-Pierre (883).
VIEUX-CHASLIN (713) by Coco (712) out of Poule by Sandi.
Coco (712) by Mignon (715) ont of Pauline by Vieux-Coco.
MIGNON (715) by Jean-le-Blanc (739).
MADEIRA 1546 (770) by Vidocq 483 (732), etc., out of Jeanne by Favori I (711), etc.

Bred to BRILLIANT 1271 (755), July 8, 1887.

·

(Hoof No. 141.) **ZILLAH 2279.**

[Recorded with pedigree in the Percheron Stud-Book of America.]

Dark dapple grey ; foaled April 23, 1883 ; bred at Oaklawn ; got by BRILLIANT 1271 (755); dam Fulida 1456 (1435) by DÉCIDÉ 126 (720) out of a daughter of DUKE OF PERCHE 173 (740).

BRILLIANT 1271 (755) by Brilliant 1899 (756) out of Ragont by Favori I (711).
BRILLIANT 1899 (756) by Coco II (714) out of Rosette by Mina, belonging to the French government.
Coco II (714) by Vieux-Chaslin (713) out of La Grise by Vieux-Pierre (883).
VIEUX-CHASLIN (713) by Coco (712) out of Poule by Sandi.
Coco (712) by Mignon (715) out of Pauline by Vieux-Coco.
MIGNON (715) by Jean-le-Blanc (739).
DÉCIDÉ 126 (720) by Superior 454 (730) he by Favori I (711), out of Pauline by Vieux-Chaslin (713), etc.
FAVORI I (711) by Vieux-Chaslin (713), etc., out of L'Amie by Vieux-Pierre (894), he by Coco (712), etc.
DUKE OF PERCHE 173 (740) by Favori I (711), etc., out of Franconie by Vieux-Pierre (883).

Bred to LA FERTÉ 5144 (452), August 23, 1887

(Hoof No. 231.) **ZOÉ 6930 (3032).**

[Recorded with pedigree in the Percheron Stud-Books of France and America.]

Black ; foaled April 1, 1884 ; imported 1887 ; bred by M. Louis Surcin, commune of Souancé, canton of Nogent-le-Rotrou, department of Eure-et-Loir ; got by VOLTAIRE 3540 (443); dam Lisette (1729) by PORTHOS, belonging to the French government, out of Malice by ROLAND, belonging to the French government.

VOLTAIRE 3540 (443) by Brilliant 1271 (755) out of Cocotte by Coco II (714).
BRILLIANT 1271 (755) by Brilliant 1899 (756) out of Ragout by Favori I (711), he by Vieux-Chaslin (713) out of L'Amie by Vieux-Pierre (894), he by Coco (712).
BRILLIANT 1899 (756) by Coco II (714) out of Rosette by Mina, belonging to the French government.
Coco II (714) by Vieux-Chaslin (713) out of La Grise by Vieux-Pierre (883).
VIEUX-CHASLIN (713) by Coco (712) out of Poule by Sandi.
Coco (712) by Mignon (715) out of Pauline by Vieux-Coco.
MIGNON (715) by Jean-le-Blanc (739).

Bred to BLACK CHIEF (6634), February 4, 1887.

ZULA 7318.

[Recorded with pedigree in the Percheron Stud-Book of America.]

Grey ; foaled July 22, 1887 ; bred at Oaklawn ; got by PRODUCTEUR 4280 (68); dam Zillah 2279 by BRILLIANT 1271 (755); 2d dam Fulida 1456 (1435) by DÉCIDÉ 126 (720); 3d dam by DUKE OF PERCHE 173 (740).

PRODUCTEUR 4280 (68) by Madeira 1546 (770) out of Gentille (4062) by Porthos.
MADEIRA 1546 (770) by Vidocq 483 (732), etc., out of Jeanne by Favori I (711).
VIDOCQ 483 (732) by Coco II (714) out of a daughter of Chéri, he by Rustique.
Coco II (714) by Vieux-Chaslin (713) out of La Grise by Vieux-Pierre (883).
VIEUX-CHASLIN (713) by Coco (712) out of Poule by Sandi.
Coco (712) by Mignon (715) out of Pauline by Vieux-Coco.
MIGNON (715) by Jean-le-Blanc (739).
BRILLIANT 1271 (755) by Brilliant 1899 (756) out of Ragout by Favori I (711).
BRILLIANT 1899 (756) by Coco II (714), etc., out of Rosette by Mina, belonging to the French government.
DÉCIDÉ 126 (720) by Superior 454 (730), he by Favori I (711) out of Pauline by Vieux-Chaslin (713), etc.
FAVORI I (711) by Vieux-Chaslin (713), etc., out of L'Amie by Vieux-Pierre (894), he by Coco (712), etc.
DUKE OF PERCHE 173 (740) by Favori I (711), etc., out of Franconie by Vieux-Pierre (883).

CATALOGUE FOR 1888.

PERCHERON STALLIONS

IMPORTED, BRED AND OWNED BY ME SINCE 1872.

The number in parentheses is the number of animal as recorded in the Percheron Stud-Book of France; the other number, as recorded in the Percheron Stud-Book of America.

ABDEL, bl., fo. 81, imp. 81. Rec. 1372.
ABDEL-KADER, gr., fo. 78, imp. 86. 5155 (5699).
ABOUKIR, gr., fo. 82, imp. 84. Rec. 3651 (1735).
ABOUKIR, bl., fo. 83, imp. 85. Rec. 4296 (2225).
ABSALON, bl., fo. 79, imp. 83. Rec. 2513 ('000).
ABSALON, gr., fo. 85, imp. 87. Rec. 7017 (8605).
ACCOLEDE, gr., fo. 80, imp. 81. Rec. 1285.
ACHILLE, gr., fo. 82, imp. 85. Rec. 2676 (1228).
ACHILLE, gr., fo. 79, imp. 84. Rec. 3708 (421).
ACHILLES, gr., fo. 74, imp. 77. Rec. 615.
ACTON, gr., fo. 79, imp. 83. Rec. 2364 (1258).
ACTON, bl., fo. 78, imp. 84. Rec. 3514 (2138).
ACTOR, bl., fo. 80, imp. 80. Rec. 907 (846).
ADOLPH, gr., fo. 82, imp. 83. Rec. 2666 (1180).
ADONIS, b., fo. 74, imp. 79. Rec. 851 (801).
ADORATEUR, bl., fo. 83, imp. 87. Rec. 6361 (10857).
AFRICAN, bl., fo. 77, imp. 82. Rec. 2136 (805).
AFRICUS, bl., fo. 75, imp. 75. Rec. 3 (802).
AGAMEMNON, gr., fo. 82, imp. 85. Rec. 2513 (1120).
AGRICOL, gr., fo. 81, home bred. Rec. 1403.
AIMARD, gr., fo. 81, imp. 81. Rec. 1373.
ALAMET, gr., fo. 78, imp. 82. Rec. 1920 (806).
ALAMET, gr., fo. 81, imp. 84. Rec. 3700 (2291).
ALARIC, bl., fo. 76, imp. 80. Rec. 905 (818).
ALARIC, gr., fo. 84, imp. 87. Rec. 6932 (6256).
ALBATROSS, gr., fo. 80, imp. 80. Rec. 908 (845).
ALBION, gr., fo. 81, imp. 81. Rec. 1395.
ALCALDE, gr., fo. 78, imp. 82. Rec. 1992 (897).
ALCEDO, gr., fo. 80, imp. 84. Rec. 3498 (888).
ALDUS, bl., fo. 80, imp. 80. Rec. 1257.
ALEDO, gr., fo. 80, imp. 82. Rec. 1929 (898).
ALENCON, gr., fo. 80, imp. 84. Rec. 3487 (885).
ALESANDRO, b., fo. 81, imp. 81. Rec. 1374.
ALEXANDER, gr., fo. 78, imp. 81. Rec. 1287 (804).
ALEXANDRE, b., fo. 81, imp. 84. Rec. 3724 (2360).
ALEXANDRE, bl., fo. 82, imp. 84. Rec. 3745 (2766).
ALEXANDRE, gr., fo. 83, imp. 84. Rec. 3785 (1758).
ALEXIS, bl., fo. 82, imp. 84. Rec. 3325 (2561).
ALFRED, gr., fo. 75, imp. 80. Rec. 905.
ALFRED, gr., fo. 83, imp. 84. Rec. 3774 (2637).
ALI BABI, bl., fo. 84, imp. 85. Rec. 4316 (2625).
ALLEMAGNE, gr., fo. 79, imp. 83. Rec. 2358 (1272).
ALLEPPO, gr., fo. 77, imp. 77. Rec. 618.
ALLEZAN, gr., fo. 78, imp. 81. Rec. 1204.
ALMADA, gr., fo. 78, imp. 78. Rec. 619.
ALMO, gr., fo. 79, imp. 82. Rec. 1989 (899).
ALMONT, gr., fo. 76, imp. 80. Rec. 988.
ALPHA, bl., fo. 74, imp. in dam. Rec. 8.
ALTA, gr., fo. 78, imp. 82. Rec. 1995 (900).
ALTIMO, gr., fo. 79, imp. 82. Rec. 1984 (901).
ALVAREZ, bl., fo. 81, imp. 81. Rec. 1375.
AMADIS, gr., fo. 84, imp. 87. Rec. 6863 (3946).
AMBER, b., fo. 77, imp. 82. Rec. 2131 (902).
AMBERCOURT, b., fo. 78, imp. 81. Rec. 1286.
AMBOIS, gr., fo. 76, imp. 81. Rec. 1282 (820).
AMEER, bl., fo. 80, imp. 82. Rec. 1977 (903).
AMELIAN, gr., fo. 72, imp. 76. Rec. 11.

AMERIGO, bl., fo. 77, imp. 82. Rec. 1979 (904).
AMILLY, gr., fo. 82, imp. 85. Rec. 4217 (2228).
AMIRAL, gr., fo. 83, imp. 84. Rec. 3744 (2150).
AMPERE, bl., fo. 82, imp. 83. Rec. 2977 (1274).
ANATOLE, bl., fo. 82, imp. 85. Rec. 2628 (1258).
ANATOLE, gr., fo. 81, imp. 84. Rec. 3730 (2166).
ANCHORITE, gr., fo. 78, imp. 81. Rec. 1370 (805).
ANDRE, gr., fo. 84, imp. 87. Rec. 6034 (16531).
ANGELO, gr., fo. 79, imp. 81. Rec. 1382.
ANGELO, gr., fo. 81, imp. 83. Rec. 2603 (1437).
ANNIBAL, gr., fo. 81, imp. 84. Rec. 3556 (2441).
ANTINONI, gr., fo. 82, imp. in dam. Rec. 2199.
APOLLO, gr., fo. 69, imp. 75. Rec. 14.
APOLLON, gr., fo. 80, imp. 84. Rec. 3515 (2151).
ARABI, gr., fo. 80, imp. 82. Rec. 1981 (905).
ARAMIS, gr., fo. 82, imp. 85. Rec. 4221 (226).
ARBITOR, b., fo. 79, home bred. Rec. 806.
ARBO, gr., fo. 79, imp. 82. Rec. 1955 (1051).
ARCADIAN, gr., fo. 80, home bred. Rec. 911.
ARCHDUKE, gr., fo. 78, imp. 80. Rec. 909 (844).
ARCOLA, gr., fo. 74, imp. 79. Rec. 850 (819).
ARCOLE, gr., fo. 84, imp. 86. Rec. 5172 (3494).
ARCOLE, gr., fo. 84, imp. 87. Rec. 6905 (3626).
ARCOLE, gr., fo. 85, imp. 87. Rec. 7018 (6346).
ARDELU, gr., fo. 82, imp. 83. Rec. 2950 (1237).
ARDENNES, gr., fo. 81, imp. 83. Rec. 2361 (1).
ARDOR, b., fo. 76, imp. 76. Rec. 15 (851).
ARGENTINE, b., fo. 80, imp. 82. Rec. 1972 (507).
AIGOSSA, gr., fo. 76, imp. 81. Rec. 1430.
AIGOSTA, bl., fo. 80, imp. 82. Rec. 1949 (1032).
ARIAN, gr., fo. 80, imp. 82. Rec. 2151 (908).
ARISTOS, gr., fo. 78, imp. 82. Rec. 1985 (909).
ARMAGNAC, gr., fo. 86, imp. 87. Rec. 7020 (8295).
ARMENIAN, bl., fo. 82, imp. 82. Rec. 2150 (910).
ARMITAGE, gr., fo. 76, imp. 81. Rec. 1289.
ARNO, bl., fo. 77, imp. 80. Rec. 905 (849).
ARRIGO, gr., fo. 80, imp. 82. Rec. 1975 (911).
ARROU, bl., fo. 82, imp. 83. Rec. 2329 (1235).
ARTHUR, gr., fo. 80, imp. 80. Rec. 904 (847).
ARTHUR, bl., fo. 82, imp. 84. Rec. 5038 (2168).
ARTHUR, gr., fo. 85, imp. 86. Rec. 5546 (6520).
ARTISAN, gr., fo. 85, imp. 86. Rec. 5695 (7427).
ASPIRATION, gr., fo. 81, imp. 81. Rec. 1483.
ASSYRIAN, br., fo. 81, imp. 83. Rec. 1571.
ASTEROID, gr., fo. 72, imp. 77. Rec. 620.
ASTOR, gr., fo. 74, imp. 77. Rec. 621 (850).
ATHENES, gr., fo. 81, imp. 83. Rec. 2358 (6).
ATHLETE, br., fo. 81, imp. 84. Rec. 1376.
ATHOS, gr., fo. 76, imp. 80. Rec. 916.
ATHOS, b., fo. 81, imp. 83. Rec. 2308 (1169).
ATHOS, gr., fo. 82, imp. 85. Rec. 4230 (225).
ATILLA, gr., fo. 84, imp. 87. Rec. 7015 (6201).
AUBEPIN, gr. fo. 84, imp. 87. Rec. 7019 (9204).
AUBRY, gr., fo. 85, imp. 87. Rec. 7014 (11542).
AUDOBON, gr., fo. 77, imp. 80. Rec. 1255.
AUGERON, gr., fo. 78, home bred. Rec. 719.
AUGUSTE, gr. fo. 82, imp. 84. Rec. 3684 (2794).

AUGUSTINE, b., fo. 78, imp. 81. Rec. 1290 (793).
AUNAIS LES BOIS, gr., fo, 82, imp. 84. 3494 (2504).
AUNEAU, bl., fo. 80, imp. 83. Rec. 2561 (1263).
AURELIAN, gr., fo. 78, imp. 83. Rec. 1945 (1033).
AUSTERLITZ, gr., fo. 76, imp. 80. Rec. 1256.
AUSTERLITZ, gr., fo. 78, imp. 83. Rec. 2715 (1282).
AUSTERLITZ, gr., fo. 83, imp. 85. Rec. 4243 (2228).
AUTOCRAT, r., fo. 63, imp. 75. Rec. 18.
AVALANCHE, gr., fo. 73, imp. 79. Rec. 849.
AVATA, bl., fo. 78, imp. 82. Rec. 1966 (912).
AVENIR, gr., fo. 85, imp. 86. Rec. 5526 (7220).
A'VENTURE, gr., fo. 78, imp. 81. Rec. 1448 (803).
BACCHUS, gr., fo. 74, imp. 78. Rec. 622.
BADER, gr., fo. 82, imp. 85. Rec. 4206 (4927).
BADGER BOY, gr., fo. 83, home bred. Rec. 2490.
BAILLEAU, gr., fo. 79, imp. 83. Rec. 2583 (1137).
BAILLEUL, bl., fo. 80, imp. 83. Rec. 2705 (1127).
BAJARDO, gr., fo. 78, imp. 82. Rec. 1991 (913).
BAJIZET, bl., fo. 78, imp. 81. Rec. 1292.
BALFOUR, bl., fo. 76, imp 81. Rec. 1445.
BALLIETT, bl., fo. 87, home bred. Rec. 7161.
BALSORA, ? ., fo. 71, imp. 80. Rec. 917.
BALTHAZ_R, gr., fo. 82, imp. 85. Rec. 4261 (2296).
BALZAAC, bl., fo. 80, imp. 83. Rec. 2716 (1283).
BALZAC, gr., fo. 83, imp. 85. Rec. 4299 (1756).
BAMBINAS, gr., fo. 83, imp. 87. Rec. 6366 (6428).
BANBURY, gr., fo. 83, imp. 84. Rec. 3786 (1853).
BANCROFT, b., fo. 84, home bred. Rec. 3667.
BANKER, gr., fo. 80, imp. 82. Rec. 1909 (1054).
BANLIEU, gr., fo. 87, home bred. Rec. 7222.
BANQUO, bl., fo. 77, imp. 82. Rec. 1987 (914).
BANQUO, gr., fo. 87, home bred. Rec. 7325.
BAPTISTE, bl., fo. 72, imp. 75. Rec. 22 (737).
BAPTISTE, gr., fo. 86, imp. 87. Rec. 7029 (10088).
BARABAS, bl., fo. 84, imp. 87. Rec. 6937 (6027).
BARABOSA, bl., fo. 77, imp. 81. Rec. 1491.
BARBANSON, bay, fo. 85, imp. 87. Rec. 7028 (8312).
BARBARIAN, gr., fo.80, imp. 80. Rec. 841.
BARBEAU, gr., fo. 84, imp. 85. Rec. 4317 (4216).
BARCINO, gr., fo. 85, home bred. Rec. 4341.
BARDINO, gr., fo. 76, imp. in dam. Rec. 23.
BARNOT, gr., fo. 80, imp. 83. Rec. 2563 (1290).
BARONET, gr., fo. 78, imp. 81. Rec. 1293.
BARRETT, bl., fo. 87, home bred. Rec. 7237.
BARTHOLDI, bl., fo. 84, home bred. Rec. 3695.
BARVILLE, gr., fo. 80, imp. 83. Rec. 2795 (1129).
BASCEDO, gr., fo. 80, imp. 82. Rec. 1957 (915).
BASILE, bl., fo. 87, home bred. Rec. 4339.
BASSANIO, b., fo. 85, home bred. Rec. 4339.
BASTA, bl., fo. 82, imp. 84. Rec. 3466 (521).
BATAILLE, bl., fo. 84, imp. 86. Rec. 5367 (6858).
BAUTE, bl., fo. 80, imp. 83. Rec. 2708 (1129).
BAVARD, gr., fo. 84, imp. 85. Rec. 4318 (4221).
BAVARDO, bl., fo. 87, home bred. Rec. 7236.
BAY, b., fo. 82, imp. 85. Rec. 4263 (650).
BAYADERE, b., fo. 77, imp. 82. Rec. 2147 (916).
BAYARD, b., fo. 68, imp. 74. Rec. 26 (717).
BAYARD, gr., fo. 82, imp. 84. Rec. 3483 (550).
BAYARD, gr., fo. 80, imp. 84. Rec. 3555 (687).
BAYARD, gr., fo. 82, imp. 84. Rec. 5337 (691).
BAYARD, gr., fo. 81, imp. 84. Rec. 3760 (2422).
BAYARD, gr., fo. 82, imp. 85. Rec. 4240 (1772).
BAYARD II, br., fo. 70, imp. 73. Rec. 29.
BAY BRILLIANT, b., fo. 77, imp. 80. Rec. 912 (842).
BAYMONT, b., fo. 81, imp. 82. Rec. 2148 (917).
BAYWOOD, b., fo. 80, imp. 82. Rec. 1978 (918).
BEAUCERON, bl., fo. 79, imp. 84. Rec. 3481 (1999).
BEAU-CŒUR, gr., fo. 80, imp. 83. Rec. 2680 (1125.)
BEAUFORT, gr., fo. 77, imp. 82. Rec. 1988 (919).
BEAULIEU, bl., fo. 83, imp. 84. Rec. 3551 (1763).
BEAUMONT, gr., fo. 71, imp. 75. Rec. 30.
BEAUMONT, bl., fo. 83, imp. 85. Rec. 4221 (488).

BEAU NOIR, bl., fo. 75, imp. 80. Rec. 943.
BEAU NOIR, gr., fo. 85, home bred. Rec. 5741.
BECKET, gr., fo. 85, imp. 86. Rec. 5600 (7381).
BECKLAND, gr., fo. 82, imp. 85. Rec. 4256 (91).
BEDEAU, gr., fo. 77, imp. 81. Rec. 1291 (864).
BEDIVERE, gr., fo. 74, imp. 80. Rec. 1211 (751).
BEDOUIN, w., fo. 65, imp. 73. Rec. 32.
BEIDLER, bl., fo. 87, home bred. Rec. 7276.
BELDEMEER, gr., fo. 80, imp. 82. Rec. 2134 (920).
BELFORT, gr., fo. 86, imp. 87. Rec. 7031 (8308).
BELLAIRE, bl., fo. 79, imp. 82. Rec. 2130 (921).
BELLAIRE, bl., fo. 79, imp. 82. Rec. 2133 (1089).
BELLEFONTAINE, gr., fo. 70, imp. 73. Rec. 33.
BELLERUS, bl., fo. 74, imp. 75. Rec. 34.
BELLIEVRE, gr., fo. 80, imp. 83. Rec. 2382 (1285).
BELLOT, gr., fo. 83, imp. 87. Rec. 6368 (1635).
BELLVIEW, gr., fo. 77, imp. 77. Rec. 625 (843).
BELLWOOD, gr., fo. 78, imp. 82. Rec. 1994 (922).
BEMBO, gr, fo. 85, imp. 87. Rec. 7024 (7946).
BENONI, bl., fo. 73, imp. 78. Rec. 626.
BEPPO, bl., fo. 76, imp. 80. Rec. 914.
BERDHUIS, gr., fo. 81, imp. 83. Rec. 2534 (1188).
BERDHUIS, gr., fo. 81, imp. 83. Rec 2546 (1386).
BERNARD, gr., fo. 83, imp. 84. Rec. 5592 (5052).
BERON, bl., fo. 80, imp. 83. Rec. 2565 (1139).
BERRARD, bl., fo. 79, imp. 84. Rec. 3689 (2663).
BERTON, bl., fo. 82, imp. 83. Rec. 3625 (1290).
BERTRAND, gr., fo. 80, imp. 80. Rec. 916.
BERTRAND, gr., fo. 82, imp. 83. Rec. 4253 (2356).
BERTRAND, gr., fo. 84, imp. 87. Rec. 7164 (2924).
BICHE, bl., fo. 81, imp. 84. Rec. 3480 (2588). .
BIENVENU, bl., fo. 85, home bred. Rec. 4337.
BIJOU, gr., fo. 83, imp. 84. Rec. 3775 (2601).
BIJOU, gr., fo. 81, imp. 85. Rec. 4286 (162).
BINOIS, bl., fo. 81, imp. 85. Rec. 2587 (1200).
BISMARK, gr., fo. 83, imp. 85. Rec. 4250 (4925).
BLACK, bl., fo. 84, imp. 85. Rec. 4258 (4674).
BLACK BART, bl., fo. 85, home bred. Rec. 4259.
BLACK PRINCE, bl., fo. 75, imp. 80. 990 (752).
BLASON, gr., fo. 82, imp. 83. Rec. 2656 (1171).
BLASON, bl., fo. 87, home bred. Rec. 7230.
BLENHEIM, gr., fo. 76, imp. 80. Rec. 1365.
BLEUET, gr., fo. 84, imp. 87. Rec. 6970 (3712).
BLEVY, gr. fo. 82, imp. 83. Rec. 3062 (1249).
BLOIS, gr., fo. 85, home bred. Rec. 5695.
BLUCHER, gr, fo. 82, imp. 83. Rec. 2631 (1173).
BOABDIL, gr., fo. 76, imp. 79. Rec. 852 (802).
BOCARDO, gr., fo. 76, imp. 81. Rec. 1294.
BOCCACCIO, bl., fo. 80, imp. 80. Rec. 1251.
BOERHAAVE, gr., fo. 82, imp. 83, Rec. 2634 (1174).
BOHEMIAN, bl., fo. 85, home bred. Rec. 4538.
BOHEMOND, fo 82, imp. 86. Rec. 5508 (92).
BOIS, gr., fo. 80, imp. 83. Rec. 2558 (1291).
BOISJOLY, bl., fo 80, imp. 83. Rec. 2578 (1327).
BOKHARA, b., fo. 76, imp. 80. Rec. 987.
BOLIDE, bl., fo. 84, imp. 86. Rec. 5508 (6700).
BOLINDA, gr., fo. 87, home bred. Rec. 7241.
BON-BON, gr., fo. 81, imp. 81. Rec. 1274.
BONCŒUR, gr., fo. 82, imp. 82. Rec. 2100 (923).
BONCŒUR, bl., fo. 81, imp. 84. Rec. 3479 (367).
BONCŒUR, gr., fo. 82, imp. 84. Rec. 3088 (2544).
BONCŒUR, bl., fo 82, imp. 84. Rec. 3743 (1824).
BONCŒUR, gr., fo. 82, imp. 85. Rec. 4248 (440).
BONCŒUR II, bl., fo. 82, imp. 86. Rec. 5584 (7000).
BONCOURT, gr., fo. 81, imp. 83. Rec. 2539 (1135).
BON ESPOIR, gr., fo. 73, imp. 79. Rec. 853.
BON ESPOIR, br., fo. 76, imp. 81. Rec. 1370 (753).
BON ESPOIR, gr., fo. 83, imp. 87. Rec. 7022 (5618).
BONGARD, gr., fo. 77, imp. 80. Rec. 1384.
BONIFACE, bl., fo. 79, imp. 82. Rec. 1958 (924).
BON LURON gr. fo. 85, imp. 87. Rec. 7027 (9408).
BONNEFOI, gr., fo. 81, imp. 83. Rec. 2598 (1196).

BONNEVAL , gr., fo. 80, imp. 83. Rec. 2929 (1124).
BON-TON, bl., fo. 77, imp. 81. Rec. 1441.
BORDEAUX, gr., fo. 84, imp. 85. Rec. 4235 (4168).
BORDEAUX, gr., fo. 82, imp. 86. Rec. 5499 (5546).
BORDELAISE, gr., fo. 86, home bred. Rec. 5528.
BORDINE, gr., fo. 75, imp. 80. Rec. 908 (754).
BOULEVARD, gr., fo. 81, imp. 81. Rec. 1547.
BOULLAY, gr., fo. 80, imp. 83. Rec. 2789 (1147).
BOURBON, gr., fo. 80, imp. 83. Rec. 2589 (1257).
BOUTIGNY, gr., fo. 80, imp. 83. Rec. 2713 (1241).
BOUVILLE, gr., fo. 81, imp. 83. Rec. 2531 (1148).
BRABANT, bl, fo. 84, imp. 86. Rec. 5345 (7979).
BRACARIA, gr., fo. 85, home bred. Rec. 4580.
BRACHELLE, gr., fo. 78, imp. 84. Rec. 1205.
BRACONNIER, bl., fo. 81, imp. 84. Rec. 3758 (450).
BRAGANZA, bl., fo. 70, imp. 75. Rec. 62.
BRAMBLE, gr., fo. 80, imp. 82. Rec. 1967 (923).
BRANCHARD, gr., fo. 81, imp. 83. Rec. 2292 (1232).
BRANDON, bl., fo. 85, home bred. Rec. 5329.
BRANNOCK, b., fo. 86, home bred. Rec. 5088.
BRANT, bl., fo. 86, home bred. Rec. 5696.
BRASTIN, bl., fo. 86, home bred. Rec. 5689.
BRAVADE, gr., fo. 87, home bred. Rec. 7227.
BRAVO, gr., fo. 72, imp. 77. Rec. 650.
BRAVO, gr., fo. 84, imp. 87. Rec. 6940 (6617).
BRAZZOLA, gr., fo. 80, imp. 82. 1968 (926).
BREBIO, gr., fo. 87, home bred. Rec. 7231.
BREEZE, gr., fo. 87, home bred. Rec. 7224.
BREGENT, gr., fo. 82, imp. 83. Rec. 3652 (1175).
BREME, gr., fo. 87, home bred. Rec. 7223.
BREMUS, gr., fo. 83, imp. 83. Rec. 2637 (1176).
BRESLEAU, gr., fo. 84, imp. 86. Rec. 5516 (6841).
BRETTE, gr., fo. 87, home bred. Rec. 7278.
BREVET, bl., fo. 87, home bred. Rec. 7228.
BREVIAIRE, bl., fo. 87, home bred. Rec. 7225.
BREZE, gr., fo. 79, imp. 83. Rec. 2519 (1101).
BREZOLLES, bl., fo. 80, imp. 83. Rec. 2573 (1245).
BRIALMONT, gr., fo. 78, imp. 81. Rec. 1296.
BRIANT, bl., fo. 87, home bred. Rec. 7225.
BRIARD, bl., fo. 82, imp. 86. Rec. 5317 (1630).
BRIARDO, gr., fo. 87, home bred. Rec. 7234.
BRIDAH, gr., fo. 82, imp. 83. Rec. 2642 (1172).
BRIGADIER, gr., fo. 87, home bred. Rec. 7277.
BRIGAND, bl., fo. 72, imp. 77. Rec. 651.
BRIGHT STAR, gr., fo. 80, imp. 82. Rec. 2138 (927).
BRILLANT, gr., fo. 81, imp. 84. Rec. 3712 (361).
BRILLANT, gr., fo. 82, imp. 84. Rec. 3767 (607).
BRILLANT, gr., fo. 84, imp. 85. Rec. 4285 (2252).
BRILLANT, gr., fo. 85, imp. 86. Rec. 5588 (5441).
BRILLANT, gr., fo. 85, imp. 87. Rec. 7021 (9797).
BRILLIANT, gr., fo. 69, imp. 74. Rec. 65 (718).
BRILLIANT, bl., fo. 76, imp. 81. Rec. 1271 (755).
BRISKE, gr., fo. 87, home bred. Rec. 7226.
BRISOIR, gr., fo. 87, home bred. Rec. 7233.
BRISSON, gr., fo. 85, home bred. Rec. 4594.
BRISSON, gr., fo. 83, imp. 86. Rec. 5553 (7199).
BRISUDAN, bl., fo. 86, home bred. Rec. 5530.
BRITANICUS, gr., fo. 85, imp. 87. Rec. 7025 (9294).
BROCANTEUR, gr., fo. 85, imp. 87. Rec. 7079 (9496).
BROUARD, gr., fo. 81, imp. 83. Rec. 2381 (1209).
BROUHO, gr., fo. 82, imp. 84. Rec. 3756 (556).
BRUNO, gr., fo. 71, imp. 75. Rec. 65.
BRUTUS, gr., fo. 81, imp. 83. Rec. 2709 (22).
BRUTUS, bl., fo. 82, imp. 84. Rec. 3742 (351).
BRUTUS, gr., fo. 83, imp. 84. Rec. 3772 (1314).
BRUTUS, gr., fo. 84, imp. 87. Rec. 6941 (6619).
BUCCANEER, gr., fo. 80, imp. 82. Rec. 2145 (928).
BUCENTAURE, gr., fo. 79, imp. 83. Rec. 2578 (1097).
BUCEPHALOS, bl., fo. 84, imp. 86. Rec. 5591 (6949).
BUCKEYE BRILLIANT, bl., fo. 78. 1851 (1655).
BUFFON, bl., fo. 80, imp. 83. Rec. 2398 (1098).
BUFFON, bl., fo. 84, imp. 86. Rec. 5336 (7100).

BULLON, gr., fo. 82, imp. 83. Rec. 2654 (1239).
BURATTI, bl., fo. 79, imp. 83. Rec. 2704 (1262).
BUREAUCRATE, bl., fo. 87, home bred. 7332.
BURGLAR, gr., fo. 81, imp. 81. Rec. 1454.
BURIDAN, gr., fo. 84, imp. 85. Rec. 4750 (3902).
BUSIRUS, bl., fo. 85, home bred. Rec. 4555.
BUTOR, gr., fo. 85, imp. 87. Rec. 7023 (9052).
CADMUS, bl., fo. 82, imp. 82. Rec. 2462 (929).
CÆSAR, gr., fo. 74, imp. 79. Rec. 856 (757).
CAGET, gr., fo. 82, imp. 83. Rec. 2915 (1253).
CAILLAUX, gr., fo. 82, imp. 83. Rec. 2633 (1178).
CALIGULA, gr., fo. 82, imp. 85. Rec. 4329 (2156).
CALIN, gr., fo. 83, imp. 84. Rec. 3780 (247).
CALINO, gr., fo. 83, imp. 84. Rec. 3736 (236).
CALIPH, gr., fo. 71, imp. 76. Rec. 74.
CALYPSO, gr., fo. 77, imp. 82. Rec. 1980 (900).
CALYPSO, gr., fo. 83, imp. 84. Rec. 3773 (208).
CAMANCHE, gr., fo. 79, imp. 79. Rec. 854.
CAMBRONNE, gr., fo. 85, imp. 86. Rec. 5297 (7484).
CAMEMBERT, gr., fo. 82, imp. 86. Rec. 5415 (93).
CAMILLE, bay, fo. 83, imp. 87. Rec. 7034 (9280).
CANADIEN, gr., fo. 84, imp. 87. Rec. 7033 (9653).
CANROBERT, gr., fo. 85, imp. 87. Rec. 7037 (9290).
CAPITAINE, gr., fo. 85, imp. 87. Rec. 6942 (6240).
CAPORAL, gr., fo. 84, imp. 87. Rec. 4943 (5568).
CAPUCINES, gr., fo. 82, imp. 85. Rec. 2539 (1335).
CARBONNIER, bl., fo. 82, imp. 83. Rec. 2659 (1179).
CARDINAL, gr., fo. 70, imp. 76. Rec. 78.
CARDINO, gr., fo. 78, imp. 81. Rec. 1444.
CARLIER, gr., fo. 80, imp. 83. Rec. 2500 (1297).
CARLO, gr., fo. 80, imp. 80. Rec. 918.
CARLOS, gr., fo. 84, imp. 87. Rec. 7035 (9276).
CARLOVIN, gr., fo. 76, imp. 81. Rec. 1297.
CARNI, bl., fo. 79, imp. 82. Rec. 1900 (1056).
CARNIVAL, gr., fo. 78, imp. 81. Rec. 1533.
CARNOT, bl., fo. 76, imp. 75 in dam. Rec. 79.
CAROLUS, gr., fo. 86, imp. 87. Rec. 7032 (8858).
CARRATTI, bl., fo. 82, imp. 83. Rec. 2649 (1263).
CASEY, bl., fo. 81, imp. 83. Rec. 2327 (1196).
CASTEL, gr., fo. 84, imp. 87. Rec. 6944 (6678).
CASTILLON, bl., fo. 80, imp. 83. Rec. 2585 (1900).
CATALAN, gr., fo. 84, imp. 87. Rec. 6945 (10508).
CATO, gr., fo. 79, imp. 82. Rec. 2002 (561).
CAVAIGNAC, gr., fo. 83, imp. 86. Rec. 5523 (6250).
CAVALIER, gr., fo. 70, imp. 75. Rec. 81.
CAZIQUE, gr., fo. 81, imp. 81. Rec. 1498.
CEDRIC, gr., fo. 80, imp. 82. Rec. 1995 (922).
CENTENNIAL, b., fo. 72, imp. 76. Rec. 82.
CERIGO, gr., fo. 79, imp. 82. Rec. 1944 (1037).
CERNAY, gr., fo. 82, imp. 83. Rec. 2648 (1295).
CERVANTES, gr., fo. 79, imp. 82. Rec. 2119 (933).
CESAR, gr., fo. 82, imp. 84. Rec. 3526 (631).
CESAR, gr., fo. 82, imp. 85. Rec. 4280 (468).
CESAR, bl., fo. 83, imp. 86. Rec. 5537 (7470).
CETON, bl., fo. 81, imp. 83. Rec. 2579 (1217).
CEVALIO, gr., fo. 82, imp. 82. Rec. 2461 (934).
CHARANAIS, gr., fo. 82, imp. 83. Rec. 2672 (1204).
CHABOT, gr., fo. 81, imp. 83. Rec. 2905 (1211).
CHAILLOT, bl., fo. 82, imp. 83. Rec. 2664 (1005).
CHALDEAN, bl., fo. 77, imp. 77. Rec. 637 (854).
CHALDEAN, JR., gr., fo. 84, home bred. Rec. 5874.
CHALIGNY, bl., fo. 80, imp. 83. Rec. 2559 (1501).
CHALLENGE, gr., fo. 76, imp. 80. Rec. 987 (758).
CHAMBERTIN, gr., fo. 80, imp. 83. 2565 (1502).
CHAMOUNIX, gr., fo. 81, imp. 83. Rec. 2587 (1250).
CHAMPAGNE, b., fo. 79, imp. 83. Rec. 2512 (1117).
CHAMPAGNE, gr., fo. 79, imp. 83. Rec. 2546 (17).
CHAMPAGNE, gr., fo. 81, imp. 84. Rec. 3715 (78).
CHAMPAION, gr., fo. 82, home bred. Rec. 5678.
CHAMPION, gr., fo. 69, imp. 73. Rec. 84.
CHAMPLAIN, gr., fo. 79, imp. 83. Rec. 2670 (1304).
CHANDON, b., fo. 82, imp. 83. Rec. 2660 (32).

CHANTILLY, gr., fo. 84, imp. 87. Rec. 7041 (8311).
CHAPTAL, gr., fo. 85, imp. 87. Rec. 7038 (9288).
CHARLE, gr., fo. 79, imp. 82. Rec. 1910 (1058).
CHARLEMAGNE, gr., fo. 71, imp. 76. Rec. 87.
CHARLEMAGNE, gr., fo. 85, home bred. Rec. 4290.
CHARLES, gr., fo. 78, imp. 85. Rec. 2365 (1354).
CHARLES, gr., fo. 81, imp. 83. Rec. 2557 (1250).
CHARLES, gr., fo. 82, imp. 84. Rec. 3729 (2797).
CHARLES, gr., fo. 83, imp. 84. Rec. 3784 (2655).
CHARLESTOWN, gr., fo. 82, imp. 84. Rec. 3504 (1790).
CHARMANT, bl., fo. 81, imp. 87. Rec. 7042 (7334).
CHARPONT, gr., fo. 82, imp. 83. Rec. 2670 (1181).
CHARTEIN, gr., fo. 81, imp. 83. Rec. 2530 (1181).
CHARTRES, gr., fo. 82, imp. 4. Rec. 3567 (1695).
CHASLIN II, bl., fo. 78, imp. 83. Rec. 2692 (1513).
CHASSANT, gr., fo. 82, imp. 83. Rec. 2644 (51).
CHASSEUR, b., fo. 80, imp. 84. Rec. 3522 (689).
CHATILLON, gr., fo. 81, imp. 83. Rec. 2576 (1297).
CHECKMATE, bl., fo. 81, imp. 81. Rec. 1199.
CHEERE, gr., fo. 69, imp. 73. Rec. 90 (801).
CHERE, gr., fo. 75, imp. 79. Rec. 855.
CHERI, bl., fo. 80, imp. 83. Rec. 2384 (18).
CHERI, bl., fo. 83, imp. 84. Rec. 3528 (709).
CHERI, gr., fo. 83, imp. 84. Rec. 3781 (1847).
CHERI, gr., fo. 82, imp. 85. Rec. 4216 (65).
CHERI, b., fo. 82, imp. 86. Rec. 5148 (5614).
CHERI, gr., fo. 83, imp. 86. Rec. 5506 (1922).
CHERRY, gr., fo. 80, imp. 83. Rec. 2363 (1093).
CHERUBIN, bl., fo. 83, imp. 87. Rec. 6946 (11241).
CHEVALIER BAYARD, b., fo. 79, imp. 81. 1279.
CHEVRAY, gr., fo. 82, imp. 83. Rec. 2668 (1240).
CHICAGO, gr., fo. 76, imp. 81. Rec. 1225.
CHICAGO, bl., fo. 83, imp. 87. Rec. 6947 (7485).
CHILPERIC, b., fo. 82, imp. 84. Rec. 3744 (96).
CHILDEBERT, bl., fo. 81, imp. 85. Rec. 4283 (451).
CHILTON, gr., fo. 79, imp. 83. Rec. 2688 (1255).
CHIVALRY, gr., fo. 79, imp. 82. Rec. 1960 (933).
CHOUNARD, gr., fo. 79, imp. 81. Rec. 1281.
CHRAM, bl., fo. 84, imp. 87. Rec. 6948 (9466).
CINQ-MARS, gr., fo. 80, imp. 83. Rec. 2693 (1153).
CLEMENCEAU, gr., fo. 83, imp. 86. Rec. 5548 (7255).
CLEMENT, gr., fo. 79, imp. 82. Rec. 1965 (935).
CLEREMONT, bl., fo. 78, imp. 81. Rec. 1298.
CLIMAX, gr., fo. 78, home bred. Rec. 640.
CLODIUS, gr., fo. 82, imp. 85. Rec. 4219 (2242).
CLODOMAR, b., fo. 82, imp. 85. Rec. 4281 (98).
CLOTAIRE, gr., fo. 84, imp. 86. Rec. 5461 (5742).
CLOTHAIRE, gr., fo. 79, imp. 82. Rec. 1961 (937).
CLOVIS IV, gr., fo. 85, imp. 87. Rec. 7056 (11350).
CLUNY, gr., fo. 82, imp. 85. Rec. 2069 (1306).
COCO, gr., fo. 73, imp. 76. Rec. 98.
COCO, gr., fo. 76, imp. 81. Rec. 1209 (762).
COCO, gr., fo. 83, imp. 84. Rec. 3533 (697).
COCO, gr., fo. 82, imp. 85. Rec. 4250 (234).
COCO V, gr., fo. 84, imp. 86. Rec. 5611 (2022).
COGNAC, gr., fo. 82, imp. 84. Rec. 3729 (621).
COLANDO, gr., fo. 80, imp. 83. Rec. 2539 (1192).
COLAS, gr., fo. 81, imp. 83. Rec. 2683 (1208).
COLBERT, br., fo. 84, imp. 86. Rec. 5508 (6551).
COLBERT, bl., fo. 85, imp. 87. Rec. 7059 (9410).
COLEMAN, gr., fo. 81, imp. 83. Rec. 2639 (1395).
COLENZO, gr., fo. 81, imp. 82. Rec. 2204 (1294).
COLICHON, gr., fo. 83, imp. 84. Rec. 3543 (344).
COLIN, gr., fo. 81, imp. 84. Rec. 3549 (2461).
COLIN, gr., fo. 83, imp. 84. Rec. 3762 (1840).
COLIN, gr., fo. 83, imp. 86. Rec. 5501 (1619).
COLIN, gr., fo. 83, imp. 87. Rec. 6949 (10833).
COLIN II, bl., fo. 83, imp. 84. Rec. 3558 (339).
COLINO, bl., fo. 84, imp. 84. Rec. 3557 (257).
COLOSSUS, gr., fo. 69, imp. 73. Rec. 101.
COMBLOT, bl., fo. 81, imp. 83. Rec. 2697 (1185).
COMMODORE, gr., fo. 78, imp. 82. Rec. 1946 (1029).

COMPERE, gr., fo. 83, imp. 85. Rec. 4331 (5075).
COMPERE, bl., fo. 84, imp. 86. Rec. 5523 (6684).
COMTE DE CHAMBORD, bl., fo. 80. 3708 (1142).
COMTE LOBAU, gr., fo. 82, imp. 86. Rec. 5531 (5490).
COMVICI, gr., fo. 83, imp. 83. Rec. 2671 (1233).
CONDE, gr., fo. 84, imp. 86. Rec. 5163 (5628).
CONFIDENCE, gr., fo. 77, imp. 80. Rec. 920 (763).
CONFIDENT, bl., fo. 81, imp. 84. Rec. 3647 (397).
CONGO, bl., fo. 80, imp. 82. Rec. 2156 (936).
CONNOUGHT, gr., fo. 78, imp. 82. Rec. 1908 (1048).
CONQUERANT, bl., fo. 82, imp. 84. 3751 (1798).
CONQUEROR, gr., fo. 67, imp. 73. Rec. 110.
CONSTANTINE, gr., fo. 80, imp. 83. 2547 (1309).
CONSUL, bl., fo. 77, imp. 80. Rec. 901 (840).
CONSUL, gr., fo. 83 imp. 85. Rec. 4225 (4046).
COQUET, bl., fo. 84, imp. 85. Rec. 5175 (5746).
CORANA, gr., fo. 74, imp. 80. Rec. 1428.
CORDALINO, gr., fo. 81, imp. 83. Rec. 2595 (1335).
CORNEILLE, gr., fo. 81, imp. 83. Rec. 2611 (1093).
CORSAIR, gr., fo. 67, imp. 72. Rec. 113.
CORSICAN, b., fo. 78, imp. 81. Rec. 1209 (800).
CORUBERT, bl., fo. 84, imp. 87. Rec. 6950 (10239).
COSTOU, gr., fo. 79, imp. 83. Rec. 2367 (1314).
COUNT, gr., fo. 73, imp. 78. Rec. 643 (736).
COUNT DE PARIS, gr., fo. 71, imp. 75. Rec. 118.
COUNT MONTHOLON, gr., fo. 85. 919 (839).
COUNT OF PERCHE, bl., fo. 75, imp. 80. Rec. 905.
COUNT ROTROU, gr., fo. 75, imp. 80. Rec. 959.
COURCERAULT, gr., fo. 85, imp. 87. 7049 (9327).
COURIER, gr., fo. 69, imp. 74. Rec. 159.
COURTOMER, gr., fo. 82, imp. 84. Rec. 3488 (2537).
CROMWELL, gr., fo. 80, imp. 82. Rec. 1958 (999).
CRUSADER, gr., fo. 77, imp. 81. Rec. 1437 (799).
CYGNE, gr., fo. 83, imp. 87. Rec. 6951 (6356).
CYLO, gr., fo. 78, imp. 83. Rec. 2719.
CYRIL, gr., fo. 80, imp. 82. Rec. 2135 (940).
DAGOBERT, bl., fo. 82, imp. 86. Rec. 5151 (2431).
DALAROCHE, gr., fo. 81, imp. 81. Rec. 1381.
DANIEL, gr., fo. 81, imp. 83. Rec. 2562 (1190).
DANTE, gr., fo. 82, imp. 82. Rec. 2156 (941).
DAPLON, gr., fo. 81, imp. 83. Rec. 2541 (1108).
DARDANELLE, gr., fo. 82, imp. 82. 2189 (942).
DARE, gr., fo. 79, imp. 79. Rec. 557 (858).
DARIUS, bl., fo. 80, imp. 83. Rec. 2720.
DARLING, gr., fo. 78, imp. 78. Rec. 647.
DARQUIER, gr., fo. 81, imp. 81. Rec. 1380.
D'ARTAGNAN, bl., fo. 82, imp. 84. Rec. 3462 (1771).
D'ARTAGNAN, gr., fo. 82, imp. 85. Rec. 4255 (277).
D'ARTAGNAN, gr., fo. 83, imp. 86. Rec. 5142 (6399).
DAUNEY, gr., fo. 81, imp. 83. Rec. 2557 (1315).
DAUNTLESS, gr., fo. 75, imp. 78. Rec. 648 (823).
DAVID, gr., fo. 85, imp. 87. Rec. 7045 (9059).
DAVILO, bl., fo. 80, imp. 82. Rec. 1971 (943).
DEBILLE, gr., fo. 81, imp. 83. Rec. 2376 (5).
DEBONAIRE, gr., fo. 76, imp. 81. Rec. 1302.
DECIDE, gr., fo. 73, imp. 76. Rec. 136 (720).
DECIDE, bl., fo. 83, imp. 84. Rec. 3532 (695).
DECIDE, gr., fo. 81, imp. 84. Rec. 3719 (54).
DECIDE, bl., fo. 82, imp. 85. Rec. 4284 (233).
DECIDE, gr., fo. 83, imp. 85. Rec. 4275 (1925).
DECIDE, gr., fo. 82, imp. 86. Rec. 5574 (1666).
DECIDE, gr., fo. 83, imp. 87. Rec. 6952 (9325).
DEFENSEUR, gr., fo. 84, imp. 86. Rec. 5573 (6184).
DEFIANCE, gr., fo. 69, imp. 73. Rec. 649.
DEGOURDI, gr., fo. 81, imp. 84. Rec. 3685 (52).
DEGOURDI, gr., fo. 83, imp. 86. Rec. 5558 (6468).
DE LACROIX, gr., fo. 80, imp. 83. Rec. 2507 (1321).
DE LAPIERRE, bl., fo. 78, imp. 81. Rec. 1305.
DELESSE, bl., fo. 78, imp. 81. Rec. 1304.
DELGARDO, bl., fo. 80, imp. 82. Rec. 2116 (344).
DELOS, gr., fo. 79, imp. 82. Rec. 1950 (1040).
DEL SUR, gr., fo. 77, imp. 81. Rec. 1365.

DELVINO, gr., fo. 84, imp. 87. Rec. 6957 (6923).
DEMOSTHENE, gr., fo. 85, imp. 87. Rec. 6354 (5730).
DEO, gr., fo. 82, imp. 82. Rec. 2163 (945).
DE PEER, gr., fo. 77, imp. 81. Rec. 1551.
DE PROVINCE, b., fo. 82, imp. 83. Rec. 3691 (1365).
DESIRA, gr., fo. 84, imp. 85. Rec. 4323 (4225).
DESIRUS, gr., fo. 84, imp. 85. Rec. 4341 (4218).
DESPRE, gr., fo., 78, imp. 82. Rec. 1912 (1041).
D'ESTAING, gr., fo. 81, imp. 81. Rec. 1592.
DEVELLE, gr., fo. 85, imp. 86. Rec. 5549 (6997).
DEY, gr., fo. 85, imp. 86. Rec. 5556 (6572).
DIAMANT, bl., fo. 82, imp. 84. Rec. 3545 (1856).
DIAMANT, gr., fo. 84, imp. 84. Rec. 3754 (2418).
DIAMOND, gr., fo. 84, imp. 84. Rec. 1879.
DIAVOLO, bl., fo. 82, imp. 82. Rec. 2182 (946).
DICTATOR, gr., fo. 80, home bred. Rec. (921).
DICTATOR, gr., fo. 77, imp. 84. Rec. 1220.
DIOCLES, gr., fo. 82, imp. 85. Rec. 2422 (1165).
DIOMEDE, gr., fo. 78, imp. 85. Rec. 2323 (1118).
DIPLOMACY, gr., fo. 78, imp. 82. Rec. 1915 (1042).
DISTINGUE, bl., fo. 82, imp. 86. Rec. 5309 (66).
DISTINGUE, gr., fo. 85, imp. 87. Rec. 7043 (9574).
DOCILE, gr., fo. 70, imp. 75. Rec. 141.
DOCILE, gr., fo. 81, imp. 84. Rec. 3386 (228).
DOCILE, gr., fo. 81, imp. 84. Rec. 3715 (1779).
DOCILE, bl., fo. 83, imp. 84. Rec. 3791 (2630).
DOCILE, b., fo. 82, imp. 85. Rec. 4324 (5255).
DOCILE, gr., fo. 83, imp. 85. Rec. 4232 (4925).
DOCILE, gr., fo. 85, imp. 85. Rec. 4332 (1067).
DOLPHE, gr., fo. 81, imp. 84. Rec. 3554 (2146).
DOMINANT, gr., fo. 82, imp. 85. Rec. 5146 (3017).
DOMINANT, bl., fo. 84, imp. 87. Rec. 6955 (6776).
DOMINGO, gr., fo. 78, imp. 83. Rec. 2721.
DOMPTEUR, gr., fo. 84, imp. 87. Rec. 6959 (9765).
DON, bl., fo. 71, imp. 76. Rec. 143.
DON CARLOS, gr., fo. 83, imp. 86. Rec. 5510 (1759).
DON CESAR, gr., fo. 84, imp. 86. Rec. 5587 (6242).
DONDOLA, gr., fo. 76, imp. 80. Rec. 1201.
DONIMOINE, br., fo. 81, imp. 84. Rec. 1578.
DONIZETTE, gr., fo 76, imp. 81. Rec. 1306.
DON JUAN, bl., fo. 76, imp. 79. Rec. 865.
DON VEGUS, bl., fo. 84, imp. 81. Rec. 1577.
D'OR, gr., fo. 82, imp. 82. Rec. 2186 (947).
DORMEAU, gr., fo. 83, imp. 85. Rec. 4332 (4749).
DOURO, gr., fo. 80, imp. 82. Rec. 1952 (1043).
DRACO, gr., fo. 80, imp. 82. Rec. 2003 (948).
DRACO, gr., fo. 82, imp. 85. Rec. 4215 (2203).
DUBOIS, gr., fo. 82, imp. 83. Rec 2947 (1275).
DUC D'AVEZE, gr., fo. 85, imp. 85. Rec. 4222 (480).
DUC DE BROGLIE, bl., fo. 81, imp. 83. 2808 (1145).
DUC D'ORLEANS, gr., fo. 81, imp. 84. 3519 (890).
DUC-NOIR, bl., fo. 84, imp. 87. Rec. 6957 (1939).
DUKE DE LEVOY, bl., fo. 78, imp. 82. 2117 (949).
DUKE OF ARNO, fo. 79, imp. 82. 1953 (144).
DUKE OF BERNAY, gr., fo. 69, imp. 73. Rec. 158.
DUKE OF PERCHE, gr., fo. 68, imp. 73. 173 (749).
DUMAS, gr., fo. 85, imp. 87. Rec. 7046 (10340).
DUNOIS, gr., fo. 82, imp. 83. Rec. 2640 (1276).
DUROC, gr., fo. 80, imp. 84. Rec. 2335 (1316).
DUROC, gr., fo. 81, imp. 84. Rec. 3768 (453).
DU-ROCHER, gr. fo. 85, imp. 87. Rec. 7044 (8864).
DUVAL, gr., fo. 77, imp. 82. Rec. 1970 (950).
DUVEYRIER, gr., fo. 78, imp. 81. Rec. 1307.
DUVIVERE, bl., fo. 81, imp. 83. Rec. 2559 (1317).
EBLOUISSANT, gr., fo. 84, imp. 86. 5513 (6678).
EBONY, bl., fo. 78, imp. 77. Rec. 656.
ECLIPSE, gr., fo. 78, imp. 82. Rec. 1924 (1045).
ECONOMIST, gr., fo. 81, imp. 81. Rec. 1295.
EDMOND, gr., fo. 84, imp. 86. Rec. 5517 (6844).
ELDORADO, bl., fo. 72 imp. 78. Rec. 657.
ELKADER, gr., fo. 82, imp. 82. Rec. 2157 (951).
ELWYN, gr., fo. 76, imp. 81. Rec. 1308.

ELYSEE, gr., fo. 80, imp. 83. Rec. 2551 (1318).
EMAN, bl., fo. 80, imp. 83. Rec. 2548 (1146).
EMANUEL, gr., fo. 85, imp. 86. Rec. 5555 (7390).
EMERALD, bl., fo. 82, imp. 82. Rec. 2164 (952).
EMIGRANT, gr., fo. 77, imp. 81. Rec. 1741 (764).
ENCHANTER, gr., fo. 74, imp. 77. Rec. 659 (817).
ENCHANTEUR, br., fo. 83, imp. 86. Rec. 5535 (7352).
ENDYMION, bl., fo. 77, imp. 80. Rec. 1249 (852).
ENGARDINE, bl., fo. 73, imp. 79. Rec. 860.
ENOCH ARDEN, gr., fo. 74, imp. 78. Rec. 669 (798).
ENQUIRER, bl., fo. 81, imp. 81. Rec. 1408.
ENVOY, gr., fo. 76, imp. 79. Rec. 858.
EPERNON, gr., fo. 80, imp. 83. Rec. 2548 (1320).
EPERNON, b., fo. 82, imp. 83. Rec. 3617 (1121).
EPINETTE, br., fo. 80, imp. 81. Rec. 3628 (1267).
ERIC, bl., fo. 81, imp. 83. Rec. 2306 (1229).
ERNEST, bl., fo. 72, imp. 75. Rec. 185.
ESAU, gr., fo. 68, imp. 73. Rec. 186.
ESTRABA, gr., fo. 67, imp. 74. Rec. 187 (799).
ETHIOPIAN, gr., fo. 80, imp. 82. Rec. 2125 (953).
ETINNE, bl., fo. 78, imp. 81. Rec. 1309 (850).
EUGENE, gr., fo. 78, imp. 83. Rec. 2359 (1279).
EUREKA, gr., fo. 74, imp. 79. Rec. 839.
EUREKA, bl., fo. 77, imp. 81. Rec. 1234.
EXCELSIOR, gr., fo. 69, imp. 73. Rec. 192.
EXCELSIOR, gr., fo. 76, bred in Ohio. Rec. 1500
EXILE, gr., fo. 69, imp. 74. Rec. 193 (724).
EXTRADOR III, bl., fo. 85, imp. 87. 6958 (11224).
FABIAN, gr., fo. 79, imp. 82. Rec. 1996 (954).
FABIUS, gr., fo. 84, imp. 86. Rec. 5519 (6981).
FABRICUS, bl., fo. 81, imp. 83. Rec. 2394 (1140).
FACEY, gr., fo. 83, imp. 84. Rec. 3542 (251).
FAIRLIGHT, gr., fo. 78, imp. 82. Rec. 1905 (1046).
FAIRMONT, gr., fo. 76, imp. 81. Rec. 1310.
FAISAN, bl., fo. 85, imp. 84. Rec. 3334 (1764).
FAISANT, gr., fo. 80, imp. 83. Rec. 2407 (1130).
FANFAROY, gr., fo. 83, imp. 84. Rec. 3777 (1995).
FARAOUCK, gr., fo. 85, imp. 87. Rec. 7052 (3009).
FARDIN, bl., fo. 82, imp. 84. Rec. 3750 (348).
FASCENO, gr., fo. 82, imp. 82. Rec. 2165 (955).
FASOU, bl., fo. 80, imp. 84. Rec. 3759 (2388).
FAURIEL, gr., fo. 78, imp. 81. Rec. 1311 (816).
FAVORA, gr., fo. 72, imp. 77. Rec. 696 (735).
FAVORI, gr., fo. 81, imp. 84. Rec. 3680 (89).
FAVORI, gr., fo. 85, imp. 86. Rec. 5467 (1835).
FAVORI, gr., fo. 82, imp. 86. Rec. 5612 (6771).
FAVRIL, gr., fo. 80, imp. 83. Rec. 2387 (1122).
FAYETTE, gr., fo. 82, imp. 83. Rec. 2355 (1162).
FELIX, gr., fo. 78, imp. 81. Rec. 1283.
FENELON, bl., fo. 80, imp. 83. Rec. 2682 (38).
FERDINAND, bl., fo. 78, imp.78. Rec. 669 (803).
FERRAND, gr., fo. 83, imp. 86. Rec. 5452 (6390).
FERTOIS, bl., fo. 83, imp. 86. Rec. 5105 (6578).
FIDELIO, bl., fo. 84, imp. 86. Rec. 5542 (6532).
FIER, gr., fo. 84, imp. 87. Rec. 6959 (10932).
FIGARO, gr., fo. 81, imp. 83. Rec. 2315 (33).
FIGARO, bl., fo. 79, imp. 79. Rec. 861 (835).
FIGARO II, gr., fo. 76, imp. 80. Rec. 922.
FILBERT, gr., fo. 77, imp. 80. Rec. 1247.
FILLETTE II, gr., fo. 84, imp. 85. Rec. 4322 (4374).
FINAL, gr., fo. 73, imp. 76. Rec. 199.
FINESSE, gr., fo. 78, imp. 78. Rec. 670.
FIRMIN, gr., fo. 85, imp. 87. Rec. 7047 (8911).
FLACEY, bl., fo. 80, imp. 83. Rec. 2432 (1125).
FLEURY, gr., fo. 82, imp. 83. Rec. 2508 (1164).
FLORAIN, bl., fo. 81, imp. 83. Rec. 2402 (1130).
FLORAINE, gr., fo. 76, imp. 81. Rec. 1312.
FOLLEMBRAY, b., fo. 79, imp. 83. Rec. 2722.
FONTAINE, gr., fo. 81, imp. 81. Rec. 1385.
FONTAINEBLEAU, gr., fo. 77, imp. 84. 3469 (891).
FONTANELLE, gr., fo. 78, imp. 81. Rec. 1218 (705).
FONTENOY, bl., fo. 75, imp. 80. Rec. 1248.

FORABE, bl., fo. 81, imp. 85. Rec. 4327 (628).
FORABEL, gr., fo. 81, imp. 84. Rec. 3546 (629).
FORBAN, gr., fo. 83, imp. 84. Rec. 3778 (1849).
FORBAN, gr., fo. 84, imp. 86. Rec. 5417 (7026).
FORGE, bl., fo. 81, imp. 82. Rec. 2579 (1199).
FORRESTER, gr., fo. 75, imp. 78. Rec. 674 (741).
FORTUNE, bl., fo. 78, imp. 82. Rec. 1983 (956).
FOSCOLA, gr., fo. 81, imp. 81. Rec. 1386.
FOURNEAUX, bl., fo. 80, imp. 83. Rec. 2568 (1324).
FRANCIS, gr., fo. 80, imp. 83. Rec. 2701 (16).
FRANC CŒUR, gr., fo. 85, imp. 87. 7048 (10829).
FRANCŒUR, gr., fo. 81, imp. 83. Rec. 2039 (1135).
FRANCOIS I, gr., fo. 85, imp. 87. Rec. 7051 (8772).
FRANCONI, gr., fo. 82, imp. 85. Rec. 4241 (2182).
FRANCONI, gr., fo. 83, imp. 86. Rec. 5578 (6401).
FRANCONI, gr., fo. 84, imp. 87. Rec. 6960 (10203).
FRANC PICARD, gr., fo. 81, imp. 84. 3706 (2469).
FRANC TIREUR, bl., fo. 82, imp. 84. 3726 (2470).
FRANKLIN, bl., fo. 71, imp. 74. Rec. 200 (843).
FRAZE, gr., fo. 85, imp. 87. Rec. 7050 (9449).
FREDERICK, gr., fo. 80, imp. 83. Rec. 2541 (1138).
FRENCH EMPEROR, gr., fo. 63, imp. 68. 203.
FRENCH MONARCH, gr., fo. 75, imp. 80. 992 (824).
FREYCINET, b., fo. 84, imp. 85. Rec. 5550 (6998).
FRIPOLIN, gr., fo. 82, imp. 85. Rec. 4220 (82).
FRISE, gr., fo. 82, imp. 84. Rec. 3473 (545).
FRISSON, bl., fo. 85, imp. 86. Rec. 5559 (6613).
FRITZ, bl., fo. 84, imp. 87. Rec. 6961 (5458).
FROISSART, gr., fo. 77, imp. 84. Rec. 1314.
FROSINO, gr., fo. 78, imp. 81. Rec. 1315.
FULGIDO, gr., fo. 82, imp. in dam. Rec. 1796.
FULGIDO, gr., fo. 80, imp. 84. Rec. 3402 (2260).
FULMINANT, gr., fo. 85, imp. 87. Rec. 7049 (11916).
GABRIEL, gr., fo. 81, imp. 83. Rec. 2096 (40).
GALLARDON, gr., fo. 80, imp. 83. Rec. 2311 (1144).
GARDA, bl., fo. 77, imp. 81. Rec. 1228.
GARIBALDI, gr., fo. 81, imp. 83. Rec. 2597 (28).
GARIBALDI, gr., fo. 81, imp. 84. Rec. 3649 (396).
GARLAND, gr., fo. 78, imp. 78. Rec. 679.
GARNAY, br., fo. 79, imp. 83. Rec. 2324 (1148).
GASTRONOME, gr., fo. 85, imp. 87. Rec. 7058 (8052).
GASTRONOME, gr., fo. 86, imp. 87. Rec. 7054 (8270).
GAUDAINE, bl., fo. 82, imp. 83. Rec. 2037 (1247).
GAUTIER, gr., fo. 81, imp. 83. Rec. 2375 (1204).
GENDARME, gr., fo. 76, imp. 79. Rec. 662.
GENDARME, bl., fo. 85, imp. 86. Rec. 5130 (6443).
GENDINO, gr., fo. 82, home bred. Rec. 2192.
GENERAL, gr., fo. 82, imp. 82. Rec. 2105 (957).
GENERAL MOREAU, gr., fo. 81. 2517 (1184).
GENERAL ROSECRANS, bl., fo. 80. 1947 (1047).
GENTIL, br., fo. 83, imp. 86. Rec. 5554 (3010).
GEORGE, gr., fo. 81, imp. 83. Rec. 2329 (1339).
GERMAIN, gr., fo. 82, imp. 86. Rec. 5595 (6225).
GEROME, gr., fo. 80, imp. 84. Rec. 3355 (456).
GESTATOR, gr., fo. 84, imp. 87. Rec. 6962 (8957).
GIBRALTAR, gr., fo. 78, imp. 82. Rec. 2241.
GIBRALTAR, gr., fo. 86, imp. 87. Rec. 7055 (7826).
GIL BLAS, bl., fo. 77, imp. 83. Rec. 1982 (958).
GILDINO, gr., fo. 77, imp. 82. Rec. 2008 (959).
GILLE, bl., fo. 83, imp. 85. Rec. 4297 (4894).
GLADIATEUR, gr., fo. 82, imp. 84. Rec. 3727 (2158).
GLADIATEUR, gr., fo. 83, imp. 84. Rec. 3779 (1757).
GLADIATOR, b., fo. 72, imp. 78. Rec. 683 (742).
GLENMORE, gr., fo. 76, imp. 81. Rec. 1316.
GLORIOUS, gr., fo. 81, imp. 83. Rec 2579 (1109).
GLORIOUX, gr., fo. 78, imp. 82. Rec. 1997 (1049).
GODICHON, bl., fo. 85, imp. 87. Rec. 7056 (6324).
GOLIATH, gr., fo. 83, imp. 85. Rec. 4302 (2944).
GOLIATH, gr., fo. 82, imp. 85. Rec 4298 (632).
GOLIATH, bl., fo. 85, imp. 87. Rec. 7057 (9200).
GONDOLIER, gr., fo. 77, imp. 80. Rec. 923 (836).
GOOD HOPE, gr., fo. 80, imp. 82. Rec. 2127 (900).

GOUVERNEUR, gr., fo. 78, imp. 83. 2700 (1330).
GRANADA, gr., fo. 80, imp. 80. Rec. 924 (835).
GRAND DUKE, gr., fo. 72, imp. 78. Rec. 215.
GRANDEE, bl., fo. 74, imp. 77. Rec. 686 (743).
GRANDPERE, gr., fo. 78, imp. 82. Rec. 2242 (1050).
GRAND VIZIER, gr., fo. 72, imp. 77. Rec. 685.
GRENADIER, gr., fo. 72, imp. 77. Rec. 688 (796).
GREY HAWK, gr., fo. 72, imp. 77. Rec. 689 (815).
GREY MARQUIS, gr., fo. 72, imp. 77. 690 (818).
GRINGALET, gr., fo. 84, imp. 86. Rec. 5530 (6349).
GRIS GRIS, gr., fo. 84, imp. 87. Rec. 6963 (9012).
GRIT, gr., fo. 82, imp. 83. Rec. 2673 (1276).
GUILLEMIN, gr., fo. 83, imp. 85. Rec. 4236 (1880).
GUIZOT, bl., fo. 82, imp. 83. Rec. 2026 (1177).
GUSTAVE, bl., fo. 81, imp. 83. Rec. 2513 (1141).
HAMLET, gr., fo. 80, imp. 80. Rec. 1244.
HANLAN, gr., fo. 82, imp. 83. Rec. 2616 (1226).
HANNIBAL, gr., fo. 71, imp. 76. Rec. 222.
HARKAWAY, gr., fo. 80., imp. 80. Rec. 926.
HAROLD, gr., fo. 86, imp. 87. Rec. 7000 (8386).
HARPSBURG, gr., fo. 81, imp. 81. Rec. 1282.
HARRY LIVINGSTONE, bl., fo. 76. Rec. 928.
HECLA, b., fo. 80, imp. 86. Rec. 1245.
HECTOR, gr., fo. 71, imp. 77. Rec. 692.
HELOS, gr., fo. 76, imp. 81. Rec. 1317.
HELVETIUS, br. b., fo. 86, imp. 87. Rec. 7061 (8854).
HENCHMAN, gr., fo. 81, imp. 81. Rec. 1387.
HENGIS, gr., fo. 78, imp. 81. Rec. 1318.
HENRI, gr., fo. 82, imp. 84. Rec. 3475 (333).
HENRI, b., fo. 82, imp. 84. Rec. 3557 (571).
HENRI, gr., fo. 83, imp. 84. Rec. 3771 (2638).
HENRI, gr., fo. 83, imp. 87. Rec. 6964 (8129).
HERCULANUM, bl., fo. 84, imp. 87. 6965 (4027).
HERCULE, gr., fo. 79, imp. 80. Rec. 1260.
HERCULE, gr., fo. 79, imp. 82 Rec. 1903 (1651).
HERCULE, gr., fo. 76, imp. 82. Rec. 1959 (361).
HERCULE, gr., fo. 81, imp. 84. Rec. 3463 (53).
HERCULE, bl., fo. 81, imp. 84. Rec. 3714 (2354).
HERCULE, gr., fo. 79, imp. 84. Rec. 3723 (2692).
HERCULE, gr., fo. 82, imp. 84. Rec. 3718 (2288).
HERCULE, gr., fo. 81, imp. 85. Rec. 4251 (4204).
HERCULE, gr., fo. 81, imp. 85. Rec. 4239 (1230).
HERCULE, gr., fo. 83, imp. 86. Rec. 5145 (5955).
HERCULES, gr., fo. 65, imp. 72. Rec. 225.
HERMIT, bl., fo. 72, imp. 77. Rec. 695.
HERNANDO, gr., fo. 81, imp. 82. Rec. 2154 (932).
HESPERIS, gr., fo. 82, imp. 82. Rec. 2167 (965).
HIAWATHA, gr., fo. 81, imp. 81. Rec. 1392.
HIGHLANDER, bl., fo. 81, imp. 81. Rec. 1388.
HIGHLANDER, gr., fo. 84, imp. 86. 5570 (5922).
HILDARE, gr., fo. 75, imp. 79. Rec. 863.
HILDEBRAND, gr., fo. 80, imp. 80. Rec. 925.
HILGARD, gr., fo. 76, imp. 81. Rec. 1319.
HINDOO, bl., fo. 79, imp. 82. Rec. 2129 (964).
HOCHE, gr., fo. 80, imp. 80. Rec. 1246.
HOLOPHERNE, gr., fo. 85, imp. 87. 7059 (8542).
HOMER, bl., fo. 80, imp. 82. Rec. 1955 (1052).
HOTSPUR, gr., fo. 82, home bred. Rec. 2243.
HUBERT, gr., fo. 81, imp. 81. Rec. 1389.
HUGUENOT, gr., fo. 81, home bred. Rec. 2244.
HUMBER, gr., fo. 80, imp. 82. Réc. 2140.
HUMBERT, gr., fo. 82, imp. 83. Réc. 2669 (1195).
HUNTINGTON, gr., fo. 82, imp. 81. Rec. 2245.
HUNTOON, gr., fo. 82, home bred. Rec. 2246.
HURRICANE, gr., fo. 82, home bred. Rec. 2247.
HUSSAH, gr., fo. 76, imp. 80. Rec. 927.
IAGO, gr., fo. 77, imp. 80. Rec. 995 (768).
IDLEWILD, bl., fo. 79, imp. 79. Rec. 864.
IDOL, gr., fo. 68, imp. 73. Rec. 233.
ILLUSTRIOUS, gr., fo. 81, imp. 81. Rec. 1481.
INCAS, gr., fo. 76, imp. 80. Rec. 1243.
INDECIS, gr., fo. 84, imp. 86. Rec. 5539 (7230).

INDUS, gr., fo. 75, imp. 80. Rec. 1212.
INGOMAR, bl., fo. 77, imp. 81. Rec. 1339.
INTREPIDE, bl., fo. 82, imp. 84. Rec. 3544 (1857).
INTROUVABLE, gr., fo. 85, imp. 86. 5464 (5620).
INVADER, gr., fo. 77, imp. 81. Rec. 1321 (769).
IOLIAN, gr., fo. 82, imp. 82. Rec. 2108 (945).
IRON DUKE, gr., fo. 69, imp. 75. Rec. 234.
IRONSIDES, gr., fo. 69, imp. 72. Rec. 235.
ISENGRIAN, gr., fo. 77, imp. 81. Rec. 1322.
ISENLO, gr., fo. 81, imp. 81. Rec. 1204.
ISSY, gr., fo. 85, imp. 85. Rec. 5557 (6582).
IVANHOE, gr., fo. 81, imp. 81. Rec. 1202.
JAPONAIS, gr., fo. 84, imp. 87. Rec. 6006 (6536).
JEAN, bl., fo. 82, imp. 84. Rec. 3491 (2437).
JEAN BART, gr., fo. 70, imp. 76. Rec. 237.
JEAN BART, gr., fo. 78, imp. 81. Rec. 1431.
JEAN BART, gr., fo. 82, imp. 84. Rec. 3501 (1723).
JEAN BART, bl., fo. 80, imp. 84. Rec. 3320 (1787).
JEAN BART, gr., fo. 85, imp. 86. Rec. 5502 (6789).
JEAN JACQUES, bl., fo. 85, imp. 87. 7052 (10205).
JEAN-LE-BON, bl., fo. 84, imp. 87. 6907 (6547).
JENEREUX, gr., fo. 81, imp. 83. Rec. 2200 (1185).
JEROME, bl., fo. 81, imp. 81. Rec. 1393 (3242).
JOHN A. LOGAN, gr., fo. 1885, home bred. 4111.
JOKER, bl., fo. 76, imp. 80. Rec. 929.
JOLI-COEUR, gr., fo. 85, imp. 85. Rec. 4397 (2362).
JOLY, gr., fo. 80, imp. 84. Rec. 3551 (2327).
JUCHET, bl., fo. 80, imp. 84. Rec. 3512 (2142).
JUGURTHA, gr., fo. 82, imp. 84. Rec. 3305 (1699).
JULES, gr., fo. 83, imp. 84. Rec. 3790 (3028).
JULIAN, gr., fo. 81, imp. 81. Rec. 1304.
JULIUS, gr., fo. 80, imp. 84. Rec. 3701 (2442).
JUMBO, gr., fo. 80, imp. 82. Rec. 2110 (966).
JUPITER, gr., fo. 74, imp. 80. Rec. 1206.
JUPITER, gr., fo. 78, imp. 83. Rec. 2540 (1111).
JUPITER, gr., fo. 81, imp. 84. Rec. 3292 (216).
JUPITER, gr., fo. 82, imp. 85. Rec. 4301 (2243).
JUPITER, gr., fo. 84 imp. 86. Rec. 5544 (4166).
JURA, gr., fo. 78, imp. 81. Rec. 1280.
JUSTIN, bl., fo. 85, imp. 84. Rec. 3788 (2651).
KABYLE, bl., fo. 85, imp. 86. Rec. 5560 (6574).
KAISAR, gr., fo. 70, imp. 76. Rec. 516.
KANSAS, bl., fo. 87, home bred. Rec. 7246.
KENMORE, gr., fo. 77, imp. 81. Rec. 1323.
KENNETH, bl., fo. 80, imp. 80. Rec. 1240.
KIMO, gr., fo. 81, imp. 81. Rec. 1306 (859).
KIMRIS, b., fo. 78, imp. 81. Rec 1324.
KING, bl., fo. 82, imp. 82. Rec. 2169.
KLEBER, gr., fo. 79, imp. 83. Rec. 2317 (1213).
KLEBER, bl., fo. 85, imp. 87. Rec. 7053 (10270).
KNIGHT, gr., fo. 74, imp. 79. Rec. 805.
KOLOMA, bl., fo. 77, imp. 80. Rec. 803.
LABRIE, gr., fo. 87, home bred. Rec. 7247.
LACEDEMONE, gr., fo. 81, imp. 83. Rec. 2399 (27).
LACLEDE, gr., fo. 81, imp. 81. Rec. 1399.
LAERTIS, gr., fo. 81, imp. 81. Rec. 1398.
LAFAYETTE, gr., fo. 67, imp. 73. Rec. 254.
LA FERTE, gr., fo. 81, imp. 83. Rec. 2986 (1202).
LA FONTAINE, bl., fo. 82, imp. 84. Rec. 3749 (550).
LAIGLE, gr., fo. 81, imp. 83. Rec. 2714 (1261).
LALEU, gr., fo. 81, imp. 83. Rec. 2522 (1491).
LAMARTINE, b., fo. 76, imp. 80. Rec. 951.
LAMBRA, gr., fo. 83, imp. 84. Rec. 3653 (117).
L'AMI, gr., fo. 83, imp. 87. Rec. 6908 (6775).
L'AMI, gr., fo. 84, imp. 87. Rec. 7068 (8522).
L'AMIRAL, bl., fo. 83, imp. 87. Rec. 7067 (9570).
L'AMOUR, b., fo. 81, imp. 81. Rec. 1297.
L'AMOUREUX, gr., fo. 82, imp. 85. 4274 (5097).
LANNERAY, gr., fo. 82, imp. 83. Rec. 2615 (1248).
LA RUE, gr., fo. 81, imp. 83. Rec. 2504 (1187).
LAUNAY, gr., fo. 82, imp. 83. Rec. 2712 (1239).
LAUNCELOT, gr., fo. 73, imp. 78. Rec. 708.

LAUREATE, gr., fo. 80, imp. 80. Rec. 1237.
LAUREL, gr., fo. 78, imp. 80. Rec. 1280.
LAZARE, gr., fo. 82, imp. 85. Rec. 4399 (2119).
LE BEAUX, gr., fo. 77, imp. 80. Rec. 932.
LE BLOND, gr., fo. 84, imp. 87. Rec. 7064 (7270).
LE BOIS, gr., fo. 80, imp. 83. Rec. 4305 (1336).
LECEANO, gr., fo. 81, imp. 81. Rec. 1401.
LECOMTE, bl., fo. 80, imp. 83. Rec. 2323 (1353).
LE COUNT, gr., fo. 70, imp. 74. Rec. 258.
LE DUC, gr., fo. 81, imp. 83. Rec. 2203 (25).
LE DUC, bl., fo. 82, imp. 84. Rec. 3168 (542).
LE GATE, gr., fo. 78, imp. 82. Rec. 1361 (667).
LE GOUPIE, gr., fo. 80, imp. 83. Rec. 2512 (1243).
LE GRAND, gr., fo. 77, imp. 82. Rec. 2252 (1654).
LE GRAND, gr., fo. 82, imp. 83. Rec. 2616 (1299).
LE GROS, gr., fo. 69, imp. 74. Rec. 260.
LE MAITRE, gr., fo. 81, imp. 83. Rec. 2994 (1134).
LEMAN, gr., fo. 78, imp. 82. Rec. 1954 (1055).
LE MISLE, gr., fo. 76, imp. 80. Rec. 2196.
LEMNOS, gr., fo. 86, imp. 87. Rec. 7071 (8329).
LEMOINE, gr., fo. 81, imp. 83. Rec. 2516 (1296).
LENA ROUX, gr., fo. 76, imp. 80. Rec. 994.
LE NOIR, bl., fo. 71, imp. 75. Rec. 262 (744).
LE NOIR, bl., fo. 82, imp. 85. Rec. 4305 (631).
LEO, bl., fo. 70, imp. 76. Rec. 265.
LEONARD, bl., fo. 79, imp. 82. Rec. 1918 (1056).
LEONARDO, bl., fo. 80, imp. 80. Rec. 955 (854).
LEONI, bl., fo. 81, imp. 81. Rec. 1400.
LEONIDAS, bl., fo. 79, home bred. Rec. 867.
LEONOWEN, gr., fo. 78, imp. 81. Rec. 1324.
LEOPARD, gr., fo. 71, imp. 77. Rec. 714.
LE PELLETIER, gr., fo. 80, imp. 83. 2374 (1244).
LERIDA, gr., fo. 84, imp. 87. Rec. 6909 (6780).
L'ERMITAGE, br., fo. 85, imp. 87. Rec. 7050 (3437).
LE ROI, bl., fo. 84, imp. 85. Rec. 4399 (4839).
LEROUX, gr., fo. 81, imp. 83. Rec. 2572 (1909).
LEROUX, bl., fo. 82, imp. 84. Rec. 3748 (2429).
LEROY, w., fo. 67, imp. 73. Rec. 263.
LESBOS, bl., fo. 81, imp. 83. Rec. 2610 (7).
LESEUR, br., fo. 80, imp. 83. Rec. 2307 (11).
LE TASSE, gr., fo. 79, imp. 83. Rec. 2514 (1114).
L'ETOILE, gr., fo. 82, imp. 84. Rec. 3467 (538).
LEVASSEUR, gr., fo. 78, imp. 81. Rec. 1296.
LEVIATHAN, w., fo. 73, imp. 78. Rec. 209 (728).
LIBERATOR, bl., fo. 81, imp. 81. Rec. 1343.
LIMONNIER, gr., fo. 85, imp. 86. Rec. 5143 (6447).
LION D'OR, gr., fo. 84, imp. 87. Rec. 6970 (8583).
LLION, bl., fo. 86, imp. 82. Rec. 2115 (909).
LOCHIEL, gr., fo. 80, imp. 80. Rec. 1238.
LODI, gr., fo. 84, imp. 87. Rec. 6971 (9451).
LOFTY, gr., fo. 76, imp. 82. Rec. 1996 (1957).
LOKE, gr., fo. 84, imp. 87. Rec. 7065 (5885).
LOMBARD, bl., fo. 84, imp. 83. Rec. 2586 (1728).
LONGFELLOW, gr., fo. 76, imp. 81. Rec. 1229.
LORD BYRON, bl., fo. 81, imp. 84. Rec. 3648 (336).
LORENZO, gr., fo. 82, imp. 82. Rec. 2170.
LOSIER, b., fo. 81, imp. 84. Rec. 3489 (2538).
LOTHAIR, gr., fo. 77, imp. 81. Rec. 1327.
LOTO, bay, fo. 85, imp. 87. Rec. 7054 (10540).
LOUIS, bl., fo. 81, imp. 83. Rec. 2521 (1212).
LOUIS, gr., fo. 80, imp. 83. Rec. 2309 (1187).
LOUIS, gr., fo. 81, imp. 84. Rec. 3721 (2292).
LOUIS BLANC, gr., fo. 82, imp. 84. 3303 (1729).
LOUIS LE BLANC, gr., fo. 81, imp. 84. 3328 (2432).
LOUIS PHILIPPE, gr., fo. 67, imp. 72. Rec. 283.
LOUVOIS, bl., fo. 80, imp. 83. Rec. 2319 (1119).
LUBIN, bl., fo. 82, imp. 84. Rec. 3681 (554).
LUCAS, gr., fo. 80, imp. 83. Rec. 2310 (1105).
LUCIAN, gr., fo. 77, imp. 82. Rec. 2141 (971).
LUCIEN, gr., fo. 85, imp. 87. Rec. 7072 (8081).
LUCIUS, br., fo. 82, imp. 87. Rec. 7010 (8875).
LUCO, b., fo. 78. imp. 82. Rec. 1940 (1058).

LUCULLUS, gr., fo. 81, imp. 83. Rec. 2324 (1104).
LUISANT, gr., fo. 81, imp. 83. Rec. 2536 (1312).
LUSTY, gr. fo. 79, imp. 83. Rec. 5570 (5928).
LUNEVILLE, gr., 79, imp. 83. Rec. 2309 (1331).
LURON, bl., fo. 85, imp. 87. Rec. 7039 (6346.)
LUTHER, ch. fo. 77, imp. 81. Rec. 1273 (1384).
LUTHER, b., fo. 80, imp. 83. Rec. 1932 (1059).
LUTHER, bl., fo. 79, imp. 83. Rec. 2301 (10).
LUTHER, gr., fo. 82, imp. 84. Rec. 3190 (2436).
LUTHER, gr., fo. 81, imp. 84. Rec. 3496 (1890).
LUTHER, gr., fo. 80, imp. 85. Rec. 4273 (3239).
LYONAIS, bl., fo. 80, imp. 83. Rec. 2386 (1332).
MADERE, gr., fo. 77, imp. 81. Rec. 1263 (772).
MADERE, bl., fo. 81, imp. 84. Rec. 3556 (70).
MADERE, gr., fo. 80, imp 83. Rec. 3093 (424).
MADERE, gr., fo. 82, imp. 85. Rec. 4271 (2928).
MADERE, gr., fo. 80, imp. 86. Rec. 5407 (5613).
MADRID, bl., fo. 82, imp. 84. Rec. 5153 (441).
MAGENDIE, gr., fo. 80, imp. 83. Rec. 2462 (1103).
MAGENTA, gr., fo. 84, imp. 87. Rec. 6972 (10476).
MAGENTA, bl., fo. 86, imp. 87. Rec. 7075 (7817).
MAGLOIRE, gr., fo. 79, imp. 83. Rec. 2334 (1102).
MAGNUS, gr., fo. 68, imp. 73. Rec. 290.
MAHDI, gr., fo. 84, imp. 86. Rec. 5524 (6171).
MAINTENON, b., fo. 82, imp. 83. Rec. 2455 (1252).
MAINTERNE, b., fo. 81, imp. 83. Rec. 2399 (1251).
MAJOR, gr., fo. 83, imp. 84. Rec. 3634 (2419).
MAJOR, gr., fo. 81, imp. 85. Rec. 4254 (636).
MAJOR CLARK, gr., fo. 81, imp. 83. 2513 (1784).
MAJORDOME, bl., fo. 83, imp. 85. Rec. 4395 (110).
MALEDA, gr., fo. 78, imp. 82. Rec. 2121 (972).
MALO, w., fo. 68, imp. 73. Rec. 294.
MALVOLI, bl., fo. 77, imp. 82. Rec. 2132 (973).
MAMELUCK, gr., fo. 83, imp. 86. Rec. 5178 (111).
MANDRIN, gr., fo. 86, imp. 87. Rec. 7979 (10582).
MANOIR, bl., fo. 78, imp. 81. Rec. 1331.
MARCEAU, gr., fo. 83, imp. 83. Rec. 2614 (1259).
MARCEAU, gr., fo. 79, imp. 84. Rec. 3510 (2383).
MARCIUS, gr., fo. 81, home bred. Rec. 1488.
MARCOU, bl., fo. 82, imp. 84. Rec. 3720 (524).
MARCUS, gr., fo. 81, imp. 85. Rec. 4740 (2247).
MARDINO, gr., fo. 78, imp. 82. Rec. 1934 (1000).
MARGO, bl., fo. 77, imp. 83. Rec. 2571 (1143).
MARGOT, gr., fo. 71, imp. 75. Rec. 255.
MARGOT, bl., fo. 82, imp. 84. Rec. 3679 (349).
MARGOT, b., fo. 82, imp. 84. Rec. 3734 (1079).
MARGOT, bl., fo. 83, imp. 85. Rec. 4257 (1877).
MARGOT, bl., fo. 84, imp. 85. Rec. 4314 (2232).
MARGOT, gr., fo. 83, imp. 86. Rec. 5102 (1845).
MARGRAVE, gr., fo. 77, imp. 80. Rec. 934.
MARION, bl., fo. 81, imp. 83. Rec. 1497.
MARJOY, gr., fo. 85, imp. 87. Rec. 7978 (11088).
MARMADUKE, gr., fo. 72, imp. 75. Rec. 297.
MARMION, gr., fo. 81, imp. 83. Rec. 1406.
MARMONTEL, gr., fo. 80, imp. 83. Rec. 2099 (1112).
MARQUIS, gr., fo. 75, imp. 79. Rec. 868 (774).
MARQUIS, bl., fo. 81, imp. 83. Rec. 2595 (24).
MARQUIS, gr., fo. 82, imp. 84. Rec. 3705 (549).
MARQUIS, gr., fo. 83, imp. 84. Rec. 3793 (3504).
MARTIGNY, gr., fo. 81, imp. 83. Rec. 2528 (1271).
MARTIN, bl., fo. 81, imp. 83. Rec. 2580 (5).
MARTINE, gr., fo. 76, im. 81. Rec. 1261.
MARTON, gr., fo. 79, imp. 83. Rec. 2395 (1299).
MARVEL, bl., fo. 78, imp. 82. Rec. 1922 (1061).
MASSARD, gr., fo. 81, imp. 83. Rec. 2543 (1206).
MASSARD, gr., fo. 83, imp. 84. Rec. 3787 (2650).
MASSOIT, b., fo. 81, imp. 81. Rec. 1409.
MASTER, gr., fo. 81, imp. 83. Rec. 4272 (3233).
MASTODON, gr., fo. 75, imp. 77. Rec. 721.
MATCHLESS, bl., fo. 75, imp. 80. Rec. 902.
MATHIAS, gr., fo. 83, imp. 86. Rec. 5532 (6444).
MATHURIN, gr., fo. 82, imp. 84. Rec. 3470 (519).

MAYGAR, gr., fo. 77, imp. 80. Rec. 1235.
MAZAMET, gr., fo. 77, imp. 80. Rec. 1332.
MAZARINE, br., fo. 81, imp. 81. Rec. 1408.
MAZEPPA, bl., fo. 76, imp. 80. Rec. 937 (775).
MAZRARAMIA, gr., fo. 81, imp. 81. Rec. 1404.
McMAHON, gr., fo. 70, imp. 74. Rec. 289.
MEAUCE, gr., fo. 84, imp. 87. Rec. 6073 (7410).
MECHE, gr., fo. 85, imp. 86. Rec. 5558 (6576).
MEDALLIST, gr., fo. 76, imp. 81. Rec. 1330.
MEDARD, gr., fo. 84, imp. 87. Rec. 7076 (7065).
MELOS, gr., fo. 79, imp. 82. Rec. 1974 (974).
MENDECINO, gr., fo. 80, imp. 83. Rec. 1383.
MENDOZA, bl., fo. 80, imp. 80. Rec. 1429.
MENELAUS, gr., fo. 76, imp. 82. Rec. 2003 (975).
MERCURE, gr., fo. 82, imp. 85. Rec. 4234 (403).
MERCUTIO, gr., fo. 81, imp. 81. Rec. 1405 (3241).
MEREDITH, b., fo. 79, imp. 83. Rec. 2549 (1322).
MERLIN, gr., fo. 74, imp. 78. Rec. 723.
MESQUIN, gr., fo. 85, imp. 86. Rec. 5547 (7393).
MESSIDOR, bl., fo. 82, imp. 84. Rec. 3753 (685).
MESSINA, gr., fo. 76, imp. 82. Rec. 2142 (976).
METACOMET, gr., fo. 84, imp. 83. Rec. 2906 (1224).
METEOR, gr., fo. 76, imp. 80. Rec. 1210.
METIDJAH, b., fo. 81, imp. 81. Rec. 1402 (977).
MIARD, gr., fo. 80, imp. 82. Rec. 1900 (978).
MIDI, gr., fo. 83, imp. 85. Rec. 4229 (4587).
MIDNIGHT, bl., fo. 79, imp. 80. Rec. 1000 (776).
MILANO, gr., fo. 82, imp. 83. Rec. 2654 (1200).
MILO, gr., fo. 79, imp. 82. Rec. 1942 (1052).
MILOR, gr., fo. 69, imp. 74. Rec. 500.
MINARD, bl., fo. 82, imp. 84. Rec. 3717 (467).
MINGO, gr., fo. 78, imp. 82. Rec. 2133 (979).
MIRABEAU, gr., fo. 84, imp. 86. Rec. 5591 (6043).
MIZA, gr., fo. 77, imp. 80. Rec. 939.
MODENA, bl., fo. 80, imp. 82. Rec. 2143 (980).
MODESTA, bl., fo. 77, imp. 80. Rec. 1204.
MOGUL, gr., fo. 77, home bred. Rec. 726.
MOKENA, gr., fo. 80, imp. 82. Rec. 2114 (981).
MOLDENO, gr., fo. 78, imp. 82. Rec. 1937 (1063).
MOLIERE, gr., fo. 75, imp. 80. Rec. 894.
MOLO, gr., fo. 75, imp. 82. Rec. 2007 (982).
MOLOCH, gr., fo. 76, imp. 80. Rec. 935.
MONACO, gr., fo. 80, imp. 80. Rec. 1443.
MONARCH, gr., fo. 65, imp. 72. Rec. 313.
MONARQUE, gr., fo. 79, imp. 84. Rec. 3496 (1784).
MONARQUE, gr., fo. 82, imp. 84. Rec 3493 (2503).
MONARQUE, gr., fo. 82, imp. 84. Rec. 3747 (1884).
MONARQUE, bl., fo. 82, imp. 86. Rec. 4911 (2428).
MONARQUE, bl., fo. 84, imp. 86. Rec. 5009 (7321).
MONETOILLE, gr., fo. 83, imp. 85. Rec. 4242 (4160).
MONITOR, gr., fo. 80, imp. 82. Rec. 2152 (983).
MONOLOA, bl., fo. 78, imp. 82. Rec. 2133 (98).
MONTAGNARD, gr., fo. 86, imp. 87. 7077 (10281).
MONTAGUE, b., fo. 79, imp. 82. Rec. 1927 (1064).
MONTALVAN, gr., fo. 81, imp. 81. Rec. 1410.
MONT D'OR, gr., fo. 85, imp. 87. Rec. 7074 (10884).
MONTE CHRISTO, gr., fo. 76. Rec. 318.
MONTEZUMA, b., fo. 81, imp. 83. Rec. 2364 (1254).
MONTIBELLO, gr., fo. 77, imp. 82. Rec. 1362 (985).
MONTIGNY, gr., fo. 79, imp. 83. Rec. 2395 (1).
MONTJADOR, bl., fo. 79, imp. 83. Rec. 2510 (1308).
MONTROSE, gr., fo. 80, imp. 80. Rec. 938 (833).
MOKANO, gr., fo. 81, imp. 82. Rec. 1933 (1065).
MORDAUNT, b., fo. 70, imp. 75. Rec. 842.
MORDICEAU, b., fo. 82, imp. 82. Rec. 2171 (986).
MOREAU, gr., fo. 81, imp. 83. Rec. 2544 (1186).
MOREAU, gr., fo. 84, imp. 86. Rec. 5367 (5481).
MORO, gr., fo. 73, imp. 76. Rec. 319.
MORTAGNE, gr., fo. 82, imp. 84. Rec. 3500 (1716).
MOUSQUETAIRE, bl., fo. 83, imp. 85. 4294 (1984).
MOUSSE, gr., fo. 82, imp. 84. Rec. 3842 (2058).
MOUSSE, gr., fo. 82, imp. 85. Rec. 4232 (458).

MOUSTACHE, gr., fo. 79, imp. 84. Rec. 3709 (2547).
MOUTON, gr., fo. 80, imp. 84. Rec. 3710 (1780).
MOUTON, b., fo. 81, imp. 85. Rec. 4287 (455).
MOUTON, bl., fo. 82, imp. 85. Rec. 4264 (5231).
MOUTON, bl., fo. 82, imp. 87. Rec. 6974 (6598).
MOUTON, gr., fo. 85, imp. 87. Rec. 6975 (10475).
MOUVETTE, gr., fo. 82, imp. 87. Rec. 6976 (599).
MURAT, gr., fo. 71, imp. 75. Rec. 329.
MUSCADIN, gr., fo. 84, imp. 85. Rec. 5545 (4173).
MYDIAN, bl., fo. 84, home bred. Rec. 4325.
MYLORD, gr., fo. 80, imp. 84. Rec. 3521 (2186).
XYLORD, bl., fo. 81, imp. 84. Rec. 3547 (627).
MYLORD, gr., fo. 82, imp. 86. Rec. 5264 (2188).
NABOB, gr., fo. 77, home bred. Rec. 731.
NAPOLEON III, gr., fo. 69, imp. 18—. Rec. 900.
NARBONNE, gr., fo. 76, imp. 81. Rec. 3534 (777).
NAUDRIE, gr., fo. 78, imp. 81. Rec. 1335.
NAUTICUS, gr., fo. 82, imp. 85. Rec. 2641 (1222).
NAUTILUS, gr., fo. 84, imp. 86. Rec. 5511 (6884).
NAVARDO, gr., fo. 79, imp. 81. Rec. 1356.
NAVARIN, gr., fo. 84, imp. 86. Rec. 5903 (5948).
NAVARRE, gr., fo. 77, imp. 80. Rec. 1219.
NAVARRO, gr., fo. 77, imp. 81. Rec. 1857.
NEGRINO, bl., fo. 82, imp. 84. Rec. 3524 (1899).
NEMO, b., fo. 77, home bred. Rec. 737.
NEPTUNE, b., fo. 78, imp. 83. Rec. 2555 (123).
NEPTUNE, gr., fo. 86, imp. 87. Rec. 7080 (8862).
NERON, gr., fo. 83, imp. 85. Rec. 4309 (2656).
NEVOY, gr., fo. 80, imp. 82. Rec. 2004 (987).
NEY, gr., fo. 70, imp. 74. Rec. 342.
NIMOUR, gr., fo. 80, imp. 82. Rec. 2251 (1095).
NINO, gr., fo. 80, imp. 82. Rec. 2146 (988).
NIVOSE, gr., fo. 82, imp. 84. Rec. 3575 (686).
NOCE, bl., fo. 82, imp. 84. Rec. 3731 (1795).
NOGENT, bl., fo. 80, imp. 84. Rec. 3709 (455).
NOGENTAIS, bl., fo. 83, imp. 85. Rec. 5414 (2257).
NOMAD, gr., fo. 82, imp. 82. Rec. 2172 (988).
NONPAREIL, b., fo. 76, imp. 81. Rec. 1579.
NORMAND, gr., fo. 81, imp. 83. Rec. 2574 (23).
NORMONT, gr., fo. 81, imp. 82. Rec. 1997 (990).
NORVAL, bl., fo. 76, imp. 81. Rec. 1369 (794).
NORWAY, gr., fo. 84, home bred. Rec. 5091.
NYANZA, gr., fo. 79, home bred. Rec. 869.
OBERON, gr., fo. 82, imp. 82. Rec. 2184 (991).
OCTAVIUS, gr., fo. 77, imp. 81. Rec. 1340.
ODALISQUE, bl., fo. 82, imp. 83. Rec. 2678 (1095).
OGANILLA, bl., fo. 79, imp. 81. Rec. 1541.
OLIVIER, gr., fo. 81, imp. 84. Rec. 3722 (2543).
OMEGA, gr., fo. 76, imp. 86. Rec. 949.
ONNISSIME, br., fo. 78, imp. 78. Rec. 1342.
ONTARIO, bl., fo. 84, imp. 86. Rec. 5592 (5365).
OPAL, gr., fo. 78, home bred. Rec. 740.
ORESTES, gr., fo. 82, imp. 82. Rec. 2173 (992).
ORESTO, gr., fo. 79, imp. 81. Rec. 1282 (778).
ORGUEILLEUX, gr., fo. 84, imp. 87. Rec. 7013 (6051).
ORIENTAL, bl., fo. 81, imp. 83. Rec. 2545 (2277).
ORIENTAL, gr., fo. 80, imp. 85. Rec. 4210 (225).
ORIGENE, gr., fo. 82, imp. 84. Rec. 3573 (3100).
ORION, gr., fo. 79, imp. 82. Rec. 2128 (993).
ORIZABA, bl., fo. 84, imp. 86. Rec. 5008 (7325).
ORMOND, bl., fo. 78, imp. 84. Rec. 1278.
ORPHELIN, gr., fo. 84, imp. 86. Rec. 5521 (6980).
ORPHEUS, gr., fo. 78, imp. 82. Rec. 2144 (994).
ORTIGAL, gr., fo. 80, imp. 82. Rec. 2129 (995).
OSCEOLA, bl., fo. 79, imp. 82. Rec. 2137 (996).
OSPREY, gr., fo. 75, imp. 81. Rec. 1358 (779).
OSWALD, gr., fo. 76, imp. 81. Rec. 1344.
OTHELLO, gr., fo. 79, imp. 79. Rec. 870 (812).
OVANDO, gr., fo. 79, imp. 82. Rec. 1956 (1097).
OVEDO, gr., fo. 78, imp. 82. Rec. 1973 (997).
OZEANZE, bl., fo. 81, imp. 83. Rec. 2525 (1210).
PACHA, b., fo. 81, imp. 83. Rec. 2555 (1311).

PACHA, bl., fo. 81, imp. 86. Rec. 5577 (5961).
PACHA, gr., fo. 84, imp. 87. Rec. 6267 (4390).
PACIFIC, bl., fo. 81, imp. 86. Rec. 5506 (454).
PADAGIO, b., fo. 84, imp. 81. Rec. 1411.
PALADIN, gr., fo. 82, imp. 82. Rec. 2175 (998).
PALAGE, gr., fo. 82, imp. 83. Rec. 2677 (1108).
PALEFRENIER, gr., fo. 81, imp. 87. Rec. 6968 (6344).
PALLADINO, gr., fo. 82, imp. 83. Rec. 2672 (1193).
PAMPEIRO, gr., fo. 82, imp. 86. Rec. 5561 (5369).
PANORAMA, bl., fo. 85, imp. 87. Rec. 7085 (13010).
PANORAMA, gr., fo. 85, imp. 87. Rec. 7094 (7269).
PANTECOTE, gr., fo. 80, imp. 83. Rec. 1518 (1116).
PANTHEON, bl., fo. 82, imp. 85. Rec. 2693 (1223).
PAOLO, gr., fo. 83, imp. 84. Rec. 3674 (249).
PAPILLON, gr., fo. 79, imp. 84. Rec. 3531 (2141).
PAPILLION, bl., fo. 80, imp. 84. Rec. 3559 (3759).
PAPILLION, gr., fo. 84, imp. 84. Rec. 3711 (2793).
PAPILLON, gr., fo. 83, imp. 86. Rec. 5505 (2222).
PAPILLON, gr., fo. 84, imp. 87. Rec. 6269 (6672).
PAPILLON, gr., fo. 82, imp. 87. Rec. 7080 (5759).
PAPILLON III, gr., fo. 85, imp. 87. Rec. 7080 (11409).
PARAGON, b., fo. 78, imp. 81. Rec. 1345.
PARENT, gr., fo. 82, imp. 84. Rec. 3746 (1977).
PARISIEN, bl., gr., fo. 84, imp. 86. Rec. 5544 (6744).
PAROLE, gr., fo. 87, home bred. Rec. 7240.
PAROLI, gr., fo. 84, imp. 87. Rec. 6960 (6321).
PAROS, gr., fo. 79, imp. 82. Rec. 1943 (1008).
PARTHENON, gr., fo. 87, home bred. Rec. 7241.
PASCAL, gr., fo. 82, imp. 83. Rec. 2638 (1196).
PAS LOUIS, gr., fo. 82, imp. 84. Rec. 3472 (327).
PAS NOMME, gr., fo. 86, imp. 87. Rec. 7083 (9799).
PASSE AVANT, b., fo. 82, imp. 84. Rec. 3471 (328).
PASSE PARTOUT, gr., fo. 80, imp. 83. Rec. 2502 (1202).
PASSE-PERE, gr., fo. 83, imp. 85. Rec. 4235 (124).
PASSE POURTANT, bl., fo. 82, imp. 84. Rec. 3476 (540).
PAS SOT, gr., fo. 83, imp. 84. Rec. 3541 (245).
PATCHOULI, gr., fo. 84, imp. 87. Rec. 6981 (6541).
PATHFINDER, gr., fo. 81, imp. 81. Rec. 1267.
PATRIOTE, gr., fo. 80, imp. 83. Rec. 2717.
PATROCLE, gr., fo. 82, imp. 83. Rec. 2629 (1167).
PATU, gr., fo. 82, imp. 85. Rec. 4330 (2908).
PATURIN, gr., fo. 85, imp. 87. Rec. 7087 (9292).
PAUL, gr., fo. 76, imp. 81. Rec. 1252.
PAUL, gr., fo. 84, imp. 84. Rec. 3478 (364).
PAUL, b., fo. 83, imp. 84. Rec. 3761 (248).
PAUL, bl., fo. 82, imp. 85. Rec. 4367 (58).
PAUL, gr., fo. 83, imp. 87. Rec. 7084 (10071).
PAUL JONES, gr., fo. 84, imp. 85. Rec. 2554 (1251).
PAULUS, gr., fo. 82, imp. 85. Rec. 4297 (6053).
PAULUS, gr., fo. 85, imp. 87. Rec. 7081 (10085).
PAX, gr., fo. 84, imp. 86. Rec. 5535 (6926).
PEER, gr., fo. 80, home bred. Rec. 1256.
PEER, gr., fo. 86, home bred. Rec. 6008.
PELLERAY, gr., fo. 80, imp. 83. Rec. 2515 (1333).
PELLICO, bl., fo. 82, imp. 84. Rec. 3506 (1715).
PENSIF, gr., fo. 84, imp. 86. Rec. 5558 (6728).
PENTHIEVRE, gr., fo. 82, imp. 83. Rec. 2645 (1169).
PEPIN, b., fo. 82, imp. 83. Rec. 2657 (1170).
PERFECT, gr., fo. 81, imp. 83. Rec. 2788 (1319).
PERROT, gr., fo. 82, imp. 85. Rec. 4212 (4156).
PERTINAX, gr., fo. 83, imp. 84. Rec. 5524 (1087).
PERVENCHERES, gr., fo. 85, imp. 86. Rec. 5704 (7420).
PETROCLEUS, bl., fo. 80, imp. 82. Rec. 1904 (9926).
PHILIBERT, gr., fo. 80, imp. 83. Rec. 2684 (2340).
PHILIBERT IV, gr., fo. 84, imp. 87. Rec. 6982 (11249).
PHILIPPE I, bl., fo. 83, imp. 85. Rec. 4304 (4558).
PHILIPPE, bl., fo. 84, imp. 84. Rec. 5552 (4200).
PHILIPPE AUGUST, bl., fo. 85, imp. 87. Rec. 7088 (8042).
PHILLISIDES, gr., fo. 81, imp. 81. Rec. 1414.
PHILOGENE, gr., fo. 85, imp. 86. Rec. 5595 (5269).
PHONECIAN, bl., fo. 78, imp. 82. Rec. 1923 (1079).
PHONECIAN, bl., fo. 82, imp. 82. Rec. 2174 (909).

PHOTOGRAPHIE, gr., fo. 84, imp. 85. 4321 (4238).
PICADOR, b., fo. 76, imp. 81. Rec. 1254 (780).
PICADOR, gr., fo. 80, imp. 84. Rec. 5517 (2359).
PICADOR, gr., fo. 83, imp. 84. Rec. 3680 (207).
PICADOU, bl., fo. 81, imp. 85. Rec. 4211 (2909).
PIERRE, gr., fo. 81, imp. 84. Rec. 5046 (382).
PIERRE, gr., fo. 84, imp. 86. Rec. 5571 (5325).
PIERRE PIERRE, gr., fo. 72, imp. 76. Rec. 373.
PIERROT, b., fo. 82, imp. 85. Rec. 4382 (1935).
PILGRIM, gr., fo. 74, imp. 78. Rec. 746.
PILLIER, gr., fo. 83, imp. 85. Rec. 5177 (6445).
PILLON, bl., fo. 84, imp. 87. Rec. 6083 (4227).
PILOT, b., fo. 78, imp. 83. Rec. 2718.
PITON, bl., fo. 81, imp. 83. Rec. 2600 (1196).
PIZARRO, gr., fo. 78, imp. 81. Rec. 1253.
PLANET, gr., fo. 80, imp. 80. Rec. 941 (811).
PLESSIS, gr., fo. 83, imp. 84. Rec. 3696 (2234).
PLUTARQUE, gr., fo. 80, home bred. Rec. 5220.
PLUVIOSE, gr., fo. 82, imp. 84. Rec. 3755 (683?.
POLISSON, gr., fo. 83, imp. 86. Rec. 5306 (6611).
POLLUX, gr., fo. 84, imp. 87. Rec. 6084 (6860).
POMPADOUR, gr., fo. 77, imp. 81. Rec. 1239 (781).
POMPEY, gr., fo. 82, imp. 83. Rec. 2655 (1127).
PONCEAU, gr., fo. 84, imp. 86. Rec. 5512 (6882).
PON PON, bl., fo. 85, imp. 80. Rec. 5963 (5171).
PONTIFF, rn., fo. 72, imp. 76. Rec. 378.
PORTHOS, gr., fo. 81, imp. 83. Rec. 2556 (1199).
PORTHOS, gr., fo. 82, imp. 84. Rec. 3652 (2170).
POTENTAT, bl., fo. 84, imp. 86. Rec. 5520 (7202).
POULO, gr., fo. 82, imp. 84. Rec. 3480 (510).
POURQUOI PAS, b., fo. 81, imp. 84. 3047 (2147).
POURQUOI PAS, bl., fo. 83, imp. 86. 5582 (7184).
PREAUX, gr., fo. 83, imp. 84. Rec. 3753 (2329).
PRECEPT, gr., fo. 87, home bred. Rec. 7230.
PREMIER, gr., fo. 79, imp. 80. Rec. 1208 (782).
PREMIER II, gr., fo. 79, imp. 81. Rec. 1151.
PRIDE OF CAYUGA, gr., fo. 73, imp. 78. Rec. 848.
PRIEUR, gr., fo. 82, imp. 85. Rec. 4214 (2149).
PRIMAL, gr., fo. 77, imp. 81. Rec. 1493.
PRIMATE, gr., fo. 71, imp. 76. Rec. 331.
PRINCE, bl., fo. 81, imp. 81. Rec. 1097.
PRINCE D'IGE, bl., fo. 83, imp. 86. Rec. 5489 (7483).
PRINCE NOIR, bl., fo. 82, imp. 85. 4215 (2363).
PRINCE NOIR, bl., fo. 85, imp. 85. 4333 (5003).
PRIZE, gr., fo. 79, imp. 79. Rec. 871.
PROCOPE, gr., fo. 83, imp. 86. Rec. 5507 (6992).
PRODIGE, gr., fo. 87, home bred. Rec. 7238.
PRODUCTEUR, gr., fo. 79, imp. 82. Rec. 1936 (1071).
PRODUCTEUR, gr., fo. 79, imp. 83. Rec. 2371 (1256).
PRODUCTEUR, gr., fo. 81, imp. 85. Rec. 4280 (?8).
PRODUCTEUR, gr., fo. 87, home bred. Rec. 7242.
PROMETHEE, gr., fo. 81, imp. 83. Rec. 2592 (29).
PROMISE, gr., fo. 76, imp. 81. Rec. 1346.
PROMPTER, gr., fo. 77, imp. 81. Rec. 1329.
PROSPER, gr., fo. 82, imp. 83. Rec. 2501 (1155).
PROSPERO, gr., fo. 81, imp. 81. Rec. 1413.
PROTEAN, bl., fo. 80, imp. 82. Rec. 1901 (1072).
PROTECTEUR, gr., fo. 83, imp. 87. Rec. 7082 (9272).
PROTEINE, gr., fo. 80, imp. 82. Rec. 2118 (1000).
PROTEUS, gr., fo. 81, imp. 81. Rec. 1412.
PROUDHON, gr., fo. 86, imp. 87 Rec. 7090 (10643).
PROVIN, gr., fo. 82, imp. 84. Rec. 3474 (563).
PROVOST, gr., fo. 81, imp. 83. Rec. 25.2 (1301).
PUMANOIR, gr., fo. 82, imp. 84. Rec. 3689 (7161).
PYLADE, gr., fo. 81, imp. 83. Rec. 2601 (1091).
PYRAME, gr., fo. 80, imp. 83. Rec. 2533 (1308).
PYRAME, gr., fo. 81, imp. 83. Rec. 2592 (1093).
QUANTREL, gr., fo. 82, imp. 82. Rec. 2176 (1001).
QUAZZOLA, b., fo. 78, imp. 80. Rec. 1222 (825).
QUINTON, bl., fo. 79, imp. 79. Rec. 872.
QUIPROQUE, bl., fo. 85, imp. 87. Rec. 7092 (9602).
QUIXOTE, gr., fo. 75, imp. 80. Rec. 942.

QUIXOTE, bl., fo. 80, imp. 80. Rec. 1290 (860).
RADIGUET, bl., fo. 83, imp. 84. Rec. 3789 (470).
RAJAH, gr., fo. 76, imp. 80. Rec. 1209.
RAMBLER, gr., fo. 77, imp. 81. Rec. 1338.
RANGER, gr., fo. 79, home bred. Rec. 807.
RAPHAEL, gr., fo. 84, imp. 87. Rec. 6985 (11242).
RAPPORTEUR, gr., fo. 82, imp. 85. 4247 (5037).
RASPAIL, gr., fo. 82, imp. 85. Rec. 4223 (1939).
RASPAIL, gr., fo. 82, imp. 85. Rec. 4227 (4611).
RASSELIN, gr., fo. 82, imp. 83. Rec. 2612 (1305).
RATISBONNE, gr., fo. 83, imp. 85. 4231 (2851).
RAVAGEUR, gr., fo. 85, imp. 87. Rec. 7034 (8675).
RAVEN, bl., fo. 74, imp. 79. Rec. 874.
RAVENNA, bl., fo. 80, imp. 82. Rec. 2153 (1002).
RAVENSTEIN, bl., fo. 79, imp. 81. Rec. 1301.
RAVENSWOOD, bl., fo. 81, imp. 81. Rec. 1489.
RECLUSE, bl., fo. 77, imp. 81. Rec. 1348.
REFORMER, gr., fo. 81, imp. 81. Rec. 1476.
REGAL, gr., fo. 74, imp. 80. Rec. 943 (983).
REGENT, bl., fo. 85, imp. 87. Rec. 7095 (5167).
REGI, gr., fo. 78, imp. 81. Rec. 1221.
REGISSEUR, gr., fo. 80, imp. 84. (B. S. B.) (11).
REGLEMENT, gr., fo. 85, imp. 86. Rec. 5523 (7225).
REGLIER, gr., fo. 84, imp. 86. Rec. 5171 (5735).
REGULUS, b., fo. 79, imp. 82. Rec. 2240 (1073).
RELIANCE, gr., fo. 78, imp. 82. Rec. 1911 (1074).
RENALDO, bl., fo. 81, imp. 81. Rec. 1415.
RENFORTH, b., fo. 82, imp. 83. Rec. 2639 (1225).
REQUIN, gr., fo. 84, imp. 87. Rec. 6086 (6514).
REVOLTE, gr., fo. 84, imp. 87. Rec. 6387 (5485).
RIALTO, gr., fo. 78, imp. 80. Rec. 1202 (825).
RICHARD, br., fo. 77, imp. 81. Rec. 1350.
RICHELIEU, gr., fo. 86, imp. 87. Rec. 7096 (7803).
RIENZI, gr., fo. 77, imp. 81. Rec. 1349.
RIGOLO, bl., fo. 85, imp. 86. Rec. 5561 (5165).
RIGOLOT, gr., fo. 82, imp. 84. Rec. 3794 (2287).
RIGOT, gr., fo. 83, imp. 84. Rec. 3792 (2333).
RINALDO, bl., fo. 84, imp. 86. Rec. 5540 (6730).
RINGLET, gr., fo. 81, imp. 81. Rec. 1273.
RIVAL, gr., fo. 71, imp. 75. Rec. 408.
RIVAL, gr., fo. 76, imp. 80. Rec. 906.
RIVOLI, gr., fo. 80, imp. 83. Rec. 2370 (1202).
ROBERT, gr., fo. 84, imp. 85. Rec. 4312 (4236).
ROBESPIERRE, gr., fo. 81, imp. 83. 2570 (1149).
ROBINSON, gr., fo. 82, imp. 86. Rec. 5500 (5544).
ROBINSON, gr., fo. 82, imp. 86. Rec. 5535 (7313).
ROCHEFORT, gr., fo. 69, imp. 74. Rec. 412.
ROCHAMBORT, gr., fo. 82, imp. 85. Rec. 4328 (172).
RODANT, gr., fo. 77, imp. 81. Rec. 1450.
RODERICK, bl., fo. 78, imp. 78. Rec. 758.
RODRIGUEZ, gr., fo. 78, imp. 81. Rec. 1352.
ROI, gr., fo. 77, imp. 81. Rec. 1284 (784).
ROITELET, gr., fo. 85, imp. 87. Rec. 7003 (11222).
ROLAND, gr., fo. 79, imp. 82. Rec. 1911 (1075).
ROLLO, bl., fo. 80, imp. 80. Rec. 2105 (1003).
ROMAIN, gr., fo. 83, imp. 86. Rec. 5157 (6449).
ROMAINE, bl., fo. 80, imp. 82. Rec. 1902 (1076).
ROMAN, bl., fo. 82, imp. 84. Rec. 3794 (2032).
ROMANI, bl., fo. 78, imp. 82. Rec. 1906 (1077).
ROMANO bl., fo. 85, imp. 87. Rec. 7095 (11000).
ROMEO, gr., fo. 71, imp. 75. Rec. 423.
ROMEO, gr., fo. 83, imp. 86. Rec. 5595 (4325).
ROMERO, gr., fo. 78, imp. 81. Rec. 1265.
ROMULUS, gr., fo. 73, imp. 79. Rec. 873 (785).
ROMULUS, gr., fo. 76, imp. 81. Rec. 1300.
ROMULUS, gr., fo. 78, imp. 82. Rec. 1938 (1078).
ROMULUS, gr., fo. 80, imp. 83. Rec. 2306 (1391).
ROMULUS, gr., fo. 79, imp. 84. Rec. 3525 (223).
ROMULUS, gr., fo. 83, imp. 84. Rec. 3529 (608).
ROMULUS, gr., fo. 79, imp. 84. Rec. 3752 (2175).
ROMULUS, bl., fo. 82, imp. 84. Rec. 3766 (534).
ROMULUS, bl., fo. 83, imp. 86. Rec. 5595 (7070).

ROSNY, gr., fo. 85, imp. 85, Rec. 4238 (2869).
ROSSITER, gr., fo. 77, imp. 84. Rec. 1353.
ROUGEMONT, gr., fo. 76, imp. 84. Rec. 1354.
ROULAND, gr., fo. 85, imp. 87. Rec. 7480 (1033G).
ROUSSEAU, bl., fo. 81, imp. 83. Rec. 2361 (1150).
ROUSTAN, gr., fo. 83, imp. 87. Rec. 4088 (4165).
ROUVIER, gr., fo. 85, imp. 87. Rec. 7097 (10631).
ROVER, gr., fo. 69, imp. 74. Rec. 437.
ROVIGNO, gr., fo. 80, imp. 82. Rec. 2123 (1000).
ROYAL, gr., fo. 75, imp. 80. Rec. 1307 (822).
RUNNYMEDE, gr., fo. 81, imp. 84. Rec. 1693.
RUSTICO, gr., fo. 83, imp. 86. Rec. 5579 (7203).
SAILLANT, bl., fo. 83, imp. 86. Rec. 5575 (4180).
ST. CYR, gr., fo. 82, imp. 85. Rec. 1238 (929).
ST. GERMAIN, bl., fo. 80, imp. 85. Rec. 2567 (1325).
ST. GERMAIN, gr., fo. 85, imp. 85. Rec. 4228 (2855).
ST. HILAIRE, gr., fo. 78, imp. 84. Rec. 1355.
ST. JEAN, gr., fo. 83, imp. 84. Rec. 2570 (701).
ST. LAWRENCE, gr., fo. 76, imp. 80. Rec. 909.
ST. LAZARE, gr., fo. 86, imp. 85. Rec. 2383 (39).
ST. LEON, bl., fo. 81, imp. 81. Rec. 1416.
ST. MAURICE, bl., fo. 81, imp. 83. Rec. 2337 (1182).
ST. VICTOR, gr., fo. 81, imp. 83. Rec. 2710 (1189).
SALADO, gr., fo. 77, imp. 80. Rec. 1229.
SALERNO, gr., fo. 78, imp. 81. Rec. 1356.
SALLUSTE, r., fo. 80, imp. 83. Rec. 2393 (1113).
SALOMON, b., fo. 79, imp. 84. Rec. 3793 (2500).
SALUTE, bl., fo. 82, imp. 82. Rec. 2112 (1005).
SALVADOR, gr., fo. 84, imp. 87. Rec. 6389 (4370).
SALVATOR, gr., fo. 83, imp. 85. Rec. 4295 (701).
SALVINI, gr., fo. 78, imp. 84. Rec. 1357.
SAMSON, gr., fo. 83, imp. 87. Unrecorded.
SANCHO, gr., fo. 71, imp. 75. Rec. 441.
SANDY, gr., fo. 78, imp. 82. Rec. 1059 (1079).
SANDY, gr., fo. 81, imp. 84. Rec. 3464 (55).
SANDY, gr., fo. 80, imp. 86. Rec. 3462 (2225).
SANDY, gr., fo. 83, imp. 87. Rec. 6290 (7801).
SANSCRIT, gr., fo. 84, imp. 86. Rec. 5495 (6553).
SANSCRIT, bl., fo. 84, imp. 85. Rec. 5380 (7206).
SANS-FACON, gr., fo. 83, imp. 85. Rec. 4306 (2848).
SANSONNET, bl., fo. 81, imp. 84. Rec. 3345 (51).
SANSONNET, gr., fo. 79, imp. 84. Rec. 3552 (2467).
SANSONNET, bl., fo. 83, imp. 85. Rec. 4300 (1939).
SANSONNET, gr., fo. 82, imp. 85. Rec. 4279 (115).
SANSONNET, gr., fo. 82, imp. 86. Rec. 5581 (7503).
SANSONNET, bl., fo. 84, imp. 87. Rec. 6591 (8811).
SANS-PEUR, gr., fo. 84, imp. 85. Rec. 4310 (4334).
SANS SOUCI, gr., fo. 81, imp. 87. Rec. 7100 (6970).
SANS TACHE, gr., fo. 86, imp. 87. 7114 (10075).
SARACEN, b., fo. 78, imp. 82. Rec. 1976 (1035).
SARCAS, gr., fo. 82, imp. 82. Rec. 2183 (1007).
SARDONICUS, gr., fo. 82, imp. 83. Rec. 2676 (1218).
SARGOSSA, gr., fo. 80, imp. 82. Rec. 2122 (1008).
SATELLITE, bl., fo. 85, home bred. Rec. 4734.
SATRAPE, gr., fo. 83, imp. 86. Rec. 5509 (127).
SATURN, gr., fo. 74, imp. 80. Rec. 1238.
SATURNE, gr., fo. 79, imp. 84. Rec. 3387 (625).
SATURNE, bl., fo. 85, imp. 87. Rec. 7102 (6750).
SATURNE, gr., fo. 81, imp. 83. Rec. 2577 (20).
SAUMUR, bl., fo. 83 imp. 84. Rec. 3327 (702).
SAVARIN, gr., fo. 85, imp. 87. 7117 (11544).
SCIPION, bl., fo. 83, imp. 87. Rec. 6992 (10359).
SCYTHIAN, gr., fo. 80, imp. 82. Rec. 1986 (1009).
SEBASTIAN, gr., fo. 79, imp. 82. Rec. 2001 (1010).
SEDAN, gr., fo. 73, imp. 76. Rec. 445.
SEDUCTEUR, gr., fo. 79 imp. 84. Rec. 3518 (2556).
SEDUCTEUR, gr., fo. 82, imp. 84. Rec. 3582 (2157).
SEEZ, gr., fo. 82, imp. 83. Rec. 2618 (1246).
SELIM, bl fo. 78, imp. 78. Rec. 764.
SELIM, gr., fo. 81, imp. 84. Rec. 3594 (2302).
SEM, gr., fo. 79, imp. 84. Rec. 3515 (2137).
SENANTES, gr., fo. 81, imp. 83. Rec. 2575 (1172).

SENATOR, gr., fo. 80, imp. 80. Rec. 944 (939).
SENATOR, gr., fo. 81, imp. 86. Rec. 5303 (4120).
SENSATION, w., fo. 65, imp. 73. Rec. 446.
SEPOY, gr., fo. 80, imp. 82. Rec. 2131 (1011).
SEQUIM, gr., fo. 78, imp. 81. Rec. 1358.
SERAGLIO, gr., fo. 75, imp. 81. Rec. 1476.
SERGOT, bl., fo. 83, imp. 85. Rec. 4241 (2955).
SERPIN, gr., fo. 78, imp. 83. Rec. 2781 (1261).
SILVER DUKE, gr., fo. 79, imp. 82. Rec. 1946 (1040).
SIMONEAU, bl., fo. 85, imp. 87. Rec. 7104 (9429).
SIMPLON, b., fo. 82, imp. 83. Rec. 2656 (1259).
SINBAD, gr., fo. 81, imp. 81. Rec. 1479.
SINNA, b., fo. 79, imp. 84. Rec. 2552 (2009).
SIPERIAN, gr., fo. 82, imp. 82. Rec. 2188 (1012).
SOLFERINO, gr., fo. 77, imp. 80. Rec. 1321 (821).
SOLFERINO, gr., fo. 81, imp. 83. Rec. 2588 (30).
SOLFERINO, gr., fo. 81, imp. 84. Rec. 3650 (2245).
SOLIDE, bl., fo. 83, imp. 84. Rec. 3752 (2695).
SOLIDE, gr., fo. 83, imp. 85. Rec. 4308 (2364).
SOLIDE, gr., fo. 81, imp. 85. Rec. 4324 (438).
SOLIDE, bl., fo. 82, imp. 87. Rec. 7101 (8649).
SOLIMAN, gr., fo. 83, imp. 86. Rec. 5565 (5504).
SOLIMAN, br., fo. 85, imp. 87. Rec. 7109 (8052).
SOPHOCLE, bl., fo. 82, imp. 84. Rec. 3495 (1689).
SOPHOCLE, gr., fo. 84, imp. 87. Rec. 7105 (4548).
SORUS, gr., fo. 81, imp. 84. Rec. (B. B. B.) No. (10).
SOUANCE, gr., fo. 85, imp. 87. Rec. 7111 (9104).
SOUDAN, b., fo. 82, imp. 84. Rec. 3484 (2154).
SOUDAN, bl., fo. 82, imp. 84. Rec. 3508 (1724).
SOUVENIR, bl., fo. 75, imp. 80. Rec. 1223.
SOUVENIR, gr., fo. 83, imp. 86. Rec. 5560 (1791).
SOUVENIR, gr., fo. 84, imp. 87. Rec. 6903 (4500).
SOUVERAIN, gr., fo. 85, imp. 87. Rec. 7106 (6214).
SPARTACUS, bl., fo. 81, imp. 83. Rec. 2670 (21).
SPARTACUS, gr., fo. 85, imp. 87. Rec. 7107 (6290).
SPARTAN, bl., fo. 81, imp. 81. Rec. 1417.
SPOSO, gr., fo. 84, imp. 85. Rec. 5598 (6543).
STEHR, bl., fo. 82, imp. 83. Rec. 2775 (1194).
STRADAT, bl., fo. 80, imp. 87. Rec. 7112 (2465).
STRANGER, gr., fo. 73, imp. 78. Rec. 771.
STROGOFF, bl., fo. 83, imp. 83. Rec. 5554 (6812).
SUCCESS, w., fo. 64, imp. 68. Rec. 452.
SUCCESS, gr., fo. 82, imp. 86. Rec. 5613 (6904).
SULTAN, bl., fo. 80, imp. 82. Rec. 1925 (1084).
SULTAN, gr., fo. 81, imp. 84. Rec. 3548 (356).
SULTAN, gr., fo. 82, imp. 84. Rec. 3381 (1640).
SULTAN, bl., fo. 82, imp. 84. Rec. 3257 (603).
SULTAN, gr., fo. 85, imp. 85. Rec. 4291 (4032).
SULTAN, gr., fo. 82, imp. 85. Rec. 4237 (1665).
SULTAN IV., bl., fo. 85, imp. 87. Rec. 7103 (9798).
SUPERBE, bl., fo. 82, imp. 84. Rec. 3509 (1038).
SUPERBE, bl., fo. 83, imp. 84. Rec. 3555 (699).
SUPERBE, gr., fo. 82, imp. 84. Rec. 3553 (2154).
SUPERIOR, w., fo. 68, imp. 74. Rec. 454 (730).
SUPERIOR, gr., fo. 78, imp. 81. Rec. 1259.
SUPERIOR, gr., fo. 81, imp. 85. Rec. 4313 (2923).
SUPERIOR II, bl., fo. 82, imp. 85. Rec. 4289 (4423).
SURPRENANT, gr., fo. 82, imp. 84. Rec. 3732 (692).
SURPRISE, gr., fo. 75, imp. 80. Rec. 980.
SYLLA, gr., fo. 83, imp. 84. Rec. 5299 (7383).
SYLVAIN, gr., fo. 84, imp. 85. Rec. 4319 (4177).
SYLVIO, gr., fo. 83, imp. 87. Rec. 7110 (10710).
TACHEAU, gr., fo. 81, imp. 85. Rec. 2356 (4197).
TACITE, gr., fo. 80, imp. 83. Rec. 2380 (1136).
TACOMA, gr., fo. 79, imp. 79. Rec. 877 (808).
TACONET, bl., fo. 79, imp. 83. Rec. 2381 (4397).
TAITBOUT, bl., fo. 82, imp. 83. Rec. 2453 (1234).
TALISMAN, gr., fo. 75, imp. 80. Rec. 1212.
TALMA, gr., fo. 83, imp. 85. Rec. 4225 (2885).
TAMARIN, gr., fo. 85, imp. 87. Rec. 7114 (10945).
TAMBOUR MAJOR, gr., fo. 85, imp. 87. 7119 (10094).

TAMERLANE, gr., fo. 78, imp. 82. Rec. 2155 (1915).
TAMPON, gr., fo. 82, imp. 86. Rec. 5589 (6794).
TARQUIN, bl., fo. 75, imp. 80. Rec. 947.
TARSUS, bl., fo. 79, imp. 82. Rec. 2150.
TAUPIN, bl., fo. 82, imp. 84. Rec. 3725 (2468).
TARTARY, gr., fo. 85, imp. 86. Rec. 5545 (6518).
TEJON, bl., fo. 81, imp. 81. Rec. 1330.
TEMERAIRE, gr., fo. 84, imp. 85. Rec. 5567 (6371).
TEMPEST, bl., fo. 71, imp. 76. Rec. 458.
TEMPLAR, gr., fo. 80, imp. 83. Rec. 945.
TENOCOA, gr., fo. 76, imp. 81. Rec. 1369.
THE MOOR, gr., fo. 76, imp. 81. Rec. 1361.
THEODORE, bl., fo. 78, imp. 83. Rec. 2372 (1280).
THEON, gr., fo. 81, imp. 81. Rec. 1418.
THEOPHILE, bl., fo. 82, imp. 84. Rec. 3746 (2795).
THESIS, bl., fo. 80, imp. 80. Rec. 2113 (1015).
THIRON, gr., fo. 82, imp. 83. Rec. 2974 (1221).
THOMAS, gr., fo. 80, imp. 83. Rec. 2356 (1128).
THOMAS, gr., fo. 80, imp. 83. Rec. 2397 (1228).
THOMPSON, gr., fo. 80, imp. 83. Rec. 2339 (1215).
THORSTINE, gr., fo. 81, imp. 81. Rec. 1449.
TIBER, bl., fo. 78, imp. 82. Rec. 2112 (1016).
TIC TAC, bl., fo. 83, imp. 86. Rec. 5158 (6784).
TIGER, gr., fo. 78, imp. 77. Rec. 778.
TIMOLINE, b., fo. 82, imp. 82. Rec. 2180 (1017).
TIMONNIER, gr., fo. 85, imp. 87. Rec. 7116 (8716).
TIRO, gr., fo. 81, imp. 81. Rec. 1419.
TOBIE, b., fo. 78, imp. 81. Rec. 1227 (826).
TOBIE, gr., fo. 83, imp. 86. Rec. 5550 (7013).
TOCSIN, gr., fo. 83, imp. 86. Rec. 5534 (6223).
TOPAZ, bl., fo. 76, imp. 80. Rec. 946.
TOP GALLANT, gr., fo. 75, imp. 79. Rec. 876.
TORNADO, gr., fo. 76, imp. 75. Rec. 467.
TOULON, b., fo. 80, imp. 80. Rec. 948 (857).
TRAGEDIEN, gr., fo. 84, imp. 87. Rec. 6094 (10126).
TRIANO, gr., fo. 78, imp. 82. Rec. 1924 (1087).
TRIANON, gr., fo. 83, imp. 86. Rec. 5525 (6508).
TRILBY, gr., fo. 85, imp. 87. Rec. 7115 (8417).
TRISTAM, gr., fo. 76, imp. 82. Rec. 1980 (1018).
TRIUMPH, gr., fo. 71, imp. 75. Rec. 466.
TRIUMPH, gr., fo. 78, imp. 83. Rec. 2711.
TROCU, gr., fo. 78, imp. 84. Rec. 3497 (884).
TROJAN, bl., fo. 77, imp. 80. Rec. 1205 (832).
TROJUS, gr., fo. 77, imp. 81. Rec. 1332 (827).
TROMPETTE, b., fo. 84, imp. 85. Rec. 4396 (2603).
TROMPEUR, gr., fo. 84, imp. 86. Rec. 5572 (3749).
TROPHY, bl., fo. 85, home bred. Rec. 4906.
TROUBADOUR, gr., fo. 83, imp. 86. Rec. 5532 (475).
TROUBADOUR, bl., fo. 85, imp. 86. Rec. 5562 (5169).
TUDOR, gr., fo. 82, imp. 82. Rec. 2178 (1019).
TUDUC, gr., fo. 83, imp. 86. Rec. 5156 (474).
TURBULENT, gr., fo. 85, imp. 86. Rec. 5404 (5204).
TURCO, gr., fo. 82, imp. 85. Rec. 4208 (2255).
TURCOMAN, bl., fo. 84, imp. 86. Rec. 5515 (7336).
TURENNE, gr., fo. 82, imp. 84. Rec. 3764 (336).
TURK, gr., fo. 73, imp. 76. Rec. 470 (855).
UBRIQUE, gr., fo. 83, imp. 86. Rec. 5161 (5654).
ULAN, gr., fo. 76, imp. 80. Rec. 949.
ULRIC, gr., fo. 82, imp. 82. Rec. 2179 (1020).
ULSTER, gr., fo. 83, imp. 86. Rec. 5506 (7576).
ULYSSE, gr., fo. 85, imp. 86. Rec. 5551 (6747).
ULYSSES, bl., fo. 79, home bred. Rec. 878.
URIEL, gr., fo. 81, imp. 81. Rec. 1450.
VAILLANT, gr., fo. 81, imp. 84. Rec. 3931 (2145).
VAILLANT, gr., fo. 82, imp. 84. Rec. 3702 (2539).
VAILLANT, bl., fo. 82, imp. 84. Rec. 3738 (2901).
VAILLANT, bl., fo. 82, imp. 85. Rec. 4776 (4304).
VAINQUEUR, gr., fo. 80, imp. 83. Rec. 2691 (1197).
VAINQUEUR, bl., fo. 82, imp. 84. Rec. 3745 (1798).
VAINQUEUR, gr., fo. 81, imp. 85. Rec. 4288 (284).
VALDEMAR, gr., fo. 82, imp. 84. Rec. 3716 (1955).
VALDEMEER, bl., fo. 83, home bred. Rec. 2271.

VALENCIENNE, gr., fo. 82, imp. 83. Rec. 2323 (1163).
VALENTIN, bl., fo. 83, imp. 86. Rec. 5349 (471).
VALENTINE, gr., fo. 74, imp. 78. Rec. 781.
VALERIAN, gr., fo. 78, imp. 82. Rec. 2009 (1021).
VALIANT, gr., fo. 66, imp. 74. Rec. 471 (746).
VALJEAN, bl., fo. 73, imp. 79. Rec. 879.
VALLEE, gr., fo. 81, imp. 83. Rec. 2008 (8).
VALLEE, b., fo. 83, imp. 85. Rec. 4233 (1879).
VALLIDOLI, gr., fo. 77, imp. 80. Rec. 1438.
VALMOND, bl., fo. 82, imp. 83. Rec. 2624 (1273).
VALOIS, gr., fo. 73, imp. 75. Rec. 474.
VALOR, gr., fo. 76, imp. 86. Rec. 951 (828).
VAMBREY, gr., fo. 77, imp. 81. Rec. 1364.
VANDAL, bl., fo. 76, imp. 80. Rec. 950.
VANQUER, br., fo. 79, imp. 82. Rec. 1941 (1683).
VAPEUR, bl., fo. 79, imp. 83. Rec. 2685 (1158).
VARGRAVE, bl., fo. 83, home bred. Rec. 2272.
VARRO, gr., fo. 81, home bred. Rec. 1365.
VASQUES, gr., fo. 80, imp. 82. Rec. 1963 (1022).
VASSORA, gr., fo. 81, home bred. Rec. 1366.
VAUBAN, gr., fo. 80, imp. 80. Rec. 954 (807).
VAUCLAIR, gr., fo. 84, imp. 87. Rec. 7122 (6274).
VAUGIRARD, bl., fo. 84, imp. 86. Rec. 5537 (6862).
VENDEE, gr., fo. 78, imp. 82. Rec. 2126 (1023).
VENDOME, gr., fo. 76, imp. 80. Rec. 952.
VENTEUR, gr., fo. 84, imp. 87. Rec. 6095 (6182).
VERCINGETORIX, gr., fo. 84, imp. 86. Rec. 5360 (6186).
VERIGNY, gr., fo. 81, imp. 83. Rec. 2397 (1131).
VERMONT, gr., fo. 73, imp. 76. Rec. 475 (747).
VERMOUTH, gr., fo. 81, imp. 84. Rec. 3695 (2471).
VERMOUTH, gr., fo. 82, imp. 84. Rec. 3735 (2235).
VERMOUTH, gr., fo. 84, imp. 85. Rec. 4218 (76).
VERMOUTH, gr., fo. 82, imp. 85. Rec. 4296 (608).
VERO, bl., fo. 83, home bred. Rec. 2273.
VERT GALLANT, gr., fo. 80, imp. 84. 3350 (2464).
VESUVIUS, gr., fo. 80, imp. 83. Rec. 2508 (1152).
VICI, bl., fo. 70, imp. 75. Rec. 476 (844).
VICTOR, gr., fo. 67, imp. 73. Rec. 477.
VICTOR, bl., fo. 80, imp. 83. Rec. 2509 (1115).
VICTOR I, gr., fo. 84, imp. 86. Rec. 5602 (4112).
VICTOR HUGO, gr., fo. 70, imp. 74. Rec. 478.
VICTOR HUGO II, bl., fo. 83, imp. 86. Rec. 5355 (6735).
VICTORY, gr., fo. 80, imp. 82. Rec. 2194 (1088).
VIDAL, gr., fo. 69, imp. 74. Rec. 481.
VIDOCQ, gr., fo. 69, imp. 74. Rec. 483 (732).
VIDOCQ, fo. 78, imp. 82. Rec. 1917 (1684).
VIDOCQ, b., fo. 81, imp. 84. Rec. 3461 (75).
VIDOCQ, gr., fo. 81, imp. 84. Rec. 3477 (434).
VIDOCQ, gr., fo. 81, imp. 84. Rec. 3702 (1908).
VIDOCQ II, gr., fo. 77, imp. 79. Rec. 880 (788).
VIDOU, gr., fo. 80, imp. 80. Rec. 953 (858).
VIGO, gr., fo. 69, imp. 74. Rec. 485.
VIGOUREUX, gr., fo. 79, imp. 83. Rec. 2357 (1234).
VIGOUREUX, bl., fo. 79, imp. 84. Rec. 3516 (2372).
VIGOUREUX, bl., fo. 82, imp. 85. Rec. 4292 (405).
VIKING, gr., fo. 76, imp. 80. Rec. 1731 (829).
VILLERNEUVE, gr., fo. 79, imp. 83. 2351 (1161).
VILLROY, bl., fo. 82, imp. 83. Rec. 2624 (1157).
VIMOUTIER, gr., fo. 81, imp. 83. Rec. 2377 (1156).
VINCENT, bl., fo. 80, home bred. Rec. 1328.
VINDEX, gr., fo. 83, imp. 86. Rec. 4295 (130).
VINDEX, gr., fo. 85, imp. 86. Rec. 5527 (7318).
VINDICATOR, gr., fo. 82, imp. 82. Rec. 2181 (1024).
VIPSANIUS, b., fo. 81, imp. 81. Rec. 1421.
VIRGIL, gr., fo. 78, imp. 82. Rec. 2000 (1025).
VIRGINIAN, gr., fo. 81, imp. 83. Rec. 2532 (9).
VIVEY, gr., fo. 82, imp. 83. Rec. 2645 (1286).
VIVIAN, gr., fo. 73, imp. 78. Rec. 785 (831).
VLADIMIR, gr., fo. 73, imp. 78. Rec. 786 (748).
VOL-AU-VENT, gr., fo. 77, imp. 81. Rec. 1233 (830).
VOLCANI, gr., fo. 78, imp. 82. Rec. 1928 (1026).
VOLGA, gr., fo. 80, imp. 82. Rec. 1951 (1085).

VOLNA, bl., fo. 80, imp. 80. Rec. 957 (855).
VOLNEY, gr., fo. 80, imp. 83. Rec. 2584 (2).
VOLTA, gr., fo. 84, imp. 87. Rec. 6266 (6277).
VOLTAIRE, gr., fo. 77, imp. 81. Rec. 1277.
VOLTAIRE, gr., fo. 79, imp. 84. Rec. 3485 (1931).
VOLTAIRE, gr., fo. 83, imp. 84. Rec. 3556 (3491).
VOLTAIRE, gr., fo. 80, imp. 84. Rec. 3540 (4413).
VOLTAIRE, gr., fo. 80, imp. 84. Rec. 3556 (2496).
VOLTAIRE, gr., fo. 83, imp. 84. Rec. 3770 (1983).
VOLTAIRE, gr., fo. 82, imp. 85. Rec. 4213 (64).
VOLTAIRE, gr., fo. 83, imp. 87. Rec. 7121 (5431).
VOLTAIRE II, gr., fo. 84, imp. 87. Rec. 6267 (2809).
VOLTAIRE III, b., fo. 84, imp. 85. Rec. 4320 (2985).
VOLTAIRE VII, gr., fo. 82, imp. 87. 7123 (1948).
VOLTIGUER, gr., fo. 82, imp. 82. Rec. 2187 (1027).
VOLTIGEUR, gr., fo. 82, imp. 87. Rec. 6808 (6402).
VOLTIGEUR, gr., fo. 84, imp. 87. Rec. 7129 (6778).
VOUILLE, gr., fo. 83, imp. 86. Rec. 5630 (6312).
VOYAGEUR, gr., fo. 85, imp. 87. Rec. 6999 (5467).
VULCAIN, gr., fo. 80, imp. 83. Rec. 2348 (1288).
VULCAIN, gr., gr. 82, imp. 84. Rec. 3302 (1758).
VULCAIN, gr., fo. 84, imp. 85. Rec. 4315 (4175).
VULCAIN, gr., fo. 85, imp. 87. Rec. 7124 (5515).
VULCAN, gr., fo. 69, imp. 75. Rec. 488.
WAGRAM, gr., fo. 75, imp. 80. Rec. 955.
WALLENSTEIN, gr., fo. 82, imp. 82. Rec. 2185.

WAMBA, gr., fo. 80, imp. 82. Rec. 2111 (1028).
WARRIOR, gr., fo. 76, imp. 80. Rec. 955.
WARSAW, bl., fo. 81, imp. 84. Rec. 1422.
WASHINGTON, gr., fo. 80, imp. 85. 2353 (1216).
WATERLOO, gr., fo. 81, imp. 84. Rec. 2733 (1694).
WATERLOO, gr., fo. 84, imp. 84. Rec. 3892 (2329).
WEBER, gr., fo. 85, imp. 87. Rec. 7125 (6016).
WESTERMAN, b., fo. 84, imp. 87. Rec. 7060 (6302).
WILDAIR, gr., fo. 66, imp. 72. Rec. 468.
WILFRED, gr., fo. 79, imp. 79. Rec. 881.
WILIAM, gr., fo. 83, imp. 86. Rec. 5583 (6333).
WOLFORD, b., fo. 85, home bred. Rec. 2274.
YEOMAN, bl., fo. 71, imp. 76. Rec. 591.
YOLO, gr., fo. 80, imp. 80. Rec. 958.
YOUNG AMERICA, gr., fo. 78, imp. 81. Rec. 1967.
YOUNG MONARCH, gr., fo. 78, imp. 81. Rec. 1526.
ZACH TAYLOR, gr., fo. 79, imp. 82. Rec. 2241.
ZAMA, br., fo. 81, home bred. Rec. 1968.
ZANTE, gr., fo. 77, imp. 82. Rec. 1948 (1086).
ZANTO, gr., fo. 79, imp. 83. Rec. 4747 (4583)
ZIMO, bl., fo. 81, imp. 81. Rec. 1422.
ZINGARI, gr., fo. 72, imp. 76. Rec. 502.
ZOLA, gr., fo. 79, imp. 79. Rec. 894.
ZOPHIEL, gr., fo. 79, imp. 82. Rec. 2149.
ZULOA, gr., fo. 80, imp. 82. Rec. 2256 (1087).
ZULU, bl., fo. 77, imp. 82. Rec. 2005 (1029).

SUCCESS.

The number in parenthesis is the number of animal as recorded in the Percheron Stud-Book of France; the other number, as recorded in the Percheron Stud-Book of America.

ABSALA, bl., fo. 81, imp. 86. Rec. 5651 (6718).
ABYDOS, gr., fo. 80, imp. 86. Rec. 900 (899).
ACACIA, gr., fo. 81, imp. 81. Rec. 1495.
ACTINE, bl., fo. 87, home bred. Rec. 7316.
ACTRESS, gr., fo. 77, imp. 80. Rec. 561 (1400).
ADELAIDE, bl., fo. 72, imp. 75. Rec. 549 (1407).
ADELAIDE, gr., fo. 86, home bred. Rec. 5221
ADELE, gr., fo. 76, imp. 82. Rec. 2217 (1408).
ADELIA, bl., fo. 81, home bred. Rec. 1487.
ADRIENNE, b., fo. 80, imp. 83. Rec. 2781 (1565).
AGNES, gr., fo. 77, imp. 81. Rec. 1477 (1406).
AGRIPPINE, bl., fo. 85, imp. 86. Rec. 5652 (6489).
ALBANIA, gr., fo. 77, imp. 82. Rec. 2395 (1410).
ALBERTINE, bl., fo. 85, imp. 87. Rec. 6923 (10782).
ALDINE, gr., fo. 81, imp. 81. Rec. 1424 (1411).
ALENE, bl., fo. 85, home bred. Rec. 4392.
ALENIA, bl., fo. 82, imp. 83. Rec. 2737 (1389).
ALEXANDRINE, gr., fo. 84, imp. 85. 4355 (4846).
ALICE, gr., fo. 80, imp. 84. Rec. 3677 (1375).
ALMA, bl., fo. 84, home bred. Rec. 3672.
ALVENA, gr., fo. 87, home bred. Rec. 7319.
AMAZON, b., fo. 74, imp. 79. Rec. 882 (1412).
AMAZONIA, gr., fo. 81, home bred. Rec. 1482.
AMIE, bl., fo. 87, home bred. Rec. 7357.
AMIRAUTE, gr., fo. 84, imp. 86. Rec. 5646 (6719).
ANGELE, gr., fo. 85, imp. 85. Rec. 4542 (4850).
ANGELIC, gr., fo. 87, home bred. Rec. 7356.
ANGELICA, gr., fo. 77, imp. 81. Rec. 1452 (1413).
ANNA, gr., fo. 85, imp. 85. Rec. 4371 (4362).
ANNA, gr., fo. 84, imp. 85. Rec. 4347 (4438).
ANNETA, gr., fo. 80, imp. 80. Rec. 1218 (897).
ARIA, gr., fo. 77, imp. 82. Rec. 2207 (1414).
ARIANE, gr., fo. 85, home bred. Rec. 4385.
AURELIA, gr., fo. 82, home bred. Rec. 1472.
AURORA, gr., fo. 82, imp. 83. Rec. 2728 (1482).
AVENA, gr., fo. 81, imp. 83. Rec. 2783 (1561).
AVENA, b., fo. 87, home bred. Rec. 7102.
AVENANTE, b., fo. 82, imp. 83. Rec. 2783 (1562).
BABIE, gr., fo. 85, imp. 87. Rec. 7127 (9508).
BABIE, bl., fo. 84, imp. 87. Rec. 7129 (8721).
BALSAMINE, gr., fo. 85, imp. 87. Rec. 6224 (5508).
BARBICHE, gr., fo. 82, imp. 86. Rec. 5337 (6488).
BASQUINE, gr., fo. 81, imp. 83. Rec. 2788 (1581).
BATHILDE, gr., fo. 85, imp. 86. Rec. 5639 (4087).
BAVOLETTE, gr., fo. 81, imp. 83. Rec. 2789 (1560).
BEATRICE, gr., fo. 84, imp. 85. Rec. 4348 (4848).
BEATRICE, bl., fo. 84, imp. 86. Rec. 5661 (6671).
BEAUANNA, gr., fo. 81, imp. 83. Rec. 2353 (1373).
BEAUTE, gr., fo. 85, imp. 86. Rec. 5638 (7092).
BEAUTY, gr., fo. 81, home bred. Rec. 1376.
BELINDA, gr., fo. 87, home bred. Rec. 7334
BELLA, bl., fo. 87, home bred. Rec. 7335.
BELLE, bl., fo. 84, imp. 85. Rec. 4352 (4852).
BELLETTE, bl., fo. 81, imp. 83. Rec. 2790 (1579).
BELLINA, gr., fo. 81, imp. 83. Rec. 2801 (1543).
BELLORA, bl., fo. 82, imp. 82. Rec. 2257 (1415).
BERENGERE, gr., fo. 79, imp. 83. Rec. 2800 (1549).
BERENICE, gr., fo. 82, imp. 83. Rec. 2799 (1550).
BERESINE, gr., fo. 80, imp. 83. Rec. 2738 (1552).

BERGERE, gr., fo. 83, imp. 87. Rec. 7130 (6046).
BERINGIA, gr., fo. 81, imp. 81. Rec. 1425.
BERNICE, bl., fo. 78, home bred. Rec. 792.
BERTHA, bl., fo. 81, imp. 86. Rec. 5340 (7008).
BERTHE, gr., fo. 85, imp. 85. Rec. 4394 (5095).
BERTHINE, gr., fo. 87, home bred. Rec. 7355.
BETHOUNE, bl., fo. 87, home bred. Rec. 7332.
BERTINE, gr., fo. 82, imp. 82. Rec. 2235 (1416).
BEULAH, gr., fo. 75, imp. 79. Rec. 883 (1417).
BIANA, bl., fo. 82, imp. 82. Rec. 2225 (1418).
BIANCA, bl., fo. 82, imp. 82. Rec. 2234 (1419).
BIBI, bl., fo. 86, imp. 87. Rec. 7128 (10248).
BICHETTE, gr., fo. 79, imp. 84. Rec. 3664 (2579).
BICHONNE, gr., fo. 82, imp. 86. Rec. 5644 (6721).
BIJOU gr., fo. 82, imp. 84. Rec. 3658 (2085).
BIJOU, bl., fo. 79, imp. 83. Rec. 2349 (1481).
BIJOU, bl., fo. 81, imp. 86. Rec. 5657 (7025).
BIJOU, gr., fo. 85, imp. 87. Rec. 7136 (10031).
BIJOURIE, gr., fo. 82, imp. 83. Rec. 2750 (1557).
BLANCHE, w., fo. 69, imp. 74. Rec. 525.
BLEUETTE, gr., fo. 85, imp. 86. Rec. 5621 (6148).
BOBINETTE, gr., fo. 83, imp. 86. Rec. 5649 (6715).
BODECIA, bl., fo. 82, imp. 82. Rec. 2223 (1420).
BONELLE, bl., fo. 81, imp. 83. Rec. 2785 (1560).
BOSCORA, gr., fo. 82 imp. 82. Rec. 2227 (1421).
BRAZETTE, gr., fo. 82, imp. 82. Rec. 2232 (1422).
BRAZOLLA, bl., fo. 82, home bred. Rec. 1473.
BRAZZONIA, gr., fo. 82, imp. 82. Rec. 2224 (1424).
BREBIA, gr., fo. 86, home bred. Rec. 5292.
BREBIS, gr., fo. 80, imp. 83. Rec. 4395 (1753).
BRETOLINE, bl., fo. 77, imp. 83. Rec. 2786 (1574).
BIHARIA, gr., fo. 82, imp. 83. Rec. 2760 (1492).
BRIE, gr., fo. 77, imp. 83. Rec. 2777 (1508).
BRILLANTE, gr., fo. 84, imp. 85. Rec. 4354 (4065).
BRILLANTE, bl., fo. 83, imp. 86. Rec. 5634 (4067).
BRILLANTINE, gr., fo. 84, imp. 86. 5675 (6348).
BRILLETTE, gr., fo. 87, home bred. Rec. 7343.
BRUNETTE, bl., fo. 80, imp. 80. Rec. 962 (882).
CALECIA, bl., fo. 82, imp. 83. Rec. 2776 (1496).
CALITTE, bl., fo. 82, imp. 83. Rec. 2341 (1509).
CALETTE, bl., fo. 86, home bred. Rec. 5696.
CAMILLE, gr., fo. 85, home bred. Rec. 4582.
CAMILLE, gr., fo. 84, imp. 86. Rec. 5339 (6804).
CAMILLE, gr., fo. 86, imp. 87. Rec. 7134 (5561).
CANADIENNE, d. g., fo. 85, home bred. 5701.
CAPITOLA, gr., fo. 77, imp. 77. Rec. 793 (873).
CARAVANE, b., fo. 85, home bred. Rec. 4385.
CARITA, gr., fo. 85, home bred. Rec. 4390.
CARLOTTA, bl., fo. 78, imp. 78. Rec. 794 (879).
CAROLINE, bl., fo. 85, imp. 86. Rec. 5674 (7054).
CARRESADRIA, gr., fo. 77, imp. 81. 1453 (1424).
CELESTE, bl., fo. 80, imp. 80. Rec. 963.
CENI, gr., fo. 82, imp. 83. Rec. 2723 (1480).
CHALOUPE, gr., fo. 85, imp. 87. Rec. 7131 (9507).
CHANSONNETTE, bl., fo. 84, imp. 86. 5650 (6394).
CHARMANTE, gr., fo. 79, imp. 83. 2754 (1540).
CHARMEUSE, gr., fo. 84, imp. 86. 5683 (7342).
CHEVRETTE, gr., fo. 78, imp. 83. 2344 (1569).
CINDA, gr., fo. 79, home bred. Rec. (855).

CINNA, bl., fo. 85, imp. 87. Rec. 7137 (10121).
CLARA BELLE, gr., fo. 74, imp. 78. Rec. 7.6
CLAUDIA, gr., fo. 77, imp. 81. Rec. 1475.
CLEOPATRA, bl., fo. 76, imp. 80. Rec. 951.
CLOTHILDE, gr., fo. 85, imp. 87. Rec. 1332 (10455).
COCODETTE, bl., fo. 83, imp. 85. Rec. 4342 (4658).
COCOTTE, gr., fo. 82, imp. 87. Rec. 6295 (16598).
COLETTA, b., fo. 82, imp. 83. Rec. 2330 (1557).
COLINE, bl., fo. 87, home bred. Rec. 7339.
CONSTANCE, b., fo. 78, imp. 81. Rec. 1478 (1425).
COQUETTA, gr., fo. 82, imp. 86. Rec. 5677 (7599).
COQUETTE, gr., fo. 10, imp. 80. Rec. 965 (850).
COQUETTE, gr., fo. 82, imp. 83. Rec. 2774 (1558).
COQUETTE, gr., fo. 79, imp. 84. Rec. 3956 (3039).
COQUETTE, b., fo. 83, imp. 85. Rec. 4303 (5310).
COQUILLE, b., fo. 87, home bred. Rec. 7331.
CORBEILLE, bl., fo. 84, imp 86. Rec. 5645 (6971).
CORINNE, b., fo. 85, imp. 86. Rec. 5024 (7090).
COUNTESS, gr., fo. 71, imp. 75. Rec. 537.
COUNTESS, gr., fo. 71, imp. 77. Rec. 796.
COZETTE, gr., fo. 75, imp. 79. Rec. 854.
CYNTHIA, gr., fo. 82, imp. 83. Rec. 2764 (1509).
DAHLIA, b., fo. 81, imp. 80. Rec. 1455.
DAISY, gr., fo. 76, imp. 80. Rec. 966 (871).
DAISY, bl., fo. 82, home bred. Rec. 186.
DAMEMARIE, gr., fo. 85, imp. 87. 7145 (11298).
DELORA, bl., fo. 81, imp. 83. Rec. 2156 (1530).
DELIGHT, bl., fo. 87, home bred. Rec. 7539.
DELPHINE, gr., fo. 85, imp. 86. Rec. 5425 (7008).
DELPHINETTE, bl., fo. 83, imp. 85. 4875 (4982).
DIANA, bl., fo. 82, imp 83. Rec 2767 (1515).
DIANA, gr., fo. 79, home bred. Rec. 885.
DINDINETTE, bl., fo. 81, imp. 81. Rec. 1427.
EDNA, bl., fo. 82, imp. 82. Rec. 2215 (1426).
EGALITE, bl., fo. 84, imp. 86. Rec. 5685 (7233).
EGERIE, gr., fo. 85, imp. 83. Rec. 5642 (6748).
EGLANTINE, bl., fo. 81, imp. 84. Rec. 3338 (7028).
ELBERTA, gr., fo. 75, imp. 80. Rec. 1215.
ELDORADO, br., fo. 81, imp. 86. Rec. 5425 (7178).
ELEANORE, gr., fo. 82, home bred. Rec. 1797.
ELECTRA, gr., fo. 81, imp. 83. Rec. 2740 (1586).
ELLEN, gr., fo. 78, home bred. Rec. 720.
ELISE, gr., fo. 84, imp. 86. Rec. 5648 (7094).
ELISE, gr., fo. 84, imp. 86. Rec. 5680 (7357).
ELOISE, gr., fo. 75, imp. 80. Rec. 1216 (1427).
ELPHIN, gr., fo. 80, home bred. Rec. 908.
ELSIE, gr., fo. 78, imp. 81. Rec. 545.
EMOLIA, gr., fo. 82, imp. 82. Rec. 2230 (1426).
EMPRESS, gr., fo. 67, imp. 73. Rec. 543.
EMPRESS, gr., fo. 71, imp. 75. Rec. 544.
ENCHANTRESS, bl., fo. 74, imp. 77. Rec. 801 (870).
ENTERPRISE, gr., fo. 84, imp. 86. Rec. 5648 (6455).
ERCILLA, gr., fo. 79, imp. 82. Rec. 2241 (1429).
ESPERANCE, gr., fo. 79, imp. 83. Rec. 2313 (1557).
ETELKA, gr., fo. 75, imp. 80. Rec. 1217 (1430).
ETOILE DU PERCHE, gr., fo. 84, imp. 87. Rec. 6926 (8887).
EUGENIA, gr., fo. 75, imp. 75. Rec. 547 (865).
EUGENIA, gr., fo. 69, imp. 72. Rec. 967.
EULALIE, gr., fo. 84, home bred. Rec. 3670.
EUNICE, gr., fo. 82, home bred. Rec. 2205.
EVANGELINE, gr., fo. 76, home bred. Rec. 532.
FADETTE, bl., fo. 80, imp. 83. Rec. 2780 (1558).
FAIRY, gr., fo. 81, imp. 83. Rec. 2794 (1592).
FANNIE, gr., fo. 80, imp. 83. Rec. 2730 (1552).
FANTINE, bl., fo. 74, imp. 79. Rec. 887.
FATIMA, gr., fo. 79, home bred. Rec. 951.
FATMA, bl., fo. 86, imp. 87. Rec. 7136 (9512).
FAULTLESS, b., fo. 77, home bred. Rec. 804.
FAUSTINE, gr., fo. 76, imp. 80. Rec. 1314 (1431).
FAUVETTE, bl., fo. 85, home bred. Rec. 4388.
FAVORITA, bl., fo. 82, imp. 85. Rec. 4359 (4410).

FENELLA, gr., fo. 82, imp. 82. Rec. 2750 (4408).
FLEUR DE LIS, gr., fo. 76, imp. 80. Rec. 971 (1432).
FLIRT, gr., fo. 76, imp. 80. Rec. 950 (1306).
FLORA, gr., fo. 75, home bred. Rec. 806.
FLOREDA, gr., fo. 79, imp. 81. Rec. 1409 (1433).
FLORENA, gr., fo. 78, home bred. Rec. 1181.
FLORENCE, gr., fo. 74, imp. 79. Rec. 895 (1470).
FLORENTINE, gr., fo. 77, imp. 80. Rec. 924 (875).
FLORINDA, gr., fo. 81, home bred. Rec. 1692.
FORMOSA, gr., fo. 78, imp. 83. Rec. 1865.
FORNICK, bl., fo. 81, home bred. Rec. 1692.
FORTUNA, bl., fo. 85, home bred. Rec. 1364.
FOSTORIA, gr., fo. 81, imp. 81. Rec. 1430 (1431).
FRANCAISE, gr., fo. 81, home bred. Rec. 3420.
FRANCESCA, gr., fo. 87, home bred. Rec. 7338.
FRANCINE, gr., fo. 78, imp. 81. Rec. 2741 (1577).
FRASIE, bl., fo. 85, imp. 85. Rec. 4358 (4740).
FREDONNE, gr., fo. 85, imp. 86. Rec. 5673 (7000).
FREGATE, gr., fo. 84, imp. 85. Rec. 5635 (5674).
FRIPPONNE, gr., fo. 83, imp. 81. Rec. 2732 (1458).
FROSINE, b., fo. 81, imp. 85. Rec. 4756 (4856).
FULIDA, gr., fo. 77, imp. 81. Rec. 1456 (1455).
FULVIA, gr., fo. 77, imp. 81. Rec. 1457 (1456).
GAIL, gr., fo. 77, got in France. Rec. 807.
GALLIMA, gr., fo. 81, imp. 86. Rec. 5667 (6991).
GEM, gr., fo. 67, imp. 73. Rec. 555.
GENEVIEVE, gr., fo. 79, home bred. Rec. 888.
GENTILLE, gr., fo. 83, imp. 85. Rec. 5655 (1756).
GENTILLETTE, gr., fo. 84, imp. 86. Rec. 5542 (4650).
GENTILLETTE, bl., fo. 84, imp. 87. 7137 (9841).
GERALDINE, gr., fo. 78, imp. 81. Rec. 1431 (1437).
GERMAINE, gr., fo. 83, imp. 86. Rec. 5681 (6855).
GERVAISE, gr., fo. 85, imp. 86. Rec. 5620 (6145).
GIARIA, bl., fo. 82, imp. 83. Rec. 2735 (1551).
GIPSY GIRL, bl., fo. 87, home bred. Rec. 7329.
GLENORA, gr., fo. 81, imp. 81. Rec. 1432.
GRACE, gr., fo. 74, imp. 77. Rec. 809 (872).
GRACIA, gr., fo. 81, home bred. Rec. 1485.
GUERANDE, gr., fo. 85, imp. 86. Rec. 5641 (6568).
GYPSEY GIRL, gr., fo. 77, home bred. Rec. 808.
HAZEL KIRKE, gr., fo. 85, imp. 81. Rec. 2792.
HEBE, bl., fo. 74, imp. 80. Rec. 972 (898).
HEBE, gr., fo. 85, imp. 86. Rec. 5826 (2089).
HEIRESS, gr., fo. 79, imp. 81. Rec. 1458.
HELENA, gr., fo. 81, imp. 81. Rec. 1454.
HELENE, bl., fo. 85, imp. 86. Rec. 5627 (7050).
HINDA, gr., fo. 82, imp. 83. Rec. 2765 (1519).
HIRONDELLE, gr., fo. 86, imp. 87. 7138 (10298).
HONORA, gr., fo. 80, imp. 82. Rec. 2204 (1458).
HORTENSE, gr., fo. 86, imp. 84. Rec. 3670 (1374).
IANTHE, gr., fo. 86, imp. 80. Rec. 973 (881).
IDABEL, gr., fo. 78, imp. 82. Rec. 2233.
IDEALITY, gr., fo. 82, imp. 81. Rec. 2248.
IDEALITY, gr., fo. 83, imp. 87. Rec. 4326.
IDELIA, gr., fo. 86, home bred. Rec. 5424.
ILDA, bl., fo. 80, imp. 83. Rec. 2787 (1575).
IMO, bl., fo. 75, imp 73. Rec. 810 (878).
IMPATIENTE, gr., fo. 84, im. 87. Rec. 5650 (2005).
INFELICE, gr., fo. 82, imp. 82. Rec. 2225 (1439).
IN NUCE, gr., fo. 79, imp. 82. Rec. 2234.
IOLA, bl., fo. 80, home bred. Rec. 981.
IONE, gr., fo. 78, imp. 82. Rec. 2291 (1440).
IRENA, gr., fo. 78, imp. 83. Rec. 2739 (1587).
ISADORE, gr., fo. 79, home bred. Rec. 889.
ISADORE, gr., fo. 81, imp. 84. Rec. 1455.
ISIS, gr., fo. 81, home bred. Rec. 1574.
ISNIA, gr., fo. 82, imp. in dam. Rec. 2243.
ISTRIA, gr., fo. 80, imp. 82. Rec. 2239 (1441).
ISUDA, bl., fo. 82, imp. 84. Rec. 2214 (1442).
ISUDINE, bl., fo. 87, home bred. Rec. 7327.
ITALA, gr., fo. 81, imp. 81. Rec. 1456.
ITASCA, gr., fo. 81, home bred. Rec. 2250.

JANECIA, b., fo. 82, imp. 83. Rec. 2705 (1510).
JENA, bl., fo.82, imp. 83. Rec. 2753 (1491).
JENNY, gr., fo. 86. Rec. 7157 (8553).
JOUVENCELLE, bl., fo. 84, imp. 87. 7158 (8896).
JOYEUSE, gr., fo. 84, imp. 86. Rec. 5682 (2839).
JULIA, bl., fo. 77, imp. 83. Rec. 2731 (1536).
JULIA, bl., fo. 79, imp. 78 in dam. Rec. 890.
JULIA, bl., fo. 85, imp. 86, Rec. 5676 (7015).
JULIE, gr., fo. 80, imp. 84. Rec. 3637 (2394).
JULIE, bl., fo. 83, imp. 86. Rec. 5656 (2961).
JUNO, gr., fo. 75, imp. 79. Rec. 891.
KATRINA, bl., fo. 79, home bred. Rec.892.
LA BELLE, gr., fo. 74, imp. 85. Rec. 974.
LA BOURDONNIERE, gr., fo. 85, imp. 87. Rec. 7139 (8842).
LACETTE, gr., fo. 85, imp. 86. Rec 5672 (6994).
LADORA, gr., fo. 76, imp. 82. Rec. 1932.
L'AMIE, bl., fo. 81, imp. 84. Rec. 306 (2347).
LAURETTA, gr., fo. 74, imp. 78. Rec. 822 (880).
LEA, gr., fo. 85, imp. 87. Rec. 7141 (8841).
LENA, gr., fo. 82, imp. 83. Rec. 2336 (1570).
LENORE, gr., fo. 70, imp. 74. Rec. 571.
LEONA, gr., fo. 85, imp. 87. Rec. 7144 (9768).
LEONIA, gr., fo. 82, imp. 83. Rec. 2335 (1538).
LETA, gr., fo. 81, imp. 81. Rec. 1440.
LEVRETTE, gr., fo. 84, imp. 87. Rec. 7140 (8638).
LIBERIA, gr., fo. 85, imp. 86. Rec. 5620 (7046).
LILIANE, bl., fo. 86, imp. 87. Rec. 7145 (8854).
LINDA, gr., fo. 81, 4imp. 83. Rec. 2751 (1521).
LIZETTE, gr., fo. 75, imp. 82. Rec. 1910 (1471).
L'OEIL, gr., fo. 81, imp. 81. Rec. 1442.
LOISELLE, gr., fo. 85, imp. 87. Rec. 7143 (8661).
LOUISE, bl., fo. 82, imp. 83. Rec. 2727 (1490).
LOULOUTE, bl., fo. 86, imp. 87. Rec. 7142 (10993).
LUCILLE, gr., fo. 74, imp. 80. Rec. 976 (1443).
LULA, gr., fo. 74, imp. in dam. Rec. 573.
LULIA, gr., fo. 81, home bred. Rec. 1494.
LURA, bl., fo. 82, imp. 83. Rec. 2799 (37).
LUTINE, bl., fo. 82, imp. 83. Rec. 2802 (1547).
LYDIA, gr., fo. 78, home bred. Rec. 826.
MABEL, gr., fo. 82, imp. 82. Rec. 1913 (2671).
MACARIA, gr., fo. 78, imp. 83. Rec. 2797 (35).
MADAME ANGOT, gr., fo. 73, imp. 75. Rec. 576.
MADAME MAINTENON, gr., fo. 80. 980.
MADELON, gr., fo. 85, imp. 86. Rec. 5699 (2174).
MAITRESSE, gr., fo. 77, imp. 83. Rec. 2778 (1590).
MARALIA, gr., fo. 82, imp. 83. Rec. 2769 (1499).
MARGOT, bl., fo. 83, imp. 85. Rec. 4351 (1350).
MARGOT, bl., fo. 85, imp. 86. Rec. 5656 (7021).
MARGOT, gr., fo. 82, imp. 86. Rec. 5662 (3734).
MARGUERITA, b., fo. 74, imp. 80. 978 (1444).
MARGUERITE, gr., fo. 85, imp. 85. 4746 (4897).
MARIE ANTOINETTE, gr., fo. 79. Rec. 580.
MARIE THERESE, gr., fo. 85, imp. 85. 4278 (5084).
MARINDA, gr., fo. 79, imp. 83. Rec. 2315 (1484).
MARITA, bl., fo. 83, imp. 85. Rec. 4353 (4290).
MARTHA, gr., fo. 86, imp. 87. Rec. 7148 (11965).
MASCOTTE, gr., fo. 81, imp. 81. Rec. 1446.
MASCOTTE, gr., fo. 82, imp. 87. Rec. 6927 (4365).
MATHILDE, gr., fo. 82, imp. 84. Rec. 3662 (416).
MATHILDE, gr., fo. 86, imp. 87. Rec. 7149 (11927).
MATIE, gr., fo. 82, imp. 83. Rec. 2795 (1591).
MATINE, gr., fo. 86, home bred. Rec. 5695.
MAZOLIA, gr., fo. 79, imp. 82. Rec. 1920.
McEDEAH, br., fo. 85, home bred. Rec. 4381.
MEDICI, gr., fo. 82, imp. 82. Rec. 2221 (1445).
MEDORA, bl., fo. 85, home bred. Rec. 4386.
MEDUSA, bl., fo. 80, imp. 82. Rec. 2263 (1446).
MERE, gr., fo. 82, imp. 83. Rec. 2775 (1497).
MERINE, bl., fo. 86, home bred. Rec. 5628.
MERIT, bl., fo. 87, home bred. Rec. 7326.
MIDA, gr., fo. 84, imp. 85. Rec. 4350 (4909).

MID-OCEAN, gr., fo. 75, imp. 75. Rec. 583.
MIGNONETTE, gr., fo. 70, imp. 76. 584 (1447).
MIGNONNE, gr., fo. 80, imp. 85. Rec. 2798 (1551).
MIGNONNE, gr., fo. 78, imp. 83. Rec. 2342 (1541).
MIGNONNE, gr., fo. 77, imp. 83. Rec. 1518.
MIGNONNE, bl., fo. 81, imp. 85. Rec. 45-9 (2962).
MILDA, gr., fo. 81, imp. 83. Rec. 2806 (1548).
MILDRED, bl., fo. 79, imp. 78 in dam. Rec. 893.
MILLICENT, gr., fo. 81, imp. 83. Rec. 2791 (1578).
MINDA, gr., fo. 77, imp. 83. Rec. 2354 (1516).
MINDELE, bl., 85, home bred. Rec. 4387.
MINERVA, bl., fo. 60, imp. 75. Rec. 585.
MINETTE, gr., fo. 84, imp. 87. Rec. 7150 (4059).
MINNA, gr., fo. 77, imp. 82. Rec. 2308 (1448).
MINNIE, gr., fo. 74, imp. 80. Rec. 977.
MINNIE, gr., fo. 85, home bred. Rec. 5693.
MIRA, gr., fo. 84, imp. 87. Rec. 7146 (8627).
MIRANE, bl., fo. 85, home bred. Rec. 4579.
MISS, bl., fo. 86, imp. 87. Rec. 7147 (10083).
M'LLE D'AUGUAISE, gr., fo. 80, imp. 87. Rec. 7151 (2171).
MODESTINE, bl., fo. 82, imp. 83. Rec. 2779 (1580).
MODJESKA, bl., fo. 80, imp. 82. Rec. 2212 (1449).
MORCENA, gr., fo. 82, imp. 82. Rec. 2222 (1450).
MORENA, bl., fo. 80, home bred. Rec. 979.
MOUCHETTE, gr., fo. 81, imp. 83. Rec. 2804 (1553).
MOUVANTE, bl., fo. 84, imp. 87. Rec. 7163 (10003).
MOUVETTE, gr., fo. 81, imp. 85. Rec. 2805 (1544).
MUSETTE, gr., fo. 81, imp. 81. Rec. 1447 (1451).
MYDIA, bl., fo. 78, imp. 82. Rec. 2200 (1452).
MYRA, bl., fo. 85, imp. 86. Rec. 5623 (7099).
MYRTLE, bl., fo. 77, home bred. Rec. 828.
MANETTE, gr., fo. 80, home bred. Rec. 86.
NAOMI, gr., fo. 80, imp. 82. Rec. 2218 (1453).
NATHALIA, gr., fo. 81, imp. 81. Rec. 1450 (2793).
NAVETTE, gr., fo. 80, imp. 83. Rec. 2746 (1572).
NAVOLIA, gr., fo. 78, imp. 82. Rec. 2209 (1451).
NEMEA, bl., fo. 77, imp. 83. Rec. 2748 (1582).
NEVA, gr., fo. 81, imp. 83. Rec. 2345 (1583).
NIAMI, gr., fo. 82, imp. 82. Rec. 2220 (1455).
NINA, bl., fo. 79, home bred. Rec. 809.
NINDA, gr., fo. 82, imp. 83. Rec. 2748 (1532).
NINICHE, bl., fo. 81, imp. 85. Rec. 4245 (4603).
NITA, gr., fo. 84, home bred. Rec. 3071.
NITANTE, bl., fo. 87, home bred. Rec. 7325.
NONETTE, gr., fo. 81, imp. 83. Rec. 2801 (1546).
NORA, br. b., fo. 87, home bred. Rec. 7324.
NORVA, bl., fo. 81, imp. 82. Rec. 2219 (1456).
NORVALINE, br., fo. 82, imp. 82. Rec. 2233 (1457).
NORVETTE, b., fo. 86, home bred. Rec. 5699.
NUBIE, gr., fo. 85, imp. 86. Rec. 5640 (6503).
NUDA, bl., fo. 81, imp. 83. Rec. 2761 (1491).
NUDINE, bl., fo. 87, home bred. Rec. 7323.
OCTAVIE, gr., fo. 83, imp. 86. Rec. 5631 (7048).
ONDINE, gr., fo. 85, imp. 87. Rec. 7152 (8859).
OPHELIA, gr., fo. 70, imp. 78. Rec. 590 (1472).
ORANGE, gr., fo. 85, imp. 86. Rec. 5619 (7056).
OUIDA, bl., fo. 80, imp. 80. Rec. 982 (807).
PALLAS, gr., fo. 84, imp. 86. Rec. 5636 (2258).
PALMA, gr., fo. 82, imp. 85. Rec. 4359 (4929).
PANDORA, bl., fo. 83, imp. 86. Rec. 5555 (6669).
PANDORE, gr., fo. 86, imp. 87. Rec. 7153 (10780).
PAQUERETTE, gr., fo. 80, imp. 83. 2724 (1478).
PAQUERETTE, bl., fo. 82, imp. 86. 5680 (6834).
PASTOURELLE, gr., fo. 84, imp. 86. 5654 (2569).
PAULINE, gr., fo. 78, imp. 83. Rec. 2540 (1535).
PECADIE, gr., fo. 81, imp. 85. Rec. 4356 (1712).
PEERLESS, gr., fo. 72, imp. 77. Rec. 744.
PEERLESS, bl., fo. 86, home bred. Rec. 5322.
PELOTE, gr., fo. 79, imp. 83. Rec. 2763 (1487).
PELOTE, bl., fo. 81, imp. 83. Rec. 2762 (1489).
PELOTE, b., fo., fo. 78, imp. 84. Rec. 3659 (1809).

CATALOGUE

OF

FRENCH COACH HORSES.

INDEX.

FRENCH COACH STALLIONS.

FRENCH COACH MARES.

FRENCH COACH HORSES.

INFLUENCE OF THE GOVERNMENT STUDS UPON THEIR DEVELOPMENT.

The following history of the government studs of France, and their effect upon the horses of that country will give a person a fair idea of the quality of horses the scientific breeders of later periods were provided with, from which, by mingling the blood of the Arab, Barb and Thoroughbred, they formed that magnificent *race* of coach horses that so admirably meets the demands of the fastidious purchasers of high-stepping, fine-styled, smooth-formed horses of sufficient weight to draw the heavy European coaches of the present day.

The liberal aid in supplying the finest stallions, and generous encouragement extended by the government to the breeders of fine coach horses in France since the establishment of the government stud-book, by Louis Phillip, in 1833, has done much to secure that combination of power, elegance and endurance that has placed the French Coach Horse in the front rank of excellence among the carriage breeds of the world.

The need of this class of horses in America has been grievously felt, and the demand for them is constantly increasing, and their raising will undoubtedly prove a lucrative branch of horse breeding. The eagerness that information is sought after on this subject is the best evidence we can have that the introduction of French coachers into America will meet with a favorable reception.

THE GOVERNMENT STUDS OF FRANCE.

The French Government has taken an interest in the improvement of horses never equaled by that of any other nation.

That the French people have, from the earliest periods, been ardent lovers of equine perfection, is evinced in the early superiority of the horses of that country, and the popularity of every movement made by the government tending toward their improvement.

As early as the Middle Ages the horses of France had a recognized superiority over those of any other country, which may be partially attributed to its peculiar system of government. Upon the accession of Hugh Capet, in the tenth century, France was divided into about 70,000 fiefs governed by nobles. The constant dissensions among these petty lords made a military education a necessity for self-protection. In those days of chivalry, when the success of battle depended chiefly upon the prowess of mounted knights, the strength and endurance of their horses was of more importance and more highly appreciated than at any other period of the world's history. Under these necessities a most powerful and intense impulse was given to the development of horses suited to the requirements of the period.

We thus see in the feudal ages the improvement of horses based upon individual necessity, but as this system disappeared in the centralization of the government in the CROWN, the powers of the state slowly absorbing feudal sovereignty, the government itself became interested in all movements tending toward the production of a superior class of horses, so necessary at that time for a thorough military equipment, upon which its safety depended.

The most effective and energetic action in establishing permanent government studs was taken under the administration of that great French minister, Colbert, in 1665, and was so well managed that in 1690 statistics show the number of *Royal* and *approved* stallions standing in France to have been 1,600. The government stallions kept at the Haras were called *the King's* stallions, and were selected from among the finest and best breeds to be found in France, and many were brought from Barbary, Turkey, Spain and latterly from England. The approved stallions were the produce of government stallions and the best mares of the country.

Two large government Haras were established by Louis XV, that of Pin 1714, located near the borders of La Perche, which was the first and largest establishment of the kind ever created, and where the finest stallions belonging to the government have been kept up to the present day. It is to this establishment that the Percherons owe much of their superiority, as here was kept the Arab Gallipoli, from which is descended the famous Jean le Blanc 739, the progenitor of many of the finest Percherons of the present time. In 1775 the Haras of Pompadour were established with twelve depots, and placed under the superintendence of the administration of the Haras.

In 1789, there were in France 3,239 approved and government stallions, which served, according to regulations, 115,000 mares, producing 55,000 living colts. From 1815 to 1833 the government bought for service in their studs 1,902 stallions; of these 223 came from Arabia and other foreign countries, 853 from the northern departments of France, principally from Calvados and Le Perche, and 826 were selected from the finest of the improved breeds from government stallions. In 1831 a most notable advance was made toward the improvement of the light breeds suitable for coach and cavalry purposes, which was followed in 1833 by a royal decree establishing a government studbook for the preservation of pedigrees; this was placed under the supervision of the Minister of Agriculture. After the establishment of this stud-book more critical judgment was exercised in the selection of stallions for government use than ever before, and large prizes were offered for colts produced by the finest mares of the country. Since the establishment of this stud-book a very decided improvement has taken place in the character of the horses of the entire country, between 11,000 and 12,000 owned by the government having been recorded. No animal is given a number unless belonging to the government studs.

May 5, 1870, the management of the government Haras or studs was vested in the Department of Agriculture and Commerce under the immediate supervision of a director-general, eight inspectors, twenty-six sub-directors, ten superintendents and twenty-six veterinaries.

In order to be eligible to an appointment to one of the above offices, the candidate must be a graduate of the "Ecole de Haras du Pin," a school located at the Haras of Pin for the education of men to whom shall be confided the future management of this department of the government.

In 1874 the number of stallions owned by the government throughout France was ordered increased 200 per year until they should reach 2,500, and the credit necessary for prizes awarded to breeding animals should reach 1,500,000 francs per annum, and a special sum of 50,000 francs per year was granted to make experiments with Arab and Anglo-Arab, and for this purpose 60 finely bred mares were placed at the Haras of Pompadour.

In the organization by the government of the administration of the Haras, there has been one central object constantly kept in view, that is the encouragement of the people by every means possible, to a higher standard of breeding, and at the same time to furnish them the means by which to accomplish this purpose, by the introduction into every locality of the finest of the different breeds and types, which are offered for use to the mare owners at a nominal fee of service. These consist, first, of stallions owned by the government itself; second, stallions belonging to private individuals inspected and approved by the government, such approved stallions receiving from the government as long as they are so kept, from 300 to 3,000 francs per annum, according to their breeding and superior excellence; third, authorized stallions, animals that by government inspection are pronounced of good quality and worthy of public patronage. To farther prevent the use of inferior individuals a decree was issued in 1885, excluding from public service all stallions not authorized by the government.

By a decree of December 9, 1860, a subsidy or prize of from 100 to 600 francs each (according to breeding and quality), was authorized to be given to approved mares with colts by government stallions. Besides this, large sums are given in prizes at the annual regional exhibitions and races held under the auspices of the government.

We thus see the French Government the most liberal patron of the breeder and the stallioner, but farther yet than this, it becomes an important factor in sustaining the prices of the finest types of all breeds, as the hundreds of stallions of the very highest order of merit that they are obliged to buy annually to supply the Haras, creates a constant demand for the best types at very high prices.

The valuable qualities claimed for the French Coach horses over those of other Coach breeds are based upon a system of breeding not possessed by any other race.

The breeding of all classes of domestic animals in every other country is conducted by individual enterprise and the outgrowth of individual ideas. Therefore the fixity of type is greatly affected or destroyed altogether by the variety of opinions entertained by the large number of people of different tastes engaged in the breeding; hence so general a lack of that uniformity of character so highly esteemed and so necessary in every successful breeding animal. The French Coach breed, instead of being the product of a multiplicity of ideas, has been developed under the exclusive guidance of the Director General of the National Studs of France; and as these officials are educated in the same school from generation to generation, are taught to value the same form, seek for the same qualities and pursue the same system, we can understand how it has been possible for them to attain such high perfection and great uniformity in the horses of the country. The power exercised by the Inspector-General is extraordinary, controlling, as he does, the selection of the 2,500 stallions owned exclusively by the government, and the thousands of others annually inspected, which must obtain his approval before receiving

their permits and subsidy ; and further, all breeders are confined exclusively
to the use of animals inspected and licensed by this department. This places
horse-breeding entirely under government control, as far as the stallions,
which so greatly control results, can do.

The Coach stallions, as will be seen by the pedigrees given in the following pages (which are transcripts from the government record, the original
certificate of birth accompanying each individual), are the descendants, and
possess a combination of the Arab, the famous breed of the Merlerault, and the
French and English thoroughbreds.   The most famous trotting families of
this breed are the result of the mingling of the blood of the Norfolk trotters,
a breed that through imported Belfounder has given to American trotters
much of their renown, imported Phenomenon in France corresponding to
imported Belfounder in the United States.

The uniting of all the valuable qualities of the various breeds, and con-
centrating them through several generations under the direction of a single
mind, has developed a race of such size and perfect symmetry, and a wonder-
ful endurance that makes it possible for them to trot, as three and four-year
olds, the three to seven mile races common to that country. Although they
do not attain the high rate of speed as American trotters do, when we consider
the size of the animals, many of them attaining a weight of 1,300 to 1,400
pounds, in trotting condition, their cumbersome vehicles or heavy-weight
riders, and inferior tracks, we cannot but recognize that they possess qualities
unequaled by any other breed. The National Studs are supplied with these
stallions from various parts of France, where the breed has attained its highest perfection. The mares are owned by the breeders of the country, and the
stallions are in use by the government which buys large numbers to keep up
its supply.

The finest of these horses are bred in the department of Calvados, where,
in the fall of every year, the government purchases are made. In order to
secure the very finest to supply the trade of Oaklawn, we make our purchases
in the summer, before the government stallions are selected, thus securing the
choicest of every year's production, the government always buying three-year
olds. While this system has the advantage of securing the very best animals,
it also necessitates the payment of larger prices in order to obtain them. The
policy of this course has never for a moment been doubted by me. My patrons
have never been of a class seeking to purchase animals of an inferior quality,
even though they may be obtained at low prices.

Confident that no horses of this breed that have ever been brought from
France have been accompanied by the records of finer lineage or possess
higher individual qualities than those described in the following pages, I
submit them to the criticism of all who desire to inspect or purchase, with full
confidence that they will prove as valuable and successful in America as their
ancestors have in France.

                                        M. W. DUNHAM.

Oaklawn, November 1, 1887.

FRENCH COACH HORSES.

ARPENTEUR.

Bay; foaled May 24, 1883; imported 1886; bred by M. Denis Duverger, of Brocottes, department of Calvados; got by the government stallion ULBACH; dam CERES by CENTAURE out of a daughter of GREAT WESTERN.

ULBACH, by Glaneur out of a daughter of John Bull, he by Taconnet out of a daughter of Sultan, he by Tipple Cider out of a daughter of Dupleix, he by Pickpocket out of Marquise by Young Rattler, he by Rattler out of the Snap Mare.

TACONNET, by Idalis out of a daughter of Faust I, he by Biron out of a daughter of Lucholl, he by Old Lucholl.

BIRON, by Captain Candid out of Helene by Eastham, he by Sir Oliver out of Cowslip by Alexander.

CAPTAIN CANDID, by Cerberus out of Mandane by Pot-8-os.

IDALIS, by Don Quichotte out of a daughter of Chapman, he by Trotteur, he by Chapman.

DON QUICHOTTE, by Sylvio out of Moina by Tigris, he by Quitz out of Persepolis by Alexander.

SYLVIO, by Trance out of Hebe by Rubens.

TIPPLE CIDER, by Defence out of Deposit by Blacklock.

PICKPOCKET, by St. Patrick out of the Hedley Mare.

GLANEUR, by Buckthorn out of Alma by Prime Warden.

BUCKTHORN, by Venison out of Zelia by Emilius, he by Emilius out of Cobweb, by Phantom.

CENTAURE, by Seducteur out of a daughter of Merlerault, he by Royal Oak out of a daughter of Sylvio, etc

ROYAL OAK, by Caton out of Smolensko Mare.

SEDUCTEUR, by Noteur out of a daughter of Fatibello, he by Sylvio, etc., out of a daughter of Y, he by Norfolk Phenomenon out of Henriette by Invincible, he by Hoemus out of Regatta by Camel.

NOTEUR, by Eylau out of a daughter of Diomed, he by Young Rattler, etc., out of a daughter of Young Topper, he by Topper.

EYLAU, by Napoleon out of Delphine by Massoud (pure Arab).

NAPOLEON, by Bob Booty out of the Pope Mare.

GREAT WESTERN, by The Steamer out of a daughter of The General.

(Hoof No. 47.)   # ALPHA.

Chestnut; foaled September 27, 1887; bred at Oaklawn; got by DON JUAN; dam MARGUERITE by TEMPETE out of Mouvette by UGOLIN; 3d dam by URSIN.

DON JUAN, by Tigris out of Glaneuse by Buci, he by Solide out of a daughter of Eylau, he by Napoleon out of Delphine by Massoud (pure Arab).

  SOLIDE, by Nestor out of a daughter of Jaggard, he by Mailhand-Schols.

  NESTOR, by Hospodar out of a daughter of Captain Candid, he by Cerberus out of Mandane by Pot-8-os.

  CERBERUS, by Roland (English thoroughbred).

  HOSPODAR, by Imperieux out of a daughter of Young Rattler, he by Rattler out of the Snap Mare.

  IMPERIEUX, by Young Rattler, etc., out of a daughter of Volontaire, he by Eclipse (English thoroughbred).

  NAPOLEON, by Bob Booty out of the Pope Mare.

TIGRIS, by Lavater out of a daughter of The Heir of Linné, he by Galaor out of Mrs. Walker by Jereed.

LAVATER, by Y out of Candelaria (English thoroughbred).

Y, by the Norfolk Phenomenon out of Henriette by Invincible.

NORFOLK PHENOMENON, by Old Phenomenon.

TEMPETE, by Conquerante out of a daughter of Abrantes, he by Pledge out of a daughter of Noteur, he by Eylau, etc., out of a daughter of Diomed, he by Young Rattler, etc., out of a daughter of Young Topper, he by Topper.

  PLEDGE, by Royal Oak out of a daughter of Young Rattler, etc.

  ROYAL OAK, by Catton out of Smolensko Mare.

CONQUERANTE, by Kapirat out of Elisa by Corsair, he by J. C. Knox's Corsair out of a daughter of Cleveland.

KAPIRAT, by Voltaire out of a daughter of The Juggler, he by Wamba out of Pantechnetheca by Master Henry.

VOLTAIRE, by Imperieux out of a daughter of Pilot, he by Octavius (English thoroughbred).

UGOLIN, by Parisien, he by Ganymede out of a daughter of Biron, he by Captain Candid, etc., out of Helene by Eastham, he by Sir Oliver out of Cowslip by Alexander

GANYMEDE, by Xerxes out of La Louve by Chasseur, he by Eastham, etc., out of Marquise by Young Rattler, etc.

XERXES, by Young Rattler, etc., out of a daughter of Young Highflyer, he by Highflyer out of a daughter of Young Docteur, he by Docteur out of a daughter of Mignon, he by Glorieux (English thoroughbred).

URSIN, by Ramsay out of a daughter of Ganymede, etc.

RAMSAY, by Sylvio out of Emelina by Emilius, he by Emilius out of Cobweb by Phantom.

SYLVIO, by Trance out of Hebe by Rubens.

(Hoof No. 43.)   **BRAVO.**

Black; 16¾ hands; weight, 1,350 lbs.; foaled February 26, 1883; imported 1886; bred by M. Paul Lemeland, of Valgnes, department of La Manche; got by the government stallion UTRECHT; dam CASTILLE by SNAP.

UTRECHT, by Palm out of a daughter of Pretender.

PALM, by Centaure out of a daughter of Torigny, he by Merlerault out of a daughter of Hector, he by Quebec out of a daughter of Buffalo, he by Holme out of a daughter of Little Isaac.

  MERLERAULT, by Royal Oak out of a daughter of Sylvio, he by Trance out of Hebe by Rubens.

  ROYAL OAK, by Catton out of Smolensko Mare.

  QUEBEC, by Oscar, he by Young Rattler out of a daughter of Bacha (pure Arab).

  YOUNG RATTLER, by Rattler out of the Snap Mare.

CENTAURE, by Seducteur out of a daughter of Merlerault, etc.

SEDUCTEUR, by Noteur out of a daughter of Fatibello, he by Sylvio, etc., out of a daughter of Y, he by Norfolk Phenomenon out of Henriette by Invincible, he by Hoemus out of Regatta by Camel.

  NORFOLK PHENOMENON, by Old Phenomenon.

NOTEUR, by Eylau out of a daughter of Diomed, he by Young Rattler, etc., out of a daughter of Young Topper, he by Topper.

EYLAU, by Napoleon out of Delphine by Massoud (pure Arab).

NAPOLEON, by Bob Booty out of the Pope Mare.

SNAP, by Anghton Merry Leggs.

(Hoof No. 46.)   # CLERMONT.

Bay ; foaled May 10, 1884 ; imported 1886 ; bred by M. Nicholas Viel, of Fresville, department of La Manche ; got by the government stallion AVEYRON ; dam Castille.

AVEYRON, by Kaolin out of a daughter of Seduisant, he by Lagopede out of a daughter of Koulikham, he by Voltaire out of a daughter of Proselyte, he by Proselyte.

LAGOPEDE, by Voltaire out of a daughter of the Juggler, he by Wamba out of Pantechnetheca by Master Henry.

VOLTAIRE, by Imperieux out of a daughter of Pilot, he by Octavius (English thoroughbred).

IMPERIEUX, by Young Rattler out of a daughter of Volontaire, he by Eclipse (English thoroughbred).

YOUNG RATTLER, by Rattler out of the Snap Mare.

KAOLIN, by Zouave out of Dainty by Ionian.

ZOUAVE, by the Baron out of Dacia by Gladiator, he by Partisan out of Pauline by Moses.

PARTISAN, by Lucholl, he by Old Lucholl.

(Hoof No. 42.)

EBLOUISSANT.

Chestnut; 16¼ hands; weight, 1,300 lbs.; foaled March 2, 1883; imported 1886; bred by M. Goupil, of Leaupartie, department of Calvados; got by the government stallion MONTFORT; dam NOIRETTE by MATCHLESS II.

MONTFORT, by Arc-en-Ciel (English thoroughbred) out of Fougeres by Faugh-a-Ballagh, he by Sir Hercules out of Guiccioli by Bob Booty.

MATCHLESS II, by Matchless out of a daughter of Flying Buck, he by Lucain, he by Eylau out of Desiree by Talma.

EYLAU, by Napoleon out of Delphine by Massoud (pure Arab).

NAPOLEON, by Bob Booty out of the Pope Mare.

MATCHLESS, by Willesdin (English thoroughbred).

(Hoof No. 12.)   **FAN FAN.**

Brown ; 16 hands ; weight, 1,275 lbs. ; foaled April 29, 1883 ; imported 1887 ; bred by M. Guerard, of St. Pierre-du-Jonquet, department of Calvados ; got by the government stallion ACQUILA ; dam RACHAEL by IRLANDAIS out of a daughter of ESCULAPE.

ACQUILA, by Niger out of a daughter of Centaure, he by Seducteur out of a daughter of Merlerault, he by Royal Oak out of a daughter of Sylvio, he by Trance out of Hebe by Rubens.

SEDUCTEUR, by Noteur out of a daughter of Fatibello, he by Sylvio, etc., out of a daughter of Y., he by the Norfolk Phenomenon out of Henriette by Invincible, he by Hoemus out of Regatta by Camel (English thoroughbred).

NOTEUR, by Eylau out of a daughter of Diomed, he by Young Rattler out of a daughter of Young Topper, he by Topper.

EYLAU, by Napoleon out of Delphine by Massoud (pure Arab).

NAPOLEON, by Bob Booty out of the Pope Mare.

YOUNG RATTLER, by Rattler out of the Snap Mare

NORFOLK PHENOMENON, by Old Phenomenon.

ROYAL OAK, by Catton out of Smolensko Mare.

NIGER, by Elu out of a daughter of Tipple Cider, he by Defence out of Deposit by Blacklock.

ELU, by Idalis out of a daughter of Tipple Cider, etc.

IDALIS, by Don Quichotte out of a daughter of Chapman, he by Trotteur, he by Chapman.

DON QUICHOTTE, by Sylvio, etc., out of Moina by Tigris, he by Quitz out of Persepolis by Alexander.

IRLANDAIS, by Seducteur, etc., out of a daughter of Homère, he by Imperieux out of a daughter of D. I. O., he by Whitworth out of Hambletonian Mare.

IMPERIEUX, by Young Rattler, etc., out of a daughter of Volontaire, he by Eclipse (English thoroughbred).

GIDEON.

See page 221.

(Hoof No. 23).   FAVORI.

Brown bay; 16 hands; weight, 1,305 lbs.; foaled May 20, 1884; imported 1887; bred by M. Debois, of Percy-en-Auge, department of Calvados; got by the government stallion TURCO; dam LISETTE by ESCULAPE out of a daughter of ESTAFETTE.

TURCO, by Hick out of a daughter of Ignace, he by Centaure out of a daugher of Lanercost, he by Liverpool out of Otis by Bustard.

CENTAURE, by Seducteur out of a daughter of Merlerault, he by Royal Oak out of a daughter of Sylvio, be by Trance out of Hebe by Rubens.

ROYAL OAK, by Catton out of Smolensko Mare.

SEDUCTEUR, by Noteur out of a daughter of Fatibello, he by Sylvio, etc., out of a daughter of Y., he by Norfolk Phenomenon out of Henriette by Invincible, he by Hoemus out of Regatta by Camel.

NORFOLK PHENOMENON, by Old Phenomenon.

NOTEUR, by Eylau out of a daughter of Diomed, he by Young Rattler out of a daughter of Young Topper, he by Topper.

YOUNG RATTLER, by Rattler out of the Snap Mare.

EYLAU, by Napoleon out of Delphine by Massoud (pure Arab).

NAPOLEON, by Bob Booty out of the Pope Mare.

HICK, by Centaure, etc., out of a daughter of Tipple Cider, he by Defence out of Deposit by Blacklock.

ESCULAPE, by Utrecht out of a daughter of Koenisberg, he by Frejus out of a daughter of Achille, he by Young Rattler, etc., out of a daughter of Jaggard, he by Mailhand-Schols.

FREJUS, by Eastham out of a daughter of Imperieux, he by Young Rattler, etc., out of a daughter of Volontaire, he by Eclipse.

EASTHAM, by Sir Oliver out of Cowslip by Alexander.

UTRECHT, by Prince out of a daughter of Eylau, etc.

PRINCE, by Don Quichotte out of a daughter of Marengo, he by Napoleon out of Cloris by Aslan.

DON QUICHOTTE, by Sylvio, etc., out of Moina by Tigris, he by Quitz out of Persepolis by Alexander.

ESTAFETTE, by Ottoman out of a daughter of Telegraph, he by Old Phenomenon.

OTTOMAN, by Faliero, out of a daughter of Basly, he by Eastham, etc., out of a daughter of Valient, he by Equator.

FALIERO, by Sylvio, etc., out of a daughter of Dart, he by Dart out of a daughter of Loadstone.

(Hoof No. 15.)

FERRON.

Dark bay ; 16¾ hands ; weight, 1,320 lbs. ; foaled April 30, 1883 ; imported 1887 ; bred by M. Lecanu, of Brucheville, department of La Manche ; got by the government stallion IDOMENEE ; dam PER-FECTION by PERFECTION.

IDOMENEE, by Serenader out of a daughter of Eylau, he by Napoleon out of Delphine by Massoud (pure Arab).

NAPOLEON, by Bob Booty out of the Pope Mare.

SERENADER, by The Troubadour.

PERFECTION, by Imperieux out of a daughter of Friedland, he by Napoleon, etc., out of Cloton by Eastham, he by Sir Oliver out of Cowslip by Alexander.

IMPERIEUX, by Young Rattler out of a daughter of Volontaire, he by Eclipse (English thoroughbred).

YOUNG RATTLER, by Rattler out of the Snap Mare.

(Hoof No. 11.)

FLEURON.

Brown ; 16½ hands ; weight, 1,375 lbs.; foaled April 25, 1883 ; imported 1887 ; bred by M. Compere, of Coquenauville, department of La Manche ; got by the government stallion GIBERT; dam RAPIDE.

GIBERT, by Pompier out of Florida by Florin.

POMPIER, by Josaphat out of a daughter of Kapirat, he by Voltaire out of a daughter of the Juggler, he by Wamba out of Pantechnetheca by Master Henry.

VOLTAIRE, by Imperieux out of a daughter of Pilot, he by Octavius (English thoroughbred).

IMPERIEUX, by Young Rattler out of a daughter of Volontaire, he by Eclipse (English thoroughbred).

YOUNG RATTLER, by Rattler out of the Snap Mare.

JOSAPHAT, by Ugolin, he by Parisien, he by Ganymede out of a daughter of Biron, he by Captain Candid out of Helene by Eastham, he by Sir Oliver out of Cowslip by Alexander.

CAPTAIN CANDID, by Cerberus out of Mandane by Pot-8-os.

GANYMEDE, by Xerxes out of La Louve by Chasseur, he by Eastham, etc., out of Marquise by Young Rattler, etc.

XERXES, by Young Rattler, etc., out of a daughter of Young Highflyer, he by Highflyer out of a daughter of Young Docteur, he by Docteur out of a daughter of Mignon, he by Glorieux (English thoroughbred).

(Hoof No. 17.)

FLORISSANT.

Brown; 16 hands; weight, 1,250 lbs.; foaled May 10, 1883; imported 1887; bred by M. Thomas Edmond, of Bazoches, department of Orne; got by the government stallion TRISTAN; dam CLEMENTINE by QUOTIES out of a daughter of EXTASE.

TRISTAN, by Interprete out of a daughter of West Australian, he by Melbourne out of a daughter of Mowerina, he by Touchstone.

INTERPRETE, by Interprete, he by Centaure out of a daughter of Tancrede, he by The Roue out of a daughter of Eylau, he by Napoleon out of Delphine by Massoud (pure Arab).

THE ROUE, by Claret out of Roulette by Philipp-the-First.

NAPOLEON, by Bob Booty out of the Pope Mare.

CENTAURE, by Seducteur out of daughter of Merlerault, he by Royal Oak out of a daughter of Sylvio, he by Trance out of Hebe by Rubens.

ROYAL OAK, by Catton out of Smolensko Mare.

SEDUCTEUR, by Noteur out of a daughter of Fatibello, he by Sylvio, etc., out of a daughter of Y., he by The Norfolk Phenomenon out of Henriette by Invincible, he by Hoemus out of Regatta by Camel (English thoroughbred).

NORFOLK PHENOMENON, by Old Phenomenon.

NOTEUR, by Eylau out of a daughter of Diomed, he by Young Rattler out of a daughter of Young Topper, he by Topper.

YOUNG RATTLER, by Rattler out of the Snap Mare.

EYLAU, by Napoleon, etc., out of Delphine by Massoud (pure Arab).

QUOTIES, by Trouville out of a daughter of Bassompierre, he by Performer out of Sylvie by Young Rattler, etc.

TROUVILLE, by Fitz Gladiator out of Clementine by The Governor, he by Royal Oak, etc., out of Lydia by Rainbow, he by Rainbow.

FITZ GLADIATOR, by Gladiator out of Sarah by Reveller, he by Reveller out of Scornful by Woful (English thoroughbred).

GLADIATOR, by Partisan out of Pauline by Moses.

PARTISAN, by Lucholl, he by Old Lucholl.

(Hoof No. 38.)　　　**FONTIBELLO.**

Chestnut; 16¼ hands; weight, 1,400 lbs.; foaled May 17, 1883; imported 1887; bred by M. F. Desir, of Lisieur, department of Calvados; got by the government stallion VAMPIRE; dam SULTANE by SULTAN out of a daughter of EYLAU.

VAMPIRE, by Legislateur out of a daughter of Désiré, he by Quasi out of a daughter of Nimrod, he by Voltaire out of a daughter of Xerxes, he by Young Rattler out of a daughter of Young Highflyer, he by Highflyer out of a daughter of Young Docteur, he by Docteur out of a daughter of Mignon, he by Glorieux (English thoroughbred).

QUASI, by Herschell, he by Eylau out of a daughter of Pretender, he by Holme.

EYLAU, by Napoleon out of Delphine by Massoud (pure Arab).

NAPOLEON, by Bob Booty out of the Pope Mare.

VOLTAIRE, by Imperieux out of a daughter of Pilot, he by Octavius (English thoroughbred).

IMPERIEUX, by Young Rattler out of a daughter of Volontaire, he by Eclipse (English thoroughbred).

YOUNG RATTLER, by Rattler out of the Snap Mare.

LEGISLATEUR, by Centaure out of a daughter of Kramer, he by Hercule out of Cybele by Chasseur, he by Eastham out of Marquise by Young Rattler, etc.

HERCULE, by Rainbow out of Aimable by Election.

EASTHAM, by Sir Oliver out of Cowslip by Alexander.

CENTAURE, by Seducteur out of a daughter of Merlerault, he by Royal Oak out of a daughter of Sylvio, he by Trance out of Hebe by Rubens.

ROYAL OAK, by Catton out of Smolensko Mare.

SEDUCTEUR, by Noteur out of a daughter of Fatibello, he by Sylvio, etc., out of a daughter of Y., he by the Norfolk Phenomenon out of Henriette by Invincible, he by Hoemus out of Regatta by Camel (English thoroughbred).

NORFOLK PHENOMENON, by Old Phenomenon.

NOTEUR, by Eylau, etc., out of a daughter of Diomed, he by Young Rattler, etc., out of a daughter of Young Topper, he by Topper.

SULTAN, by Tipple Cider out of a daughter of Dupleix, he by Pickpocket out of Marquise, by Young Rattler, etc.

PICKPOCKET, by St. Patrick out of the Hedley Mare.

TIPPLE CIDER, by Defence out of Deposit by Blacklock.

GILDAS.

See page 223.

(Hoof No. 13.)   # FORESTER.

Brown; 16¼ hands; weight, 1,360 lbs.; foaled March 10, 1883; imported 1887; bred by M. Normand, of Sallenelles, department of Calvados; got by the government stallion VIDI; dam LISETTE by GLORIEUX.

VIDI, by Quiclet out of a daughter of Inkerman, he by Jericko out of a daughter of Ai, he by Young Rattler out of a daughter of Cleveland.

JERICKO, by Biron out of a daughter of Voltaire, he by Imperieux out of a daughter of Pilot, he by Octavius (English thoroughbred).

IMPERIEUX, by Young Rattler out of a daughter of Volontaire, he by Eclipse (English thoroughbred).

YOUNG RATTLER, by Rattler out of the Snap Mare.

BIRON, by Captain Candid out of Helene by Eastham, he by Sir Oliver out of Cowslip by Alexander.

CAPTAIN CANDID, by Cerberus out of Mandane by Pot-8-os.

QUICLET, by Lumineux out of a daughter of Sultan, he by Tipple Cider out of a daughter of Dupleix, he by Pickpocket out of Marquise by Young Rattler, etc.

TIPPLE CIDER, by Defence out of Deposit by Blacklock.

PICKPOCKET, by St. Patrick out of the Hedley Mare.

LUMINEUX, by Trouville out of a daughter of Galeon, he by Voltaire, etc., out of a daughter of Young Rattler, etc.

TROUVILLE, by Fitz Gladiator out of Clementine by The Governor, he by Royal Oak out of Lydia by Rainbow, he by Rainbow.

ROYAL OAK, by Catton out of Smolensko Mare.

FITZ GLADIATOR, by Gladiator out of Sarah by Reveller, he by Reveller out of Scornful by Woful (English thoroughbred).

GLADIATOR, by Partisan out of Pauline by Moses.

PARTISAN, by Lucholl, he by Old Lucholl. .

GLORIEUX, by Solide out of a daughter of Tipple Cider, etc.

SOLIDE, by Nestor out of a daughter of Jaggard, he by Mailhand-Schols.

NESTOR, by Hospodar out of a daughter of Captain Candid, etc.

HOSPODAR, by Imperieux, etc., out of a daughter of Young Rattler, etc.

(Hoof No. 25.)

FORGERON.

Black; 15¾ hands; weight, 1,250 lbs.; foaled May 2, 1883; imported 1887; bred by M. Casimir Lepecq, of Coudray Robut, department of Calvados; got by the government stallion VERA CRUZ; dam BELLE-DE-NUIT by NOVILLE out of a daughter of D'ORIDE.

VERA CRUZ, by Phaeton out of a daughter of Abrantes, he by Pledge out of a daughter of Noteur, he by Eylau out of a daughter of Diomed, he by Young Rattler out of a daughter of Young Topper, he by Topper.

PLEDGE, by Royal Oak out of a daughter of Young Rattler.

ROYAL OAK, by Catton out of Smolensko Mare.

EYLAU, by Napoléon out of Delphine by Massoud (pure Arab).

NAPOLEON, by Bob Booty out of the Pope Mare.

YOUNG RATTLER, by Rattler out of the Snap Mare.

PHAETON, by The Heir of Linne out of a daughter of Crocus.

THE HEIR OF LINNE, by Galaor out of Mrs. Walker by Jereed.

NOVILLE, by Ipsilanty out of Therence by Turk.

IPSILANTY, by Norfolk Phenomenon out of a daughter of Sylvio, he by Trance out of Hebe by Rubens.

NORFOLK PHENOMENON, by Old Phenomenon.

(Hoof No. 16.)   # FORTUNE.

Dark bay; 16½ hands; weight, 1,420 lbs.; foaled May 15, 1883; imported 1887; bred by M. A. Votier, of Sallenelles, department of Calvados; got by the government stallion VIDI; dam NACELLE by HICK out of a daughter of GLORIEUX.

VIDI, by Quiclet out of a daughter of Inkerman, he by Jericko out of a daughter of Ai, he by Young Rattler out of a daughter of Cleveland.

JERICKO, by Biron out of a daughter of Voltaire, he by Imperieux out of a daughter of Pilot, he by Octavius (English thoroughbred).

BIRON, by Captain Candid out of Helene by Eastham.

CAPTAIN CANDID, by Cerberus out of Mandane by Pot-S-os.

IMPERIEUX, by Young Rattler out of a daughter of Volontaire, he by Eclipse (English thoroughbred).

YOUNG RATTLER, by Rattler out of the Snap Mare.

QUICLET, by Lumineux out of a daughter of Sultan, he by Tipple Cider out of a daughter of Dupleix, he by Pickpocket out of Marquise by Young Rattler, etc.

TIPPLE CIDER, by Defence out of Deposit by Blacklock.

PICKPOCKET, by St. Patrick out of the Hedley Mare.

LUMINEUX, by Trouville out of a daughter of Galion, he by Voltaire, etc., out of a daughter of Young Rattler, etc.

TROUVILLE, by Fitz Gladiator out of Clementine by Governor, he by Royal Oak out of Lydia by Rainbow, he by Rainbow.

ROYAL OAK, by Catton out of Smolensko Mare.

FITZ GLADIATOR, by Gladiator out of Sarah by Reveller, he by Reveller out of Scornful by Woful (English thoroughbred).

GLADIATOR, by Partisan out of Pauline by Moses.

PARTISAN, by Lucholl, he by Old Lucholl.

HICK, by Centaure out of a daughter of Tipple Cider, etc.

CENTAURE, by Seducteur out of a daughter of Merlerault, he by Royal Oak, etc., out of a daughter of Sylvio, he by Trance out of Hebe by Rubens.

SEDUCTEUR, by Noteur out of a daughter of Fatibello, he by Sylvio, etc., out of a daughter of Y, he by the Norfolk Phenomenon out of Henriette by Invincible, he by Hoemus out of Regatta by Camel.

NORFOLK PHENOMENON, by Old Phenomenon.

NOTEUR, by Eylau out of a daughter of Diomed, he by Young Rattler, etc., out of a daughter of Young Topper, he by Topper.

EYLAU, by Napoleon out of Delphine by Massoud (pure Arab).

NAPOLEON, by Bob Booty out of the Pope Mare.

GLORIEUX, by Solide out of a daughter of Tipple Cider, etc.

SOLIDE, by Nestor out of a daughter of Jaggard, he by Mailhand-Schols.

NESTOR, by Hospodar out of a daughter of Captain Candid, etc.

HOSPODAR, by Imperieux, etc., out of a daughter of Young Rattler, etc.

(Hoof No. 14.)

FRANCAIS.

Bay; 16 hands; weight, 1,310 lbs; foaled May 20, 1883; imported 1887; bred by M. Bree, of Henevez, department of La Manche; got by the government stallion QUINTE CURCE; dam COCOTTE by RIVOLI.

QUINTE CURCE, by Elu out of a daughter of Thesee, he by Gainsborough (he by Gainful) out of a daughter of Xerxes, he by Young Rattler out of a daughter of Young Highflyer, he by Highflyer out of a daughter of Young Docteur, he by Docteur.

YOUNG RATTLER, by Rattler out of the Snap Mare.

ELU, by Idalis out of a daughter of Tipple Cider, he by Defence out of Deposit by Blacklock.

IDALIS, by Don Quichotte out of a daughter of Chapman, he by Trotteur, he by Chapman.

DON QUICHOTTE, by Sylvio out of Moina by Tigris, he by Quitz out of Persepolis by Alexander.

SYLVIO, by Trance out of Hebe by Rubens.

RIVOLI, by Ramsay out of a daughter of Junot, he by Friedland out of a daughter of Chasseur, he by Eastham out of Marquise by Young Rattler, etc.

FRIEDLAND, by Napoleon out of Cloton by Eastham, he by Sir Oliver out of Cowslip by Alexander.

NAPOLEON, by Bob Booty out of the Pope Mare.

RAMSAY, by Sylvio out of Emelina by Emilius, he by Emilius out of Cobweb by Phantom.

SYLVIO, by Trance out of Hebe by Rubens.

(Hoof No. 1.)

GALBA.

Brown; 16 hands; weight, 1,275 lbs.; foaled June 20, 1884; imported 1887; bred by M. Legoupil, of Emondeville, department of La Manche; got by the government stallion VITAL; dam LAPOULE by IGNORE out of a daughter of ARGONAUT.

VITAL, by Montfort out of a daughter of Interprete, he by Centaure out of a daughter of Tancrede, he by Eylau out of a daughter of Gall, he by Kapirat out of a daughter of Sir Henry Dimsdale, he by Old President out of a daughter of Camel (English thoroughbred).

CENTAURE, by Seducteur out of a daughter of Merlerault, he by Royal Oak out of a daughter of Sylvio, he by Trance out of Hebe by Rubens.

ROYAL OAK, by Catton out of Smolensko Mare.

SEDUCTEUR, by Noteur out of a daughter of Fatibello, he by Sylvio, etc., out of a daughter of Y, he by Norfolk Phenomenon out of Henriette by Invincible, he by Hoemus out of Regatta by Camel (English thoroughbred).

NORFOLK PHENOMENON, by Old Phenomenon.

NOTEUR, by Eylau out of a daughter of Diomed, he by Young Rattler out of a daughter of Young Topper, he by Topper.

YOUNG RATTLER, by Rattler out of the Snap Mare.

EYLAU, by Napoleon out of Delphine by Massoud (pure Arab).

NAPOLEON, by Bob Booty out of the Pope Mare.

KAPIRAT, by Voltaire out of a daughter of the Juggler, he by Wamba out of Pantechnetheca by Master Henry.

VOLTAIRE, by Imperieux out of a daughter of Pilot, he by Octavius (English thoroughbred).

IMPERIEUX, by Young Rattler, etc., out of a daughter of Volontaire, he by Eclipse (English thoroughbred).

MONTFORT, by Arc-en-Ciel out of Fougeres by Faugh-a-Ballagh, he by Sir Hercules out of Guiccioli by Bob Booty.

IGNORE, by Uzel out of a daughter of Ugolin, he by Parisien, he by Ganymede out of a daughter of Biron, he by Captain Candid out of Helene by Eastham, he by Sir Oliver out of Cowslip by Alexander.

GANYMEDE, by Xerxes out of La Louve by Chasseur, he by Eastham, etc., out of Marquise by Young Rattler, etc.

XERXES, by Young Rattler, etc., out of a daughter of Young Highflyer, he by Highflyer out of a daughter of Young Docteur, he by Docteur out of a daughter of Mignon, he by Glorieux (English thoroughbred).

CAPTAIN CANDID, by Cerberus out of Mandane by Pot-8-os.

UZEL, by Myrthe out of a daughter of Ramsay, he by Sylvio, etc., out of Emelina by Emilius, he by Emilius out of Cobweb by Phantom.

MYRTHE, by Homere out of a daughter of Voltaire, etc.

HOMERE, by Imperieux, etc., out of a daughter of D. I. O., he by Whitworth out of Hambletonian Mare.

ARGONAUT, by Stockwell out of Aphrodite by Bay Middleton.

GILDINO.

See page 224.

GASCON.

Bay; 16½ hands; weight, 1,500 lbs.; foaled April 8, 1884; imported 1887; bred by M. Sauvages, of St. Pellerin, department of La Manche; got by the government stallion BANYULS; dam BREBIS by PARTISAN out of a daughter of UGOLIN.

BANYULS, by Quiclet out of a daughter of Solide, he by Nestor out of a daughter of Jaggard, he by Mailhand-Schols.

NESTOR, by Hospodar out of a daughter of Captain Candid, he by Cerberus out of Mandane by Pot-8-os.

HOSPODAR, by Imperieux out of a daughter of Young Rattler, he by Rattler out of the Snap Mare.

IMPERIEUX, by Young Rattler, etc., out of a daughter of Volontaire, he by Eclipse (English thoroughbred).

QUICLET, by Lumineux out of a daughter of Sultan, he by Tipple Cider out of a daughter of Dupliex, he by Pickpocket out of Marquise by Young Rattler, etc.

TIPPLE CIDER, by Defence out of Deposit by Blacklock.

PICKPOCKET, by St. Patrick out of the Hedley Mare.

LUMINEUX, by Trouville out of a daughter of Galion, he by Voltaire out of a daughter of Young Rattler, etc.

VOLTAIRE, by Imperieux, etc., out of a daughter of Pilot, he by Octavius (English thoroughbred).

TROUVILLE, by Fitz Gladiator out of Clementine by Governor, he by Royal Oak out of Lydia by Rainbow, he by Rainbow.

ROYAL OAK, by Catton out of Smolensko Mare.

FITZ GLADIATOR, by Gladiator out of Sarah by Reveller, he by Reveller out of Scornful by Woful (English thoroughbred).

GLADIATOR, by Partisan out of Pauline by Moses.

PARTISAN, by Lucholl, he by Old Lucholl.

PARTISAN, by Galba out of a daughter of Wanderer.

GALBA, by Pledge out of a daughter of Sylvio, he by Trance out of Hebe by Rubens.

PLEDGE, by Royal Oak, etc., out of a daughter of Young Rattler, etc.

UGOLIN, by Ugolin out of a daughter of Ursin, he by Ramsay out of a daughter of Ganymede, he by Xerxes out of La Louve by Chasseur, he by Eastham out of Marquise by Young Rattler, etc.

RAMSAY, by Sylvio, etc., out of Emelina by Emilius, he by Emilius out of Cobweb by Phantom.

XERXES, by Young Rattler, etc., out of a daughter of Young Highflyer, he by Highflyer out of a daughter of Young Docteur, he by Docteur out of a daughter of Mignon, he by Glorieux (English thoroughbred).

EASTHAM, by Sir Oliver out of Cowslip by Alexander.

UGOLIN, by Parisien, he by Ganymede, etc., out of a daughter of Biron, he by Captain Candid, etc., out of Helene by Eastham, etc.

(Hoof No. 37.)

GENDINO.

Brown; 16 hands; weight, 1,205 lbs.; foaled May 1, 1884; imported 1887; bred by M. Vesiel, of Magny, department of Calvados; got by the government stallion LE DARD; dam MIGNONNE by ORIENTAL.

LE DARD, by Wingrave out of La Dheune by Black Eyes, he by Malton out of Rosabelle by Terror.

ORIENTAL, by Jactator out of a daughter of Emir (pure Arab).

JACTATOR, by Elu out of a daughter of Idomenee, he by Serenader out of a daughter of Eylau, he by Napoleon out of Delphine by Massoud (pure Arab).

SERENADER, by The Troubadour.

NAPOLEON, by Bob Booty out of the Pope Mare.

ELU, by Idalis out of a daughter of Tipple Cider, he by Defence out of Deposit by Blacklock.

IDALIS, by Don Quichotte out of a daughter of Chapman, he by Trotteur, he by Chapman.

DON QUICHOTTE, by Sylvio out of Moina by Tigris, he by Quitz out of Persepolis by Alexander.

SYLVIO, by Trance out of Hebe by Rubens.

GENERAL.

Chestnut; 16 hands; weight, 1,210 lbs.; foaled April 10, 1884; imported 1887; bred by M. Clement Levaillant, of Gatteville, department of La Manche; got by the government stallion VENDOME; dam MOUVETTE by BANDIT.

VENDOME, by Abrantes out of a daughter of Praticien, he by Monarque out of Papillotte, by Gladiator, he by Partisan out of Pauline by Moses.

PARTISAN, by Lucholl, he by Old Lucholl.

ABRANTES, by Pledge, out of a daughter of Noteur, he by Eylau out of a daughter of Diomed, he by Young Rattler out of a daughter of Young Topper, he by Topper.

EYLAU, by Napoleon out of Delphine by Massoud.

NAPOLEON, by Bob Booty out of the Pope Mare.

YOUNG RATTLER, by Rattler out of the Snap Mare.

PLEDGE, by Royal Oak out of a daughter of Young Rattler, etc.

ROYAL OAK, by Catton out of Smolensko Mare.

BANDIT, by Lully out of a daughter of Incomparable, he by Oliver Cromwell out of a daughter of Pickpocket, he by St. Patrick out of the Hedley Mare.

LULLY, by Tipple Cider out of Pecora by Sylvio, he by Trance out of Hebe by Rubens.

TIPPLE CIDER, by Defence out of Deposit by Blacklock.

(Hoof No. 18.)   # GENEREUX.

Bay; 16 hands; weight, 1,350 lbs.; foaled May 22, 1884; imported 1887; bred by M. Alfred Yoray, of Formigny, department of Calvados; got by the government stallion PHARE; dam ORPHELINE by ORPHELIN out of DRAGON (English thoroughbred).

PHARE, by Pater out of a daughter of Isolier, he by Nunnykirk out of Deception by Defense.

NUNNYKIRK, by Touchstone out of Doctor-Snytax-Mare.

PATER, by Victorieux out of a daughter of Assault, he by Touchstone out of Ghuznee by Pantaloon (English thoroughbred).

VICTORIEUX, by Pledge out of a daughter of Incomparable, he by Oliver Cromwell out of a daughter of Pickpocket, he by St. Patrick out of Hedley Mare.

PLEDGE, by Royal Oak out of a daughter of Young Rattler, he by Rattler out of the Snap Mare.

ROYAL OAK, by Catton out of Smolensko Mare.

ORPHELIN, by Jovial out of a daughter of Trouville, he by Fitz-Gladiator out of Clementine by Governor, he by Royal Oak, etc., out of Lydia by Rainbow.

FITZ-GLADIATOR, by Gladiator out of Sarah by Reveller, he by Reveller out of Scornful by Woful (English thoroughbred).

GLADIATOR, by Partisan out of Pauline by Moses.

PARTISAN, by Lucholl, he by Old Lucholl.

JOVIAL, by Pledge, etc., out of a daughter of Myrthe, he by Homere out of a daughter of Voltaire, he by Imperieux out of a daughter of Pilot, he by Octavius (English thoroughbred).

IMPERIEUX, by Young Rattler, etc., out of a daughter of Volontaire, he by Eclipse (English thoroughbred).

HOMERE, by Imperieux, etc., out of a daughter of D. I. O., he by Whitworth out of Hambletonian Mare.

(Hoof No. 36.)   # GERANT.

Brown bay ; 16½ hands ; weight, 1,400 lbs. ; foaled April 30, 1884 ; imported 1887 ; bred by M. Montee, of St. Leger-du-Cosq, department of Calvados ; got by the government stallion Uzos ; dam SOPHIE.

Uzos, by Ignore out of a daughter of Auguste, he by Monarque out of Etoile-du-Nord by The Baron.

IGNORE, by Uzel out of a daughter of Ugolin, he by Parisien, he by Ganymede out of a daughter of Biron, he by Captain Candid out of Helene by Eastham, he by Sir Oliver out of Cowslip by Alexander.

GANYMEDE, by Xerxes out of La Louve by Chasseur, he by Eastham, etc., out of Marquise by Young Rattler, he by Rattler out of the Snap Mare.

XERXES, by Young Rattler, etc., out of a daughter of Young Highflyer, he by Highflyer out of a daughter of Young Docteur, he by Docteur out of a daughter of Mignon, he by Glorieux (English thoroughbred).

CAPTAIN CANDID, by Cerberus out of Mandane by Pot-8-os.

UZEL, by Myrthe out of a daughter of Ramsay, he by Sylvio out of Emelina by Emilius, he by Emilius out of Cobweb by Phantom.

SYLVIO, by Trance out of Hebe by Rubens.

MYRTHE, by Homere out of a daughter of Voltaire, he by Imperieux out of a daughter of Pilot, he by Octavius (English thoroughbred).

HOMERE, by Imperieux out of a daughter of D. I. O., he by Whitworth out of Hambletonian Mare.

IMPERIEUX, by Young Rattler. etc., out of a daughter of Volontaire, he by Eclipse (English thoroughbred).

(Hoof No. 9.)

GERONIMO.

Black; 16½ hands; weight, 1,275 lbs.; foaled April 23, 1884; imported 1887; bred by M. P. Simon, of Nacqueville, department of La Manche; got by the government stallion ALSACIEN; dam BIJOU by SEDUISANT out of a daughter of RIVOLI.

ALSACIEN, by Ignore out of a daughter of Pater, he by Victorieux out of a daughter of Assault, he by Touchstone out of Ghuznee by Pantaloon.

VICTORIEUX, by Pledge out of a daughter of Incomparable, he by Oliver Cromwell out of a daughter of Pickpocket, he by St. Patrick out of the Hedley Mare.

PLEDGE, by Royal Oak out of a daughter of Young Rattler, he by Rattler out of the Snap Mare.

ROYAL OAK, by Catton out of Smolensko Mare.

IGNORE, by Uzel out of a daughter of Ugolin, he by Parisien, he by Ganymede out of a daughter of Biron, he by Captain Candid out of Helene by Eastham, he by Sir Oliver out of Cowslip by Alexander.

GANYMEDE, by Xerxes out of La Louve by Chasseur, he by Eastham, etc., out of Marquise by Young Rattler, etc.

XERXES, by Young Rattler, etc., out of a daughter of Young Highflyer, he by Highflyer out of a daughter of Young Docteur, he by Docteur out of a daughter of Mignon, he by Glorieux (English thoroughbred).

CAPTAIN CANDID, by Cerberus out of Mandane by Pot-8-os.

UZEL, by Myrthe out of a daughter of Ramsay, he by Sylvio out of Emelina by Emelius, he by Emelius out of Cobweb by Phantom.

SYLVIO, by Trance out of Hebe by Rubens.

MYRTHE, by Homere out of a daughter of Voltaire, he by Imperieux out of a daughter of Pilot, he by Octavius (English thoroughbred)

IMPERIEUX, by Young Rattler, etc., out of a daughter of Volontaire, he by Eclipse (English thoroughbred).

HOMERE, by Imperieux, etc., out of a daughter of D. I. O., he by Whitworth out of Hambletonian Mare.

SEDUISANT, by Lagopede out of a daughter of Koulikan, he by Voltaire out of a daughter of Proselyte.

VOLTAIRE, by Imperieux, etc., out of a daughter of Pilot, etc.

LAGOPEDE, by Voltaire, etc., out of a daughter of the Juggler, he by Wamba out of Pantechnetheca by Master Henry.

RIVOLI, by Ramsay, etc., out of a daughter of Junot, he by Friedland out of a daughter of Chasseur, etc.

FRIEDLAND, by Napoleon out of Cloton by Eastham, etc.

NAPOLEON, by Bob Booty out of the Pope Mare.

(Hoof No. 4.)   GERVASE.

Dark bay ; 16¾ hands ; weight, 1,375 lbs. ; foaled March 25, 1884 ; imported 1887 ; bred by M. Laillier, of Bieville-en-Auge, department of Calvados ; got by the government stallion KAOLIN ; dam GRISETTE by MONTMORENCY.

KAOLIN, by Zouave out of Dainty by Ionian.

ZOUAVE, by The Baron out of Dacia by Gladiator, he by Partisan out of Pauline by Moses.

   PARTISAN, by Lucholl, he by Old Lucholl.

MONTMORENCY, by Conquerant out of a daughter of Bavent, he by Lucain out of a daughter of Jericko, he by Biron out of a daughter of Voltaire, he by Imperieux out of a daughter of Pilot, he by Octavius (English thoroughbred).

   LUCAIN, by Eylau out of Desiree by Talma.

   EYLAU, by Napoleon out of Delphine by Massoud (pure Arab).

   NAPOLEON, by Bob Booty out of the Pope Mare.

   BIRON, by Captain Candid out of Helene by Eastham, he by Sir Oliver out of Cowslip by Alexander.

   CAPTAIN CANDID, by Cerberus out of Mandane by Pot-8-os.

   IMPERIEUX, by Young Rattler out of a daughter of Volontaire, he by Eclipse (English thoroughbred).

   YOUNG RATTLER, by Rattler out of the Snap Mare.

CONQUERANT, by Kapirat out of Elisa by Corsair, he by J. C. Knox's Corsair out of a daughter of Cleveland.

KAPIRAT, by Voltaire, etc., out of a daughter of the Juggler, he by Wamba out of Pantechnetheca by Master Henry.

GITANO.

See page 225.

(Hoof No. 31.)   # GIBOYEUX.

Chestnut; 16 hands; weight, 1,325 lbs.; foaled April 6, 1884; imported 1887; bred by M. Chaventre, of Dozule-Putot, department of Calvados; got by the government stallion MONTFORT; dam COLINETTE by INTERPRETE out of a daughter of BUCI.

MONTFORT, by Arc-en-Ciel out of Fougeres by Faugh-a-Ballagh, he by Sir Hercule out of Guiccioli by Bob Booty.

INTERPRETE, by Centaure out of a daughter of Tancrede, he by The Roue out of a daughter of Eylau, he by Napoleon out of Delphine by Massoud (pure Arab).

THE ROUE, by Claret out of Roulette by Philipp-the-First.

NAPOLEON, by Bob Booty out of the Pope Mare.

CENTAURE, by Seducteur out of a daughter of Merlerault, he by Royal Oak out of a daughter of Sylvio, he by Trance out of Hebe by Rubens.

ROYAL OAK, by Catton out of Smolensko Mare.

SEDUCTEUR, by Noteur out of a daughter of Fatibello, he by Sylvio, etc., out of a daughter of Y, he by the Norfolk Phenomenon out of Henriette by Invincible, he by Hoemus out of Regatta by Camel (English thoroughbred).

NORFOLK PHENOMENON, by Old Phenomenon.

NOTEUR, by Eylau, etc., out of a daughter of Diomed, he by Young Rattler out of a daughter of Young Topper, he by Topper.

YOUNG RATTLER, by Rattler out of the Snap Mare

BUCI, by Solide out of a daughter of Eylau, etc.

SOLIDE, by Nestor out of a daughter of Jaggard, he by Mailhand-Schols.

NESTOR, by Hospodar out of a daughter of Captain Candid, he by Cerberus out of Mandane by Pot-8-os.

HOSPODAR, by Imperieux out of a daughter of Young Rattler, etc.

IMPERIEUX, by Young Rattler, etc., out of a daughter of Volontaire, he by Eclipse (English thoroughbred).

(Hoof No. 32.)

GIDEON.

Black ; 16¼ hands ; weight, 1,365 lbs.; foaled March 14, 1884 ; imported 1887 ; bred by M. H. Blandamour, of Balognes, department of La Manche ; got by the government stallion UTRECHT ; dam MINE-D'OR by L'INCROYABLE out of a daughter of JOSAPHAT.

UTRECHT, by Palm out of a daughter of Pretender.

PALM, by Centaure out of a daughter of Torigny, he by Merlerault out of a daughter of Hector, he by Quebec out of a daughter of Buffalo, he by Holme (thoroughbred).

MERLERAULT, by Royal Oak out of a daughter of Sylvio, he by Trance out of Hebe by Rubens.

ROYAL OAK, by Catton out of Smolensko Mare.

QUEBEC, by Oscar, he by Young Rattler out of a daughter of Bacha (pure Arab).

YOUNG RATTLER, by Rattler out of the Snap Mare.

CENTAURE, by Seducteur out of a daughter of Merlerault, etc.

SEDUCTEUR, by Noteur out of a daughter of Fatibello, he by Sylvio, etc., out of a daughter of Y, he by Norfolk Phenomenon out of Henriette by Invincible, he by Hoemus out of Regatta by Camel (English thoroughbred).

NORFOLK PHENOMENON, by Old Phenomenon.

NOTEUR, by Eylau out of a daughter of Diomed, he by Young Rattler, etc., out of a daughter of Young Topper, he by Topper.

EYLAU, by Napoleon out of Delphine by Massoud (pure Arab).

NAPOLEON, by Bob Booty out of the Pope Mare.

L'INCROYABLE, by The Nabob out of La Tosa by Chevalier-d'Industrie.

THE NABOB, by The Nob out of Hester by Camel.

JOSAPHAT, by Ugolin, he by Parisien, he by Ganymede out of a daughter of Biron, he by Captain Candid out of Helene by Eastham, he by Sir Oliver out of Cowslip by Alexander.

CAPTAIN CANDID, by Cerberus out of Mandane by Pot-8-os.

GANYMEDE, by Xerxes out of La Louve by Chasseur, he by Eastham, etc., out of Marquise by Young Rattler, etc.

XERXES, by Young Rattler, etc., out of a daughter of Young Highflyer, he by Highflyer out of a daughter of Young Docteur, he by Docteur out of a daughter of Mignon, he by Glorieux (English thoroughbred).

(Hoof No. 28.)   ## GIL BLAS.

Bay ; 16½ hands ; weight, 1,475 lbs. ; foaled March 12, 1884 ; imported 1887 ; bred by M. Jean Baptiste Gasselin, of St. Marie-du-Monts, department of La Manche ; got by the government stallion UZERCHE ; dam BIJOU by VOLANT.

UZERCHE, by Normand out of a daughter of Extase, he by Thesee out of a daughter of Kramer, he by Hercule out of Cybele by Chasseur, he by Eastham out of Marquise by Young Rattler.

THESEE, by Gainsborough (he by Gainful) out of a daughter of Xerxes.

HERCULE, by Rainbow out of Aimable by Election.

EASTHAM, by Sir Oliver out of Cowslip by Alexander.

NORMAND, by Divus out of a daughter of Kapirat, he by Voltaire out of a daughter of the Juggler, he by Wamba out of Pantechnetheca by Master Henry.

VOLTAIRE, by Imperieux out of a daughter of Pilot, he by Octavius (English thoroughbred).

IMPERIEUX, by Young Rattler out of a daughter of Volontaire, he by Eclipse (English thoroughbred).

DIVUS, by Quebec out of a daughter of Electrique, he by Young Emilius out of Kermesse by Camel (English thoroughbred).

YOUNG EMILIUS, by Emilius (by Fortune) out of Cobweb by Phantom.

QUEBEC, by Ganymede out of a daughter of Voltaire, etc.

GANYMEDE, by Xerxes out of La Louve by Chasseur, etc.

XERXES, by Young Rattler out of a daughter of Young Highflyer, he by High-flyer out of a daughter of Young Docteur, he by Docteur out of a daughter of Mignon, he by Glorieux (English thoroughbred).

YOUNG RATTLER, by Rattler out of the Snap Mare.

VOLANT, by Noteur out of a daughter of ,Tipple Cider, he by Defence out of Deposit by Blacklock.

NOTEUR, by Eylau out of a daughter of Diomed, he by Young Rattler, etc., out of a daughter of Young Topper, he by Topper.

EYLAU, by Napoleon out of Delphine by Massoud (pure Arab).

NAPOLEON, by Bob Booty out of the Pope Mare.

(Hoof No. 19.)

GILDAS.

Brown; 16 hands; weight, 1,300 lbs.; foaled April 12, 1884; imported 1887; bred by M. Cabourg, of Troarn, department of Calvados; got by the government stallion VALPARAISO; dam LISETTE by RAIFORT out of a daughter of IRLANDAIS.

VALPARAISO, by Noville out of a daughter of Affidavit, he by Javelot out of Dahlia by Caravan.

   JAVELOT, by Gladiator out of Rhinoplastie by Royal Oak, he by Catton out of Smolensko Mare.

   GLADIATOR, by Partisan out of Pauline by Moses.

   PARTISAN, by Lucholl, he by Old Lucholl.

NOVILLE, by Ipsilanty out of Therence by Turk.

IPSILANTY, by Norfolk Phenomenon out of a daughter of Sylvio, he by Trance out of Hebe by Rubens.

NORFOLK PHENOMENON, by Old Phenomenon.

RAIFORT, by Glorieux out of a daughter of Succes, he by Telegraph out of a daughter of the Juggler, he by Wamba out of Pantechnetheca by Master Henry.

   TELEGRAPH, by Old Phenomenon.

GLORIEUX, by Solide out of a daughter of Tipple Cider, he by Defence out of Deposit by Blacklock.

SOLIDE, by Nestor out of a daughter of Jaggard, he by Mailhand-Schols.

NESTOR, by Hospodar out of a daughter of Captain Candid, he by Cerberus out of Mandane by Pot-8-os.

HOSPODAR, by Imperieux out of a daughter of Young Rattler, he by Rattler out of the Snap Mare.

IMPERIEUX, by Young Rattler, etc., out of a daughter of Volontaire, he by Eclipse (English thoroughbred).

(Hoof No. 34.)   **GILDINO.**

Chestnut ; 15¾ hands ; weight, 1,275 lbs. ; foaled May 12, 1884 ; imported 1887 ; bred by M. Luce, of Vierville, department of La Manche ; got by the government stallion IDOMENEE ; dam BELLA by FELIBIEN out of a daughter of RACINE.

IDOMENEE, by Serenader out of a daughter of Eylau, he by Napoleon out of Delphine by Massoud (pure Arab).

NAPOLEON, by Bob Booty out of the Pope Mare.

SERENADER, by The Troubadour.

FELIBIEN, by Perfection out of a daughter of Boucanier, he by Chasseur, he by Eastham out of Marquise by Young Rattler, he by Rattler out of the Snap Mare.

EASTHAM, by Sir Oliver out of Cowslip by Alexander.

PERFECTION, by Imperieux out of a daughter of Friedland, he by Napoleon, etc., out of Cloton by Eastham, etc.

IMPERIEUX, by Young Rattler, etc., out of a daughter of Volontaire, he by Eclipse (English thoroughbred).

RACINE, by Sylvio out of a daughter of Young Rattler, etc.

SYLVIO, by Trance out of Hebe by Rubens.

(Hoof No. 5.)   # GITANO.

Dark bay ; 16½ hands ; weight, 1,425 lbs.; foaled June 20, 1884 ; imported 1887 ; bred by M. Leon Truffer, of Angoville, department of La Manche ; got by the government stallion ARISTOCRATE ; dam IDOMENEE by IDOMENEE out of a daughter of NANTEUIL.

ARISTOCRATE, by Quiclet out of a daughter of Extase, he by Thesee out of a daughter of Kramer, he by Hercule out of Cybele by Chasseur, he by Eastham out of Marquise by Young Rattler, he by Rattler out of the Snap Mare.

THESEE, by Gainsborough out of a daughter of Xerxes, he by Young Rattler, etc., out of a daughter of Young Highflyer, he by Highflyer out of a daughter of Young Docteur, he by Docteur out of a daughter of Mignon, by Glorieux (English thoroughbred).

GAINSBOROUGH, by Gainful (English thoroughbred).

HERCULE, by Rainbow out of Aimable by Election.

EASTHAM, by Sir Oliver out of Cowslip by Alexander.

QUICLET, by Lumineux out of a daughter of Sultan, he by Tipple Cider out of a daughter of Dupleix, he by Pickpocket out of Marquise by Young Rattler, etc.

TIPPLE CIDER, by Defence out of Deposit by Blacklock.

PICKPOCKET, by St. Patrick out of the Hedley Mare.

LUMINEUX, by Trouville out of a daughter of Galion, he by Voltaire out of a daughter of Young Rattler, etc.

VOLTAIRE, by Imperieux out of a daughter of Pilot, he by Octavius (English thoroughbred).

IMPERIEUX, by Young Rattler, etc.

TROUVILLE, by Fitz Gladiator out of Clementine by Governor, he by Royal Oak out of Lydia by Rainbow, he by Rainbow.

ROYAL OAK, by Catton out of Smolensko Mare.

FITZ GLADIATOR, by Gladiator out of Sarah by Reveller, he by Reveller out of Scornful by Woful (English thoroughbred).

GLADIATOR, by Partisan out of Pauline by Moses.

PARTISAN, by Lucholl, he by Old Lucholl.

IDOMENEE, by Serenader out of a daughter of Eylau, he by Napoleon out of Delphine by Massoud (pure Arab).

NAPOLEON, by Bob Booty out of the Pope Mare.

SERENADER, by The Troubadour.

NANTEUIL, by Ignace out of a daughter of Vol-au-Vent, he by Kabin out of a daughter of Tamerlan, he by Gainsborough, etc., out of Miss Allen by Captain Candid, he by Cerberus out of Mandane by Pot-8-os.

KABIN, by Uzel out of a daughter of Urus, he by Coleraine (he by Coleraine) out of a daughter of Lucain, he by Eylau, etc., out of Desiree by Talma.

UZEL, by Myrthe out of a daughter of Ramsay, he by Sylvio out of Emelina by Emilius, he by Emilius out of Cobweb by Phantom.

SYLVIO, by Trance out of Hebe by Rubens.

MYRTHE, by Homere out of a daughter of Voltaire, etc.

HOMERE, by Imperieux, etc., out of a daughter of D. I. O., he by Whitworth out of Hambletonian Mare.

IGNACE, by Centaure out of a daughter of Lanercost, he by Liverpool out of Otis by Bustard.

CENTAURE, by Seducteur out of a daughter of Melerault, he by Royal Oak, etc., out of a daughter of Sylvio, etc.

SEDUCTEUR, by Noteur out of a daughter of Fatibello, he by Sylvio, etc., out of a daughter of Y, he by Norfolk Phenomenon out of Henriette by Invincible, he by Hoemus out of Regatta by Camel (English thoroughbred).

NORFOLK PHENOMENON, by Old Phenomenon.

NOTEUR, by Eylau, etc., out of a daughter of Diomed, he by Young Rattler, etc., out of a daughter of Young Topper, he by Topper.

(Hoof No. 33.)

GLADIATEUR.

Dark bay; 16 hands; weight, 1,275 lbs.; foaled April 15, 1884; imported 1887; bred by M. J. Castel, of Trouville-le-Houlle, department of Eure; got by the government stallion RIVOLI; dam ORDONNANCE by Y.

RIVOLI, by Conquerant out of a daughter of Coleraine, he by Coleraine (English thoroughbred).

CONQUERANT, by Kapirat out of Elisa by Corsair, he by J. C. Knox's Corsair out of a daughter of Cleveland.

KAPIRAT, by Voltaire out of a daughter of The Juggler, he by Wamba out of Pantechnetheca by Master Henry.

VOLTAIRE, by Imperieux out of a daughter of Pilot, he by Octavius (English thoroughbred).

IMPERIEUX, by Young Rattler out of a daughter of Volontaire, he by Eclipse (English thoroughbred).

YOUNG RATTLER, by Rattler out of the Snap Mare.

Y, by Norfolk Phenomenon out of Henriette by Invincible, he by Hoemus out of Regatta by Camel.

NORFOLK PHENOMENON, by Old Phenomenon.

GODFREY.

See page 230.

(Hoof No. 39.)   GLANEUR.

Brown ; 16¼ hands ; weight, 1,450 lbs.; foaled April 10, 1884 ; imported 1887 ; bred by M. Pitrais Hervien, of Pont L'Eveque, department of Calvados ; got by the government stallion TIGRIS ; dam CERIRETTE by UMBER out of a daughter of COLERAINE.

TIGRIS, by Lavater out of Modestie by The Heir of Linne, he by Galaor out of Mrs. Walker by Jereed.

LAVATER, by Y, he by the Norfolk Phenomenon out of Henriette by Invincible, he by Hoemus out of Regatta by Camel (English thoroughbred).

NORFOLK PHENOMENON, by Old Phenomenon.

UMBER, by Pledge out of a daughter of Polecat, he by Bay Middleton out of Pussy by Pollio.

PLEDGE, by Royal Oak out of a daughter of Young Rattler, he by Rattler out of the Snap Mare.

ROYAL OAK, by Catton out of Smolensko Mare.

COLERAINE, by Coleraine (English thoroughbred).

(Hoof No. 40.)

GLORIEUX.

Bay; 16½ hands; weight, 1,400 lbs.; foaled April 12, 1884; imported 1887; bred by M. Cornet, of Coudray Rabus, department of Calvados; got by the government stallion TIGRIS; dam ESPOIR by CONQUERANT out of a daughter of USAGER.

TIGRIS, by Lavater out of Modestie by The Heir of Linne, he by Galaor out of Mrs. Walker by Jereed.

LAVATER, by Y, he by the Norfolk Phenomenon out of Henriette by Invincible, he by Hoemus out of Regatta by Camel (English thoroughbred).

NORFOLK PHENOMENON, by Old Phenomenon.

CONQUERANT, by Kapirat out of Elisa by Corsair, he by J. C. Knox's Corsair out of a daughter of Cleveland.

KAPIRAT, by Voltaire out of a daughter of The Juggler, he by Wamba out of Pantechnetheca by Master Henry.

VOLTAIRE, by Imperieux out of a daughter of Pilot, he by Octavius (English thoroughbred).

IMPERIEUX, by Young Rattler out of a daughter of Volontaire, he by Eclipse (English thoroughbred).

YOUNG RATTLER, by Rattler out of the Snap Mare.

USAGER, by Proportionne out of a daughter of Imperial, he by Eylau, he by Napoleon out of Delphine by Massoud (pure Arab).

NAPOLEON, by Bob Booty out of the Pope Mare.

PROPORTIONNE, by Ganymede out of a daughter of Young Rattler, etc.

GANYMEDE, by Xerxes out of La Louve by Chasseur, he by Eastham out of Marquise by Young Rattler, etc.

EASTHAM, by Sir Oliver out of Cowslip by Alexander.

XERXES, by Young Rattler, etc., out of a daughter of Young Highflyer, he by Highflyer out of a daughter of Young Docteur, he by Docteur out of a daughter of Mignon, he by Glorieux (English thoroughbred).

(Hoof No. 29.)   **GODFREY.**

Chestnut; 16½ hands; weight, 1,450 lbs.; foaled June 4, 1884; imported 1887; bred by M. Alfred Le Drouet, of Revenoville, department of La Manche; got by the government stallion VITAL; dam LA PELOTTE by DANIEL.

VITAL, by Montfort out of a daughter of Interprete, he by Centaure out of a daughter of Tancrede, he by The Roue out of a daughter of Eylau, he by Napoleon out of Delphine by Massoud (pure Arab).

CENTAURE, by Seducteur out of a daughter of Melcrault, he by Royal Oak out of a daughter of Sylvio, he by Trance out of Hebe by Rubens.

ROYAL OAK, by Catton out of Smolensko Mare.

SEDUCTEUR, by Noteur out of a daughter of Fatibello, he by Sylvio, etc., out of a daughter of Y, he by the Norfolk Phenomenon out of Henriette by Invincible, he by Hoemus out of Regatta by Camel (English thoroughbred).

NORFOLK PHENOMENON, by Old Phenomenon.

NOTEUR, by Eylau, etc., out of a daughter of Diomed, he by Young Rattler out of a daughter of Young Topper, he by Topper.

YOUNG RATTLER, by Rattler out of the Snap Mare.

THE ROUE, by Claret out of Roulette by Philipp-the-First.

NAPOLEON, by Bob Booty out of the Pope Mare.

MONTFORT, by Arc-en-Ciel out of Fougeres by Faugh-a-Ballagh, he by Sir Hercule out of Guiccioli by Bob Booty.

DANIEL, by Paternal out of a daughter of Boucanier, he by Chasseur, he by Eastham out of Marquise by Young Rattler, etc.

EASTHAM, by Sir Oliver out of Cowslip by Alexander.

PATERNAL, by Tipple Cider out of a daughter of Dupleix, he by Pickpocket out of Marquise by Young Rattler, etc.

PICKPOCKET, by St. Patrick out of the Hedley Mare.

TIPPLE CIDER, by Defence out of Deposit by Blacklock.

(Hoof No. 35.)   **GONDOLIER.**

Brown; 16¼ hands; weight, 1,360 lbs.; foaled March 20, 1884; imported 1887; bred by M. Ceram Maillard, of Turqueville, department of La Manche; got by the government stallion AGNADEL; dam PLANETE by IDOMENEE out of a daughter of KAPIRAT.

AGNADEL, by Lavater out of a daughter of the Heir of Linne, he by Galaor out of Mrs. Walker by Jereed.

LAVATER, by Y, he by the Norfolk Phenomenon out of Henriette by Invincible, he by Hoemus out of Regatta by Camel (English thoroughbred).

NORFOLK PHENOMENON, by Old Phenomenon.

IDOMENEE, by Serenader out of a daughter of Eylau, he by Napoleon out of Delphine by Massoud (pure Arab).

NAPOLEON, by Bob Booty out of the Pope Mare.

SERENADER, by The Troubadour.

KAPIRAT, by Voltaire out of a daughter of the Juggler, he by Wamba out of Pantechnetheca by Master Henry.

VOLTAIRE, by Imperieux out of a daughter of Pilot, he by Octavius (English thoroughbred).

IMPERIEUX, by Young Rattler out of a daughter of Volontaire, he by Eclipse (English thoroughbred).

YOUNG RATTLER, by Rattler out of the Snap Mare.

(Hoof No. 24.)

GOVERNOR.

Black; 16 hands; weight, 1,315 lbs.; foaled May 9, 1884; imported 1887; bred by M. Millot, of St. Julien-sur-Calonne, department of Calvados; got by the government stallion TIGRIS; dam DIVA by NORMAND out of Miss Mowbray.

TIGRIS, by Lavater out of Modestie by the Heir of Linne, he by Galaor out of Mrs. Walker by Jereed.

LAVATER, by Y, he by the Norfolk Phenomenon out of Henriette by Invincible, he by Hoemus out of Regatta by Camel (English thoroughbred).

NORFOLK PHENOMENON, by Old Phenomenon.

NORMAND, by Divus out of a daughter of Kapirat, he by Voltaire out of a daughter of The Juggler, he by Wamba out of Pantechnetheca by Master Henry.

VOLTAIRE, by Imperieux out of a daughter of Pilot, he by Octavius (English thoroughbred).

IMPERIEUX, by Young Rattler out of a daughter of Volontaire, he by Eclipse (English thoroughbred).

YOUNG RATTLER, by Rattler out of the Snap Mare.

DIVUS, by Quebec out of a daughter of Electrique, he by Young Emilius out of Kermesse by Camel (English thoroughbred).

YOUNG EMILIUS, by Emilius (he by Fortune) out of Cobweb by Phantom.

QUEBEC, by Ganymede out of a daughter of Voltaire, etc.

GANYMEDE, by Xerxes out of La Louve by Chasseur, he by Eastham out of Marquise by Young Rattler, etc.

EASTHAM, by Sir Oliver out of Cowslip by Alexander.

XERXES, by Young Rattler, etc., out of a daughter of Young Highflyer, he by Highflyer out of a daughter of Young Docteur, he by Docteur out of a daughter of Mignon, he by Glorieux (English thoroughbred).

(Hoof No. 2.)

GRANCEY.

Black; 16½ hands; weight, 1,325 lbs; foaled May 5, 1884; imported 1887; bred by M. V. Villiers, of Lison, department of Calvados; got by the government stallion BEAU SEIGNEUR; dam COQUETTE by LEOTARD out of a daughter of TORTICOLIS.

BEAU SEIGNEUR, by Ribaud out of a daughter of Uzel, he by Myrthe out of a daughter of Ramsay, he by Sylvio out of Emelina by Emilius, he by Emilius out of Cobweb by Phantom.

MYRTHE, by Homere out of a daughter of Voltaire, he by Imperieux out of a daughter of Pilot, he by Octavius (English thoroughbred).

HOMERE, by Imperieux out of a daughter of D. I. O., he by Whitworth out of Hambletonian Mare.

IMPERIEUX, by Young Rattler out of a daughter of Volontaire, he by Eclipse (English thoroughbred).

YOUNG RATTLER, by Rattler out of the Snap Mare.

SYLVIO, by Trance out of Hebe by Rubens.

RIBAUD, by Ugolin out of a daughter of Vandermulin, he by Von Tromp out of Muley-Moloch Mare.

UGOLIN, by Parisien, he by Ganymede out of a daughter of Biron, he by Captain Candid out of Helene by Eastham, he by Sir Oliver out of Cowslip by Alexander.

CAPTAIN CANDID, by Cerberus out of Mandane by Pot-8-os.

GANYMEDE, by Xerxes out of La Louve by Chasseur, he by Eastham, etc., out of Marquise by Young Rattler, etc.

XERXES, by Young Rattler, etc., out of a daughter of Young Highflyer, he by Highflyer out of a daughter of Young Docteur, he by Docteur, out of a daughter of Mignon, he by Glorieux (English thoroughbred).

LEOTARD, by Despote out of a daughter of Ballinkeele, he by Irish-Birdcatcher out of Perdita by Langar.

DESPOTE, by Succes out of a daughter of Adolphus, he by Royal Oak out of Anna by Godolphin (pure Arab).

ROYAL OAK, by Catton out of Smolensko Mare.

SUCCES, by Telegraph out of a daughter of The Juggler, he by Wamba out of Pantechnetheca by Master Henry.

TELEGRAPH, by Old Phenomenon.

TORTICOLIS, by Royal Quandmeme out of Defiance by Royal Oak, etc.

ROYAL QUANDMEME, by Giges out of Eusebia by Emilius, etc.

(Hoof No. 10.)   **GRANDEE.**

Bay; 16½ hands; weight, 1,375 lbs.; foaled April 1, 1884; imported 1887; bred by M. Victor Groud, of Mesnil Garnier, department of La Manche; got by the government stallion TUDIEU; dam LISA by BEAU-MANOIR, out of a daughter of GUELFE.

TUDIEU, by Estafette out of a daughter of Jactator, he by Elu out of a daughter of Eylau, he by Napoleon out of Delphine by Massoud (pure Arab).

    ELU, by Idalis out of a daughter of Tipple Cider, he by Defence out of Deposit by Blacklock.

    IDALIS, by Don Quichotte out of a daughter of Chapman, he by Trotteur, he by Chapman.

    DON QUICHOTTE, by Sylvio out of Moina by Tigris, he by Quitz out of Persepolis by Alexander.

    SYLVIO, by Trance out of Hebe by Rubens.

    NAPOLEON, by Bob Booty out of the Pope Mare.

ESTAFETTE, by Ottoman out of a daughter of Telegraph, he by Old Phenomenon.

OTTOMAN, by Faliero out of a daughter of Basly, he by Eastham out of a daughter of Valient, he by Equator (thoroughbred).

    EASTHAM, by Sir Oliver out of Cowslip by Alexander.

FALIERO, by Sylvio, etc., out of a daughter of Dart, he by Dart (English thoroughbred) out of a daughter of Loadstone (English thoroughbred).

BEAUMANOIR, by Sancho out of a daughter of Turpin, he by Hangton-Merry-Leggs.

SANCHO, by Don Quichotte, etc., out of a daughter of Vautour, he by Young Rattler out of a daughter of Lattitat, he by Lattitat out of a daughter of Volontaire, he by Eclipse (English thoroughbred).

    YOUNG RATTLER, by Rattler out of the Snap Mare.

GUELFE, by Isolier out of a daughter of Ramsay, he by Sylvio, etc., out of Emelina by Emilius, he by Emilius out of Cobweb by Phantom.

ISOLIER, by Nunnykirk out of Deception by Defence.

NUNNYKIRK, by Touchstone out of Doctor-Syntax-Mare.

GOVERNOR.

See page 232.

(Hoof No. 20.)   # GRENADA.

Bay; 16 hands; weight, 1,350 lbs.; foaled April 25, 1884; imported 1887; bred by M. Chedeville, of Argentan, department of Orne; got by the government stallion SAINT RIGOMER; dam VESTA by ORPHEE.

SAINT RIGOMER, by Gall out of a daughter of Tipple Cider, he by Defence out of Deposit by Blacklock.

GALL, by Kapirat out of a daughter of Sir Henry Dimsdale, he by Old President out of a daughter of Camel (English thoroughbred).

KAPIRAT, by Voltaire out of a daughter of The Juggler, he by Wamba out of Pantechnetheca by Master Henry.

VOLTAIRE, by Imperieux out of a daughter of Pilot, he by Octavius (English thoroughbred).

IMPERIEUX, by Young Rattler out of a daughter of Volontaire, he by Eclipse (English thoroughbred).

YOUNG RATTLER, by Rattler out of the Snap Mare.

ORPHEE, by the Heir of Linne out of a daughter of Ugolin, he by Parisien, he by Ganymede out of a daughter of Biron, he by Captain Candid out of Helene by Eastham, he by Sir Oliver out of Cowslip by Alexander.

GANYMEDE, by Xerxes out of La Louve by Chasseur, he by Eastham, etc., out of Marquis by Young Rattler, etc.

XERXES, by Young Rattler, etc., out of a daughter of Young Highflyer, he by Highflyer out of a daughter of Young Docteur, he by Docteur out of a daughter of Mignon, he by Glorieux (English thoroughbred).

CAPTAIN CANDID, by Cerberus out of Mandane by Pot-8-os.

HEIR OF LINNE, by Galaor out of Mrs. Walker by Jereed.

(Hoof No. 21.)   **GRIVOIS.**

Bay; 16½ hands; weight, 1,400 lbs.; foaled April 5, 1884; imported 1887; bred by M. Brion, of Gerrots, department of Calvados; got by the government stallion HIPPOMENE; dam NEUSTRIA by NORMAND out of a daughter of ECLIPSE.

HIPPOMENE, by Bagdad out of Barbe D'Or by Mogador, he by Hlavie (Arab) out of a daughter of Spy (English thoroughbred).

NORMAND, by Divus out of a daughter of Kapirat, he by Voltaire out of a daughter of The Juggler, he by Wamba out of Pantechnetheca by Master Henry.

VOLTAIRE, by Imperieux out of a daughter of Pilot, he by Octavius (English thoroughbred).

IMPERIEUX, by Young Rattler out of a daughter of Volontaire, he by Eclipse (English thoroughbred).

YOUNG RATTLER, by Rattler out of the Snap Mare.

DIVUS, by Quebec out of a daughter of Electrique, he by Young Emilius out of Kermesse by Camel (English thoroughbred).

YOUNG EMILIUS, by Emilius (he by Fortune) out of Cobweb by Phantom.

QUEBEC, by Ganymede out of a daughter of Voltaire, etc.

GANYMEDE, by Xerxes out of La Louve by Chasseur, he by Eastham out of Marquise by Young Rattler, etc.

EASTHAM, by Sir Oliver out of Cowslip by Alexander.

XERXES, by Young Rattler, etc., out of a daughter of Young Highflyer, he by Highflyer out of a daughter of Young Docteur, he by Docteur out of a daughter of Mignon, he by Glorieux (English thoroughbred).

(Hoof No. 26.)   GUELFE.

Dark bay ; 16 hands ; weight, 1,300 lbs. ; foaled March 27, 1884 ; imported 1887 ; bred by M. Charles Carre, of Tamerville, department of La Manche ; got by the government stallion ROMANO ; dam COCOTTE by INVARIABLE out of a daughter of EGESIPPE.

ROMANO, by Auguste out of a daughter of Agenda, he by Lucain out of a daughter of Imperial, he by Eylau out of a daughter of Talma.

Lucain, by Eylau out of Desiree by Talma.

Eylau, by Napoleon out of Delphine by Massoud (pure Arab).

Napoleon, by Bob Booty out of the Pope Mare.

Auguste, by Monarque out of Etoile-du-Nord by The Baron.

Invariable, by Divan out of a daughter of Brocardo, he by Touchstone out of Brocarde by Pantaloon.

Divan, by Utrecht out of a daughter of Noteur, he by Eylau, etc., out of a daughter of Diomed, he by Young Rattler out of a daughter of Young Topper, he by Topper.

Young Rattler, by Rattler out of the Snap Mare.

Utrecht, by Prince out of a daughter of Eylau, etc.

Prince, by Don Quichotte out of a daughter of Marengo, he by Napoleon, etc., out of Cloris by Aslam (pure Arab).

Don Quichotte, by Sylvio out of Moina by Tigris, he by Quitz out of Persepolis by Alexander.

Sylvio, by Trance out of Hebe by Rubens.

Egesippe, by Lucain, etc., out of a daughter of Tipple Cider, he by Defence out of Deposit by Blacklock.

(Hoof No. 30.)

GUERRIER.

Black ; 16¼ hands ; weight, 1,350 lbs. ; foaled May 15, 1884 ; imported 1887 ; bred by M. Louis Lefauconnier, of Flottmanville, department of La Manche ; got by the government stallion QUINTE CURCE ; dam LISETTE by FEU-DE-JOIE out of a daughter of TALLEY-RAND.

QUINTE CURCE, by Elu out of a daughter of Thesee, he by Gainsborough (son of Gainful) out of a daughter of Xerxes, he by Young Rattler out of a daughter of Young Highflyer, he by Highflyer out of a daughter of Young Docteur, he by Docteur out of a daughter of Mignon, he by Glorieux (English thoroughbred).

YOUNG RATTLER, by Rattler out of the Snap Mare.

ELU, by Idalis out of a daughter of Tipple Cider, he by Defence out of Deposit by Blacklock.

IDALIS, by Don Quichotte out of a daughter of Chapman, he by Trotteur, he by Chapman.

DON QUICHOTTE, by Sylvio out of Moina by Tigris, he by Quitz out of Persepolis by Alexander.

SYLVIO, by Trance out of Hebe by Rubens.

FEU-DE-JOIE, by Seducteur out of a daughter of The Repealer.

SEDUCTEUR, by Noteur out of a daughter of Fatibello, he by Sylvio, etc., out of a daughter of Y, he by the Norfolk Phenomenon out of Henriette by Invincible, he by Hoemus out of Regatta by Camel (English thoroughbred).

NORFOLK PHENOMENON, by Old Phenomenon.

NOTEUR, by Eylau out of a daughter of Diomed, he by Young Rattler, etc., out of a daughter of Young Topper, he by Topper.

EYLAU, by Napoleon out of Delphine by Massoud (pure Arab)

NAPOLEON, by Bob Booty out of the Pope Mare.

TALLEYRAND, by Tipple Cider, etc., out of a daughter of Young Rattler, etc.

(Hoof No. 3.) # GUSTAVE.

Black ; 16½ hands ; weight, 1,375 lbs. ; foaled March 30, 1884 ; imported 1887 ; bred by M. Gustave Buisson, of Authieux-du-Puits, department of Orne ; got by the government stallion UN ; dam LUCRECE by THESEE out of a daughter of CENTAURE.

UN, by Niger out of a daughter of Telegraph, he by Telegraph, he by Old Phenomenon.

NIGER, by the Norfolk Phenomenon out of Miss Bell (English thoroughbred).

NORFOLK PHENOMENON, by Old Phenomenon.

THESEE, by Gainsborough out of a daughter of Xerxes, he by Young Rattler out of a daughter of Young Highflyer, he by Highflyer out of a daughter of Young Docteur, he by Docteur out of a daughter of Mignon, he by Glorieux (English thoroughbred).

YOUNG RATTLER, by Rattler out of the Snap Mare.

GAINSBOROUGH, by Gainful (English thoroughbred).

CENTAURE, by Seducteur out of a daughter of Merlerault, he by Royal Oak out of a daughter of Sylvio, he by Trance out of Hebe by Rubens.

ROYAL OAK, by Catton out of Smolensko Mare.

SEDUCTEUR, by Noteur out of a daughter of Fatibello, he by Sylvio, etc., out of a daughter of Y, he by Norfolk Phenomenon, etc., out of Henriette by Invincible, he by Hoemus out of Regatta by Camel (English thoroughbred).

NOTEUR, by Eylau out of a daughter of Diomed, he by Young Rattler, etc., out of a daughter of Young Topper, he by Topper.

EYLAU, by Napoleon out of Delphine by Massoud (pure Arab).

NAPOLEON, by Bob Booty out of the Pope Mare.

GRANDEE.

See page 234.

(Hoof No. 7.)   # HARKAWAY.

Dark bay ; 16 hands ; weight, 1,290 lbs. ; foaled April 28, 1885 ; imported 1887 ; bred by Madame Ballois, of Montviron, department of La Manche ; got by the government stallion BLACK ; dam LISETTE by ST. POIS out of a daughter of OURSON.

BLACK, by Ximenes out of a daughter of Marignan, he by Norfolk Phenomenon, he by Old Phenomenon.

XIMENES, by Noteur out of a daughter of Usbekyeh (pure Arab).

NOTEUR, by Eylau out of a daughter of Diomed, he by Young Rattler out of a daughter of Young Topper, he by Topper.

YOUNG RATTLER, by Rattler out of the Snap Mare.

EYLAU, by Napoleon out of Delphine by Massoud (pure Arab).

NAPOLEON, by Bob Booty out of the Pope Mare.

ST. POIS, by Navigateur, he by Herschell out of a daughter of Oliver Cromwell.

HERSCHELL, by Eylau, etc., out of a daughter of Pretender, he by Yorkshire Hero.

OURSON, by Ursin out of a daughter of Balthazar, he by Royal Oak out of Amenaide by Napoleon, etc.

ROYAL OAK, by Catton out of Smolensko Mare.

URSIN, by Ramsay out of a daughter of Ganymede, he by Xerxes out of La Louve by Chasseur, he by Eastham out of Marquise by Young Rattler, etc.

XERXES, by Young Rattler, etc., out of a daughter of Young Highflyer, he by Highflyer out of a daughter of Young Docteur, he by Docteur out of a daughter of Mignon, he by Glorieux (English thoroughbred).

EASTHAM, by Sir Oliver out of Cowslip by Alexander.

RAMSAY, by Sylvio out of Emelina by Emilius, he by Emilius out of Cobweb by Phantom.

SYLVIO, by Trance out of Hebe by Rubens.

(Hoof No. 8.)

HELVETIUS.

Bay; 16 hands; weight, 1,360 lbs.; foaled April 8, 1885; imported 1887; bred by M. Auguste Mahier, of Camerville, department of La Manche; got by the government approved stallion ANTIPODE; dam COCOTE by MIRLITON.

ANTIPODE, by Pancrace out of a daughter of Forey, he by Urus out of a daughter of Orgueilleux, he by Homere out of a daughter of Royal George, he by Royal Oak out of Destiny by Centaure, he by Seducteur out of a daughter of Merlerault, he by Royal Oak out of a daughter of Sylvio, he by Trance out of Hebe by Rubens.

URUS, by Coleraine (he by Coleraine) out of a daughter of Lucain, he by Eylau out of Desiree by Talma.

EYLAU, by Napoleon out of Delphine by Massoud (pure Arab).

NAPOLEON, by Bob Booty out of the Pope Mare.

HOMERE, by Imperieux out of a daughter of D. I. O., he by Whitworth out of Hambletonian Mare.

IMPERIEUX, by Young Rattler out of a daughter of Volontaire, he by Eclipse (English thoroughbred).

YOUNG RATTLER, by Rattler out of the Snap Mare.

ROYAL OAK, by Catton out of Smolensko Mare.

SEDUCTEUR, by Noteur out of a daughter of Fatibello, he by Sylvio, etc., out of a daughter of Y, he by the Norfolk Phenomenon out of Henriette by Invincible, he by Hoemus out of Regatta by Camel (English thoroughbred).

NORFOLK PHENOMENON, by Old Phenomenon.

NOTEUR, by Eylau, etc., out of a daughter of Diomed, he by Young Rattler, etc., out of a daughter of Young Topper, he by Topper.

PANCRACE, by Centaure, etc., out of a daughter of Prince-Colibri, he by Sylvio, etc., out of Fraga by Harlequin, he by Cervantes out of Flora by Camillus.

MIRLITON, by Matinal out of Chique-A-Voine.

MATINAL, by Bourgeois Gentilhomme, he by Lully out of a daughter of Diomed, etc.

LULLY, by Tipple Cider out of Pecora by Sylvio, etc.

TIPPLE CIDER, by Defence out of Deposit by Blacklock.

(Hoof No. 44.)   # HENRI.

Brown; 15½ hands; weight, 1,200 lbs.; foaled April 7, 1885; imported 1887; bred by M. Barbier, of Guilderville, department of La Manche; got by the government approved stallion DARTOS, he by UNAU; dam MIGNONNE by IGNORE.

IGNORE, by Uzel out of a daughter of Ugolin, he by Parisien, he by Ganymede out of a daughter of Biron, he by Captain Candid out of Helene by Eastham, he by Sir Oliver out of Cowslip by Alexander.

GANYMEDE, by Xerxes out of La Louve by Chasseur, he by Eastham, etc.

XERXES, by Young Rattler out of a daughter of Young Highflyer, he by Highflyer out of a daughter of Young Docteur, he by Docteur out of a daughter of Mignon, he by Glorieux (English thoroughbred).

YOUNG RATTLER, by Rattler out of the Snap Mare.

CAPTAIN CANDID, by Cerberus out of Mandane by Pot-8-os.

UZEL, by Myrthe out of a daughter of Ramsay, he by Sylvio out of Emelina by Emilius, he by Emilius out of Cobweb by Phantom.

SYLVIO, by Trance out of Hebe by Rubens.

MYRTHE, by Homere out of a daughter of Voltaire, he by Imperieux out of a daughter of Pilot, he by Octavius (English thoroughbred).

HOMERE, by Imperieux out of a daughter of D. I. O., he by Whitworth out of Hambletonian Mare.

IMPERIEUX, by Young Rattler, etc., out of a daughter of Volontaire, he by Eclipse (English thoroughbred).

(Hoof No. 6.)

HILAIRE.

Dark bay ; 16¼ hands ; weight, 1,500 lbs.; foaled March 21, 1885 ; imported 1887 ; bred by M. Clermont Godey, of St. Croix-de-St. Lo, department of La Manche ; got by the government stallion SERIEUX ; dam RAGOT by VIOLENT.

SERIEUX, by Ugolin out of a daughter of Jarnac, he by Kapirat out of a daughter of Ursin, he by Ramsay out of a daughter of Ganymede, he by Xerxes out of La Louve by Chasseur, he by Eastham out of Marquise by Young Rattler, he by Rattler out of the Snap Mare.

KAPIRAT, by Voltaire out of a daughter of The Juggler, he by Wamba out of Pantechnetheca by Master Henry.

VOLTAIRE, by Imperieux out of a daughter of Pilot, he by Octavius (English thoroughbred).

IMPERIEUX, by Young Rattler, etc., out of a daughter of Volontaire, he by Eclipse (English thoroughbred).

RAMSAY, by Sylvio out of Emelina by Emilius, he by Emilius out of Cobweb by Phantom.

SYLVIO, by Trance out of Hebe by Rubens.

XERXES, by Young Rattler, etc., out of a daughter of Young Highflyer, he by Highflyer out of a daughter of Young Docteur, he by Docteur out of a daughter of Mignon, he by Glorieux (English thoroughbred).

EASTHAM, by Sir Oliver out of Cowslip by Alexander.

UGOLIN, by Ugolin out of a daughter of Ursin, he by Ramsay, etc., out of a daughter of Ganymede, etc.

UGOLIN, by Parisien, he by Ganymede, etc., out of a daughter of Biron, he by Captain Candid out of Helene by Eastham, etc.

CAPTAIN CANDID, by Cerberus out of Mandane by Pot-8-os.

VIOLENT, by Orgueilleux out of a daughter of Vautour, he by Young Rattler, etc., out of a daughter of Lattitat, he by Lattitat out of a daughter of Volontaire, he by Eclipse (English thoroughbred).

ORGUEILLEUX, by Homere out of a daughter of Royal George, he by Royal Oak out of Destiny by Centaure, he by Seducteur out of a daughter of Merlerault, he by Royal Oak out of a daughter of Sylvio, etc.

ROYAL OAK, by Catton out of Smolensko Mare.

SEDUCTEUR, by Noteur out of a daughter of Fatibello, he by Sylvio, etc., out of a daughter of Y, he by Norfolk Phenomenon out of Henriette by Invincible, he by Hoemus out of Regatta by Camel (English thoroughbred).

NORFOLK PHENOMENON, by Old Phenomenon.

NOTEUR, by Eylau out of a daughter of Diomed, he by Young Rattler, etc., out of a daughter of Young Topper, he by Topper.

EYLAU, by Napoleon out of Delphine by Massoud (pure Arab).

NAPOLEON, by Bob Booty out of the Pope Mare.

HOMERE, by Imperieux, etc., out of a daughter of D. I. O., he by Whitworth out of Hambletonian Mare.

(Hoof No. 45.)   ## ST. LEGER.

Bay ; 16¼ hands ; weight, 1,365 lbs.; foaled May 4, 1883 ; imported 1886 ; bred by M. Desmannetaux, of St. Marie-du-Monts, department of La Manche ; got by the government stallion ARISTOCRATE ; dam FLORA, by PRETTY BOY out of a daughter of URSIN.

ARISTOCRATE, by Quiclet out of a daughter of Extase, he by Thesee out of a daughter of Kramer, he by Hercule out of Cybele by Chasseur, he by East-ham out of Marquise by Young Rattler, he by Rattler out of the Snap Mare.

THESEE, by Gainsborough (by Gainful) out of a daughter of Xerxes, he by Young Rattler, etc., out of a daughter of Young Highflyer, he by High-flyer out of a daughter of Young Docteur, he by Docteur out of a daughter of Mignon, he by Glorieux (English thoroughbred).

HERCULE, by Rainbw out of Aimable by Election.

EASTHAM, by Sir Oliver out of Cowslip by Alexander.

QUICLET, by Lumineux out of a daughter of Sultan, he by Tipple Cider out of a daughter of Dupleix, he by Pickpocket, out of Marquise by Young Rattler, etc.

TIPPLE CIDER, by Defence, out of Deposit by Blacklock.

PICKPOCKET, by St. Patrick out of the Hedley Mare.

LUMINEUX, by Trouville out of a daughter of Galion, he by Voltaire out of a daughter of Young Rattler, etc.

VOLTAIRE, by Imperieux out of a daughter of Pilot, he by Octavius (English thoroughbred).

IMPERIEUX, by Young Rattler, etc., out of a daughter of Volontaire, he by Eclipse (English thoroughbred).

TROUVILLE, by Fitz Gladiator out of Clementine by Governor, he by Royal Oak out of Lydia by Rainbow, he by Rainbow.

ROYAL OAK, by Catton out of the Smolensko Mare.

FITZ GLADIATOR, by Gladiator out of Sarah by Reveller, he by Reveller out of Scornful by Woful (English thoroughbred).

GLADIATOR, by Partisan out of Pauline by Moses.

PARTISAN, by Lucholl by Old Lucholl.

PRETTY BOY, by Idle Boy out of Lena by Glaucus.

URSIN, by Ramsay out of a daughter of Ganymede, he by Xerxes out of La Louve by Chasseur, etc.

RAMSAY, by Sylvio out of Emelina by Emilius, he by Emilius out of Cobweb by Phantom.

SYLVIO, by Trance out of Hebe by Rubens.

FRENCH COACH MARES

ADALIE.

Bay ; foaled April 28, 1885 ; imported 1887 ; bred by M. Charles Du Hays, of St. Germain-de-Clairefeuille, department of Orne ; got by the government stallion GEDEON ; dam ADA.

GEDEON, by Harami (pure Arab) out of the Stockwell Mare.

BARBILLONNE.

Bay ; foaled May 2, 1884 ; imported 1887 ; bred by M. Crochet, of St. Hilaire-du-Recy, department of Vendee ; got by the government stallion TERME ; dam NINETTE by HENRI IV out of a daughter of NECKER.

TERME, by Gouverneur out of a daughter of Egesippe, he by Lucain out of a daughter of Tipple Cider, he by Defence out of Deposit by Blacklock.

    LUCAIN, by Eylau out of Desiree by Talma.

    EYLAU, by Napoleon out of Delphine by Massoud (pure Arab).

    NAPOLEON, by Bob Booty out of the Pope Mare.

GOUVERNEUR, by Bisson out of a daughter of Navigateur, he by Herschell out of a daughter of Oliver Cromwell.

    HERSCHELL, by Eylau, etc., out of a daughter of Pretender, he by Holme (English thoroughbred).

BISSON, by Nemrod out of a daughter of Cominges, he by Captain Candid out of Helene by Eastham, he by Sir Oliver out of Cowslip by Alexander.

    CAPTAIN CANDID, by Cerberus out of Mandane by Pot-8-os.

    CERBERUS, by Roland (English thoroughbred).

NEMROD, by Voltaire out of a daughter of Xerxes, he by Young Rattler out of a daughter of Young Highflyer, he by Highflyer out of a daughter of Young Docteur, he by Docteur out of a daughter of Mignon, he by Glorieux (English thoroughbred).

VOLTAIRE, by Imperieux out of a daughter of Pilot, he by Octavius (English thoroughbred).

IMPERIEUX, by Young Rattler out of a daughter of Volontaire, he by Eclipse (English thoroughbred).

YOUNG RATTLER, by Rattler out of the Snap Mare.

NECKER, by Ganymede out of a daughter of Young Rattler, etc.

GANYMEDE, by Xerxes, etc., out of La Louve by Chasseur, he by Eastham, etc., out of Marquise by Young Rattler, etc.

(Hoof No. 53.)   ·   # GAZELLE.

Bay; foaled March 12, 1884; imported 1887; bred by M. Batard, of St. Gervais, department of Vendee; got by the government stallion ROMNALD; dam DIANE by KAPIRAT II out of a daughter of NECKER.

ROMNALD, by La Hire out of a daughter of Jambe-d'Argent, he by Centaure out of a daughter of Torigne, he by Merlerault out of a daughter of Hector, he by Quebec out of a daughter of Buffalo, he by Holme out of a daughter of Little Isaac.

CENTAURE, by Seducteur out of a daughter of Merlerault, he by Royal Oak out of a daughter of Sylvio, he by Trance out of Hebe by Rubens.

ROYAL OAK, by Catton out of Smolensko Mare.

SEDUCTEUR, by Noteur out of a daughter of Fatibello, he by Sylvio, etc., out of a daughter of Y, he by the Norfolk Phenomenon out of Henriette by Invincible, he by Hoemus out of Regatta by Camel (English thoroughbred).

NORFOLK PHENOMENON, by Old Phenomenon.

NOTEUR, by Eylau out of a daughter of Diomed, he by Young Rattler out of a daughter of Young Topper, he by Topper.

YOUNG RATTLER, by Rattler out of the Snap Mare.

EYLAU, by Napoleon out of Delphine by Massoud (pure Arab).

NAPOLEON, by Bob Booty out of the Pope Mare.

QUEBEC, by Oscar, he by Young Rattler, etc., out of a daughter of Bacha (pure Arab).

LA HIRE, by Noteur, etc., out of a daughter of Solide, he by Nestor out of a daughter of Jaggard, he by Mailhand-Schols.

NESTOR, by Hospodar out of a daughter of Captain Candid, he by Cerberus out of Mandane by Pot-8-os.

CERBERUS, by Roland (English thoroughbred).

HOSPODAR, by Imperieux out of a daughter of Young Rattler, etc.

IMPERIEUX, by Young Rattler, etc., out of a daughter of Volontaire, he by Eclipse (English thoroughbred).

KAPIRAT II, by Kapirat out of a daughter of Perfection, he by Imperieux, etc., out of a daughter of Friedland, he by Napoleon, etc., out of Cloton by Eastham, he by Sir Oliver out of Cowslip by Alexander.

KAPIRAT, by Voltaire out of a daughter of The Juggler, he by Wamba out of Pantechnetheca by Master Henry.

VOLTAIRE, by Imperieux, etc., out of a daughter of Pilot, he by Octavius (English thoroughbred).

NECKER, by Ganymede out of a daughter of Young Rattler, etc.

GANYMEDE, by Xerxes out of La Louve by Chasseur, he by Eastham, etc., out of Marquise by Young Rattler, etc.

XERXES, by Young Rattler, etc., out of a daughter of Young Highflyer, he by Highflyer out of a daughter of Young Docteur, he by Docteur out of a daughter of Mignon, he by Glorieux (English thoroughbred).

(Hoof No. 54.)

GOELETTE.

Brown bay; foaled April 15, 1884; imported 1887; bred by M. A. Lebaudy, of Cagny, department of Calvados; got by the government approved stallion RIVOLI; dam NAAIDE by TIGRIS out of a daughter of ESCULAPE.

RIVOLI, by Tabac out of Berenice by Vermouth, he by Nabob out of Vermeille by The Baron (English thoroughbred).

TIGRIS, by Lavater out of Modestie by the Heir of Linne, he by Galaor out of Mrs. Walker by Jereed.

LAVATER, by Y out of Candelaria (English thoroughbred).

Y, by Norfolk Phenomenon out of Henriette by Invincible.

NORFOLK PHENOMENON, by Old Phenomenon.

ESCULAPE, by Utrecht out of a daughter of Kœnisberg, he by Frejus out of a daughter of Achille, he by Young Rattler out of a daughter of Jaggard, he by Mailhand-Schols.

    FREJUS, by Eastham, out of a daughter of Imperieux, he by Young Rattler out of a daughter of Volontaire, he by Eclipse (English thoroughbred).

    EASTHAM, by Sir Oliver out of Cowslip by Alexander.

    YOUNG RATTLER, by Rattler out of the Snap Mare.

UTRECHT, by Prince out of a daughter of Eylau, he by Napoleon out of Delphine by Massoud (Pure Arab).

    NAPOLEON, by Bob Booty out the Pope Mare.

PRINCE, by Don Quichotte out of a daughter of Marengo, he by Napoleon out of Cloris by Aslam (Pure Arab).

DON QUICHOTTE, by Sylvio out of Moina by Tigris, he by Quitz out of Persepolis by Alexander.

SYLVIO, by Trance out of Hebe by Rubens.

Bred to FORTUNE, September 12, 1887.

HIRONDELLE.

Bay; foaled April 27, 1885; imported 1887; bred by M. Le Chaudelier, of Baraville, department of Calvados; got by the government stallion NIGER; dam by KAOLIN out of a daughter of NORMAND.

NIGER, by Norfolk Phenomenon out of Miss Bell.

NORFOLK PHENOMENON, by Old Phenomenon.

KAOLIN, by Zouave out of Dainty by Ionian.

ZOUAVE, by The Baron out of Dacia by Gladiator, he by Partisan out of Pauline by Moses.

  PARTISAN, by Lucholl, he by Old Lucholl.

NORMAND, by Introuvable out of a daughter of Emule, he by Eastham out of a daughter of Young Rattler, he by Rattler out of the Snap Mare.

  EASTHAM, by Sir Oliver out of Cowslip by Alexander.

INTROUVABLE, by Diomed out of a daughter of Jaggard, he by Mailhand-Schols.

DIOMED, by Young Rattler, etc., out of a daughter of Cleveland.

Bred to FORTUNE, October 13, 1887.

(Hoof No. 56.)

MADAME ANGOT.

Black; foaled May 4, 1882; imported 1886; bred by M. Gustave Buisson, of Authieux, department of Orne; got by the government stallion VOUZIERS; dam ETOILE-DU-NORD, by MARX (Orloff) out of a daughter of PHENOMENON.

VOUZIERS, by Ignore out of a daughter of Pater, he by Victorieux out of a daughter of Assault, he by Touchstone out of Ghuznee by Pantaloon.

    VICTORIEUX, by Pledge out of a daughter of Incomparable, he by Oliver Cromwell, out of a daughter of Pickpocket, he by St. Patrick out of the Hedley Mare.

    PLEDGE, by Royal Oak out of a daughter of Young Rattler, he by Rattler out of the Snap Mare.

    ROYAL OAK, by Catton out of Smolensko Mare.

IGNORE, by Uzel out of a daughter of Ugolin, he by Parisien, he by Ganymede out of a daughter of Biron, he by Captain Candid out of Helene by East-ham, he by Sir Oliver out of Cowslip by Alexander.

    GANYMEDE, by Xerxes out of La Louve by Chasseur, he by Eastham, etc., out of Marquise by Young Rattler, etc.

    XERXES, by Young Rattler, etc., out of a daughter of Young Highflyer, he by Highflyer out of a daughter of Young Docteur, he by Docteur out of a daughter of Mignon, he by Glorieux (English thoroughbred).

    CAPTAIN CANDID, by Cerberus out of Mandane by Pot-8-os.

    CERBERUS, by Roland (English thoroughbred).

UZEL, by Myrthe out of a daughter of Ramsay, he by Sylvio out of Emelina by Emilius, he by Emilius out of Cobweb by Phantom.

    SYLVIO, by Trance out of Hebe by Rubens.

MYRTHE, by Homere out of a daughter of Voltaire, he by Imperieux out of a daughter of Pilot, he by Octavius (English thoroughbred).

    IMPERIEUX, by Young Rattler, etc., out of a daughter of Volontaire, he by Eclipse (English thoroughbred).

HOMERE, by Imperieux, etc., out of a daughter of D. I. O., he by Whitworth out of Hambletonian Mare.

PHENOMENON, by Wildfire, he by Old Phenomenon.

    Bred to FORTUNE, October 4, 1887.

MARGUERITE.

Brown ; foaled May 24, 1881 ; imported 1886 ; bred by M. Auguste Capey, of Meautes, department of La Manche ; got by the government stallion TEMPETE ; dam MOUVETTE by UGOLIN, out of a daughter of URSIN.

TEMPETE, by Conquerante out of a daughter of Abrantes, he by Pledge out of a daughter of Noteur, he by Eylau out of a daughter of Diomed, he by Young Rattler out of a daughter of Young Topper, he by Topper.

PLEDGE, by Royal Oak out of a daughter of Young Rattler, he by Rattler out of the Snap Mare.

ROYAL OAK, by Catton out of Smolensko Mare.

EYLAU, by Napoleon out of Delphine by Massoud (pure Arab).

NAPOLEON, by Bob Booty out of the Pope Mare.

CONQUERANTE, by Kapirat out of Elisa by Corsair, he by J. C. Knox's Corsair out of a daughter of Cleveland.

KAPIRAT, by Voltaire out of a daughter of The Juggler, he by Wamba out of Pantechnetheca by Master Henry.

VOLTAIRE, by Imperieux out of a daughter of Pilot, he by Octavius (English thoroughbred).

IMPERIEUX, by Young Rattler, etc., out of a daughter of Volontaire, he by Eclipse (English thoroughbred).

UGOLIN, by Parisien, he by Ganymede out of a daughter of Biron, he by Captain Candid out of Helene by Eastham, he by Sir Oliver out of Cowslip by Alexander.

CAPTAIN CANDID, by Cerberus out of Mandane by Pot-8-os.

GANYMEDE, by Xerxes out of La Louve by Chasseur, he by Eastham, etc., out of Marquise by Young Rattler, etc.

XERXES, by Young Rattler, etc., out of a daughter of Young Highflyer, he by Highflyer out of a daughter of Young Docteur, he by Docteur out of a daughter of Mignon, he by Glorieux (English thoroughbred).

URSIN, by Ramsay out of a daughter of Ganymede, etc.

RAMSAY, by Sylvio out of Emelina by Emilius, he by Emilius out of Cobweb by Phantom.

SYLVIO, by Trance out of Hebe by Rubens.

Bred to GIL BLAS, November 20, 1887.

(Hoof No. 57.)

PENELOPE.

Brown ; foaled May 10, 1882 ; imported 1886 ; bred by M. Gustave Buisson, of Authieux, department of Orne ; got by the government stallion VOUZIERS; dam CERES by PHENOMENON out of a daughter of PLEDGE.

VOUZIERS, by Ignore out of a daughter of Pater, he by Victorieux out of a daughter of Assault, he by Touchstone out of Ghuznee by Pantaloon.

VICTORIEUX, by Pledge out of a daughter of Incomparable, he by Oliver Cromwell out of a daughter of Pickpocket, he by St. Patrick out of the Hedley Mare.

PLEDGE, by Royal Oak out of a daughter of Young Rattler, he by Rattler out of the Snap Mare.

ROYAL OAK, by Catton out of Smolensko Mare.

IGNORE, by Uzel out of a daughter of Ugolin, he by Parisien, he by Ganymede out of a daughter of Biron, he by Captain Candid out of Helene by Eastham, he by Sir Oliver out of Cowslip by Alexander.

GANYMEDE, by Xerxes out of La Louve by Chasseur, he by Eastham, etc., out of Marquise by Young Rattler, etc.

XERXES, by Young Rattler, etc., out of a daughter of Young Highflyer, he by Highflyer out of a daughter of Young Docteur, he by Docteur out of a daughter of Mignon, he by Glorieux (English thoroughbred).

CAPTAIN CANDID, by Cerberus out of Mandane by Pot-8-os.

CERBERUS, by Roland (English thoroughbred).

UZEL, by Myrthe out of a daughter of Ramsay, he by Sylvio out of Emelina by Emilius, he by Emilius out of Cobweb by Phantom

SYLVIO, by Trance out of Hebe by Rubens.

MYRTHE, by Homere out of a daughter of Voltaire, he by Imperieux out of a daughter of Pilot, he by Octavius (English thoroughbred).

IMPERIEUX, by Young Rattler, etc., out of a daughter of Volontaire, he by Eclipse (English thoroughbred).

HOMERE, by Imperieux, etc., out of a daughter of D. I. O., he by Whitworth out of Hambletonian Mare.

PHENOMENON, by Wildfire, he by Old Phenomenon

Bred to FORTUNE, September 3, 1887

(Hoof No. 55.)   # VESTA.

Bay ; foaled April 10, 1880 ; imported 1887 ; bred by M. A. Fontaine, of Cricqueville, department of Calvados ; got by the government stallion TAMAR ; dam by PIMPANT, out of a daughter of INTERPRETE.

TAMAR, by Jactator out of a daughter of Francais, he by Abrantes out of a daughter of Tipple Cider, he by Defence out of Deposit by Blacklock.

ABRANTES, by Pledge out of a daughter of Noteur, he by Eylau out of a daughter of Diomed, he by Young Rattler out of a daughter of Young Topper, he by Topper.

PLEDGE, by Royal Oak out of a daughter of Young Rattler, he by Rattler out of the Snap Mare.

ROYAL OAK, by Catton out of Smolensko Mare.

EYLAU, by Napoleon out of Delphine by Massoud (pure Arab).

NAPOLEON, by Bob Booty out of the Pope Mare.

JACTATOR, by Elu out of a daughter of Eylau, etc.

ELU, by Idalis out of a daughter of Tipple Cider, etc.

IDALIS, by Don Quichotte out of a daughter of Chapman, he by Trotteur, he by Chapman.

DON QUICHOTTE, by Sylvio out of Moina by Tigris, he by Quitz out of Persepolis by Alexander.

SYLVIO, by Trance out of Hebe by Rubens.

PIMPANT, by Vice Roi out of a daughter of Navigateur, he by Herschell out of a daughter of Oliver Cromwell.

HERSCHELL, by Eylau, etc., out of a daughter of Pretender, he by Holme (English thoroughbred).

VICE ROI, by Gainsborough (he by Gainful) out of a daughter of Merlerault, he by Royal Oak, etc., out of a daughter of Sylvio, etc.

INTERPRETE, by Centaure out of a daughter of Tancrede, he by The Roué out of a daughter of Eylau, etc.

THE ROUÉ, by Claret out of Roulette by Philipp-the-First.

CENTAURE, by Seducteur out of a daughter of Merlerault, etc.

SEDUCTEUR, by Noteur, etc., out of a daughter of Fatibello, he by Sylvio, etc., out of a daughter of Y, he by the Norfolk Phenomenon out of Henriette by Invincible, he by Hoemus out of Regatta by Camel (English thoroughbred).

NORFOLK PHENOMENON, by Old Phenomenon.

Bred to the government stallion SIR QUID PIGTAIL, April 9, 1887.

OAKLAWN.